Three Cases for

Mr. Campion

This is the second omnibus of Margery Allingham mysteries and contains three of her most distinguished novels of suspense and detection.

THE FASHION IN SHROUDS: A superb story involving the theft of dress designs, sixty cages of canaries, and blackmail, as Albert Campion investigates a three-year-old murder.

TRAITOR'S PURSE: The man could not remember anything, yet he knew he had to do something of immense consequence quickly. An exciting study in suspense for Mr. Campion.

THE GYRTH CHALICE MYSTERY: A thrilling mystery for Mr. Campion of the secret in the locked room of Gyrth Tower.

Scene: England

Margery Allingham

Three Cases

for Mr. Campion

Doubleday & Company, Inc., Garden City, New York

*All of the characters in this book are fictitious, and any resemblance to
actual persons, living or dead, is purely coincidental.*

CONTENTS

508

The Fashion

in Shrouds

". . . there reigned throughout their whole world a special sort of snobbism and a conscious striving for effect which were the very parents of Fashion."—PAUL POIRET

CHAPTER ONE

Probably the most exasperating thing about the Fashion is its elusiveness. Even the word has a dozen definitions, and when it is pinned down and qualified, as "the Fashion in woman's dress," it becomes ridiculous and stilted and is gone again.

To catch at its skirts it is safest to say that it is a kind of miracle, a familiar phenomenon. Why it is that a garment which is honestly attractive in, say, 1910 should be honestly ridiculous a few years later and honestly charming again a few years later still is one of those things which are not satisfactorily to be explained and are therefore jolly and exciting and an addition to the perennial interest of life.

When the last Roland Papendeik died, after receiving a knighthood for a royal wedding dress—having thus scaled the heights of his ambition as a great couturier—the ancient firm declined and might well have faded into one of the amusing legends Fashion leaves behind her had it not been for a certain phoenix quality possessed by Lady Papendeik.

At the moment when descent became apparent and dissolution likely Lady Papendeik discovered Val, and from the day that the Valentine cape in Lincoln-green facecloth flickered across the salon and won the hearts of twenty-five professional buyers and subsequently five hundred private purchasers Val climbed steadily, and behind her rose up the firm of Papendeik again like a great silk tent.

At the moment she was standing in a fitting room whither she had dragged a visitor who had come on private business of his own and was surveying herself in a wall-wide mirror with earnest criticism.

Like most of those people whose personality has to be consciously expressed in the things they create, she was a little more of a person, a little more clear in outline than is usual. She had no suggestion of overemphasis, but she was a sharp, vivid entity, and when one first saw her the immediate thing one realised was that it had not happened before.

As she stood before the mirror considering her burgundy-red suit from every angle she looked about twenty-three, which was not the fact. Her slenderness was slenderness personified and her yellow hair, folding softly into the nape of her neck at the back and combed into a ridiculous roll in front, could have belonged to no one else and would have suited no other face.

It occurred to her visitor, who was regarding her with the detached affection of a relation, that she was dressed up to look like a female, and he said so affably.

She turned and grinned at him, her unexpectedly warm grey eyes, which saved her whole appearance from affectation, dancing at him happily.

"I am," she said. "I am, my darling. I'm female as a cartload of monkeys."

"Or a kettle of fish, of course," observed Mr. Albert Campion, unfolding his long thin legs and rising from an inadequate gilt chair to look in the mirror also. "Do you like my new suit?"

"Very good indeed." Her approval was professional. "Jamieson and Fellowes? I thought so. They're so mercifully uninspired. Inspiration in men's clothes is stomach-turning. People ought to be shot for it."

Campion raised his eyebrows at her. She had a charming voice which was high and clear and so unlike his own in tone and colour that it gave him a sense of acquisition whenever he heard it.

"Too extreme," he said. "I like your garment, but let's forget it now."

"Do you? I was wondering if it wasn't a bit 'intelligent.'"

He looked interested.

"I wanted to talk to you before these people come. Aren't we lunching alone?"

Val swung slowly round in only partially amused surprise. For a moment she looked her full age, which was thirty, and there was character and intelligence in her face.

"You're too clever altogether, aren't you?" she said. "Go away. You take me out of my stride."

"Who is he? It's not to be a lovely surprise, I trust?" Campion put an arm round her shoulders and they stood for a moment admiring themselves with the bland unself-consciousness of the nursery. "If I didn't look so half-witted we should be very much alike," he remarked presently. "There's a distinct resemblance. Thank God we took after Mother and not the other side. Red hair would sink either of us, even Father's celebrated variety. Poor old Herbert used to look like nothing on earth."

He paused and considered her dispassionately in the mirror, while it occurred to him suddenly that the relationship between brother and sister was the one association of the sexes that was intrinsically personal.

"If one resents one's sister or even loathes the sight of her," he remarked presently, "it's for familiar faults or virtues which one either has or hasn't got oneself and one likes the little beast for the same rather personal reasons. I think you're better than I am in one or two ways, but I'm always glad to note that you have sufficient feminine weaknesses to make you thoroughly inferior on the whole. This is a serious, valuable thought, by the way. See what I mean?"

"Yes," she said with an irritating lack of appreciation, "but I don't think it's very new. What feminine weaknesses have I got?"

He beamed at her. In spite of her astonishing success she could always be relied upon to make him feel comfortingly superior.

"Who's coming to lunch?"

"Alan Dell—Alandel aeroplanes."

"Really? That's unexpected. I've heard of him, of course, but we've never met. Nice fellow?"

She did not answer immediately and he glanced at her sharply.

"I don't know," she said at last and met his eyes. "I think so, very." Campion grimaced. "Valentine the valiant."

She was suddenly hurt and colour came into her face.

"No, darling, not necessarily," she objected a little too vehemently. "Only twice shy, you know, only twice, not forever."

There was dignity in the protest. It brought him down to earth and reminded him effectively that she was after all a distinguished and important woman with every right to her own private life. He changed the conversation, feeling, as he sometimes did, that she was older than he was for all her femininity.

"Can I smoke in this clothespress without sacrilege?" he enquired. "I came up here once to a reception when I was very young. The Perownes had it then as their town house. That was in the days before the street went down and a Perowne could live in Park Lane. I don't remember much about it except that there were golden cream horns bursting with fruit all round the cornice. You've transformed the place. Does Tante Marthe like the change of address?"

"Lady Papendeik finds herself enchanted," said Val cheerfully, her mind still on her clothes. "She thinks it a pity trade should have come so near the park, but she's consoling herself by concentrating on 'our mission to glorify the Essential Goddess.' This is a temple, my boy, not a shop. When it's not a temple it's that damned draughty hole of

Maude Perowne's. But on the whole it's just exactly what she always wanted. It has the grand manner, the authentic Papa Papendeik touch. Did you see her little black pages downstairs?"

"The objects in the turbans? Are they recent?"

"Almost temporary," said Val, turning from the mirror and slipping her arm through his. "Let's go up and wait. We're lunching on the roof."

As he came through the wide doorway from a hushed and breathless world whose self-conscious good taste was almost overpowering to the upper, or workshop, part of the Papendeik establishment, Mr. Campion felt a gratifying return to reality. A narrow uncarpeted corridor, still bearing traces of the Perowne era in wallpaper and paint, was lit by half-a-dozen open doorways through which came a variety of sounds, from the chiming of cups to the hiss of the pressing iron, while above all there predominated the strident, sibilant chatter of female voices, which is perhaps the most unpleasant noise in the world.

An elderly woman in a shabby navy-blue dress came bustling along towards them, a black pincushion bumping ridiculously on her hip-bone as she walked. She did not stop but smiled and passed them, radiating a solid obstinacy as definite as the clatter of her old-lady shoes on the boards. Behind her trotted a man in a costume in which Campion recognised at once Val's conception of the term "inspired." He was breathless and angry and yet managed to look pathetic, with doggy brown eyes and the cares of the world on his compact little shoulders.

"She won't let me have it," he said without preamble. "I hate any sort of unpleasantness, but the two girls are waiting to go down to the house and I distinctly promised that the white model should go with the other. It's the one with the draped corsage."

He sketched a design with his two hands on his own chest with surprising vividness.

"The vendeuse is in tears."

He seemed not far off them himself and Mr. Campion felt sorry for him.

"Coax her," said Val without slackening pace and they hurried on, leaving him sighing. "Rex," she said as they mounted the narrow uncarpeted staircase amid a labyrinth of corridors. "Tante says he's not quite a lady. It's one of her filthy remarks that gets more true the longer you know him."

Campion made no comment. They were passing through a group of untidy girls who had stepped aside as they appeared.

"Seamstresses," Val explained as they came up on to the landing. "Tante prefers the word to 'workwomen.' This is their room."

She threw open a door which faced them and he looked into a vast attic where solid felt-covered tables made a mighty horseshoe whose well was peopled with dreadful brown headless figures each fretted with pinpricks and labelled with the name of the lady whose secret faults of contour it so uncompromisingly reproduced.

Reflecting that easily the most terrifying thing about women was their practical realism, he withdrew uneasily and followed her up a final staircase to a small roof garden set among the chimney-pots, where a table had been laid beneath a striped awning.

It was early summer and the trees in the park were round and green above the formal flower beds, so that the view, as they looked down upon it, was like a coloured panoramic print of eighteenth-century London, with the houses of the Bayswater Road making a grey cloud on the horizon.

He sat down on a white basketwork settee and blinked at her in the sunlight.

"I want to meet Georgia Wells. You're sure she's coming?"

"My dear, they're all coming." Val spoke soothingly. "Her husband, the leading man, Ferdie Paul himself and heaven knows who else. It's partly mutual publicity and partly a genuine inspection of dresses for *The Lover*, now in rehearsal. You'll see Georgia all right."

"Good," he said and his lean face was unusually thoughtful. "I shall try not to be vulgar or indiscreet, of course, but I must get to know her if I can. Was she actually engaged to Portland-Smith at the time he disappeared, or was it already off by then?"

Val considered and her eyes strayed to the doorway through which they had come.

"It's almost three years ago, isn't it?" she said. "My impression is that it was still on, but I can't swear to it. It was all kept so decently quiet until the family decided that they really had better look for him, and by then she was stalking Ramillies. It's funny you never found that man, Albert. He's your one entire failure, isn't he?"

Apparently Mr. Campion did not care to comment.

"How long has she been Lady Ramillies?"

"Over two years, I think."

"Shall I get a black eye if I lead round to Portland-Smith?"

"No, I don't think so. Georgia's not renowned for good taste. If she stares at you blankly it'll only mean that she's forgotten the poor beast's name."

He laughed. "You don't like the woman?"

Val hesitated. She looked very feminine.

"Georgia's our most important client, 'the best-dressed actress in the world gowned by the most famous couturier.' We're a mutual benefit society."

"What's the matter with her?"

"Nothing." She glanced at the door again and then out over the park. "I admire her. She's witty, beautiful, predatory, intrinsically vulgar and utterly charming."

Mr. Campion became diffident.

"You're not jealous of her?"

"No, no, of course not. I'm as successful as she is—more."

"Frightened of her?"

Val looked at him and he was embarrassed to see in her for an instant the candid-eyed child of his youth.

"Thoroughly."

"Why?"

"She's so charming," she said with uncharacteristic naïveté. "She's got *my* charm."

"That's unforgivable," he agreed sympathetically. "Which one?"

"The only one there is, my good ape. She makes you think she likes you. Forget her. You'll see her this afternoon. I like her really. She's fundamentally sadistic and not nearly so brilliant as she sounds, but she's all right. I like her. I do like her."

Mr. Campion thought it wisest not to press the subject and would doubtless have started some other topic had he not discovered that Val was no longer listening to him. The door to the staircase had opened and her second guest had arrived.

As he rose to greet the newcomer Campion was aware of a fleeting sense of disappointment.

In common with many other people he cherished the secret conviction that a celebrity should look peculiar, at the very least, and had hitherto been happy to note that a great number did.

Dell was an exception. He was a bony thirty-five-year-old with greying hair and the recently scoured appearance of one intimately associated with machinery. It was only when he spoke, revealing a cultured mobile voice of unexpected authority, that his personality became apparent. He came forward shyly and it occurred to Campion that he was a little put out to find that he was not the only guest.

"Your brother?" he said. "I had no idea Albert Campion was your brother."

"Oh, we're a distinguished family," murmured Val brightly, but an underlying note of uncertainty in her voice made Campion glance at her shrewdly. He was a little startled by the change in her. She looked younger and less elegant, more charming and far more vulnerable. He looked at the man and was relieved to see that he was very much aware of her.

"You've kept each other very dark," said Dell. "Why is that?"

Val was preoccupied at the moment with two waiters who had arrived with the luncheon from the giant hotel next door, but she spoke over her shoulder.

"We haven't. Our professions haven't clashed yet, that's all. We nod to each other in the street and send birthday cards. We're the half of the family that is on speaking terms, as a matter of fact."

"We're the bones under the ancestral staircase."

Campion embarked upon the explanation solely because it was expected of him. It was a reason he would never have considered sufficient in the ordinary way, but there was something about Alan Dell, with his unusually bright blue eyes and sudden smile, which seemed to demand that extra consideration which is given automatically to important children, as if he were somehow special and it was to everyone's interest that he should be accurately informed.

"I was asked to leave first—in a nice way, of course. We all have charming manners. Val followed a few years later, and now, whenever our names crop up at home, someone steps into the library and dashes off another note to the family solicitor disinheriting us. Considering their passion for self-expression, they always seem to me a little unreasonable about ours."

"That's not quite true about me." Val leant across the table and spoke with determined frankness. "I left home to marry a man whom no one liked, and after I married I didn't like him either. Lady Papendeik, who used to make my mother's clothes, saw some of my designs and gave me a job——"

"Since when you've revolutionised the business," put in Campion hastily with some vague idea of saving the situation. He was shocked. Since Sidney Ferris had died the death he deserved in a burnt-out motorcar with which, in a fit of alcoholic exuberance, he had attempted to fell a tree, he had never heard his widow mention his name.

Val seemed quite unconscious of anything unusual in her behaviour. She was looking across at Dell with anxious eyes.

"Yes," he said, "I've been hearing about you. I didn't realise how long Papendeik's had been going. You've performed an extraordinary feat in putting them back on the map. I thought change was the essence of fashion."

Val flushed.

"It would have been easier to start afresh," she admitted. "There was a lot of prejudice at first. But as the new designs were attractive they sold, and the solidarity of the name was a great help on the business side."

"It would be, of course." He regarded her with interest. "That's true. If the things one makes are better than the other man's, one does get the contracts. That's the most comforting discovery I've ever made."

They laughed at each other, mutually admiring and entirely comprehending, and Campion, who had work of his own to do, felt oddly out of it.

"When do you expect Georgia Wells?" he ventured. "About three?"

He felt the remark was hardly tactful as soon as he had made it, and Val's careless nod strengthened the impression. Dell was interested, however.

"Georgia Wells?" he said quickly. "Did you design her clothes for *The Little Sacrifice*?"

"Did you see them?" Val was openly pleased. Her sophistication seemed to have deserted her entirely. "She looked magnificent, didn't she?"

"Amazing." He glanced at the green treetops across the road. "I rarely go to the theatre," he went on after a pause, "and I was practically forced into that visit, but once I'd seen her I went again alone."

He made the statement with a complete unself-consciousness which was almost embarrassing and sat regarding them seriously.

"Amazing," he repeated. "I never heard such depth of feeling in my life. I'd like to meet that woman. She had some sort of tragedy in her life, I think? The same sort of thing as in the play."

Mr. Campion blinked. Unexpected naïveté in a delightful stranger whose ordinary intelligence is obviously equal to or beyond one's own always comes as something of a shock. He glanced at Val apprehensively. She was sitting up, her mouth smiling.

"She divorced her husband, the actor, some years ago, and there was a barrister fiancé who disappeared mysteriously a few months before she married Ramillies," she said. "I don't know which incident reminded you of the play."

Alan Dell stared at her with such transparent disappointment and surprise that she blushed, and Campion began to understand the attraction he had for her.

"I mean," she said helplessly, "*The Little Sacrifice* was about a woman relinquishing the only man she ever loved to marry the father of her eighteen-year-old daughter. Wasn't that it?"

"It was about a woman losing the man she loved in an attempt to do something rather fine," said Dell and looked unhappy, as if he felt he had been forced into an admission.

"Georgia was brilliant. She always is. There's no one like her." Val was protesting too much and realising it too late, in Campion's opinion, and he was sorry for her.

"I saw the show," he put in. "It was a very impressive performance, I thought."

"It was, wasn't it?" The other man turned to him gratefully. "It got one. She was so utterly comprehendable. I don't like emotional stuff as a rule. If it's good I feel I'm butting in on strangers, and if it's bad it's unbearably embarrassing. But she was so—so confiding, if you see what I mean. There *was* some tragedy, wasn't there, before she married Ramillies? Who was this barrister fiancé?"

"A man called Portland-Smith," said Campion slowly.

"He disappeared?"

"He vanished," said Val. "Georgia may have been terribly upset; I think she probably was. I was only being smart and silly about it."

Dell smiled at her. He had a sort of chuckleheaded and shy affection towards her that was very disarming.

"That sort of shock can go very deep, you know," he said awkwardly. "It's the element of shame in it—the man clearing off suddenly and publicly like that."

"Oh, but you're wrong. It wasn't that kind of disappearance at all." Val was struggling between the very feminine desire to remove any misapprehension under which he might be suffering and the instinctive conviction that it would be wiser to leave the subject altogether. "He simply vanished into the air. He left his practice, his money in the bank and his clothes on the peg. It couldn't have been anything to do with Georgia. He'd been to a party at which I don't think she was even present, and he left early because he'd got to get back and read a brief before the morning. He left the hotel about ten o'clock and didn't get to his chambers. Somewhere between the two he disappeared. That's the story, isn't it, Albert?"

The thin young man in the horn-rimmed spectacles did not speak at once, and Dell glanced at him enquiringly.

"You took it up professionally?"

"Yes, about two years later." Mr. Campion appeared to be anxious to excuse his failure. "Portland-Smith's career was heading towards a recordership," he explained, "and at the time he seemed pretty well certain to become a county court judge eventually, so his relatives were naturally wary of any publicity. In fact they covered his tracks, what there were of them, in case he turned up after a month or so with loss of memory. He was a lonely bird at the best of times, a great walker and naturalist, a curious type to have appealed so strongly to a successful woman. Anyway, the police weren't notified until it was too late for them to do anything, and I was approached after they'd given up. I didn't trouble Miss Wells because that angle had been explored very thoroughly by the authorities and they were quite satisfied that she knew nothing at all about the business."

Dell nodded. He seemed gratified by the final piece of information, which evidently corroborated his own convinced opinion.

"Interesting," he remarked after a pause. "That sort of thing's always happening. I mean one often hears a story like that."

Val looked up in surprise.

"About people walking out into the blue?"

"Yes," he said and smiled at her again. "I've heard of quite half-a-dozen cases in my time. It's quite understandable, of course, but every time it crops up it gives one a jolt, a new vision, like putting on a pair of long-sighted spectacles."

Val was visibly puzzled. She looked very sane sitting up and watching him with something like concern in her eyes.

"How do you mean? What happened to him?"

Dell laughed. He was embarrassed and glanced at Campion for support.

"Well," he said, the colour in his face making his eyes more vivid, "we all do get the feeling that we'd like to walk out, don't we? I mean we all feel at times an insane impulse to vanish, to abandon the great rattling caravan we're driving and walk off down the road with nothing but our own weight to carry. It's not always a question of concrete responsibilities; it's ambitions and conventions and especially affections which seem to get too much at moments. One often feels one'd like to ditch them all and just walk away. The odd thing is that so few of us do, and so when one hears of someone actually succumbing to that most familiar impulse one gets a sort of personal jolt. Portland-Smith is probably selling vacuum cleaners in Philadelphia by now."

Val shook her head.

"Women don't feel like that," she said. "Not alone."

Mr. Campion felt there might be something in this observation but he was not concerning himself with the abstract just then.

Months of careful investigation had led him late the previous afternoon to a little estate in Kent where the young Portland-Smith had spent a summer holiday at the age of nine. During the past ten years the old house had been deserted and had fallen into disrepair, creepers and brambles making of the garden a Sleeping Beauty thicket. There in a natural den in the midst of a shrubbery, the sort of hide-out that any nine-year-old would cherish forever as his own private place, Mr. Campion had found the thirty-eight-year-old Portland-Smith, or all that was left of him after three years. The skeleton had been lying face downward, the left arm pillowing the head and the knees drawn up in a feather bed of dried leaves.

CHAPTER TWO

Val's office was one of the more original features of Papendeik's new establishment in Park Lane. Reynarde, who had been responsible for the transformation of the mansion, had indulged in one of his celebrated "strokes of genius" in its construction and Colin Greenleaf's photographs of the white wrought-iron basket of a studio slung under the centre cupola above the well of the grand staircase had appeared in all the more expensive illustrated periodicals at the time of the move.

In spite of its affected design the room was proving unexpectedly useful, much to everyone's relief, for its glass walls afforded a view not only of the visitors' part of the building but a clear vision down the two main workshop corridors and permitted Lady Papendeik to keep an eye on her house.

Although it was technically Val's own domain and contained a drawing table, Marthe Papendeik sat there most of the day "in the midst of her web," as Rex had once said in a fit of petulance, "looking like a spider, seeing itself a queen bee."

When Marthe Lafranc had come to London in the days when Victorian exuberance was bursting through its confining laces and drawing its breath for the skyrocketing and subsequent crash which were to follow, she had been an acute French businesswoman, hard and brittle as glass and volatile as ether. Her evolution had been accomplished by Papendeik, the great artist. He had taken her as if she had been a bale of tinsel cloth and had created from her something quite unique and individual to himself. "He taught me how to mellow," she said once with a tenderness which was certainly not Gallic, "the *grand seigneur*."

At sixty she was a small, dark, ugly woman with black silk hair, a lifted face and the gift of making a grace of every fold she wore. She was at her little writing table making great illegible characters with a ridiculous pen when Mr. Campion wandered in after lunch and she greeted him with genuine welcome in her narrow eyes.

"The little Albert," she said. "My dear, the ensemble! Very distinguished. Turn round. Delightful. That is the part of a man one remembers always with affection, his back from the shoulders to the waist. Is Val still on the roof with that mechanic?"

Mr. Campion seated himself and beamed. They were old friends and without the least disrespect he always thought she looked like a little wet newt, she was so sleek and lizardlike with her sharp eyes and swift movements.

"I rather liked him," he said, "but I felt a little superfluous so I came down."

Tante Marthe's bright eyes rested for a moment on two mannequins who were talking together some distance down the southern corridor. The glass walls of the room were soundproof so there was no means of telling if they were actually saying the things to each other which appearances would suggest, but when one of them caught sight of the little figure silhouetted against the brightness of the further wall there was a hurried adjournment.

Lady Papendeik shrugged her shoulders and made a note of two names on her blotting pad.

"Val is in love with that man," she remarked. "He is very masculine. I hope it is not merely a most natural reaction. We are too many women here. There is no 'body' in the place."

Mr. Campion shied away from the subject.

"You don't like women, Tante Marthe?"

"My dear, it is not a question of liking." The vehemence in her deep, ugly voice startled him. "One does not dislike the half of everything. You bore me, you young people, when you talk about one sex or the other, as if they were separate things. There is only one human entity and that is a man and a woman. The man is the silhouette, the woman is the detail. The one often spoils or makes the other. But apart they are so much material. Don't be a fool."

She turned over the sheet of paper on which she had been writing and drew a little house on it.

"*Did* you like him?" she demanded suddenly, shooting a direct and surprisingly youthful glance at him.

"Yes," he said seriously, "yes. He's a personality and a curiously simple chap, but I liked him."

"The family would raise no difficulty?"

"Val's family?"

"Naturally."

He began to laugh.

"Darling, you're slipping back through the ages, aren't you?"

Lady Papendeik smiled at herself.

"It's marriage, my dear," she confided. "Where marriage is concerned, Albert, I am still French. It is so much better in France. There marriage is always the contract and nobody forgets that, even in the beginning. It makes it so proper. Here no one thinks of his signature until he wants to cross it out."

Mr. Campion stirred uneasily.

"I don't want to be offensive," he murmured, "but I think all this is a bit premature."

"Ah." To his relief she followed him instantly. "I wondered. Perhaps so. Very likely. We will forget it. Why are you here?"

"Come about a body." His tone was diffident. "Nothing indelicate or bad for business, naturally. I want to meet Georgia Wells."

Tante Marthe sat up.

"Georgia Wells," she said. "Of course! I could not think if Portland-Smith was the name of the man or not. Have you seen the evening paper?"

"Oh, Lord, have they got it already?" He took up the early racing edition from the desk and turned it over. In the Stop Press he found a little paragraph in blurred, irregular type.

SKELETON IN BUSHES. Papers found near a skeleton of a man discovered in the shrubbery of a house near Wellferry, Kent, suggest that body may be that of Mr. Richard Portland-Smith, who disappeared from his home nearly three years ago.

He refolded the paper and smiled at her wryly.

"Yes, well, that's a pity," he said.

Lady Papendeik was curious but years of solid experience had taught her discretion.

"It is a professional affair for you?"

"I found the poor chap."

"Ah." She sat nibbling her pen, her small back straight and her inquisitive eyes fixed upon his face. "It is undoubtedly the body of the fiancé?"

"Oh yes, it's Portland-Smith all right. Tante Marthe, was that engagement on or off when he vanished? Do you remember?"

"On," said the old lady firmly. "Ramillies had appeared upon the scene, you understand, but Georgia was still engaged. How long after he disappeared did the wretched man die? Can you tell that?"

"Not from the state of the body . . . at least I shouldn't think so. It must have been fairly soon but I don't think any pathologist could swear to it within a month or so. However, I fancy the police will be able to pin it down because of the fragments of the clothes. He seems to have been in evening dress."

Tante Marthe nodded. She looked her full age and her lips moved in a little soundless murmur of pity.

"And the cause? That will be difficult too?"

"No. He was shot."

She moved her hands and clicked her tongue.

"Very unpleasant," she pronounced and added maliciously: "It will be interesting to see Ferdie Paul turn it into good publicity."

Campion rose and stood looking down at her, his long thin figure drooping a little.

"I'd better fade away," he said regretfully. "I can't very well butt in on her now."

Lady Papendeik stretched out a restraining hand.

"No, don't go," she said. "You stay. Be intelligent, of course; the woman's a client. But I'd like someone to see them all. We are putting up some of the money for Caesar's Court. I would like your advice. Paul and Ramillies will be here and so will Laminoff."

"Caesar's Court?" Campion was surprised. "You too? Everyone I meet seems to have a finger in that pie. You're sitting pretty. It's going to be a Tom Tiddler's ground."

"I think so." She smiled complacently. "London has never had that kind of luxury on the doorstep and we can afford it. It was never possible in the old days because of the transport difficulty and when the transport did come there wasn't the money. Now the two have arrived together. Have you been out there yet? It's hardly a journey at all by car."

"No," said Mr. Campion, grinning. "I don't want to picnic in Naples, take a foam bath, improve my game, eat a lotus or mix with the elite. Also, frankly, the idea of spending six or seven hundred on a week-end party makes me feel physically sick. However, I realise that there are people who do, and I must say I like the wholesale magnificence of the scheme. These things usually flop because the promoters will rely on one or two good features to carry the others. This show *is* solid leather all through. The chef from the Virginia, Teddy Quoit's band, Andy Bullard in charge of the golf course, the Crannis woman doing the swimming and Waugh the tennis, while it was genius to make the place the headquarters of the beauty king chap, what's-his-name."

"Mirabeau," she supplied. "He's an artist. Ditto, his coiffeuse, designed my hair. Yes, the idea was excellent, but the execution has been extraordinary. That's Laminoff. Laminoff was the maître d'hôtel at the Poire d'Or. Bjornson let him in when he crashed. He's incredible, and Madame is no fool. It was Laminoff who insisted that the flying field must be made a customs port. Alan Dell arranged that."

"Dell? Is he in it too?"

"Naturally. All the club planes are Alandel machines and his pilots are in charge. His works are only a mile or so away on the other side of the river. He has a big interest in the whole hotel. That's how Val met him."

"I see." Mr. Campion blinked. "It's quite a neat little miracle of organisation, isn't it? Who's the clever lad in the background? Who woke up in the night with the great idea?"

Tante Marthe hesitated.

"Ferdie Paul. Don't mention it. It's not generally known." She pursed her lips and looked down her long nose. "Do you know Paul?"

"No. I thought he was a stage man. He's a producer, surely?"

"He's very clever," said Lady Papendeik. "He made Georgia Wells and he holds the leases of the Sovereign and the Venture theatres. The Cherry Orchard Club is his and he has a half share in the Tulip Restaurant."

Campion laughed. "And that's all you've been able to find out about him?"

She grimaced at him. "It's not enough, is it?" she said. "After all, we're not made of money—who is? Oh, they're here, are they? We'll go down."

She nodded and dismissed a page boy who had barely entered the room and had not had time to open his mouth.

"Now," she said without the slightest trace of conscious affectation, "we will see what beautiful dresses can do to a woman. One of these gowns is so lovely that I burst into tears when I first saw it and Rex would have fainted if he hadn't controlled himself, the poor neurotic."

Finding himself incapable of suitable comment, Mr. Campion said nothing and followed her dutifully down the grand staircase.

CHAPTER THREE

It was never Mr. Campion's custom to make an entrance. In early youth he had perfected the difficult art of getting into and out of rooms without fuss, avoiding both the defensive flourish and the despicable creep, but he swept into Papendeik's grand salon like the rear guard of a conqueror, which in a way, of course, he was.

Lady Papendeik at work was a very different person from Tante Marthe in Val's office. She appeared to be a good two inches higher, for one thing, and she achieved a curious sailing motion which was as far removed from ordinary walking as is the goose step in an exactly opposite direction. Mr. Campion found himself stalking behind her as though to fast and martial music. It was quite an experience.

The salon was golden. Val held that a true conceit is only a vulgarity in the right place and had done the thing thoroughly.

The room itself had been conceived in the grand manner. It was very long and high, with seven great windows leading out on to a stone terrace with bronzes, so that the general effect might easily have become period had not the very pale gold monotone of the walls, floor and furnishings given it a certain conscious peculiarity which, although satisfactory to the eye, was yet not sufficiently familiar to breed any hint of ignorant contempt.

The practical side of the colour scheme, which had really determined the two ladies to adopt it and which was now quite honestly forgotten by both of them, was that as a background for fine silk or wool material there is nothing so flattering as a warm, polished metal. Also, as Tante Marthe had remarked in an unguarded moment, "gold is so *comforting*, my dears, if you can really make it unimportant."

So Mr. Campion tramped through pale golden pile and was confronted at last by a vivid group of very human people, all silhouetted, framed and set and thus brought into startling relief against a pale golden wall. He was aware first of a dark face and then a fair one, a small boy of all unexpected things and afterwards, principally and completely, of Georgia Wells.

She was bigger than he had thought from the auditorium and now, without losing charm, more coarse. She was made up under the skin, as it were, designed by nature as a poster rather than a pen drawing.

He was aware that her eyes were large and grey, with long strong lashes and thick pale skin round them. Even the brown flecks in the grey irises seemed bolder and larger than is common and her expression was bright and shrewd and so frank that he felt she must have known him for some time.

She kissed Lady Papendeik ritualistically upon both cheeks but the gesture was performed absently and he felt that her attention was never diverted an instant from himself.

"Mr. Campion?" she echoed. "Really? Albert Campion?"

Her voice, which, like everything else about her, was far stronger and more flexible than the average, conveyed a certain wondering interest and he understood at once that she knew who he was, that she had seen the newspapers and was now considering if there was some fortunate coincidence in their meeting or if it were not fortunate or not a coincidence.

"Ferdie, this is Mr. Campion. You know. Mr. Campion, this is Ferdie Paul."

The dark face resolved itself into a person. Ferdie Paul was younger than Mr. Campion had expected. He was a large, plumpish man who looked like Byron. He had the same dark curling hair that was unreasonably inadequate on crown and temples, the same proud, curling mouth which would have been charming on a girl and was not on Mr. Paul, and the same short, strong, uniform features which made him just a little ridiculous, like a pretty bull.

When he spoke, however, the indolence which should have been a part and parcel of his make-up was surprisingly absent. He was a vigorous personality, his voice high and almost squeaky, with a nervous energy in it which never descended into irritability.

There was also something else about him which Campion noticed and could not define. It was a peculiar uncertainty of power, like pinking in a car engine, a quality of labour under difficulties which was odd and more in keeping with his voice than his appearance or personality.

He glanced at Campion with quick, intelligent interest, decided he did not know or need him, and dismissed him from his mind in a perfectly friendly fashion.

"We can begin at once, can't we?" he said to Lady Papendeik. "It's absolutely imperative that they should be quite right."

"They are exquisite," announced Tante Marthe coldly, conveying her irrevocable attitude in one single stroke.

Paul grinned at her. His amusement changed his entire appearance. His mouth became more masculine and the fleeting glimpse of gold stopping in his side teeth made him look for some reason more human and fallible.

"You're a dear, aren't you?" he said and sounded as if he meant it. Lady Papendeik's narrow eyes, which seemed to be all pupil, flickered at him. She did not smile but her thin mouth quirked and it occurred to Campion, who was watching them, that they were the working brains of the gathering. Neither of them were artists but they were the masters of artists, the Prosperos of their respective Ariels, and they had a very healthy admiration for one another.

By this time new visitors had arrived and were drifting towards the quilted settees between the windows. Rex was very much in evidence. He had lost his anger but retained his pathos, interrupting it at times with little coy exuberances always subdued to the right degree of ingratiating affability.

Campion noticed one woman in particular, a very correctly dressed little matron whose excellent sartorial taste could not quite lend her elegance, finding him very comforting. He wondered who she was and why she should receive such deference. Rex, he felt certain, would genuinely only find charm where it was politic that charm should be found, yet she did not by her manner appear to be very rich nor did she seem to belong to anybody. He had little time to observe her or anyone else, however, for Georgia returned to him.

"I'm so interested in you," she said with a frankness which he found a little overwhelming. "I'm not at all sure you couldn't be useful to me."

The naïveté of the final remark was so complete that for a second he wondered if she had really made it, but her eyes, which were as grey as tweed suiting and rather like it, were fixed on his own and her broad, beautiful face was earnest and friendly.

"Something rather awful has happened to me this afternoon," she went on, her voice husky. "They've found the skeleton of a man I adored. I can't help talking about it to somebody. Do forgive me. It's the shock, you know."

She gave him a faint apologetic smile and it came to him with surprise that she was perfectly sincere. He learnt a great deal about Georgia Wells at that moment and was interested in her. The ordinary hysteric who dramatises everything until she loses all sense of proportion and becomes a menace to the unsuspecting stranger was familiar to him, but this was something new. For the moment at any rate Georgia Wells was genuine in her despair and she seemed to be regarding him not as an audience but as a possible ally, which was at least disarming.

"I ought not to blurt it out like this to a stranger," she said. "I only realise how terrible these things are when I hear myself saying them. It's disgusting. Do forgive me."

She paused and looked up into his face with sudden childlike honesty.

"It is a frightful shock, you know."

"Of course it is," Campion heard himself saying earnestly. "Terrible. Didn't you know he was dead?"

"No. I had no idea." The protest was hearty and convincing but it lacked the confiding quality of her earlier announcements and he glanced at her sharply. She closed her eyes and opened them again.

"I'm behaving damnably," she said. "It's because I've heard so much about you I feel I know you. This news about Richard has taken me off my balance. Come and meet my husband."

He followed her obediently and it occurred to him as they crossed the room that she had that rare gift, so rare that he had some difficulty in remembering that it was only a gift, of being able to talk directly to the essential individual lurking behind the civilised façade of the man before her, so that it was impossible for him to evade or disappoint her without feeling personally responsible.

"Here he is," said Georgia. "Mr. Campion, this is my husband."

Campion's involuntary thought on first meeting Sir Raymond Ramillies was that he would be a particularly nasty drunk. This thought came out of the air and was not inspired by anything faintly suggestive of the alcoholic in the man himself. From Ramillies' actual appearance there was nothing to indicate that he ever drank at all, yet when Campion was first confronted by that arrogant brown face with the light eyes set too close together and that general air of irresponsible power the first thing that came into his mind was that it was as well that the fellow was at least sober.

They shook hands and Ramillies stood looking at him in a way that could only be called impudent. He did not speak at all but seemed amused and superior without troubling to be even faintly antagonistic.

Mr. Campion continued to regard him with misgiving and all the odd stories he had heard about this youthful middle-aged man with the fine-sounding name returned to his mind. Ramillies had retired from a famous regiment after the Irish trouble, at which times fantastic and rather horrible rumours had been floating about in connection with his name. There had been a brief period of sporting life in the shires and then he had been given the governorship of Ulangi, an unhealthy spot on the West Coast, a tiny serpent of country separating two foreign possessions. There the climate was so inclement that he was forced to spend three months of the year at home, but it was hinted that he contrived to make his exile not unexciting. Campion particularly remembered a pallid youngster who had been one of a party to spend a month at the Ulangi Residency and who had been strangely loth to discuss his adventures there on his return. One remark had stuck in Campion's mind: "Ramillies is a funny bird. All the time you're with him you feel he's going to get himself hanged or win the V.C. then and there before your eyes. Wonderful lad. Puts the wind up you."

Ramillies was quiet enough at the moment. He had made no remark of any kind since their arrival, but had remained standing with his feet apart and his hands behind him. He was swinging a little on his toes and his alert face wore an expression of innocence which was blatantly deceptive. Campion received the uncomfortable impression that he was thinking of something to do.

"I've just blurted out all my misery about Richard." Georgia's deep voice was devoid of any affectation and indeed achieved a note of rather startling sincerity. "I had no idea how frightfully shaken up I am. You know who Mr. Campion is, don't you, Raymond?"

"Yes, of course I do." Ramillies glanced at his wife as he spoke and his thin sharp voice, which had yet nothing effeminate about it, was amused. He looked at Campion and spoke to him as though from a slight distance. "Do you find that sort of thing terribly interesting? I suppose you do or you wouldn't do it. There's a thrill in it, is there, hunting down fellows?"

The interesting thing was that he was not rude. His voice, manner and even the words were all sufficiently offensive to warrant one knocking him down, but the general effect was somehow naïve. There was no antagonism there at all, rather something wistful in the final question.

Mr. Campion suddenly remembered him at school, a much older boy who had gone on to Sandhurst at the end of Campion's first term, leaving a banner of legend behind him. With a touch of snobbism which he recognised as childish at the time he refrained from mentioning the fact.

"The thrill is terrific," he agreed solemnly. "I frequently frighten myself into a fit with it."

"Do you?" Again there was the faint trace of real interest.

Georgia put her arm through Campion's, an unself-conscious gesture designed to attract his attention, which it did.

"Why did you come to see this dress show?"

He felt her shaking a little as she clung to him.

"I wanted to meet you," he said truthfully. "I wanted to talk to you."

"About Richard? I'll tell you anything I know. I want to talk about him."

While there was no doubt about her sincerity there was a suggestion of daring in her manner, an awareness of danger without the comprehension of it, which gave him his first real insight into her essential character and incidentally half startled the life out of him.

"You said he was dead, Raymond." There was a definite challenge in her voice and Campion felt her quivering like a discharging battery at his side.

"Oh yes, I knew the chap was dead." Ramillies was remarkably matter of fact and Campion stared at him.

"How did you know?"

"Thought he must be, else he'd have turned up once I'd gone back to Africa and Georgia was alone." He made the statement casually but with conviction and it dawned upon the other man that he was not only indifferent to any construction that might be put upon his words, but incapable of seeing that they might convey any other meaning.

Georgia shuddered. Campion felt the involuntary movement and was puzzled again, since it did not seem to be inspired purely by fear or disgust. He had the unreasonable impression that there was something more like pleasure at the root of it.

"If it wouldn't upset you to talk about him," he ventured, looking down at her, "I'd like to hear your impression of his mental condition the last time you saw him . . . if you're sure you don't mind."

"My dear, I *must* talk!" Georgia's cry came from the heart, or seemed to do so, but the next instant her grip on his arm loosened and she said in an entirely different tone: "Who's that coming over here with Val?"

Campion glanced up and was aware of a faint sense of calamity.

"That?" he murmured guiltily. "Oh, that's Alan Dell, the aeroplane chap."

"Introduce us," said Georgia. "I think he wants to meet me."

Val came across the room purposefully and it occurred to Mr. Campion that she looked like the Revenge sailing resolutely into battle with her pennants flying. She looked very fine with her little yellow coxcomb held high and every line of her body flowing with that particular kind of femininity which is neat and precisely graceful. He sighed for her. He was prepared to back the Spanish galleon every time.

Alan Dell came beside her. Having once met the man, Campion discovered that his shy and peculiarly masculine personality was now

completely apparent and that his first superficial impression of him
had vanished.

Georgia put about.

"My pretty," she said, stretching out both hands. "Come and comfort me with clothes. I'm in a tragedy."

Her fine strong body was beautiful as she swung forward and a
warmth of friendliness went out to meet the other girl. Val responded
to it cautiously.

"I've got just the dress for it, whatever it is," she said lightly. "The
ultimate garment of all time."

Georgia drew back. She looked pathetically hurt behind her smile.

"I'm afraid it's a real tragedy," she said reproachfully.

"My pet, I'm so sorry. What is it?" Val made the apology so unjustly
forced from her and her eyes grew wary.

Georgia glanced over her shoulder before she spoke. Ramillies still
stood swinging on his toes, his glance resting consideringly upon the
small boy in the corner. Georgia shook her head.

"Tell me about the lovely dresses," she said, and added before Val
or Campion could speak, "Who is this?" a demand which brought
Dell forward with the conviction that there had been a general dis-
inclination to present him.

He shook hands with unexpected gaucherie and stood blinking at
her, suffering no doubt from that misapprehension so common to shy
folk, that he was not quite so clearly visible to her as she was to him.

Georgia regarded him with that glowing and intelligent interest
which was her chief weapon of attack.

"The second last person on earth to find in a dress shop," she said.
"My dear, are you going to enjoy all this? Have you ever been to this
sort of show before?"

"No," he said and laughed. "I stayed to see you."

Georgia blushed. The colour flowed up her throat and over her face
with a charm no seventeen-year-old could have touched.

"That's very nice of you," she said. "I'm afraid I'm going to be very
dull. Something rather beastly has happened to me and I'm just behaving disgustingly and blurting it out to everyone."

It was a dangerous opening and might well have proved disastrous
but that her gift of utter directness was a lodestone. Dell's sudden
gratified sense of kindly superiority was communicated to them all and
he murmured something bald about seeing her in trouble once more.

"*The Little Sacrifice?*" she said quickly. "Oh, I adored that woman
Jacynth. I found myself putting all I'd ever known or ever felt into
her, poor sweetie. It was very nice of you to go and see me."

From that moment her manner changed subtly. It was such a gradual metamorphosis, so exquisitely done, that Campion only just noticed it, but the fact remained that she began to remind him strongly of the heroine in *The Little Sacrifice*. Touches of the character crept into her voice, into her helpless little gestures, into her very attitude of mind, and he thought ungenerously that it would have been even more interesting, besides being much more easy to follow, if the original part had only been played in some strong foreign accent.

Dell was openly enchanted. He remained watching her with fascinated attention, his blue eyes smiling and very kind.

"It was a long time ago and all very sad and silly even then." Georgia sounded both brave and helplessly apologetic. "He was such a dear, my sweet moody Richard. I knew him so awfully well. We were both innately lonely people and . . . well, we were very fond of one another. When he simply vanished I was brokenhearted, but naturally I couldn't admit it. Could I?"

She made a little fluttering appeal to them all to understand.

"One doesn't, does one?" she demanded with that sudden frankness which, if it is as embarrassing, is also as entirely disarming as nakedness. "I mean, when one really is in love one's so painfully self-conscious, so miserably mistrustful of one's own strength. I'm talking about the real, rather tragic thing, of course. Then one's so horribly afraid that this exquisite, precious, deliriously lovely sanctuary one's somehow achieved may not be really solid, may not be one's own for keeps. One's so conscious all the time that one can be hurt beyond the bounds of bearing that in one's natural pessimism one dreads disaster all the time, and so when something does happen one accepts it and crawls away somewhere. You do know what I mean, don't you?"

They did, of course, being all adult and reasonably experienced, and Mr. Campion, who was shocked, was yet grudgingly impressed. Her tremendous physical health and that quality which Dell had called "confiding" had clothed an embarrassing revelation of the ordinary with something rather charming. He glanced at Val.

She looked past him and did not speak aloud, although her lips moved. He thought he read the words "strip tease," and regarded her with sudden respect.

Georgia did not let the scene drop.

"I'm so sorry," she said helplessly. "This is all so disgustingly vulgar of me, but oh, my dears!—suddenly to see it on the placards, to make Ferdie leap out of the car and get a paper, to snatch it away from him and then to look and find it all true! They've found his skeleton, you see."

Her eyes were holding them all and there was real wretchedness in the grey shadows.

"You never think of people you know having skeletons, do you?"

"My dear, how horrible!" Val's ejaculation was startled out of her. "When did all this happen?"

"Now," said Georgia miserably. "Now, just as I was coming here. I'd have gone home, my pet, but I couldn't let you and everybody else down just when we were all so rushed. I didn't realise it was going to have this dreadful loquacious effect upon me."

"Darling, what are you talking about?" Ferdie Paul slipped his arm round her and drew her back against him. His face over her shoulder was dark and amused, but there was more in his voice than tolerance. "Forget it. You'll upset yourself."

Georgia shivered, smiled and released herself with a gentle dignity, directed, Campion felt, at himself and Dell. She glanced at her husband, who came forward promptly, his natural springy walk lending him a jauntiness which added considerably to his disturbing air of active irresponsibility.

"That's right, Georgie," he said in his flat staccato voice. "Forget the fellow if you can, and if you can't don't make an ass of yourself."

Even he seemed to feel that this admonition might sound a trifle harsh to the uninitiated, for he suddenly smiled with that transfiguring, sunny happiness usually associated with early childhood. "What I mean to say is, a lovely girl looks very touching grizzling over a corpse but she looks damned silly doing it over a skeleton. She's missed the boat. The great lover's not merely dead, dearest; he's dead and gone. Should I be a bounder if I asked for a drink?"

The last remark was directed towards Val with a quick-eyed charm which was ingratiating.

"Certainly not. You must all need one." Val sounded thoroughly startled. She glanced at Rex, who had been hovering on the edge of the group, and he nodded and disappeared. Ferdie Paul resumed his hold on Georgia. He had a gently contemptuous way with her, as if she were a difficult elderly relative of whom he was fond.

"We're going to see the great dress for the third act first," he said. "I want to make sure that when Pendleton gets you by the throat he can only tear the left shoulder out. It's got to be restrained and dignified. I don't want you running about in your brassière. The whole danger of that scene is that it may go a bit *vieux jeu* if we don't look out . . . nineteen twenty-sixish or so. Lady Papendeik wants us to see the dress on the model first because apparently it's pretty hot. Then I want you to get into it and we'll run through that bit."

Georgia stiffened.

"I'm not going to rehearse here in front of a lot of strangers," she protested. "God knows I'm not temperamental, sweetheart, but there are limits. You're not going to ask me to do that, Ferdie, not this afternoon of all times?"

"Georgia." Paul's arm had tightened, and Campion saw his round brown eyes fixed firmly upon the woman's own with a terrifying quality of intelligence in them, as if he were trying to hypnotise some sense into her. "Georgia, you're not going to be silly, are you, *dear?*"

It was an idiotic little scene, reminding Campion irresistibly of a jockey he had once heard talking to a refractory horse.

"We'll go. Mr. Campion and I will go, Miss Wells." Alan Dell spoke hastily and Paul, looking up, seemed to see him for the first time.

"Oh no, that's all right," he said. "There's only a few of us here. It's a purely technical matter. You're going to be reasonable, aren't you, darling? You're only a bit jittery because of the boy friend."

Georgia smiled at him with unexpected tolerance and turned to Dell with a little deprecating grimace.

"My nerves have gone to pieces," she said and it occurred to Mr. Campion that she might easily be more accurate than she realised.

It was at this moment that Tante Marthe came over with one of her small coloured pages at her elbow.

"The *Trumpet* is on the phone, my dear," she said. "Will you speak to them?"

Georgia's hunted expression would have been entirely convincing if it had not been so much what one might have expected.

"All right," she said heavily. "This is the horrible part of it all. This is what I've been dreading. Yes, I'll come."

"No." Ramillies and Paul spoke together and paused to look at one another afterwards. It was the briefest interchange of glances and Mr. Campion, who was watching them both, became aware for the first time that the undercurrent which he had been trying to define throughout the entire afternoon was an unusual, and in the circumstances incomprehensible, combination of alarm and excitement.

"No," said Ramillies again. "Don't say a thing."

"Do you mean that?" She turned to him almost with eagerness and he did not look at her.

"No, dear, I don't think I would." Ferdie Paul spoke casually. "We'll put out some sort of statement later if it's necessary. It's not a particularly good story so they won't get excited. Tell them Miss Wells is not here. She left half an hour ago."

The page went off obediently and Paul watched the child until it disappeared, his figure drooping and his prominent eyes thoughtful. Georgia looked at Dell, who moved over to her.

"That must be a very great relief to you," he said.

She stared at him. "You understand, don't you?" she said with sudden earnestness. "You really do."

Mr. Campion turned away rather sadly and became aware of Val. She was looking at the other woman and he caught her unawares. Once again she surprised him. Jealousy is one emotion but hatred is quite another and much more rare in a civilised community. Once it is seen it is not easily forgotten.

CHAPTER FOUR

The gentle art of putting things over had always interested Mr. Campion, but as he sat down beside Alan Dell to watch the house of Papendeik at work he was aware of a sudden sense of irritation. There was so much going on under his nose that needed explanation. The strangers were vivid personalities but not types he recognised and at the moment he did not understand their reactions at all.

Meanwhile an impressive if informal performance was beginning. Val and Tante Marthe were staging an act and he was entertained to note that they worked together with the precision of a first-class vaudeville turn.

Tante Marthe had seated herself on the largest of the settees between the two most central windows and had made room for Ferdie Paul beside her, while Georgia had been provided by Rex with a wide-seated gilt chair thrust out into the room a little.

She sat in it regally, her dark head thrown back and her lovely broad face tilted expectantly. Even so she contrived to look a little tragic, making it clear that she was a woman with a background of deep emotional experience.

Val stood behind her, slender and exquisite and very much the brilliant young artist about to display something that might well prove to be the masterpiece of a century.

The rest of the conversation piece was furnished by the staff. Every available saleswoman had assembled together at one end of the room, as though for prayers in an old-fashioned houschold. There was a flutter of expectancy among them, a gathering together to admire a creation for which they all took a small degree of personal responsibility. Their very presence indicated a big moment.

Dell caught Campion's eye and leant forward.

"Wonderfully interesting," he whispered with professional appreciation.

There was a moment of silence and Rex slid forward to give an entirely unnecessary flick to the folds of a curtain. Lady Papendeik glanced round her and raised a small dark paw. The staff sighed and the dress appeared.

At this point Mr. Campion felt somewhat out of his depth. He looked at the dress and saw that it was long and white, with a satisfactory arrangement of drapery at the front, and that it had an extraordinary-looking girl in it. She caught his attention because she was beautiful without being in any way real or desirable. She had a strong superficial likeness to Georgia inasmuch as she was not small and was dark with broad cheekbones, but there all similarity ended. Where Georgia was coarse the newcomer was exquisite, where Georgia was vital the other girl was dead.

Campion glanced at Tante Marthe and was delighted to see her sitting back, her hands in her lap, her eyes half closed and an outrageous expression of fainting ecstasy on her face. Ferdie Paul looked thoughtful but by no means unimpressed and the staff whispered and preened itself.

Campion and Alan Dell looked at the gown again, each trying to discover why it should be so particularly pleasing, and were both on the verge of making the same thundering mistake by deciding that its charm lay in its simplicity when Georgia dropped the bomb.

"Val, my angel," she said, her lovely husky voice sounding clearly through the room, "it's breath-taking! It's *you*. It's *me*. But, my pet, it's not *new*. I saw it last night at the Dudley Club."

There was a moment of scandalised silence. The Greek chorus in the corner gaped and Rex's nervous giggle echoed inopportunely from the background. The formal conversation piece had turned into a Gluyas Williams picture.

Lady Papendeik rose.

"My dear," she said, "my dear." Her voice was not very loud or even particularly severe but instantly all the humour went out of the situation and Georgia was on the defensive.

"Oh, my dear, I'm so sorry." She turned to Val impulsively and the most ungenerous among them could not have doubted her honesty.

"There's been some hideous mistake, of course. This whole day is like a nightmare. I did see it. I saw it last night and it fascinated me. I can even prove it, unfortunately. There's a photograph of the Blaxill woman wearing it in one of the morning papers . . . the *Range Finder*, I think . . . on the back page. She's dancing with a cabinet minister. I noticed it, naturally. It wiped the floor with everything else."

Val said nothing. Her face was quite expressionless as she nodded to the horrified group at the other end of the room. There was a discreet scurrying towards the door and a rustle of chatter as they reached the hall. Georgia stood up. Her tall, graceful body towered over Val, making the other girl look as if she belonged to some smaller and neater world.

"Of course it hadn't your cut," she said earnestly, "and I don't think it was in that material, but it was white."

Lady Papendeik shrugged her shoulders.

"That is Bouileau's *Caresse*," she said, "woven to our design."

Georgia looked like helpless apology personified.

"I had to tell you," she said.

"Of course you did, my dear," murmured Lady Papendeik without thawing. "Of course."

There was no doubt that the incident was a major catastrophe. Everybody began to talk and Paul crossed the room to Val's side, with Ramillies, casual and unaccountable, at his heels.

Mr. Campion was puzzled. In his experience the duplication of a design, although the most dispiriting of all disasters to the artist concerned, is seldom taken seriously by anyone else, unless hard money has already been involved, and he began to wonder if this explosion was not in the nature of a safety valve, seized upon gratefully because it was a legitimate excuse for excitement actually engendered by something less politic to talk about.

The other person who might possibly have shared Mr. Campion's own Alice in Wonderland view of the situation was the small boy. He sat staring into the inside of his Haverleigh cap, his forehead wrinkled, and was apparently unaware of any crisis.

The return of Rex was dramatic. He came hurrying in with a perfectly white face, a newspaper in his outstretched hand. Lady Papendeik stood looking at the photograph for some moments and when she spoke her comment was typical.

"Only a thief would permit a woman with a stomach to commit such sacrilege. Who dresses her?"

The others crowded round and Dell turned to Campion again.

"It's a leakage," he murmured. "You can't stop it in any show where designs are secret. It's an infuriating thing."

"It's a miracle the photograph is so clear," said Georgia forlornly. "They're usually so vague. But you can't miss that, can you? It was in ribbed silk. I couldn't take my eyes off it." She put an arm round Val's shoulders. "You poor sweet," she said.

Val released herself gently and turned to Rex.

"Who is that woman's couturier?"

"Ring her up." Ramillies made the outrageously impolitic suggestion with all the vigorous irresponsibility which turned him into such a peculiarly disturbing element. "Say you're a magazine. Georgia, you do it . . . or I will. Shall I?"

"No, darling, of course not. Don't be an ass." Georgia had spoken casually and he turned to her.

"Ass be damned!" he exploded with a violence which startled everyone. "It's the only intelligent suggestion that's been put forward so far. What's the woman's name? She'll be in the book, I suppose."

His fury was so entirely unexpected that for a moment the main disaster was forgotten. Campion stared at him in astonishment. His thin jaws were clenched and the little pulses in them throbbed visibly. The reaction was so entirely out of proportion to the occurrence that Campion was inclined to suspect that the man was drunk after all, when he caught a glimpse of Ferdie Paul. Both he and Georgia were eyeing Ramillies with definite apprehension.

"Wait a moment, old boy." Paul sounded cautious. "You never know. We may be able to pin it down here."

"You may in an hour or so of fooling about." Ramillies' contempt was bitter. "But that's the straightforward, elementary way of finding a thing out . . . ask."

"Just one little moment," murmured Tante Marthe over her shoulder. "This is not a thing that has never happened before."

Ramillies shrugged his shoulders. "As you please. But I still think the intelligent thing to do is to get on the phone to the woman. Tell her all about it if you must. But if I was doing it myself I should say I was a magazine and get it out of her that way. However, it's nothing to do with me, thank God."

He swung on his heel and made for the door.

"Ray, where are you going?" Georgia still sounded apprehensive.

He paused on the threshold and regarded her with cold dislike which was uncomfortably convincing.

"I'm simply going downstairs to see if they've got a telephone book," he said and went out.

Val glanced at Georgia, a startled question in her eyes, but it was Ferdie Paul who answered her.

"Oh no, that's all right. He won't phone," he said and looked across at the small boy, who nodded reassuringly and, sliding off his chair, passed unobtrusively out of the room. It was an odd incident and Dell glanced at Campion.

"Astonishing chap," he said under his breath and regarded Georgia with increased interest.

Meanwhile Rex, who had been permitted to get a word in at last, was talking earnestly to Tante Marthe. He had a nervous habit of wriggling ingratiatingly and now, all the time he was talking, he seemed to be making surreptitious attempts to stroke his calves by leaning over backwards to get at them. But his observations were to the point.

"I know Leonard Lôke used to dress her," he said, "and if the design has gone there, of course it means it'll be turned over to the worst kind of wholesalers and produced by the hundred. It's a tragedy."

"The premier who made it, the vendeuse, Mrs. Saluski, the child in the fitting room, you, myself and Val," murmured Lady Papendeik, shooting her little lizard head up. "No one else saw the finished dress. The sketch was never completed. Val cut it on the living model."

Rex straightened.

"Wait," he said in an altered voice. "I've remembered. Leonard Lôke is two partners, Pretzger and Morris. Pretzger had a brother-in-law in the fur trade. You may remember him, madame; we've dealt with him once or twice. A fortnight ago I saw that man dining at the Borgia in Greek Street and he had Miss Adamson with him."

The dramatic point of this statement was not clear to Mr. Campion at first but, as all eyes were slowly turned upon the one person in the room who had hitherto taken no interest whatever in the proceedings, the inference dawned slowly upon him.

The mannequin had remained exactly where she was when the general attention had first been distracted from her. She was standing in the middle of the room, beautiful, serene and entirely remote. Her lack of reality was almost unpleasant and it occurred to Campion that her personality was as secret as if she had been a corpse. Now, with everyone staring at her rather than her dress, she did not come to life but remained looking at them blankly with brilliant, foolish eyes.

"Caroline, is this true?" demanded Tante Marthe.

"Is what true, madame?" Her voice, a jew's-harp with a Croydon accent, came as a shock to some of them. Campion, who knew from experience that the beauty of porcelain lies too often in the glaze, was not so much surprised as regretfully confirmed in an opinion.

"Don't be a fool, my dear." Lady Papendeik betrayed unexpected heartiness. "You must know if you've eaten with a man or not. Do not let us waste time."

"I didn't know whose brother-in-law he was," protested Miss Adamson sulkily.

"Did you describe the model? Did it slip out by accident? These things have happened."

"No, I didn't tell him, madame."

"You understand what has occurred?"

Miss Adamson did not change her expression. Her dark eyes were liquid and devastatingly unintelligent.

"I didn't tell him anything. I swear it, I didn't."

Tante Marthe sighed. "Very well. Go and take it off."

As the girl floated from the room Val made a gesture of resignation.

"That's all we shall ever know," she said to Dell, who was standing beside her. "There's a direct link there, of course, but she was quite emphatic."

Campion joined them.

"I thought I noticed a certain clinging to the letter," he ventured.

"That was the diagnosis that leapt to my mind but I didn't care to mention it," Dell said, and added with the smile which made him attractive, "She's too lovely to be that kind of fool."

"No one's too lovely to be mental, in my experience," remarked Lady Papendeik briskly. "What diagnosis is this?"

"We thought she might be a letter-of-the-law liar," Dell said, glancing at Campion for support. "She didn't tell the man, she drew it for him. They're the most impossible people in the world to deal with. If you pin them down they get more and more evasive and convince themselves all the time that they're speaking the literal truth . . . which they are, of course, in a way. In my experience the only thing to do is to get rid of them, however valuable they are. Still, I shouldn't like to convict the girl on that evidence alone."

Tante Marthe hesitated and it went through Campion's mind that she was suppressing a remark that might possibly turn out to be indiscreet.

Ferdie Paul, who had remained silent throughout the interview, looked down at her.

"Send her to Caesar's Court," he said. "She's too lovely to lose. Margaret is down there, isn't she? Turn this kid over to her. She can talk about the gowns there as much as she likes; she won't see them until they're ready to be shown."

"Perhaps so," said Tante Marthe and her black eyes wavered.

Georgia resumed her seat.

"I think you're very generous, Val," she began. "I'm brokenhearted. I could weep. You'll never make me anything so deliriously lovely again."

"No," Val said, a cloud passing over her face, "I don't suppose I ever shall."

Georgia stretched out a strong hand and drew the other girl towards her.

"Darling, that was mean," she said with a sweet gentleness which was out of period, let alone character. "You're upset because your lovely design has been stolen. You're naturally livid and I understand that. But you're lucky, you know. After all, Val, it's such a little thing. I hate to repeat all this but I can't get it off my mind. Richard's poor murdered body has been found and here are we all fooling about with stupid idiot dresses for a stupid idiot play."

She did not turn away but sat looking at them and her eyes slowly filled with tears and brimmed over. If she had only sounded insincere, only been not quite so unanswerably in the right, the outburst would have been forgivable: as it was, they all stood round uncomfortably until Mr. Campion elected to drop his little brick.

"I say, you know, you're wrong there," he said in his quiet, slightly nervous voice. "I don't think the word 'murder' has gone through any official mind. Portland-Smith committed suicide; that's absolutely obvious, to the police at any rate."

Val, who knew him, guessed from his expression of affable innocence that he hoped for some interesting reaction to this announcement, but neither of them was prepared for what actually took place. Georgia sat up stiffly in her chair and stared at him, while a dark stream of colour rose up her throat, swelling the veins in her neck and passing over her expressionless face.

"That's not true," she said.

With what appeared to be well-meaningness of the most unenlightened kind, Mr. Campion persisted in his point, ignoring all the danger signals.

"Honestly," he said. "I can reassure you on that question. I'm hand in glove with the fellow who found the body. As a matter of fact I was actually on the spot myself this morning. The poor chap had killed himself all right. . . . At least that's what the coroner will decide; I'm sure of it."

The quiet plausible voice was conversational and convincing.

"No." Georgia made the word a statement. "I don't believe it. It's not true." She was controlling herself with difficulty and when she stood up her body was trembling with the effort. There was no doubt at all about her principal emotion and it was so unaccountable and unreasonable in the circumstances that even Mr. Campion showed some of the astonishment he felt. She was angry, beside herself with ordinary, unadulterated rage.

Campion looked to Ferdie Paul for assistance, but he did not intervene. He stood regarding her speculatively, almost, it seemed to Campion, with the same sort of puzzled conjecture that he felt himself.

It was left to Tante Marthe to make the enquiry that was on the tip of everybody's tongue.

"My dear child," she said with faint reproof in her tone, "why be so annoyed? The poor man has been dead these three years. Had he been murdered it must have meant that someone killed him and that would entail trouble for everyone who knew him. If he killed himself no one need think of him with anything except pity."

"Oh, don't be so silly, angel." Georgia turned on the old woman in exasperation. "Can't you see the damage a story like that can do once it gets about? I won't believe it. I know it's not true."

"You *know?*" Campion's eyes were mild behind his spectacles but they did not disarm her into answering him impulsively.

"Richard was not a suicidal type," she said after a pause which lasted too long. "This is the final insufferable straw. I can't bear it. You must all forgive me and manage as best you can. I must go home."

"Going home?" Ramillies' voice sounded disappointed in the doorway. "Why? What's the matter now?" He seemed to have forgotten his flamboyant exit of ten minutes before, and came in jauntily pleased with himself as ever.

Georgia stood looking at him steadily.

"Albert Campion says Richard committed suicide. He seems to think there's no doubt about it."

"Oh?" Ramillies' casualness was remarkable and Campion wished he knew the man better. From what he had seen of him so far the reaction might mean absolutely anything, even genuine disinterest. Since no one else spoke it came to Ramillies somewhat belatedly that further comment was expected. "It's a long time ago, anyhow," he remarked with singularly unhappy effect. "There'll be no ferreting about either, which is one good thing. That's the one advantage of suicide; everyone knows who did it," he ended lamely, and remained looking at his wife.

Georgia kept her eyes upon him for almost a minute and, having subdued him, turned to Dell.

"Would you be most terribly kind and drive me home?"

"Why, yes. Yes, of course." He looked a little startled. "Of course," he repeated. "I'd like to."

"Bless you," said Georgia and smiled at him faintly.

"Oh, I'll take you home if you really want to go," put in Ramillies without much enthusiasm.

She drew away from him.

"I'm not sure if I ever want to speak to you again," she said distinctly and went out, taking Dell with her.

"What on earth did she mean by that?" demanded Ferdie Paul.

Ramillies turned to look at him and there was, incongruously, the suggestion of a smile in the many creases round his eyes.

"God knows, my dear fellow," he said. "God knows."

CHAPTER FIVE

There is a distinct difference between the state of believing something to be true and knowing it to be so with the paid stamp of an official opinion affixed to the knowledge.

When the embarrassed foreman of the coroner's jury stood up in the cool dark village hall at Wellferry and stated that he and his confreres were convinced that the skeleton found in the bushes at Eves Hall on the Shelley road was the skeleton of Richard Portland-Smith, who had died by his own hand—a hand which had first thrust the barrel of a revolver into his mouth and then pulled the trigger—and that in their considered opinion he must have been of unsound mind at the time to have done such a thing, Mr. Campion felt aware of a distinct wave of relief, a comforting confirmation and a full stop, as it were.

He was sitting beside the man who was his friend and client at the end of a row of church chairs arranged against a wall of the converted army hut, and the scene before him was melancholy and very human. It was a coroner's court in essence, the bare practical bones of that judicial proceeding which has remained sound and useful from far-off simple times. A man had died mysteriously and nine of his countrymen had met together on the common ground of their patrial birth to decide how such a calamity had befallen him. There had been no decoration, no merciful arabesques of judicial pomp to smother the stark proceedings. The witnesses had come to the T-shaped table and muttered their depositions with nervous humility, while the jury had listened stolidly and afterwards shuffled out to the little cloakroom behind the stage on which the Conservative Concerts were held in the spring, and had returned, self-conscious and unhappy, to give their verdict.

Now the coroner with the patchy pink face and the unfortunate air of being unaccustomed to his job wriggled in his chair. He glanced shyly at the four pressmen at the far end of the table, almost, it would seem, in the hope of getting a little appreciation from them, or at least some indication that he had been "all right," and returned to his formalities with the jury.

The witnesses, who had been sitting with their friends around the walls, began to file out into the sunlight and the inspector came across to ask Mr. Campion's companion about the funeral. He was not tactful but he was kindly, and his pleasant Kentish voice rumbled on, explaining with simple practicalness that the shed where the remains now lay was not public property and the owner needed it for his handcart, whose paint was even now blistering in the sun. He added that the local builder, who had been on the jury, was also the undertaker and he had no doubt but that he would be over in a minute, so that no time would be lost.

While the sad little details were being arranged Mr. Campion had leisure to reflect on the evidence which had brought the Sunday-suited jury, with their perpetual jingle of darts medals and their solid, sensible faces, to their conclusions.

The identification had provided the most interesting fifteen minutes of the morning. The brown paper parcels of grey-green rags, the mildewed wallet complete with discoloured notes and visiting cards, and the rusty gun had been first displayed and sworn to by tailor and manservant. Afterwards, even more gruesome, had come the evidence of the self-important little dentist, who had rushed in to rattle off his formidable list of degrees and testify that the dental work in the remains of the dead man's jaw was his own and that it corresponded to his records of Portland-Smith's mouth. He had given place to the county pathologist, who had described the wound in detail and given his opinions on the length of time during which the body must have lain undiscovered.

Finally Mr. Campion's companion had walked to the table, his enormous shoulders held erect and the light from a window high in the wall falling on his white hair, which was silky and theatrically handsome. He had given his word that as far as he knew his son had no worries of sufficient magnitude to drive him to take his life. That had been all. The coroner had summed up and the jury had shambled out. Richard Portland-Smith had retired from the round dance of life while his measure in it was yet incomplete and nobody knew why.

Mr. Campion and his companion walked down the road to the inn where lunch was awaiting them. It was bright and clean in the sunlight, with summer in the air and all that promise of breathless festivity just round the corner which is the spirit of that time of year.

Campion did not speak, since his companion showed no desire to do so, but he glanced at the man out of the corner of his eye and thought that he was taking it very well.

In his own sphere Sir Henry Portland-Smith was a great man. In his hospital in South London he was a hard-working god whose every half-hour was earmarked for some separate and important purpose. This was probably the first morning he had set aside for purely personal considerations during the past twenty years.

Like many great physicians, he had a fine presence allied to enormous physical strength, and although he was nearly seventy his movements were vigorous and decisive. He did not talk until they sat down together in an alcove of the big dining room, which smelt faintly of creosote and plaster from recent restoring. The place was very quiet. They were early and a fleet of little tables, which looked homely and countrified in spite of an effort at sophistication, spread out before them.

"Satisfied?" the old man looked at Campion directly. He had taken off his spectacles and his cold but rather fine grey eyes had that pathetic, naked look which eyes which are normally hidden behind lenses achieve when the barrier is down.

"I think it was a true verdict."

"Unsound mind?"

Campion shrugged his shoulders.

"What *is* unsound mind?" he said helplessly. "It means nothing."

"Merely a form to get round the Christian burial difficulty?" There was bitterness in the query, which was unusual and slightly shocking to find in the old, and Campion, looking up, found himself thinking irrelevantly that if over-busy people keep young they also keep raw, retaining the prejudices and sophistries of their first period. He prepared to listen to an outburst against the hypocrisy of the law and the Church, but it did not come. Sir Henry planted his great elbows on the table and pushed his hands over his face as if he were cleansing it. He had the long, fine hands of the man who does not use them and the younger man remembered that he was not a surgeon.

"I'm trying to make up my mind," he said presently. "I appreciate what you've done, Albert. I like your reticence and your quiet persistence. I'm grateful to you for finding the boy. It's all over now with the least possible scandal. In a few months now he might never have been born."

This time the bitterness was savage and Campion, meeting those old, chilly, naked eyes, was suddenly ashamed of himself for his smugness. He caught one of those sudden panoramic glimpses of a whole thirty-eight-year life and was aware for an instant of the paralysingly infuriating tragedy of waste.

"I want to know," said the old man. "For my own satisfaction I want to know. Now look here, my boy, this is a private matter between you and me. The public aspect of this affair is fixed and finished. Richard is dead. Everybody knows he shot himself. And that is the end. But I want to know why he did it and I want you to find out."

Mr. Campion's pale eyes were intelligent behind his spectacles but he looked uncomfortable.

"You're thinking he may have had a brainstorm?" Sir Henry made the query an accusation. "You're ready to believe in the form, are you? Well, you may be right. But I want to know."

Mr. Campion was an adroit young man and the present situation was not one he had not encountered before.

"I'll do anything I can," he said slowly. "But, after all, we've covered a lot of ground already. You say yourself he must have been very extravagant. He was earning money and could have carried on, but he *had* no money when he died. You think he spent all his mother's legacy on Miss Wells? That is very probable but it is a thing we shall never find out. No one can find out how a man spent the money he drew out in cash three years before. I will do all I can but I can't promise results."

Sir Henry leant back in his chair and surveyed his companion consideringly. He was smiling a little and his magnificent head had never looked more imposing.

"My boy," he said, "I'm going to tell you something. This is a secret. Never let it out of your mouth, whatever happens, but when I tell you, you'll see why I am so anxious that you should carry on."

He hesitated and Campion was puzzled. It was impossible not to be impressed by the other man's manner, nor had he any reason to suspect him of anything faintly theatrical or unsound. In his experience Sir Henry was a sophisticated and in many ways a hard man.

"Yes?" he invited.

"You've seen this girl Georgia Wells, as I asked you?"

"Yes."

"Are you taken with her?"

The question was so unexpected that Campion blinked.

"No," he said truthfully. "I see her attraction but I should never be bowled over by her myself."

"Did she strike you as being a clever woman? Not a bluestocking, of course, but a really clever woman? Clever in the extraordinary way women sometimes are? Clever enough to get a man to do anything she wanted him to by reasoning with him?"

Campion gave the matter serious consideration.

"Not unless he was a fool," he said at last.

"Ah!" The old man pounced on the admission. "I thought not. That's what makes this so very interesting. Richard was not a fool. I would admit it if he was. I haven't been a physician all my life without learning that you can't make a true diagnosis if you falsify the symptoms. Richard was not a fool in that way. He was a virile type, the type to lose his head over a woman for a night but not for a month or two. Once he got his mind working again it would work, whatever his physical inclinations were. Do you follow me?"

"Yes," said Mr. Campion dubiously. "But—forgive me—I don't think this is getting us very far. You see, there's no evidence even of a quarrel. She seems to have been happily engaged to him right up to the time he disappeared."

"Campion"—the old man was leaning across the table—"you've seen that girl and you know her history. Do you honestly think she was the type of woman to be engaged to anybody?"

The younger man stared at him. The question had jerked him round to face a problem which had been chipping away at the back of his mind for some time. Now that it was out, unprotected by the automatic acceptance that is given to a fact that is known to everybody, the whole matter did strike him as extraordinary.

"A woman once through the divorce courts, important in a bohemian profession, doesn't go and get herself involved in a long engagement." Sir Henry's voice was contemptuous. "She gets married, my boy. She gets married."

Campion sat up.

"They were married!" he said blankly. "But that's incredible. She married again. What about Ramillies?"

"Yes, that was six months after Richard disappeared." The old man was speaking earnestly. "After he disappeared, mind you, not after he died. No one knows when he died, although the likelihood is that the two events coincided. But the point I want you to realise is that the

woman knew Richard was dead more than two years before we did.
She must have known it. Why was she so quiet about it?"

He leant back in his chair and surveyed Campion steadily, his fierce
cold eyes hard and intelligent.

Mr. Campion passed his hand over his fair hair.

"Are you sure of this?"

"Absolutely."

"You could prove it?"

"Yes."

"Why didn't you tell me before?"

"I didn't know it for certain until three or four weeks ago and by
then I felt sure the boy was dead. Now that I know roughly when he
died, I am wondering. Whatever we find out, I don't want it made
public. I see no point in that. The publicity would hardly hurt me or
his memory, but I have daughters and they have children, so I see no
reason why the tale should linger on. Let it die with Richard. But I
want to know."

Mr. Campion did not look at ease. His thin, good-humoured face
with the twisted mouth was grave and his eyes thoughtful.

"You put me in a very awkward position," he said at last. "When
I undertook this search for your son I simply felt I was making myself
useful to an old friend of Belle Lafcadio's, and I've been more than
glad to do it, but now I'm afraid I can't go any farther. This woman
Georgia Wells is an important client of my sister's. To get hold of
her I must abuse hospitality there. You see how it is."

He paused apologetically, and the old man watched him, a faint
smile playing round the corners of his mouth.

"I'm hardly contemplating revenge," he observed.

"No. I did realise that." Campion was hesitating and unhappy. "But
this marriage alters the whole complexion of the business."

"I think so. It makes it very curious."

Campion was silent, and after a while Sir Henry went on.

"My boy," he said, "I'm an old man who's seen a great deal, and I
don't like mysteries. My son's death was a shock to my affections, of
course, but it was also a shock of surprise. I simply want to know what
the circumstances were that induced Richard, who was no neurotic,
to take his life, and why that woman should never have told what she
must have known. Don't make a mouthful of it, but if you should
ever find out, remember I want to know."

Campion raised his head.

"I'll do what I can," he said, "but don't rely on me."

"Very well," said the old physician, and changed the subject abruptly.

For the rest of the meal they discussed the Abominable Snowman and other sedate fripperies, but as Campion drove back to London a thought slipped quietly into his mind and sat there nagging at him.

Georgia Wells had not been sure of Portland-Smith's death until the day on which the discovery of his body had been reported in the newspapers: of that Campion was only fairly certain; but there was one point upon which he was prepared to stake his all, and that was that she had no idea that her ex-husband had committed suicide until Campion himself had told her.

CHAPTER SIX

It was a little over six weeks later, one evening when the summer was at its height and London was sprawling, dirty and happily voluptuous, in the yellow evening sun, that Mr. Campion, letting himself into the flat, was accosted by a hoarse voice from the bathroom.

"Your sis rang up. She's coming round with a Frog of some sort."

Not wishing to snub, but at the same time hoping to convey some disapproval at the lack of ceremony, Mr. Campion passed on to the sitting room without comment.

He had seated himself at the desk, found some cigarettes and pulled a sheet of notepaper towards him before there was a lumbering in the passage outside and a vast, melancholy figure in a black velvet coat surged breathily into the room.

Mr. Lugg, Mr. Campion's "male person's gentleman," regarded his employer with reproachful little black eyes.

"You 'eard," he said, and added with charming confiding, "I was cleanin' meself up. You'd do well to put on a dressing gown and a belt."

"A belt?" enquired Campion, taken off his guard.

"Braces is low, except when worn with a white waistcoat for billiards." Lugg made the pronouncement with justifiable pride. "I picked that up down at the club today. You'll 'ave to get a new robe, too. Mr. Tuke's young feller has a different-coloured one for every day of the week. What d'you say to that idea?"

"Slightly disgusting."

Lugg considered, his eyes flickering.

"I tell 'im it was pansy," he admitted, "but I couldn't be sure. It was a shot in the dark. 'Robe,' though; make a note of that. 'Robe's' the new name for dressing gown. I'm learnin' a lot from Mr. Tuke. He lent me 'is book, for one thing."

Campion threw down his pen.

"You're learning to read, are you?" he said pleasantly. "That's good. That'll keep us both quiet."

Mr. Lugg let down the flap of the cocktail cabinet with elaborate care before he deigned to reply.

"Silence is like sleep," he observed with unnatural solemnity. "It refreshes wisdom."

"Eh?" said Mr. Campion.

A slow, smug smile passed over the great white face and Mr. Lugg coughed.

"That give you something to think about," he said with satisfaction. "D'you know 'oo thought of it? Walter Plato."

"Really?" Mr. Campion was gratified. "And who was he?"

"A bloke." The scholar did not seem anxious to pursue the matter further, but afterwards, unwilling to lessen any impression he might have made, he spurred himself to a further flight. "'Im what give 'is name to the term 'platitude.'" He threw the piece of information over his shoulder with all the nonchalance of the finest academic tradition and peered round to see the effect.

He was rewarded. Mr. Campion appeared to have been stricken dumb.

"Is that in the book?" he enquired humbly after a pause.

"I expec' so," said Lugg, adding magnificently, "I read it somewhere. Mr. Tuke's getting me interested in education. Education is the final stamp of good class, that's what 'e says."

"And a belt," murmured Campion. "Don't forget that."

The fat man heaved himself towards the desk.

"Look 'ere," he said belligerently, "I expected somethin' like this. Every step I've took in an upward direction you've done your best to nark. Now I'm on to somethin' useful. I'm goin' to educate myself, and then I'll never feel inferior, not with anybody, see?"

"My dear chap——" Mr. Campion was touched. "You don't feel inferior with anybody now, surely, do you? Lay off, Lugg. This is a horrible line."

The other man regarded him shrewdly. His little black eyes were winking, and there was a certain sheepishness in his expression which was out of character.

"Not with you, of course, cock," he conceded affectionately. "But I do with Mr. Tuke. 'E thinks about it. Still, let 'im wait."

"Is it *all* in the book?" enquired Mr. Campion, whom the idea seemed to fascinate.

"A ruddy great lot of it is." Mr. Lugg wrestled with his pocket. "I'll be as hot as most when I get this on board." He produced a small dictionary of quotations and laid it metaphorically at Mr. Campion's feet. "I'm leavin' out the Yiddish," he remarked as they turned over the pages together. "See that bit there? And there's another over 'ere."

Campion sighed.

"It may be Yiddish to you, guv'nor," he murmured, "but it's Greek to me. These two lads Milt and Shakes get an unfair look-in, don't they?"

"They're all all right." Lugg was magnanimous. "But when I get good I'll do me own quotations. A quotation's only a short neat way of sayin' somethin' everybody knows, like '*It's crackers to slip a rozzer the dropsy in snide.*' That's the sort of thing. Only you want it to be about somethin' less 'omely . . . women and such."

Mr. Campion seemed rather taken with the idea of running a line in personal quotations on the system of "every man his own poet," and Lugg was gratified.

"I don't often get you goin'," he observed with satisfaction. "Lucky I 'it on this; it might have been religion. There's a bloke at the club——"

"No," said Mr. Campion, pulling himself together. "No, old boy. No, really. Not now."

"That's what I tell 'im." Lugg was cheerful. "I'll come to it, I says, but not now. I'm sorry, mate, but I don't see yer as a brother yet. Which reminds me—what about your sis? She'll be 'ere any minute. What's she up to? She's in with a funny crowd, isn't she?"

"Val? I don't think so."

Lugg sniffed. "I do. Mr. Tuke tell me in confidence that 'e 'eard someone pass a remark about seein' 'er at a luncheon party at the Tulip with a very funny lot . . . that bloke Ramillies, for one."

Once more Mr. Campion pushed his letter aside, faint distaste on his face.

"Of course we don't want to go listenin' to servants' gossip," continued Lugg happily, "but I like that girl and I wouldn't like to see 'er mixed up with a chap like Ramillies."

He pronounced the name with such a wealth of disgust that his employer's interest was stirred in spite of himself.

"I've met Sir Raymond Ramillies," he said.

"'Ave yer?" The black eyes expressed disapproval. "I ain't and I don't want to. A ruddy awful chap. 'Ide your wife in a ditch rather than let 'im set eyes on her. 'E's a proper blot. I tell you what, if you 'ad to set in public court and 'ear a beak talkin' to 'im after the sentence you'd 'ave to turn your 'ead away. You'd blush; that's a fact."

"That's slander," said Campion mildly. "The man's never been in the dock in his life."

"And wot's that?" Lugg was virtuous. "As you very well know, there's a lot of people walkin' about today 'oo ought to be in the jug by rights. 'E 'appens to be one of them, that's all."

Long experience had taught Mr. Campion not to argue with his aide in this mood, but he felt bound to protest.

"You mustn't drivel libel about people. You're like a woman."

"Ho!" The insult penetrated the skin and Mr. Lugg's mountainous form quivered. "You've got no right to say a thing like that, cock," he said earnestly. "I know what I'm sayin'. Sir Ramillies is mud, not so good as mud. He's done one man in, to my certain knowledge, and the army tales about 'im make my 'air curl, wherever it may be now. 'Ere's an instance. Take the time of the Irish trouble. There was a couple of fellers come over to England after 'im. They were lookin' for 'im, I admit that, but neither of 'em 'ad a gun. They lay for 'im up in Hampstead where 'e used to live. 'E spotted 'em and went for 'em quick as a flash. 'E caught one chap and killed 'im with 'is bare 'ands—broke 'is neck. The bloke was on the run, mind you, but Ramillies got 'im by the 'air and forced 'is chin up until 'e 'eard 'is neck go. 'E was only a little feller. It was 'ushed up when they found out the lads were reely after 'im and it was self-defence, and Ramillies was ruddy pleased with 'imself. Saw 'imself a Tarzan. I don't know what you think about it but it don't sound quite nice to me; not at all the article. It's downright brutish, look at it how you like. Put me off the chap for life. It's not respectable to lose your temper like that. Makes you no better than an animal. It's dangerous, for one thing."

The story was certainly not attractive, and it occurred to Mr. Campion that it was unfortunate that, having met Ramillies, it did not strike him as being obviously untrue.

"Do you know this for a fact?"

"Of course I do." Lugg was contemptuous. "I 'ad a drink with the other bloke. 'E *was* in a state—not frightened, you know, but shook. There's other tales about Ramillies not as pretty as that. I wouldn't soil yer ears with 'em. 'E's not the bloke for your sis to sit down to table with, not if she was in Salvation Army uniform, take it from me."

Mr. Campion said no more. He remained sitting at his desk with his head slightly on one side and an introspective expression in his eyes.

He was still there, drumming idly on the blotter with his long thin fingers, when the doorbell buzzed and a subtle change came over Mr. Lugg.

He straightened his back from his ministrations at the cocktail cabinet and padded over to the wall mirror, where he settled his collar, arranging his chins upon its white pedestal with great care. Having thus set the stage, he pulled a silk handkerchief out of his side pocket and gave his glistening head a good rub with it, using it immediately afterwards to give a flick to the toe of each patent-leather pump. Then he pulled himself up to attention and, turning all in one piece with his plump hands flat against his sides, he tottered from the room.

A moment or so later he returned with an expressionless face and the words "This way, please. 'E'll see you and be 'appy to," uttered in a voice so affected in tone and quality that the announcement was barely comprehensible.

Val came in hurriedly. She looked very charming in her black suit with the faintly military air about it, and with her came all that fragrance and flutter which has been the hallmark of the "lovely lady" since Mme. de Maintenon discovered it. She was so vivacious and determinedly gay that Campion did not notice any change in her for some time.

Behind her came a stranger whose personality was instantly and engagingly apparent.

Georgy Laminoff, or Gaiogi, as his friends called him, with the g's hard, was a delightful person. The art of being delightful was with him a life study, and, since he was no fool and at heart a prince, he achieved an excellence in it. To look at, he was round and gracious, with a small white beard and bright circular eyes in sockets as arched and sombre as Norman gateways.

He took Mr. Campion's hand with a murmur of apology which came from his soul. It was an intrusion, he insisted, an abominable and disgusting thing, but Val had assured him that it would be forgiven and he was happy to note from the very amiability of his host's expression that it was indeed miraculously so. He seated himself when bidden, conveying without saying so that the chair was incomparably comfortable and that he knew and appreciated the superb quality of the sherry which had been offered him.

Within five minutes of his arrival they were sitting round in pleasant intimacy. The ice had melted rather than broken, and yet his behaviour had never deviated for a moment from that exact formality which is the rightful protection of every man against the stranger within his doors.

Val leant back in the winged chair, unaware that she was irritating her brother, who, for some reason of his own, did not like to see a woman sitting in it.

"We've got a nice new job for you, my lamb," she said. "Something easy and vulgar. How would you like to bring your boots and have a slap-up week end with all the comforts of the rich, and the rare intellectual treat of mingling with the best people—all for nothing? What about it?"

Laminoff made a deprecating gesture with a spade-shaped hand. "I am embarrassed," he said. "We are unpleasant, ignorant people. I shall commit suicide." He chuckled with sudden happiness. "I talk like all the best plays."

"Anything except divorce," said Campion cheerfully. "Divorce and the joke's over. I'd rather go back to my people."

"Oh no." Gaiogi was shocked. "No, no, we are not indecent. Good God, no. This is at least honest vulgarity. Mr. Campion, will you come and stay in my house over the week end? I ask you so that, should I have need to call upon my guest for assistance, assistance he cannot by all the laws of hospitality refuse me, I shall have in him someone who will be an asset and not an encumbrance."

He leant back and laughed until his eyes were shining with tears. "I rehearsed that coming along. It sounds a little false."

They both looked at him, Val with tolerant amusement and Mr. Campion with simple interest.

"Having trouble?"

"No." Gaiogi was still laughing, and he glanced at Val with that shyness which comes from the intellect rather than from any social embarrassment. "We are here on false pretences."

"Not at all." Val spoke briskly, her voice a little harder than usual. "It's Ramillies," she said.

"Really?" Mr. Campion hoped he did not sound cautious. "What's he done now?"

"Nothing yet, thank God." Val was obstinately bright. "He's going to Boohoo Land, or wherever it is, on Sunday, in a gold aeroplane, and we just thought we'd like you about to see he does go."

"In a gold aeroplane?"

"Gold. The propeller hub may be studded with diamonds." Gaiogi made the announcement gravely and Campion raised his eyebrows. "Quite the gent," he commented politely. "How serious is all this?" Val rose, and as the light fell upon her face her brother looked at her sharply. He had not seen her quite so fine drawn before.

"I'm not very clear about all this," he said. "Explain it all to me without effects. Ramillies is going back to Ulangi, is he? Alone?"

"Yes. Georgia is going out to join him in six weeks time, with a wild party. The Taretons and that lot."

"That should be jolly." Campion spoke without enthusiasm.

"Riotous," she agreed. "Paul Tareton is taking 'three girls from totally different environments,' and Mrs. has selected one rather beastly little boy called Waffle. Still, that's their *après-midi*, not ours. Our concern is that nothing goes wrong with the flight. Gaiogi was telling Tante Marthe his troubles and she sent us both along to you."

"Ah yes, the flight," said Campion. "Start at the flight."

"The flight is not exactly an attempt upon the record"—Val's brightness was growing more and more artificial—"except that no one has ever taken the trouble to fly from England to Ulangi before. I wonder you haven't heard about all this, Albert. There's been enough publicity."

At the mention of the magic word Campion began to see a little daylight.

"The plane is being sent out as a present to the native ruler," she said. "It's an Alandel machine, and it's taking off from the Caesar's Court flying ground at six o'clock on Sunday night. In it go the pilot and a navigator and Ramillies. He insisted that they paint it gold. He said the man would like it better, and pointed out that if you paint a thing silver there's no reason why you shouldn't paint it gold. I think Gaiogi made up the diamonds. Anyway, the airmen will stay and instruct the coloured gentleman how not to break his neck, and Ramillies will tidy the house up ready for Georgia. On Sunday there is to be a semiofficial send-off, with Towser from the Colonial Office and one or two other bigwigs, and the whole thing is to be stage-managed gracefully. Gaiogi is anxious that nothing shall go wrong."

"I can understand that." Campion sounded sympathetic. "Is there any reason why anything should?"

Val glanced at the Russian before she spoke.

"No," she said at last but without conviction. "No, I don't think so. No, none at all. You just come down for the week end. We shall all be there. You can even bring Lugg, if he'll behave."

"I'm sorry, my dear. It sounds fishy." Campion filled her glass as he spoke. "Don't think me inquisitive, but I must have a bit more to go on. It's my luggage I'm worrying about. Do I bring a knuckle-duster and a chloroform spray, or merely my etiquette book?"

"The chloroform spray, I should say, wouldn't you, Gaiogi?" Val was not entirely flippant, and the old man laughed at her before he turned his round eyes towards Campion.

"I hope not," he said, "but who can tell? That is the difference between the world of my youth and the world of today. Then I was bored because nothing could happen; now I am apprehensive because nothing couldn't. I am living my life backwards, my exciting youth last."

"Gaiogi doesn't feel Ramillies is quite safe," Val remarked. "I know what he means."

So did Campion, but he made no comment and she continued.

"There's been some little trouble about a gun already. He wants to take one out with him and the flying people are jibbing about the weight. Anyhow, it's not the sort of thing he ought to want out there, is it?"

"I don't know. It's not a cannon, I suppose?"

"Sir Raymond wishes to take out a Filmer 5A," said Laminoff calmly. "He does not see why he should not take it to pieces and stow it under the seat, together with enough ammunition to kill every elephant in Africa. Do you know the new 5A, Mr. Campion?"

"Good Lord, that's not the big one, is it? The mounted one with the magazine? Really? What does he want that for?"

"No one likes to ask," said Val dryly. "Anyway, he can't take it. Alan Dell had to make that clear to him himself. Ramillies flew into one of his idiotic rages, came out of it, and is now sulking with a watch-what-I'm-going-to-do air about him, which is disturbing. We don't want him making a scene just when everything is set for the take-off, or getting tight and trying to take the machine up himself ten minutes before the official time. I'd like you down there anyway. Don't be a cad."

"My dear girl, I'm coming. Nothing would keep me away." Campion sounded sincere. "The suggestion is that Ramillies is slightly barmy, I take it?"

"No, no, spoilt," murmured Gaiogi tolerantly. "Too much money all his life, mental age thirteen. A superb soldier, no doubt."

Val wriggled her shoulders under her severe little coat.

"He's abnormal," she said. "I dislike having him in the house in case something awful happens to him while he's there. A thunder-bolt, perhaps. You know what I mean."

Gaiogi was delighted.

"Val is right. He has an impious challenge," he agreed, grinning at the phrase. "That is the analysis of my own alarm. He should be exorcised."

"He should be watched," said Val, who seemed to have set her heart on being practical at all costs. "That's fixed then, is it, Albert? We can rely on you to come on Saturday? You're a pet. We're terribly grateful. Gaiogi has to rush off now to catch Ferdie Paul, but I'll stay half an hour with you if I may."

Her announcement was so brusque that it constituted a dismissal and Campion regarded her with respectful astonishment. Laminoff rose.

"We shall be delighted to see you," he said earnestly. "My wife and I have a little cottage in the grounds and we will entertain you there." He glanced at Val and smiled shyly. "It is more comfortable than in the hotel."

"It's the loveliest house in the world," she assured him and he seemed pleased.

He left them gracefully, making the awkward business of departure a charming experience for everyone concerned, and went away, leaving them liking him and, for some inexplicable reason, gratified by the interview, although it had simply served to arrange something he desired.

"Nice old boy," Mr. Campion observed when they were alone.

"A dear. The only genuine Russian prince I've ever met." Val wandered down the room to look out of the window as she spoke. "He lived in Mentone before the Revolution, toddling home now and again for the wolfing or the ballet or whatever they had at home. His wife said that they were miserable, really miserable; you know what wet blankets Russians were."

"Cried each other to sleep every night," suggested Mr. Campion helpfully.

"That sort of thing." Val was not listening to him. "Then they lost all and life began anew. Gaiogi has princely ideas, real ones. He understands organisation as well as magnificence. Just the man for a luxury hotel. He's a prince with a point to him and he's hysterically happy. I'd hate anything really unpleasant to happen in that little kingdom."

Mr. Campion took up the decanter.

"Sit down," he said. "I'm not being critical but do you think you're being a bit nervy? I mean, old Ramillies may have a spot of the devil in him, but the horns haven't actually appeared yet. He evidently understands his job. That gilded aeroplane idea shows a certain amount of practical insight. You can't convince a Gold Coast nigger that silver isn't an inferior metal. He's probably quite all right in a limited way, once you get to know him. Don't think I'm not going down to Caesar's Court; I am. I want to. I only felt it was a bit hysterical, this roaring round here yourself to bring Laminoff and making a great to-do about it. You could have phoned me."

Val sat down on the couch and closed her eyes.

"It's amazing about relations," she observed after a pause. "You're a pleasant, reasonable person. You'd never be so cruelly hypercritical of any other woman. Why shouldn't I be hysterical? I'm not, as it happens, but if I was why shouldn't I?"

Mr. Campion was temporarily taken aback.

"One naturally expects one's relatives to behave with the decorum one demands of oneself," he said primly. "Hysteria doesn't run in our family."

"Oh, doesn't it?" said Val. "Like to hear me scream the place down? Give me something to drink."

"Have some gin in it and have a lovely sick?" he suggested.

She laughed and sat up. She had pulled off her ridiculous hat and her yellow hair was very slightly dishevelled. She looked young and clever and tolerantly disgusted with herself. She glanced up at him and spoke wearily.

"'Ardy, 'Ardy, I am wownded."

"Not seriously, I 'ope?" enquired Campion solicitously, dropping into the nursery joke of their youth without noticing it.

"Mort-u-ally, I fear."

"Really? What's up?"

"Unrequited love." She was still speaking lightly but with a certain breathlessness which made the words uncertain.

"Oh?" He did not sound very sympathetic. "If I may say so without being indelicate, it looked very healthy last time I saw you both."

"Did it? You're a detective of some sort, aren't you?" A change in her voice, a certain hardness, almost a cheapness, that was a stranger there, caught Mr. Campion's attention and silenced the flippant remark on his lips. He had known that sickening deterioration himself in his time and, while he still found it infuriating in himself or anyone else who might be part of his own personal secret dignity, he was not entirely without pity for it.

"These things happen," he said awkwardly, trying to sound sympathetic without inviting confidence. "It's all part of the dance."

Val laughed at him. She was genuinely amused and he was relieved to notice a slackening of the emotional tension in her voice.

"You're just the person not to come and cry to, aren't you?" she said. "You look as though you're going to be ill already. I'm all right, ducky. I'm only telling you I'm feeling like suicide because Georgia Wells has pinched my young man. You might at least say you're sorry. If I told you I was broke or had a twisted ankle you'd be flapping about like a mother chicken."

"Hen," said Campion absently. "Hen is the word you want. What do you mean when you say pinched? Has Georgia merely abducted Dell? Or has she dazzled him? I mean, has the situation come about because the fellow wants to hang round or because he's too polite to slash his way out of the palisade?"

Val lay back again. She was having great difficulty with the cigarette between her lips and her eyes were startled at her own weakness.

"No," she said at last. "No, I think it's quite genuine. It does happen, you know. She's simply knocked him off his feet. He's rather added what he *knows* of me to what he's *seen* of her, if you see what I mean."

Mr. Campion did see and he looked at her with one of those sharp glances which betrayed his surprise. Her insight was always astonishing him. It was misleading, he reminded himself hastily; a sort of inspired guesswork or, rather, an intermittent contact with truth.

"He certainly didn't know much about women," he remarked. "He'll learn a bit from Georgia."

Val did not speak and he went on without thinking of her in any objective way. He was aware of her, of course, but only as of someone whom he considered another facet of himself.

"A man like that ought to fall in love a few times. It matures the mind. He can't marry her, of course, because of Ramillies. In a way that's almost a pity because, in a case like that, that type of decent, rather sentimental chap is apt to go off and nurse a lovely pie-eyed dream of tragical frustration for a hell of a time."

He caught sight of her white face with the two tears on her cheekbones and jerked himself up with sudden contrition.

"My dear girl, forgive me. I was thinking aloud. I forgot you were in this. I'm mental. Oi! Val! Val, I'm sorry. I'm a tick. What shall we do? Go and chuck the woman in the Regent's Canal? What's she doing, by the way? Accepting it all with fashionable languor?"

"Oh no." Val's lips twisted. "You underestimate her. Georgia doesn't do things like that. Georgia loves. She always does. She's riotously, deliriously, ecstatically in love at the moment. She's a fire, a whirlwind. She comes and tells me about it by the hour. I rushed off with Gaiogi this afternoon to get away from her. She's so heart-rend-ingly genuine, Albert, like all the worst in one's self."

Mr. Campion looked scandalised and his sympathy for his sister in-creased.

"That's not quite decent," he remarked. "How startlingly vulgar you women are."

"It's not vulgarity. It's cheating," said Val calmly. "You do so hope you're not really hurting, but you do want to do it so much. I know the instinct. It's a feeling, not a 'think' at all."

Mr. Campion made no direct comment.

"Is Ramillies in on all this?" he enquired at last.

"Oh yes. Georgia's like a house on fire. It can't be kept a secret for the rest of the street, much less from the master in the library. Ramil-lies knows more about it than anyone."

"What's he doing? Anything?"

"I don't know." Val sounded uneasy. "He's a very curious person. When I can bring myself to listen to her Georgia seems to be taking him very seriously. She says he's frightfully jealous and frighteningly quiet, but that may mean anything or nothing. He seems to have set his heart on having this party out there with the Taretons. Georgia's not so keen. She says that once she gets out there he'll make her stay. That'll be awkward because *The Lover* looks like settling down, and whereas they could risk dropping her out for a month, if it was running away, I doubt whether it would carry on for a full season without her. It might, of course. It's a success."

"In six weeks time," said Mr. Campion thoughtfully. "I'm not at all sure that my estimation of Sieur Ramillies doesn't go up. The grand passion should just about reach the wobbling point by then. These thundering fires die down pretty fast, don't they?"

He paused. Val was looking at him with a speculative expression that was not altogether sympathetic.

"You've forgotten Alan," she said. "Alan's in it too. He's a different kettle of fish altogether. It's not so simple, my dear. Frankly I wish it were. They're not children. It might so easily be very serious."

"You mean Ramillies might divorce her?"

"Not because of Alan. He'd never get grounds. You don't know Alan at all. He's an idealist."

"Well, then, it'll come to a quiet, uncomfortable end and you'll have to stand by and pick up the pieces," said Campion, a little irri-tated by what he felt was an unjust estimation of his powers of com-prehension.

"Yes," said Val slowly. She shivered and stretched herself with a graceful, furtive movement like a little cat. "I envy those women who just love normally and nobly with their bodies," she observed unexpectedly. "Then they're only engulfed by a sort of lovely high tragedy. The hero persists. That's at least decent. Once you cultivate your mind you lay yourself open to low tragedy, the mingy, dirty little tragedy of making an ass of yourself over an ordinary poor little bloke. Female women love so abjectly that a reasonable hard-working mind becomes a responsibility. It's a cruelty that shouldn't have to be endured. I tell you I'd rather die than have to face it that he was neither better nor even more intelligent than I am!"

Her passionate sincerity demanded his consideration and he looked at her helplessly.

"You're asking rather a lot of him, old girl, aren't you?"

"Yes, I know." Val rose to her feet. "That's what I'm kicking at. I'm asking much too much of most men. I've so constructed myself that I've either got to ask too much or go maternal. Anyway, that's how it looks to me when I pull myself together and remember that I'm one of the most important business women in Europe, with a reputation to keep up and a staff to look after."

She looked very slim and small standing on his hearthrug and it came to him with something of a shock that she was not overestimating herself.

"Do you always see your—er—passion in this slightly inhuman light?"

"No." She glanced down at her exquisitely cut shoes, which a Viennese manufacturer had materialised from her design. "No, my other viewpoint is ordinary and howlingly undignified. I wish she were dead."

She met his eyes with sudden fire.

"My God, I hate her," she said.

Mr. Campion blinked. "I can't do her in," he said.

"Of course not. Don't be an ape." She was laughing. "Don't take any notice of me. I am nervy, very nervy. I had no idea I could behave like this. It's come rather late—I ought to be twenty-two to feel like this and enjoy it—and it's frightened me for the time being. Look here, all I want you to do is to see that Ramillies goes quietly out of the country without any fuss on Sunday. Then Georgia will follow him in six weeks time and meanwhile——"

She broke off so sharply that he was startled.

"Meanwhile what?"

"Meanwhile Alan will at least be safe physically."

"Who from? Ramillies? My poor girl, you're cuckoo. Husbands

don't go around pigsticking their rivals these days. They seize another woman and sit showing off with her at the other end of the drawing room until the wife's boy friend leaves out of sheer embarrassment."

Val was not disarmed.

"You're *vieux jeu*, my pet," she said. "Like most men you're between three and five years out of date. Don't you notice a change in the fashion? Gaiogi's right. Today anything can happen. People can wear *anything*, say *anything*, do *anything*. It's the motif of the moment; look at the waistline. Besides, consider Ramillies. He's a man who might have taken up a blasé attitude if he thought it would be in any way shocking. Nowadays it's not. It's dull, it's ordinary, it's provincial. D'you know, last week the most fashionable woman in London rushed in to tell me that her husband had thrashed her within an inch of her life and pitched her boy friend through a first-story window into a holly hedge. She was scandalised but terribly excited."

"Dear me," said Mr. Campion mildly. "You matched up her black eye in your new *peau de pêche noir*, I hope? Oh well, you surprise me. The old man must catch up on his homework. Let me get this straight. You seriously think that Sir Raymond Ramillies is capable of making a physical assault on Alan Dell?"

"I know he's capable of it," said Val bluntly. "I'm telling you that I'm haunted by the idea that it's likely. Naturally I'm bothered because I can't tell if my worry is reasonable or just some silly physical reaction. I do have to explain things in detail to you. I thought you were so hot on understanding people."

"I've been cheating all these years. I'm really Alice in Wonderland," said Mr. Campion humbly. "Still, I'm picking up a crumb or two now in my fiddling little way. What am I expected to do? Stand by to plant my body between them to stop the bullet?"

"Oh, darling, don't be a lout." Val was at her sweedling best. "I don't know what I want. Can't you see that? Just be about. I'm frightened of Ramillies. I don't think he'd simply hit out like a Christian, but I think he might do something—something—well, elaborate. That's the impression he gives me. I'm uneasy with him. After all, there was Portland-Smith, you know."

Mr. Campion's eyelids drooped.

"What about Portland-Smith?" he said. "He committed suicide."

"How do you know?"

"I do. There's no doubt about it."

Val shrugged her shoulders.

"It was very convenient for Ramillies, wasn't it?" she said, sweeping away the facts with a carelessness that left him helpless. "There's been no end of chatter about it in the last few weeks."

"Then someone will get into trouble," Campion insisted firmly. "That's pure slander."

"You can't have smoke without fire, my dear," said Val, and he could have slapped her because she was both unreasonable and quite right. "Now I'm going," she said. "Don't come down with me. I'm sorry I've behaved like a neurotic. You ought to fall in love yourself sometime and get the angle."

He did not answer her immediately but when he looked up his eyes were apologetic.

"It wouldn't take me like that, you know," he remarked seriously.

"Evidently not."

"Why?"

"Well, where is she?" Val's glance round the room was expressive and she went off, leaving him reflecting that the gentle, conservative dog with his taboos, his conscience and his ideals was a rather pathetic, defenceless animal beside his ruthless, hag-ridden sister, the cat.

Lugg's stomach appeared round the doorway.

"Sex rearin' its ugly 'ead again, eh?" he remarked, coming into fuller view. "I didn't 'ear 'er speak because I kep' in the kitchen like a gent, but you can see it in 'er face, can't you? Funny, we seem to 'ave struck a patch of it lately. It's pitch, sex is. Once you touch it, it clings to you. Why don't you sneak off and come on this cruise we're always talking about? Crime's vulgar enough, but sex crime is common. There's no other word for it. 'Oo's she in love with? 'Andle to 'is name?"

Mr. Campion regarded him with disgust.

"You turn my stomach," he said. "I believe if you had a fortune you'd try to buy a title."

"No, I wouldn't." Lugg appeared to be giving the suggestion more serious thought than it warranted. "Not a title. I wouldn't mind being a councillor of a nice classy little burrow. That's about my mark. I'm sorry about your sis but we can't 'elp 'er troubles. You look out. I don't like sex. Remember the setout we 'ad down in the country. Which reminds me, I 'ad a note from my little mate the other day. Like to see it? She's at boarding school."

He waddled over to the bureau and pulled open the bottom drawer.

" 'Ere you are," he said with the nonchalance that ill disguises bursting pride. "Not bad for a kid, is it?"

Mr. Campion took the inky square of expensive notepaper and glanced at the embossed address.

The Convent of the Holy Sepulchre
Lording
Dorset

DEAR MR. LUG [the handwriting was enormous and abominable] *I am
at scool. Here we speak French. Some of the nuns like the tricks you
showed me and some do not. I have written "I must not swindle"
50 times for S. Mary Therese but S. Mary Anna laffed. I am going
to read the Gompleat works of William Shakespeare.*

> *Lots and lots of love from*
> SARAH.

Mr. Lugg put the note back among his better shirts, which he insisted on keeping in the bureau in defiance of all objections.

"I could 'ave done a lot with that poor little bit if I'd 'ad the edu-
catin' of 'er," he remarked regretfully. "Still, she'd 'ave bin a nuisance,
you know. Per'aps she's better off, reelly, with them nuns."

"Indeed, perhaps so," said Mr. Campion not without derision.

Lugg straightened his back and regarded his employer under fat
white eyelids.

"I found this 'ere in one of yer suits," he said, feeling in his waistcoat pocket. "I've bin waitin' for an opportunity to give it to you. There
you are: a little yeller button. It came off one of Mrs. Sutane's dresses,
I think. Correc' me if I'm wrong."

Mr. Campion took the button, turned it over and pitched it out of
the open window into the street below. He said nothing and his face
was an amiable blank.

Mr. Lugg's complacent expression vanished and he pulled his collar
off.

"I'm more comfortable without it," he remarked in the tone of one
making pleasant conversation under difficulties. "Now the company's
gone I can let out the compression. Blest came in while you was talkin'
to your sis. I tell 'im you was busy. I give 'im the end of one of my
old bottles and made 'im leave a message."

"Oh?" Mr. Campion seemed mildly interested. "And how did the
ex-inspector take that from the ex-Borstal prefect?"

"Drunk up every drop like a starvin' kitty." Mr. Lugg's conversational powers increased with his anxiety. "It did me good to see 'im.
''Ave another mite of the wages of virtue, mate,' I said, smellin' another 'arf empty, but he wouldn't stop. Said 'e'd phone you, and meanwhile you might like to know that 'e'd found a little church down in
Putney with some very interesting records of a wedding three and a

'alf years ago. 'E wouldn't tell me 'oo the parties were; said you'd
know and that it was all okay, he'd got the doings."

"Anything else?"

"Yus. Wait a minute. 'Ullo, that's the bell. It would be." Mr. Lugg
fumbled with his collar again. "It's comin' back to me," he said breathlessly in the midst of his struggle. "He said did you know there was
someone else snouting around for the same information less than a
week ago, and if it was news to you, did you think it funny?"

He lumbered out into the passage. Mr. Campion's eyebrows rose.

"Damn funny," he said.

He was still lost in unquiet thought when the fat man reappeared,
his face shining.

"Look 'ere," he said with even less ceremony than usual, "look 'ere.
Look what I've found on the doorstep. 'Ere's a bottle o' milk for you."

Mr. Campion raised his eyes to the newcomer and for an instant
he did not recognise the heart-shaped face with the triangular smile
and the expression that was as resourceful, as eager and as infinitely
young as when he had last seen it six years before.

"Hullo, Orph," said Amanda Fitton. "The lieut. has come to report.
This is a nice thing to get in my face when I look up at your window
for the first time in six years."

She held out a small brown paw and displayed a yellow button
with a rose painted on it lying in the palm.

"Thank you, Amanda." Mr. Campion took the button and pocketed
it. "It burst off my waistcoat as my heart leapt at your approach. A
most extraordinary phenomenon. I wondered what on earth it was.
Why did you come? I mean, nothing wrong, I hope?"

Amanda pulled off her hat and the full glory of the Pontisbright
hair glowed in the evening light.

"It's about my chief, Alan Dell," she said, "and frightfully confidential. I say, Albert, you don't know a man called Ramillies, do you?"

CHAPTER SEVEN

Mr. Campion leant back in the taxicab, which smelt like the inside
of the dressing-up trunk in the attic of his childhood's home, and
glanced at the shadowy form beside him with a return of a respect he
had forgotten. The six years between eighteen and twenty-four had

certainly not robbed Amanda of her pep. On the whole he was inclined to think they must have added power to her elbow.

It was now a little after twelve, and the night, it seemed, was yet a babe.

"What I still don't understand is how you got there," he said. "I thought aeroplane works were holies of holies."

"So they are." Amanda sounded cheerful in the darkness. "It took me three and a half years to do it, but I'm a pretty good engineer, you know. I went straight into the shops when I got some money. I hadn't a sufficiently decent education to take an ordinary degree so I had to go the back way. My title helped, though," she added honestly.

"Did it? What does your brother say about it?"

"The little earl?" Lady Amanda Fitton's respect for young Hal did not seem to have increased. "He's still at Oxford. He seemed to be dying of old age last time I saw him. He's given me up for the time being. Aunt Hat says he's gathering strength. Meanwhile don't take your mind off the business in hand. This is serious. I'm up here on a sacred mission. You don't seem to realise that. The man Ramillies and his crowd must be called off A.D. What am I going to tell the boys?"

Mr. Campion stirred.

"Amanda," he enquired, "was I a hero in my youth?"

"A hero? No, of course not. What's the matter with you?" She was surprised. "You've got introspective or had a serious illness or something. You were a useful, dependable sort of person and the only soul I could think of to come to in this idiotic mess. Besides, in view of one thing and another, I thought you might know something about it already. Look here, you forget about yourself for a minute and consider the situation. Here's a man—a genius, Albert; there's no one like him—and in the middle of serious and important work he's got hold of by the wretched Ramillies and his crowd and taken completely off his course. It's a frightful calamity; you must see that. We can't get on without him. The whole machine room is held up. Drawings are waiting for his okay. Specimen parts are ready to be tried out. All kinds of details you wouldn't understand. . . . And it's not only that. There's the morale of the whole place to consider. He's endangering it. We stuck it as long as we could and then Sid sent me up to find out how bad things really were. We talked it all over and decided that real loyalty isn't just sentimental and unpractical. A.D. has been got at. He's a child in some things. He must be persuaded back to work."

Mr. Campion, thirty-eight next birthday, was aware of a chill. It began in the soles of his feet and swept up over him in a tingling wave. Behind Amanda's story he had caught a glimpse of a world which he had practically forgotten. In many ways it was an idiotic, exasperating but tremendously exciting world wherein incredible dreams fed fine enthusiasms and led to fierce consultations, pathetically noble sacrifices and astounding feats of endeavour, to say nothing of heights of impudence which made one giddy even in considering them.

"You're all pretty young down there, I suppose?" he ventured.

"A lot of us are. A.D.'s wonderful like that." Amanda's eyes were shining in the dusk. "It's just ability that counts with him. Of course there are a few old people too, but they're all fanatically keen on the work and that keeps them young. We're all so helplessly worried, Albert, or at least all those of us are who realise what's up. It's such a wizard show. We're all behind him, you see. We'd do anything for the work, absolutely anything. We all would. He *couldn't* let us all down, could he?"

Her voice was wonderfully young and clear and he was reminded of the first time he had ever heard it in the drawing room at Pontisbright Mill when the curtains had been drawn to hide the tears in the furniture. A lot of water had gone through the wheel since then, he reflected.

"It all depends," he said cautiously. "A man has a private life, you know, apart from his work."

"Not A.D." Amanda was vehement. "His work's his life and he's a very great man. That's why we all depend on him so. He's a genius."

It went through Mr. Campion's mind that he had had a spot of trouble with geniuses before but he thought it politic not to say so. He continued with his diffident questioning.

"What put you on to Ramillies?"

"That's the only telephone number that seems to reach Dell. He's got some money in Caesar's Court, you know, and he must have picked up that crowd down there. Ramillies is all right really, I believe; I mean his family is all right and he's a governor on the West Coast somewhere; but he's wild and in with a wild crowd. A.D. has probably never met anything like him before and is going into some idiotic scheme for setting up an airport in an African swamp. He gets wrapped up in things like that sometimes. The only alarming thing is that he's never neglected us before and we are so hoping that there aren't any sharks in Ramillies' lot. You don't know, do you? Sometimes these clever crooks get hold of wild hearties like Ramillies and impress them. A.D. wouldn't fall in the ordinary way but if they approached him through a county mug he might just possibly be taken in."

Mr. Campion's eyebrows rose in the darkness.

"I say," he murmured, "don't you think you may be getting a bit melodramatic? No offence, of course, but if a lad doesn't turn up at the office for a day or two it doesn't always mean that he's in the hands of what counsel calls 'a wicked and unscrupulous gang.'"

"An office, yes," conceded Amanda with contempt, "but not our works. You don't seem to understand at all. He's neglecting his *work*. We haven't seen him at all for a fortnight and before then he was vague and preoccupied. Sid and I diagnosed a succession of hangovers. It really is serious. Sid has sent me to find out and I must. Then if things don't improve we must have it out with him and get him back to normal."

"I see," said Mr. Campion a little helplessly. "Who is Sid?"

Amanda chuckled. "Sid's my immediate boss. A grand chap. He was born in Wallington and went to the Polytechnic and starved through the shops, finally got his M.I.M.E. and is one of the finest men in his own line in the kingdom. He's only twenty-nine and an awful snob, but so absolutely honest as a workman."

"A snob?"

"Yes, bless him. He's batty about my title. He's always getting at me for it just so he can hear himself use it. I like Sid. He's got enthusiasm. Where is this place, the Tulip? What makes you think they may be there?"

"Intuition backed by the law of elimination." Mr. Campion sounded dogged. "If they're not here, my child, we shall have to start knocking at doors and asking. London is a largish town for that method, but since you've made up your mind I see no other course."

"I hope you're not getting old," said Amanda dubiously. "If the worst comes to the worst we'll begin at Hampstead and work our way south."

The Tulip had been flowering for a little over seven months and was therefore nearing its zenith in the fashionable sunlight. Jules Parroquet, whose golden rule for the exploitation of a successful restaurant and night club was simple—a new name and orchestra to every two changes of paint—already considered it one of his triumphs. The ceiling of flowers was still noticed and admired and the silly little striped canvas canopies every now and again were as fresh and piquant as when they had first been erected.

Mr. Campion and Amanda stood for a moment looking over the broad silver rail above the orchestra before going down to the dance-floor level, where Campion was relying on the headwaiter, the lean Ulysse, the one permanent husbandman in Parroquet's ever-changing flower garden, to find them a respectably prominent table.

He did not find Georgia immediately but was relieved to see that the place was filled with likely people. Stage and society were well represented and Money hung about with Art in the corners, while the mass attempt at complete unself-consciousness provided the familiar atmosphere of feverish effort.

Young Hennessy, sitting at a table with a duchess, an actor-manager and two complete strangers, made an importunate attempt to attract his attention, and it was not until then that Campion, normally the most observant of men, glanced at Amanda and noticed that she had grown astonishingly good to look at. She saw his expression and grinned.

"I put my best frock on," she said. "Hal chooses all my things. Hal says good undergraduate taste is the only safe criterion of modern clothes. He takes it terribly seriously. Do you see anybody you know or have we got to go on somewhere else?"

"No, this'll do." Mr. Campion's tone contained not only relief but a note of resignation. Amanda, he foresaw, was about to discover the worst.

Ulysse received them with all that wealth of unspoken satisfaction which was his principal professional asset and conducted them to the small but not ill-placed table which he swore he had been keeping up his sleeve for just such an eventuality. The worst of the cabaret was over, he confided with that carefully cultivated contempt for everything that interfered with beautiful food, which was another of his more valuable affectations. He also spent some time considering the best meal for Amanda at that time of night.

As soon as they were at peace again Mr. Campion took it upon himself to rearrange his companion's chair so that her view across the room was not impeded. Then he sat down beside her.

"There you are, lady," he said. "Once more the veteran conjuror staggers out with the rabbit. There's the situation for you in the proverbial nut."

Georgia and Alan Dell had a table on the edge of the dance floor and from where she now sat Amanda had clear view of the two profiles. Georgia's slightly blunt features and magnificent shoulders were thrown up against the moving kaleidoscope of colour, and Dell sat staring at her with fifteen years off his age and the lost, slightly dazed expression of the man who, whether his trouble be love, drink or merely loss of blood, has honestly no idea that he is surrounded by strangers.

Infatuation is one of those slightly comic illnesses which are at once so undignified and so painful that a nice-minded world does its best to ignore their existence altogether, referring to them only under provocation and then with apology, but, like its more material brother, this boil on the neck of the spirit can hardly be forgotten either by the sufferer or anyone else in his vicinity. The malady is ludicrous, sad, excruciating and, above all, instantly diagnosable.

Mr. Campion glanced at Amanda and was sorry. Illusions may deserve to be broken, young enthusiasts may have to take what is coming to them, and heroes may desert their causes as life dictates, but it is always an unhappy business to watch. Amanda sat up, her round white neck very stiff and the jut of her flaming curls dangerous. Her face was expressionless, and the absence of any animation brought into sudden prominence the natural hauteur stamped into the fine bones of her head. She regarded the two for a long candid minute and then, turning away, changed the conversation with that flat deliberation which is a gift.

"This is excellent fish," she said.

Mr. Campion, who had the uncomfortable feeling that he had been a little vulgar, laboured to make amends.

"It's dudgeon," he said. "Very rare. They have great difficulty in keeping it. Hence the term 'high——' "

"Yes, I know." Amanda met his eyes. "We lived on it down at the mill one year. Do you remember? Who is that woman?"

"Georgia Wells, the actress."

Amanda's fine eyebrows rose.

"I thought that was Lady Ramillies?"

"Yes," said Mr. Campion.

She was silent. There was no possible way of divining what was in her mind, but he reflected that the younger generation was notoriously severe.

"It wears off, you know," he said, trying not to sound avuncular. "He can't help the out-in-the-street-in-the-nude effect, poor chap, at the moment. Nothing can be done. The work will have to wait."

"No, nothing can be done," agreed Amanda politely. "That's what I have to explain to Sid. Thank you very much for bringing me."

She moved her chair a little to shut out Dell, and set herself to be entertaining. Mr. Campion approved. He remembered enough of the hard-working, hero-worshipping, ecstatic days of his own youth to realise some of the shame, the sneaking jealousy and horrified sense of injustice and neglect that comes when the great man lets his fiery disciples down. But if Amanda was conscious of any of this she was not inflicting it upon him. Her manners were irreproachable. Amanda was, as ever, the perfect gent.

It occurred to him also that both Val and Amanda had intrinsically the same quarrel with Dell inasmuch as they both dreaded his loss of dignity. He sighed. The man had his sincere sympathy.

He glanced across the dance floor and caught a fleeting glimpse of Georgia dancing. It was only a momentary impression but he recognised her by her distinctive silver dress and the ridiculous but charming spray of swallows on her dark crown. His astonishment was considerable, therefore, when his glance, travelling back, lighted upon her still sitting at the table, her face radiant, her eyes shining, and the whole warmth of her magnificent, fraudulent personality glowing at the man before her. He sat up and looked out at the floor again and his expression changed. His mistake was triumphantly justified.

Another woman of Georgia's type was wearing a replica of Georgia's silver dress and Georgia's silver swallows. Her dark curls were dressed in Georgia's style and at that distance the two faces were indistinguishable. Mr. Campion recognised Miss Adamson with difficulty and reflected that the girl was a fool as well as a knave. Then he caught sight of her partner, and once again experienced that faint sense of outrage which thundering bad taste invariably produced in him.

Dancing with Miss Adamson, his small head held at a slight angle and his whole body expressing his tremendous satisfaction, was Sir Raymond Ramillies.

CHAPTER EIGHT

Ulysse had settled Sir Raymond and Miss Adamson safely at the table immediately behind Georgia, and Ramillies was grinning happily at his success in acquiring it before the good maître d'hôtel noticed the phenomenon of the two Miss Wells.

Mr. Campion, who found himself watching the scene with the fascinated apprehension of a village idiot at a dangerous crossing, almost laughed aloud at the expression of incredulity which spread over Ulysse's face as his glance took in the two women. His small bright eyes flickered and he thrashed the menu card which he happened to be holding as if it had been a tail and he a labrador. It was a comic moment but it passed too soon, leaving only a growing sense of embarrassment as half-a-dozen diners at other tables swung round to stare with that insolence which comes from an attempt to look casual, or perhaps invisible, before they returned to warn their companions not to look round immediately.

Amanda looked at Campion and for the first time in their entire acquaintance he saw her rattled.

"That *is* Ramillies," she said. "What can we do?"

"Fire at the lights," he suggested, his wide mouth twisting with brief amusement. "No, it's no good, old lady; this is grown-up vulgarity. We sit and watch. Oh, Lord!"

The final exclamation was occasioned by a movement at Georgia's table. Alan Dell had dragged his dazzled eyes away from Lady Ramillies for an instant, only to be confronted immediately by Miss Adamson, seated directly behind her. Georgia noted the sudden deflection of interest and turned her head impulsively. Ramillies met her eyes and grinned with bland self-satisfaction.

She gave him a single offended and reproving glance, natural if unreasonable in the circumstances, and turned her eyes to his companion with an expression half condescending, half curious. The next moment, however, as the full insult became apparent, she was reduced to elementary emotions. The colour rose over her chest and flowed up her neck to her face in an angry flood. There was a sudden cessation of conversation at all the tables round about and she sat for a moment in a little oasis of silence in the desert of hissing sound.

Mr. Campion dropped his hand over Amanda's but she drew it away from him and began to eat as resolutely and angrily as her Victorian grandfather might have done in similar circumstances.

Ramillies bent forward and said something to his wife and she pushed back her chair, her face as pale as it had been red, while Alan Dell sprang up and fumbled for her bag and flowers.

It was a dangerous moment. There was something not quite ordinary in the quality of the contretemps—an ultimate degree of outrage, the quintessence of going a bit too far—so that the situation became vaguely alarming even to those least concerned. At the very instant when the clash of many emotions was still tingling in the air and everyone in that half of the room was waiting uncomfortably for Georgia's exit, a preserving angel appeared somewhat heavily disguised as Solly Batemann.

When Solly was described as an ornament to the theatrical profession, the word was never meant to be taken in its literal or decorative sense. He looked like a cross between a frog and a bulldog and was reputed to have the hide and warts of a rhino, but his personality was as full and generous as his voice, which was sweet and caressing without any of the oiliness which one was led to expect from his appearance. He was very pleased with himself at the moment. Three of his theatres were playing to capacity and the fourth production, which had flopped, had been by far the least expensive of them all. He surged across the floor to Georgia, his great stomach thrown out, his little eyes popping out of the top of his head, and his many grey-blue jowls quivering with bonhomie.

"Ah, my darling, you are a clever girl," he said when he was within hailing distance. "If we were only alone I should kiss you. I saw the show tonight. I sat and cried all over my shirt. Fact. No, not that spot; that's minestrone—this one."

Solly's irresistibility was the irresistibility of a tidal wave. Even Georgia could only succumb. She had no need to speak. He swept a chair from another table and planted it squarely between her and Dell. Then, with one elephantine knee resting on its velvet seat, he held forth, pouring unstinted praise upon her as though from some vast cornucopia. It was a performance and its genuineness was Georgia's own. In spite of herself she warmed under it and within three minutes he had her laughing.

Mr. Campion was bewildered. Since Solly's interests were concentrated solely upon musical and spectacular shows and Georgia was well known to be under a long contract with Ferdie Paul, there could scarcely be any ulterior motive in the display, so that the tribute became sincere and heaven sent.

Mr. Campion glanced at the other table and his eyebrows rose. In fact heaven seemed to be sending all sorts of things. As soon as general interest had become focussed upon Solly, Ramillies had turned in his chair like an unnoticed child with every intention of joining in the new conversation, but now a waiter appeared at his elbow with a card on a salver. Ramillies took the pasteboard absently. His interest was still centred on his wife, but a glance at the message distracted him. He looked up eagerly, his dazzling childlike smile appearing, and, making a brief excuse to Miss Adamson, he set off across the room after the waiter without a backward glance. The next moment, as if these two dispensations of Providence were not enough, Ramon Starr, the Tulip's most promising gigolo, sidled over to the deserted girl and she jumped at his murmured proposal. They floated away together to the strains of "Little Old Lady."

Dell himself had remained standing, regarding the exuberant Solly with growing disapproval, but before Georgia could become preoccupied with his discomfort yet another minor miracle occurred, taking the whole thing out of the happy-coincidence class altogether. Tante Marthe herself came sweeping by, looking like a famous elderly ballerina in her severe black gown, her head crowned by a ridiculous little beaded turban which only Val could have devised.

She nodded to Georgia, who did not see her, which was not surprising since Solly still filled every arc of her horizon, and, passing on,
pounced upon Alan. She said something to him in which the name of
"Gaiogi" alone was audible and laid her small yellow hand familiarly
on his arm. From the little distance at which Campion and Amanda
sat it was not possible to hear his reply, but Lady Papendeik's lizard
glance darted round the room and came to rest on the two with a
sparkle of satisfaction. A minute or two later she bore down upon
them with Alan Dell following reluctantly at her heels, but she still
had him by the cuff so that he could hardly escape her without
brusquerie.

There was no time to warn Amanda with words and Campion
kicked her gently under the table as he rose to greet the newcomer.

"Albert, my dear, I hear you're going to join our party at Caesar's
Court. I am so glad, my dear boy. You and Mr. Dell have met, I
think?"

Tante Marthe looked him full in the eyes as she spoke and he read
there a command that he should be helpful. He made a suitable re-
joinder and turned to Dell.

The conventional words faded on his lips as he saw the other man's
face, however, and once more the whole situation became real and
painful. Dell was staring helplessly at Amanda. There was colour in his
face and his eyes were indescribably hurt, almost bewildered, as if he
could scarcely credit the astonishing cruelty of the mischance. Mr.
Campion felt very sorry for him.

Amanda took the situation in hand.

"Hallo, A.D.," she said with charming embarrassment. "I'm having
a night on the tiles. This is my fourth meal this evening. The food
is good. Come and have some. You haven't eaten yet, have you?"

"I'm afraid I have." He was looking at her suspiciously. "I've been
sitting just over there all the evening."

"Really? Where?" She stared across the room with such regretful
astonishment that she convinced even Mr. Campion, who thought for
an instant that she was out of her mind. "I'm so sorry. I didn't notice
you. I was engrossed in my fiancé. Do you know him?"

Mr. Campion received a mental thump between the shoulder blades
and saved himself from blinking just in time.

"Albert?" Lady Papendeik was startled. "My children, congratulations! Why haven't we heard of this before? It's Amanda Fitton,
isn't it? My dears, this is great news. Does Val know?"

"Engaged?" Alan Dell peered at Amanda. "You? Really? Is it recent? Tonight?"

Mr. Campion glanced at his companion from under his eyelashes. He hoped she knew what she was doing and would let him in on it. So far she had certainly succeeded in changing the conversation, albeit somewhat drastically.

"But how long has this been a fact?" Dell persisted, seizing on the point as though it had been the only solid spar in the conversational sea.

Amanda glanced at Campion demurely.

"We shall have to explain," she said.

"I think so," he agreed affably. "You do it."

"Well, it's my brother," she confided unexpectedly. "Do sit down. We ought to drink some champagne to this, you know, darling," she added, looking Campion firmly in the face and rubbing her chin thoughtfully with one finger, a gesture that fogged him utterly until he recollected that it was a secret sign in the Fitton family indicating that the speaker was there and then possessed of sufficient funds to cover the proposed extravagance.

Tante Marthe seated herself at once, and Dell, with a backward glance at Georgia, who was still monopolised, sat down in the opposite chair. As they drank, Mr. Campion met Lady Papendeik's eyes. He read vigorous approval in them and was alarmed.

Dell was even more embarrassing.

"You're extremely lucky, Campion," he said seriously. "She's a very remarkable girl. We shall feel the draught without her. When is the wrench to be, Amanda?"

"Not for quite a time, I'm afraid." The bride-to-be spoke regretfully. "It's Hal, you know. He's young and frightfully self-opinionated. Of course he's head of the family and I don't want to hurt him by flouting his authority. He'll come round in time. Meanwhile the engagement is more or less secret—as much as these things ever are. It's simply not announced; that's what it amounts to. It's a howling pity but we're both such very busy people that we can—er—bear to wait about a bit."

Lady Papendeik approved.

"So sensible," she said. "So French. You have been very sly, Albert. This has been going on some time. You're both so composed, so friendly. The coy period is over, thank God. When was the grande passion?"

Amanda smiled at her and her honey-brown eyes were guileless.

"That's all a bit shy-making in a crowd," she said. "I'll leave you with Albert for a bit. He'll tell you the worst. A.D., would you like to dance with me?"

Dell carried her off unwillingly and Tante Marthe looked after their retreating figures. "Well, that's astonishing but very nice," she said with a sigh. "You took our breath away. She is so fresh, so charming, so really young. Val will design her a wedding dress that will make her look like a Botticelli angel. She has taste, too. That is a Lelong she is wearing."

Campion regarded the old woman thoughtfully.

"You came along remarkably opportunely just now," he observed.

"I?" Her face was completely innocent but the narrow black eyes flickered. "Oh, to hear your news? Yes. I shall have some gossip again at last."

"I didn't mean that, as you know very well. You and Solly Batemann did a remarkably neat stroke of peace-preserving between you just now, didn't you? That wasn't pure act of God, was it?"

Lady Papendeik stared at him, her thin mouth widening.

"You detectives," she said with good-humoured contempt. "What a lot you see. My dear, I was simply sitting over there with the Bensons and Donald Tweed when I caught sight of Alan Dell across the room. I wanted to make sure that he was coming down on Saturday to Ramillies' farewell party at Caesar's Court and so I stepped across to speak to him. Georgia looks very exuberant, doesn't she? A woman who wears birds in her hair ceases to look like Primavera after thirty and simply reminds one of that song they will keep playing."

Mr. Campion reflected.

"You're thinking of a nest of robins, my dear," he said. "A very different caper; someone didn't consult his nature notes when he wrote that. Miss Adamson also favours swallows, I saw."

Lady Papendeik did not look at him. She sat up, her small shoulders compact and severe.

"That is the end of that little girl," she remarked briefly. "Tell me about your engagement. It is so entirely unexpected."

"It is, rather, isn't it?" he agreed. "Still, Amanda's an unexpected young person."

"She's sweet." Tante Marthe glanced across the tables to the dance floor. "She looks so lovely. Her figure is completely natural. How does she keep her stockings up?"

Mr. Campion gave the matter his serious consideration.

"I tremble to think. Two magnets and a dry battery, if I know her, or perhaps something complicated on the grid system."

The old woman leant back in her chair.

"Delightful," she murmured. "You love her so comfortably. There is no unhappy excitement. I am so glad, my dear boy. I hope the brother is reasonable. What is his objection?"

"Age," supplied Mr. Campion promptly. He made the first excuse that came into his head and was amused to find that he was irritated when she accepted it without incredulity.

"You are old for your years," she said. "You'll grow out of it. My God, I nearly died of old age when I was thirty-three, yet look at me now. There they are."

Campion glanced round and saw that Dell and Amanda had paused at Georgia's table. Ramillies was still absent and Miss Adamson seemed to have disappeared altogether, since there was no sign of her on the dance floor. He watched the little scene round Georgia with interest. It was not possible to hear any remark save from Solly, but his were enlightening.

"When I was married you know what my mama said? She said: 'Have your photograph taken, Solly; you'll never look the same again.' Such a pretty little flower! It is a pity to pick her so soon."

He almost chucked Amanda under the chin, and Lady Papendeik laughed softly at Campion's side as he changed his mind and the plump hand, fluttering uncertainly, accomplished the chucking an inch or so above the red head.

Amanda appeared to be enjoying herself. She smiled at Solly, whom she seemed to like, and was gracefully deferential to Georgia. The brief gathering broke up with Lady Ramillies embracing the younger girl with a sort of fine, generous spirituality which made Mr. Campion think of Britannia in the cartoons of Sir Bernard Partridge, and Solly trotting off across the dance floor waving and nodding like a Bacchus in a triumphal car.

Dell and Georgia settled down again and Amanda came back to her seat. Lady Papendeik rose.

"Good night, my dears," she said. "This is only a secret, isn't it? I mean, I can tell it in confidence? Felicitations, Albert. You are a very clever young man."

Amanda watched her depart before she spoke.

"He *is* in a mess, isn't he?" she said gloomily. "It wasn't too good over there. He was hoping I wouldn't notice anything and she was trying to tell me all about it. I concentrated on the hearty old party with the chins and talked about my own engagement. I'm afraid that Georgia woman's a sweep."

"I think she's genuinely very much in love at the moment." Campion put forward the excuse in all fairness.

"She's not," said Amanda. "If you're in love with a man the one thing you're frightened of is doing him any harm. That's the whole principle of the thing. She's not thinking of A.D. at all. She's using him to make herself feel emotional and that means that there are at least two or three hundred other men who would do just as well. I don't mind her going on in her natural way if she's that sort of person, but she's a sweep to pick on A.D., who has work to do."

Mr. Campion regarded her with amusement.

"Taking up philosophy in your old age?"

"That's not philosophy; that's elementary common sense," said Amanda. "Have you got enough money on you to pay for the champagne? If you haven't, that's going to be the next problem. I thought I had thirty bob with me but I see it's only ten."

"No, it's all right. They know me," he assured her, reflecting that Hal and his colleagues must find her a relief to entertain. "That was inspirational."

"It was, wasn't it?" Amanda was never modest in her self-appreciation. "There's nothing to take your mind off an embarrassing situation of your own like being asked to celebrate someone else's engagement. It's partly the champagne and partly the feeling that you're not responsible in any way for the setout. Poor chap, I thought he was going to be sick when he saw me. I felt like the blue-eyed toddler who had staggered in when Daddy was making a beast of himself. Look here, we've got to go. I excused you from that crowd by saying that you had to be in bed early after your illness."

"What illness?" demanded Mr. Campion, startled into bald enquiry.

Amanda sat looking at him, her round brown eyes curious.

"You have been rather ill, haven't you?" she enquired seriously. "You're quieter than you used to be and you look a bit bleached. I took it you'd had tonsillitis or something on the chest."

"I'm perfectly healthy and always have been," declared Mr. Campion with an outraged dignity that was at least half genuine, "and I'll thank you, miss, to keep your dispiriting remarks to yourself. I'm damned if I want to be rejuvenated, either," he added, a note of genuine resentment which he had not quite intended creeping into his tone.

"Perhaps you're sickening for something," she murmured with intent to comfort. "Come on. We shall have to stay engaged for a week or two. It was a nuisance in a way but it seemed the best thing to do. I couldn't let A.D. feel we'd been spying on him. I thought he was simply being rooked, you see. I didn't dream it was anything like this. I knew you'd back me up so I got out of the situation as neatly as possible. We can let the betrothal excitement die down gradually. I've got a ring of Aunt Flo's somewhere, so you needn't bother about that."

"Splendid." Mr. Campion seemed relieved. "Then it's just my wife to square and we're all set."

"Yes, well, you can do that," said Amanda. "I've done all the dirty work so far. Put me in a cab and I'll go down to Boot's Hotel on my own. It's right out of your way. You do look rather tired, you know."

Mr. Campion prepared to depart.

"You're stewing up for a thick ear," he remarked. "I never raise my hand against a woman save in anger."

Amanda sighed and he had the uncomfortable impression that it was with relief. Her smile vanished immediately, however, and he caught her looking a trifle older herself.

"I'm behaving like a goat mainly because I feel so miserable, you know," she remarked presently. "Can you see the sort of blazing shame this all is?"

"Yes," he said gravely, catching her mood. "It's not good. Rotten for Sid and all of you. The death of a hero but not a hero's death, so to speak."

"Oh, you're still all right." She was grinning at him with a warmth that no Georgia could ever counterfeit. "Up here, away from it all, I can understand some people feeling that this angle of ours is all a bit 'footy' and small, but down there. . . ! We all *live* from him, Albert. He's the spark that lights the fires. That woman's not so much a sweep, you know, as an enemy. Ramillies is a bit of a tick, too, isn't he? That incident might have been most indelicate. It was rather miraculous how it all cleared up in a moment."

"Rather miraculous? My poor young woman . . ." Mr. Campion regarded her with affection. "That was not merely a miracle; that was fishy. I've never actually believed in a guardian angel, but when I observe such a veritable cloud of feathers I do suspect something of the sort. You don't seem to realise I've been sitting here watching a conjuring trick that leaves Caligari cold. There's someone around here to whom I take off my hat—all my hats."

He was still pondering over the phenomenon as they went out and as they crossed into the wide aisle behind the pillars someone nodded to him from a table not too well placed in a corner. He returned the nod and comprehension came to him with recognition.

Ferdie Paul lay back idly in his chair looking more like a bored gilt Byron than ever. There was an air of great weariness and disinterest about him, but his smile was friendly and he raised a pale hand in salute. There were two women at his table and a deserted chair. Campion recognised one of his companions as the very well-dressed but ill-at-ease little person whom Rex had been so anxious to placate at

Papendeik's dress show, while the other, a big-boned good-tempered blonde, was unmistakably Mrs. Solly Batemann. At the moment she was talking to Gaiogi, who was standing at her side.

Campion glanced round him. As he thought, Tante Marthe was seated not so very far away.

CHAPTER NINE

When the seventh Earl Hurrell rebuilt Caesar's Court in the late eighteenth century he incorporated a great many of the brighter ideas of the day into the construction of the house and grounds. The Pinery, the ice house, the Vine Palace and the useful gazebo were all much admired at the time, and the sloping lawn, which not only ran down to the Thames but presumably continued under it, since it reappeared on the opposite bank and went on and on for the best part of a mile like a strip of gigantic stair carpet, had been commented on by George IV ("Impressive, Hurrell, an't it? What? What?").

Since that time the succeeding Hurrells had been fully occupied keeping the monstrous property a going concern, let alone improving it, so that when Gaiogi Laminoff took charge the place was, as the estate agent said, delightfully unspoilt.

At eleven o'clock on the Sunday morning following the farewell party given for Sir Raymond Ramillies, Mr. Campion sat on a little footbridge over the river and considered Gaiogi's alterations with sober admiration.

The rosy building itself had retained the dignity of a great private palace but had miraculously lost its pomposity. Even at this distance it exuded a party atmosphere and it occurred to Mr. Campion that it looked like some millionaire child's play pen magnified up to an impossible scale. There were expensive toys everywhere. Little silver aeroplanes taxied off the green turf on the other side of the river. Glossy hacks and shiny motorcars paraded on the gravel drives and everywhere there were flowers and casually elegant clothes, with a suggestion of music in the background. The general effect was expensive, exclusive and very pleasant; the Royal Enclosure at Home sort of atmosphere.

There was much activity on the flying field, especially round the hangar where the new plane had been housed the night before, and Campion did not notice the two who came striding towards him until

Amanda spoke. She looked very like herself in a brown suit, better cut than her working clothes of old but the same in general effect, and her heart-shaped face was alive and interested with all the freshness of a sixteen-year-old.

"Hallo," she said. "Has the old cad turned up yet?"

"Ramillies? No, I'm afraid not."

"Where on earth is he? Oh, Albert, I quite forgot. This is Sid."

They had reached the middle of the bridge by this time and Mr. Campion found himself confronted by a tall, bull-necked young man with very black hair, which he wore practically shaved save for a solid thatch on the very top of his head. He shook hands with deep resentment and said with patent insincerity that he was pleased to meet Mr. Campion.

"Well, I'll get back," he said immediately with an assumption of ease which was ridiculous or heroic according to the way one's mind worked. "If you can find out when Sir Raymond returns, Lady Amanda, send a message over to us. The broadcasting blokes are twittering away like spadgers over there."

"I thought you were coming up to the bar?" Amanda was surprised. "He'll be there if he's back."

"No, I don't think I will, thanks awfully." Sid had his hands in his pockets and the skirts of his brown jacket, which were a trifle too fluted, jutted out behind him like a cape. "I'll get back. So long. Take care of yourself."

He seemed to mistrust the social tone of the final admonition as soon as he had made it, for he reddened and, nodding to Campion without looking at him, strode off with his broad shoulders hunched and his trousers flapping. Amanda looked after him, her eyebrows raised. She glanced at Campion appealingly.

"He's all right, really," she said. "Or don't you think so?"

"Dear chap," murmured Mr. Campion. "Not quite sure of himself, that's all. That's nothing."

"Don't you believe it," said Amanda gloomily. "Class is like sex or the electric light supply, not worth thinking about as long as yours is all right but embarrassingly inconvenient if there's anything wrong with it. Sid *will* feel he's lowish, and so he is, and nothing much can be done about it. It doesn't worry other people at all, of course, but it's lousy for him. What about Ramillies?"

"He hasn't shown up yet but I don't think there's much point in worrying. He'll appear when the time comes."

She glanced at him sharply. "You think he's simply doing this to put everybody in a flap?"

"It wouldn't be astounding, would it?"

"No. Disgustingly likely. What a crowd they all are. . . ." Amanda sounded tolerant. "It was a bad show clearing off in the middle of his own farewell do like that. He's too old to go roaring off into the night at two o'clock in the morning as if he were twenty. It's so old-fashioned."

Mr. Campion was inclined to agree but he could not forget that there had been extenuating circumstances.

"Georgia wasn't helping," he ventured.

Amanda sniffed. She was wandering along beside him, her hands clasped behind her and her head bent.

"D'you know, I can't believe it of A.D.," she said suddenly. "When I actually see it I can't believe it. It's—well, it's shocking, isn't it? That's a spoilt word but you see what I mean."

He laughed.

"What's the reaction among the disciples?"

"I don't know. I mentioned it to Sid but he didn't believe me until yesterday when he came over here and got the gossip. He's just murderous towards the woman, of course. Sid sees things in black and white. It doesn't seem to be a bad idea. It saves him no end of bother. Where are we going?"

They had turned aside and taken a path which led through a rose garden to a shrubbery interspersed with several high trees, all very brave and gay in their summer finery.

"I'm staying with the Laminoffs," he explained. "They're having a small hangover party at a quarter to twelve. I promised I'd bring my fiancée if I could find her. You're getting on nicely with my family, aren't you?"

"I think I do you credit," agreed Amanda complacently. "You asked me to marry you at the Olympia Circus last year. It was just like the pictures. We came together over a game of darts in the amusement park afterwards. I don't suppose Val will ask you about it but you may as well know what she's talking about if she does. I like Val. I came to you about this business in the first place because I had an idea that A.D. was a friend of hers. He was, wasn't he?"

"They seemed to like each other."

Amanda sighed. "Then you do know about it. I only wondered. Relations are sometimes dense. It shows, you know. I noticed it as soon as I saw them together. That makes Georgia more of a sweep than ever, don't you think?"

Mr. Campion had not the opportunity to reply. They had turned a corner in the shrubbery path and now came to an unexpected wicket

gate which gave on to one of the seventh earl's prettier follies. The
seventh earl had seen the Petit Trianon and it had taken his fancy.
His recollection had been by no means accurate, however, and perhaps his purse had been shorter than the French king's, but he had
achieved a little house. It sat solid and white, like an upended box of
bricks, with pillars and steps and a fine flat lead roof. The little trees,
which had once matched its miniature magnificence, had now grown
to big trees and the tiny terrace was moss grown and charming.

So much for the earl. Gaiogi had added gaiety. The pompous windows were wide, and pink and apple-green curtains billowed in their
dark eyes. There were chairs on the steps, and cushions and great
stone urns of flowers. It was a party house and Gaiogi was the perfect
party host. His head appeared through a window as soon as they entered the gate.

"The sun has come out," he shouted to Amanda. "How are you?"

"Excited," said Amanda obligingly.

Gaiogi met her eyes and laughed, and it occurred to Campion that
it was the meeting and mutual recognition of two persons of resource.

Mme. Laminoff met them in the hall, which would have been a grim
box with a black-and-white squared marble floor if Gaiogi had not
taken it into his head to have a set of red chessmen painted on the
stones and to enliven an alcove with a red glass lobster in place of
the seventh earl's bust of Cicero.

Sofya Laminoff was herself unexpected. She was plump and gracious and succeeded in looking like a very exotic film star unsuccess-
fully disguised as Queen Victoria. She was far more placid than her
husband, but her eyes, which were theatrically black against her magnificent white hair, had a twinkle in them and her small fat hands
fluttered charmingly as she talked.

"Still no news of him?" Her anxious enquiry stood out from the
flurry of welcome as though it had leapt into blacker type. "No? Never
mind. He'll come. I tell Gaiogi he will come. He is simply a man
who likes to make himself interesting. Come in."

She swept them into the salon, where the hangover party was already in progress. The room itself was charming. It ran through to
the back of the house and ended in wide windows giving on to a small
formal garden. Here again the seventh earl had not been so much
suppressed as made a little tipsy. His graceful fireplace and flat-fluted
columns remained, while much of the furniture was pure Georgian,
but the rest was Gaiogi's own collection of interesting pieces, many
of which were of the frankly bought-for-fun variety. It was all remarkably comfortable. Tante Marthe sat in a rocking chair in a patch of

sunlight, and Val, looking like one of her own advertisements in *Vogue*, was curled up on a Mme. Récamier chaise longue. There were four or five strangers present: an affable young man from the B.B.C., a gloomy youngster with a big nose whose name was Wivenhoe and who seemed to be something to do with Towser of the Colonial Office, two quiet little men who talked together respectfully and might have had "Money" neatly embroidered on sashes round their middles, and a large gentleman with a Guardee moustache who devoted himself to Val and turned out most unexpectedly to be the managing editor of one of the larger dailies.

Gaiogi himself was happy, playing apothecary, and he dispensed his three sovereign remedies, champagne, tea or iced draught beer, according to the condition of the individual patient.

Campion wandered over to him.

"I've phoned his house, his clubs and every Turkish bath in London," he said quietly. "We'll give him another couple of hours and then I'll go to town and get the bloodhounds out. We can't very well do a thing like that too soon. I also tried to get hold of a Miss Adamson but apparently Annie doesn't live there any more."

"Ah? Oh yes, *that* girl." Gaiogi hunched his shoulders and looked vaguely introspective. "Yes, a pretty girl. No head. No perception. No, she doesn't live here or at Papendeik's any more."

"Nor with her aunt Maggie either, it would appear."

"Really?" Gaiogi did not seem interested. "That may be. Very likely. We will give him until after lunch. Meanwhile, my dear fellow, don't let it distress you. What will you drink? Let us all forget the miserable chap. Towser is coming to the lunch. He wants a round of golf before the ceremony. I had hoped that Ramillies would be here to help entertain him, but from what Wivenhoe tells me perhaps it is almost as well. Not all these charming people like one another."

He exploded with laughter on the last word and his round brown eyes met Campion's shyly.

"That fellow Wivenhoe is a bit of a stick. Marthe Papendeik keeps talking to him about his chief, Pluto. He is quite offended. She is innocent. It is a natural slip. I thought I'd warn you."

"Thank you. I'll remember that." Campion spoke gravely and it went through his mind that more than half Gaiogi's secret lay in his naïveté and the rest was deep understanding of important fun. There was an air of magnificent goings on about this morning's party, much of which was justified if one accepted the all-importance of the success of Caesar's Court.

"I talked to Ferdie Paul on the telephone just now," Gaiogi went on. "He says don't worry. In his opinion the fellow is something of an exhibitionist. He knows him well. That is between friends, of course. He says like all these people, when the moment on which their job depends actually arrives, they are always there."

"There's a lot in that," said Campion. "Is Paul coming down this afternoon?"

"No, unfortunately no. He is just off to Paris. He has interests over there and must be back in London tomorrow."

"He's a clever chap," Campion remarked absently.

"Oh, extraordinary." Gaiogi pronounced each syllable of the word in his admiration. "Brilliant. If only he weren't so lazy he'd be a force, a power."

"Lazy? I should hardly have thought that."

Gaiogi filled a glass.

"There is a phrase for him in English," he said. "Do you know it? He is 'born tired.' He never does anything at all if he can get someone to do it for him. Will your beautiful betrothed drink champagne?"

Mr. Campion glanced at his beautiful betrothed with a certain amount of apprehension. She was talking to Val and Tante Marthe and the older woman's little lizard head was cocked on one side and her eyes were dancing.

"You're both darling to want to help," Amanda was saying firmly, "but you don't know my brother. We've decided to let him grow. His mind will expand. Meanwhile we're perfectly happy, aren't we, Albert?"

"You have your aeroplanes, my dear," said Mr. Campion with caddish resignation.

Amanda blinked. "That's terribly true," she agreed earnestly. "I must try not to be selfish—or vulgar," she added warningly.

Campion caught Val's eye and turned away hastily. She had looked a little sorry for him.

"You didn't find him?" Tante Marthe put the question in an undertone and she grimaced when he shook his head. "He expected to find that girl here last night. That is why he went off. He was piqued, like a child. I told Gaiogi so. Georgia was being thoughtless, I know, but he's been married to her for over two years. He must be used to that sort of thing by this time. Who's that coming now?"

There was a stir in the room and Gaiogi hurried to the window and they caught over his plump shoulders a fleeting vision of a small vehicle passing up the drive. It was a calash, one of the pneumatic-tired electric cars like glorified bath chairs for two which Gaiogi had acquired to transport his lazier lotus-eaters about the grounds and which were proving very popular in this little world of toys. Val glanced at Campion questioningly and once again he avoided her eyes.

"Georgia," he said briefly.

"And Alan?"

"Yes, I think so."

She did not speak but glanced out across the little flower garden as if she were half a mind to escape into it, but there was no sign of any emotion on her face.

With the sound of Georgia's warm happy voice in the hall outside a flatness passed over the company. For the first time the title of the party became apt, as though everyone had just remembered that he had taken part in an uproarious ceremony the night before.

Georgia came in with Dell in attendance. She was beautiful, alive and blatantly triumphant. In any other circumstances her naïve delight in her captive would have been disarming, but this morning, in view of everything, it was not quite forgivable and succeeded in striking a démodé note in that aware community. Campion caught Amanda regarding them speculatively and, as was his gift, saw them for a moment through her eyes. He was startled. She was thinking that they were poor old things.

Georgia crossed the room, her white silk sports suit emphasising the warmth of her skin and the strong grace of her figure. She kissed Tante Marthe, nodded to the two decent young men and sat down beside Val with an arm round her shoulders. Dell remained by the door talking to Gaiogi. There was a distinct air of defiance about him which was young and sat oddly upon him, destroying his dignity, but when he came over at Georgia's imperious command they saw that his eyes were bewildered and unhappy.

"Something will have to be done," said Georgia clearly above the chatter. "He's got to go in that plane. Where on earth is he?"

It was the first time that the subject of Ramillies' absence had been mentioned in any tone above a whisper and the effect upon the whole room was interesting. Everybody stopped talking and Campion realised for the first time that every member of the party had a definite reason for being present. It was another evidence of Gaiogi's celebrated diplomacy and was, for some obscure psychological reason, faintly disturbing, as if one had accidentally discovered that the floor was laid over a well.

"Didn't he leave any message when he went off last night, Lady Ramillies?" enquired Wivenhoe, who seemed constitutionally incapable of grasping the unconventional. "Surely he said something to somebody? I mean a man doesn't go off into the night like that without a word."

Georgia looked at him steadily, holding his eyes while she laughed.

"It does sometimes happen, my pet," she said, and the large man with the moustache chuckled and the two little men who had been talking about money smiled at each other.

"Well, darlings," said Georgia, looking round the room and conveying, most unjustifiably, that they were all in the family, "we were all at the party last night, weren't we? Did anyone notice anything peculiar about the old villain? I rather lost sight of him myself." She glanced under her lashes at Dell, who blushed. The colour rushed into his face and suffused his very eyes. He was so mature for such an exhibition, so entirely the wrong sort of person for the reaction, that he could scarcely have been more obvious or caused more embarrassment if he had burst into tears. Everybody began to talk again.

As Mr. Campion turned his head he saw two profiles, Amanda as red as her hero and Val so white that her face looked stony. Georgia seemed surprised.

"It's all all right," she said. "He probably realised he was getting a bit tight and trotted off to a Turkish bath in town. He'll turn up very clean and hungry half an hour late for lunch. He hasn't been frightfully fit, as a matter of fact. He went to a specialist a fortnight ago. He knows he ought not to drink. His sins are finding him out, wicked old thing."

Why these revelations should set everyone's mind at rest was not very clear, but conversation became general again, indicating that everyone had found out that no one knew much more than he did and had decided to wait a little longer.

Georgia's attention returned to Dell, who was standing by the windows looking into the little garden. He came when she called him and paused before her. Georgia appeared to have forgotten what she wanted him for and was clearly about to tell the tasselled gentle so when Val intervened.

"What's that in your coat?" she said. "I've been trying to place it. May I ask?"

The ordinary question was a relief to him and he seized on it.

"This?" he enquired, pulling his lapel and squinting down at it. "That's the Quentin Clear."

"Good heavens, I never noticed it." Georgia's tone was vigorously possessive and her arm tightened about the other woman unconsciously, so that she was virtually holding Val back by main force.

"My dear man, you can't go about like that. You look like a darts champion. Whatever is it, pet? Give it here."

She held out her free hand and, after fidgeting with the split pin that held it in place, he gave it to her unwillingly. It was a small silver medallion, not particularly distinguished in design but of exquisite workmanship, as these things sometimes are. Georgia turned it over.

"It's rather sweet," she said. "I like the little propeller things, don't you, Val? But you can't wear it, dear, you simply can't. I'll keep it."

Dell hesitated. He looked profoundly uncomfortable.

"I'm afraid you mustn't," he said awkwardly. "I'll put it back."

"You won't." Georgia was laughing. "If anyone wears it I will. It looks rather sweet on this revers."

There was a force in her voice that he seemed to find unanswerable and Mr. Campion felt himself led firmly out into the garden.

"Sorry, but I thought I was going to protest," said Amanda, striding across the grass plot. "That's the Quentin Clear. The woman must be nuts. He is, God knows."

"That's rather special, isn't it?"

"Special?" Amanda made a noise like an angry old gentleman. "It's it. It's *the* one. Only about three men in the world have it. A.D. wouldn't wear it if it wasn't for this 'do' this afternoon. She's simply ignorant, of course, and evidently doesn't understand that he isn't just anybody, which is what I've complained of all along. He ought to be taken home and given a sedative, of course, but if Sid or any of the boys see her wearing that thing there'll be a riot. It's a howling insult. Can't we tell her?"

"I'm afraid that's his pigeon, my dear." Mr. Campion spoke mildly. "Anything we do reflects on him, doesn't it?"

Amanda kicked the edge of the lawn with a small neat toe and glanced up at him.

"The older one gets the more one understands and the smaller the things are that matter," she remarked. "It doesn't get easier, does it? I'm sorry I cleared out. I suddenly felt it was all a bit beyond me. Hullo."

Her final remark was addressed to a small boy who was seated on a wooden settle against a southern wall. He had been hidden from them as they came out by the angle of the house and was sitting very quietly all by himself, a book on his knee. He rose politely and pulled off his Haverleigh cap as Amanda spoke and Campion recognised him as the child he had seen at Papendeik's. He looked now much as he had done then, self-contained and patient, like somebody waiting on a railway station.

"It's very pleasant out here in the sun," he remarked, more, they felt, in an attempt to put them at their ease than in an attempt to cover any embarrassment of his own. "I like this little garden."

He was an undersized fourteen, Campion judged, and he tried somewhat hurriedly to remember his own mentality at that age. Meanwhile, however, Amanda came to the rescue.

"Haverleigh is shut, isn't it?" she said. "What was it? I.P. in the village? Do you think you'll get back at half?"

He shrugged his shoulders and smiled wryly.

"We hope so. The last case was reported three weeks ago. Meanwhile one can only wait. It's rather rotten. It's only my second term."

The confidence was the first sign of immaturity he had shown and Campion was relieved to notice it.

"I saw you in town the other day," he said, trying to avoid the accusing tone one so often uses to children.

The boy looked up with interest.

"With Georgia and Raymond at Papendeik's?" he said. "Yes, I remember you. I'm afraid I'm not as interested in clothes as I should be," he added apologetically. "Mother—that's Georgia, you know—is doing her best with me but I'm not really keen. That sort of interest grows on one later, don't you think?"

"It's not a thing you're born with, necessarily," remarked Amanda cheerfully. "We're going back to the party. Are you coming?"

"No, I don't think I will, thank you very much," he said, reseating himself. "I've got this that I must read, and it's very warm out here in the sun."

Amanda eyed the solid green volume on his knee.

"Holiday task?"

He nodded. "*Ivanhoe*," he admitted, a touch of amused embarrassment in his eyes.

"Heavy going?" enquired Campion sympathetically.

"Well, he wrote in a hurry, didn't he?" There was no affectation in the pronouncement, nor did he censure, but appeared to be offering an explanation merely. "It's a bit theatrical, you know, or at least I think so. The people aren't like anyone I've met." He paused and added, "So far," with a cautiousness which gave his age away again.

"That's all very true," said Mr. Campion, "but I shouldn't put it in your essay if I were you."

The child met his eyes with a startled expression.

"Good Lord, no," he said fervently and smiled at Campion as if he felt they shared a secret about schoolmasters.

They had been longer in the garden than they realised and the party had broken up when they returned. The room was deserted and the debris of empty glasses and overfilled ash trays made it look forlorn in spite of its essential gaiety. Through the front window the departing crowd was visible, straggling towards the wicket gate.

Amanda turned aside to look for her handbag and Campion went on to the hall alone. In the doorway he paused. Georgia was standing with her back to him looking up the staircase, and as he appeared she spoke to Dell over her shoulder.

"I shan't be a moment. You start the little bath chair thing."

With some vague idea of allowing them to get away first Campion remained where he was and he was still in the salon doorway when Val came hurrying downstairs, a small square box in her outstretched hand.

"There's only one left," she said. "You know how to take it? Soften it in water and gulp it down."

"Bless you, darling, you've saved my life." Georgia took the box without glancing at the other woman. "I must fly. He's waiting for me like a little dog on the step, the sweetie. Thanks so much."

She hurried across the hall and Val stood on the lowest stair looking after her. There was a startled expression upon her face and her lips were parted. Campion stared at her and she turned and saw him.

She did not speak but started violently, made a little inarticulate sound and, turning, fled up the staircase, leaving him bewildered and, in spite of every ounce of common sense that he possessed, alarmed. He had half a mind to follow her, and would, of course, have altered a great many things had he obeyed the impulse, but Georgia's precipitate return drove the incident from his mind.

"Where's Gaiogi?" she demanded, flying into the hall, her eyes bright with excitement. "My dear, he's turned up! Raymond's back. They say he's tight as forty owls, the abominable old brute. He must have been drinking like a fish all night. He's gone straight to his room. He says he'll sleep for an hour. I think it's best to let him, don't you? He's got to go on that plane. If it's the last thing he does he's got to go back today."

CHAPTER TEN

The Ulangi Flight Luncheon given by Alan Dell in the Degas Room at Caesar's Court was, as is the fashion, strictly informal. In spite of the fact that Towser spoke, Dell spoke, the heads of the various departments in the huge Alandel works responsible for the machine spoke, a wit from Towser's party who *could* speak spoke, and even the pilot drawled a few shy, halting words, the informality was strictly preserved. In spite of the amusing aeroplane of flowers suspended in a block of ice on a pillar in the centre of the horseshoe table, in spite of the silver-gilt souvenirs that Gaiogi had so thoughtfully provided, in spite of the Ulangi pears, a rather dreadful fruit imported at great trouble and expense for the occasion and served mercifully soaked in kirsch to deaden their own unpalatable flavour, the happy family party atmosphere was firmly maintained.

The one genuinely unconventional note was provided by Ramillies' absence and a great many excuses were offered, both publicly and privately, for that omission.

Towser, who was one of the older school of politicians with a big head and such an affectation of plain-mannishness on top of a natural bent in that direction that one automatically suspected him, most unjustly, of every sort of insincerity, explained at laborious length what he honestly understood about Sir Raymond's slight indisposition. It came out an overpowering story, hinting at sickly relatives dying in inaccessible parts of the island, cross-country journeys, and a noble if exhausted Ramillies crawling gamely home to be persuaded by an adoring wife to snatch what rest he might before attempting the feat of endurance which lay before him as a passenger on an almost epic flight.

It was unfortunate that the impression which this recital conveyed to that experienced audience was even worse than the facts. By the time the distinguished speaker had gone on to something else there was a universal conviction that Sir Raymond had been brought in drunk on a police stretcher and was even now lying unconscious on the floor of a private cell in the barber's shop. The pilot and the navigator exchanged glances and shrugged their shoulders philosophically. They were both lean stringy youngsters with faded hair and the curious clear-eyed, unimaginative stare of that new and magnificent breed that seems to have been created by or for the air. So long as their cargo avoided delirium tremens they did not care.

Sir Raymond's adoring wife, who was getting on very nicely in her place of honour between the minister and the host, looked properly tolerant of her husband's misfortunes, and the meal progressed happily with everyone being as charming as possible to the one uncertain element in their midst, the bored but ungullible Press.

Mr. Campion was not present. He lunched alone in the open-air restaurant in the water garden and avoided the eyes of more acquaintances than he had realised he possessed. Caesar's Court was flourishing. Gaiogi's principality was in its golden age.

With Ramillies safely in his room recovering from a night out, his own immediate charge was at a standstill. Like all professionals who are doing a little work on the side to oblige a friend, he felt at a disadvantage. Friendship is a hampering thing at the best of times, and the demands made in its name are often unreasonable. As far as he could see, everybody in his immediate circle was beseeching him to avert something different. Looking round this pleasant and expensive scene, it struck him forcibly that such universal alarm was quite extraordinary. Ramillies appeared to be the focal point of the general anxiety. Ramillies was clearly expected to do something spiteful or sensational or both. So far, it seemed to Campion, he had simply behaved like a spoilt undergraduate with a gift for the offensive, yet neither Val nor Gaiogi was unduly nervous or even inexperienced. He reminded himself that he knew all these decorative, volatile people very slightly. They were all such natural exhibitionists, all so busy presenting various aspects of themselves, that to meet them was like watching a play in which by the end of the evening all the actors seem old friends and yet in the back of one's mind there is the conviction that ten minutes behind the scenes would make them all strangers again. He decided to wander up and take a look at the patient.

He located the bedroom and was bearing down upon the door when it opened six inches or so and remained dark and ajar. He paused. Of all the minor incidents of life a door which opens at one's approach is perhaps the most disconcerting. An eye regarded him through the aperture.

"Campion."

"Yes?"

"Come in. Are the others still eating? Come in, will you?"

The thin sharp voice was not so strident as usual but the note of insolence was still there. Campion walked into a room whose only light crept in round the edges of drawn curtains and the door closed behind him. A shadowy figure laid an unsteady hand on his arm.

"I'm going to take my things down to the plane now." Ramillies sounded excited and the confidential tone was new in him. "I'm not travelling much. They're sticky about the weight because she's carrying so much extra juice. My man's gone on by sea and rail like a Christian and I don't want any damned hotel servants touching my stuff. That's natural, isn't it?"

A querulous anxiety in the question confirmed the general diagnosis, and his visitor made haste to reassure him. Ramillies tittered. It was an unpleasant sound in the gloom and reminded Mr. Campion that he never had liked the man.

"I'm going to shift it myself," Georgia's husband continued huskily. "You come down with me and see it weighed. You bear witness that I haven't got that gun. I've had my head talked off about that gun and I'm bloody sick of it. You come along. I've been on the lookout for a stranger but you're better. You'll do nicely."

Campion disengaged himself from the gripping fingers.

"Anything you like," he said easily. "Are you all right? I thought you weren't feeling too good."

"I've been drunk. God, I've been drunk!" He made the words a breathy little prayer of satisfaction. "I'm sobering up now. It's rotten sobering up but it won't last. Nothing gets me down for long. Besides, I've got something to do. I've got something on. I can always snap out of it if I've got something on. It doesn't really affect me."

The bravado sounded a trifle forlorn to Campion.

"Have you packed?" he enquired.

"Lord, yes, packed in town. What the hell are we doing chattering here in the dark?"

This was a question which had occurred to Mr. Campion himself and he said so.

"Georgia pulled the curtains to keep the blasted light out of my eyes." Ramillies was blundering slowly across the room as he spoke. "She's full of wifely concern, isn't she? Have you noticed it?"

He turned round suspiciously on the last word, letting in a shaft of sun with the same movement, but apparently the younger man's expression was satisfactory, for he seemed content.

"I've only got one little case and some coats," he said. "We'll take them down and show them. Then I'll come back and sleep. I'll be all right by the time we leave. We go at five, they say, not four; weather or something damned silly. What are you looking at? Do I show it much? I do sometimes."

He lurched unsteadily towards a mirror and stared at himself, and

Campion felt a twinge of pity for him. The man was grey and positively sweating, and his eyes had sunk into his head.

"Where on earth did you get the stuff at two in the morning?" he demanded involuntarily.

Ramillies looked round and for an instant there was a flicker of his old childlike smile.

"She had a cellar," he said. "Come on. I'm going to put on one coat. They'll weigh me as well as the baggage. I dislike those fellows. I dislike people who live for machinery. I dislike Dell himself. Not for the reason you think, Campion. Not for that reason. I dislike Dell because he's a mechanic and a blasted prig."

He found the coat he wanted and struggled slowly into it.

"A blasted sentimental petrol-scented prig," he added, standing swaying in the shaft of sunlight with the ulster flapping against his calves. "Georgia needs a sense of proportion. She'll get one when she comes out to me with the Taretons. I shall probably have my gun by then. I'm going to show them some sport. You're not the kind of chap who'd like what I call sport, Campion."

"No," said Mr. Campion, remembering him at school. "No, I don't think I am."

Ramillies began to laugh but thought better of it and presently they began a weary descent. Side by side in a calash they set off for the footbridge and a hangar. Ramillies looked like a great tweed parcel and a death's-head, and sat balancing a small suitcase on his knee while Campion drove the flimsy machine. It was nearly three quarters of a mile over gravel and turf and they took it slowly to avoid jolting. Ramillies sat silent, hunched up in his coat in the blazing sun, and Campion glanced at his beaded forehead with apprehension.

"I should take that thing off if I were you," he remarked. "You'll suffocate yourself."

"That would suit Dell, wouldn't it?" said Ramillies. "I expect he prays, don't you? That sort of chap hugs his virtue and prays I'll die —blasted prig! Damned fool, too. I'll tell you something, Campion. You're sitting there thinking I'm more offensive drunk than sober, aren't you?"

"Well," said Mr. Campion, not wishing to be offensive himself, "roughly that sort of thought, you know."

"I am," said Ramillies modestly, as if he had received a much-prized compliment. "I am. D'you know why I ever thought of leaving my wife here with that fellow hanging around her? Nobody knows Georgia. That's the cream of the joke. She's out of date. She's the 1902 chorus-girl type. It's damned low-class blood in her. She's got the careful-virgin mentality. I know. My God, I know! She wears a *ceinture de chasteté* with a wedding-ring key. She'll come out with the Taretons in six weeks time and when I get her there she'll give up the stage. This is a prophecy. You listen to it. Write it down somewhere. Georgia won't come back to the stage. I've got something on, you know. I'm not the complacent husband. I've got a surprise for Georgia and that fellow Dell. Sorry I'm being so vulgar. I don't know you well, do I?"

"We're not buddies," said Mr. Campion mildly. "You're tight."

"Yes," Sir Raymond agreed in his thin flat voice. "I'm very, very tight." He laughed. "These government fellows," he said, "they wouldn't stand me for ten minutes if it wasn't for one thing. Do you know what that is? I'm a genius with my niggers. My province is the most damned degenerate hole in the entire creation. My niggers would make your hair stand on end. They even startle me at times and I like 'em. The rest of the West Coast doesn't mention us when it writes home. It doesn't want to be associated with us. But my niggers and I understand one another. I suit them and they suit me. I'm not afraid, you know. I'm not afraid of anything on earth."

"Jolly for you," murmured Mr. Campion politely.

Ramillies nodded. "I've never tolerated fear. There's only one thing I'm afraid of and I've overcome that," he said earnestly and with that naïveté which Campion had noticed in him once before, "and I have just a touch of the miraculous with my two dirty little tribes. You look at this plane."

They were admitted somewhat grudgingly into the hangar. The plane stood half in and half out of the shed and was certainly something to see. It was a pretty four-seater single-engined machine of the Alandel Seraphim class, with the typical sharp nose and a specially designed undercarriage in anticipation of the Ulangi landing grounds, but by far the most sensational feature to the lay observer was the yellow metal paint which transformed the whole thing into a gaudy toy.

The mechanics who surrounded her each wore the slightly sullen expression reserved by the conscientious workman for anything unconventional in the way of decoration and one of them made so bold as to comment upon it.

"'Is Coloured 'Ighness will find this 'ere all colours o' the rainbow in three months," he observed ostensibly to a colleague but with a sidelong glance at Ramillies.

"He'll have broken his neck in it long before then or sold it to a dangerous relation," muttered Sir Raymond under his breath to Campion. "Where do I get myself weighed?"

Since practically everyone of authority was at the lunch there was a certain amount of confusion over this preliminary, and Mr. Campion fancied that he detected a certain transparency in his charge's motive in choosing this particular moment to make his arrangements. There was a brief delay, and he had leisure to observe the preparations for the official send-off. A narrow wooden platform had been erected against the wall just inside the hangar, and while at the moment this was smothered in cables and batteries in anticipation for the broadcast, a cut-glass water carafe and two enormous pots of hydrangeas standing precariously in a corner indicated the general effect desired.

Meanwhile Ramillies had got himself in the centre of a small group and Campion was summoned to be a witness to the fact that his small suitcase contained nothing to which anyone could possibly take exception. It was also sealed, an unnecessary precaution embarrassing to everyone except its owner, who insisted upon it being taken. Ramillies then clambered upon the scales himself while the old dangerous and irresponsible expression returned to his pallid face.

Since there appeared to be no deception here, either, everything was being very satisfactorily concluded when there was an unexpected interruption as Georgia appeared, very sweet and gracious and maternal.

"Darling," she said earnestly, hurrying over to her husband, "you ought to be lying down. I nearly had a fit when I found you'd gone. I'm going to take you back at once. My dear man, you're starting in a couple of hours. You must get some rest. Mr. Campion, you do agree, don't you?"

It was a charming little domestic scene and the group of interested minor officials were properly impressed. Ramillies proclaimed "night out" as clearly as if the words had been stamped all over him, and Georgia did much to counteract the gossip which had been floating about by as charming an exhibition of wifely devotion as the most sentimental British workingman could have wished to see. She no longer wore the Quentin Clear, Campion was relieved to notice.

Ramillies eyed her narrowly and Campion, who was watching him, was startled to see a sudden docility come into his face. He smiled at her happily, almost triumphantly, and tucked her arm into his.

"We'll go back together," he said. "Campion won't mind us taking the calash."

They went off arm in arm and Mr. Campion added another interesting and contradictory fact to his collection. Ramillies was genuinely in love with his wife and was therefore, presumably, deeply jealous of her.

He was strolling back across the turf when he encountered Amanda, who greeted him enthusiastically and seemed disposed to gossip.

"A.D.'s gone golfing with Towser," she said, "and I've just passed Georgia and Ramillies sitting side by side in a bath chair. It was very pretty. 'Having ten minutes to spare, I spent them with my husband.' I almost like her, don't you? She's so comfortingly obvious. The lunch was good—the food, I mean. Did you like the plane? It's only one of the Seraphim, of course. You should come and see the new Archangels we're building."

"I'd like it," he said gravely. "Tell me, do you do Cherubim as well?"

"Yes, we did, but the model wasn't too satisfactory." She shook her head over the failure.

"Too short in the tail, perhaps?" he suggested sympathetically.

"Nothing to—er—catch hold of."

"That's right," she agreed, eyeing him admiringly. "You're picking up, aren't you? The pink feathers came off the wings, too, just as you were going to say. Did you know Val was ill?"

"Ill?"

Amanda nodded and her big honey-coloured eyes were thoughtful.

"Not seriously. But she looked pretty white and sort of hunted at lunch and afterwards she went off to lie down." She hesitated and shot him one of those odd direct glances which were peculiarly her own. "It's terrifying and ludicrous and ugly, isn't it?" she said. "Not Val, of course, but the thing itself; cake love."

"Cake love?" he enquired, remembering her interest in food. Amanda raised her eyebrows at him.

"Oh, use your head," she said. "Don't embarrass me. This thing they've all got that's hurting them so and making us all feel they may blow up. Cake love as opposed to the bread-and-butter kind."

"Oh, I see. You're plumping for bread and butter, are you, my young hopeful?"

"I'm full of bread and butter," said Amanda with content.

Campion looked down at her. "You're very young," he remarked. She grunted contemptuously.

"Please God I'll stay like it, you poor old gent," she said. "Let's sit on the terrace and digest. We can keep our eye on 'em all from there. Ramillies is up to something, isn't he? You don't think he's going to pop his head out of the plane and pick Georgia off just as they start to taxi?"

"Relying on the engine row to hide the shot?" Campion laughed. "That would be rather pretty. If he wasn't seen doing the deed the body wouldn't be noticed till they were away, and nobody would suspect him."

"Except us," agreed Amanda complacently. "It's not such a batty idea. It's the kind of childish thing he might do. Fancy dressing that girl up as his wife the other night."

They sat chatting on the edge of the terrace until the sun passed over the edge of the house. Amanda was a stimulating conversationalist. Her complete lack of self-consciousness rendered no subject taboo, and he found her philosophy, which appeared to be part common sense and part mechanics, refreshing after the purely medical variety on which his generation had fed so long.

The ceremony was timed for a quarter to five, and by four o'clock there was a fair-sized crowd round the hangar, far away over the river at the end of the lawn. Amanda sat silent, considering the view. The scene was peaceful, there was a light wind, and the treetops were golden against an eggshell sky.

"There goes Ramillies," she said, nodding towards his tweed-coated figure gliding over the gravel in a calash. "He's in good time. Since he's alone, I suppose that means that A.D. is back."

Mr. Campion looked surprised. Traces of femininity in Amanda were rare. She smiled at him.

"I'm not one of your beastly 'kind women,'" she said. "I don't go round shedding grace. That was quite justified. There goes that little ape Wivenhoe with his nose."

They sat where they were for another half-hour, and then, when Georgia and Dell, Tante Marthe, Gaiogi and the rest of the morning's party had joined the stream winding over the bridge and across the turf, they rose themselves and wandered after the others. Campion was content. He felt rested and at ease. The air was soft and pleasant, and that tranquil mood which is induced by the contemplation of the derring-do of others was upon him.

The two boys with the faded hair and level eyes were going to fly Ramillies over the Sahara, and all Mr. Campion had to do was to watch them go. The hundred-year-old turf was spongy beneath his feet, and Amanda, the least exacting woman in the world to entertain, was by his side. In his own mind he had dismissed Ramillies as a possible source of disturbance. He felt sure that any project Ramillies had in mind was being preserved for his party with the Taretons.

The awakening came a minute or two later. Dell appeared, hurrying back with Georgia just behind him.

"Have you seen Ramillies?" he demanded. "We thought he was down here. The—the fellow seems to have gone again. The ceremony begins in a minute."

"Oh, but he's there," said Amanda inexplicitly. "We saw him go into the hangar, didn't we, Albert?"

"He certainly came down this way just over half an hour ago, just before Wivenhoe," said Campion more cautiously. "Are you sure you haven't missed him?"

"There's a lot of people there, darling," said Georgia nervously, pulling at Dell's sleeve. "He may be among them."

"My dear girl, that's impossible." Dell stood hesitating. "Time's so short," he said.

"But I saw him," insisted Amanda, and set off for the aeroplane shed at a run, with Campion behind her.

There was the usual excitement in the crowd round the entrance, and the platform was a seething jumble of privileged guests, guests who were not privileged, and experts who were trying to protect their untidy paraphernalia. Everyone seemed to have heard that Ramillies was missing again, and the long sibilant name sounded from all sides. Campion hoisted himself on the dais and looked around him. It seemed impossible that the man should be there unobserved. He pushed his way over to a mechanic.

"He *was* 'ere." The man looked over his shoulder as if he expected to find the lost sheep behind him. " 'E come in about 'alf an hour ago, just before the gentleman from the government who wanted everything altered. No, I ain't seen 'im since."

"Albert." Amanda came round from behind the plane, which had been wheeled out into the sunlight. She was dragging behind her a bespectacled young man in oily dungarees. "Jimmy says Ramillies *was* here," she said. "He wanted to see the seating accommodation again, and they let him in the plane. Then Wivenhoe came along and took everyone's attention, and they think Ramillies went off then."

Campion glanced at the gaudy little Seraphim spreading its golden wings to the evening.

"Let's have a look," he suggested.

"He's not *in* there," said Jimmy, revealing a stammer and a public-school accent. "Don't be absurd, old man. I've c-c-called him."

"Let's have a look."

They found Ramillies cramped in the back seat. His tweed ulster billowed round him, and beneath it, strapped to his body, were the dismantled parts of the Filmer 5A together with two hundred rounds of ammunition. He was quite dead.

CHAPTER ELEVEN

Mr. Campion's first thought as he looked down at the body was that if Ramillies merely intended to reawaken his wife's interest he had overdone the effort considerably. After that he had little time for reflection.

A dead man in a gilded aeroplane in the midst of a crowd, with a broadcast imminent, an African flight about to begin, and in authority a cabinet minister who does not wish to be convinced that anything unpleasant has occurred, is a responsibility which absorbs all one's attention.

The magic words "taken ill" circulated through the inquisitive gathering inside the hangar and acted, as they always do, as a temporary sedative. No doctor appeared but Georgia hurried forward, all grace and anxiety, and the photographers obtained their one useful picture of the afternoon when she stood looking up at Wivenhoe in the doorway of the plane.

It was Wivenhoe, supported by Dell and a white-faced Gaiogi, who made the situation clear to Campion.

"My dear fellow, he can't die here," he whispered urgently, indicating by a single expressive lift of his shoulder the fidgety crowd, the weaving pressmen, and the mechanics and groundsmen who were at bay round their precious plane. "He can't. The Old Man wouldn't stand for it for a moment. Sir Ray must be taken up to the house and a doctor must see him there." He leant forward, his big nose bringing his face much nearer the other man's own than he seemed to realise. "He's alive. The Old Man is convinced that he's alive. I'll bring Lady Ramillies along after you. I'll explain he's very ill, so she'll be prepared for anything."

Mr. Campion said no more. He was barely on speaking terms with himself, let alone anyone else. To spend an entire day watching a man to see that he does not make a nuisance of himself and, in the furtherance of one's object, to connive at the most obvious piece of smuggling one has ever seen, only to be so entirely frustrated at the eleventh hour, is an exasperating experience. His frame of mind did not encourage him to insist on the letter of police procedure. He hoped he knew a corpse when he saw one, but if the government wished its servant, Sir Raymond Ramillies, to die in a bed, who was Albert Campion to protest? He was, also, very sorry for Ramillies.

Actually there seemed little reason why this particular body should not be moved. There were no signs of wounding, and the possibility that the man had been shot in that confined space, firstly without sound and secondly without any smell of cordite, seemed more than unlikely.

The lean head with the doormat hair lolled forward on the chest, the weight of the skull dragging the tendons of the neck horribly. The skin was still clammy with sweat and the flesh was not quite cold. Campion was curious to see the eyes and as he lifted one flaccid lid he was surprised to find the pupil almost normal. There were one or two other curious circumstances and he made a note of them.

The arrival of the ambulance provided a few grim moments. All that had to be done was accomplished in whispers, since the broadcast, which waits for no man, had begun and Towser's resonant voice, a trifle shaken but otherwise normally monotonous, had embarked upon the prearranged speech.

Georgia climbed into the ambulance and was persuaded out of it by the resourceful Wivenhoe, while Mr. Campion took her place on the spare leather bench. The stretcher was hoisted gently into position, the doors closed, and the wheels began to move. It was a very discreet departure.

Ramillies lay on his back beside the dark glass windows and Mr. Campion and the attendant sat and looked at him.

A uniform can make a man the next best thing to invisible, and when someone sucked a tooth with a sound both human and ingratiating Mr. Campion started and turned to see, for the first time, a small, sharp-featured, red face lit with the bright ghoul's eyes of the professional calamity fancier.

"You're a relative, I expect," observed a wistful voice.

"No, no, I'm not, I'm afraid." Campion felt for a cigarette and changed his mind.

The attendant got up and stood looking down at Ramillies with fascination.

"You're just a friend, are you?" he said regretfully. "Well, I dare say it'll be a bit of a shock for you. You've got to prepare yourself, you know. I thought that as soon as I set eyes on 'im. I've seen too many of 'em. You get used to 'em in our work. As soon as I see 'im I said to myself, 'This is goin' to be a shock for someone.' I thought it might be you."

He conveyed considerable reproach and unconsciously Mr. Campion did his best for him, as was his nature.

"I knew him quite well."

"Knew? So you know he's a goner?" Reproach had become disappointment. "You're right. 'E is dead. I see it the moment I saw 'im. 'E's nearly cold. Still, you can't be too sure. When we git up to the 'ouse we'll do one or two of the tests, although I expect there'll be a doctor there by then."

There was not so much relief as contempt in the last phrase.

"Once a doctor gets 'old of a patient you're nowhere. They think they know everything. And yet a man like me, who's seen serious cases every day of 'is life, he knows quite as much as any doctor. Look at this chap 'ere, now. D'you know what I notice about 'im? I wouldn't say it if you were a relative, but as you're only a friend I shan't 'ave to be so tactful. (We're taught that, you know: be tactful with relatives. That's part of our training.) Looking at 'im, I should say, 'You've 'ad a seizure, my lad, a sort of fit, and, though I couldn't say for certain without openin' you up, in my opinion you've got a clot of blood over the 'eart or in the 'ead, and if it's not that, then it's fatty degeneration. You've had trouble with your arteries for a long time and you've bin livin' a bit too 'ard and now the excitement of getting ready for this 'ere trip's bin too much for you, and I'd give you my certificate . . . after I'd done the tests to see you *was* dead.' "

He paused and looked at Mr. Campion brightly.

"That's what I'd say and I'd be right," he said.

Mr. Campion considered him with distaste, but there was something forgivable in those bright, excited eyes. The man was a ghoul, but a good-natured one, and the dreadful thought came to Campion that if Ramillies' truculent spirit should by chance be hanging about its late abode its reply to the address might be worth hearing. There is a lot of talk about the dignity of death, yet it is but a negative kind of dignity. Ramillies alive would have made short work of this impertinence.

Meanwhile the ambulance had bumped off the flying field onto the lower road and had passed the main entrance gates of Caesar's Court.

"We're goin' round to the cottage, you know," said the ghoul. "That's standing orders. Nothing unpleasant near the main 'otel. It's very sensible reelly. As soon as you get a bit o' class there's no sympathy with illness. 'Ave you noticed that? In a different neighbour'ood a thing like this'd be an attraction, but not with the smart people you get 'ere. No, it's all 'ush, 'ush 'ere. Coo, 'e's ill! Shut 'im in a nursing 'ome and don't let me see 'im. That's the cry every time. Did you know this gentleman very well, sir? Would you say 'e was an 'ard liver? I don't want to sound inquisitive. It's just a professional question. I like to know if my diagnosis is correct. 'E's bit 'is tongue. That's a seizure, isn't it?"

Mr. Campion breathed deeply.

"I really can't tell you," he said. He was not naturally squeamish, but a ghoul is a ghoul and to suffer them gladly is not in everybody's capacity.

"I'm sorry, I'm sure," said the attendant stuffily and was silent for a while.

Presently, however, Mr. Campion, who had forgotten him, turned to find him looking down at one of the rather fine brown hands which lay upon the cover. He had tied a small piece of string very tightly round the lower phalanx of the forefinger and was studying the effect.

"That's the only test you can do in the ambulance," he said. "You can't go mucking about with saucers of water on the chest in 'ere. There you are, you see; there's no pinky glow. 'E's dead. I knew 'e was dead as soon as I saw 'im. I expect 'e was all right this afternoon, was 'e? Must 'ave been a shock for you."

"Yes, he was all right this afternoon." A certain lack of decision in Mr. Campion's tone brought the bright eyes up again.

"Then you did notice something? 'E was 'eavy, was 'e? Very likely. P'raps 'e was a bit appre'ensive? A lot of people are 'oo die sudden. It's a funny thing and the doctors say there's nothing in it, but I've noticed it time and again. Time and again I've 'ad a sobbing relative sittin' where you're sittin' now and they've told me the same thing. Just before a seizure, just before someone's took off sudden, they've bin overcast, as you might say. Felt there was somethin' 'angin' over them. Of course that's psychic; that's not medicine; and I don't suppose there's anything in it. But it does 'appen. Would you say it 'ad 'appened in this case? Would you say this gentleman 'ad any premonition? D'you think it went through 'is 'ead that 'e was goin' to die?"

"No," said Mr. Campion soberly. "No. I don't think it occurred to him for a moment."

The heavy tires scrunched on gravel and the ghoul looked out of the window.

"'Ere we are," he said. "Well, there'll be a doctor 'ere, but 'e'll tell you the same as me and get paid more for it."

It was during the next twenty minutes that Mr. Campion received the key to the entire story. At the time he did not recognise it, but afterwards, when he looked back, he saw that it was then that the shadowy words were formed and spread out for him to recognise.

Gaiogi was waiting on the cushion-strewn steps of his doll's house when the ambulance arrived and only the presence of a calash, abandoned on the path, indicated that he had not flown there. Already evidences of his extraordinary organisation were apparent. There was even a woman in nurse's uniform in the doorway behind him and a houseman, with blankets and hot-water bottles, appeared in the hall as the two ambulance men carried the stretcher inside.

"I'm afraid all that is useless," murmured Campion, trying not to be nettled by the reproachful expression in his host's shiny brown eyes. "He was quite dead when I found him."

Gaiogi took his arm.

"Oh no, my dear fellow," he said pleadingly. "Oh *no*. Be careful, be careful, you two men. Take the stairs carefully—carefully. No jolting, please."

The nurse superintended the ascent and he watched her critically, still holding Campion's arm.

"His doctor will be here in a moment," he whispered. "Then we shall see. I've been talking to him on the phone. He's coming at once."

"From town?"

"No. Oh no. He was here this afternoon, playing tennis. He's Buxton-Coltness, of Upper Brook Street, a very distinguished fellow. Very good. Do you know him? He's just coming."

Gaiogi made the announcement blandly and with the faintest suggestion of a smile behind his anxiety. He was like a man throwing off a small conjuring trick in the midst of some other major manœuvre.

"Wasn't it fortunate that he should have been here?"

"Miraculous," said Mr. Campion involuntarily. "One's every want anticipated. There'll be an inquest, of course."

"An inquest? An inquest at Caesar's Court?"

There is one expression that is the same upon every countenance. It is the slow, incredulous stare of disgust which is reserved for him who reveals the ultimate depths, the mortal insult, the utterly unforgivable error of taste or morals. Gaiogi wore it now and Mr. Campion was almost apologetic until he pulled himself together and grasped at his fleeting sense of proportion.

"My dear chap, it's a sudden death," he protested.

"I doubt it," said Gaiogi calmly. "You are a good chap, Campion, a sensible fellow, but you jump to conclusions. We do not know if this man is dead. Let us hope he is not. It is for his doctor to say."

Mr. Campion blinked and was prevented from implicating himself still further by the arrival of a second calash bearing Georgia and Wivenhoe. Georgia came to Campion, her hands outstretched. She was pale but controlled, and there was something about her manner that made him think of suppressed excitement before he put the idea aside as unworthy.

"My dear, how is he?" she said, her eyes meeting his frankly. "Don't be afraid to tell me. Is it terribly bad? I'm being as sensible as I possibly can and you can rely on me. This dear boy here has been preparing me for the worst and I'm not a child. I can stand it if you tell me. How is he?"

"Georgia, we don't know." Gaiogi seemed to have caught her mood and for the first time Mr. Campion felt slightly nauseated. Everybody was behaving too well for anything. "The doctor is coming. Don't go up yet. There is a nurse with him, an excellent girl. You are wonderfully brave. You are taking it just as I knew you would. Look, we will go into my little room and sit down."

"He's quite right, you know, Lady Ramillies." Wivenhoe's solicitude was charming. "You can see the door from the window. The moment the doctor arrives we shall know everything."

The living room had been tidied after the hangover party and a decanter of old brandy and glasses had been set out on a small table as though ready for some emergency. Gaiogi dispensed the cordial with an air.

"I've told Dell to keep everybody down here," he said. "Meanwhile this house is positively surrounded, so we shan't have any Press for a little while at least. Ah, there is someone now. That will be Doctor Buxton-Coltness."

Everyone so far forgot his manners as to stare out of the window at the newcomer. Even in flannels and a blazer Dr. Harvey Buxton-Coltness managed to convey that he was a distinguished man. The white scarf round his throat was folded with precision and his step was firm and purposeful. His voice floated in to them from the hall. It was deep and reassuring. Here, at any rate, was a man with a manner, the kind of doctor who was entirely in keeping with Caesar's Court.

Georgia and Gaiogi hurried out to him. Wivenhoe gave them two minutes and then went out himself to bring her back. There was something familiar about her when she returned. Campion was reminded forcefully of the heroine in *The Little Sacrifice*. There was the same quiet, only-just-balanced movement, the same air of suppressed tragedy.

"I think I'll sit down," she said. She glanced at Campion and smiled wanly. "They've promised to send for me the instant he's conscious."

It was a horrible moment. The complete insincerity of the entire scene sickened Campion and he looked at Wivenhoe steadily. The young man frowned at him and bent over his glass.

Georgia went on playing her part for some little time. It was not an inspired performance; rather, a trifle mechanical, as if her thoughts were not on it.

"I can't imagine Ray ill," she said. "He's not the kind of person who ought to suffer. Haven't you noticed it? There's something so vital about him, like a child. I think that's what I fell in love with first of all. He's been going the pace terribly lately. I persuaded him to go and see Buxton-Coltness only a little while ago. He didn't tell me what he said. He wouldn't, you know, not if it was anything serious. That's where Ray's rather sweet."

Mr. Campion was not given to hating people but at that moment he conceived an active dislike for Georgia Ramillies and surprised himself in an impulse to take her by the shoulders and shake her till her teeth rattled. He felt she knew as well as he did, as well as Wivenhoe knew, as well as the ghoul knew, as well as Buxton-Coltness must know by this time, that Ramillies was dead, dead as mutton, and in appallingly fishy circumstances. He knew now what Val had meant when she had described Georgia as vulgar. Georgia's vulgarity was staggering. It was the overpowering, insufferable vulgarity to which nothing is sacred. It was also, he found, the vulgarity which breeds vulgarity; his own inclination to stand and shout the brutal truth at her until he forced her out of her performance was almost uncontrollable, and when someone came in he turned towards the door with physical relief.

It was Val. She had evidently just made up her face but her pallor made the colour look artificial and there were shadows round her large light eyes. She glanced from one to the other enquiringly.

"I met a servant on the landing," she said, "and he told me something quite incredible. Is it true?"

The direct question in the clear, startled voice brought a draught of reality into the room. Georgia looked up at her and became, miraculously, a human being again.

"It's Ray," she said bluntly. "He was taken ill in the plane. The doctor is with him now. Everyone's being awfully kind but I'm afraid it's serious."

It was an odd situation. For a moment it was Georgia who was softening a staggering blow to the other woman. There was alarm in her eyes and something dreadfully like apology in her tone.

Like most men Mr. Campion was at heart conventional, and when he saw brutal, practical reality thrust under his very nose he could not bring himself to recognise it. He watched the two women with growing bewilderment. They were both entirely female, both sharp-witted, both realists, but whereas the one had a balanced intellect in control the other was as wanton and unexpected as a rudderless steamboat in a gale. Val sat down.

"Is he dead?"

Wivenhoe, even more out of his depth than Campion, made a disparaging sound, but for once Georgia did not respond to him. She seemed to be absorbed by the other woman.

"I think so," she said. "They've been preparing me for it. Oh, Val, isn't it *fantastic*? I mean it's frightful, terrible, the most ghastly thing that could have happened! But—it's amazing, isn't it?"

Mr. Campion felt his eyes widening. Now it was impossible to misunderstand. He and Wivenhoe had been forgotten as completely as if they had been children, to be ignored as soon as a grownup entered. Georgia was doing no play acting for Val. They were equals coming down to essentials in the face of the unexpected.

Val was sitting on a low chair, her hands folded in her lap. She was wearing a bright red dress of some smooth material which had been designed for her, and in it she made a complete and finished work of art, as artificial in appearance as any other ornament in that mannered room, but her personality was vivid and entirely human. She alone expressed that sense of shock and calamity which her brother now realised was the element he had missed throughout the entire incident.

"What happened?" she enquired quietly.

"I don't know." Georgia glanced at Wivenhoe. "What was it? Some sort of stroke? How did he die?"

"I say, you know—really. We—we must wait for the doctor." The young man was flustered. "I mean, we don't actually know yet, do we? He was breathing in the plane. I'm sure of it. That is definite. Otherwise he couldn't have been moved, do you see? It was probably some sort of embolism. He was getting on for fifty, wasn't he? I know that sort of thing does happen. An uncle of mine died the same way. It's dreadful when it does occur but it's very much kinder for the old boys. . . ."

He was drivelling and seemed to realise it. Neither of the two women was looking at him. Val's eyes were holding Georgia's.

"You saw him when he came in today, didn't you?" she said. "How was he? I thought he seemed so well last night."

There was no hint of accusation in her voice or in the words, but Georgia recoiled.

"He was in a fearful state this afternoon," she said sharply. "He'd been drinking all night. He said so. He was thick and loquacious and —oh, Val, don't look at me like that! I'm brokenhearted, really I am. I'm holding myself together with tremendous difficulty, darling. I am sorry. I *am*. I am sorry. When you're married to a man, whatever you do, however you behave to one another, there is an affinity. There is. It's a frightful shock. I haven't begun to realise it yet. When I do I——"

"My dear Lady Ramillies!" Wivenhoe's startled voice was what she needed. She swung towards him, put both her hands in his and began to cry. Val blushed. The slow resentful colour spread over her face and neck and her eyes were sombre.

"You poor, poor darling," she said.

Georgia wiped her eyes.

"I hate hysterical women," she murmured, smiling wryly at Campion. "I'm all right, I'm all right now." She patted Wivenhoe's hands and released them. Then, rising, she went over to Val and sat down beside her with an arm round her shoulders. "You see, dearest, I don't know what's happened," she said earnestly. "Nobody knows yet. It's all so—so utterly extraordinary. It's incredible. But, Val, incredible things do happen to me, don't they? You know that, don't you? We're always commenting on it, aren't we?"

She seemed to be pleading with the fair girl, striving to force some reassurance out of her, and Campion saw the strong, capable fingers pressing into the shoulder of the red dress. Val laid a hand on Georgia's knee but she did not speak. She was rigid, and there was a short, unhappy silence before it was mercifully broken by footsteps in the hall.

Gaiogi and the doctor came in solemnly and shut the door behind them.

CHAPTER TWELVE

The personal humility of all medical men is jeopardised throughout their career by the fact that one of the disadvantages of their profession is that they should be treated with much greater seriousness than any other visitor to the normal household. Their lightest words are hung upon and they receive every hour the flattery of absorbed attention. Some noble natures can stand up to this and some cannot, but there is a small class which turns a disadvantage into an asset and thrives upon the thing that should defeat it.

Dr. Harvey Buxton-Coltness was one of these. Critical colleagues told each other bitterly that it was Buxton-Coltness' conceit alone which kept him on the register. His head, they said, was like a balloon which lifted him gently over morass and crevice, bearing him gracefully from cocktail party to ducal bedroom, from exorbitant nursing home to fashionable funeral, with a grace and ease not afforded to any man with his feet set firmly upon the ground.

Mr. Campion recognised his type as soon as he saw him and another little detail in the key of the problem flickered under his nose.

The doctor was a large man with what is called a fine presence. His light grey eyes were entirely without humour in spite of the laughter lines beside them, and his shapely pink hands were graceful and expressive. He waited for Gaiogi to introduce him to Georgia and bestowed a general nod upon the rest of the room. When he judged the right moment had come he made his announcement tactfully.

"Lady Ramillies," he said, "I am afraid I have bad news for you. Can you bear it?"

Georgia nodded. Even she seemed to feel that a return to artificiality would be indecorous.

"I was so afraid," she said simply. "What—what was it, Doctor? His heart?"

"His heart—yes." Dr. Buxton-Coltness conveyed that he was making a very difficult thing very simple. He also seemed considerably relieved. "Yes, I think we may say in actual fact his heart." He took the hand which she had stretched out to him and stood looking down at her, his cold eyes cautious in spite of his general air of contented omnipotence. "Tell me, Lady Ramillies," he began, his voice rolling melodiously round the room, "is this quite the shock it might have been? Did Sir Raymond tell you nothing which might just conceivably have made you apprehensive?"

There was a pause and he glanced round him enquiringly.

"We are all in committee, are we not?"

"Oh yes," said Georgia hastily. "We're all very close friends."

She made some perfunctory introductions and returned to his question.

"He told me he'd been to see you. He'd been worried about himself and some of our friends advised him to go to you. He told me you thought he ought to go slow."

"I did. I did, most emphatically." The deep voice was thick with sad conviction. "There were distinct symptoms of chronic nephritis, a considerably raised blood pressure, and I diagnosed cardiovascular trouble. I warned Sir Raymond to be very careful of himself. I told him to avoid every sort of excess. I can't put it plainer than that, can I? Every sort of excess. I impressed it upon him that alcohol was definitely dangerous to him and I advised a visit to a spa. Now Mr. Laminoff tells me he can hardly have been said to have taken my advice. Do you agree with that?"

Georgia looked at him blankly and he, mistaking her reaction, fell back upon his charm.

"Forgive me," he said. "Of course this is a very great shock for you. Surely it's not necessary for you to give me these details yourself, is it? Isn't there some member of the family you can depute to act for you? If I might prescribe for *you*, Lady Ramillies, I should go to bed immediately. Keep warm. Take a sedative. What do you usually use? Aspirin? Or do you like luminol? Anything like that. Wrap yourself up. Get your maid to bring you plenty of hot-water bottles."

"No," said Georgia with sudden decision. "No, I'm all right. I can tell you. We can all tell you. Ray hasn't been looking after himself. He's been very gay during the last week or so—more, I think, than usual."

She glanced round at them for confirmation, and Gaiogi, who was watching the scene with the bright anxiety of a squirrel, made a reassuring noise. Georgia went on steadily.

"Then last night, in the middle of a farewell party, he went rushing off somewhere and came back this morning about lunchtime. He said he'd been drinking all night, and frankly that was obvious. He didn't come to the farewell luncheon and when I saw him afterwards I thought he was even worse. He was unsteady, you know, and pale, and frightfully talkative and—well . . ." She threw out her hands expressively and the doctor nodded.

He glanced round at his small audience with sad resignation.

"There you are," he said. "There you are."

Georgia opened her mouth but did not speak. She stood staring at him. The matter-of-fact expression which he had used seemed to have jolted her. Presently she turned to Val, her eyes wide and dark.

"Dead," she said. "Ray is dead. Val, do you realise it? Ray is dead." The doctor moved to her side with unexpected agility.

"Now, my dear lady," he began warningly, "my dear lady, sit down. I foresaw this. It was only to be expected. Sit down. Mr. Laminoff, I want some water, please."

"No." Georgia pushed him away. "No, really. I'm not hysterical. I suddenly saw it. That was all. Why did he die? What was it?"

She listened to his recital with deep attention and so did Campion. The full medical definition of the words "arterial thrombosis" is impressive to the lay mind. It is one of those simple mechanical disasters which are easily comprehensible to anybody, and as Mr. Campion sat listening to the full, confident voice his brows rose.

In a well-ordered society it is easy to think of some things as concrete when they are nothing of the kind. After long years of experience Mr. Campion had come to consider a sudden and suspicious death as synonymous with a post-mortem and a coroner's inquest, but now for the first time it was brought strongly to his mind that this was not so in actual fact. No ordinary hard-working general practitioner would dream of giving a certificate of natural death in the present case, for the excellent reason that should any talk arise afterwards, as well it might in ordinary circumstances, the consequences would be thunderingly inconvenient for him, and whereas he would have everything to lose he would have precious little to gain. But there was no earthly reason why a man like Harvey Buxton-Coltness should not give a certificate; rather, every reason that he should.

Buxton-Coltness' practice was not bounded by any district. His patients were all wealthy folk recommended to him by each other. The more influential friends he made the better for him, and here he was in a nest of influential people. It was clearly to everyone's advantage that there should be no fuss over Ramillies' death. Towser, for one, would be more than grateful to hear that it was a natural tragedy. Gaiogi, Georgia herself, nobody wanted publicity. The ghoul's words returned to him forcefully:

"It's all 'ush, 'ush 'ere. . . . Coo, 'e's ill! Shut 'im in a nursing 'ome and don't let me see 'im. That's the cry every time."

It was horribly true and nobody could possibly know it better than the fashionable doctor with his partnership in Mayfair, his colossal fees and his magnificent manner. There was no reason why he should not issue a certificate of death from thrombosis of a main artery following kidney disease and cardiodilation, and attend the funeral at Willesden Cemetery, fixing himself in yet another twenty useful minds as that charming man who was "so clever and considerate when poor Ray died after getting so abominably tight." And if there was a little talk afterwards, what was the real danger? It would only be talk among people who would never risk seeing themselves in court on a slander charge. At worst it would be frivolous and meaningless talk, and not in any case detrimental to the doctor.

Mr. Campion blinked. He saw how it was going to be done. Buxton-Coltness was going to give the certificate and there was only one thing that would stop him. That was immediate talk. Talk now. He glanced round the room. He saw Gaiogi, Wivenhoe, Georgia and Val. Even Val was financially interested in the preservation of the peace and privacy of Caesar's Court. There remained himself. He was the sole representative of the general public who might demand to know more definitely the cause of Raymond Ramillies' extraordinarily opportune death. He alone was unsatisfied. He alone was curious to know exactly what sort of seizure had caused those last convulsions. It was up to him. He was the only disinterested agent.

The hesitant words were on the tip of his tongue when he saw the pitfall, and as it opened beneath his feet he experienced for the first time that deep anger which altered him so and changed him from the affable universal uncle to the man with an intolerable personal affront to avenge. How could he protest? He was the guest of a host who had expressly invited him to prevent just such trouble as he was preparing to make. Moreover, he had spent the day watching a man who had died under his nose. If the circumstances were suspicious, had he not had every opportunity to alter them as they occurred? Both his professional dignity and his natural ingrained reluctance to abuse his position as a guest prevented him from speaking. They were his two vulnerable spots, his two vanities. It was almost as though someone had sized him up and sized him up accurately, a degrading experience for anybody at the best of times.

Most people dislike to be made use of and resent being forced into a position wherein their hands are tied, but in some folk the experience raises a devil. Mr. Campion was one of these. Had he been sure of his ground, he flattered himself, he would have conquered his weaknesses and taken the strong, if oafish, course, but he was not sure. If Providence's celebrated Mysterious Ways Department was actually as blatantly at work as it appeared to be, then Ramillies might have died from a thrombosis, a cerebral hæmorrhage or any other natural thunderbolt known to medicine.

As it was, Campion would do nothing. He saw that at once and his sense of personal outrage grew. He was trapped by himself, fettered by his own personality. The thing was mental jujitsu. The plaything-of-fate sensation was bad enough but he had an uncomfortable feeling that the fate in question had a human brain behind it, and there was insult as well as inconvenience to counter.

Mr. Campion's amiable brown face became dangerously blank and he stood looking at the company, his hands deep in his pockets and his pale eyes narrowed behind his spectacles.

The unexpected development came from Georgia. She was sitting on a corner of the couch under the window, her hands between her knees and her dark head bowed.

"I couldn't have done anything, could I?" she demanded, looking up.

"Nothing." Dr. Buxton-Coltness managed to give the word sympathy as well as conviction.

Georgia sighed.

"It's so extraordinary," she said. "It's so utterly extraordinary."

"It's very terrible." Gaiogi substituted the better word with gentle firmness.

"Of course," said Georgia sharply. "Of course. No one knows that better than I do, Gaiogi. But it is extraordinary, too, isn't it, Val?"

The fair woman did not reply and she hurried on.

"He didn't even take anything. He had nothing at all. He didn't even take a sleeping powder. I gave him a cachet blanc when I first saw him and he decided not to come down to lunch."

She seemed to find something surprising in her own words, for she broke off abruptly and sat up.

"It was that cachet you gave me, Val. I meant to take it myself. But when I saw him it seemed only charitable to hand it over. He took it at once. That's all he had."

Val regarded her steadily. She was cold and slightly contemptuous.

"It was a perfectly ordinary cachet blanc," she said.

"My dear, of course it was." Georgia was eyeing her. "Of course." She laughed and covered her face with her hands immediately afterwards. "I'm completely off my balance. I only suddenly remembered that that was the only thing he did take, and that you had meant it for me."

The words were out of her mouth before she realised their full significance and she looked as startled by them as anyone else in the room.

Val rose.

"You don't mean that, do you?" she said.

"No," said Georgia hastily. "No. No, of course not." But she spoiled the denial a moment afterwards by allowing a glimmer of ill-timed mischief to pass over her face. "After all, my pet, why should you want to get rid of me?"

That was all, but the trouble was made. The little flame flickered and grew. It flared in Gaiogi's eyes, passed over Wivenhoe's head, and revealed itself to Buxton-Coltness, who recognised it and retreated hastily, his cautious expression deepening. He coughed.

"Lady Ramillies," he began, "I've been thinking. This is a sudden death, you know, and if Sir Raymond had not been a patient I could never have considered giving a certificate. In that case a post-mortem and an inquest would have been automatic. You realise that, don't you?"

Georgia looked at him blankly.

"Don't you know how he died?" she said.

Dr. Buxton-Coltness smiled faintly with his small mouth and Gaiogi turned away.

"My dear lady." The doctor's beautiful voice was kind. "I am satisfied, but in a case of this sort there are certain formalities which can hardly be ignored. These things are very painful but they have to be endured."

Georgia saw Gaiogi's face.

"Not an inquest," she said. "Doctor, can't you have a post-mortem without an inquest? Isn't that possible?"

Wivenhoe cleared his throat.

"In such exceptional circumstances, sir," he said, "couldn't—I mean, couldn't the certificate be held up for an hour or two while the P.M. was rushed through?"

Campion watched the doctor curiously. The man was very tempted. After all, his entire scheme of life was to be obliging to the right people.

"I suppose it might be arranged," he was saying dubiously. "My partner, Rowlandson Blake, the surgeon, might possibly be persuaded. I don't know, really. I should have to telephone, of course."

It was at that moment that Campion caught sight of Val and her fixed expression and white face sent a thrill of unreasoning alarm trickling down his spine. He moved over to her, and, taking her by the arm, led her out into the little walled garden, lying smug in the warm evening sun. She went with him obediently, her hands clasped limply behind her back, but she did not speak and he missed her direct, confiding glance. They walked over the grass plot in silence and after a while he spoke himself.

"What are you thinking?"

"I'm not."

"Bad business."

"Frightful."

"I say, Val?"

"Yes?"

"What did you give that woman?"

"A cachet blanc."

There was a long pause and when Campion spoke again his tone was very casual.

"They're things in rice-paper cases, aren't they?"

"You know they are." The icy quality in her voice did not warn him, as it might have done. There is nothing like the blood tie to render ordinary sympathetic comprehension void.

"One could open a thing like that?"

"One could, easily."

"She simply asked for it, I suppose, and you just handed it over?"

"You know exactly what happened. You saw me."

"Yes," he said. "I did. That's what's worrying me. I did. Val, you wouldn't be an utter fool?"

"My God!" Her outburst startled him and he turned to her so that they faced each other on the turf.

"My dear girl," he said, "you behaved like an amateur actress registering stealth. It's no good being angry with me."

"I'm sorry." To his relief there was a glimmer of a smile on her mouth, although her eyes were heavy with an old pain which he was embarrassed to recognise and remember. "I'm sorry," she repeated. "But it all seems so blazingly silly. I gave Georgia a perfectly ordinary cachet blanc. She asked me if I had any after the party this morning, and I went up to get her one. When I put it into her hand I had one of those dreadful mad thoughts; insane impulses they call them, don't they? Anyway it went through my mind that a good dose of cyanide in that thing would silence her beastly, predatory vulgarity forever. And then, of course, as soon as I'd thought it I looked up and saw your ridiculous face. I felt I *was* mad and I suppose I shuddered or recoiled, as one would naturally. However, it doesn't matter. It was only one of those things."

Campion was silent and she laughed at him.

"Good heavens, you believe me, don't you?"

"I? Oh, Lord, yes." His tone was still troubled. "I was only thinking. If they find a good narcotic poison in that chap's belly you'll be very awkwardly placed. That woman has a mind like a demented eel; does she always say any mortal thing that comes into her head?"

"Usually, I think." Val spoke lightly. "It was the fashion to be daring some years ago, and the women who grew up at that period seem to have got it incorporated in their general make-up. The trouble is that when it's natural like that it becomes a negative thing. When it was deliberate it was considered a decoration, or at least a weapon. Now that it's natural it's just an ordinary unbridled tongue. It's dangerous, of course."

"Dangerous? My good girl, it's terrifying. If they find——"

Val laid a restraining hand on his arm.

"They won't find anything," she said.

Her complacency was irritating and he shrugged his shoulders and was silent.

Presently she shuddered. He felt the tremor run through the arm against his side.

"They won't find anything suspicious," she went on quietly. "I know that. I'm certain of it. If there was any real danger of that the whole thing would have worked out differently."

"Do you know what you're talking about, my sweet?"

"Yes, I do." He had succeeded in nettling her. "I know that Portland-Smith died very conveniently for Georgia, and now Ramillies has done the same thing. I know that it has been proved that Portland-Smith committed suicide, and I know it will be proved that Ramillies died naturally. There's no danger of a row because danger has been carefully eliminated. It's all working out. There's a superstition in the theatre that everything works out for Georgia. You must never cross Georgia. If you go with her you're on wheels. This is another evidence of the truth of it, that's all."

Campion frowned at his sister. His masculine mind revolted from this in-touch-with-the-stars attitude and he said so.

"This is all very fine and large," he added, "but there's obviously going to be a P.M.—Georgia brought that on her own head—and if the fellow died unnaturally everybody's going to know."

Val shook her head.

"I don't think so."

"But, my dear good girl!" Mr. Campion was restraining an impulse to jitter at her with difficulty. No one else in the world save the whole skein of his blood relations had this undignified effect upon him. "What do you mean? Do you think that that pompous ass of a doctor is going to risk his reputation saving anybody's skin? He'll spaniel round as long as everything is pretty, but did you see him when the first flicker of awkwardness showed? Did you see him?"

"I did. Don't shout at me."

"Darling, *am* I shouting?" The injustice of the accusation took his breath away. "You saw him. You know as well as I do that he's only going to be obliging as far as it suits him, and it doesn't suit any doctor on earth to hush up anything really serious unless he's personally involved. It's an ordinary question of value for risk. If Ramillies was poisoned, as I'm open to bet he was, the P.M. will uncover it and there'll be an almighty row."

"I don't agree with you."

Mr. Campion breathed deeply.

"Are you getting any fun out of baiting me or are you just not listening?"

She squeezed his arm and her head touched his shoulder.

"I can't argue," she said. "I'm only telling you. However Ramillies died, there won't be a row."

"If you think that doctor could be bribed I very much doubt it."

"I don't think that."

"Well then, Val, Val darling, put me out of my misery; how's it going to be done?"

"I don't know," she said frankly. "I just realise that if a P.M. will reveal anything unpleasant or dangerous there won't be a P.M."

"But there's *going* to be a P.M., woman!"

"Then they won't find anything."

"Do you think it was a natural death?"

She closed her eyes.

"I think someone hoped very much it would happen."

Mr. Campion sniffed. "And administered some dangerous drug unknown to science, no doubt," he murmured.

Val's expression was infuriatingly vague.

"Perhaps so," she agreed absently.

He looked down at her with a mixture of rage and affection and finally slid an arm round her shoulders.

"You're a dear little bloody, aren't you?" he said. "Let's be practical. You've got no access to anything dangerous yourself, have you? Nothing anyone could get silly about in case the dangerous drug wasn't unknown to science after all?"

Val considered and finally glanced up at him.

"I've got about half a pound of morphine crystals at the Park Lane house," she said.

"How much?"

"An enormous amount. About half a pound. A little under, perhaps."

"Don't play the fool, Val. This is fairly serious."

"I'm not, my dear. I'm telling you the literal truth. Tante Marthe knows about it. It's in a drawer at the back of my desk in a big cigarette tin. It's been there for two years at least."

She looked up at him and laughed softly.

"It came over from Lyons in the cardboard cylinder of a roll of taffeta which we hadn't ordered," she said. "Rex found there was one odd bale and the silk was put in my office to be returned. Tante

Marthe knocked it over and the cap fell off. There were about twenty-five little packets of this stuff inside. We talked it over and decided that it was quite obvious that someone was using us as a cover, and we suspected a woman on the buying side. Naturally we didn't want a fuss, police in the place and that sort of horror, so we sacked the woman, kept the material and stuck the stuff in a drawer, where it still is, as far as I know."

"How do you know it was morphine?"

Val raised her eyebrows.

"I sent a little down to a chemist and asked, naturally."

"Weren't they curious?"

"No. I told some likely story about finding it in an old medicine chest I'd bought. I sent very little. And when I had the report I told them they needn't return it."

"I see," said Mr. Campion a trifle blankly. "You're an alarmingly matter-of-fact lot, you businesswomen, aren't you?"

"I suppose so." The depth of bitterness in her voice startled him and he felt again that old bewilderment at her range of thought and her staggering inconsistencies. His common sense reasserted itself.

"Look here," he said seriously, "I'm going to collect that stuff immediately and you forget you ever had it unless I tell you to come out with the whole story. I hope to God you can substantiate it."

"All right." He had the impression that she was laughing at him a little and he regarded her helplessly.

"I don't understand you," he said. "You come roaring to me in town, making a mountain out of a positive worm cast, and yet when a situation which is really unpleasant does arise you behave as if I were an overexcited Boy Scout."

"I'm sorry. I'm really very grateful." The clear high voice sounded flat and she bestirred herself. "It's a question of proportion," she said. "When I came to you in London I was afraid of losing something really important for always; now I think I have lost it. It's altered my entire perspective."

"Perspective?" he ejaculated, resenting the intolerance which she engendered in him without being able to suppress it. "Do you know the meaning of the word? Val, you're an intelligent woman. Your mind works, so do use it, darling. This may be a beastly situation."

"If there's a P.M. they won't find anything," she repeated placidly. He caught his breath and resisted the impulse to shake her.

"How can you possibly know that?"

"I do. You must leave it at that. Whatever we're up against, it's not something childish or careless. But I can't discuss it now. I can't be

bothered with it. As far as I'm concerned it doesn't matter. I'm full,
satiate, with my own personal aspect of this affair. I've got to pull
myself together and behave, and I'm funking it. Now do you see what
I mean by perspective?"

"I think you're off your head," said Mr. Campion frankly.

She looked at him with surprise.

"I am," she said. "I thought I'd explained all that pretty thoroughly.
Oh, Albert, my dear good ape, do try and understand. You're a sensible, reasonable, masculine soul. If you fell in love and something went
wrong you'd think it all out like a little gent and think it all quietly
away, taking the conventional view and the intelligent path and saving
yourself no end of bother because your head plus your training is
much stronger than all your emotions put together. You're a civilised
masculine product. But when it happens to me, when it happens to
Georgia, our entire world slides round. We can't be conventional or
take the intelligent path except by a superhuman mental effort. Our
feeling is twice as strong as our heads and we haven't been trained for
thousands of years. We're feminine, you fool! I'm trying to use my
head constructively: she isn't. She's sailing with the tide."

"Oh," said Mr. Campion furiously, "this is damned silly introspective rot. What you need, my girl, is a good cry or a nice rape—either, I
should think."

Val's laughter was spiteful.

"There's a section of your generation who talks about rape as a cure
for all ills, like old Aunt Beth used to talk about flannel next to the
skin," she said witheringly. "This mania for sex-to-do-you-good is
idiotic. You'd far better get back to bloodletting or cod liver oil. No,
my dear, you may have the mental discipline, but we're the realists.
At least we don't kid ourselves even if we try to put on a decent performance for everyone else. When I heard Ramillies was dead I didn't
think 'Oh, poor man, what a shock for his wife!' I thought, 'My God,
now Georgia will be able to marry Alan.' I'm still thinking that. And
so is she. It's disgusting and shocking to the sentimental or conventional mind, but at least it's not false. Georgia may change round
suddenly. It all depends on whether she happens to see herself in
some new dramatic situation which demands a genuine regret for
Ramillies."

"Hush," said Mr. Campion and swung her gently round. Georgia
was advancing towards them across the grass. She was crying unaf-
fectedly. There were tears on her cheeks and tears swimming in her
eyes. She held out her hands to Val with a gesture that was oddly
youthful.

"Val darling, where are you? Come and help me. I don't know what to do. I can't bear it alone—I can't! I've got to get on to Ferdie in Paris and I've got to tell Ray's half-brother, and there are some old aunts somewhere. Alan's still down at the hangar. They're not putting off the flight. There's no one, no one I can rely on at all. You must come. You must. Whatever you feel about me, you can't desert me. I couldn't help falling in love any more than you could."

Mr. Campion stared, wondering if his ears had deceived him. Georgia had flung her arms round Val and was crying like a child.

"Oh, come in," she sobbed, "do come in! There's a dreadful nurse there. She seems to think I ought to go up and look at him, and I don't want to. I'm terrified of him. What shall I do? What shall I do?"

"I'll come." Val sounded very cool and quiet after her revealing outburst of five minutes before and Campion saw that she looked as comfortingly calm and matter of fact as ever she did.

"When Alan comes he'll look after everything." There was a naïve warning in Georgia's tearful announcement. "But until then you can't leave me, Val. You can't. I've no one to turn to."

"There, there," said Val. "There, there," and they went into the house together.

Campion stood looking after them. From the depth of his memory came a remark of old Belle Lafcadio's: "Women are terribly shocking to men, my dear. Don't understand them. Like them. It saves such a lot of hurting one way and the other."

That was all very well, he reflected, but in the present situation this feminine inability to adjust the viewpoint was appallingly dangerous. Now, without Val's level-eyed gaze to help convince him, her story of the morphine was terrifying, more especially when, having glimpsed her state of heart, he saw Georgia rubbing caustic into the wounds with a wanton recklessness which no man in his senses would risk. He shook his head impatiently. Val was getting him muddled with her intuitive convictions and airy statements. The facts were the thing. Had Ramillies died naturally? It seemed most unlikely. If he had been murdered, who had done it? Who had any motive? Georgia? Alan Dell? If, on the other hand, he had died from some noxious thing intended for his wife, who then?

He was pacing down the grass plot trying to force all personal considerations out of his reckoning when another thought occurred to him. To whose interest was it that Ramillies should be avenged if he deserved vengeance? Who in his entire circle minded if Ramillies died? Who, during the two hours since his death, had thought for an instant of Raymond Ramillies suddenly and tragically ended? Who cared?

As it happened it was at that particular moment that he heard the shuddering breaths in the shrubbery. Someone was weeping.

CHAPTER THIRTEEN

The boy sat on the edge of an ornate marble love seat hidden in the shrubbery. His feet were set squarely on the ground and his head rested in his hands. He was crying in that steady absorbed fashion which is peculiar to childhood. His grief engrossed him and he was blind and deaf to everything else in the world.

The hopvine growing over the high wall behind the seat made a yellow curtain and its scented folds hung down to spill over the stone. There were birds about and the lazy grumble of bees. Art was out of the way for once and Fashion might never have existed. There was life and reality in the garden and this ridiculous weeping figure was a part of it. Mr. Campion felt suddenly grateful to him. He sat down on the stone step and took out a cigarette. *Ivanhoe* lay at his feet and presently he turned over the pages, looking for the Black Knight.

He had been reading for several minutes when the shuddering breaths ceased and he glanced up to find a pair of fiery red eyes regarding him.

"It happens," he said when the silence had to be broken. "It's one of the things that do. It's beastly, but it's part of the experience of being alive."

"I know." The boy wiped his face and kicked the foot of the bench with his heel. "I know." He spoke with the resignation of a much older person. "This is silly. I just felt like it. That was all."

"My dear chap, it's perfectly natural. The weakness part of it is only shock. It's physical. That's nothing."

"Is it?" There was quick relief in the question. "One doesn't *know*, you know," he added presently and summed up the whole misery of youth in the statement.

Mr. Campion did his best to recount the physical effects of shock and Georgia's son listened to him with interest.

"That does explain it," he said at last. "That makes it understandable anyway. How about Georgia? Do you think I ought to go in to her? I don't want to. This—er—this shock might make me blub again and anyhow I should probably be in the way. Is Mr. Dell with her?"

"I don't know. She had my sister there with her the last time I saw her."

"Your sister? Oh, that's good. That's all right then. I'll get over the wall and sneak back to the hotel to wash in a minute. I'd better pack. She may want to get back to town."

Mr. Campion glanced at the small pointed face with interest. It was not unattractive but the son would never have his mother's dark handsomeness nor her magnificent physique. All his life he would be small and in age would look very much as he did now. He was a funny sort of child.

They sat in silence for a long time, both of them unexpectedly at ease.

"Ray wasn't my father, you know." The announcement was made bluntly and sounded like a confession. "My name's Sinclair."

"Fine. I didn't know what to call you. What's the other name?"

Campion was sorry for the question as soon as it was out of his mouth. His companion's embarrassment was considerable.

"I was christened 'Sonny,'" the boy said with a protective formality which was clearly of some years growth. "It seems to have been all right then. Fashionable, you know. Now, of course, it's ghastly. Everyone calls me Sinclair, even Mother."

"I was christened Rudolph," said Mr. Campion. "I get people to call me Albert."

"You have to, don't you?" said Sinclair with earnest sympathy. "Georgia says my father insisted on the name in case I went on the stage." His lip trembled and he scrubbed his face angrily with a sodden handkerchief.

"You're not attracted to the stage?"

"Oh, it's not that." The voice broke helplessly. "I wouldn't care, really. I wouldn't care about anything. I'd be *anything*, only—only I did think it was all settled at last. That's why I'm blubbing. It ought to be about Ray, but it's not. He was all right really—friendly, you know, and rather exciting when he got on to his adventures in Ireland, but he was an awful worry to you. You had to follow him around the whole time and play up to him and coax him into being reasonable and doing what Georgia wanted. I liked him sometimes and sometimes I got jolly tired of him. I was frightened when I heard he was dead. I mean I thought I was going to cat, like you said. But I was blubbing because of myself."

He sniffed violently and kicked the bench for support again.

"I thought I'd better tell you—not that I think you'd care, of course

—but after all it's the truth and it's ghastly to have someone sympathise with you because he thinks you're cut up about your stepfather dying when you're really being selfish. I don't really care frightfully for anyone except Bunny Barnes-Chetwynd and old Grits. Grits is Georgia's housekeeper. She looked after me when I was a kid."

"Who is Bunny?"

Sinclair brightened.

"Bunny's a good chap. We came on from Tolleshurst Prep to Haverleigh last term. He has trouble with his people too. They keep on starting divorces and changing their minds. Bunny's all right. He'd be able to explain this better than I can. It's all so stinkingly mouldy. I don't want to be a snob or a squirt but when you're *in* a thing you've got to *be* in it, haven't you?"

The last question was a plea from the heart and Mr. Campion, who was ever honest, gave a considered reply.

"It's very unsettling if you're not."

"That's what I mean." There was despair in the red eyes. "Before Ray turned up I was always in such a *mess*. It began at Tolleshurst. It's a snoop sort of prep and at first I was a sort of curiosity because of Georgia being so well known, and then . . ." He paused. "Oh, things happened, you know," he said vaguely.

"Scandal, you mean?"

"Yes, I suppose so."

"About Georgia?"

"Yes. Nothing beastly, of course." Sinclair was scarlet with shame. "I didn't follow it very well at first, of course, because I was a little kid, but you know what prep schoolmasters are. They talk like a lot of old women and fellows' people take their kids on one side and put them off you and that sort of thing. It wasn't anything beastly. It was just a sort of feeling that we were a bit low. My father appeared in a rather hot sort of farce in the town one term while Georgia was having a lot of publicity and being photographed with one of the fighters."

He took a deep breath and leant forward.

"I didn't really care," he said earnestly, "but I wish they'd sent me to a lower place. I don't want to be bogus and pretend. I only want to be something definite. I find things awfully confusing anyway. It's not the work; I like that. But it's not knowing ordinary things, like that shock business, for instance, and why you suddenly feel you must go and do something silly even though you know it's silly, like telling barmy lies or pretending you're awfully keen on poetry when you're not. *You* know."

"Yes, I know," said Mr. Campion and saw for the first time the use of Raymond Ramillies. The advent of Ramillies must have made a great difference to Sinclair. Ramillies sounded all right. His family was good and his position unquestionable. As a stepfather he must have been a rock. Much has been said against the English system of moulding young gentlemen to a certain pattern, but, whatever the arguments for and against it may be, the system itself when in operation is a formidable machine. The passage through it is painful anyway if one's corners are stubborn but to be jerked in and out of it by the capricious tricks and antics of one's parents' fluctuating whims or incomes is a mangling process not to be endured.

"Do you like Haverleigh?" he asked.

Sinclair stared at his feet. His eyes were swimming.

"It's marvellous," he said. "It's pretty good."

"We used to play you," Mr. Campion observed. "You were very strong in those days. You are still, aren't you?"

The boy nodded. "We're the top," he said. "It was foul at Tolleshurst, being not quite sound—presentable, you know—but here it would be hell. You'd let the place down, you see. They wouldn't chuck it at you, of course, but you'd feel you were doing it."

Since the talk was an intimate one and complete frankness seemed in order Mr. Campion put forward a comforting suggestion somewhat baldly.

"Perhaps you'll get someone as good."

"Yes," said Sinclair and let the air sizzle through his teeth. There was a flicker of hope in his eyes, stifled immediately, which was among the most genuinely pathetic sights Campion had ever seen. "Mother was engaged to Portland-Smith once," the boy remarked presently. "I liked him. He was hopelessly stiff and conventional but he did know what he wanted and what he was going to do next. He was going to be a county court judge. Georgia would have to have left the stage if she'd married him. I hoped she would but that was pretty low of me. I was only thinking of myself. He was a moody person, though. He shot himself. Did you know?"

"Yes. I found him, as a matter of fact."

"Did you?" Sinclair hesitated over the obvious question, instinctive to everyone and yet always false to the ear. Campion answered it for him.

"In a place very much like this," he said, looking round at the leaves.

Sinclair considered the astounding vagaries of life for some time and finally reverted to his own problems, which were at least concrete.

"It's filthy to sit and blub about oneself," he remarked. "A lot of what I've been saying is filthy. But I've started, you see. I've started to be one sort of chap. Ray said if I worked I could go to Oxford and have a shot at the diplomatic. I meant to hold him to that if it was possible. I tried to make it square with him by trailing round and doing what I could. It's putrid talking like this when he's just dead, and I liked him. I did like him, but it's my *life*, you see. It's all I've got. Now I may have to change everything again, and anyway I won't know what I'm doing for a bit. I wish I'd started on something where none of this mattered a hang. That's not quite true. I love Haverleigh and I'd miss Bunny."

The name made him laugh.

"Bunny would burst if he heard me talking like this," he said with a chuckle. "Bunny's 'fearfully decent.' Sorry I told you. I'll go and pack. She'll be going back to town, and if I'm not there when the car's ready I'll have to cadge a lift from someone. There's not a train for miles. Good-bye, Mr. Campion. Thank you for the tip about shock."

Having no other convenient place to carry it, he stuffed Sir Walter's great romance into the seat of his flannels and hoisted himself up the wall. Perched on the top, he looked down at Campion.

"I've been talking like Ray did when he was tight," he said with a bravado which deceived neither of them. "Forget it, please, won't you? It was seeing things working again that put the wind up me. It does, doesn't it?"

"Things working again?" echoed Mr. Campion sharply.

Sinclair seemed surprised.

"Things do work, don't they?" he said. "Things happen and link up rather peculiarly. Haven't you noticed it? They do round Georgia and me anyway. Don't they do it everywhere?"

"I don't know," said Mr. Campion slowly.

"I think they do," persisted Sinclair. "You'll jolly well see it if you watch, or at least I think you will. I do. I say, this wall's giving. Good-bye, sir."

Raymond Ramillies' chief mourner dropped out of sight and Mr. Campion was left alone, thinking.

He was still there, sitting with his arms clasping his bent knees, when Amanda found him. She was dishevelled and almost weary, for once in her life.

"Gone to ground?" she enquired, pausing before him. "I don't altogether blame you. The plane's off at last. Nearly an hour late. What a show!"

She sat down on the step beside him and retied her shoelace, her red hair hanging over her face.

"How did that chap die?"

Mr. Campion related the entire story truthfully, omitting only Val's incredible admission about the morphine. He knew from experience that there was not much which could be hidden from Amanda for long and so made the rest of the tale as exact as possible.

She listened to him in complete silence and when he had finished began to whistle a little tune, very flat and breathy.

"Albert," she said suddenly, "I'll tell you something. I can *hear machinery*."

He turned his head.

"It's getting a bit obvious, isn't it?" he murmured. "Even my great ears began to throb. Who's the little god in charge?"

Amanda hesitated, her hand still on her shoe and her skinny young body arched forward.

"Could she have the nerve?"

"Has she the organising ability? I know poison is supposed to be sacred to women, but she brought that P.M. on herself. Buxton-Coltness would have signed up like a lamb."

Amanda grunted.

"Perhaps she overplayed the part," she said. "Or perhaps she knows she's safe."

"How can she know she's safe? The Buxton-Coltness combine may be a gaggle of quacks, but they're not criminal and presumably they can do a P.M. between them."

Amanda opened her mouth and thought better of it.

"I don't care about Ramillies," she said at last. "I thought the chap was close to being a bounder and he was certainly a dreadful old cad, but I don't like us being used. It's this Old Testament touch that frightens me. I don't like being caught up in the cogwheels if I think someone's doing it. It's bad enough when it's the Lord."

"Organised machinations of fate," murmured Mr. Campion, and felt for the first time that old swift trickle down the spine. It was astounding that three such very different people should have expressed so unusual a thought to him within the hour.

Meanwhile Amanda was still talking.

"What's going to happen next?" she said. "Something's up. When the pilot got into the Seraphim he found this lying on his seat and he gave it to me to attend to."

Campion glanced at the little silver model in her outstretched hand. It was the Quentin Clear. Amanda's brown fingers closed over it.

"I thought I'd better hang on to it, for a while anyway," she said. "What do you know about that?"

"Georgia wasn't wearing it when she came down to the hangar after lunch."

"I know she wasn't. Nor was A.D. And why should it be lying on the seat, right under the nose of one of the few men who would know what it was and whose it was when he saw it? It's a plant, another 'mysterious way.'"

Mr. Campion stirred.

"It's so damned insulting," he said. "Amanda, we'll get the impious god in this machine."

CHAPTER FOURTEEN

The post-mortem examination on the body of Sir Raymond Ramillies was performed and an examination of certain organs was rushed through, the Richmond Laboratories performing in twenty-four hours a task over which the public analyst might have been expected to take three weeks.

After the reports had been made Dr. Harvey Buxton-Coltness saw no reason to withdraw the certificate which he had given, and the funeral took place on the fifth day, Messrs. Huxley and Coyne, the big furnishing and warehouse people, making an excellent job of the arrangements.

The details in the box headed "Cause of Death" in the registrar's oblong black book read "Cardiac failure due to myocardial degeneration. Other conditions present: chronic nephritis," and meant, in much plainer English, that Sir Raymond's heart had ceased to beat and that there was no really satisfactory reason, as far as Dr. Buxton-Coltness, Mr. Rowlandson Blake, F.R.C.S., and the Richmond Laboratories could ascertain, why on earth this should have been so. It also meant, of course, that these three authorities were prepared to bet that no other experts could ascertain more, and there the official side of the matter rested.

Several people were surprised, Amanda among them, but Mr. Campion was also angry. His sense of outrage grew. His personal and professional dignity had been assailed, his reputation had been utilised, and Val's prophetic judgment confirmed. Moreover, the "mysterious drug unknown to science" seemed to have materialised at last. He became very affable and friendly and he and Amanda went everywhere together.

They went to the memorial service at St. Jude's-by-the-Wardrobe, near the Old Palace, and Val saw them there looking very charming and sleek in their black clothes, two rows behind Gaiogi. Val went with the widow. Georgia had phoned her in the morning.

"Darling, you must. I'm relying on you, Val. The only women in the family are the aunts and the half-brother's wife and they're all definitely hostile besides being frightful females who smell like puppy's breath. I've got Sinclair, of course, but I must have a woman, mustn't I? I thought of having Ferdie sit with me, but somehow I don't think . . . do you? He's not old enough. Alan's to go alone. He must appear but I can't have him near me. That would be too filthy. Darling?"

"Yes."

"Isn't it *amazing*?"

"Extraordinary."

"I'm terribly upset, you know."

"I'm sure you are."

"You don't sound as though you were. But I am, Val. I've cried myself to sleep every night since. I *have*. I really have. I did love him. Not like Alan, of course, but I did love Ray. Poor Ray! I miss him terribly. Come with me. I'll call for you at a quarter to. Not late or early, I think, don't you? Just on time."

"It's safest."

"Val, you sound chilly, almost distant. You're not angry with me by any chance, are you?"

"Angry with you? My dear, why should I be? What have you been up to?"

There had been a light, relieved laugh.

"Nothing. Of course not. I only wondered." And then, in a burlesqued cockney accent, "We girls are funny sometimes, duck. We imagine things, don't we? It's our natures, I suppose. Val?"

"Yes."

"You do like me a little bit, don't you? We are friends?"

"Darling, of course." Val was not a great actress and a hint of dogged determination came through the words.

"Honestly?"

"Oh, don't be a fool, woman. I'm at work. Of course we are."

"All right. You needn't be so very brittle, need you? It's a memorial service to my dead husband, you know. You don't understand, do you, pet? You're hard, Val."

The word had done the work it always does, and Val's face betrayed her, but the telephone had only carried her cool, high voice to the other woman.

"Am I? I don't think so. I don't know."

"Take it from me, then. But I don't blame you. I admire you for it. You don't know how much you save yourself by it. You miss a lot but you save more, I think. Look here, what about Lady Papendeik? Would she come with us? We don't want to look like a couple of floozies. Not that we should, of course. But we both do look so young. Who is she coming with?"

"She's not going, I'm afraid."

"Oh? Why not? I think she ought to."

"She doesn't feel like it," said Val. Tante Marthe had actually said that she knew Ramillies well enough to realise that mere praying for him was a waste of her own and the Bon Dieu's time, but there seemed no point in repeating it.

"Oh, I see. Then it's just you and me and, of course, Sinclair. I've tried on the entire ensemble again and I like it enormously. You don't think those millions of little black butterflies on the cap are a tiny bit pert for the occasion?"

"No, I don't think so. . . . After all, he liked you to look lovely."

"Are you laughing at me?"

"My dear, why should I?"

"I never know with you. You don't understand. I loved him. I adore Alan but I loved Ray. I did. I really did."

"You love us all," said Val. "God bless you. Good-bye, my pet."

"Good-bye, darling. A quarter to three, then. I say, Val, don't wear all black. I'm the widow. You don't mind me saying that, do you? I thought you wouldn't. That's why I love you. I can be myself with you. Val, do you think I'm vulgar?"

"Not more than we all are. Good-bye, my dear."

The memorial service was charmingly devised and, since the church specialised in such offices, well carried out. Glancing round the ancient greystone nave, it occurred to Mr. Campion that the familiar "friends of the bride" and "friends of the groom" division had been aptly translated into "relations and officials" and "friends of the deceased."

Towser, representing royalty, and a small brigade of supporters presumably representing Towser, sat on one side of the aisle with the aunts, the half-brother and a host of army and club folk, while Georgia and the Caesar's Court contingent formed the flower of the opposition. Sinclair stood by his mother, his small drawn face stoical.

Val had given her mind to her clothes and her femininity had triumphed. She was exquisite. Georgie's dark galleon was for once a little heavy, a little funereal, beside this dainty mourning skiff. Val had conceded to the not-all-black request in her own way, and carried, instead of the more ordinary enamel compactum, a pochette made from the chased silver binding of an old German missal, with three or four large real violets threaded through its solid clasp.

Many people looked at her and there were some who nudged their neighbours and pointed her out. Much of this notice was an ordinary tribute to a distinguished and beautiful woman, but not all. Val was sublimely unconscious of the general interest. She was acutely aware of Alan Dell seated five or six rows behind her and of Georgia kneeling and rising at her side, but save for them the rest of the church might have been empty as far as she was concerned.

Mr. Campion was aware of Dell also.

The vicar of St. Jude's-by-the-Wardrobe had been a soldier himself in his time and had decided to give an address. He was an oldish man with a failing memory, and once or twice during his discourse it became apparent that he had confused Ramillies with some other warrior, but his parsonical intonation robbed most of his words of any meaning whatsoever and fortunately embarrassment was thus avoided.

The homily provided an interlude, however, and during it Campion had leisure to look at Dell.

He was sitting forward, his silk hat hanging from his hand and his face clearly outlined against a pillar. From time to time he glanced towards the backs of the two women sitting far in front of him. Amanda kicked Campion.

"A.D. looks like that at work," she murmured.

He nodded and glanced at the face again. There was no shyness there now, nor was there weakness or uncertainty. The Alan Dell at Ramillies' memorial service was the Alan Dell of Alandel planes, Val's love, Sid's hero and Amanda's boss. Mr. Campion felt more than sorry for him.

He could just see Georgia, looking unapproachable in her beauty, her elegance and her grief. Val, he knew, was beside her, and the thought of her reminded him of the uncanny accuracy of her guesses. Most women were alarming in that way, he reflected again. They muddled through to truth in the most dangerous and infuriating fashion. All the same they were not quite so clever as they thought they were, which was as it should be, of course, but odd considering their remarkable penetration in most other practical matters.

It was astonishing how the simple, direct reactions of the ordinary male eluded them. In many cases he was their main interest and yet they invariably boggled over him, approaching a machine of the relative size and simplicity of a bicycle with an outfit which one might be expected to need to take a watch to pieces.

He glanced at Dell again and picked up some of the other man's thought; he recognised the pail-of-water-over-the-head experience which Ramillies' sudden death and Georgia's sudden release must have been to him. That shock had been physical, of course, while the decent, well-behaved mind, which is always being bewildered by the body's antics, had no doubt reacted conventionally. The beloved was free and the beloved must therefore be claimed and married, so that, after making all allowances for natural regret at another human being's untimely end, the heart should be bounding. And yet did Dell's heart bound? Mr. Campion was inclined to bet his all that it did no such thing. In Mr. Campion's opinion Dell was probably disgusted, and, if he was as inexperienced as he appeared to be, disconcerted by himself. In his idle mind Mr. Campion addressed him across the church. "You'll ask the woman to marry you, old boy, insistently if you're pigheaded and half-heartedly if you're not, and if she agrees to do so with sufficient speed you will marry her, and you'll become one of the half-resentful, half-obstinately optimistic husbands that the Georgias of this world acquire. But, ever since Ramillies died, ever since the moment when the first word of his death reached you, although Georgia's body has remained sickeningly desirable and will remain so for some time, every other word that has escaped her, every little offensive trick of mind which she has betrayed and which until now has been muffled by you automatically because her deficiencies were not your affair, has suddenly become italicised. In fact, ever since Ramillies died Georgia has got on your nerves and you cannot bring yourself to believe that you are such an outsider, or love is so fragile, that the two events have any connection."

Mr. Campion read the label in his hat. It gave him a childish sense of satisfaction to reflect that this elementary mental process was one that neither Val nor Georgia would ever grasp until it had been bitten into their minds with the slow acid of the years. They would both of them pry and probe with their delicate little forceps, they would weigh intonations and pore over letters, forcing little pieces of jigsaw to fit into fantastic theories as ingenious and delightful as Chinese puzzles, and yet the elementary fact would sit and stare them in the face, defeating them by its very simplicity.

He looked down at Amanda. She was reading in a very old Prayer Book she had found in the pew a Form of Service for Thanksgiving for the Delivery of King James from the Gunpowder Plot.

It was raining a little as they came out of the church and they

paused for a moment in the half cupola of the pillared porch. Ferdie
Paul joined them. He looked profoundly mournful and his curling
mouth was drawn down. His eyes lit up at the sight of Amanda and
he congratulated Campion heartily on his engagement, about which
he seemed to know a good deal; but having completed these formalities, his gloom returned.

"It's bad," he said, his unexpectedly thin voice irritable. "Damn bad
luck all round. Too near the other business. It's bad for Georgia. People will begin to think she's poisonous or something, poor girl. It's
amazing what people *will* think, you know."

The last remark was uttered with sudden directness and the full
brown eyes were intelligent.

"I don't know how half the lunatics in this world arrive at their
beliefs. By the way, how is Val?"

The connection between the two remarks was not apparent and Mr.
Campion looked blank. Ferdie Paul, who was watching him closely,
seemed startled and then, if such a thing had been possible, almost
confused.

"She's here, is she? That's good. Oh, with Georgia? Really? That's
splendid. She's been a great comfort there, I know. Georgia's far more
cut up than she shows. I can tell it when she's working. She's put up
a stronger performance in some respects than I've ever heard her give
these last few nights, but you can tell she's running on her nerves."

He paused and a faint smile passed over his face.

"Thank God it's not a farce," he said, "or we'd have to come off.
As it is, the 'gallant little woman' can carry on with entire propriety."

Mr. Campion was mildly surprised. The reference to Val had not
been lost upon him in spite of the adroit cover-up.

"The whole thing was a great shock to everyone concerned," he said.

"Oh, my dear chap, frightful! Frightful!" There was no doubting
Ferdie Paul's sincerity. The nervous energy in his voice was almost a
touchable thing. "Frightful! I nearly had apoplexy myself when
Georgia phoned me. I mean, think of the publicity. If poor old Ray
had wanted to make a stink he couldn't have fixed it better, could he?"

"I suppose not. Gaiogi seemed upset."

"Oh, Gaiogi?" Ferdie laughed. "He took to his bed for three days
afterwards. Did you know? He's in love with that hotel. My God, the
fellow sleeps with it. It's indecent. Here he is. Czar Gaiogi, representing Caesar's Court."

The dig was unkind, but apt. Gaiogi Laminoff came out of the
church door with the dignity of a sorrowing emperor. He bowed
gravely to them and came over.

"Not a good address, did you think?" he remarked seriously as he joined them.

"Rotten. Not an ad in it," said Ferdie maliciously.

Gaiogi raised his eyebrows and turned to Amanda.

"You are a lovely thing on a sad day," he said simply. "I am so glad to see you."

Somewhat ungallantly Mr. Campion deserted his betrothed to deal with this sort of impasse as best she could and was relieved to hear her confessing that much the same notion had come into her head at the sight of Gaiogi. He went forward with Ferdie to meet Georgia, who had just appeared.

Val had become separated from her charge during their passage down the aisle and she was waiting with the rest of the fashionable crowd, on whom enforced silence had inflicted a certain simmering quality, when she caught sight of Dell looking at her anxiously.

Her first fleeting impression was that he had been waiting for her, but she dismissed it irritably and favoured him with a faint, cool smile of recognition. He came over to her, edging his way through the group clumsily, and was by her side as the crowd began to move. She was aware that he was making up his mind to speak to her and was suddenly unreasonably and degradingly elated, but when the words did come, blurted out huskily as they stepped into the rain, she was only puzzled by them.

"Val," he said, "you've got intelligence, my dear. You wouldn't blame the wrong person, would you?"

She had time to stare at him blankly and then Georgia was before them.

"Come with us, Val. We'll drop you. For God's sake don't smile. You know what photographs are. Where's Sinclair? Oh well, never mind. He can take a taxi. Come, we can't stand here. It looks terrible. Come, Alan. Sinclair is a little beast. I told him to stick to me."

Sir Raymond's chief mourner was in a pew at the back of the church. A thought had been tormenting him all the way down the aisle and at the last moment he had weakened and given way to it.

"O God, dear God," he prayed, "if so be it You do exist, hear me. I know they say there isn't a hell, but if there is, O God, dear God, kind God, don't let Ray burn. He was only silly, O God, dear God, only stinkingly silly. Don't let him burn."

Then, this last orison performed, he scrambled up, caught a verger looking at him suspiciously, and hurried out, his ears burning. The car had gone and he looked about for a cab and would have taken one had not Amanda and Campion met him on a street island and carried him off to tea with them.

Meanwhile Val and Georgia sat side by side in Georgia's car and Alan Dell sat opposite them.

Georgia was on edge. There was a certain quality of defence about her also which was new in her in Val's experience. She was working hard. Every ounce of her physical magnetism was forced into service and, because this was hardly necessary and even a large car is a confined space, the effect was overwhelming and uncomfortable.

Val became very quiet, almost sedate. She sat gracefully in her corner, one knee tucked up under her and the four-inch heel of her little shoe showing against the grey rep-covered seat.

Dell looked preoccupied and morose but Georgia was irresistibly warm. Her life flowed over him, forcing him to respond to it in spite of his inclination, which was towards peace.

"Oh, darlings, this is the first time that I've felt happy since that dreadful afternoon. You're the two people I rely on most. I couldn't live without either of you. I know I say and do the filthiest things but I don't mean it. Do you think I could take my hat off, Val? No one could see in here, could they? Not to recognise me, I mean."

Dell took her hat from her outstretched hand and put it down on the seat beside him. The little black butterflies on the crown attracted him and he filliped one of them idly. Georgia laughed.

"They're like aeroplane wings, aren't they?" she said. "Val's a genius. She's entirely brilliant. Do you realise that, Alan?"

He looked at the two of them dispassionately, his bright blue eyes reproving.

"Val is a good friend," he said. "The best friend you have."

Georgia shrank back like an abashed baby and there was new colour in her cheeks.

"Oh, but, darling, I *know*," she said with passionate reproach in her tone. She laid a hand on Val's wrist possessively. "I do know. Don't I know? Alan, why do you say that? I adore Val and Val likes me, don't you, Val? You do like me. We've been friends for years. We're all frightfully upset. The service was terribly emotional. That's why I dread these things. Let's stop and have a cocktail somewhere. Oh no, I suppose we can't like this. My God, I suppose we can't be seen out at all tonight. Where shall we go?"

"I must go back to Tante Marthe. She's waiting for me at Park Lane," said Val.

"Oh, must you." Georgia did not make the words a question. "What a frightful nuisance. I don't know what we shall do. Alan?"

"Yes."

"Take me up in a plane."

"What, now?"

"Yes, as soon as we've changed. Drive me out to Caesar's Court and take me up in a plane. I want to get away, right away, just for a little tiny while. Do. Please, Alan, because I ask you."

"All right," he said dubiously. "It'll be frightfully cold, you know, and it's raining."

"Oh, all right." Georgia shrugged her shoulders. "We'll light a fire and sit round it and talk, or dress up in old clothes and go to some dirty little Soho restaurant where we shan't be recognised. What shall we do?"

Val glanced at Dell. He was watching the other woman gravely. There was no telling what was the thought in his mind. He was regarding her earnestly and with evident interest, but his opinion was secret. Val blinked and turned her head.

"Here we are," she said with relief. "Will you come in? No? All right. I'll see you soon, Georgia. Good-bye, Alan."

Her small gloved hand rested in each of their own for an instant and then she was gone. Georgia looked after her and smiled with genuine sadness.

"Poor pretty Val," she said. "Isn't she a dear?"

Dell did not answer her directly. He moved over into the seat Val had vacated and laid a hand on Georgia's arm.

"I'm going to take you home now and then I'm going to leave you," he said. "I'll phone you tomorrow."

"Oh, but why?" She moved away and sat looking at him with the wide-open eyes of an injured child. It was Georgia at her most appealing, her warmest and most vulnerable. He hesitated.

"Don't you think I ought to?" he said at last.

"Ought to?" She was honestly bewildered and he laughed uneasily.

"I think I will," he said.

Georgia could see herself faintly mirrored in the glass between them and the chauffeur's dark back. It was a flattering reflector and she was reassured after a momentary misgiving. His obvious reason, which was a natural conventional distaste for the proximity of love and death, escaped her and she was puzzled. She slid an arm through his.

"I want to be with you this evening, Alan," she said. "I'm not playing tonight, you know, because of the service. No, my dear, this is the first time, the very first time, I've felt free." There was no mistaking her confiding. It was genuine, voluptuous and entirely generous.

He did not speak and she felt him stiffen. She looked up and was amazed. She had caught him unawares and there had been nausea on his face.

"All right," she said, releasing him. She was laughing but obviously deeply hurt. "All right. I shall be terribly rushed tomorrow. Phone me the day after."

He sighed and rubbed his hard, scrubbed hands over his face.

"You don't understand at all, do you?" he said.

"My dear, I do, of course I do," said Georgia with more conviction than truth, and sat looking at him with patent speculation in her tweed-grey eyes, so that he felt like a medical specimen and was revolted and ashamed of himself and very unhappy.

Meanwhile Val proceeded calmly to her office. Rex met her in the hall with two queries concerning dresses which she had forgotten and she dragged her mind out of its self-protective coma and considered them intelligently. He noticed nothing unusual about her and when she stepped into the little wrought-iron gazebo of a room, Lady Papendeik, who was sitting at her desk, thought she looked particularly well and was grateful for the circumstance in view of the letter before her.

They talked of trivialities for some moments and touched on business. Val pulled off her small black hat and her yellow hair shone in a stray shaft of sunlight cutting through to them from the west landing window, where the sun was breaking through after the rain.

"It was tiring," she explained, smiling in faint apology.

Tante Marthe's little black eyes glinted.

"Georgia played the leading part well, no doubt? Did she enjoy herself?"

"Oh, I think so. She behaved excellently."

"Did she? That must have been a comfort to her husband's ghost."

"Mustn't it?" Val agreed absently.

She had not seated herself and there was an undercurrent of restlessness in her movements which did not escape the old woman.

"Are you feeling irritable?"

"No, not particularly."

"Good." Lady Papendeik sniffed over the word. "I had a letter this afternoon from Emily."

"From Mother?" There is nothing like surprise to ease emotional tension and Val moved over to the desk with her natural step.

Lady Papendeik spread her small hands over the blotter.

"It is annoying."

"I can imagine it."

"I wonder. I hope not." Tante Marthe shrugged her shoulders. "Oh, read it," she said. "It must be true or she could never have heard of it. No one can do anything."

Val took up the thick cream double sheet with the well-known crimson heading, the single arrogant house name and county which had once been so familiar and which even now brought a far-off memory of a peach tree of all things, a sprawling peach tree on a rosy wall.

DEAR LADY PAPENDEIK,

I am an old woman [the letter had originally begun "We are both," but the three words had been struck out with a single broad line from the hard steel pen and remained a shining example of British county tact at its unhappiest], *and I am writing to you instead of to my daughter because I feel that you at least will appreciate to the full my natural reactions to the monstrous situation which has arisen. This morning I received a letter from Dorothy Phelps. She is a fool, of course, but I am sure she wrote me out of the kindest of motives. She is a distant relation of my husband's, a collateral branch of his mother's family, and I am sure she would never do anything to wound me maliciously. I enclose her letter, which I hope you will return to me. You will see she says "everyone is talking about it." This is quite intolerable. I have suffered enough from my children, God knows, but even they must see that this is the last straw. Will you kindly see that Val has nothing more to do with this woman? Val should never again visit this hotel, Caesar's Court, and must be brought to realise that, even if she has obstinately thrown away every advantage to which her birth has entitled her, she cannot escape from the* responsibility *which is hers as much as it is mine or any other owner of our name or those few names like ours which are left. They tell me times have changed, but they have not changed here. This precious little part of England is as it ever was, thank God, and until I die it will remain so. After that I dare not contemplate. Of course no action is possible. Val, I am sure, will recognise this in spite of the subversive influences of the past few years, but in my opinion a threatened action might have some effect, and I am instructing our solicitors to put themselves at her disposal. I do not want to hear from Val. Explanations do not interest me, as all my children know. In my world explanations and excuses have ever been taken, rightly or wrongly, as signs of guilt or weakness. This abominable slander should never have been uttered. No daughter of ours should ever have put herself into a position which made its utterance possible. Since*

*it has been uttered, I am forced to take steps to see that it is
silenced and I appeal to you to bring Val to her sense of responsibility in the matter. If she can do nothing she should at least go
abroad for six months. Meanwhile, you will oblige me by refusing,
of course, to have any future transactions with this woman
Georgia Ramillies.*

> *Believe me,*
> *Yours sincerely,*
> EMILY K——

The rest of the signature was illegible.

Val put the letter down quietly and picked up the enclosure, which
was written on single sheets with a club address and was in an 1890
calligraphy.

DEAREST AUNT EMILY,

*I do not know how to write to you, darling, without hurting
you much more than you could ever deserve, but something has
come to my ears which Kenneth and I feel we ought to let you
know about. I was playing bridge here yesterday and a Mrs. Fellowes—her husband is one of the Norfolk people, I think—was
talking about poor Val. Of course I listened and said nothing.
Amy Fellowes has a daughter who is in the stage set (many quite
good young people play at this nowadays, you know, dear) and
when the conversation turned to the death of Raymond Ramillies
(no doubt you read about it; it was very sudden) Mrs. Fellowes
came out with an extraordinary story. According to this, Lady
Ramillies, who is Georgia Wells, the actress, actually said to Amy
Fellowes' daughter, in front of several other people, that it was a
very extraordinary thing that her husband should have died so
suddenly after taking some aspirin which Val had given Lady
Ramillies for herself. What made it worse is that she hinted that
Val and this Ramillies woman had some quarrel over a man
whose name I did not hear although several were mentioned.
Of course this cannot be true. Neither Kenneth nor I would believe it for a moment. But I felt it was my duty to write to
you because it is the kind of gossip which should be stopped.
Everyone is talking about it. Val, I know, is very clever and probably very foolish. I am sure if she realised the pain she gave you
she would be more careful. Forgive me for sending you such bad
news but I thought it best to come out in the open, and so did
Kenneth.*

I expect your dear garden is very beautiful now. How you must love it!

> *Very affectionately, dear Auntie, yours,*
> DOROTHY PHELPS

Val let the paper drop and her fingers fluttered over it in a little gesture of distaste.

"A frightful old woman," she said. "I remember her. Yes, well, that accounts for it."

"Accounts for what?" demanded Tante Marthe sharply.

"Oh—things." Val walked down the room and stood looking across the landing to the west window blazing in the evening sun.

"Georgia must have said this thing to someone," remarked Tante Marthe.

"Oh, Lord, yes, she's said it." Val sounded weary. "She's said it to everyone she's become confidential with in the last fortnight. There must be dozens of them. You know what Georgia is. She doesn't really mean it. She doesn't think I tried to poison her. She simply knows it's a good story but doesn't realise how good. She doesn't actually think at all. She goes entirely by feel."

"It's dangerous, my dear."

"Is it?" The younger woman spoke bitterly. "There's been a P.M. Ramillies is safely buried. It's all perfectly normal. Am I likely to sue her?"

"You could."

"I could. But am I likely to? If she weren't one of our most important clients would I be likely to admit I've even heard that I am so much in love with Alan Dell that I attempted to murder the woman he preferred?"

Lady Papendeik did not speak for a moment.

"It's very naughty of Georgia," she observed somewhat inadequately, when the silence had gone on long enough. "What shall one say to Emily?"

"She's seventy." Val sounded tolerant. "Say you'll do all you can. She's a hundred and fifty miles away and a hundred and fifty years off. She's living in the past, somewhere just before the Napoleonic Wars. You get like that down there. The house hasn't changed and neither has she. If she weren't so gloriously hard it would be pathetic. Still, it's idiotic. You can't behave like Queen Charlotte just because you live in a Georgian pile."

Lady Papendeik nodded regretfully.

"Will you mention this to Georgia?"

"Oh no." Val was standing with her back to the room, the sun turning her hair into a blazing halo. "No. She'll forget it in a day or so. If I talk to her it'll give her something else to add to it, or else she'll be brokenhearted and contrite and have to confess to someone terribly confidentially, and the whole thing'll blaze up again."

"You're very wise for your age." Lady Papendeik seemed to find the fact a pity. "Perhaps this niece of Emily's has exaggerated."

"Perhaps so. Let us look on the bright side by all means."

"You are afraid the man will hear of it?"

"I'm afraid he has." Val's tone was commendably matter of fact. Ever since she had read Dorothy Phelps's letter the full significance of Dell's muttered injunction on the church step had been slowly sinking into her mind. It is the little unexpected nicenesses which creep through the armour chinks, and suddenly her restraint shivered. She laid her forehead against the pane.

My dear, oh, my dear, my dear, my love, oh, sweet, sweet, oh, my dear. The idiotic refrain made existence just bearable until the moment was over.

She turned away from the window and glanced at Tante Marthe.

"It passes," said the old woman, answering her thought. "Of all the things that pass that passes most completely. Enjoy it while you can."

"Enjoy it?"

Lady Papendeik looked down at her hands with the little brown mottles on them.

"There's a great deal to be said for feeling anything," she remarked. "I don't."

Val sat down at her table and began to scribble. Presently the other woman rose to look over her shoulder.

"What's that?" she demanded. "A nightgown?"

Val ran a pencil through the design. She looked up, her cheeks red and her eyes laughing.

"A tiddy little shroud," she said. "It should be made in something rather heavy and expensive. Berthé's new corded chîne-chîne, I think."

"Morbid and silly," said Lady Papendeik. "I like the little bows. What's the pocket for?"

"Indulgences," said Val cheerfully. "They're always in fashion."

CHAPTER FIFTEEN

"I tell you wot, cock," said Mr. Lugg, looking at an enormous gold hunter which had been entirely ruined, from his point of view, by an engraved tribute in the back which rendered it of little interest to pawnbrokers. "I tell you wot. She's not coming."

Mr. Campion turned away from his sitting-room window and wandered across the carpet, his lean dinner-jacketed shoulders hunched.

"A nasty little girl," he observed. "Take the crème-de-menthe away. Drink it if you like."

"And smell like a packet o' hiccorf suckers. I know." Lugg waddled to the coffee table and restored the offending bottle to the cocktail cabinet. "You treat me as a sort of joke, don't you?" he remarked, his great white face complacent. "I'm a regular clown. I make you laugh. I say funny things, don't I?"

His employer regarded him dispassionately. In his velvet house coat, his chins carelessly ranged over a strangling collar and his little black eyes hopeful, he was not by any means an uncomic figure.

"Well, go on, say it. I'm a laugh, ain't I?"

"Not to everyone."

"Wot?" He seemed hurt and also incredulous.

"Not to everyone. A lot of my friends think you're overrated."

"*Overrated?*" The black eyes wavered for a moment before a faint smile spread over the great face. "Reelly?" he said at last, adding tolerantly, "It takes all sorts to make a world, don't it? It's a funny thing, I often give meself a laugh. I think we'd better give 'er up, don't you? It's no use me sitting around dressed like a parcel if company's not expected. That's *makin'* trouble. Mr. Tuke advises me to wear lower collars. One inch above the shirtband, in 'is opinion, is quite sufficient if a gentleman 'as an 'eavy neck. What would you say?"

"What's the time?"

"Close on arf-past. She's not comin'. She's led you up the gardin. That's a woman all over. I don't know what you want to bother with them for. Two blokes 'ave died and are tucked up tidy, and what if there is a lot of talk about your sis and a sleepin' tonic? That's nothin'. Leave it alone. Fergit it. Be a gent and look it in the face and don't see it."

"A sleeping tonic?" Mr. Campion's pale eyes were cold behind his spectacles and Mr. Lugg perceived the pitfall too late.

"A naspirin, then," he said defiantly. "Fergit it. Don't roll in the mud. Don't *bathe* yourself in it."

"When did you hear this?"

"Oh, ages ago. Months, it was. Last week per'aps." Mr. Lugg was throwing the subject about until he lost it. "I changed the conversation, if you want to know, same as any gent would 'oo 'adn't fergot 'isself."

"Where was this? At your beastly pub?"

"I may 'ave 'eard a careless word at the club. I really fergit." Mr. Lugg's eyes were veiled and his dignity was tremendous.

"The club!" said Mr. Campion with a force and bitterness which were unusual in him. "All the blasted clubs. Oh, my God, what a mess! There's the bell at last. Let her in, there's a good chap. Where on earth has she been?"

Mr. Lugg raised his eyebrows, or rather the ridge of fat where his eyebrows should have been, and shuffled out of the room. His voice came back from the passage a moment or so later.

"No luck. It's only Miss Amanda. This way, yer ladyship. She's let 'im down. No, 'asn't showed up at all."

Amanda came in full of sympathy. She did not take off the thick ivory silk coat which covered her from throat to toe but seated herself on the arm of a chair and regarded her host enquiringly.

"What do we do now?"

He grinned at her. Her enthusiasm was infectious and comforting and it occurred to him then that she would retain it all her days. It was part of her make-up and sprang from a passionate and friendly interest in all the many and exciting surfaces of life.

"I was considering," he said seriously. "At the moment we face an impasse. The old maestro allows beautiful suspect to slip through nicotine-stained fingers. I had been all over London for that wretched girl and I was lying harmlessly in bed this morning, wondering if the Salvation Army wasn't the next most likely hunting ground after all, when she phoned me. I recognised the jew's-harp voice immediately and promptly fell out of the bed onto the bear I shot in the Afghanistan campaign. She gave her name at once and plunged into business. 'It's Miss Caroline Adamson speaking. Is that Mr. Albert Campion? Oh, it is?' *Light laugh.* 'I don't know if you remember me?' *Pause.* 'Oh, you do? That's divine of you.' *Gasp.* 'Well, Mr. Campion, would you be in tonight about eight if I was to call round? I think you've been looking for me and I think I know what you're interested in. You want me to tell you something, don't you?' *Seductive upward inflection.* 'I'll call then. Oh no, no, thanks, that's sweet of you. No, I won't dine. I just want a little business chat. You understand it will be business, don't you?' *Firm, straight-from-the-shoulder tone.* 'Oh, you do? I thought you did.' *Relief.* 'I've only seen you once to speak to but I thought I was right about you.' *Unnecessary laugh.* 'Well, I've got your address so I'll drop in about eight, then. What d'you want to know where I live for?' *Hur hur hur.* 'I'll come round to you. No, really, I'm on a diet, I am really. About eight then. Righty-ho.' "

He finished his impersonation with a realistic giggle.

"There you are," he said. "I couldn't discover where the call came from. Never try to trace a London telephone call unless you're a superintendent of police. So I washed my hands and face, bought three pennyworth of mimosa for the desk vase, lassoed Lugg into a collar and sat down to wait. When I asked you to come along at half-past nine I thought we'd have some jolly gossip to discuss. Instead of that the little canine has ditched me and here I am, disconsolate and foolish."

"You'd look more foolish if she'd fixed up to meet you outside the Leicester Square tube. It's raining like stink," said Amanda with typical practicalness. "What does she know? It must be something fairly good or she'd never approach you. She must have some sort of information to sell."

Campion glanced at her with mild surprise.

"Without wanting to wound your finer susceptibilities, I should have thought that was fairly obvious," he said at last. "I take it that Miss Adamson knows where Ramillies went when he rushed away from his farewell party at Caesar's Court, and where he got the alcoholic drenching which was so tactfully avoided in Doctor Buxton-Coltness' report."

Amanda looked up. She was quietly pleased with herself, he noticed.

"She may, of course," she said, "but I doubt it. I know where Ramillies went that night. He went to Boot's Hotel."

"Boot's?" Mr. Campion was frankly incredulous.

Boot's Hotel is one of those curious survivals which still eke out a failing existence in odd corners of London's mysterious western end. It had been founded early in the nineteenth century by a retired royal servant, and something of the stuffy, homely dignity of the court of Silly Billy still persisted inside its dusty crimson walls. The place had possessed a distinguished clientele in the days when a fine country lady and her husband were at a disadvantage if their relatives were out of town and could not offer them hospitality for their visit, since hotels which were not also public houses were scarce. But now its period was long past and only its tremendously valuable freehold and the sentiment of its owners stood between it and the housebreaker. So far as

Mr. Campion knew, the Fitton family were the only people wealthy enough to face the tariff yet sufficiently hardy to stand the discomfort. There was a legend that hip baths were still provided in the vast bedrooms and were filled from small brass cans by ancient personages in livery, but Amanda said it was a good hotel and gave it as her opinion that once they got rid of the rats it would be very healthy.

"Boot's?" Campion repeated. "Boot's and Ramillies? Ramillies left Caesar's Court and beetled off back down the years to Boot's? Why?"

"To get a little peace, perhaps," suggested Amanda. "He wasn't awfully young. Love and the dance band may have got him down between them. It's not unlikely. Anyway he was there on the nineteenth because I saw his name in the book when I signed mine tonight. It was on the top of the page before mine. (I don't think they're doing very well.) I asked George about it. He's that old man in the office place, and he remembers him coming in very well. Ramillies arrived fairly late and went up to his room, and, what's more, George doesn't think he came down again until the next morning, rather late. He's going to find that out for certain. Also—and this is the funny thing—George doesn't think he was drunk then."

"My dear child, he must have been." Mr. Campion was almost dogmatic. "Otherwise no man on earth could have done it in the time. I diagnosed at least a twelve-hour blind when I saw him after lunch. The whole story sounds fantastic. He may have taken a quart of whisky to bed with him at Boot's and privately drunk himself pallid. It's a form of vice which I don't understand myself, but, having seen Ramillies, I'm open to concede that such a form of perversion might conceivably appeal to him. I say, are you sure you've got the right date and the right man?"

"Raymond Ramillies, The Residency, Ulangi," said Amanda, "*and* George described him."

"George also says he wasn't tight," objected Mr. Campion.

"George is a wonderful smart old man." She dropped into her native Suffolk by way of emphasis. "If George said you were tight now I'd take his word for it against yours, and as for the date, if Ramillies went and stayed alone on any other night at Boot's for no good reason whatever, that *would* be astonishing. But if he suddenly got fed up with Caesar's Court and Georgia and the noise and wanted somewhere quiet to sleep, then it would be a perfectly normal thing to go to Boot's, where there's not even any plumbing to uggle-guggle at you from inside the walls. That's all right. That's the kind of thing I'd do myself."

Campion was silent. There was a great deal of common sense in

Amanda's remarks. It was the kind of thing Amanda would do herself, and Ramillies, for all his vagaries, came from much the same background as Amanda. He stood frowning down at her.

"Suppose you're right," he said. "Suppose all this is true. Where and when did he get in the condition in which he arrived at Caesar's Court and what in the name of good fortune has Miss Adamson to tell us that is sufficiently interesting for her to think we might buy it?"

"That's what I was wondering," said Amanda. "We ought to get hold of her, you know. This is a filthy tale that's going round about Val."

Campion raised his head sharply.

"It's reached you too, has it?" he said. "Isn't that jolly? New York will get it tomorrow when the Queen Mary docks and Uncles Henry and Edwin will mail their protests from the outposts of empire a couple of months from now. That's Georgia. That's what comes of emancipating the wrong type of female. For a thousand years they breed a species to need a keeper and then they let it off the chain and expect it to behave. Progress has made things damned difficult. Twenty years ago Val would have been forced to bring an action for slander, but nowadays, when we have decided that quarrelling is childish, friendship is the fashion, and we're all one big unhappy family, there's nothing to be done at all except to produce an even better story to contradict the first, and that, let me tell you, is not so frightfully easy."

Amanda slid down into the chair and sat looking up at him gravely. Her heart-shaped face was intelligent and he noticed again in an absent-minded fashion how much her appearance had improved. She would never have Val's extraordinary elegance but there was strength and breeding in her fine bones and her personality was as refreshing as the small clear streams of her own county.

"It's this hand-of-fate method that's the trouble," she remarked. "We can't get at anything, not even the body. I suppose those doctors were all right?"

"Oh, I think so." He smiled at her seriousness. "They'd hardly risk their own necks. Why should they? No, I fancy they were genuinely fogged, just as I am, and I think that whoever arranged that Ramillies should die (and I'm open to bet that somebody did) knew that any ordinary doctor would be taken in. The P.M. didn't disclose anything at all, you see, not even why the fellow died. I wish that Adamson girl had turned up."

"You think she meant to come?"

"Well, I wondered," he began and shot her a glance which was half amused and half genuinely grateful. "What a pleasant girl you are, Amanda. Did you deduce that from my reported telephone conversation? You comfort me. Thank you. I need it. I wasn't quite my usual coruscating self this morning. But when she phoned I admit it did go through my mind that she might have a girl friend in the box with her. There was a distinct flavour of third person in the air and if so, you see, the whole thing may be a discreet enquiry to find out just how much I'm interested."

"In that case there's something definite to know, which is a comfort, and the sooner we find her the better." Amanda rose with determination. "What are you looking like that for?"

Mr. Campion had taken off his spectacles and was staring absently at the carpet. He looked older and, as Amanda had said, a trifle bleached.

"I was thinking," he said slowly, "I was thinking that suppose we do find out who got rid of Sieur Ramillies, and supposing when we do it's not quite such a good telling story after all?"

"Then we shut up about it, of course," said Amanda cheerfully. "It's our hanging. Where do we go from here? If you know anything you'd better tell me. It'll save time and I'm bound to find out in the end."

He sighed. "I don't know much. During my little mug round after the elusive Miss Adamson I picked up a crumb here and there. Nothing sensational like your Boot's Hotel bomb. That's the irony of life. Poor old Blest and I go nosing about like a pair of bloodhounds for days on end and discover practically nothing, and you go dancing into your horrible home from home and discover Ramillies' name and address in the visitors' book. Just before you descended on me and we went to the Tulip that night Blest had been round with the useful information that someone besides myself had been looking into a trifling matter in Georgia's past, and since then I have discovered that it was Caroline Adamson. That's one crumb. I then found out from various Aunt Maggies that our Caroline was the daughter of a former employee of Gaiogi Laminoff's and that she began her career at the Old Beaulieu when Gaiogi was managing it. She was the girl who sat in a box in the vestibule and exchanged one's hat and coat for a ravishing smile and an artificial gardenia. After that he seems to have got Ferdie Paul to give her a chance on tour, and when everyone was perfectly certain that although the flesh was beautiful the voice was foul, she landed a mannequin job at Papendeik's. That's the other crumb."

"It's a bit," said Amanda. "Have you been to see Gaiogi?"

"About Miss Adamson? No."

"But why not? He's the obvious person to go to. He knows more about her than anyone. Let's go now."

She was already halfway to the door, but paused, when he did not follow her, to stand regarding him with open suspicion in her eyes.

"Can I say something rather rude?" she said. "If you're thinking that there's the least chance that the story about Val is true you're nuts. You don't mind me putting it like that, do you?"

"Not at all. I agree with you."

"Thank goodness for that. Let's go to Gaiogi at once."

"I don't think I would."

"Why not?"

Mr. Campion looked uncomfortable beneath her steady gaze.

"It's a little question of self-advertisement," he explained evasively. "While I admire your forthrightness, Amanda, it gives me pins and needles in the soles of my feet. In view of everything I think Ferdie Paul is our most likely bet. He'll know who she was on tour with. In situations like this the girl friends have a tendency to cling together."

"All right." Amanda sounded dubious. "He has a flat over the Sovereign Theatre, the one Sir Richard built for Lucy Gay. He's not likely to be in at this hour of the night but we can try."

"How true, my sweet, how true," said Mr. Campion and reached for the telephone.

Ferdie was not only in, but in cheerful mood. His thin voice, which suited so ill with his appearance, squeaked heartily over the wire.

"I've got to leave town in forty minutes. Come round and have a drink. I'll tell you all I know about the bit, which isn't much. Is young Amanda with you? She is? Good God, what are you worrying about another woman for? I'll expect you both then, in five minutes. Fine. Good-bye."

The flat, which a great actor-manager had built for a charming leading lady on top of the Sovereign Theatre, was, if sumptuous in the main, a trifle furtive about the entrance. The back of the theatre possessed a yard, now used by privileged persons as a car park, and in the yard beside the stage door was another, smaller and even meaner in appearance, giving on to a flight of uninviting concrete stairs. Once inside, however, the atmosphere changed, and Campion and Amanda came up in a small hand-worked passenger lift to a front door as impressive as any in Victorian London.

They were admitted by a Japanese manservant, who led them across a narrow hallway to the main living room, which was a quarter as large as a church and not at all unlike one in structural design.

Ferdie Paul, who had employed most of the great décor men of the day in his productions, had not permitted their work to get into his home. The vast untidy room had grown. No man on earth could have sat down in cold blood and visualised such jolly chaos.

Ferdie himself sat on a gigantic chesterfield with his feet up, and around him were manuscripts, books, papers, sketches and even patterns of material, in happy confusion.

On the floor before an open suitcase knelt a now familiar figure. She rose as they came in and stood waiting to be introduced with the same hidden discomfort which Campion had noticed in her when he had first seen her at Papendeik's dress show and later with Ferdie at the Tulip.

"Haven't you met Anna? Surely? Oh, you must meet Anna. She's the most extraordinary woman in London."

Ferdie rose lazily.

"Lady Amanda, Mrs. Fitch. Anna, the Lady Amanda Fitton. Anna, Mr. Albert Campion; Campion, Mrs. Fitch. And now, darling, I shan't need four pairs of socks for twelve hours in Frogland. Would you like to be barmaid?"

He sank down on the couch again, moved a pile of loose papers to make room for Amanda beside him, and waved Campion to an armchair opposite. Mrs. Fitch mixed the drinks. As she moved about her home her position in it was as clear as if she had announced it in lights round her head, and it was odd that the fashionable little hat which she wore on one side of her carefully waved hair, and the fact that her bag and gloves lay conspicuously on the side table, should have made this position even more apparent. She was self-contained and polite without being friendly, yet conveyed that because they were friends of Ferdie's they were delightful and exalted beings on whom it was her duty and privilege to wait.

She was the mistress of the house and the handmaid of Ferdie Paul, and it occurred suddenly to Mr. Campion that what she really represented was an old-fashioned, pre-Chaucerian wife, entirely loyal, completely subject, her fortunes inescapably her husband's own. The notion amused him, since he reflected that in view of all the excitement in the past century over the legal status of females the only way for a man to achieve this natural if somewhat elementary relationship with a woman at the present time was to persuade her to love him and never to marry her.

He glanced at her with interest. She could never have been beautiful and the cut of her dark gown showed ugly little spaniel haunches and plump elbows, but her face was placid and there was a veiled expression in her pretty diamond-shaped eyes which might have hidden intelligence. Ferdie was supremely unaware of her save as an added comfort.

"I won't drink, if you'll forgive me," he said to Campion. "I may have a bumpy crossing tonight. I've got to run down to Caesar's Court to catch one of their planes. Bellairs is going over at ten-thirty and we fixed up to share a machine. Do you know Bellairs, the furniture man? That gives me six hours sleep when I get to Paris and then a couple of appointments and I can catch the evening plane back. It's very convenient, this service. I used to have to stagger backwards and forwards once every six weeks. Now I can nip over every three and do the whole thing inside twenty-four hours."

He glanced at his watch and laughed at the other man, his round brown eyes impudent.

"Is your car downstairs? You wouldn't like to run me down to Caesar's Court? It wouldn't take you fifty minutes there and back."

"Not at all. I'd like to." Campion glanced at Amanda questioningly and she answered at once. "I'll wait for you here if I may." She looked at Mrs. Fitch, who smiled politely.

"That's grand," said Ferdie, obviously delighted at getting his own way. "My car's laid up. I hate cabs. We'll start in ten minutes. Anna, no one's drinking. Give me a brandy."

"I shouldn't." It was the first definite statement they had heard her make. She spoke flatly and placidly.

"Shouldn't be blowed! She treats me as though I was ill already. One small brandy."

She refused to hear him and there was quite a tussle between them, Ferdie laughing and the woman mutely obstinate. In the end he got his drink and sat sipping it, laughing at her over the glass.

"It may be the best thing for me," he said. "It hasn't proved so in the past, but still, one never knows. That's the exciting part of life. Isn't that so, Campion?"

"It adds to the general gaiety," agreed Campion affably. "What about Miss Caroline Adamson?"

"Zut! Before the jeune fille?" Ferdie set down his glass and raised his eyebrows. He looked more baroque and Byronic even than usual, with his dark-skinned face shining and his eyes dancing. "Oh, I didn't know. I was trying to be discreet. I don't know where she's living at the moment but I remember the bit well. She got the sack from Papendeik's when poor old Ray dressed her up as Georgia and took

her to the Tulip to annoy his wife. She ran around with Ray a bit, I
believe. I say, we ought to go, old man. I'll tell you all I know about
Caroline on the way down, and when you get there you can talk to
Gaiogi about her. He'll know where she is. If Gaiogi feels like it he
can put his hands on anyone in London within twenty-four hours. (Is
that case packed, Anna? Send Yusai down with it.) What do you want
Caroline for, Campion, or aren't you telling?"

"She phoned me this morning and made an appointment with me
which she didn't keep," said Mr. Campion mildly and with perfect
truth.

Ferdie Paul stared at him, a questioning smile curling his mouth.

"And when you called the number she gave you they put you on to
the zoo?" he suggested, grinning at Amanda.

"That's right, and I answered the phone," she said cheerfully. "He
has had a beastly evening. You'd better hurry. Don't smash the car
up. We may go to the races tomorrow."

"Oh no, be careful." The words had escaped the other woman before she could stop them and they saw her for a moment with the
visor up. The expression in her eyes was not intelligent. Its mute, adoring stupidity was startling.

Ferdie laughed at her good-humouredly.

"She has a theory I'm going to drop to pieces at any moment," he
said, inviting them to join in his amusement at her. "We must go.
Have I got everything? Is that contract in the portfolio, Anna? And
the sketches? Good. Right. Last plane tomorrow if I don't miss it.
Good-bye. Come on, Campion."

He did not kiss the woman but rubbed her solid shoulder affectionately as he passed her and, having said farewell to Amanda,
bustled out of the room, taking an atmosphere of nervous excitement
which was somehow backless and ephemeral, like a methylated spirit
flame, with him. As he descended the few steps to the lift they heard
his thin voice rising heartily.

"I warn you of one thing; Caroline's a good deal older than you
think."

Mrs. Fitch stood watching the door for a moment. In the arrested
movement she looked shorter and stockier than ever, but with Ferdie's
going her poise increased. The handmaid vanished and the mistress
of the house remained.

"He's in a good mood tonight," she remarked. "I do hope he has a
flat crossing. A bad one takes it out of him so."

She hesitated and glanced at Amanda, who was still sitting on the chesterfield, looking a trifle over sixteen and very comfortable and content.

"I'm going to have some tea," she said. "Would you like some? You haven't drunk your gin and lime."

Her visitor accepted the suggestion with genuine enthusiasm and, when the tray arrived with a small tin of ginger biscuits, settled down to enjoy them. They made a funny pair, and Mrs. Fitch slid unconsciously into the half-sentimental, half-patronising frame of mind that the consciously sophisticated keep up their sleeves for extreme youth and foolish innocence.

"You're getting married," she said. "That's going to be exciting, isn't it?"

"Staggering, I should think," agreed Amanda, swallowing a piece of biscuit. "Tolerance is the great secret, don't you think?" she added with a graceful effort to keep the ball rolling. "Tolerance and three good meals a day."

Mrs. Fitch did not laugh. Her diamond-shaped eyes narrowed and she looked for a moment almost frightened. She had a curious habit of moving her lips as if she were trying out words and finding them unsuitable, and she sat for a moment holding her teacup and staring over it consideringly.

"You don't want to be too tolerant," she said at last and added feelingly, "if you can help it."

"I suppose not."

"No. Do you know this girl, Caroline Adamson?"

"I've seen her once. She's rather like Lady Ramillies, isn't she?"

"Yes," said Mrs. Fitch and suddenly laughed. The laugh altered her personality entirely. It was revealing and intimate and made her less of an unknown quantity, and Amanda, who was one of those optimists who confidently expect every new person to be a delightful surprise, was disappointed once again.

"I shouldn't be too tolerant where Caroline Adamson is concerned," repeated Mrs. Fitch. "She's not the type of girl you know much about, I should say." She glanced at her visitor dubiously as she spoke, as though she wondered if there was anything on earth of which Amanda knew much. "When you asked me if she was like Georgia Wells I laughed because you're not the first person who's noticed the likeness. You were in the Tulip, weren't you, when Ray Ramillies brought her in with those swallows in her hair? When I saw those two women together I laughed until I cried. Gaiogi Laminoff was so cross with me but I couldn't stop. There they were, the two of them, with Ramillies in the middle and Georgia with her new man. It was funny."

She laughed again at the picture re-created in her mind and Amanda echoed her, since it would have been impolite not to do so. Of all the band of personal traitors the sense of humour is the most dangerous. Mrs. Fitch's sense of humour disarmed her and made her careless.

"Oh, Lord, that was funny!" she said. "And that wasn't the only thing. I knew something else, you see. Don't you ever tell Georgia this because she doesn't know, only it does make the story. Long ago there was another man who was taken with Caroline because she looked like Georgia. That makes it funnier, doesn't it?"

She went off into paroxysms of laughter again and uncertainly Amanda laughed with her.

"I ought not to have told you that," said Mrs. Fitch, wiping her eyes before she poured herself another cup of tea, "but I happened to know Caroline long ago when she was a cloakroom attendant trying to get on the stage, and that night at the Tulip I was the only person who knew the other story. That's what made me laugh. Two men! Both Georgia's specials! It *is* funny."

"Who was the first man?"

"Oh, you wouldn't know him. He was long before your time. You were in the cradle when all that happened. Besides, he's dead now. He was a very stuck-up chap. Saw himself as a judge or something. Not at all Georgia's type, nor Caroline's either. But she could tell you something about him if she liked. She's a naughty girl."

She laughed again.

"Don't you repeat this, though. I don't know why I told you except that it was so funny. I've been dying to tell somebody."

"Was Ferdie amused?"

"Mr. Paul? Oh, I wouldn't tell him." Mrs. Fitch looked shocked but the sight of Amanda's face seemed to amuse her again. "There's a great difference between the things you tell men and the things you tell another woman. You'll have to learn that when you get married. Women think the same things are funny while men often don't see anything in them at all."

"Don't you like Georgia?" enquired Amanda innocently, still in quest of the joke.

"Yes, I do, as much as I like any actress." Mrs. Fitch was clearly truthful. "She's very clever. Did you see her in *The Little Sacrifice?* My dear, in that last scene, although it was so farfetched, she was wonderful. I had to sit in the theatre and wait till everyone else had gone. I couldn't go out into the foyer with my face. It was in a state. Georgia is an artist. I spotted her as a winner years before I met her up here."

She paused and added, as Amanda looked puzzled, "I used to buy for the Old Beaulieu at one time. That's where I met Caroline."

"Buy?"

"Yes. Linen. Silver. Electric-light bulbs. Novelties. It all has to be done, you know. These places have to be looked after, the same as a house."

"Of course they do. I never realised that." Amanda seemed astounded by the discovery and there was a brief pause in the conversation. A chiming clock in the hall struck the half-hour and Mrs. Fitch sighed.

"They'll be just taking off," she observed. "I do hope they have a good crossing. Your boy will be back by eleven. He looks strong."

"Oh, very healthy," said Amanda heartily and hesitated, as the conversation seemed to have reached an impasse. "That's very important," she added heroically.

"It saves a lot of worry," murmured Mrs. Fitch. "You're always fidgeting if you feel they're not well."

"Ferdie looks disgustingly fit." Amanda made the remark sound inconsequential.

"So he may, but all the same he's not strong." There was a new tenderness in the woman's voice which was unexpected and her lips moved soundlessly again. "Not really strong," she repeated. "He'll see Doctor Peugeot this time, I expect. He usually does. He's too clever and he works too hard. Think, think, think; that's all there is in his work. Some people imagine it doesn't take anything out of one, but it does. The brain uses blood just like the muscles do. It stands to reason."

She spoke of Ferdie's mind as if it were an incomprehensible mystery to her and it occurred to Amanda that it probably was.

"Have you got a clever man?" Mrs. Fitch was still misled by Amanda's youth and her tone was gently chaffing.

"Brilliant," said Amanda, who believed in taking a firm line.

Mrs. Fitch chuckled.

"Isn't that sweet?" she said to no one in particular. "Go on believing that and you'll always be happy. Never see round your own man, that's the secret." She laughed again a little spitefully. "Even if you have to blind yourself."

Amanda looked hurt and the other woman handed her the biscuit tin. It was a conciliatory gesture and her stupid eyes were kind.

"Never mind. You won't have to worry about that sort of thing for a long time yet," she said, "if you ever do. But once you've met a really clever man he spoils you for everyone else."

Amanda said nothing but sat up digesting this piece of dubious information and nibbling her third biscuit.

"Oh, I hope they have a good trip," Mrs. Fitch repeated. "There *is* a clever man for you. Ferdie Paul is in a class by himself. If he told me to jump off the roof I'd know he was right."

Amanda looked up.

"Are you sure that's his brains or is it . . . ?"

She broke off delicately and the woman stared at her.

"No, my dear," she said with sudden sharpness. "It's his brains. There's no silly love stuff about me. I'm far too old a bird." She shook her head, stupidity and pride and a certain doggedness all apparent in her expression.

"I wonder if he's got to the coast yet," she added as she relaxed. "The weather report said 'fair.'"

Mr. Campion and Amanda spent the last hour of the evening driving slowly round the outskirts of the town, which were fresh after the rain.

"Gaiogi wasn't there," he said. "He's come to town and isn't expected back until late. I put Ferdie on the plane. I wondered why he was so pleased when we rang up. He hadn't much to tell about Miss Adamson except what I already knew. You seem to have been more successful. Suppose you repeat that conversation word for word as far as you can?"

Amanda lay in the Lagonda, her head resting on the back of the seat, and the street lamps shining on her triangular mouth as she talked. She made a very good job of her report, cutting out only the extraneous matter.

"It was Portland-Smith, of course," she said. "Georgia simply couldn't have had two boy friends who wanted to be judges."

"One would seem to be enough."

Amanda stirred.

"Two women, two Georgias," she announced. "And two men, Ramillies and Portland-Smith, both dead. It's funny, isn't it?"

"That depends on your sense of humour, my girl," said Mr. Campion. "It's frightening me to death. We'll find Miss Adamson tomorrow."

But the following day an Essex constable made a discovery.

To the police a corpse is a corpse and murder is a hanging matter, and the whole affair slid out of the shrouding mists of the fashionable world and the gossip of the bridge clubs and came under the glare of a thousand bulls'-eyes and the ruthlessly indelicate curiosity of the Press.

CHAPTER SIXTEEN

Superintendent Stanislaus Oates of the Central Investigation Department, New Scotland Yard, was one of those happy people who retain throughout their lives a childlike belief in a sharp dividing line between that which is wrong and that which is right. It is this peculiarity which is common to all the great English policemen and is probably the basis of their reputation both for integrity and for stupidity. In his thirty-five years in the force he had acquired a vast knowledge of the incredible weaknesses and perversities of his fellow men, but, while these were all neatly tabulated in his pleasant country mind, his sense of what was black and what was white remained static and inviolate. He was a gentle man, quiet in speech and possessed of a charming yokel sense of fun, but in spite of this he was as hard, as clear-eyed, and therefore often as cruel, as a child of five.

Mr. Campion, who had known him for eleven years and was very fond of him, still paid him that respect which has a modicum of fear in it.

At a little after five on the day following Amanda's enlightening interview with Mrs. Fitch, Mr. Campion came up on the carpet in Oates's office. Although he was so well known to the superintendent his invitation to "step up for a few words" had been as formal as if he had never set his nose inside the place before, and he was conducted to the visitors' chair with considerable ceremony. He looked round him with quick interest. There was quite a gathering. Besides Oates himself, whose bony smile was even less expansive than usual, there was present Chief Detective Inspector Pullen, a great lump of a man with a squat nose and bright eyes who had spent much of his earlier service in the W Division and was one of the Yard's best bets of the year. He sat, solid and solemn, on the superintendent's right hand, looking, in his dark clothes and unnatural gravity, like a bearer at a funeral.

Detective Sergeant Flood was with him, Campion was relieved to see, but his face, which was kite-shaped, did not lighten as the visitor appeared.

A police stenographer sat in the background and they all four looked up silently as the lean man in the horn-rimmed spectacles came quietly in.

Mr. Campion surveyed the scene, his face amiably blank and a head-master's-study feeling gripping the back of his neck.

"Well, who's been riding a bicycle without a reflector?" he said in a well-meaning effort to lighten the atmosphere.

Oates shook his closely cropped head at him.

"It's not a very nice business, Mr. Campion," he said. "It was good of you to come. Just one or two questions, if you don't mind."

Campion was familiar with the superintendent's brand of under-statement and his eyebrows rose. "Not a very nice business" was un-usually strong.

"Oh," he said cautiously. "What's up?"

Pullen glanced at his chief and cleared his throat.

"Mr. Campion," he said, "a young woman has been found dead in circumstances which suggest violence. In the back of a powder com-pactum in her handbag we found a slip of paper with some figures on it. The superintendent here recognised them as forming your tele-phone number, although only the first letter of the exchange was given. I will now read you a description of the deceased. If you think you recognise it I shall be compelled to ask you to come with me to view the body."

He had a curious, staccato delivery which was not unlike the rattle of a tape machine and gave the official words an inhuman quality.

Mr. Campion preserved his famous half-witted expression. It was not quite so misleading as it once had been, since the last ten years had etched lines of character in his face, but it was still serviceable.

"Height five seven, slender build, eyes grey, hair very dark brown, hands and feet well cared for. Age at present doubtful, between twenty-five and thirty-five. Exceptionally well dressed."

Oates leant over the desk.

"That's tall for a woman," he said. "A tall dark girl with grey eyes who was very smart. I asked you to come round because I have a fancy that *was* your telephone number. Do you know her?"

"Yes," said Mr. Campion slowly. "Yes, I think I do. Hadn't she any other papers?"

"None at all. Not a card, not a letter, not a mark on her clothes. This scrap in the powder box may have been overlooked."

He was waiting expectantly and Mr. Campion hesitated. He knew from experience that complete openness is the only thing to offer the police once one is convinced that one's affairs are also their own, but while there is still a chance that things may not be as bad as that it is wisest not to awaken their insatiable curiosity.

"I'd like to see the body before I mention any name," he said.

"Naturally." Oates looked disappointed. "Perhaps you'd like to go along with the inspector now? The identification is holding us up," he continued, relapsing into a more natural manner for a moment. "We can't very well turn her over to Sir Henry until we get that done."

Mr. Campion stirred. Sir Henry Wryothsley, the eminent pathologist, was not called in for the obvious or mediocre.

Pullen heaved himself out of his chair.

"It's a little way out of town, I'm afraid, sir," he said. "Do you mind?"

"Not at all. How long is it going to take me?"

"It all depends on how much you know, my boy." Oates grinned as he spoke. "I think I'll come down with you if you don't mind, Pullen. If she does turn out to be a friend of Mr. Campion's I may be able to give you a hand with him. He's a slippery witness."

There was general laughter at this, none of it ringing quite true, and Mr. Campion found himself checking up on dangerous points, considering Val's position, Gaiogi's and his own. He had time to notice that the inspector took his superior officer's co-operation in very good part. The two men had worked together for some years and were fortunate in possessing different faults and qualities. As he sat jammed in the back of a police car between the two of them he reflected that they made a formidable team and hoped devoutly that he was going to be on their side.

"It's technically an Essex crime," Oates remarked as they swung down the Embankment. "The corpse was found on a common at a little place called Coaching Cross. Where is it exactly, Inspector?"

"Half a mile off the Epping and Ongar main road."

Pullen rattled the words more cheerfully. In the open air, away from the official atmosphere of the Yard, both policemen seemed to have experienced a humanising change, a loosening of the belt, as it were, and there was even just a hint of the "outing" spirit in their smiles, but Mr. Campion was no more misled by them than they by him.

"It's hardly a common. More of a wood," the inspector continued more conversationally. "A sort of thicket. It's a bit of the old forest, I should say. It's full of brambles and hasn't done my trousers any good. I'm a London cop and my clothes aren't constructed for a cross-country beat. Still, the Essex police say it's a London crime and I think they're right. They called us in straight away, not but what an hour or so earlier wouldn't have hurt 'em."

"Anyway, it's our body from now on," Oates remarked complacently. "If they call us in within three days we pay the cost of the enquiry; if not, it's their county council's pigeon." He paused. "We're talking lightly and there's a poor girl lying dead. I hope we're not hurting you, Mr. Campion?"

The naïveté of the question was disarming and Campion smiled. "No," he said. "No. If it turns out to be the girl I think it may be, I know her name and that's about all. She was a very beautiful person with a terrible voice."

"This young woman is good looking," said Pullen dubiously, "but she hasn't much voice left, poor kid, with a damned great wound clean through her chest. It's a funny wound. I don't know if I've ever seen anything quite like it except once, and that was made by a sword. However, that's for Sir Henry to say."

The rest of the drive took place in comparative silence, both parties having indicated quite clearly just how far they were prepared to talk, but as soon as they entered the long cool room at the back of the police station at Coaching Cross Mr. Campion realised that the mischief was done. The canker had come to the surface. Now there was no hiding, no saving of faces nor guarding of reputations. The realisation thrust a little thin stab of alarm behind his diaphragm, but in the back of his mind he was aware of a sense of relief. The pseudo-Nemesis had slipped up at last. The hand of Providence so seldom has a knife in it.

The detective sergeant of the Essex constabulary, who had lifted the sheet from the sharp-angled mass on the table, looked at him enquiringly and he nodded.

It was Caroline Adamson. Rigour had set in before the body had been moved and she lay in a dreadful, unnatural attitude, with one knee a little bent and her spine curved. Her face lay on the sheet so that he had to stoop to see it properly. She was still beautiful, even with the greying flesh shrinking away from the cosmetics on her face and her long eyelashes stiff with mascara, and Mr. Campion, who had never quite got over his early astonishment at the appalling waste when death comes too soon, drew back from her with pity.

"Do you recognise her?" Oates was touching his elbow.

"Yes," he said and was aware of a general sigh of relief from the assembled policemen. One more step in the enquiry had been accomplished.

There was an immediate adjournment to the Charge Room, where there was an embarrassment of important police officials. The Essex superintendent, who, etiquette demanded, should receive a place of honour, sat on Oates's right hand at the solid kitchen table which half filled the room. Pullen was beside him, while Flood and the Essex detective sergeant stood behind. A constable perched at the desk, pen in hand.

Mr. Campion sat on the other side of the table before this impressive array and gave Miss Adamson's name and a list of addresses where he had sought her without success.

Oates listened to him with his head a little on one side. He looked like a very old terrier at a promising rathole, and Mr. Campion spoke casually and with engaging candour.

"I didn't know the girl at all," he said. "I only had one conversation with her in my life and that was over the phone yesterday morning, but I'd seen her once when she was a mannequin at Papendeik's and once or twice at various restaurants."

"Yet you knew all these former addresses of hers?" Pullen sounded puzzled rather than suspicious.

"Yes, I'd been looking for her. I thought she might be able to give me a little information on a private matter."

Mr. Campion regarded the London superintendent steadily as he spoke, and Oates, who knew better than any man the advantage of having a willing witness, hurried on with routine questions. He had the statement finished in fifteen minutes and as soon as Campion had signed it the telephone wires began to buzz and purposeful detectives in London went off to make enquiries at the houses where Miss Adamson had lodged.

Oates had a word apart with Pullen and returned to Campion with an entirely unprecedented invitation to take a stroll down the road to see the scene of the discovery of the body.

"It's only a step," he said and added charmingly, "I know you're interested in these things. I've got full instructions. I think I'll find it. Pullen will be along in a moment. He wants a word with Sir Henry on the phone."

On a less uncomfortable occasion his guest might have been amused. Oates in tactful mood was delightfully unconvincing.

They avoided the loitering sight-seers and circumnavigated the Press, and as they walked down the narrow lane together, the flint dust eddying before them and the brown grasses nodding in the hedgerows, the air was warm and clear, soft and sweet smelling. The superintendent breathed deeply.

"If I hadn't been ambitious I might still be getting a lungful of this every night," he said unexpectedly. "This isn't Dorset but it's not bad. That's what getting on does for you. Nowadays I never see a bit of uncut grass but what it leads me to a perishing corpse. What about this girl, Campion?"

"I've told you practically all I know." The younger man was speaking slowly. "She was once the hat and coat attendant at the Old Beaulieu. From there she went on the stage, where she was not successful. After that she got a job at Papendeik's where there was a spot of bother over a stolen design for a dress and she was sent down to Caesar's Court to show models there. While she was at the hotel she participated in a silly joke on a client and got the sack. This was about six weeks ago. Where she's been since then I cannot find out."

Oates trudged along in silence. His shoulders were bent and his hands were deep in his pockets, rattling his money.

"Caesar's Court," he said at last. "Seems like I've heard that name before, quite recently." He pursed his lips, and Campion, glancing up, caught him peering at him out of the corners of his eyes. The superintendent laughed, drawing back his lips from his fine narrow teeth. "I'm a terrible one for a bit of gossip," he said. "It seems to me I heard a funny story about this lad who died in an aeroplane down at Caesar's Court. He died so pretty there wasn't an inquest nor anything. It was about him and his wife and a very clever lady who's the head of Papendeik's, a very clever, pretty lady. She's a sister of yours, isn't she?"

Mr. Campion's eyelids flickered and for a long time he said nothing at all. Oates walked along, jingling his money.

"It's not far down here," he remarked conversationally. "We're to look out for a turn to the left and a cop with a bike. I don't believe all I hear," he added as his companion made no comment. "When a man's safely buried, with a certificate backed by a P.M. report and nobody making any complaints, I know he died as naturally as makes no difference. I just happened to pick up a bit of high-class scandal which fixed it in my mind. That was all. Who was this dead girl exactly? Did she know Ramillies?"

"Yes. I'm afraid she did. She got the sack from Papendeik's when he dressed her up as his wife, whom she resembles, and took her to dine at the restaurant where Lady Ramillies was having supper after her show. Ramillies got hopelessly tight the night before he died and no one knew where he spent the hours between midnight and noon. I thought he might have been entertained by Caroline Adamson. That was why I looked for her."

"Oh." The superintendent seemed relieved. "That accounts for it. That covers the telephone number very nicely. It's funny how I stumble on things, isn't it? I never seem to forget a name. Faces often mislead you but names have a way of linking up. That 'Caesar's Court' stuck in my head. You can't call to mind anyone else who knew this girl besides the landladies at these addresses? Papendeik's, of course; they knew her. What about the Caesar's Court people?"

"That place is run by Mr. Laminoff," remarked Campion without expression.

"Laminoff." Oates turned the name over on his tongue. "Gaiogi Laminoff, a naturalised British subject. He used to run the Old Beaulieu."

"Did he?"

"He did." Oates wagged his head. "It's funny, I should have thought you would have known that, somehow," he said. "There's the footpath and there's our man with his bike. Good afternoon, Constable. Detective Superintendent Oates of the Central Division here. Can you take us along?"

As Mr. Campion stood on the bald path and peered over the superintendent's shoulder through a gap between two bramble bushes at the spot where Miss Adamson had been found, a distressing sense of travesty assailed him. The scene was the traditional *Midsummer Night's Dream* set. There was the overhanging oak tree, the lumpy bank, and even the wings of thorn for Moth and Mustardseed to vanish into, but here was none of the immortal wild thyme, the sweet musk roses nor the eglantine. This was a forest which three hundred years of civilisation had laid bald and waste. The brown grass was thin and there were roughnesses and threadbare patches which suggested that the coaching of Coaching Cross was motor coaching and the place had been frequented by untidier souls than sweet Bully Bottom and his company.

The constable indicated the position of the body and the sordid joke was complete. Unlike Titania, Miss Adamson had lain head downwards on the bank, one leg drawn up and her face cushioned on a tuft of soiled twitch.

The constable, who was a cheerful countryman, forgot his awe for the distinguished London detective after the first three stultifying minutes and presently so far forgot himself as to impart a circumstance which had been delighting his bucolic soul all day. The local detective, gathering clues, had removed at least two barrow-loads of waste paper, cigarette ends, used matches, cartons, tins and other delicacies which had lain defacing the clearing for the past three years. The constable also pointed out with some glee that the ground was so turrible hard it afforded no wheel or footmarks and was so trodden over at the best of times that any information which it might yield was practically certain to be misleading. Oates listened to him with a sad smile and a patience which made Campion suspect him until he realised that the old man was merely enjoying the country accent, and finally sent him back to his post with the gentlest of snubs.

"Poor chap, he's got too much sense of humour for a policeman," he remarked when the man was out of hearing. "He'll stick to his helmet and his bicycle for the rest of his days, lucky bloke."

He looked round him and indicated a fallen tree trunk which might have been a piece of sylvan loveliness had it not been for the remnants of a dozen picnic meals strewn around it.

"Have a sit-down," he suggested, wrapping his thin grey overcoat tightly round his haunches before perching himself uncomfortably upon the wood.

Mr. Campion took up a position beside him and waited for the ultimatum. It came.

"I've always found you a particularly honest sort of a feller." The superintendent made the announcement as if it were an interesting piece of information. "You've been very fair, I've always thought. Your dad brought you up nicely too."

"A proper little Boy Scout," agreed Mr. Campion helpfully. "If you are asking me in a delicate way if I am going to play ball with you or if I would rather not because I am afraid my sister may have murdered someone by mistake and I do not want to assist in her apprehension, let me say at once, as an old reliable firm with a reputation to maintain, I play ball. I did not know the young woman who is lying in your icebox, and what I knew of her did not amuse me particularly, but I don't associate myself with anybody who sticks a breadknife into any lady. I'm against him, whoever he is. I endorse your point of view in the matter. On the other hand, I do not want to be involved in a lot of unpleasant tittle-tattle or scandal in the daily press, nor do I want my innocent friends and relations to have that degrading experience either. Do I make myself clear?"

"Yes," said Oates. "Yes, you do." He was silent for some moments and sat looking at the yellow evening light on the treetops with apparent satisfaction. "Why did you say 'breadknife'?"

"Joke," explained his companion grimly. "Why?"

"It might have been a breadknife," said Oates seriously. "A thinnish breadknife. Still, that's conjecture." He showed no desire to rise but remained with his coat wrapped round him, staring down at his feet, and presently he began to talk about the case with a lack of official discretion which Mr. Campion fully appreciated without altogether enjoying it, since any deviation from routine in such a die-hard must have some specific purpose.

"The local bobby found the corpse when he came past here on a bicycle at ten minutes past eight this morning," Oates began slowly. "He was taking a short cut to a farm down here in connection with some foot-and-mouth regulations. Now I don't know if you've noticed this place, Campion, but it's not very secret, is it? It's simply the first piece of cover which a fellow would come to if he had taken a chance on a lonely turning off the main road."

"Arguing that the fellow who dumped the body need not have had any pre-knowledge of the district?"

"That's what I thought." The superintendent nodded his appreciation of his guest's intelligence. "As a matter of fact the choice of this particular place rather argues that he didn't know the village. Do you know what this is, Campion? This is the local sitting-out acre, the petting-party field. Every decent village has something of the sort. I remember when I was a boy down in Dorset there was a little wood above a disused quarry. Go down there after tea alone and you'd feel like the one child at the party who hadn't been given his present off the Christmas tree. The place was alive with boys and girls minding their own affairs. Now wouldn't that be a silly place to turn up to with a body? You'd walk into trouble the moment you set foot on the grass with a couple of witnesses behind every bush. No, I don't think our feller knew where he was at all. I think he saw a tree or two and thought 'This'll do.' Pullen, who is a good man, saw that at once. He's got the local lads going round talking to country sweethearts now. That'll mean some delicate interviews. Well, that's one point. Then there's another. That girl was stabbed clean through the chest. Sir Henry said the heart was grazed, in his opinion, but he couldn't say for certain until he'd done his examination. We haven't found the weapon, yet she wasn't saturated with blood."

He paused and cocked an enquiring eye at his companion.

"The sword, or whatever it was, was removed some time after death?"

"Looks like it, doesn't it? They're searching for it now but somehow I don't think they'll find it. If a murderer doesn't throw away the weapon within ten minutes of the crime he's a cool hand and that means we'll never find it like as not."

The old detective was working up to his argument and Campion listened, fascinated by the placid common sense which is the essence of all good police work.

"Then there's the question of rigour." Oates sounded contemptuous. "I don't trust it. I've known it have some amazing vagaries. But we can't afford to ignore it. Rigour is now well advanced and there's no sign of it abating. That shows the chances are a hundred to one that she's not been dead thirty hours yet. So say the crime took place after one o'clock midday yesterday. She was wearing a black silk dress and a small fur cape. It didn't look to me like a morning getup. It was the kind of outfit you might go to a cinema in."

Mr. Campion blinked intelligently.

"Had rigour set in before she was put on the bank?"

"No, after. That's the expert opinion."

"So she must have been brought here within six hours of death?"

"There's no must about it, my lad, and don't you forget it." Oates sounded irritable. "We can only say that the probability is that it was round about six hours after. Yet rigour was well advanced when she was found at eight o'clock. Therefore it's fairly certain that she was killed before 2 A.M. at the latest. As we see it the poor thing was murdered somewhere, probably in London, and the weapon was left in the wound for a time, thus staunching the blood flow. Then, some little time later, say within six or seven hours at least, she was brought down here by car and dumped and the weapon removed. She was wearing high-heeled black patent shoes when she was found and these were grazed on top of the toes, indicating that she'd been carried face forward, with her legs sprawling behind her. There was also a smear on one of her stockings which looked to me like oil. None of this is proved, of course; the whole thing is pure conjecture; but that's how we see it at the moment. You follow where that takes us?"

"Nowhere at all," said Mr. Campion cheerfully, his pale eyes belying his tone.

Oates grunted.

"It takes us to *you*, mate," he said bluntly. "It takes us back to you and your pals, and you know that better than anyone. We've got to go over that girl's immediate past with a magnifying glass and we've got to have a chat with everyone who knew her. It's the motive that's going to put us on to our man and that's what we're after. That's plain speaking, isn't it?"

"Almost homely," agreed Mr. Campion absently. "I've told you all I can, I think. There's one trivial little thing which may be interesting. It's only an impression but they're sometimes useful. I don't think she was alone when she phoned me yesterday."

"An accomplice?"

"I don't know. An audience, anyway. She hadn't her entire mind on me."

The superintendent was interested.

"There you are," he said. "That's corroboration. This isn't an ordinary knifing. I said that to Pullen as soon as I heard the details.

In the normal way, when a good-looking young woman gets herself stabbed it's a perfectly straightforward human story, but this is different. This is what I call number-one murder. It's an honest, done-on-purpose killing for a reason. There was no 'Gawd-I-love-you—take-that' about that stab. Do you know, her dress was rolled down neatly off her shoulders and the weapon inserted as carefully as if she'd been on an operating table. Not torn down, mind you, but rolled."

Mr. Campion stared at him in natural astonishment at this bewildering piece of information.

"What was she doing while all this was happening?"

"The Lord alone knows." Oates shook his bowler hat over the mystery. "I tell you, Campion, the poor thing was barely untidy. Her hands weren't torn and there wasn't another mark on her skin. She hadn't defended herself at all. I've never seen anything quite like it." He hesitated and laughed because he was embarrassed at the fancifulness of his own thoughts. "There's a sort of inhuman quality about that killing," he said. "It's almost as if it had been done by a machine or the hand of fate or something. Where are you going?"

Mr. Campion had risen abruptly. His face was expressionless and he held his shoulders stiffly.

"That is a very unpleasant thought," he said.

"It's foolishness. I don't know what possessed me to say such a thing." Oates seemed genuinely surprised at himself. "I'm getting lightheaded in this country air; that's about it. Well, if he's Dracula himself we'll get him and hang him up by his neck until he's learnt his lesson, and I warn you, Campion, there'll be a lot of questions asked around your part of the world."

"I can see that."

"So long as you know." Oates was avuncular. "I'm taking you at your word," he pointed out. "You're working with us. You've never been foolish yet and I don't suppose you will be this time."

"I'm glad to hear it." Campion spoke with mild indignation. "If I may say so without offence, your rustic personality has been ruined by your association with the police. This perpetual 'I know you're a little gentleman because I've got my beady eye on you' embarrasses me. I don't want to shield any murderer. I'm not antisocial. I'm against murder on principle. I think it's unethical and ungentlemanly and also unkind."

"That's all right," said Oates. "But don't forget it. That's all I'm saying."

"I shall probably visit my sister tonight."

"Why shouldn't you?"

"Why indeed? I'm only mentioning it in case you have me tailed and your suspicious nature suspects conspiracy."

The superintendent laughed.

"It's not that I don't trust you, but I wish you were in the force," he said.

"In other words you don't doubt my honour, but you wish it was a fear of my losing my pension," commented Mr. Campion with acerbity. "You embarrass and disgust me."

Oates was still grinning, the tight skin shining on the bones of his face.

"So long as that's all I've got to do, it won't hurt," he said piously. "Do you know the party you fancy I may come after?"

"No. If I did I should tell you. Can't you see I'm not afraid that you may make an arrest? It's the dust you'll kick up snouting round the rabbit burrows which is my concern."

Mr. Campion seemed to have lost some of his composure and his friend was sympathetic.

"We'll come on tiptoe," he promised.

Campion regarded him affectionately.

"The patter of your little boots will sound like a regiment of cavalry," he said. "Rest assured I'll do everything I can. Frankly, I want this man quite as much as you do."

"Oh, you do, do you? What for?"

"A question of personal affront," said Mr. Campion with deep feeling.

Oates eyed him thoughtfully.

"You were at Caesar's Court when that fellow Ramillies died so suddenly and so naturally, weren't you?" he observed. "And you found the body of that young lawyer fellow who shot himself? He was engaged to the present Lady Ramillies at one time, if I remember. You've got no particular party in mind, you say?"

"No. No one. It may be a Malignant Fate for all I know."

"Ah." The superintendent grunted. "When fate is as malignant as this I take an interest in it. Well, Mr. Campion, since you've failed, we'll see what we can do. We may not be so delicate with our fancywork but we have one great advantage over you, you know."

Mr. Campion glanced down the footpath. Inspector Pullen was striding towards them. His heavy face was animated, for once, and the skirts of his dust coat were flapping.

"You have—The Hired Help," said Campion with feeling. "He's got something."

The inspector was delighted. Satisfaction oozed from him.

"Important new development," he announced with a rattle like a machine gun.

"Let's have it. Never mind Mr. Campion; he's going to be very useful."

Pullen opened his small eyes but he did not demur. His news was bursting from him.

"Sergeant Jenner of the local force has found a witness," he said joyfully. "She's a girl who works in the all-night carmen's café on the main road. Her boy's a milk lorry driver from Eye and apparently he's been in the habit of speeding up his schedule to get half an hour or so extra with this little miss. She can't be eighteen. (I don't know what these country girls are coming to.) Anyway, he got in here at one-thirty last night and hadn't to get to town before four, so she fetched him a meal and then they walked down here. She's going to point out the place where they were sitting. As far as I can make out it's over there behind the tree. About twenty to three, or thereabouts, because her boy was talking of having to get on to London, they heard a car stop in this lane and then there was a lot of movement behind them. The youngsters minded their own business and the girl actually saw nothing, but the young man got up, she says, and looked over a briar hedge. She doesn't know what he saw and no doubt it wasn't anything very sensational, but anyway he sat down again and said, as far as she can remember, 'They've gone.' Then she heard the car go off again and they said good night and walked back. This morning when she heard of the crime she was frightened because of the boy friend's schedule irregularities, but when Jenner put it to her direct she came out with it. We're getting on to the boy now. With luck he saw whoever it was who dumped the body. The whole thing may be in the bag within twenty-four hours."

"I wonder," said Oates and added slyly, glancing at Campion, "Don't you leave London. There may be another description for you to identify. Can you see our Nemesis fellow in a bag?"

Mr. Campion said nothing. The familiar stab behind his diaphragm was disturbing and he caught his breath.

"Nemesis?" said Inspector Pullen with disgust. "He's a two-legged Nemesis, if you ask me, and if he has two legs the chances are he also has a neck."

CHAPTER SEVENTEEN

Val and Mr. Campion were in the studio at Papendeik's; not the little office, which was only a semiprivate apartment, but the great studio at the top of the house, which was a holy of holies and looked to Mr. Campion's inexperienced eyes like the inside of a woman's handbag magnified. It seemed to contain everything except a bath, although there certainly was a businesslike sink in one corner of the room, besides a remarkable assortment of tables, cupboards, mirrors and mysterious boxes.

They had chosen this place for conversation partly because it was secret and partly because there was a gas fire and, although it was midsummer, the night was chilly.

Miss McPhail, Val's secretary, who spent her life guarding this sanctuary, had gone home, but Rex was still about in spite of the time, and the three of them were alone in the great house. Val had come back from her little Queen Ann bandbox in Hampstead at her brother's request and they had found Rex still working when they arrived a little after ten. Georgia was expected after her show and they were waiting for her.

Campion sat on the edge of a solid wooden table before the fire directly under a hanging daylight bulb. The rest of the room was in shadow, and the hard, unnatural glare shone down on his dark back and bent head.

Val walked about the room. Her dress was the bright, clear green of cooking apples and she looked young but very brave and capable, with her fine hands clasped behind her and her chin set.

Rex leant against the mantelshelf. He held a small square of chestnut velvet and was playing with it absently, feeling the yielding quality of the material and trying the light on it as he laid it on his arm. It was very quiet in the room and still cold.

"I remember her at the Old Beaulieu," Rex remarked without looking up. "She was very attractive. Not chic, never any class, but a *pièce*. Well worth looking at. Her father was Gaiogi Laminoff's accountant. His name was Wilfred Adamson. He died before she left. That was very early in '33, I think. Gaiogi Laminoff did what he could for her. He got Ferdie Paul to give her a little part on tour, and I know one September—it must have been that same year—she was hanging round the agents, very sorry for herself."

"Gaiogi didn't take her back?" enquired Campion curiously.

"No, he was shutting the Beaulieu and looking about for capital to start the Poire d'Or." Rex was still speaking in an absent fashion, as if he were working round to a point and wondering whether to make it. Mr. Campion, who was liable to moments of irrelevant observation, suddenly saw him objectively, a natty, demure little soul, only effeminate insomuch as sex shocked him for its ugliness and interested him because it shocked him.

He went on talking, still stroking the scrap of material on his cuff. "Then she came into money," he said. "I don't know if there was a man or not, but for quite a bit she was running round with the dancing boys and driving about in a little car. She even bought one of our models. I used to see her quite a bit. She never said where she got the cash but she certainly had it."

Mr. Campion looked up sharply, enlightenment on his thin face. "That was in 1934, the year Portland-Smith disappeared?"

Rex raised his head, and his eyes, which were doggy and harassed in the usual way, now had a flicker of excitement in them.

"Yes," he said. "He went off on June the eighteenth. I've always remembered that; it's the anniversary of Waterloo. Caroline Adamson had plenty of money, but long before then. It was early spring when she came round here for a model and she'd had it some time then. I noticed her particularly. She chose a very lovely grey moire which Madame admired and which passed over the heads of the buyers. It's only three years ago. She was broke again early the next autumn, when Gaiogi Laminoff recommended her. She was a good model but not a pleasant girl. She was very bitter about Gaiogi, although he did so much for her. He was having trouble of his own then. The Poire d'Or opened in April or May of '34 and Bjornson had let Laminoff in by that crash of his by the January; it had been coming some time."

"I thought Gaiogi was only the manager of the Poire d'Or?" put in Val, who had paused behind the table.

"No. He had money in it. Bjornson never put up *all* the money for anything. Besides, I knew Bud Hockey, who was running the music there, and I remember he told me that Laminoff was down for a packet. I know I wondered where the old man had got it from because there was no squeal. His backer, if he had one, was very quiet."

There was a long silence while everybody digested this information.

"You think it was Gaiogi's own money?" said Val at last.

Rex shrugged his shoulders and twisted the velvet into a rosette, holding it at arm's length to admire the effect.

"It looked like it, madame. But he had none when the Beaulieu closed. There was a little gossip about it at the time; nothing exciting, just speculation." He laughed at Campion shyly. "One talks about money," he said. "It's the other subject."

Mr. Campion considered the discovery and Val cut into his thoughts with another of the tag phrases from their childhood.

"There's no proof, but I've lost a ha'penny and you're eating nuts," she remarked.

He nodded. Portland-Smith had shot himself in June and Miss Adamson had been well supplied with money since the previous winter. After the shooting she had become poor again. He did not say the words aloud, but Val, he knew, was following his thought. As with many people of one blood, there was a curious, wordless communion between them which might have been telepathy or an identically similar mental process.

"I didn't know she knew him," said Val.

"Caroline Adamson and Portland-Smith?" Rex hesitated over the names. "I don't know that she did but I think she did. It's merely an impression; something to do with a joke about her being so like Georgia Wells. I can't remember it at all. I doubt if I ever really heard it. It wasn't much, I know; only snack-bar talk."

"You're quite the little gossip, Rex, aren't you?" Val was amused.

"A little bit here, a little bit there. It all tells up."

The man wriggled and giggled coyly and his face flushed.

"I've got a very good memory," he said primly. "Besides, I like to know what's going on. But I never put two and two together; it's too disturbing."

An electric bell over the door began to vibrate and Val hurried across the room.

"There she is," she said. "No, Rex, thank you, I'll go down myself. I want to."

The little man bowed elaborately and held the door open for her. His every movement was self-consciously gallant and there was a nervous, chuckling effrontery behind his manner which was quite out of keeping with this or any other situation. He came back to the mantelpiece to pick up his piece of velvet. It lay, a dark pool, on the white ledge, and as his hand hovered over it he suddenly drew back. Then, controlling himself, he took up the scrap and threw it into a wastepaper basket.

"She was stabbed, wasn't she?" he said. "That velvet reminded me. It's very lovely material. Very soft and beautiful to drape. But I don't care for it. Dried blood is that colour, you know. I saw a lot of it in France."

"In France?" Mr. Campion was surprised. The notion of the lady-like Rex as a warrior was incongruous.

"'Fourteen to '17." Rex spoke briskly. "The Somme and the Marne. I was a Tommy. I never got a commission. It was a long time ago but it cured me of all kinds of things. I've never put up with ugliness or discomfort since. I shall advise Madame against the velvet. All this plum and magenta which is so popular is a great pity, I think. It was the Coronation which introduced it, of course, but I still don't like it. It doesn't make *me* think of royalty."

He giggled again and smoothed his hair.

"Laminoff had some peculiar experiences in Russia, I believe. He doesn't talk about them, but he went back during the Revolution and only came through with his life. He can't stand ugliness either. Have you noticed? Everything has to be easy, delicate and elegant. He'll do anything for it. When the Poire d'Or was actually smashing he wouldn't give up the orchid on each table. Money for its comfort's sake means more than a lot to him."

He glanced at his neat wrist watch, which was gold and very delicate without being at all womanish.

"Beddy-byes," he said unexpectedly. "I shan't be home till midnight. I don't know if I've been of any use. It's only gossip, as Madame says. I don't know anything unpleasant. I don't really want to. Good night."

He giggled again and went out, adroitly avoiding the visitor by thirty seconds.

Georgia was not alone. Campion heard Ferdie Paul's excited squeak before the party reached the second floor. He came in a little in advance of the others, a great wave of nervous energy sweeping into the room with him.

"My God!" he said. "My God, what a schemozzle! One damned thing on top of another!" He sat down on a wooden chest and pulled out a cardboard packet of cigarettes, lighting one from it and pitching the spent match into the furthest corner of the room.

Georgia came in with Val. She was at her loveliest, in a black dress of some soft, transparent material draped over her bosom and flowing out into soft baby frills round the hem and train of the skirt. She looked graceful, womanly and, in some inexplicable way, pathetically bereft.

"Oh, darling," she said to Campion. "Oh, darling. How incredibly depressing. I've had a policeman in my dressing room and Ferdie's had two; one at the plane and one at the flat. What a slut of a girl!"

"Damn it, you can't blame her," said Ferdie from the background.

"It's not her fault. She's simply the person who fell through the hole in the floor. She was a good-looker, too. It's a pity."

He spoke with real regret, no doubt at the thought of beauty wasted.

Georgia sat down on the table close to Campion.

"Two deaths," she has huskily. "Two. But I'm not superstitious. I won't be superstitious. What are we going to do? What exactly does it mean to us?"

Everyone looked at Campion, who bestirred himself.

"It's an awkward position," he said slowly, thinking that it would have been easier for Val and himself to tackle Georgia on the delicate matter which they had met to discuss if a fourth party had not been present. "You see, once the police get hold of a case like this they're so infernally thorough. Everyone who knew Miss Adamson will be cross-examined for days by earnest detectives trying to sound as though they had just dropped in to talk about string. In the end they'll find out every mortal thing the wretched girl has said and done during the last six months. That doesn't matter much, of course. I promised them I would give them any information I came across, and I shall, as anyone else would. But whereas it doesn't matter what they find out if it's relevant, they may so easily get on to all kinds of things which are nothing to do with the case and which, although not criminal, have their awkward aspects. These may make the good dicks red herrings and land us all with a kettle of fish."

He paused. Ferdie Paul was looking at him with his head a little on one side and a slightly derisive smile, which was tolerant rather than contemptuous, on his curly mouth.

"Exactly!" he said. "Exactly, my dear boy. And so what?"

"It's about me," said Val, coming forward with sudden determination. "It's no good being vague and lawyer-like, Albert. You must say the words in a case like this. Now look here, Georgia my pet, you must not go telling the police that story about me and the cachet blanc. It's a good yarn and amusing and all the rest of it and it doesn't matter who else you tell it to, because everyone we know will see it as you see it and realise that you don't really mean that it's true. But the police may take it seriously and we don't want them going all hysterical and applying for exhumation orders and that sort of thing, do we? It isn't as though they could find anything, we know. There was a P.M. at the time, thank God, but there would be a frightful row which would ruin us both professionally."

Ferdie Paul, who had been sitting admiring his feet throughout this eminently straightforward statement, now glanced up.

"You're a good girl, Val," he said. "A sensible girl and a damned good sort to take it like that. I told you, Georgia, that story was stark lunacy at the time."

Georgia put her arm round Val. It was a long, slow movement, and, laying her dark head gently against the apple-green dress, she allowed two tears, and only two, to roll slowly down her cheeks. It was exquisite, the most abject, expressive and charming apology Campion had ever seen. Georgia seemed to think it was pretty good, too, for she brightened perceptibly for an instant before resuming her mood.

"I didn't realise it," she said earnestly. "I've got a blind spot. I didn't see it. That story has got me into terrible trouble, Val, more than you'll ever know, so I have been punished. But if it wasn't for you I'd be almost glad. If it hadn't been for that silly story I'd never have realised something rather awful that was happening to me. Now at least I'm sane again."

She paused.

"And my darling is dead," she said in her breath, but with a tragic depth of feeling which startled them all by its staggering sincerity.

"Who's dead?" said Val sharply.

Georgia stared at her in genuine bewilderment.

"Ray," she said. "Oh, my dear, you haven't forgotten him so soon? He was the only man I ever really loved and when he died I didn't realise it. I don't want to talk about it or I shall make a fool of myself. Forgive me."

She blew her nose on a little white handkerchief and smiled through her tears.

Ferdie sat looking at her with professional admiration. Then he glanced at the other two and laughed.

"She's a dear girl, isn't she?" he said, not without a certain pride. "That's very sweet, Georgia, but get the main idea. Don't tell the police fairy stories, even if you believe them. Val's absolutely right. This thing could make one hell of a stink if the Press decided to risk it, which they might, of course. I don't know. What do you think, Campion? Oh, Lord, what a mess! How long will the police keep at this thing?"

"Until they find out how the girl died." Mr. Campion seemed to consider the question superfluous. "The longer it takes the more ground they'll cover. They're a fairly efficient machine."

"I know." Ferdie was disgusted. "They went along to the flat and frightened Anna Fitch out of her wits. She told them where I was and they met me on the landing ground. Poor old Bellairs was in the plane, too, and he came in for it as well. Among other things we told them when we left, where we stayed in Paris, and who I'd seen during the day. I was convinced they thought I'd done it at least. Then I told them all I could remember about the blasted girl, which wasn't a lot. Apparently Anna had the same questions and so did Georgia. Two o'clock in the morning seems to be the fatal hour. I don't like to think how the girls got on, but I had a nice clean tale to tell for once in my life. Bellairs and the pilot and I were all eating respectably at the Bouton." He paused. "They asked me a lot of questions about Gaiogi. Did you put them on to him?"

Mr. Campion blinked before the implied reproach.

"She was last employed at Caesar's Court. Val's had the police round here about her. You employed her too."

"Oh, I see. Of course." Ferdie sighed. "It's bad," he said. "Thunderingly bad. Lousy. However you look at it. She was running round with Ray, you know, Georgia."

"I know." Georgia's voice was very small and quiet. "I know. That was my fault. I was infatuated with Alan Dell. That was a nightmare, a dreadful insane sort of dream. I neglected Ray horribly—don't remind me of it, Ferdie; I've been terribly punished—and he was brokenhearted and picked up that little beast because she was vaguely like me. That's all there was to that."

"Very likely," agreed Ferdie grimly, "but it's very unfortunate in view of everything, isn't it, *dear?*"

Georgia responded to the implied rebuke.

"Must you be brutal, Ferdie?"

"Darling, it's the coincidence." Val spoke with the dogged patience which the other woman seemed to inspire in her. "And it's not only that, either. There's another coincidence which may come out, isn't there? There's nothing in them. For God's sake don't think I mean that. But Caroline knew Portland-Smith too, didn't she?"

Ferdie's shiny eyes opened to their widest extent.

"Did she indeed?" he ejaculated. " 'Strewth! Where did that come from, Val?"

"Rex told me. He seemed to think there was a sort of tale about it at the time. He was very vague but that's the kind of thing the police get hold of. If they're going to ferret out everything we may as well be prepared for it."

Georgia laughed. She seemed unaccountably flattered.

"I never heard that," she said, "but it's quite possible. My dears, that girl was *like* me. That's why you let her model my frocks, Val. If a man was terribly miserable because I'd been a cat to him it was quite natural if he tried to console himself with someone who reminded him of me. Surely the police could see an elementary point like that?"

Mr. Campion, who was listening to the scene with interest, considered Superintendent Oates and wondered.

"I know, Georgia, I know." Val was helpless. "But, dearest, *they're all dead.*"

"I say, you know, I say, Georgia! I say! It's bad." Ferdie Paul rose as he spoke and strayed down the room with a peculiar jaunty gait which he adopted when excited. "Shattering publicity if it came out. For God's sake don't go talking about cachets blanc and what not. Look here, the whole thing is nothing to do with you or Val. Let 'em talk to me and Campion. Where were you last night, Campion?"

"Driving round the houses with Amanda."

"Were you? I suppose that's fairly conclusive. I like that kid. Good class is attractive when it's genuine, isn't it? Oh well, then, you're all right. So am I. I've got a blameless twenty-four hours and no extraneous odds and ends to hide, for a change. We'll talk to the police, then. You lie low, Georgia, and don't try to tell any bobby what men will do in love. It's over his head."

Georgia smiled at him affectionately.

"Common old Ferdie," she observed. "My dear, I'm not a lunatic. I may have been a little insane just lately but I've snapped out of it. I've told Val I'm sorry, or at least I've conveyed that I am, and she's forgiven me. The cachet was a silly little bit of nonsense we've both forgotten. That's over. Now none of us has anything to worry about, have we?"

Mr. Campion coughed. There was unusual determination on his face and his eyes were cold.

"I'm afraid it's not quite so simple," he said decisively, turning to Georgia. "There is one other matter which I think we ought to mention while we're about it. It's not my affair but it may come up, and if it does you must be ready for it. The police will find out everything remotely connected with Caroline Adamson. They're certain to discover that she was thought to have known Portland-Smith when he was engaged to you. That's all right, I know, but in the course of their investigations they may stumble on another fact which might make them curious. You were married to Portland-Smith, weren't you?"

The effect of the question was startling. The whole room, with its hard, unnatural light and black-shadowed corners, seemed to contract round the girl in the black dress and round Ferdie Paul, arrested in his walk behind her.

Georgia did not move a muscle. She sat looking at Campion and the colour rushed into her face as if she had been a baby, while her grey eyes were guilty and appalled.

Ferdie Paul's reaction was less restrained. For an instant his plumpish face, with its rococo curves and contours, was frozen with astonishment. Then he leapt forward and took the woman by the shoulder.

"You weren't? My God!"

He conveyed that his particular deity was insane.

"Georgia, you trollop! Why didn't you tell me? When did you marry him? When? Out with it. When? My blessed girl, don't you see how this is going to look?"

There was ferocious urgency in his thin voice and he shook her, unconsciously digging his fingers into her shoulder. Georgia pulled herself away and rubbed the place. She looked utterly pathetic and as guilty as an accused puppy.

"When?" Ferdie repeated mercilessly.

"One lovely rainy April day." The infuriating words tinkled in the quiet room.

"The year he vanished?"

"No. We were married fifteen months, the most miserable months of my life."

"Oh, for God's sake!" said Ferdie Paul.

He sat down heavily on the edge of the table and began to whistle. Georgia went over to him.

"*He* insisted on it being a secret," she protested. "It was his career. Apparently if you're going to be a county court judge the stage is still a bit low to marry into."

"Is it? What was the idea? Was he going to keep you under the dresser all his life?"

"No. When he became this judge person I was going to leave the stage. It was the getting there that might have been mucked up. Besides, we had money to think of."

"Really? You astound me."

Georgia ignored him. She was looking over his head, a half smile on her lips.

"It may sound silly now, but that was the argument at the time," she said. "It seems mad at this distance. Utterly mad. I was so hopelessly in love, Ferdie. He was such a sweet prig. I'd never met anything like him before. He was so secretive, all pompous and shut up inside himself, and gloriously narrow and conventional. It was the same thing you like in Alan, Val. You get so sick of it when you're married to it. But at first it was like a heavenly closed door, all stern and secret and mysterious."

"We'll imagine it," said Ferdie.

"Forgive me, but I don't see why you actually married the poor mysterious beast." Mr. Campion put the question diffidently.

"Why does one marry?" Georgia appealed to him for information.

"I know." A dreadful travesty of a sentimental smile spread over Ferdie's face. "So you could have a dear little baby."

Georgia eyed him. "No," she said. "Not necessarily. Look here, Ferdie, you and Val and everybody, you don't understand. I really love them. My whole life is controlled by them. I see everything from their point of view. I love them. I want to *be* them. I want to get into their lives. I'm quite sincere, Ferdie. At the time I'm terribly, desperately hurt. I can't stop it. I'm just the same as any little servant girl helplessly in love for the first time, but *it wears off*."

She hesitated, looking at them, her beautiful dark face earnest and her eyes imploring.

"It's because I'm a natural actress, of course," she continued, revealing that odd streak of realism which made her lovable. "When I've made a character I've made it and she's done. She's finished. She bores me unbearably. Val, you understand. You've made some divine gowns but you wouldn't wear any one of them for the rest of your life. I can't help it. It's my tragedy. When I feel morbid I wonder if I myself exist at all."

Ferdie regarded her. He seemed wearier and heavier. Only his eyes were animated.

"Don't worry," he said dryly. "You exist." He thrust out an arm and pulled her to his side, holding her there as if she were an obstinate child. "You're obsessed by contracts," he observed. "That's your complex. It's got its basis in ordinary inbred female funk. I don't blame you. But if you must sign documents think about them first. A marriage certificate isn't quite the same as a Guild contract. The time clause is different."

Georgia freed herself and walked slowly round the room, her black dress rippling over her strong, slender thighs.

Ferdie was silent for some time. He sat on the edge of the table, his head bowed, so that the inadequacy of his dark curling hair was revealed. He was thinking, and it occurred to Mr. Campion that he had never seen a man think more obviously. The man's brain was almost audible.

"Hey," Ferdie said suddenly, "how the hell did you know?"

He swung round and sprawled across the table, looking up into Georgia's face.

"What?"

"How did you know that you were free to marry Ray Ramillies? Portland-Smith's body's only just been found."

Georgia shied away from him and from the question, but he caught her and pulled her round to face him. There was a tremendous force in the man and his incredulity was so great that they were all as conscious of it as if it had been their own.

"Did you know he was dead?"

"Not exactly—I mean of course I knew. You're hurting me, you fool. I thought he must be."

"*You thought he must be!*" Ferdie scrambled off the table and stood before the girl, peering into her eyes as if they were keyholes. "Are you telling me that for all you knew you might have been committing bigamy? You're insane, woman. You're mad. You ought to be locked up. You're sex crazy. A nymphomaniac. You're *barmy!* You must have known."

Georgia covered her face with her hands and managed to convey the tragically adventurous innocence of an Ibsen heroine.

"I believed what Ray told me."

"Ray?" This development was a surprise to Mr. Campion and he glanced up sharply. But he had no need to question. Ferdie pounced on the admission.

"What did he know about it? He was present at the suicide, I suppose, egging the wretched chap on."

"Don't, Ferdie, don't!" It was a cry from the heart and Georgia turned to Val for support. Val submitted to the considerable weight upon her shoulder and took the quivering hand in her own.

"This is all too emotional, my children," she said, the quiet authority of her voice surprising herself a little. "Everybody sit down. Now, Georgia, you'll have to explain this. What happened?"

Seated on a hard chair, with her lovely rounded elbows resting on the worktable, in her black dress, tears in her eyes and a foil in apple-green beside her, Georgia evidently felt stronger. She raised her head and the hard light gave her black hair a blue depth and darkened the shadows beneath her eyes.

"I married Richard Portland-Smith in April 1933," she said slowly. "You know how I loved him. I've told you that. We were going to keep it a secret until we could afford to announce it and I could leave the stage. It was a ridiculous, idealistic programme and it failed. We lived apart and met in sordid hole-and-corner ways, stole week ends and did all the things that are absolutely fatal. Gradually we got on each other's nerves and by the end of the year we both realised it was a horrible, unbearable mistake. In September you put on *The Little Sacrifice*, Ferdie, and when I played that part I realised for the first time what real unhappiness means. I was caught, I was trapped. My lovely, lovely life was spoilt. I'd ruined it and there was no escape ever."

"Ramillies was over here then, wasn't he?" Ferdie made the remark without spitefulness.

"It wasn't only Ray." Georgia leapt to her own defence with child-like eagerness. "It wasn't. I'd say if it was. I'm not ashamed of love. It's a beautiful thing that one simply can't help. Ray and I did fall in love at first sight but I was desperately, helplessly miserable before. Richard was fantastically jealous and mean about it. He was petty and disgusting. He listened at doors, even, and got possessive and revolting. I begged him to let me divorce him, or even to divorce me, but he wouldn't. His filthy career came first every time. I can't tell you what it was like. He went off in October for one of his walking tours and the relief of being without him was like kicking off a pinching shoe. Ray was so very sweet. He was going back in a few weeks and he spent most of his leave hanging round the theatre. I loved him. He was so strong and happy and extroverted. When Richard came back he really had become impossible. He'd got parsimonious suddenly and was narrower than ever. After a while I began to realise the dreadful truth. He was going off his head. It must have been in his blood all the time and being piqued brought it out."

She passed her hand over her forehead and her eyes were pained and sincere.

"We had fantastic rows, dozens of them. It was unspeakably sordid and degrading. He used to try to make me jealous. It was so piteous. I never actually saw him with Caroline Adamson but he used to rave about women, reviling the whole sex and generally behaving more and more like a lunatic. I bore it as well as I could but it made life impossible. I was physically frightened of him. The subject of divorce sent him into a ferment. He wouldn't even hear the word. Finally I was so utterly miserable that I went to a firm of private detectives in Rupert Street, but they couldn't find a thing. Apparently he really was insane, and simply worked all day and lived on sardines. He sacked his servant and lived like a hermit. There's a name for that sort of mental trouble. Melancholia, or dementia praecox, or some-thing. Meanwhile the detectives were horribly expensive and quite useless, and at last in despair I called them off. And then, in June, quite suddenly, Richard disappeared. I couldn't believe it at first. I went about like a child, crossing my fingers and praying that he'd never come back. I had *suffered*, Val."

The other girl looked down at her and there was a bewildered expression in her eyes.

"She had, you know," she said to Ferdie Paul. "She really had."

He met her glance and a faint smile passed over his curly mouth. "Astounding, isn't it?" he agreed. "Go on, Georgia. I believe you're doing your best. Don't lie. Let's have the full strength."

Georgia shook her head.

"You don't know me, Ferdie," she said tolerantly. "I couldn't lie about Ray. That was my real love affair. When he came back I knew that this was the true thing. It was about six weeks after Richard had gone and I was still quivering in case he came back. Ray walked into my dressing room one night and stood looking at me. You remember how he used to stand, all lean and exciting and sort of gallant. We didn't speak. It just happened. I cried all over him. I was so —so happy."

Ferdie Paul chuckled involuntarily, and, half shamefacedly, because she was heart-rendingly sincere, they joined him.

"What a life you have!" he said. "Then what?"

"He wanted to marry me at once, of course." Georgia ignored the interruption. She was used to being misunderstood. "So I did, of course. I held him off as long as I could and then I saw it was no use, so I had to tell him everything."

"This was all after Portland-Smith had disappeared? You're sure of that?"

"Ferdie, I am not lying. My dear, can't you see I'm not? I'm being wonderfully frank. I'm telling you the absolute, literal truth. I'm not sparing myself. This is what actually happened. It was November when I told Ray I was married to Richard—on Guy Fawkes night as a matter of fact. I remember, because we'd had a party for little Sinclair, who was silly and didn't like it. Ray was adorable with him, and I suddenly saw what home life could be with them both, and it was too much for me altogether. I told Ray and he was kinder than I can possibly describe. He simply laughed in that slightly devilish way he had and said I wasn't to worry."

She pressed her handkerchief to her lips and shook her head.

"After that it wasn't so frightfully easy. I loved him with all my soul, you see, and yet . . . and yet . . ."

"And yet you do like a contract," said Ferdie easily. "You're a remarkable girl, aren't you? So respectable at heart. Ray went to find him, I suppose. Did he find him?"

"We-ell . . ." Georgia was evidently coming to the crux of her story and was considering the light in which to present it. Presently she threw out her hands in a particularly charming gesture of renunciation. "I'll tell it simply," she said. "If you don't understand you've never really loved. Ray was absolutely convinced that Richard was dead. He said he would never have left me for so long if he had been alive, and of course that was true. Besides, knowing Richard in that insane brooding mood of his, I couldn't help feeling that it would be just like him to go off and die somewhere secretly, revenging himself on me by leaving me in doubt. He was like that in the end, all mad and tied up and mean in soul."

"When you got the secret door open you found it led to the junk cupboard," Val remarked dreamily.

"The *cellar*, my dear! Old bottles and damp newspapers and frightful white crawly things." Georgia threw the bagatelle over her shoulder happily. She and Val were dear friends again and she was so glad. "Ray hurled himself into the search. He worked like a lunatic. You know how energetic he was, Ferdie. *You* saw him, Albert, over that idiotic gun. Once he wanted a thing he wanted it more than anything in the world. He scoured the country for unidentified bodies, but he couldn't find a trace of him until just before Christmas, and then he found Richard."

"Found him?"

The words were jerked from Mr. Campion, who had been standing quietly by the fireplace listening to the scene with his habitual politeness.

Georgia met his eyes steadily.

"Yes," she said. "He found him in a crevasse in Wales. He'd been mountaineering or something. People often go to mountains with broken hearts; they're so comfortingly solid. Anyway, he'd fallen and been lost for months. Ray wouldn't let me go to see him because of the filthy things that happen to bodies. He simply gave me his word of honour and I took it. We married on January the fifth, by special licence, as you know. As my marriage to Richard was secret I called myself Sinclair."

"In fact, as far as you knew, you committed bigamy." Ferdie strode down the room. "If this comes out you're done. It mustn't, of course. I don't see it need. We shall all hold our tongues for our own sakes."

Georgia rose. She was angry and her cheeks were bright.

"It *was* Richard," she said. "Ray gave me his word of honour."

"Don't be silly, dear." For the first time Ferdie betrayed an unintentional irritation. "Portland-Smith was found in Kent with a bullet through his skull. His papers were found on him. The coroner decided the bones were his. You drove the poor brute off his head and he killed himself. That's the truth of that. See a few facts now and again. Don't let 'em cramp your style but don't kid yourself all the time."

"That is not true." Georgia was gentle. "Ferdie, you're sadistic. You enjoy hurting me. My dear boy, Ray *proved* to me that the body in Wales was Richard's."

"How?"

"He went down in the train with a woman who was also travelling to identify the body. He recognised her as the wife of an old sergeant-major of his, a perfect fiend of a hag who'd led her wretched husband such a ghastly life that the poor creature ran away from her. Ray knew because the man had been to him and borrowed some money to get to Canada and Ray had lent it to him. The woman was mad to identify this body to get a widow's pension, and so of course Ray was in a cleft stick. Once this woman had decided that her husband was dead the man was free from her forever. Besides, if Ray had put his foot down and insisted that it was Richard, we couldn't very well marry immediately, could we? After all, it was only he and I who had to be satisfied. We were the only people to whom it really mattered."

"Except his parents and his clients," murmured Mr. Campion tactlessly.

"Oh? Had he got people?" Georgia was both startled and contrite. "He was over thirty. I never thought of him as being someone's child. How disgustingly selfish of me! But I was so, so terribly in love. Well, Ray saw it was Richard, and the awful woman, who was sick at the sight of the body and couldn't look at it, insisted that it was her husband, and so Ray didn't interfere. I think it was rather nice of him. He told me the whole story and even took me to see the woman, who had some dreadful little hovel in Hackney. She convinced me utterly."

"That it was her husband?"

"No, of course not. She convinced me that she had persuaded herself that it was. She was unbelievable. I sympathised with the wretched man in Canada. Then she went into the most gruesome details and Ray had to take me away. Then, of course, since I was sure, Ray and I married."

There was a long pause after her husky voice had died away. Ferdie sat looking at her, his chin resting on his hands and his face morose and inscrutable.

Mr. Campion was shocked. There are some people to whom muddled thinking and self-deception are the two most unforgivable crimes in the world.

Val patted Georgia's shoulder absently.

"How did *he* dare?" she demanded suddenly. "He had an enormous amount to lose."

"Oh, Ray was like that." Surprisingly it was Georgia herself who answered. "Ray was a natural adventurer. That's why I adored him. He risked everything all the time. He didn't care. So long as he achieved his objective he didn't care how dangerous it was."

She went on talking happily, sublimely unconscious of the tacit admission she was making.

"Ray just wanted Georgia and he didn't care what he did to get her. He was so young always, so brave, so gloriously dangerous."

"He was a damned fourflusher," said Ferdie Paul. "Dangerous is the word. What happened when Portland-Smith's body was discovered? That tarnished his word of honour a bit, didn't it?"

"Oh, I was frightfully angry with Ray." Georgia spoke involuntarily, adding with maddening gentleness, "Until I realised that there'd been another mistake, and anyway it didn't really matter then. I was so terribly upset about poor Richard at the time. I only remember the best in people, you know."

Ferdie Paul rose to his feet with what appeared to be a considerable physical effort.

"Yes, well," he said heavily, "let's all hope she never gets into the witness box. Now look here, you people, there's only one thing we need all remember and that is that this particular mess is nothing to do with us. We can be as helpful and as polite as we like. The more helpful we are the better. It looks well. But the affair is not our business. It's quite obvious what happened to Caroline Adamson. She went around with a dangerous lot, the dregs of the fur and the restaurant trade and the lower West End mob. Heaven knows what scrap she got herself into. They're a nasty crowd to monkey with and she was a pretty piece. We're all all right if we don't go and jump into it. Get that well into your head, Georgia."

"I have, my dear." There was a flicker of shrewdness in Georgia's tweed-grey eyes, but it vanished almost at once. "I should probably be very good in court, you know."

"You wouldn't." Ferdie's brown eyes were intensely earnest. "Don't for pity's sake get that idea in your head. You wouldn't. D'you remember that blank-verse play you would try one Sunday? You do? It would be like that only a million times worse. Take my word for it."

Georgia shrugged but she looked chastened.

"I see things so clearly," she said and laughed at herself. "Even when I'm wrong."

It was nearly two in the morning. Campion had the Lagonda in the drive and Val's man was waiting in her famous grey Daimler with the special body. As Georgia lived in Highgate she went home with Val, while Campion dropped Ferdie at the Sovereign.

As the two women settled down in the soft grey-quilted depths of the car, which was like a powder closet inside, shut away from the chauffeur and as exquisitely feminine as a sedan chair, Georgia linked her arm through Val's.

"Ferdie's quite right," she said with a return to the more truthful mood which she kept for the few women she recognised as her equals. "If we simply smile and do all we can for everyone without actually doing anything, it may be all all right. I do hope so. It'll all pass. We'll laugh about it when we're old women."

"I hope so," said Val soberly.

"Oh, we shall." After her ordeal Georgia's spirits were reviving and she was dangerously optimistic. "I'm so glad all that about Ray and Richard has come out at last. It's been half on my conscience. I hate secrets. It was dangerous, but it didn't matter as it happened. I simply didn't care at the time. You don't, do you? Nothing else seems to matter. That's why Ray and I got on so well together. In that respect he was feminine too. He was the only man I ever met who really understood how my mind worked. His own was the same. Oh, my dear, it's going to be hell without him."

She was speaking quite sincerely and Val glanced at her out of the corner of her eye. Georgia was aware of the scrutiny in spite of the shifting darkness.

"I've got rid of Alan," she said, adding in a burst of truthfulness which was more than half pure generosity, "In a way he got rid of me. We had a dreadful row the day after the memorial service, of all indecent moments. He simply abused me, Val. Not noisily in a way you could forgive, but quietly, almost as though he meant it. It was about that cachet story, as a matter of fact. It had come round to him again, fifteenth hand. Someone got tight and tried to tell it as a joke. I said that I was sorry and that you did understand but he was just quietly unreasonable, and suddenly, while he was talking, I came to my senses. I saw him objectively. He's not my type, Val. He's too 'all on one plane.' Then, of course, I realised what I'd done, I ought to have looked after Ray. He was the only man I ever loved and I let him die. It's terribly tragic, isn't it?"

"It has its disastrous aspects." There was humour in Val's dry little comment, which robbed it of much of its bitterness. "There's a word for you, Georgia my pet. You're a proper cough drop, aren't you?"

"Darling, how vulgar. I thought you were going to say bitch."

Georgia was laughing but broke off to sigh.

"Isn't it odd?" she said presently. "Have you noticed that women like me who have dozens of men in love with them spend such an astounding amount of time alone? Here am I, under thirty-two, a pathetic, brokenhearted widow, utterly deserted, and yet God knows I've had enough men hysterical about me. I like your brother, Val. He doesn't approve of me. Men who don't approve of me always intrigue me. I can never understand why it is and that keeps me interested in them."

"Albert?" said Val dubiously. "What about Amanda?"

"Oh yes. The pretty little red-haired child." Georgia was thoughtful. "Isn't it tragic when you think what all these babies have got to go through?" she added, sighing. "All the hurts, the heartaches, the wretched emotional agonies which make one mature."

"Darling, I don't know and I don't care. It's nearly half-past two. Don't you live somewhere along here?"

"No, it's miles further yet." Georgia peered out into the darkness. "I love my little house," she remarked. "Ray and I adored each other there. When I get sentimental I think of it as a little shrine. Don't be angry with me, Val. After all, I've given up Alan. You can have him now if you want to."

Val was silent. The car sped on down the faintly lit street and only now and again, when they passed a street lamp, was her face visible.

"Don't look like that." There was a note of panic in the childish phrase. "Val, don't look like that. You're grim. You're frightening me. Say something."

"Can you see that you've put that man out of my life forever?"

The words were spoken unemotionally and Georgia considered them.

"No," she said at last. "No, honestly I don't see that, darling. Not if you love him. Nothing in love is forever, is it? Be reasonable."

They were two fine ladies of a fine modern world, in which their status had been raised until they stood as equals with their former protectors. Their several responsibilities were far heavier than most men's and their abilities greater. Their freedom was limitless. There they were at two o'clock in the morning, driving back in their fine carriage to lonely little houses, bought, made lovely and maintained by the proceeds of their own labours. They were both mistress and master, little Liliths, fragile but powerful in their way, since the livelihood of a great number of their fellow beings depended directly upon them, and yet, since they had not relinquished their femininity, within them, touching the very core and fountain of their strength, was the dreadful primitive weakness of the female of any species. Byron, who knew something about ladies if little enough about poetry, once threw off the whole shameful truth about the sex, and, like most staggeringly enlightening remarks, it degenerated into a truism and became discountenanced when it was no longer witty.

"Love really can rot any woman up," Georgia observed contentedly. "Isn't it funny?"

"Dear God, isn't it dangerous!" said Val.

They drove on in silence, both of them thinking of a very different thing from the common disaster which they had met to discuss and which, had they been less preoccupied, must have terrified them by its imminence and its tremendous risk.

CHAPTER EIGHTEEN

Mr. Campion, arriving home a little before three in the morning full of the deepest misgivings and secretly uneasy because the police had not called upon him to identify anyone whom the amorous lorry driver might have described, found, instead of the expected detective, Lugg and Amanda in the kitchenette eating bacon and eggs.

"The poor kid's got to get to work at the factory by seven-thirty termorrow." Lugg's greeting was reproachful. "I thought at least I'd give 'er a bit of breakfast. What will you 'ave yourself? Eggs or a mite of 'erring? I've got a lovely little tin 'asn't been opened above a couple of days. I was savin' it for when I fancied it."

The kitchen was warm and odorous, and Mr. Campion, who suddenly felt he had been too long among the sophists, sat down on the other side of the enamel-topped table and glanced at his lieutenant with satisfaction. She was rosy with sleep but bright-eyed and very interested.

"I've been here since ten, sleeping in a chair. I thought I'd better wait in case you needed any help. What happened?"

He gave her the rough outline of the momentous interview, while Lugg sizzled contempt and bacon fat in the background.

"So you see," he said at last, "Portland-Smith was being blackmailed. That emerged with a blinding flash and a smell of damp fireworks. No one who heard Georgia's story of the six months before he vanished—heard it with anything beside his ears, I mean—could possibly have missed that."

"Who blackmailed him? Miss Adamson?"

Amanda's untroubled logic was comforting after the tortuous mental fancywork of the past three hours.

"She was in it; I think that's certain." He spoke decisively and paused, a shadow of embarrassment passing over his face. She caught his expression and grinned.

"I'm getting a big girl now," she said. "You can mention it in front of me. It was the usual story but 'she had her auntie Jessie underneath the kitchen sink,' I suppose? When and where did all this happen?"

"I don't know, of course." Mr. Campion sighed and his lean face looked less weary. Amanda was easy to talk to. "He went off on a walking tour in October and came back all peculiar. He seems to have been batty about his wife at this time and she evidently loathed him, so I take it that a solicitous Caroline who resembled the Dear Unkind might easily have had a walkover. That angle is a job for Blest. I'll get hold of Portland-Smith's itinerary and Blest must go round all the pubs he might have stayed in. That should put us on to it. But we must be prepared for it only leading us to the girl, and I'm more than certain she didn't do it alone. It was too opportune. The whole thing has a curious organised flavour, like everything else. Portland-Smith was caught and bled until he took the shortest way out, poor beast. All this evening I've been quaggly in the middle at the thought of that fellow. He must have had hell's delight."

"Very nice dick work, but it's unsatisfactory," remarked Mr. Lugg, flopping another egg onto the plate before his keeper. "There's no fear of blackmail nowadays. It's Mr. A. and Miss X. and three years, yes, yer lordship, thankyer very much. You don't even read the papers."

"That's where you're wrong, you with your mammy's eyes, poor hideous woman." Mr. Campion spoke without resentment. "It's because of the anonymity rule that I'm certain the whole thing was a more subtle affair than would at first appear. Miss Adamson's own methods were just plain abominable. I gathered that much when she phoned me. There usually is a third, negotiating party in this sort of case and it's pretty obvious that this particular third was the brains of the act. You see, Portland-Smith was a barrister, i.e. he had the one kind of job which makes the anonymity rule a trifle less than useless. He couldn't go into the Central Court at the Old Bailey calling himself Mr. X., at least not with any marked success, unless, of course, he wore a false beard or a cagoulard hood, either of which might so easily have been misunderstood."

"Oh well, if you say so, cock. I can't talk about trade risks." Mr. Lugg was magnanimous. "I'll do you a bit o' bacon."

"I suppose the threat was divorce information for Georgia," Amanda observed. "That might have cooked his county court ambitions. Was it done purely for the money? How much had he got?"

"I don't know exactly, but I think he must have got through about four thousand pounds in the last six months of his life. He died broke. I had taken it that he'd been wallowing in diamonds, costly furs and ballet shoes of champagne, but it seems not." Campion spoke lightly but his eyes were not amused. "All the same, I don't believe money was the primary motive, although somebody thought a lot about it. Our Caroline did, for one. I may be braying in the wilderness, but whenever I consider the events in the round I smell fish. It's fishy that Portland-Smith should have been driven to suicide just as Georgia met Ramillies, and fishier still that Ramillies should have looked up his ancestors just as Georgia fell for Dell. I may merely have a beastly mind, of course, but it shouts to heaven to me."

Amanda nodded gloomily.

"A.D.'s back at work," she observed. "He looks a bit tempered but he's making up for lost time. We're getting the old atmosphere back. Sid's like a dog who's discovered he's got his collar on after all. I say, Albert?"

She sat back from the table and remained looking at him, her face scarlet and her honey-brown eyes embarrassed.

"She couldn't possibly have persuaded *them* to do it, could she?"

"What? Persuaded each succeeding boy friend to do in the retiring chairman?" Mr. Campion was impressed. "That's a very beautiful idea, Amanda. It's got a flavour of the classics. Lovely stuff. All clean, ruthless lines and what not. But I don't fancy it for a bet. It belongs to a more artistic age."

"I find that very comforting," said Amanda candidly. "Would you like some more to eat?"

The downstairs button sounding a cuckoo-clock device in the hall outside forestalled Mr. Campion's acceptance. Lugg paused, frying pan in hand, his eye ridges raised.

"Eh?" he demanded.

"That damned owl again," said Mr. Campion. "Go and see who it is."

"Three o'clock in the mornin'?" Lugg's little black eyes were startled. "'Ere, is your aunt in London, yer ladyship?"

"My dear fellow, you could chaperone a regiment of Georgias." Amanda was cheerful. "Don't put on a collar. Decolletage is perfectly all right at this time of night. Buck up."

The cuckoo called again and Lugg surged to the door.

"I've laid them eggs there and I want to see 'em when I come back," he said warningly. "I'm coming. I'm coming."

"His mother instinct is strong, isn't it?" commented Amanda as he disappeared. "Who is this? The police?"

"I don't know." Mr. Campion looked uneasy. "I don't like this show, Amanda. I'd feel much happier if you were out of it. You don't mind, do you?"

Amanda laughed at him. "Don't drop the pilot," she said. "I'm the only disinterested intelligence in the whole outfit. My motive is nice clean curiosity. I'm valuable. Listen."

It was Lugg's breathing, of course. The noise of it came up from the stairs like a wind machine. As he reached the flat door they heard him speak.

"On a bicycle?" he protested. "That's a nice way to get about! Would you care for an egg or a nice fresh bit of 'erring?"

Mr. Campion and Amanda exchanged startled glances and were on their feet when the visitor appeared shyly round the doorpost. It was Sinclair. He looked smaller than ever in his grey suit, his hair untidy from his ride in the wind.

"It's stinkingly late," he said. "I hope you don't mind, but I thought I might find you up, and it seemed important."

He was evidently excited but his self-possession was extraordinary and he reminded them both of some little old gentleman in his old-fashioned ease. Amanda made room for him on the edge of her chair and pushed rolls and butter towards him.

"That's all right," she said affably. "What's up? New developments?"

"Well, I don't know." Sinclair glanced questioningly at Lugg and, receiving Campion's reassuring nod, hurried on. "It's about Ray. I say, they—they're not going to dig him up, are they? That's why I came at once. I didn't like to wait until the morning if there was anything I could do to stop them. It's such a filthy thing to happen."

"My dear chap, don't worry about that." Mr. Campion had caught a glimpse of the horror behind the small white face. "That's all right.

That won't happen. And even if it did there'd be a tremendous setout first. The Home Office would have to move, for one thing, and that takes weeks even if everyone there happens to be awake. What put the idea in your head?"

Sinclair looked relieved and afterwards a little foolish.

"I'm sorry to have come so soon," he said. "I didn't know this, you see, and I got worrying. Georgia came in just now. I was waiting up for her; I often do, as a matter of fact. She was a bit hysterical, I'm afraid, and she rather frightened me. I hadn't heard of the murder of this girl friend of Ray's. I read the case in the evening papers, of course, but she hadn't been identified then. Georgia wept over me and I finally got it out of her that she was afraid the police might get suspicious over Ray's death. That upset us both, naturally. Then I suddenly realised that I knew something that might help, so I got out my bicycle and came down to see you. I didn't want to go to the police if it wasn't necessary."

"Jolly sensible," encouraged Amanda. "Eat while you talk. There's nothing like food when you're rattled; even if it gives you indigestion, that takes your mind off the main trouble. It's actually about Ray, is it?"

"Yes." Sinclair accepted the plate which Lugg placed before him, showing a certain amount of enthusiasm. "It's about old Ray getting tight that morning. I've been thinking. Perhaps he wasn't so tight, you see."

They stared at him and he hurried on, wrestling with his bacon in between remarks.

"I don't know if you knew old Ray very well," he said shyly, "but I did and I saw him pretty tight dozens of times. He used to weep, as a rule, and then thresh round a bit and finally sleep. I never saw him as chatty as he was on that day and yet so sort of thick and unsteady." He hesitated. "I don't want to sneak on the old man," he said, "but he told me something one day in strict confidence which may be rather important. It was about courage."

"Courage?"

"Yes." Sinclair flushed. "He used to go a bit kiddish and earnest at times. He was nuts about courage. He thought it was the one really big thing. He'd done some pretty brave stunts, you know, and I think he was frightfully proud of them really. We were talking one night about six weeks ago when he suddenly told me something and made me swear I'd never repeat it. I don't like doing it now, but he is dead, and my hat, I'd hate them to disturb him. Ray told me that in spite of everything he did about it there was one thing that put the wind up him. He said he had a complex about flying."

"Had he, by George?" said Mr. Campion with interest.

Sinclair nodded.

"So he said, and I believed him, because he was pretty well sweating when he told me. He said he used to make himself go up now and again, but he couldn't stand it and he used to get the breeze up for days, both before and afterwards."

"There are people like that, of course," put in Amanda, "but it doesn't seem possible in Ramillies. Why on earth did he take on this big flight?"

"I asked him that," agreed Sinclair, nodding to her, "but as a matter of fact, though, I understood pretty well. It was because of the flight that he told me about the complex. He was so jolly scared that he had to tell someone. I've felt like that about other things. What he actually said was that he'd arranged the whole business because he thought that as flying was the one last thing in the world that he was afraid of he ought to make one great effort to cure himself of it once and for all." He blushed. "That wasn't true, though. Old Ray used to pretend a bit. You know how people do. As a matter of fact he didn't arrange it. The government did that. He was asked to make the flight and it would have looked stinkingly bad if he'd refused. He was simply telling me to make it sound all right to himself."

He sighed for the weaknesses of man and the perversities of circumstance.

"Your idea is that he died of shock induced by fright, I take it?" enquired Mr. Campion with interest.

"Oh no, I think he took something." Sinclair was innocent of any attempt at dramatic effect. "You see," he continued awkwardly, "he went on talking to me for quite a bit. He explained how frightfully brave he was in everything else except this, and then he said that in a way he was really extra brave over the flight, because he knew someone who could give him a drug to make him perfectly fit and confident throughout the whole thing. It was quite easy, he said. You just took it in your arm and you felt a bit rotten for four hours and then you suddenly felt magnificent and that lasted for about a day. He pointed out what a temptation it was, and then he said he wasn't going to give in to it and that he'd made up his mind to make the flight without."

"I see." Mr. Campion's pale eyes were darker than usual. "Did he mention the name of this stuff?"

"No. He wouldn't tell me. He just said he knew someone who could see he got it if he wanted it. I half thought this person, whoever it was, had found out how scared old Ray was. I think he'd told them. But he didn't want to go on talking about it to me and so naturally I didn't mention it."

"Four hours feeling rotten and then a day feeling fine?" Amanda repeated the words dubiously. "Is there such stuff, Albert?"

"I've never heard of it. It sounds to me like a tale from someone with an unpleasantly perverted sense of humour." Mr. Campion's precise tone was grim. "You think Ray succumbed to the temptation after all, then, Sinclair?"

"He might have done, mightn't he?" The young voice was very reasonable. "When I heard that he'd cleared out in the middle of the farewell party, I thought at once that it was probably because he'd suddenly realised that he couldn't face the flight after all, and had dashed up to town to get hold of this drug stuff somewhere. That would have been frightfully like him."

"There you are." Amanda was sitting up. "There you are. That's it. Sinclair's right. Ramillies left the party in a blue funk, went to Boot's to be quiet and attempt to pull himself together. In the morning he found it was no good and he went round to Miss Adamson, who gave him this stuff. He must have taken it round about noon. Probably he began to feel peculiar almost at once and told that story about being tight in order to cover up any obvious ill effects. That must be right, because the flight was timed for four. Don't you see, the murderer would have expected him to die in the air. Ramillies thought he was going to feel fine in four hours and instead of that it killed him. Miss Adamson realised what had happened and tried to blackmail the person who had given her the drug for Ramillies. She used you as a threat and got herself killed. It all fits in."

"I know, I know, my dear, but there's no proof." The words escaped Campion reluctantly. "I'm sorry to be so unhelpful but there's no proof that he went near our Caroline after he left Boot's. Besides—and this is vital—what was it? What was the stuff? There was a P.M., you know, and an analysis."

"That's irritatingly true." Amanda was deflated. "I thought we were on to it. It's frightfully good, though, Sinclair. Part of the truth is there. Don't you think so, Albert?"

"Yes." Mr. Campion still spoke cautiously. "Yes, there was no mention of alcohol in the report on the body, and the entire story points to him having been poisoned somewhere in town. And yet what about that badge in the plane?"

"The Quentin Clear?" Amanda had the grace to look startled. "I'd forgotten it. I've still got it, too. A.D.'s never enquired about it. That's odd. You're right. We shall have to consider that. And yet I don't know, though. It was an obvious plant, wasn't it? We decided that at once."

"Is that the badge of the Award?" Sinclair was interested. "It's frightfully good, isn't it? What did Mr. Dell get it for?"

"The first Seraphim." In spite of her preoccupation there was tremendous pride in Amanda's statement. "It's only given for exceptional pioneer work in aviation design. Look here, Albert, it does fit in. Whoever gave Miss Adamson the stuff to kill Ramillies would naturally be there watching him, and when they saw that the man was going to die in the plane before she went up they planted the Quentin Clear there to pin the thing on A.D. How's that?"

"Not bad, for the one 'disinterested intelligence,'" said Campion and grinned as she grew fiery at the dig. "I don't know. I don't know, my hearty young betrothed. I don't really like to think."

He leant back in his chair and sat there, his head jutting forward and his hands in his pockets. For a long time he did not look up.

At four the morning papers were on sale outside in Piccadilly and they all went down to get them. The story had made the wrong side headlines on the front pages, most of which also carried studio portraits of Miss Adamson, looking beautiful and more like Georgia than ever. Much of the published account was unusually accurate and fitted in with the superintendent's own version, but there was one interesting new development. A formal police appeal, boxed and leaded, took the pride of place in every double column.

> In connection with the death of Miss Caroline Adamson, late of Petunia House, W. 2, whose body was found yesterday morning on a piece of waste ground at Coaching Cross, Essex, the police are anxious to trace the whereabouts of two men, both of medium height and very heavy build, who are thought to be in possession of a small four-cylinder car of some considerable age. These men were observed by a witness near the scene of the discovery at 3 A.M. approximately on the morning of Wednesday, July 21st. Information should be lodged at any police station.

As they stood in the Circus, with the thin cold wind of dawn drawing its fingers up their spines, they looked up from the papers and stared at each other.

"Two shortish, very fat men in an old car?" translated Amanda in bewilderment. "They don't fit in at all. We're all wrong. It almost looks as though it was nothing to do with our business after all. It's another incredible coincidence, another manifestation of the hand of Providence."

The words struck an answering note in Lugg's mysterious consciousness. He looked over his paper with that plump, gratified satisfaction at a chance to shine which in the dog world is the peculiarity of the hound.

" 'Providence, 'aving the advantage of knowin' both the strengths and the weaknesses of men, 'as a facility for unostentatious organisation undreamed of by our generals.' Sterne," he said. "That come out of my book. What's the matter, cock?"

Mr. Campion was staring at him with fascinated excitement.

"What?" he demanded.

Mr. Lugg obligingly repeated this latest fruit of his labours in the fields of culture.

"Tell you anythink?" he enquired with interest.

Mr. Campion put an arm round each of his two younger lieutenants.

"Yes," he said and the old enthusiasm returned in his voice and in the gleam behind his spectacles. "Yes, my secondhand scholar, it does. Look here, I'll drive you down to work, Amanda, and I'll phone you in the lunch hour. We can drop Sinclair and his bicycle on the way. And when I come back, Lugg, I'll want a bath, a clean shirt, and you ready for outside work. We start, we stir, we seem to feel the thrill of life beneath our keel."

Amanda laughed with pure excitement.

"Seen his taillight?"

"Not yet," said Mr. Campion, "but the Lord be praised, I've seen his wheels go round."

CHAPTER NINETEEN

Sir Montague Paling, the chief commissioner, who was a soldier and a gentleman and everything that phrase implies, phoned his superintendent of the Central Criminal Investigation Department early in the morning.

"Oates? That you? You still there? Good man. Good man. About this girl-in-the-wood case of yours; is there a foreign element in that?"

"We don't know yet, sir." Stanislaus Oates tried to suppress any placatory tone which might have crept into his pleasant country voice.

"Pullen found a quantity of drugs in her flat last night. We're working on that angle with Wylde at the moment."

"Who?"

"Detective Inspector Wylde, sir—Narcotics."

"Oh yes, of course. I didn't catch you. Oh well, that's very promising. What is it? Cocaine?"

"No sir. Morphine. Quite a bit of it. Seven or eight ounces."

"Really? She was a distributor, I suppose? Yes, yes, that's satisfactory. I phoned you because I've had a private word from the Colonial Office. The girl was the mistress of one of their fellers who died the other day, and, while they don't want to interfere in any way, of course, they do hope we'll be discreet. No need to drag up a lot of mud if it's not necessary. We know that as well as anyone, don't we?"

"I hope so, sir."

"Good man. Good work, Oates. Advise me from time to time. Good-bye."

The superintendent in charge of the Essex side phoned Superintendent Stanislaus Oates five minutes after the commissioner had returned to his breakfast.

"We've taken Robin Whybrow, the lorry driver, over his statement again, Superintendent, and he's remembered that one man was hatless. He only saw him up against what light there was in the sky, remember, but he says the top of his head was all crinkled, like as if he had curls. I don't know if it's worth noting."

"Eh? I dunno. Every crumb means something to an empty spadger. No news of the car?"

"Not yet, there isn't. We're working on it."

"Nor the weapon?"

"No. I don't think we ever will find that. Sorry to disappoint you, but we've combed that place. Still, we're working on it. I'll give you a call the moment anything crops up. I thought I'd let you know we were keeping busy."

"Oh yes, fine, thank you very much. Good-bye."

Oates wrote down "One bloke seen in dark may have curly hair" on his blotting paper, added an exclamation mark and drew a ring round it. He glanced absently at the teapot on his desk, his sole sustenance for twenty hours, and, resisting it, took up the telephone again.

Sir Henry Wryothsley was happy to hear from him. The fine precise voice which was so impressive in the box sounded bright and enthusiastic.

"I'll bring it round myself as soon as it's finished. I've been working all night. A lovely wound. Oh yes, definitely. Obviously sole cause of death. I'm working out the specifications now. I'll read you the opinion. It gives it in one. Are you listening? Don't take it down; I'll bring the report round. Listen. '1. The cause of death was the wounding of the main blood vessel of the heart and the consequent internal bleeding. 2. The wound on the wall of the chest, penetrating the main heart bag, was caused by a sharp-pointed two-edged instrument approximately six tenths of an inch wide. 3.'—and this is interesting, Oates—'the blow was delivered practically straight.'"

"What?"

"I know. The direction is all but dead level. I'll talk to you about it when I see you, but for the present take it from me she was lying peacefully on her back when it was done, and so far I don't see any trace of an anaesthetic or anything else. I'm doing the analysis myself. The only other mark was a slight contusion high up on the left side of the neck, but it's very faint. What? Oh, I don't know, old boy. I don't know at all. Before midnight and after midday. I daren't be more specific. I'll come round. Good-bye."

Meanwhile Georgia was phoning Val.

"I simply threw myself on his mercy, my dear, and he was charming. He says he'll do all he can and I'm not to worry. He was very sensible and very sweet. Government people so often are. Did you meet him?"

"I think I did." The line was bad and Val's high voice sounded very far away.

"Old, but rather nice. Slightly doggy, with a sprouty moustache. Just like his name. Don't you remember?"

"I can't hear you."

"Oh, it doesn't matter, darling. This line is abominable. I only phoned to tell you I'd fixed everything and it's all going to be hushed up, so we needn't worry any more, thank God. Toddy Towser's going to see to everything. Isn't Toddy a perfectly vile name? Good-bye, sweet."

Val phoned Mr. Campion, and the steady buzzing echoing in the empty flat answered her. As she hung up the receiver the little white instrument in her panelled room at Hampstead rang once more and she pounced on it eagerly, but it was only Rex again.

"Lady Papendeik is with the inspector now." He was gabbling in his annoyance. "Everyone in the place is talking about drugs. I'm doing everything I can, madame, but I simply cannot guarantee that some wretched vendeuse won't blurt it out in confidence to the first trade buyer who comes in. One wouldn't think they'd be so vulgar but one can't be sure. Marguerite Zingari has had hysterics and handed in her resignation. What would you advise?"

"I'll come, Rex, I'll come. Since your last message I've been trying to phone my brother. Never mind. Keep them all quiet if you can. Don't worry. I'll come."

Val sounded calm and her authority was consoling. The little man's theatrical sigh was magnified over the wire.

"I shall be relieved," he said. "This is appalling. Such frightful disorganisation. Can I send the peach 'Fantastique' to Lady B.? I can't be more specific over the phone, can I? She's asked for it, but you know that we did say that next time, in view of the past, we ought to have a trifle on account. Lady B. B for bolero."

"I'll leave it to you, Rex." Val sounded breathless. "I should be tactful but firm. I'll come down at once."

She hung up and made one more attempt to get Campion's flat. There was still no reply, and she phoned the Junior Greys and left a message for him.

The Daimler was at the door and she was setting a small black hat at precisely the right angle over her left eye, characteristically giving the task the same intelligent care which she would have bestowed upon it had she been summoned by the Last Trump and not Rex's shrill alarum, when Papendeik's rang through again. It was Tante Marthe herself this time. The ugly voice betrayed that faint trace of accent which the telephone always seems to accentuate.

"Val, my child, there is an inspector here. He is at my side now. Do you remember that mannequin, Caroline, the one we got rid of? She has got herself murdered, wretched little girl. The police seem to think she may have had something to do with drugs, and they are enquiring about them from all former employees. Do you remember anything about some morphine? There was something, my dear, wasn't there? I seem to remember it."

No policeman on earth could have mistaken Madame's warning tone, and Val grew hot and then very cold again.

"The inspector says it is purely a matter of form," Tante Marthe concluded, speaking apparently from dictation.

"I'm coming right down, darling. I'll be with you both in fifteen minutes." The high voice was brisk and cheerful, and Val rang off.

While she was riding through the streets Gaiogi Laminoff stood in his amusing sitting room and telephoned Mr. Paul.

"Ferdie, my dear fellow, listen to me for a moment." The Russian's voice was sibilant and charged with all the emotional force of his dramatic race. "Have you seen the papers? I have had the police here at my house. Yes, here. My dear Ferdie, it is not at all funny. I am not laughing. They have found some drugs in the girl's flat at Petunia House, and they have found out that Ramillies took up the lease of that flat. I have told them nothing, naturally; it is not my affair. The abominable girl was only here for six weeks. But for everybody's sake, Ferdie, keep Georgia quiet. That story of hers about the cachet—it won't do any good, you know. Things are bad enough as they are."

"You're telling me," said Ferdie Paul and hung up.

The obliging Sinclair succeeded in getting a call through to the Alandel works and bore the instrument in triumph to his parent. Dell's secretary, who had been trying to get Papendeik's all the morning without success, put the incoming call through to the inner office in all innocence.

"Alan"—Georgia's tone was motherly—"I wouldn't have disturbed you, dear, but don't you think you ought to ring up Val?"

"Hallo, Georgia. Ring Val? Why?"

"Oh, darling"—she was reproachful—"don't you read the papers? She's frightfully worried and upset. That murdered girl was one of her mannequins, the one who stole my dress, you remember. Papendeik's are bound to be positively bristling with police. It will be frightful for her. You know how temperamental these artist people are. A phone message from you would probably help a lot."

There was a long pause from the other end of the wire, and Georgia began to feel dubious.

"This is just between ourselves, of course," she said hurriedly. "I'm only trying to help you both, my sweet. Of course I haven't said a word to her."

She heard him laugh. It was one of those short explosive laughs associated in her mind with an embarrassed expression and a change of colour.

"What a *dear* you are, Georgia, aren't you?" he said.

She was surprised and gratified. She laughed herself.

"It's funny to hear you say that. Do you know, Alan, everyone who has ever loved me has said that in the end. Oh well, you ring her, darling. She'll be frightfully pleased. Good-bye, Alan. I say, give the poor sweetie my love."

He rang off, a little abruptly, she thought, but put it down quite seriously to eagerness on his part to condole with Val. She sighed. There was a tremendous satisfaction in being magnanimous, so much satisfaction that she sometimes wondered if there wasn't a catch in it somewhere.

Val had not expected any friendly offer of assistance from Dell, but had only hoped for it. She was, therefore, not surprised when he did not ring her.

Just before noon a little girl with ferret's eyes in an innocent face stepped out of Papendeik's, where she was employed in the sewing rooms with nearly two hundred others and turned into a public telephone booth. Within a minute or two a fat young man with a superior manner and disreputable clothes was listening to her with interest in a corner of an editorial mezzanine floor.

"It's drugs. Madame was with the police an hour and they took a statement." The squeaky voice was thin with excitement. "Madame's shut up in the studio now and no one can get near her. They say she's crying and we're wondering if she's going to be arrested. If this is useful I get the usual, don't I?"

"Have I ever let you down, kiddo?" The pseudo-American accent was slick. "Step on it, baby. Keep your ears open. So long."

At about the same time, in a glass cubicle on the other side of the same floor, a far more elegant personage was listening to a far better accent.

"Well, my dear"—the instrument's voice was crisp—"that's all I know. I was actually in the Tulip when it happened. Ray Ramillies brought this girl in actually *disguised* as Georgia Wells and there was nearly a frightful scene, and then poor Ray died and now this girl. Dangerous? Of course I know it's dangerous. But isn't it exciting?"

Mr. Campion's call to Papendeik's came through to Val while her employee was still in the phone box in Oxford Street. Val was in the studio, and Miss McPhail, who was both discreet and practical, hurried out of the room and planted her solid back against the door, casting suspicious glances at anyone who ventured within twenty feet of it.

"Albert?" Campion knew at once by the very control in Val's voice that she was badly rattled. "The police have been here. They've found that morphine I told you I had. It was in Caroline Adamson's flat."

"My dear girl, you told me you'd destroyed it."

"I know I did. I couldn't find it when I came to look for it. I took it for granted that it had been mislaid. It never dawned on me that someone might have pinched it."

"Oh, I see." He sounded comfortingly unalarmed. "Oh well, it can't be helped. She saw what it was and thought it marketable, I suppose. It was all packed up in little doses, was it?"

"Yes, I'm afraid it was. I say, I told the police."

"Oh, you did? I daren't ask. Good, that's good. What did you tell them? The full strength?"

"Yes, everything. I gave the name of the woman we sacked on suspicion of smuggling it and the firm in Lyons from whom we bought the bale of silk. They took it all down and I signed it. I say, Albert?"

"Yes ma'am?"

"The men—the inspector had someone called Wylde with him—weren't exactly matey after I'd told the story."

"Old Pullen? Not offensive, surely?"

"What? Oh no, just reserved. 'Yes' and 'no' and that sort of thing."

"The atmosphere changed, you mean?"

"Yes, it did rather. Is that bad?"

"Oh, Lord, no." His tone was hearty, but not entirely convincing. "The police are always like that when they get a new bit of information. They've got to go home to Poppa and see what it means, that's all. That's all right. That's nothing. I'm glad you told them. Tell 'em every mortal thing. You haven't suppressed anything, have you?"

"No, nothing. At least, I didn't mention the cachet blanc. Ought I to have?"

"No." The word sounded considered. "No, I don't think so. If things stew up a bit more before this evening we'll go along to see Oates and have a showdown, but it may not come to that. You did tell them everything else?"

"Yes, I did. I did, dear. You sound suspicious."

"I'm not. Only you told me you destroyed that muck."

"Oh darling"—Val sounded helpless—"this really honestly is the truth, all of it."

"May all your designs fail if you lie?"

"May all my designs fail if I lie."

"Right, that's fine. Now, is Rex about? I want to know if anyone saw that girl at a night club recently."

Rex was summoned by Miss McPhail, who seemed to have got it into her head that Val was in danger of being kidnapped, for she only admitted one person at a time into the room, and then only after a keen visual "frisking."

Rex did his best, but it was not very helpful.

"I've only seen her at the Tulip," he said. "I'll enquire if you like."

"Will you? Make a list of any names and phone it to the Junior Greys. Don't leave any other message; just the list of clubs where the girl may have been seen. If you would do that? Thank you. Look after my sister. There's nothing to worry about. Good-bye."

He rang off and felt for another twopence. His face was sharper than usual, and for once his natural indolence had vanished. Oates could not speak to him at once and he waited and rang again. He rang every five minutes for half an hour, and when at last he got hold of the old man, he gathered that Pullen had been before him, for conversation was not easy.

"I'm so rushed, Mr. Campion. If you haven't anything relevant to tell me I'll have to ask you to excuse me. You know how it is. I haven't slept since it broke."

"You should take a shot of morphine," said Campion and plugged in a question while he still had the other man's attention. "Have you had the P.M. report? What was the weapon? Go on, that can't be a state secret. Damn it, man, I'm likely to help you. What was the weapon?"

"A long double-sided blade six tenths of an inch wide. That's all I can tell you, mate. Sorry. Good-bye."

Campion hung up. He was whistling a slow, mournful little tune which went painfully flat in the middle and his eyes were troubled. He went out to the hotel bookstall, obtained another pocketful of pennies, and returned, still whistling. He was soothed by getting on to the hospital immediately. Also, Sir Henry Portland-Smith was unexpectedly easily found. The old man was evidently curious and his fine voice sounded eager.

"I wondered if I should hear from you, my boy. I was thinking of you this morning. Have you any news for me?"

"No proof, sir." Campion had to drag his mind round to this half-forgotten angle of the case which yet remained the other man's main interest. "But I think it's fairly obvious now that the cause was blackmail."

"Blackmail." There was no question in the word, only enlightenment and considerable relief.

"I haven't finished by any means. It's still in the air. I can't tell you the details over the phone. I'll call on you when I've got it straightened out a bit. I really wanted to bother you for a piece of information. How long does morphine take to kill?"

"What kind of morphine?"

"I don't know. White powdery crystals."

"Diluted and taken subcutaneously?"

"No. By the mouth."

"How much?"

"God knows."

"What?"

"I have no earthly means of finding out."

The old man laughed. "I can't help you, my boy. I'm sorry. Thirty-six hours, perhaps."

"Really? As long as that? You wouldn't expect fatal results in four hours?"

"Well, I don't like to say on such vague grounds. You'd get some effect in four hours, you know. Perhaps even coma."

"I see. There would be a protracted period of coma, would there?"

"Oh yes. That is, in straight morphine poisoning. But there might be other conditions present, you see. Those would have to be considered."

"Yes, of course. But if you saw a man take—well, say a rice-paper container full of morphine crystals you wouldn't expect him to throw a fit four hours afterwards, bite his tongue and pass out?"

"No, I shouldn't. I should expect him to be sick. If not you'd get sleep, and afterwards no reflex action, slow pulse and so on, and finally coma."

"No fit?"

"No, no, no convulsions. At least I shouldn't say so. If you could be more specific I could help you. Post-mortem would find it, you know."

"It would?"

"Oh, certainly, if it was competently done. Bound to. Sorry I can't help you more. You'll come and see me, will you?"

"Yes, I will. I can't give you a date, unfortunately, but I'll come."

"Then we'll have the whole story?"

"Yes." Campion's voice was unusually sober. "The whole story. Good-bye. Thank you enormously."

"Not at all. I'm afraid I've been most unhelpful. These things depend so much on circumstances. As far as it goes the instance you give sounds most unlikely, but one can't tell. Odd things happen in medicine. Good-bye."

"Good-bye," said Mr. Campion.

Oates was eating a sandwich when Pullen's call came through to him. The superintendent's eyes were hard and bright with the nervous "second wind" which comes after the first intolerable desire for sleep has been overcome, and he held the receiver at some little distance from his ear. The inspector's machine-gun delivery was apt to be paralysing when received at short range.

"One of Wylde's men has dug up a band-boy friend of the girl's," Pullen rattled. "He has some story about her offering dope openly to anyone who seemed likely to have any money. It all sounds very amateurish. Wylde's seeing the man now. I don't like the dope angle myself. All the stuff came directly from Papendeik's. We mustn't lose sight of that."

"What?"

"All the dope we found came from Mrs. Valentine Ferris, I told you that last time I phoned, sir. There is no evidence to show that Adamson had any more than this in her possession. Wylde is inclined to believe Mrs. Ferris' story about the smuggling. His people are looking up the woman she sacked on suspicion. He thinks the name is familiar to him."

"Ah." Oates sounded unhappily convinced. "That leads us back to the swells."

"Looks like it. Still, that alibi of Laminoff's is not satisfactory, is it? He's a fat man, you know. I've got it here. Will you check it with yours? 'Six-fifteen, left Caesar's Court. Six thirty-five, Savoy cocktail bar. Seven-forty, Tulip Restaurant. Eight-fifty, the Tatler Theatre to see Mickey Mouse programme (alone). Eleven approximately the White Empress. Four-thirty A.M., left the White Empress for Caesar's Court in taxicab.' That's the White Empress Club in Grafton Street."

"I know. The high-class all-alien dive. No reliable witnesses there, you feel?"

"Not one." The machine gun was vehement. "Every one of 'em would swear each other out of hell."

"I suppose they'd try. You'll go over them, of course."

"I was going down there now. I'll ring you at two-thirty. Good-bye, sir."

By a coincidence Gaiogi Laminoff was telephoning Matvey Kuymitchov, manager of the White Empress, at the same time that the two policemen were considering his alibi. He also was a trifle worried but not over the same matter.

"Matvey," he said, "you have in your hall some little birds in a gold cage shaped like a basket. Will you tell an old friend where you got them? They are charming."

Kuymitchov was delighted to oblige. He rattled off the name of the importers of the golden canaries and explained that the firm were also part owners of the cage-making company.

"I know them very well, Excellency. They are not easy people to deal with, but if you want some, perhaps I could get them for you."

"Would you do that, Matvey? That would be kind of you. I should appreciate that." The faint note of irony was well suppressed. "Can you get me sixty cages, each containing two little birds, to be delivered here by the thirtieth?"

"Sixty cages?"

"Yes. I went through my dining room just now—not the main dining room, but the little romantic one in the flower garden—and it depressed me. It is sad, Matvey. It is almost gloomy. I want it to be essentially gay, and I thought that if over each table there was one of those little basket-shaped gold cages it would make it look a little happier. Don't you think so?"

Matvey laughed. "It is not very practical," he said. "You will get tired of them."

"Of course I shall. Then I shall get rid of them. But meanwhile they will look gay. Sixty cages by the thirtieth. You won't disappoint me? Tell the firm to send a little boy to look after them. You will see they are all there?"

"I will. You are an extraordinary person."

"Not at all." Gaiogi's laugh was infectious. "I was depressed. Now I feel quite happy."

Mr. Lugg phoned Mr. Campion by appointment. Mr. Campion was in the private office of the Boiled Owl Club and Mr. Lugg was in a small basement room which looked as though some thoughtless person had built four walls round a gipsy encampment.

"Not a sossidge, cock." The thick melancholy voice was just audible above a chatter like the din of a monkey house. "Ma Knapp was no good at all. Thos. is inside again, so he can't help, poor chap. I've been to Walkie's and to Ben's and I dropped in at Conchy Lewis'. Not a sossidge anywhere."

"Have you tried Miss King?"

"I 'ave. Just got out alive. If Mr. Tuke ever 'ears of this I'll never 'old up me 'ead again. Mud-rollin', that's what I'm doing. They was all very pleased to see me. It was like old times."

"That must have been ever so nice. Keep your mind on the job."

"I am. My Gawd, you're grateful, aren't you? Here am I with me pockets sewn up mixin' with dust I've shook orf my feet for ever. What d'you think I'm doin' it for? What luck your end?"

"Nothing yet. Phoebe gave me the Starlight, the Fish, the Newspaper, the Enraged Cow and a staggering dive called the All At Home. I've had a morning long after the night before. All a blank. Look here, try straight food with a smear."

"Smear meanin' filf?"

"Yes. I was wrapping it up for you. Ollie is the man you want. Ollie Dawson of Old Compton Street. Take him a bottle of kümmel."

"Is it kümmel? I thought 'is fancy was dressed crab? I'll take both. Righto. Any more dope?"

"Dope? Oh, I'm sorry, I was on the other book. Yes, one thing. Listen. A long two-edged knife, very narrow indeed."

"Ham and beef type?"

"That's about it. My hat, you're horrible. All right then. Phone me at four at the Dorindas' in the Haymarket. I'm keeping Pa Dorinda as a last hope. Good-bye."

"Good-bye, cock. Good hunting."

"Yoicks to you, sir. Good-bye."

Amanda, who had been sitting over the telephone in her private cubbyhole at the works for considerably over an hour, was commendably good-tempered when at last her fiancé kept his promise.

"Never mind," she encouraged with all the boundless energy of youth in her voice. "Never mind. Keep at it. I've got something. It's a bit negative. You know the Clear, the badge? I say, that was Sid. Yes, Sid. He pinched it from Georgia. The sight of her wearing it turned him up, as I thought it would, and he pinched it off her lapel during the crush after lunch. He didn't want to go into a lot of explanations, so he put it where someone who knew what it was would be bound to see it. He did that at once, while the plane was still empty."

"Did he though? That was a bit roundabout, wasn't it?"

"Not really." She sounded embarrassed. "He's only a bit touchy on the subject of his snappy pinching. He's shy about it. The accomplishment wasn't thought a lot of at his school. At your place they probably thought it was clever and funny; at his they didn't. It's a social question. I got it out of him this morning."

"I see. That means the deity in the machine may not have been near the hangar at all?"

"I know. But so few people were there before Ramillies, were they? I say, A.D. has been trying to get you all the morning, but he's out now seeing Gaiogi. I think he wants to ask if there's anything he can do."

"If there is I'll let him know. Good-bye, Lieut."

"Good-bye."

Detective Inspector Wylde of Narcotics had a soft, friendly voice and a habit of lowering it when speaking on the telephone. Superintendent Oates had to concentrate to hear him.

"I've had a little talk with Happy Carter," Wylde murmured. "I'm afraid it's not down our street at all, sir. We shall go on working on it, of course, until further orders, but I thought I'd let you know what the situation is. This girl Adamson certainly wasn't in touch with any of the big people. It looks to me as though she stole the stuff, or had it given her, from someone at Papendeik's, and simply tried to make a bit on the side."

"Oh, I see. Thank you very much, Inspector." Oates was gloomy. "You'll just cover every angle, won't you? We don't want anything to slip through our fingers at this stage, do we?"

"No, of course not, sir, but I think you'll find it's not our pigeon. All right, sir. Good-bye."

He had barely replaced the receiver when the Essex superintendent was on the line again.

"Nothing at all to report." The cheerful voice sounded unwarrantably pleased with itself. "We've practically stripped the clearing and there's no weapon of any sort, unless you'd count three tin openers and a bicycle pump. I reckon the seat of the mystery is at your end, as I said all along. Mayhap if you could get on to the motive now we might learn something."

"Mayhap we might," agreed Oates grimly. "We've had the medical report and none of the usual reasons apply."

"Fancy that, now. Oh well, we'll go on looking. So long."

"Wait a minute. No news of the car?"

"No, no, not a sign of it. The petrol stations can't help us. There's plenty of traffic on our roads just now, you know. We've been on to the lorry driver again and he can't add to his statement. He only heard it, you see. Still, he knows engines and he sticks to his story. He says it was four cylinders, missing on one, and there was a body rattle like a sackful of old iron. But there's plenty o' they about at this time of year."

"You're right, son. The woods are full of 'em. The boy's evidence isn't worth the paper it's written on as it stands. It's seeing that's believing; that's what they say."

"So they do, so they do. I don't know if it interests you, but Glasshouse for the three-thirty. It's a local horse. Sure to do well. Oh, perhaps not. I only thought it might. Good-bye."

Oates hung up, considered a few moments, sighed and recalled Sir Henry Wryothsley. The pathologist seemed surprised at his question.

"The Richmond Laboratories?" he repeated. "Why yes, I think so. I've never had any reason to doubt them. I can't give you any firsthand information, unfortunately. They don't do my stuff. But a big place like that is sure to be pretty sound. What's the trouble? Anything I can do?"

"No trouble at all." Oates was suspiciously casual. "I was only curious. It's not this affair we're on now. Another matter. If these people did a rushed analysis they'd be bound to find anything fairly obvious, would they?"

A laugh reached him. "What do you call fairly obvious?"

"Well, acute morphine poisoning, for instance."

"A fatal dose? Oh, Lord, yes, I should say so, if they tested for it. Why don't you ask 'em? Parsons is the man there. He's a good chap. Frightfully conscientious. Ask him. He's not chatty. He'll be discreet if you tell him so. Ring him up."

"Perhaps I will. Thank you very much. Sorry to trouble you."

"Not at all. Have you been through my report? It's interesting, isn't it? I've got one or two theories. I'll put them forward when I see you. I've got to rush back now. My assistant's calling. We're doing a Stass-Otto. Good-bye."

Sergeant Francis Gwynne, hopeful product of the Hendon Police College, caught Inspector Pullen just before he settled down to write his report. The young man was diffident.

"I took up the angle you suggested, sir, and I've found one interesting piece of gossip which may or may not be of some use to you. . . ."

"Come to the horses," snapped the machine gun, who was irritated by the accent which he insisted on considering, quite erroneously, as unmanly.

"Well, sir, I saw Madame Sell of the big hairdressing firm just off Bond Street and she tells me that there has been a story going about for some weeks now concerning the death of Sir Raymond Ramillies and Mrs. Valentine Ferris of Papendeik's. Apparently Lady Ramillies and Mrs. Ferris were quarrelling over the same man, and on the morning of Ramillies' death Mrs. Ferris gave Lady Ramillies a cachet blanc —a sort of aspirin in a rice-paper case—for herself, but instead of taking it the woman gave it to her husband. According to the story it was the last thing he had before he died."

"This is only gossip, you say?" Pullen was loth to show his intense interest.

"Yes sir, but I thought I'd better let you know at once in case it was useful."

"It may be. I can't say. I'm going up to the superintendent now.

I'll mention it to him. That's all right, Gwynne. Carry on. That may be of some use."

Meanwhile Rex wrestled with the newspapers.

"Lady Papendeik authorises me to state that she is extremely sorry that she cannot help you any further. The whole matter is in the hands of the police. I am really very sorry but I myself know nothing. No sir, nothing at all. Miss Caroline Adamson left our employ some weeks ago. I really cannot remember if she was dismissed or if she resigned. Yes, that is my last word, absolutely my last word."

He rang off, only to pick up the receiver again as the instrument buzzed once more.

Val's attempts to find her brother brought her in despair to Amanda's office wire.

"No, Val, not since lunch." Mr. Campion's fiancée was intensely sympathetic. "What's the matter? Reporters?"

"Oh, my dear, they're everywhere." Val sounded despairing. "We're in a state of siege. Four women have actually got into the building at various times by representing themselves as clients. The staff is hysterical. Tante Marthe's had half a bottle of champagne and gone to sleep. You don't know where he is at all?"

"No, not at the moment, but he's on the job. If you could only hang out for a bit he'll see you through. Lock the doors if you have to. Shall I collect A.D. and come and help you? We could always barricade the windows."

"No, my dear." Val was almost laughing. "It's not as bad as that yet. I'll send out an SOS when the party begins to get rough. You think Albert's doing something?"

"Doing something? He's moving heaven and earth."

"Your faith is very comforting."

"Faith nothing," said Amanda. "It's the old firm. We're invincible."

It was four o'clock when a reluctant Oates, with Pullen at his elbow, got on to Papendeik's.

"Is that Mrs. Valentine Ferris? This is Superintendent Oates of the Central Department, New Scotland Yard. Mrs. Ferris, I wonder if you'd mind coming down to see me? Yes, at once, please. I'll send a car for you. It's nothing to get worried about. We just want a little statement."

"But I've told you all I can about Caroline Adamson." The high clear voice was nervy now and very much on the defensive.

"I dare say you have, ma'am." Oates was avuncular but firm. "It's nothing alarming. I just want to have a little talk with you, that's all."

"Is it very important? The house is surrounded by reporters. I daren't set my foot outside the door."

"I'm afraid it is, ma'am. Very important. Don't worry about the press, ma'am. We'll get you through them all right. You'll be ready, will you? Thank you very much. Good-bye."

"Good-bye," said Val faintly.

At four o'clock Papendeik's phoned Mr. Campion's flat without result. At four-one Papendeik's called the Junior Greys, but Mr. Campion had not come in. At four-three Papendeik's called Mr. Campion's fiancée again, but she had not heard from him. At four-five and a half Mr. Campion called Oates and, on hearing that the superintendent could not speak to him, sent him a message which not only brought the eminent policeman to the phone, but sent him and Inspector Pullen, to say nothing of a couple of plain-clothes men, hurtling down to 91 Lord Scroop Street, Soho, like a pack on the scent. Mr. Campion's original message sounded cryptic to the secretary who took it.

"Ask him," he had said, "ask him if one of his fat suspects had curly hair."

CHAPTER TWENTY

In summertime the streets of Soho are divided into two main species, those which are warm and dirty and jolly, and those which are warm and dirty and morose. Lord Scroop Street, which connects Greek Street and Dean Street, belongs to the latter category. Number 91 was a restaurant with high brick-red window curtains and the name HAKAPOPULOUS in a large white arc on the glass. The main entrance, which was narrow and a thought greasy, had a particularly solid door with a picture of a grove of palm trees painted on the glass, while the back entrance, which gave on to Augean Passage, was, as the local divisional superintendent put it in a moment of insight, like turning over a stone.

Inside, the restaurant was strangely different from its exterior. The main room, which possessed a gilt-and-mahogany staircase rising up into mysterious blackness above, was indubitably shabby, but it was

not a bare shabbiness. There was a cold darkness, a muffled quiet in
the big curtain-hung room. All the tables were half hidden, if only
by shadows, and the carpet, the Victorian hangings and the columns
to the ceiling were all so thick and dusty that the smell of them pervaded the place like a kind of unscented incense. It was this quality
which met one as one entered. The quiet swooped down on one as
does the quiet of a church, but here there was no austerity, only
secrecy: not the exciting secrecy of conspiracy but the awful, lonely
secrecy of passion, the secrecy of minding one's own business. It was
not a pleasant room.

The divisional superintendent, a grizzled friend of Oates, who knew
and rather loved his district, arrived at the back door at the moment
that Oates and his company arrived at the front. This happy co-operation avoided the suggestion that anything so unfriendly as a raid was
intended, and the two parties, save for those four men who were left
to hang about the entrances, met in the shadows of the main dining
room, where there were only two customers, four-fifteen in the afternoon not being a busy hour with the house.

Mr. Lugg and Mr. Campion came out of their obscurity as Oates
arrived. They had been sitting in a corner and their appearance had
some of the elements of a conjuring trick, so that Pullen glanced
round him suspiciously.

"Anyone else here?"

"No one. Only this lad." Mr. Campion's murmur was as discreet
as the room itself, and they all turned to stare at the waiter on duty,
who had come sidling out from behind a column. He was a small
furtive person in an oiled tail coat and dirty tablecloth and he took in
the nature of the visit in a single wide-eyed glance. Then, shying
away from them like a field animal, he sent an odd, adenoidal shout
up into the pit of darkness above the staircase. He was answered immediately and there was a tremor in the walls above and every chin
in the room was raised to greet the newcomer. After a moment of
suspense he appeared, and a small, satisfied sigh escaped Inspector
Pullen.

Fatness and curliness are relative terms, but there is a degree at
which either condition becomes remarkable. In each case Andreas
Hakapopulous strained the description to its limit. He was nearly
spherical, and the oily black hair, which carried the line of his stupendous nose to a fine natural conclusion somewhere about six inches
above the top of the back of his head, was curly in the way that the
leaves of the kale are curly, or Italian handwriting, or the waves surrounding an ascending Aphrodite in a Pre-Raphaelite painting.

He came downstairs daintily, like a big rubber ball, bouncing a very little on each step. His welcoming smile was more than friendly. It had a quality of greasy joy in it, and he winked at the divisional superintendent with such convincing familiarity that Inspector Pullen had to glance at the other man's unbending stare to reassure himself.

"We will all 'ave a nize bot'le of wine." The newcomer made the suggestion as if he were announcing a rich gift to the Police Orphanage. "Louis, quickly. A nize bot'le of wine for everybody 'ere."

"That'll do." Oates was not amused. "We want a few words with you only, Mr. Hakapopulous. Will you please look at this photograph and tell us if you have ever seen the girl before?"

Andreas Hakapopulous was not abashed. He stood balancing on the last step but one of the staircase, exuding a strong odour of jasmine and an ingratiating affectionateness which in that particular room was almost unbearable. He put out a shapeless hand for the pasteboard and looked at it with a casual interest which, although unconvincing, was also, unfortunately, negative.

He peered at Miss Adamson's lovely, languorous face for some moments and finally carried the photograph under the window, where he held it at arm's length.

"Euh!" he said at last. "A nize little bit. Who iz shee?"

"We're asking you." The divisional superintendent put the words in briskly. "Come along, Andreas. Don't be a b.f. We're not interested in your theatricals. Have you seen her before?"

"No."

"Wait a minute." Oates was smiling sourly. "Have you seen the papers?"

The Greek perceived his mistake and rectified it jauntily.

"She might be a girl who was found dead somewheres," he said. "I don' know. I see something this morning. I don' take much account of it."

"Yes, well, you clean up your memory, my lad. Where's your brother?"

"Jock iz upstairs."

Andreas kept his smile and his soft, satisfied tone. He was neither sulky nor reproachful. A divisional plain-clothes man went up to find the other member of the firm and a minor inquisition began in the dining room.

"Now, Mr. Hakapopulous, think carefully: have you ever seen that girl in the flesh?"

"In the flesh?"

"Yes. Have you seen her?"

"No."

"You understand me, don't you? Have you ever seen the girl alive?"

"Has she been 'ere?"

"That's what I'm asking you."

Andreas smiled. "I don' know," he said. "So many girls come 'ere. I don' think I ever saw 'er before."

Pullen thrust his chin out and butted into Oates's enquiry.

"Have you seen her dead, by any chance?"

"Dead?" Andreas raised his eyebrows.

"You heard what I said."

"Dead? No."

"Look here, Hakapopulous." The name was cramping to Pullen's staccato style but he took it manfully. "Do you want to come inside and think it over? You know what the inside of a cell is like, don't you?"

Andreas laughed aloud. It was a little teetering giggle which displayed his magnificent teeth.

"Excuse me," he said. "I tell you I don' know the girl. Ask someone else. Don' let's quarrel. We understand each other. I have not seen the girl except in the papers."

"I see." Oates took up the questioning again. It made an interesting picture in the gloom, the lean grey-haired policeman with the eyes which were as bleak and honest as the North Sea, and before him, supremely happy in his security, the monstrous Latin, smiling and guileful.

"Mr. Hakapopulous"—the old super was always studiously polite—"you have several private dining rooms here, haven't you?"

"Yes, for business conferences." Andreas made the statement with unblushing simplicity.

"For business conferences?"

"Yes."

"Very well." The glimmer of a smile passed over the superintendent's thin lips. "We're not going into that now. Where are these dining rooms?"

His question was answered somewhat precipitately by the hurried return of the divisional detective, who made a startled announcement from the head of the staircase.

"Painting?"

Pullen was across the room in an instant. The Greek's smile broadened.

"That is so," he admitted placidly. "We do a little redecoration. My brother makes a 'obby of it."

"Does he?" Oates was very grim. "We'll go up there, please."
"Why not?"

The entire company mounted the staircase, Campion and Lugg
dropping in behind the procession. They came up into a dark, quiet
passage which had four solid doors on either side and a small half-
glassed one at the far end. The doors were all numbered very plainly,
odd on the left and even on the right. Number eight alone stood
open. In the passage the atmosphere so noticeable in the room below
was intensified. It was not unlike the box of a very old theatre. Muf-
fling festoons of drapery hung everywhere, and the strong smell of
turpentine issuing through the one open doorway came as a relief.
With the turpentine fumes came a little song. Jock Hakapopulous
was singing at his work.

They found him on a stepladder, his head protruding through a
hole in an old sheet which was tied about his tremendous middle
with a blind cord. Apparently he wore no shirt, for his great forearms
were naked save for a thatch of long soft black hair. He was engaged
in painting the cornice, and his head, which was exactly like his
brother's, save that it was bald, was very near the ceiling.

The room was uncompromisingly bare. There was not a vestige of
furniture in it anywhere. Even the walls had been stripped and the
dirty boards of the floor were furred where linoleum had been removed.

Oates avoided Pullen's eyes and a gloom descended on the raiding
party. Andreas indicated the visitors.

"The police," he said unnecessarily. "They want to know if we seen
a girl."

"That'll do." Pullen snapped out the admonition and the pantomime with the photograph was repeated.

Jock Hakapopulous was even blander than his brother. He too was
ingratiating but he was an older man, and there was an underlying
capability about him and a dreadful rat intelligence which was not
only not negligible but, somehow, in that atmosphere, alarming.

He too professed himself unhappy not to be able to oblige. There
were so many girls in the world, he said. One was very much like
another. He himself had no use for women.

The divisional superintendent remarked that this fact would hardly
seem to emerge from his police record, and both brothers were in-
ordinately amused.

Since there was nothing to be seen in number eight, always ex-
cluding Jock Hakapopulous in his drapery, which was a sight with
merits of its own, Mr. Campion and Mr. Lugg drifted away from the

police party and explored the other rooms. As soon as they opened the doors the story was evident. Every dining room was suspiciously clean and there were uneven, discoloured patches on the wallpaper where furniture had been removed and replaced. Every room on the floor had been recently rearranged.

"They've got the police cold." Mr. Lugg made the observation through closed lips. "There's not much those two don't know. Where are you going?"

Mr. Campion did not reply. He had opened the half-glass door and was already some way down a flight of dirty stairs which he had discovered behind it.

When Oates joined him five minutes later he was still standing at the foot of the staircase looking out of the back door into the small yard which gave on to Augean Passage. The old superintendent had left the Greeks to the pack and he came down to Campion, holding the skirts of his coat closely round him like a fastidious woman.

"Lumme," he said expressively.

Mr. Campion nodded. "A corner of our picturesque London," he observed. "Mind that swill can. See what this is?"

Oates glanced up the staircase and then out into the yard again.

"A convenient getaway," he said. "Getaway or, of course, a get-in. Trusted clients take the back stairs, I suppose. Let's get out in the air. I don't really fancy the atmosphere of this place. They're a couple o' daisies, aren't they? How did you come to stumble on them?"

"Old-fashioned footwork. Lugg and I have been round every fishy club and suspicious eatery in London. What do you think?"

"About them?" Oates jerked his head upward and smiled with his lips only. "They know something, don't they?" he said.

It was not effusive thanks but Mr. Campion knew his Oates.

He led the other man across the yard to an open shed which he and Lugg had inspected less than an hour before. The plain-clothes man inside looked up from the car which he was examining, shame-faced disappointment in his smile.

"Well, here it is, sir," he said, "such as it is. I was just coming in to report."

The superintendent walked round the machine, his shoulders hunched. There it was indeed, a nondescript four-seater Morris Twelve which had been someone's pride in 1929 and was still serviceable. The most irritating thing about it was its cleanliness. There were certainly a few traces of vegetable litter in the back, but the leather upholstery had been recently scrubbed and the paint positively scraped. Also, which was even more depressing, it possessed four new tires.

Oates said something under his breath, nodded to the man and came out into the yard again. He looked at Campion.

"I hate this kind of outfit," he said. "Did you see anyone in that house except those two and the waiter?"

"No," said Campion. "And yet, of course, there must be other people about; kitchen staff and so on."

"That's what I mean." Oates was spiteful. "They're all there somewhere. The place is full of people. We'll find 'em, of course, but it's like a rat warren. The whole house is so darned furtive you never know if the chair you're leaning on hasn't someone curled up in the bottom of it. They're all the same, these places—cold, dark, dirty and alive. They get on my nerves. Come on, we'll go in."

They picked their way to the back door through a miscellaneous collection of kitchen refuse, dirty delivery trays and fresh supplies of greengrocery. Campion was in front and in the doorway he stopped abruptly, so that the superintendent ran into him.

"I say," he said.

Oates peered over his shoulder and an exclamation escaped him. At Campion's feet was a basket half full of cabbage leaves and among them, its bright blade gleaming wickedly against the green, was a long, thin, double-edged knife, about six tenths of an inch wide at the shaft.

Oates took up the basket without a word and went upstairs. The entire company had moved down to the main room again and as they passed along the passage curtains sighed dustily around them and the carpet swallowed up their tread.

Pullen looked down at the knife and for the first time during his visit a gleam of satisfaction appeared in his face.

"Ah," he said, "that's something like, sir. Yes, indeed. Now then, you two."

The brothers Hakapopulous regarded the discovery without interest. Jock had removed his sheet and now stood clad in a torn singlet and a disreputable pair of trousers. His great neck flowed from his jowls and swelled into a double roll at the top of his spine.

"Don' you like it?" he enquired. "We got a dozen of these. Show 'im, Andreas."

Andreas Hakapopulous was delighted to oblige in any way. He threw open the drawers of his sideboard. He invited Inspector Pullen and his friends into the unholy mystery of his dreadful kitchens. Jock had underestimated his possessions. They found twenty-seven knives of the same pattern in various parts of the establishment and the elder Hakapopulous took up one of them and balanced it in his hand.

"Nize little knife," he said as the filtering light from the top of the window glistened on his shining face.

"'Andy. They're very popular just now in the trade. We get them from Loewenstein in Ol' Compton Street. He tell me the other day he sells more of these knives to restaurants than any other kind. Sharp, you know. She goes through a tough ol' chicken as though she was a little bit o' butter." He wiped the blade affectionately along his forearm and Mr. Campion, who was not unimaginative, turned away.

In the shed, where the car stood, the police held a brief conference. Pullen faced the two superintendents while Mr. Campion nosed about discreetly among the rubbish in the background.

"I'd like to pull 'em in at once, sir, all three of them." Pullen spoke earnestly. Lack of sleep had changed the key of his machine-gun rattle and his eyes were angry. "They're lying, of course, but you can't seem to get at 'em in a place like this. You can't see 'em, for one thing. I'd like to get 'em into the light. Jock has a record as long as your arm, and Andreas has been inside half-a-dozen times to my knowledge. That little waiter chap might be made to squeal too," he added, not without a certain grim anticipation. He glanced across at Campion and gave him a conciliatory smile. "It makes you wild when you see it under your nose and can't lay your hands on it, don't it?" he demanded. "The job was done here if it was done anywhere and you can see how it was done."

"Those two wouldn't kill in their own house," said the divisional superintendent, unaware that he was making a nice distinction.

"No, no, they didn't do the killing." Oates made the pronouncement out of the fund of his vast experience. "They had a corpse wished on 'em. They're accessories after the fact."

"And they've had two days to clear up the mess." Pullen was bitter. "Let's get 'em inside," he said. "No arrest, of course; just a little friendly chat. They know something."

"Of course they do." Oates was laughing in spite of his weariness. "You'll leave someone to go over the house. That's your pigeon, Super."

"Righto." The divisional man grinned. "God knows what I'll find," he said. "Half-a-dozen stiffs, I shouldn't wonder."

Pullen went off to superintend the exodus and Oates looked at Campion.

"We'll go back together, I think," he said. "Not forgetting Master Lugg either. I want to talk to you two. I was just going to see your sister when you phoned. Don't worry; I put her off." He paused. "We don't want to *make* trouble," he added presently. "You'll come along, will you?"

"Right by your side," said Mr. Campion. "I'm not leaving you."

At ten o'clock on the same evening he had not gone back on his word. Lugg had returned to the flat for sustenance and a relief from his collar and shoes, but in a corner of the superintendent's office Mr. Campion sat on, and because of his service, and because he might be even more useful, no one disturbed him. Oates remained at his desk. The hard artificial light made him look old and his shoulders were prominent under his coat.

Four hours intensive questioning in the little office next door had elicited a number of things from the Hakapopulous brothers, among them the fact that the respectability of their establishment was, in spite of several extraordinary miscarriages of justice in the past, absolutely above reproach. They agreed, moreover, that they had used their car not only in the small hours on the morning of the twenty-first, but on every other morning for the past two years. A car, they explained, was indispensable for an early visit to Smithfield or Covent Garden, and, if one was to provide one's customers with good clean wholesome food, personal marketing was the only way to avoid economic ruin. Both brothers professed themselves charmed by the photograph. It reminded them of several customers, they said, and offered names and addresses to prove it. As for the redecoration—well, it was about time. The house was just a little old-fashioned. Had the inspector noticed it? It was indeed a coincidence that they should have chosen just this particular time to make a start, but then one must begin sometime, and the summer air carried away the smell of the paint.

It was an unequal contest. The police were handicapped and knew it. Their one forlorn hope, the lorry driver, had let them down badly. He had been rushed from Coaching Cross and had arrived eager to help. For a long, wearisome hour he had watched the brothers parading in half darkness in company with half-a-dozen or so other well-nourished aliens, only to confess himself "a bit muddled" at the end of it. In despair Pullen had dismissed him and returned to the direct attack.

The brothers remained friendly, oily and untired. Although the whole story was clear for anyone to read, and no one appreciated that fact more deeply than themselves, they knew that so long as they kept their heads they had nothing worse than inconvenience to fear. They were both men of tremendous physical stamina and mental agility.

Moreover, their experience of police procedure was considerable. Nothing was new to them. Any deviation from the beaten track of police questioning brought a bland demand for their solicitor and the farce began again.

At a little after eleven Pullen came in to Oates. He was hoarse and irritable, and there was a limpness about his appearance which suggested that a portion of the grease of his captives had somehow got on to himself.

"Nothing," he said savagely. "Absolutely nothing. Something's happened to that race since they did all that marble work."

Mr. Campion grinned and looked up.

"Those two are 'wide,' are they?"

"Wide?" The inspector threw out his arms expressively. "Not only do they know all the answers, but they enjoy giving them. I've got my hands right on it, you know. Chorge! That makes me wild."

He looked like an exasperated setter and Mr. Campion sympathised with him.

"How about the other chap?" he enquired.

"Him?" Pullen showed the whites of his eyes. "Have you ever had a long serious talk with an idiot child? He ought to be in a bottle, that's where he ought to be, in a jar. Flood's got him now. He's gentle, is Flood. They were matching cigarette cards when I left 'em. God give me strength!"

Oates sighed. "Sit down, Inspector," he said. "Mr. Campion's got a fag on him. Now we'll see what Flood's up to." He took up the telephone and made the enquiry. The instrument crackled back hopefully and Pullen jumped up. "Oh." Oates was interested. "Is that so? That's better than nothing, Sergeant. *Is* he? Yes, I dare say. Yes. They often are, these fellows. Yes. Well, bring him up here." He hung up and cocked an eye at Pullen. "Flood says he's weak-minded, but his mouth is moving," he said. The inspector sat down again and bit at his cigarette.

"It's in our hands," he said. "That's what pips me."

Louis Bartolozzi came in with Flood, who treated him as if he were certified, that is to say with great tenderness.

"Sit there," he said, stretching out a great bony arm and planting a small chair in the exact centre of the room. "Put your hat under it. Now are you all right? There's the superintendent."

Louis smiled faintly at the gathering and looked as though he were going to be sick.

"His mother was half Italian and half Rumanian and his father was probably French," explained the sergeant, consulting his notebook.

"He was born in the Boro', he thinks, and he can't speak any other language than—er—what he does."

"Street Arabic," exploded Pullen and laughed unpleasantly, relapsing into bitter silence as Oates glanced at him.

"He remembers a girl in room number eight on Tuesday," Flood continued softly. "That's right, isn't it, Louis?"

"Da girl in da room, a nize pretty girl, yes."

"On Tuesday night? Last Tuesday?"

"Ver' like. Y'know we have a lot of people come there. Rich people. Nize girls, some of dem. Smart, y'know."

"In room eight on Tuesday last?"

The wide-eyed stare on the man's face became intensified. "Tuesday, yes, every day."

"That's how he keeps going, sir." Flood looked at Oates apologetically. "Perhaps I'd better read you what he's said so far. He thinks he recognises the photograph but can't be sure. He remembers a girl in room eight on Tuesday last. She came in alone and ordered a meal. She must have been expected, but he doesn't know how the rooms are booked. He took her some food and never saw her again."

"Never saw her again?"

"No sir. He can't remember if she was gone when he went in again or whether the door was locked."

"But it's only two days ago!" roared Pullen. "He *must* remember."

Flood looked at his protégé helplessly. "He doesn't seem to," he said.

Louis seemed paralysed, but after a moment of complete vacancy he burst into sudden and excited speech.

"She was annoyed," he said. "Wild, y'know. Feller hadn't come. Somethin', I don' know."

"Annoyed, was she?" Oates sat up. "When was this? What time of the evening?"

The little creature, who looked as if he had never before been above ground, gave the old man an ingratiating smile.

"In the evening, yes, tha's right."

"What time? Was it still light?"

An elaborate shrug answered him. "In the evening."

Oates turned to Flood. "Any more?"

"No sir, not really, I'm afraid. He thinks people did use the back stairs, but he doesn't seem to notice people getting in and out of the place. When they're there he waits on 'em. He works very hard, sir."

"I don't doubt it, son." Oates's smile at Flood was half amused and half affectionate. "All right, take him away. See what you can get."

The sergeant collected his charge and shepherded him out again.

"That would look nice in the witness box, wouldn't it?" Pullen spoke with feeling. "You'd throw that to counsel as you'd throw a dog a bone."

Oates shook his head. "No, I see," he said. "I see. That explains the Hakapopulous calm. There's nothing very useful there except that it's fairly clear now what actually did happen. She went there by appointment and somebody came up those back stairs and killed her, probably with one of the restaurant's own knives, leaving the body for the Greeks to deal with. One of the brothers must have found her, and, not wanting any trouble—heaven knows they understand trouble, those two—they cleaned up the mess in their own way. Frankly I'm inclined to take my cap off to them. They've been thorough. When they went to market I suppose they slung the body in the back of the car, drove a little further out, dumped it and probably returned to do their shopping without raising an eyelid. They're that kind."

Mr. Campion stirred in his corner.

"If I might suggest," he said slowly, "if your man—I take it it was a man—came into that place up the back stairs he must have known his way about. Ergo, he'd been there before. Do you think Flood's little packet of trouble could recognise a photograph?"

"That's an idea, sir." Pullen shot up. His energy was amazing and it flashed through Campion's mind that one could almost see his body pumping it out. "It won't be evidence but it might be useful. If we could only get something to jolt those greasy beggars in the next room out of their damned complacency it would be something."

Oates unlocked a drawer in his desk and took out a bundle of photographs. They were all there, taken from illustrated papers or begged or borrowed from servants; Val, Georgia, Gaiogi, Tante Marthe, Ferdie, Alan Dell, even Mr. Campion himself. Pullen gathered them up. "I'll mix 'em with the usual," he said. "We'll see."

As the door closed behind him Oates swung round in his chair and looked at Campion.

"You're still on the blacking?"

"Yes," said Campion with a complete lack of hesitation which was unusual in him. "It's blackmail all right, guv'nor. Think of it. What a place for a transaction of that kind! Complete safety. Complete secrecy. Our Caroline has used that place before for the same purpose. Andreas recognised her immediately and it wasn't a good photograph if one had only seen her dead. Besides, my dear chap, how could she get into the place alone if they didn't know her? If this little Louis

person is any good and he's been there long I should be very much
inclined to show him a photograph of Portland-Smith. Don't you see,
someone knew that place well. Whoever he was, he got Caroline Adamson to book a room there by promising her money. Then he
sneaked across the yard and slipped up the stairs. He need not have
met anybody. It was made for him. It was a place where muffled figures
were always slipping in and out. The Mazarini mob used to use it for a
paying-out place last year; did you know that? That's where Mazarini
used to pay his thugs for services rendered on the racecourse."

"Is it? I didn't know that. When did you hear that?"

"This afternoon, from the friend who gave me the name of the place
as a likely dive."

"Oh, I see." Oates glanced at the younger man with a smile that
was only part amusement. "You and your friends," he said. "*All* your
friends."

Mr. Campion's expression grew serious.

"I don't mind my friends' troubles," he remarked feelingly, "but
I draw a line when they get mixed up with the family."

They were still eyeing each other when Pullen came in. He walked
over to the desk and laid the photographs down without a word.
His heavy face was blank and his eyes looked bloodshot.

"Well, did he recognise anyone?" Oates was hopeful.

"He did." The inspector could barely trust himself to speak. "He
knew 'em all. Why shouldn't he? They're all fairly well-known people.
He knew Miss Wells and Mr. Dell and Mrs. Ferris and Laminoff, of
course. He'd waited on every one of 'em, he said. He also recognised
a photograph of the ex-Emperor of Germany, Sergeant Withers of the
K Division, and the portrait of you, sir, as an inspector. He's worse
than hopeless. Flood seems to understand about half he says, but I'm
hanged if I do. I'll go back and have one more talk to those perishing
Greeks. I can't keep 'em here all night without charging 'em and although there's plenty we could hold 'em for I don't see much point
in it. They won't run away. Why should they? I don't suppose the
boys on the car have phoned yet, sir, have they?"

"No, nothing. That's a forlorn hope, Inspector, I'm afraid. We
didn't get on to it soon enough. I'll leave you to it. I've had forty-
eight hours solid and I'm no longer intelligent. If you want me you
know where you can find me."

The phone bell answered him, and he pounced on the instrument
hopefully, all trace of weariness receding from his eyes. Mr. Campion
had seen the same phenomenon in the face of an angler who had
noticed a nibble when he was just about to wind in his line.

"What? Yes, Superintendent Stanislaus Oates here. Yes. Sanderson speaking? Yes. You have? Really? Good man. She saw 'em, did she? Splendid! Saw the two brothers lifting a girl into the car? She thought the girl was what? Oh, drunk. Yes, of course. Fine. Bring her round. She's just what we want. What? What? Oh. Oh, I see. Oh. What a pity! No, no, of course. Of course not. Well, yes, yes, you may as well. Yes, Inspector Pullen will be here. Yes, righto. Good-bye."

He replaced the receiver and grimaced at them.

"You heard that, did you? They've found a witness who saw the Greeks carry a girl out of the back door at two in the morning of the twenty-first. She thought the girl was drunk and took no notice of them. Unfortunately she's a vagrant and not a good witness. We could never put her in the box. She'd be discredited in five minutes. They're going to bring her round, but I don't see that she's going to help. There you are, Pullen. I'm sorry, but what do you expect in Augean Passage?"

The inspector thrust his hands into his pockets.

"It's always the same with these cases," he said. "Still, I'll get back to those two. This might rattle 'em. There's a chance. If only they'd play ball we might get a description of the man. That'd be something."

"If they saw him," said Mr. Campion.

Both men turned to look at him and he spread out his hands.

"With a back entrance like that, why should anyone ever have seen him? Why shouldn't he have come and gone like any other of the shadows in that rats' nest? No one need ever have seen him there that night."

"Except the girl," put in Oates. "She saw him and she knew him. We're back where we started, Mr. Campion. It's motive we want; motive and Miss Adamson's friends."

"Give me a week." The demand was out of the younger man's mouth before he realised he had spoken. "Give me a week, Oates, before you stir up the dovecotes. The chief won't like it if you do, the Colonial Office will be furious. What's the good of an exhumation order? What's the good of an unholy stink? What's the good of smearing all this appalling mud over people who don't even dream it exists? Give me a week, only a week."

"It'll take a week to get the Home Office to move," said Oates.

CHAPTER TWENTY-ONE

On the Sunday Amanda gave a formal sherry party to mark the breaking off of her engagement to Albert Campion.

It took place at her cottage on the river near the Alandel works and was one of those elaborately masochistic gestures which the modern cult for the proper sublimation of all the more commonplace emotions has made fashionable among the highly civilised.

Coming, as it did, at the end of one nightmare week and at the beginning of another, it seemed very appropriate and was almost, as Tante Marthe said, the only conceivable kind of celebration which one could decently bring oneself to face in the circumstances.

No one knew the cause of this new trouble, and most people were too worried to care, but the first impression, which was that young Pontisbright had put his foot down, was dispelled. The mischief lay between the two parties most concerned. So much was evident as soon as one set foot in the house.

Amanda's house was like Amanda inasmuch as it was both small and astonishingly rational. The main room, which, with a little kitchenette, comprised the whole of the ground floor, possessed one glass side which opened on to a steep lawn running down to the river, and was otherwise individual inasmuch as the furnishings had been taken over complete from the prim old lady who had lived there before, and had been made comfortable and attractive with anything which had taken Amanda's fancy, from a nice piece of machinery to a two-foot bowl of marigolds. The result of this marriage of tastes was a big, odd room in which a fine "tea-chest" clock and a plush-framed photograph of Edward VII in a kilt lived in harmony with an architect's drawing table and a magnificent Van Gogh.

Hal Fitton, Earl of Pontisbright, supported his sister at the gathering. He stood by her side, grave and old-fashioned as he had always been. At twenty he was a sturdy, serious young man with the family's eyes and hair and a double dose of the family's composure. The situation was one which appealed to his youthful sense of the dramatic, while appeasing his individual mania for decorum. He was very nice indeed to Mr. Campion and frequently spoke to him, making it even more clear than if he had said so in so many words that the dissolution of the proposed partnership had been a matter of mutual arrangement, and that nothing unpleasant had been said or even thought on either side.

Amanda was at ease, if a trifle brittle, but Mr. Campion was not so good. He looked hunted rather than harassed and there were fine lines running down his cheeks from ears to chin, as if his facial muscles were under particularly good control.

Val was inclined to be bitterly amused. She had come over with most of the others who had been lunching at Caesar's Court and she was, as never before, the complete professional woman, hard, experienced and aware of her responsibilities. Her tailored silk suit was a minor miracle. She looked unapproachable and, had it not been for her essential femininity, severe.

Ferdie Paul was there. He had come over with Gaiogi and his wife, and he stood in a corner, his quick brown eyes interested. Val fascinated him and the paralysing decency of the whole procedure evidently took his fancy, for he watched the brother and sister with a smile that was part genuine admiration.

Georgia arrived alone, her chauffeur driving. She caused a little sensation by appearing in white muslin, blue bows and a picture hat, which, although decorative and eminently suitable to the weather, were out of keeping both with the last mood in which anyone present had seen her and the unfortunate nature of the gathering.

"Mon Dieu!" said Tante Marthe aloud and turned away with interest, having caught sight of her own discreetly clad, silk-caped figure in a convex mirror.

Gaiogi alone seemed to appreciate the essential preposterous charm of the main idea of the party. He behaved as if he were at the funeral of an old enemy, looking about him with a kind of mock solemn relish. Too, he alone seemed to have shaken off the real bond of calamity which encompassed them all. If ruin threatened, for him it was at least not yet. He talked earnestly in a low voice about trivialities and was delighted with Hal, whom he obviously took to be a particularly interesting English "piece." But if Gaiogi could forget the main situation, the others were not so fortunate. After the first overbright five minutes the morale broke down. The room was littered with Sunday papers and by the time Dell arrived, looking if anything a little more worn than Campion himself, the post-mortem upon them was in full swing.

The cheaper press carried little new about the actual mystery. The Hakapopulous brothers had burst upon the world two days before and the photograph of "Mr. Andreas Hakapopulous, who has been questioned by the police in connection with the death of beautiful Caroline Adamson (Miss Adamson was once a mannequin at a famous dress house)" was still vivid enough in everyone's mind. So far the name of Ramillies had not appeared in print in connection with the case, and the references to Papendeik's had been most carefully confined to the bare fact that the dead girl had once been in their employ, but what the laws of libel restrained in print had not been silenced in conversation, and the feature, or magazine, sides of the family Sundays were littered with evidences of the trend of popular thought.

There was in particular an article by Lady Jevity called "My Life as a Mannequin. How I Saved Myself from the Dreaded Drug Habit. The Canker of the Upper Classes" which came as near being actionable as anyone dared go, and a catchpenny indictment headed "Hands Off Our Girls!" by Honest John McQuean, which began "In a little country morgue a lovely girl lies dead" and ended with typical inconsequentiality, "Will no one tell them drugs and lovely dresses are snares for little moths?" printed in gothic letters.

Most of the other papers had something in the same vein but *Oliphant's News* had taken another and more ominous line. They had merely written up Val very thoroughly. There was no reference to the crime in their article at all, but the house of Papendeik received a full-page spread adorned with Val's photograph and a press picture of Georgia in a Val negligee. This publicity was a trifle suspicious in itself, but the writer of the copy had infused a touch of melancholy into her account which gave the whole thing the dreadful flavour of an obituary notice and left the uninitiated reader with the uncomfortable feeling that the end of the story would be sad and that he must wait until next week for it.

Georgia brought the ball out into the open field in her own unmatchable style.

"It's very sweet of Alan, you know," she said, smiling across at him. "Most people in his position would just keep away from us all, wouldn't they? I don't mean anything personal by that, Amanda. I know you and Albert just don't want to get married and that's all there is to that. Besides, you've got a family and a village and traditions and that sort of thing. But I mean, poor Alan is nothing to do with this and he could so easily just stay away, couldn't he? We all are a bit leprous just now. It's got to be faced. Do you know, my dears, I've been astonished. Quite a lot of people have been really awfully nice. Which reminds me: what's the time?"

"Half-past six," said Ferdie, who appeared to be the only member of the party still coherent. "Got a boy friend?"

"No, just a food appointment." Georgia nodded to him but glanced out of the front windows immediately afterwards and smoothed down her muslin frills with an expression of such tender artlessness on her lovely face that several people glanced at her sharply. After her original pronouncement normal reticence seemed a little affected and people began to talk freely.

"I am ill," said Tante Marthe. "I feel the end of the world is coming, and I do not care what I wear for it. Don't you know anything at all, Albert? We haven't even seen you for two days."

"Albert's had troubles of his own," said Val absently and bit her tongue as he turned to look at her with sudden darkness in his eyes.

"Ciel! Yes. But what a time to choose!" Lady Papendeik spoke to herself, but the events of the last week had destroyed a poise which had lasted half a lifetime and the words were audible. Hal heard them and so did Amanda, and their reactions were precisely similar. Hal replenished Lady Papendeik's glass and Amanda began to talk about her house. There was not a lot to be shown, but she did the thing thoroughly, displayed the convenience of the white gas stove, the sink and the cupboard in the kitchenette, the stairs to the two little bedrooms, the bathroom, and her own newly invented electric geyser. There were several interesting labour-saving features, all of a startlingly practical rather than a merely gadgety character, and Gaiogi began to chip her gently about her domesticity, avoiding most adroitly any errors of taste which the nature of the occasion might have invited.

"But, darling, it's mad to live here *alone*," said Georgia, innocently spoiling everything. "It's all so sort of honeymoon, isn't it? What do you do about service?"

"Oh, a char, you know." Amanda spoke with determined cheerfulness. "She's a good old thing. She lives just down on the highroad and she doesn't come when I don't want her. I go away rather a lot. I'm off to Sweden tomorrow."

"Really?" It was Gaiogi who spoke, but everyone had heard and there was a moment of embarrassment as her immediate personal difficulties were recalled to everyone's mind. Hal moved over to her side.

"I have persuaded my sister to come with me to visit the Tajendie works," he said primly. "Alan, you approve, don't you?"

"Oh yes, rather. Very useful. We must keep in touch with what the other fellow's doing." Dell spoke dutifully but his eyes strayed curiously towards Mr. Campion, who met his glance with studied disinterest. Campion did nothing, nor did he speak, but at that moment everyone was aware of him. He stood looking at Dell and there was a wave of unrest in the room as it passed through most people's minds that perhaps this lean, affable person was not entirely reliable in his present mood. It was a sort of telepathic warning that he was not taking his personal disaster with quite the same decent casualism that everyone else was prepared to afford it and they were all, in spite of their own worries, a little embarrassed by it.

Georgia alone seemed unaware of the signal. As usual she was entirely occupied with her own point of view.

"You just shut the cottage when you go away, do you, Amanda?" she said.

"Yes, it's very convenient. In the country but with all the amenities of town." Amanda's satisfaction had a trace of hardness in it. "I'm off tonight. I go home to Suffolk first and we sail on Tuesday. I'm looking forward to it."

"My dear, of course you are. I wish I could do something like that, but then you haven't got children, have you?" Georgia sighed and looked out of the window again. Her beautiful face was troubled and her eyes were gentle. "I wish to God I *could* go away and get out of it all," she went on quite sincerely, forgetting the unfortunate inference. "I bet you do, too, don't you, Val? My dear, let's *rat*. Let's bunk and go to Cassis and lie in the sun."

"Darling!" The protest escaped Val before she could prevent it and as Georgia gaped at her she added with the quiet bluntness of exasperation, "For pity's sake, sweetheart, shut up. Things are bad enough."

"I wonder if you realise how bad they are, my dear." Mr. Campion's soft observation from the other side of the room made them all turn to him. He was leaning over the drawing table, his strong, sensitive hands, which no one seemed to have noticed before, gripping the sides of the board. His natural vacuity of expression had vanished and he had taken off his spectacles. He looked vigorous, deeply intelligent and by no means unhandsome in his passionate sincerity. "I don't like putting it to you as baldly as this," he said, clipping his words a little. "It's not a jolly subject to rake up at this particular party, of all times. But you terrify me. You appall me, standing around hopefully as you discount this and that little private awkwardness, packing it away in the back of your minds as not really important while you blind yourselves to the terrifying fact that these little awkwardnesses all mounting together make up one tremendous and overpowering sum, awkward enough to ruin every one of you. At the actual moment you're all comparatively safe. The libel laws protect you and the police enquiry is at its beginning. But my enquiry is nearing its end. I don't intend to rat to the police but the methods I have used are ordinary orthodox methods and what I know tonight they are bound to know soon, certainly by the end of the week. There is nothing to stop them finding out everything if they consider it necessary to pursue the enquiry, and as long as the murderer of Caroline Adamson goes free they will consider it necessary."

"What do you know?" Tante Marthe's question was sharp and unexpected, but no one in Mr. Campion's audience looked round at her.

"I know a number of interesting things." He was very earnest. "Several of them are criminal and the rest are, in varying degrees, unfortunate. For any one of them to be set down in print would be a considerable embarrassment for one of you, but for all of them to come out would be a catastrophe for the whole crowd of us. Let me tell you something. I know, and the police will eventually know, that Richard Portland-Smith was driven to suicide, not deliberately but by accident. The fact that he committed suicide was fortuitous. The idea behind that blackmailing was the desire to ruin him, to get him out of the way. I know that a carefully arranged frame-up, involving Miss Adamson, was staged for him at the Green Bottle Hotel at Shelleycomb on the Downs in October 1933. I know that one other person was present on that occasion besides Caroline Adamson and that that other person was a woman."

"A woman?" Georgia spoke faintly but Campion ignored her.

"I know," he went on, "that Portland-Smith used to meet this second woman in a back room in Hakapopulous' restaurant in Lord Scroop Street and that there he paid her all he had. I also know that this woman was not the main instigator of the plot. She merely did the work and took the money, half of it which she paid to Caroline, who threw it away, and half of which she kept herself and invested most unprofitably. I know that Ramillies was murdered. I know that he left Caesar's Court in the middle of a party because he was so frightened of the approaching flight that he couldn't bear himself any longer. He went to Boot's Hotel and spent the night there in an agony of apprehension, and in the morning he went to see someone who knew his phobia and who gave him a hypodermic injection, promising him that the effects of it would be discomfort for four hours followed by a feeling of happy irresponsibility and freedom from fear. I know that the flight was unexpectedly postponed for an hour and that therefore Ramillies died on the ground when he should have died in the air. But I also know that any accident of this sort was anticipated by the fact that his specialist was at Caesar's Court in response to an invitation to sample the amenities of the place at the management's expense. I know that Miss Adamson was killed because, having been taught to blackmail once, she saw in Ramillies' death an opportunity to blackmail again. I know that she visited Hakapopulous' restaurant thinking to receive money and met a knife instead." He paused and looked round. They were all watching him. Georgia stood with tears on her cheeks and her eyes wide, but the others were all imperturbable, their faces strained but expressionless.

"That is the criminal side," said Mr. Campion. "Now we come to the merely interesting but unfortunate. I make no apology for digging up these facts about you all. My principal care has naturally been for my sister and in her interest I have done my best to satisfy myself of the whole truth of the story. I've told you that I shan't squeal to the police, and I shan't, but, as I say, my methods of enquiry are the same as theirs and they are doing now what I did a week ago. Some of these facts are relevant and some of them aren't. I don't know yet which are which, but I shall know, and should the police come to discuss them the entire world will know. I know, for instance, that you, Gaiogi, received a small but mysterious backing for the Poire d'Or. I know that you, Dell, have an enormous sum of money invested in Caesar's Court. I know that you, Georgia, have all the money you possess in the world in the same place. You too, Ferdie, have a packet there, and so has Val and Tante Marthe. Then there's Rex. Rex has a lot of money, Tante Marthe. He's your senior partner, isn't he? Then Caroline Adamson's father was a friend of Gaiogi's and when he died Gaiogi promised to keep an eye on the girl. I know lots of little odd things which may mean nothing, but which have come out in my enquiry, personal things which perhaps don't matter very much to anyone but those concerned. I know Georgia's first husband is playing in a concert party in a third-rate watering place. I know the name of Ferdie's doctor in Paris. I know the White Empress Club is financed by Gaiogi, and I know that Val was criminally careless to leave some seven ounces of morphine where any member of her staff could steal it. None of these may matter very much, but they won't look jolly in print, with ghouls like Honest John McQuean and Lady Jevity underlining them. There's only one way to save the worst of the mess and that is to get the murderer into the hands of the police immediately. Fortunately one can only hang a murderer once. One body is sufficient to inaugurate the ceremony. If the police can only get Caroline Adamson's murderer they won't go into the death of Ramillies. That is why I am still here. I shall make one last attempt. If I fail—and I warn you I'm not too hopeful—then I'm through. I don't care what happens to me or to anyone else. I'm finished."

He glanced across at Amanda.

"God knows this business has cost me enough," he said.

Nobody spoke for a long time. Young Pontisbright was white and angry and the others were thinking the swift, absorbing, lonely thoughts of self-preservation. It was an appalling minute and the incident which ended it was mercifully ludicrous. Tires crackled in the flint road outside and Georgia started. Everybody looked out of the window and Gaiogi laughed abruptly. A long black chauffeur-driven car had pulled up outside the garden gate. The tonneau was nearly all glass and the three occupants were clearly visible. Two of them sat side by side in the back. One was Sinclair and the other was Towser. They had been to Whipsnade and had called back by appointment for Mama, forced to waste her time at a tiresome formal party. Even at that distance it was evident that the outing had been a success. Towser spoke to the chauffeur, who smiled faintly and sounded the horn. Georgia did not say good-bye. She picked up her little pale blue handbag and her long gloves and walked out of the cottage in her demure white muslin, her bows and her picture hat. She looked beautiful, sweetly feminine and virginal, as she went off on a new adventure, tears still on her cheeks.

Dell walked over to Val and led her out onto the little lawn behind the house. There was a gate leading into a flat meadow there and he piloted her through it. The atmosphere had been so electric that there seemed nothing odd in his behaviour. Her instinct had been to get away at all costs and his appearance at her elbow merely made the going easier, but out in the warm air, with the world green and rational about her, the sensation of nightmare wore off, leaving her battered but aware again of life as it was in the daylight.

"He's very cut up," Dell remarked as they stepped onto the turf.

She nodded. "I've never seen him like that before. It's rather unnerving when you see someone you know so well go all out of character. He's frightened, too, I think. Things aren't good."

"No," he said. "No. Yet they may not be as bad as he seems to think. We can only hope, you know."

He was comfortingly calm and Val glanced up at him. She was relieved to see that he was at least not embarrassed by their recent personal upheaval. She tried to consider him objectively, and saw only that his hair was going grey and that he looked tired. In common with most modern-thinking women she was pessimistic where her own emotions were concerned and she found herself acutely conscious of her attitude towards him. She was still most painfully in love with him. He still created in her that unaccountable excitement and exquisite sensitiveness which would seem to have some psychic or at least some chemical origin, since it had no birth in reason, but she still shrank from investigating him. She still recoiled from the secret door which Georgia's Pandora instinct found so irresistible in all men. A living room or a junk cupboard? The risk was too great to take. Her own exacting intelligence, her own insufferable responsible importance, weighed her down like a pack. She was desperately aware that she wanted something from him that was neither physical nor even mental, but rather a vague moral quality whose very nature escaped her. It was something of which she stood in great need and her fear was not only that he did not possess it but that no one did. Her unhappy superiority made her feel lonely and she turned from him so that she was not looking at him when he spoke.

"I wanted to talk to you, Val. Do you mind if I talk about myself?"

The question was so unlike him and yet so much to be expected that her heart sank.

"Oh, that's all right," she said. "I think we can almost take that as read, don't you?"

"What?" He was astonished and his bright blue eyes were amused. "What do you think I'm talking about? Georgia?"

"Aren't you?"

"Well, no, I wasn't exactly." He was laughing a little. "I wanted to talk about myself. This is my trouble, Val. I am in love and I want to marry, but there are difficulties, my own mainly. I don't want a mistress or a companion. I want a wife."

Val paused in her walk. She was surprised. She held her head stiffly and her eyes were interested. Her business people knew her thus and in certain Parisian quarters the attitude was viewed with deep respect. Madame was alert.

Dell smiled at her. He seemed to find her charming.

"It's not so easy," he said. "Wives are out of fashion. I love you, Val. Will you marry me and give up to me your independence, the enthusiasm which you give your career, your time and your thought? That's my proposition. It's not a very good one, is it? I realise that I've made a fine old exhibition of myself with Georgia Wells which has hardly enhanced my immediate value in the market, but I can't honestly say that I regret the experience. That woman has maturing properties. However, that is the offer. In return—and you probably won't like this either—in return, mind you (I consider it an obligation), I should assume full responsibility for you. I would pay your bills to any amount which my income might afford. I would make all decisions which were not directly in your province, although on the other hand I would like to feel that I might discuss everything with you if I wanted to; but only because I wanted to, mind you; not as your right. And until I died you would be the only woman. You would be my care, my mate as in plumber, my possession if you like. If you wanted your own way in everything you'd have to cheat it out of me, not demand it. Our immediate trouble is serious, but not so serious as this. It means the other half of my life to me, but the whole of yours to you. Will you do it?"

"Yes," said Val so quickly that she startled herself. The word sounded odd in her ears, it carried such ingenuous relief. Authority. The simple nature of her desire from him took her breath away with its very obviousness and in the back of her mind she caught a glimpse of its root. She was a clever woman who would not or could not relinquish her femininity, and femininity unpossessed is femininity unprotected from itself, a weakness and not a charm.

He pulled her towards him and her shoulders were slim and soft under his hands.

"It's the only unfashionable thing you've ever done, Val."

Her eyes were clever as a monkey's and sunny as a child's.

"My fashions are always a little in advance," she said, and laughed in that sudden freedom which lies in getting exactly what one needs to make the world that place in which one's own particular temperament may thrive.

They walked on through the meadow and, finding the road, came back to the front of the cottage. Georgia's chauffeur had driven away and the Lagonda now lay first in the line. The sight of it brought the general situation back to their minds with an overpowering sense of dismay. Dell was holding Val's elbow and he pressed it encouragingly.

"We'll get by," he said. "Come on."

Their first impression was that the party had dwindled. Ferdie was talking to Hal about jujitsu and Gaiogi and Tante Marthe were standing together in more serious consultation. The three glass doors on the lawn stood wide, and through them, on the edge of the river's bank, Mr. Campion was listening to Amanda. Ferdie looked up as Val came in and his glance followed her own to the two on the lawn.

"Hallo," he said suddenly. "What's this? A reconciliation? That lad's in a nasty state. I thought she was going to take pity on him when she took him out there."

"I don't think . . ." Hal began stiffly and paused abruptly as the conversation on the lawn took a sudden turn.

As Amanda ceased to speak Mr. Campion took her hand and raised it to his lips with a gallantry which might or might not have been derisive. Amanda recovered her hand and hit him. It was no playful salutation but a straight broadside attack delivered with anger, and the noise of the impact sounded clearly in the room.

"Indeed," murmured Gaiogi with an embarrassed laugh, and added instantly "Good God!"

Campion had picked up his ex-fiancée and they saw him poised for an instant with the girl over his head. He said something which no one caught, but which possessed that peculiar quality of viciousness which is unmistakable, and then, while they all stared at him, pitched her from him into the deep river with a splash like a waterspout. He did not wait to see what became of her, but swung away and strode up the garden, the imprint of her hand showing clearly on his white face. As they reached the water's edge they heard the roar of the Lagonda.

Amanda's comment as she swam ashore and was lifted, breathless and dripping, onto the lawn by a bewildered gathering, was typical of her new mood.

"Not everybody's form of humour," she said briefly. "Will you all go and have a drink while I change?"

Tante Marthe accompanied her and Val made helpless apologies to Hal, who was devastatingly polite.

"He's not taking it very well," he said. "Frankly I was afraid something like this might happen. Anyway, she'll be out of the country for a bit. It's really nothing to do with you, Mrs. Ferris. Please don't worry about it. Fortunately there was no one here who could make a gossip paragraph of it."

"He's obviously off his head with worry," put in Alan Dell hastily. "That résumé which he gave was most enlightening. He evidently knows what the police intend to do. I heard this morning that there was talk of an exhumation order for Ramillies' body. What he said is quite true. If there is no arrest the enquiry may turn into a long ordeal for all of us. A murder is the one and only thing which cannot be hushed up in this country."

Amanda's brother regarded him with a curious little smile on his young mouth.

"Believe me, I appreciate that," he said. "If you'll excuse me I'll just have a word with my sister."

Ferdie looked after his retreating figure.

"There's not much that that kind of kid in that kind of position couldn't hush up, is there?" he said. "What was the row about? Anybody know?"

And Gaiogi, who had been listening with his bright eyes on Ferdie's face, shrugged his shoulders.

"That is how it should be," he said.

Val laughed uneasily.

"I thought you were going to say, 'What is a little murder to disturb an aristocrat?' Gaiogi," she murmured.

The Russian looked at her steadily, his round eyes intelligent.

"Among clever aristos, what is it?" he said.

CHAPTER TWENTY-TWO

Ferdie Paul was on the telephone when Mrs. Fitch brought Campion in. The room was much tidier than usual and struck cold after the warmth of the summer streets, but Ferdie himself was slightly dishevelled in his anxiety.

"Well, do what you can, anyway, old boy, won't you?" he said into the instrument, his thin voice carrying a world of nervous force and irritability behind it. "Yes, I know, but it's not a pleasant experience for any of us, is it? You were an old friend, that was all."

He hung up and glanced at Campion, the welcoming smile fading from his face as he saw him.

"Hullo, you all right?" he enquired.

"All right?" Mr. Campion threw himself down in the armchair which Mrs. Fitch pulled up for him. He barely remembered to thank her but she did not seem to notice the omission. "Yes, I'm all right. I'm alive, anyway. The corpselike effect is induced by lack of sleep."

"It's getting you down, is it? I don't blame you." His host was grimly amused. "Have a drink. Anna, for God's sake, dear, get the man a snifter. Don't hang about. Don't hang about."

If Mrs. Fitch resented his tone she did not show it. She mixed a drink on the sideboard and carried it to the visitor, who took the glass from her absently and set it down untasted. He looked like a skeleton in a dinner jacket. There were blue hollows round his eyes, while the skin stretching over his jaws seemed to have pulled his lips back a little. His normal affability had vanished completely and a sort of spiteful recklessness, which was wrong in him, had taken its place. Ferdie watched him, his shiny eyes laughing a little contemptuously in spite of his friendliness.

"Your girl friend swam ashore last night," he remarked.

"Did she?" Mr. Campion was profoundly disinterested.

"They have nine lives, all of 'em." Ferdie was not intentionally tasteless, but the little joke amused him. "You forgot the brick," he said.

Mr. Campion did not smile.

"You said you wanted to see me?" he enquired pointedly.

Ferdie raised his eyebrows and turned round to frown at Mrs. Fitch.

"Just a moment, dear," he said, every tone in the request indicating that she and everyone else in the world exasperated him unbearably. "Shut the door behind you. I've asked Mr. Campion round here to talk. You don't mind, do you? We shan't be long."

Anna Fitch went out obediently and Ferdie got up and shook his loose clothes.

"You're taking that engagement bust of yours too hard," he said. "I was talking to Georgia on the phone just now. She said Val seemed to be very worried about you. Still, that's your affair," he added hastily as his visitor prepared to rise. "I didn't phone all over London simply to tell you that no woman's worth it. You'll discover that in your own time. I've got my hands full at the moment. This is all pretty nasty, Campion, isn't it? Where's it going to end? We're in the soup, aren't we?"

Mr. Campion sighed. "It's comforting to find that someone realises that," he said bitterly. "These silly women don't see what's stewing up for them. They haven't savoured the Hakapopulous variety of stink. They don't know what it's like. Their innocent little snouts don't register anything stronger than cheating at bridge. The home secretary is considering the exhumation petition now, I believe."

"Oh, he is, is he? I was afraid that was coming." Ferdie spoke gloomily but his eyes were still bright with interest. "I've been trying to pull a few strings myself, as a matter of fact, but there's an ominous frigidity on all sides which doesn't feel too healthy. Still, supposing the police do get the order through, what can they expect to find? Wasn't there a P.M. at the time?"

"Yes, but the police aren't satisfied." Mr. Campion made the statement wearily. "They've got the report of the first P.M. and in it there's a mention of a hypodermic puncture in the left upper arm, yet the analysis found nothing to account for this. Not unnaturally, the police feel they'd like their own man to go over the ground again. They've got the viscera from Richmond now, as a matter of fact, and it's in Wryothsley's lab, but he wants to see the rest of the cadaver." He laughed briefly at the other man's expression. "I'm sorry to be so forthright, but there you are. That's the sort of detail which next

Sunday's press is going to dish up with comment. Meanwhile, if there is anything in the body which was overlooked in the first P.M., Wryothsley will find it."

Ferdie looked up. "There's always a chance that there's nothing to find," he observed but his optimism was not convincing.

"The 'unknown drug'?" Mr. Campion sounded derisive. "Don't you believe it, guv'nor. There ain't no such thing. What they don't find they'll deduce, same as I have, and that deduction, if it doesn't give them proof, will certainly give them the lead they want. It's going to be an almighty mess."

Ferdie Paul wandered about the big cold room. His body looked heavier than usual as his shoulders drooped and his chin rested thoughtfully on his chest. After a while he came to a pause before Campion's chair and stood looking down at him.

"I haven't any illusions, you know, Campion," he said at last. "I see the danger. *I've* got the wind up all right. But, if you don't mind me saying so, my business has trained me to keep a bit quieter about it than yours has. Also, of course, I'm not personally touched by it as you are. I'm not a fool, though. I've lived with it for over three weeks and I've had my mind working. It's a question of proof now, isn't it?"

"Practically." Mr. Campion met the other man's eyes and seemed to make the reservation unwillingly.

"You mean you don't actually *know*. Is that it?" Ferdie was merciless and Mr. Campion was forced to hedge badly.

"Well," he said, "since Val is so closely involved the police don't trust me entirely. Why should they? Then this row of my own broke on Friday and, frankly, I made a fool of myself, got tight and that sort of thing, and after the exhibition I put up I fancy the super may be wondering if I'm the white-headed boy after all. Still, I'm fairly well acquainted with police movements. Just now they're concentrating on the Hakapopulous pair. Inspector Pullen has worked it out that whoever murdered Miss Adamson must have known the restaurant very well or had at least used the back entrance before. They've decided that she was killed about eight in the evening. Just now he is spending his time trying to get the Greeks to identify photographs of everyone who has ever had anything to do with the poor wretched girl. Jock Hakapopulous is still as resilient as a sphere of solid rubber, but Andreas, I understand, is showing signs of wear and tear. Those two are holding out because of the accessory-after-the-fact charge, of course."

Ferdie perched himself on the edge of the table and the light behind his thin hair made his curls look forlorn and inadequate.

"Campion," he said quietly, "who do you think it is? Does your idea coincide with mine?"

Mr. Campion raised his weary eyes.

"That's a very delicate question," he murmured cautiously.

"Because it involves a friend of mine, you mean?" Ferdie's driving force was tremendous. The air seemed to quiver with it.

"Well, yes, there is that aspect, isn't there?"

"My dear chap"—the other man was exasperated—"I have many friends but I don't stand for 'em through thick and thin. I'm not super-human nor am I a sentimental bloody fool. What put you on?"

"A quotation from a letter of Sterne's," said Mr. Campion. He spoke dreamily and when his host stared at him went on, his tired voice precise and almost expressionless. "Lugg of all people produced it at four o'clock in the morning. All through this business I've been bewildered by a curious hand-of-fate quality which has pervaded the whole thing. I noticed it first when I found young Portland-Smith so very conveniently dead and yet lying in the one spot where no murderer could possibly have put him. I said something about it being 'like Providence' and Lugg suddenly produced the key. This is the quotation. It gives it to you in one. The truth is startlingly obvious when you consider it. 'Providence, having the advantage of knowing both the strengths and the weaknesses of men, has a facility for un-ostentatious organisation undreamed of by our generals.' It's a smart-type remark and just like a sophisticated parson, but it contains the key of this business. See it? 'Unostentatious organisation.' That's the operative phrase, while the recipe for same is given earlier: 'knowing both the strengths and the weaknesses.' That is how it was all done."

"My God, you've got it, Campion!" Ferdie was watching him with fascinated interest. "I think you're right. I thought you were three parts fool but I take it back. This is what I've been groping for. This explains *how*. Yes, I see it in the main, but I thought when you were talking yesterday you said that Portland-Smith's suicide was not in-tended?"

Mr. Campion rose.

"It wasn't," he said. "The intention was merely to get him out of the way of Georgia. He was round her feet. No one knew they were married, remember. You didn't yourself, even. In the beginning it was simply a little intrigue to break up an engagement of which Georgia was obviously tired and yet which, for some reason or other, she re-fused to dissolve. There was no great underlying scheme about it. It was just a little plot to end an unwise alliance. Portland-Smith was evidently nuts about the woman and I fancy the idea was either to get it into his head that he could never afford to marry her or, failing that, to get it into *her* head that he was unfaithful and not worth worrying about. Anyway, the original plan was merely to make a decisive sort of row between them. Unfortunately the 'unostentatious organisation' technique was not then perfected and, as with many beginners, the tendency was to work too large, while of course the unknown fact that the two were married altered the whole scale of the thing. However, it provides a fine example of the method itself. The recipe lies in the strengths and the weaknesses, remember. A frame-up was arranged. Portland-Smith was in love with Georgia and she was unkind. Therefore a girl who resembled Georgia had a chance with him. That was a weakness in him. He was a barrister and therefore unable to take any real advantage of the anonymity law, so that he was peculiarly susceptible to blackmail. That was another weakness. Of the two women employed to do the dirty work the elder, who arranged the whole thing and who in my opinion needed no more than to have the idea as a money-making scheme put up to her, had a passion for money and that particular type of mind which can see the sufferings of others and regard them without comprehension, seeing them only as an interesting spectacle. That in her was a strength. Unfortunately, however, the blindness which made it possible for her to have undertaken the project at all was too much for the scheme altogether. Unconscious of the effect she was really having on Portland-Smith, she hounded the poor beast to death, and her boss, the original perpetrator of the little row, found Georgia's unwanted fiancé permanently removed. Whether this astounding success encouraged him or not I don't like to think, but I imagine that, once one has accustomed oneself to the idea of causing death, the convenient finality of that means of disposing of an obstacle might outweigh all other considerations. Anyhow, when Ramillies became a howling nuisance, the 'unostentatious organisation' method was put into practice again. Again the strengths and the weaknesses of men were all carefully utilised. Ramillies was so afraid of flying that he believed in the perfectly preposterous story of a drug which would make him feel seedy for four hours and magnificent for twenty-four. That was a weakness. Caesar's Court is one of the few places in England where the organisation is so perfect that, should anything arise there which the manager desired to hush up, every possible facility for doing so could be instantly afforded him. That was a strength. Then there were interested government officials there who could lend their influence to avoid any scan-

dal if there seemed no real cause for one. That was the strength of
the occasion. It was all very prettily thought out. Think of the doctor.
Buxton-Coltness is an unmitigated snob and he was flattered by the
invitation to Caesar's Court and availed himself of it promptly. That
was a weakness in him. He is anxious to please all important people
and is in the peculiar position of having the kind of fashionable practice which permits him to take little risks which an ordinary G.P.
might hesitate about. That is a strength. See what I mean?"

"Yes, I do. You're right, thunderingly right." Ferdie was trembling
in his interest. "What about the last case?"

"Caroline? Oh, that was the same thing. I mean it was done in the
same way. But it was a murder of necessity. Caroline attempted to
blackmail her old colleague of the Portland-Smith business and, since
anything that involved that elder woman would of necessity also in-
volve the man, the old original god in the machine, she had to be
silenced. This time the strengths and the weaknesses were brilliantly
employed. He was becoming more experienced, I suppose. Caroline
needed money badly. She had no job, no protector. This need blinded
her to the tremendous danger of going alone to the Hakapopulous
restaurant. However, she had been there before with her colleague to
interview Portland-Smith and she thought she was going to meet a
woman, the woman who had stood by the telephone while the
wretched girl rang me up as a threat. Still, real need of money was
her weakness. Then the Hakapopulous brothers could not afford an
enquiry into their business. They were people who simply could not
risk a murder investigation on their premises. That was their weakness.
But their strengths were equally useful. Those two are crooks with
the real crook temperament which half enjoys a tremendous risk. Also
they are experienced. They've cleared up a mess and destroyed evidence before. Added to this, they're both used to police cross-exami-
nation and they know all the answers.

"There you are. That's how the whole thing was done: by brilliant,
unostentatious organisation. He organised his crimes and relied on the
strengths and the weaknesses of other people, none of whom had the
least idea of the way in which they were being used, to protect him.
The fact that he could do it shows the sort of chap he is: shrewd,
sophisticated, quite without conscience and probably under the impression that he's superhuman, in which respect he's insane, of
course."

His voice died away and there was silence in the room.

"The man's a genius," said Ferdie presently and sighed. "Look how he runs that place," he added. "What a pity, Campion. What a cracking pity!"

Mr. Campion lay back in his chair again. He looked exhausted. "Have you known this long?" he enquired at last.

"It's been forcing in on me for a bit. I've been afraid of it, yes. After all, when you're in the thick of a thing like this you can't help your mind working on it, can you?"

"Got any ideas?"

"I don't know. I've been thinking." Ferdie paused and looked at his visitor. "Forgive me, old chap, but I haven't really taken you seriously before. I've been working on an idea of my own. I didn't know *how* he'd done it, you see; all I knew was that he *must* have done it, and of course I saw why."

"You did? I didn't. I don't. That's the thing I don't understand now. I can't see why on earth he should get rid of two of Georgia's boy friends, one after the other, simply because she'd set her heart on someone new. It's not feasible. That's where the whole case goes to pieces and becomes fantastic."

Ferdie laughed softly.

"You haven't got the full story, old boy. You've got some of your facts wrong," he said. "All he did was to remove two men who were dangerous to Georgia's career. That was the thing Ramillies and Portland-Smith had in common. Damn it, Georgia's had plenty of love affairs which didn't end fatally! Look at that fellow Dell. Portland-Smith was a strong-minded chap who'd set his heart on being a county court judge. You never met him, did you? I did. I can't describe that chap. He was one of those pompous, pigheaded, thick-skinned fellows. You knew he'd get his own way if it was only by nagging for it or simply sitting next it until it became his by squatter's rights. You saw that in his eyes. If he hadn't been removed he'd have removed Georgia in the end. He just happened to be that sort of chap. Ramillies was a different bloke but just as dangerous. He was the 'scatty beaver' breed; you know, half-built dams in every square foot of stream. He wanted Georgia out on that swamp of his and when he got her there he played old Harry with her. Did you see her when she came back last time? Oh, terrible. Half frightened, half demoralised, figure going, God knows what. Ramillies was wild, you know, reckless, slightly crackers. He'd have ruined her if she'd stayed out there any length of time. Besides, she was terrified of him."

He hesitated.

"Just before the flight excitement he'd got some hold on her too, I fancy. I think he got some information out of that girl."

"Out of Caroline Adamson?"

"Yes, I think so."

"About the fleecing of Portland-Smith?"

"Yes. I imagine he was using it to get Georgia out to his infernal swamp and to keep her there for some time. At least that's what I think."

"I see." Mr. Campion's hollow eyes were hard. "But why?" he demanded. "Why this concern for Georgia and her career? Why Georgia?"

Ferdie slid off the table and walked down the room. He looked unhappy and embarrassed but there was still a hint of amusement on his shining rococo face.

"She's a considerable artist, you know," he said. "She makes a lot of money. He didn't see he was running any risk, and he wasn't until he had to wipe out Caroline. She's a valuable property, Campion; a great possession."

"To *him*?" Campion was insistent.

"I think Gaiogi Laminoff had better tell you about that himself, old boy," said Ferdie Paul. "Good heavens, haven't you ever looked at 'em?"

"Do you mean that she's his daughter?" Mr. Campion seemed taken completely off his balance.

"You talk to him, old boy," said Ferdie Paul.

There was a long pause during which Mr. Campion lay back in his chair, his face blank. Ferdie was more practical.

"Campion," he said suddenly, "look here, this is a jam. We're all in it. None of us want any more of a row than we can possibly help. I'm not asking you to shield anybody. That's too darned dangerous, I see that. But if we could avoid the worst it would at least be something. We might at least save ourselves the flood of dirt in the newspapers. Let's get hold of him. Let's get him up here and get the whole truth out of him and then put it to him plainly. He's up in the clouds. He doesn't see where he stands. I bet you he doesn't realise the danger. He's probably thinking about table decorations or illuminating the bed of the river by the swimming pool. His sense of proportion has gone to pot. If we got him here, in this room, and talked to him we could get the facts into his head."

Mr. Campion passed his fine hands over his face.

"Get him to sign something, you mean?" he said dubiously. "Sign something and go to Mexico or some other place uncovered by the extradition agreement?"

"Well, yes," said Ferdie slowly, "unless, of course, he has some

other idea. . . . After all, that would be better than the police way,"
he added defensively.

"I think perhaps we ought to see him," agreed Mr. Campion hesitantly. "Between us we've got quite enough to prove the truth to
him, if not to a jury. What did he use in that hypodermic on Ramillies? Did he get Caroline to do that? She may have swallowed the
whole story, as did Ramillies himself, of course. Women will believe
anything about medicine. It was a hell of a risk."

"I suppose it was. It all depends what it was. The police may never
find out."

"That's so, but they'll do their best." Mr. Campion spoke bitterly.
"They'll go round to our pet chemists, our doctors, our personal
friends, making what they consider are discreet enquiries, until no one
will give us so much as a packet of bicarbonate of soda without looking at us as if we were buying prussic acid. That's what I mean. The
police are so damnably thorough. Our lives won't be worth living."

Ferdie took a deep breath.

"We'll get him up here," he said. "After all, Campion, once the
police are satisfied about him they'll stop hounding the rest of us. We
must do it. There's no other way, is there?"

"We could try. Is he suspicious?"

"I'm not sure." Ferdie stood considering the practical aspects of
the project. Now that the moment had come it was he who took
command. Mr. Campion remained in his chair, his head sunk between
his shoulders, weary disillusionment in every line of his thin body.
"He's at home tonight," said Ferdie at last. "He rang me up just before you came. I don't think we'll beard him there. We don't want
a row down there if we can help it. We've all got too much precious
cash in the darned place. Look here, I'll go down now and fetch him.
You'd better not come. If he sees you he'll spot something. I'll bring
him back here and we'll have it out, alone, where we can't be disturbed. How's that?"

"I'll leave it to you." Mr. Campion sounded listless. "The Lagonda's
in the yard. You can take it if you like."

"My dear good chap, pull yourself together." Ferdie was reproachful. His own energy was boundless. All trace of his old lackadaisical
manner had vanished and he seemed possessed of an enthusiasm
which might have been undergraduate had it not been for its obviously nervous origin. "Never lend your car, your shoes or your girl
friend. I've got my bus in the garage. I say, Campion?"

"Yes."

"I think we're going to pull this off with luck."

"I hope so."

Ferdie stood looking at him.

"I don't want to offend you," he said, "but I'm an experienced sort of bloke, you know. I know a lot about women. That girl of yours is going to Sweden tomorrow, isn't she? Do you know what train?"

"They're going from Harwich. They'll motor over. It's not far from their place. It's the early boat, I think." Mr. Campion made the confidence unwillingly and Ferdie did not move. He made an odd, uncouth figure standing there looking down, a quizzical expression on his face.

"Send her some flowers."

Mr. Campion began to laugh. He laughed with savage amusement for quite a long time. Ferdie appeared hurt.

"Women like that sort of thing," he said.

"I'm sorry." Mr. Campion sat up. "Forgive me. It's got its damnably amusing side. In fact it's not a bad idea. If there was time I'd do it. I could phone them, of course, couldn't I?"

"Send some from the Court. They've got the best florist in England down there. I'll do it for you myself when I collect Gaiogi, if you like." Ferdie seemed completely oblivious of any incongruity in the two errands. "What will you have? Roses?"

"A pot of basil would be nice." Mr. Campion's interest in life seemed to have revived for an instant and his smile had a curious intensity of derision.

"You're a fool, you know." Ferdie was perfectly serious. "Send a straight armful of red roses and a card with a sentimental message down to the boat and it'll work miracles. Women are like that. Their minds run on those sort of lines. Give me the card and I'll send it with the flowers. She's sailing for Sweden from Harwich tomorrow early? That's all I need know. They'll do the rest. Her name's Fitton, isn't it? Right."

Mr. Campion took out his wallet and found a card.

"You think a message, do you?" he said, a trickle of amusement in his voice.

"I do, and not a rude one either." Ferdie was emphatic. "Say 'A happy journey, my dear' or something of that sort."

Mr. Campion wrote obediently and looked up, his pencil poised.

"You're an extraordinary chap, aren't you?" he said. "You keep your mind very mobile, what with one thing and another. A murderer to be apprehended here, an engagement to be patched up there. It's amusing how you find the time, really."

Ferdie took up the card.

"You're too conscious of the personal angles, my dear fellow," he said. "You let yourself be obsessed. 'Amanda—You'll never forget me—Albert.' That's all right. Bit didactic but not bad. You know the girl, after all. Very well then, I'll send the roses from the Court, collect Gaiogi and persuade him to come back here. We shall be back before eleven. You'll wait, will you? Good man. We'll put it to him."

He hurried out, and Mr. Campion, his plans made for him, was left alone with his thoughts. The room was very quiet and still cold and the noise of the traffic below sounded far away, a remote sea in another world. He heard the front door of the flat shut behind Ferdie and then, after a long pause, Mrs. Fitch came in.

She did not speak but moved quietly about the room, tidying up odds and ends, replacing books in their shelves and plumping up the cushions on the couch. There was an indefinable air of neatness about her, a suggestion of making all safe in her very walk, and a finality in the pat of her plump hands on the upholstery.

When she came to Campion's side in her tour of orderliness she looked down at his glass.

"You haven't touched your drink," she said. "Would you like a nice cup of tea?"

"No, thanks. I'm all right."

"You don't look it. Been to bed lately?"

"No, not for a night or two."

"What a pity you lost that girl." Mrs. Fitch had gone past him now and had reached the untidy muddle on the end of the sofa table. Her tone was conversational. "She was a nice little thing. No sense of humour but very good class. Pretty hair, too, but I don't expect you want to talk about her. Now look here, the whisky is there on the side. There's some gin and French and a little Advocaat and some more siphons in the cupboard underneath. If you want more glasses ring for them and the Jap will bring them in. There's plenty of cigarettes in that red box on the shelf."

"You're not staying to meet Gaiogi?" Mr. Campion put the question idly but she looked at him sharply, her glance unnecessarily square.

"No," she said. "No, I don't think so. I'll just get my coat and then I'm off."

He heard her giving some last instructions to the Japanese boy in the kitchen and then she popped in again, a dyed ermine coat hanging from her shoulders.

"Good-bye," she said.

"Good-bye. I'll give your love to Gaiogi, shall I, or haven't you for-given him?"

"I don't know what you're talking about." She was smiling at him boldly. "Gaiogi's always been very kind to me. I worked for him long ago at the Old Beaulieu. He was very generous to work for. Always putting me on to things. He's not a bad old stick."

"Yet he lost your money for you at the Poire d'Or. It was quite a packet, wasn't it? Two or three thousand pounds. Unlucky money."

She stared at him and for a moment he thought he was going to see her angry. Bright patches appeared in her cheeks and her mouth was pale round its make-up. Suddenly, however, she laughed and a flash of the insouciance which is the keystone of her profession ap-peared in her smile.

"I've learnt a thing or two since then, ducky," she said.

She did not display her hands but his eyes were drawn to them. They were ablaze with stones. Her square ugly neck was alight, too, and the clips on her dress shone with the unmistakable watery gleam of the true diamond.

"Well, I'm off," she said and paused abruptly as the phone began to ring. She took up the receiver and listened for a moment. "Yes, all right, all right," she said. "What's the matter? I see, dear. It's Mr. Paul," she added, holding the instrument out to Campion. "He wants you. Something seems to be up."

"Hullo, Campion, is that you?" Ferdie's voice sounded loud and unsteady in his ear. "I say, can you come down here at once? Yes, I'm at Caesar's Court. I've just arrived. Look here, I can't tell you over the phone because of the girl on the house exchange. You under-stand? You come down, will you? Yes, just as soon as you can. There's an unexpected development in that business we were discussing. Very unexpected. I don't know what we'd better do, quite. What's the name of that man you know at Scotland Yard?"

"Oates?"

"Yes. I wondered if I'd ring him and tell him to come down here. No, I tell you what, you come down yourself first and then we'll have a conference. Hurry, old man, won't you? It's a question of time, I'm afraid. You'll be down at once, will you? Righto. I won't do a thing till you come."

"What is it?" The woman put the question as he hung up the re-ceiver.

"I don't know." Campion sounded puzzled. "He seems upset about something. He wants me down there at once. I'd better go, I sup-pose."

"It's not like him to get windy," said Mrs. Fitch and led the way into the hall. As they went down the stairs together she sighed. "It's a nice old flat," she said. "Are you going by car?"

"Yes, I've got the bus down here."

"Give me a lift as far as Marble Arch, or aren't you going that way? It's just as quick this time of night. Would you mind?"

"Not at all." Mr. Campion seemed almost bored.

She scrambled into the front seat beside him and he swung the car out of the dark yard into the blazing Circus. He drove recklessly and she gripped the side.

"Here, don't break *my* neck," she said, laughing. "Put me down at the cinema, will you?"

"Got a date?" he enquired.

"You mind your own business," she said. "There we are. Pull right up. What do you expect me to do? Jump for it?"

"I'm sorry." He stopped outside the cinema and the commissionaire opened the door and helped the woman out. Her jewels flashed in the lamplight and he touched his cap respectfully at the tip she gave him.

"Well, good-bye," she shouted. "Cheer up."

Campion did not answer her but let in the clutch and swung out from the curb, missing a bus by inches.

The Lagonda continued her breathless speed through the town, which was enjoying a temporary lull in the traffic before the theatres closed. Campion sat at the wheel, the light from the dashboard shining up on his expressionless face. The hooded car was like a little quiet universe inside the larger world. It possessed the same atmosphere which had been so noticeable in Ferdie's flat, a cold loneliness, an air of going away. It seemed very doubtful if Mr. Campion was thinking at all. He drove brilliantly but apparently without interest and if he was consumed with a burning interest to discover what new disaster Ferdie might have brought to light in Gaiogi Laminoff's tight little kingdom he showed no sign of it.

He left London behind and travelled through those little townships which crowd on tiptoe round her skirts, jostling each other in their efforts to get close, and yet each retaining its essential characteristics, never merging either with a neighbour or with the mother city. He shot through Maidenhead at last and came swiftly into darker Berkshire. There was less than half a mile to go now. He had one long straight strip of tree-hung road, a dip and a humpbacked bridge, and then the turning and the long drive. This was Money's Acre: quiet reserves, well-kept grounds, protected reaches of river, here and there a little cottage like Amanda's built for working folk but dressed expensively and kept for pleasure, here and there a club or a discreet roadhouse, but country air and cool, unobscured starlit sky.

For the first time the Lagonda had the road clear. Nothing passed her and there was a gap in the oncoming traffic. He raced through the tree-hung stretch, bounced over the humpbacked bridge and slowed down for the turn. It was then, just at the moment when he was aware of the silence, of the lonely peace of his little world, dark in the midst of darkness, and when the brilliant lights of the Court sprang into sight through the shrouding elms, it was then that he felt the movement so close to him, so warm, so familiar and yet so horrible in its very intimacy. Someone was breathing on his neck.

He trod on the brakes and brought the car up with a scream and a jerk which stopped the engine and sent her slewing across the bend. The steering wheel caught him in the stomach and as he turned he saw for an instant the face captured by the upward ray of the dashboard light. The soft glow touched the unfamiliar under-curves, the nostrils, the insides of the arches of the eyes.

He did not speak. There was no time. The light glancing blow which, in the illegal science of the Kempo, has a very sinister name, touched the nerve centre behind his ear and he stiffened and slid forward. As Mr. Campion went out into the darkness a single thought ripped through his mind with the dazzling clarity of revelation: *This is why the knife went in at a right angle. This is why Caroline Adamson lay so still.*

CHAPTER TWENTY-THREE

The headlights of the Lagonda described a wide arc over the grey meadows and laid yellow fingers on the boles of fine old trees as the great car swung round and crept smoothly on to the main road again.

She took the quarter mile to the winding lane with the same swift efficiency which she would have afforded had her master been in command, passed the white gate through which Val and Dell had come up out of the green field together, and slid quietly to a standstill in the dark road outside Amanda's cottage. The lights went out and the engine died away.

It was a fine night with stars and a fine rain-promising wind. The flowers in the cottage garden nodded together like small white ghosts in the shadows and there were whispers in the grass and in the leafy billowings of the trees.

The small house waited with that forlorn secrecy which is the peculiarity of all empty houses. The windows shone like beetles where the starlight touched them and the chimneys showed squat and smokeless against the cloudless sky.

The door of the car opened noiselessly and a figure remained motionless, half in and half out of the driving seat, as the twin searchlights of a traveller on the highroad behind him climbed up to the stars, sank and disappeared again, leaving an inkier blackness behind.

The wind in the trees freshened and the whispering among the leaves grew more intense. The figure moved. It vanished behind the car, melted into the uncertain silhouette and reappeared an instant later on the other side. There was a moment of tremendous noise as the door catch clicked. The tiny alien sound seemed to silence the roar in the treetops, but there was no other movement. The cottage remained dead and the fussy wind busied itself about it caressingly.

There was a long pause which seemed interminable as the figure remained wedded inextricably to the black shadow which was the car. Afterwards came the sound of effort, breathing, muscles straining, and once the single scrunch of a shoe on the loose flint road. Then out of the larger shadow came the other one. It was monstrous, horrible, a nightmare shape, topheavy and enormous, limp arms flapping, the head of an elephant, and, when it turned, the great beak of a gigantic bird ending incongruously in a shoe, vividly describable against the holey curtain of the sky.

It advanced falteringly down the path until, outside the first window, it turned miraculously into two, a long figure on the ground and a thicker one bending over it.

There was the thin, alarming sound of splintering glass, then another pause while the whole world seemed to listen, then breathing again and the swift rattle of a window sash and a scrambling sound as the upright figure pressed into the darkness of the house and was swallowed by it.

The night grew older. The wind dropped and sprang up again. On the highroad headlights climbed to heaven and shied away again. Down in the river an otter swam by and a rat paddled about in the mud. Amanda's house crouched beside the figure on the path. They were both very quiet, very lonely, very dead.

The little creak which the door made as it swung open was the creak of wood and started no shuddering questions in the night. A cedar by the field path opposite creaked back in answer.

The breathing had begun again and once more the monster rose up out of the blackness and there was the clatter of a heel on tiles. The door swung wide and the night rushed into the little house, carrying dust and a crumpled leaf or two and a white petal in its surging drapery, which floated over the tea-chest clock, brushed the Van Gogh and scattered the papers on the desk. The monster struggled on. Safe within protecting walls, it was less cautious. It moved more quickly and when it cannoned into the table ledge it whispered an imprecation. The door of the kitchenette stood open and a circle of glowing blue beads on the top of the stove cast just enough light to show the way in. The monster stooped under the lintel and bowed to the ground.

For a long time there was swift movement in the kitchen. Gloved hands fastened the small window and drew both blinds and curtains. The heavy mat was kicked up over the crack beneath the door and finally the inner door, through which the night still poured, exploring every corner in silent busyness, was closed and the blackness was almost complete.

The man lit a match and found the light switch. Mr. Campion lay on the floor. He was breathing regularly and his fair hair was tousled. He looked as if he were sleeping after being very tired. The man who bent over him laid a finger on his pulse and straightened himself immediately. Then he replaced his glove and turned off the lighted gas jet. Evidently time was precious, for he completed his arrangements hurriedly. He stripped off Campion's jacket, folded it into a pad and opened the oven door.

The shining cupboard was partitioned with iron shelves and he removed them hastily, stacking them carefully beside the sink. He arranged the pad carefully over the sharp edge of the oven's iron surround and returned to the man on the floor. It was not an easy operation to force the head and one shoulder into that tiny cavity while maintaining a fairly natural position but he accomplished it presently and settled the long thin legs with care, drawing up one knee under the body and pulling the loose trouser cuff into a likely fold.

He turned on the gas tap almost as an afterthought and stood back to look at his handiwork while the thirty jets poured choking death into the tiny space. The man he was going to kill stirred. He breathed deeply and at one time seemed to be struggling to rise. Once, even, he spoke. The thick voice was the first human sound in the cottage and it set the walls quivering, but the rushing gas was louder. It swelled up into a roar, a cascade, a relentless torrent of whispering noise. The body on the floor grew still again, the muscles relaxed, and the leg which had been drawn up slithered a little.

The man who stood watching with a handkerchief pressed over his nose drew a visiting card out of his waistcoat pocket and looked at the scribbled message it bore.

"Amanda—You won't forget me—Albert."

It seemed miraculously appropriate and he folded it in two and tucked it into the livid hand which lay across Mr. Campion's breast.

In his mind's eye he saw the headlines on the morrow. "Suicide after Broken Engagement." "Tragic Discovery in Lady Amanda Fitton's Riverside Cottage." That was the strength of the Press; it jumped to the obvious scandal in all scandals. That was the weakness of the Earl of Pontisbright's position; any scandal in his family *was* a scandal. Mr. Campion had taken his broken heart badly; that had been his weakness. The Lady Amanda Fitton was of sufficient social importance for everyone concerned to sympathise with her youth and to hurry through the inquest, with its inevitable verdict, as swiftly and decently as possible; that was her strength.

Now, however, it was still the time to hurry. The Lagonda in which the cinema commissionaire had seen Mr. Campion leave Marble Arch alone must remain where it was, a silent witness for the next passer-by to note, but Caesar's Court was less than ten minutes by the field path. He took a last look round, satisfied himself that there was no betraying sign for the first inquisitive police constable to observe, and moved quietly to the light switch.

His fingers were actually on the bakelite when he noticed the phenomenon which sent the blood streaming into his face and passed a white-hot hand over his head and spine. The door to the living room, which was not a foot away from him, was opening inwards, very slowly, and even as he stared at it the stubby nose of a police revolver crept quietly round the jamb.

At the same instant there was a commotion behind him as the food cupboard burst open, as heavy footsteps sounded in the room above, as the garden door was flung wide, as the whole house burst into sudden swarming life, and a young voice, savage with indignation, sounded clearly in his very ear.

"If you've killed the old man I'll never forgive you, Ferdie Paul," said Amanda Fitton.

CHAPTER TWENTY-FOUR

"Perhaps you'd care to be sick, sir," said the plain-clothes man help-fully.

Mr. Campion declined the invitation gracefully, and Amanda grinned at him. On the other side of the room Mr. Lugg, still padding about in stockinged feet, turned away from the Van Gogh, which seemed to fascinate him, and leant over the superintendent's chair.

"He put a lot of faith in that solicitor of 'is, didn't 'e?" he remarked. "It'll take more than a lawyer to explain that fancywork in the kitchen. No wonder the pore little legal gent looked a bit on 'is dig. It's cost the country a mint o' money, too. That'll pile it on for Mr. Paul. Still, a very nice police turnout; I will say that. If you'd done a murder, cock, you couldn't 'ave bin looked after better. Busies 'ere, busies round the Sovereign watching Mr. Paul hang about the theatre until it was time to do 'is bit of telephoning from a call box, busies in the yard watching Mr. Paul gettin' in the back of the Lagonda, busies phoning up the report, busies on motorcycles, busies at Caesar's Court, busies all round the perishin' country. And yet 'e might 'ave spiked you in that car. I don't blame you for drivin' so fast. Still, you would do it. I 'ad a look at you first thing to see if you was dead."

"They kept as near the car as they dared." Oates looked across at Campion apologetically. "You seemed fairly safe while you were go-ing at that pace. I didn't think he'd attack you, for his own sake. And don't you talk so much," he added, glancing round at Lugg. "Mr. Campion asked for police protection and I gave it to him. The way you tell the story it sounds as if we were all agents provocateurs."

"I knew he'd come here." Hal Fitton spoke from the fireplace. "Amanda and I were both convinced of it. I actually saw him take the idea yesterday. You handed it to him on a plate, of course. I thought you were going to overdo it with that river business. He's pretty shrewd."

"He's so sharp he cut hisself." Sergeant Flood could not resist the observation and hoped the lateness of the hour would excuse the breach of discipline.

"That's it exactly," said Amanda, beaming at him. "That's what we hoped. What will you do now? Will the Hakapopulous brothers split?" Oates rose.

"They might," he said. "They'd recognise Mrs. Fitch anyway. Still,

I don't think we shall have to bother much about him. He's a sick man. He may not even come to trial."

"That's what put you on to him, isn't it?" Hal glanced at Campion. Now that he had shelved his tremendous dignity of the previous afternoon his youth was very apparent.

Mr. Campion stirred himself. He looked ill and exhausted.

"Oates found it," he said. "He had the list of people Ferdie Paul had seen in Paris and one of them was Doctor Peugeot, the great diabetic biochemist. That explained a lot. If Ferdie Paul was an insulin-taking diabetic the death of Ramillies ceased to be so much of a mystery. It also explained why he was so happily convinced that he was perfectly safe."

"It's indetectable, is it?"

"Practically. A blood-sugar test must be taken within five minutes of death to trace anything unusual even. That's what I meant when I said he'd slipped into it, Oates. It was so abominably simple for him. Once Ramillies had confessed his fear of flying to him, all Ferdie Paul had to do was to tell him the kind of tale he wanted to hear. He had the method of killing in his hand twice a day. He knew enough of Ramillies' character to realise that the man would hang on until the last minute and finally give way, and he prepared accordingly. He backed his judgment as to what the other man would do. After all, that's the basis of most business methods. If Ramillies hadn't been really so frightened, or if he had been a stronger character, he wouldn't have gone creeping round to Ferdie at the eleventh hour and the scheme would have fallen through. Ferdie put his money on the chance that Ramillies was the sort of man he thought he was, and he happened to be right. I should think he gave him a dose of about two hundred D.S. units and after that nothing could have saved him, unless someone had spotted the condition and dosed him up with some sort of vasopressin, Tonephin or something. As it was, of course, the wretched Ramillies had no idea he was dying."

"Paul's a peculiar sort of chap." The old superintendent was buttoning himself into his coat as he spoke. It was nearly dawn and there was a cold mist over the water meadows. "He's got exalted ideas of his own importance. A lot of them have. It's the commonest type of what you might call the 'elaborate' killer. I've seen it before. George Joseph Smith was one of them. They honestly think a bit of their cash or a bit of their convenience is worth someone else's life. I don't suppose we shall ever know the full ins and outs of the motive, shall we?"

"We do. He told me." Mr. Campion was battling with sleep. "I'll come up in the morning and make a full report. He gave me the whole motive so frankly that I sat there with my eyes popping; terrified out of my life he was going to do me in on the spot. He told me the full truth and fastened it on to Gaiogi Laminoff with a single magnificent lie. Who are Georgia Wells's parents, by the way?"

"She's only got a father," said Amanda, who knew everything, as usual. "He runs a touring company in Australia and is a bit low, so Georgia keeps him dark. She sends him all her press cuttings. Ferdie didn't try to palm Georgia off on Gaiogi, did he? The poor little man can't be more than fifty-five. Did he?"

"He hardly committed himself." Mr. Campion spoke wearily. "It was in character, though. He told Ramillies the truth, you know, except for the one stupendous lie."

" 'After four hours you'll feel fine,' " said Amanda. "He had a sort of sense of humour, but not very kind. What about the woman? Will she stick to him? I wonder."

Mr. Campion glanced at Oates, whose thin lips curled sourly.

"I don't think we shall hear of her again," he said. "She was on her way when Mr. Campion left her at the cinema to come here. I've seen her sort before. They're not a wholly bad lot, but they get sort of used to looking after themselves. Paul knew that better than anyone. Oh, he said one funny thing, Campion. He gave me a message for you. I nearly forgot it. He said: 'Tell Campion it's interesting to see his recipe works both ways.' What did he mean by that?"

"The strengths and the weaknesses of man." Mr. Campion laughed and there was genuine regret in his tone. "He forgot the catch in it, poor lunatic," he said. "It's Providence who has the advantage. The rest of us haven't the divine facility for correct diagnosis. Providence would hardly have fallen for our broken hearts, for instance."

"Talking of our broken hearts," said Amanda when the last of the company had departed and the Earl of Pontisbright was assisting Mr. Lugg to make beds upstairs, "where is my ring? It was Aunt Flo's, you know, and the stones are thought to be real if not large."

Mr. Campion turned out all his pockets and discovered the missing token. Amanda stood balancing it in the palm of her hand and he looked up at her.

"Go on. Put it on. I'll be happy to marry you if you care for the idea," he said. "And then when I'm fifty, and feeling like a quiet life, you'll go and fall with a thud for some silly chap who'll give us both hell."

Amanda hesitated. She looked very young indeed, her red hair standing out like an aureole.

"Cake love, you mean?" she said dubiously.

"Call it what you like." He sounded irritable. "The only thing is, don't pretend that it doesn't exist or that you're immune."

Amanda regarded him with great affection.

"Cake makes some people sick," she remarked cheerfully. "I'll tell you what we'll do: we'll pop this tomorrow and buy some apples."

He brightened.

"And comfort ourselves," he said. "That's an idea. Do you know, Amanda, I'm not sure that 'Comfort' isn't your middle name."

Traitor's
Purse

This book is for
P. Y. C.

CHAPTER ONE

The muttering was indistinct. It crept down the dark ward, forcing itself upon the man who lay in the patch of light at the far end of the vast room.

It was a pleasant muttering. It made a reassuring undercurrent below the worry, that terrifying anxiety which was thrusting icy fingers deep into his diaphragm.

He tried to concentrate on the muttering. Mercifully it was recognizable. There were two distinct voices and when he could catch them the words meant something. That was good. That was hopeful.

In a little while the words might start connecting and then, please God, he would learn something and this appalling fear would recede.

From where he lay he could just see a wedge of polished floor, a section of a neat empty bed, and a tall shrouded window, fading into complete darkness at the top where the shaded light over his own head was too faint to reach it. All these were entirely unfamiliar. He was not even sure that he was in a hospital. That was part of the whole situation. He knew what a hospital was; that was comforting. They were large grey buildings, made grimly gay by enormous posters announcing scarifying debts. The recollection of those placards cheered him up. He could still read; he was sure of that. Sometimes one couldn't. Sometimes on these occasions one could only recognize spoken words. That was an odd piece of information to remember now. His mind was clear enough as far as it went . . . as far as it went.

He concentrated on the muttering. It was a long way away. They must be just outside the farther door up there in the darkness. The woman was a nurse, of course. The discovery delighted him foolishly. He was getting on. At any moment now other obvious things must occur to him.

He had no idea who the man was, but his rumble was human and friendly. He settled himself to listen.

"I shan't question him myself, you know." He heard the man's words with mild interest.

"I daresay not." She sounded acid. "It's very serious indeed. I wonder they left him alone with us here. It's not very nice."

"There's no need to worry about that, Miss." The rumble was aggrieved. "I'd like a quid for every one I've handled. He'll be quiet enough, you'll see. Probably he won't even remember what's happened—or he'll say he doesn't until he's seen a lawyer. They're like that nowadays, up to anything."

The man in bed lay very still. The muttering had ceased to be so comforting. He forgot to be glad that it was coherent. He listened avidly.

"They'll hang him, I suppose?" said the nurse.

"Bound to, Miss." The man was both apologetic and definite. "It was one of us, you see, so there's no way of getting out of it. Once a man slugs an officer of police he's for it. It's a necessary precaution for the safety of the public," he added, not without satisfaction. "This chap had all that money on him, too. That'll take a bit of explaining on its own."

"All I can say it's very unpleasant." The nurse crackled a little after she had spoken and the man in bed thought she was coming in. He closed his eyes and lay rigid. There were no footsteps, and presently she spoke again.

"It seems very strange here without any patients," she said and laughed a little unnaturally, as if she recognized the ghostliness of the great empty wards. "We're only a skeleton staff left behind to deal with emergencies like this. We're the one hospital in the town cleared for action in case of anything. All our regulars have been evacuated. I don't know how they're all getting on in the country, I'm sure."

"My missus and the kids are in the country," said the policeman unexpectedly. "It keeps me short and she's lonely. . . ." His voice died away into a murmur of confidence and at the other end of the ward the man in bed opened his eyes again.

Slugging a policeman. He knew what that meant, whatever condition his mind was in. That was pretty serious. It was so serious that it made him sweat.

He had had nightmares like that and he'd known policemen. Now he came to consider the matter it seemed to him that he had known policemen very well and had liked them.

What on earth had happened to him? The bobby outside had just said that he might not remember anything about it. Well, he didn't. He didn't remember anything about anything. That was the anxiety, or part of it. He did not remember anything at all. There was only that secret worry, that gnawing, fidgeting, terrifying anxiety, beyond any consideration of his personal safety; that awful half-recollected responsibility about fifteen. Fifteen. He had no idea what the figure signified. That part had gone completely. But it was both urgent and vital: he did know that. It towered over the rest of his difficulties, a great dim spirit of disaster.

Now, to add to everything else, he was going to be hanged for slugging a policeman. He might have slugged him too; that was the devil of it. Anyhow, there was that fool bobby talking to a nurse about it as if it were a foregone conclusion. They expected him to call in a solicitor, did they? A fine chance he had of helping any solicitor to make a case, he who didn't even know his own name!

Moved by indignation and the odd singleness of purpose symptomatic of his condition, he got out of bed.

He moved very quickly and naturally, still partly wrapped in the shrouding comfort of semi-consciousness, and therefore made no noise at all.

He chose the nearest door, since even he recognized the prudence of avoiding the mutterers, and his bare feet were silent on the tiles of the passage. It was a wide corridor, clean and yet ill lit because the bulbs were shaded heavily and cast separate circles of light on the gleaming floor.

It was in one of these circles that he saw the hairpin. He stooped to pick it up mechanically and the wave of dull pain which swept over him as he bent down frightened him. This was a fine kettle of fish. What was going to happen now? He was going to pass out, he supposed, and be dragged back and hanged for slugging a policeman. God Almighty, what a position!

The tiles, striking cold on his bare soles, pulled him together a little, and he became aware for the first time that he was undressed and the coarse hospital pyjamas were his only covering.

He glanced at the row of shining doors on his left. At any moment one of these might open and Authority emerge. It would be a dreadful supercilious Authority, too, properly clothed and antipathetic.

It was a real nightmare. This idea seemed feasible and he seized on it gratefully. The conviction relieved him of a great deal of worry. For one thing, it did not matter so much that his brain was so unreliable.

All the same, even in dreams certain problems are urgent and it was obvious that some sort of clothes were imperative if he were to have a dog's chance with the lurking Authority behind those shining doors.

He glanced round him anxiously. The walls were as bare as an empty plate save for the fire-buckets, and the alcove beneath that crimson row escaped him until he was upon it, and then the glimpse of the red-rimmed glass case within jerked him to a standstill. He stood before the cupboard transfixed. There was the usual paraphernalia inside. A black oilskin coat hung at the back and the toes of a pair of thigh-boots showed just beneath it, while the hose was draped round the ensemble in neat heraldic festoons.

The man in pyjamas ignored the invitation printed on the enamelled plate requiring him to break the glass. Instead he concentrated on the keyhole in the smooth red wood. When he lifted his hand to touch it he rediscovered the hairpin and a warmth of satisfaction spread over him. So it was one of those merciful dreams in which things came out all right—that was, if it worked.

He had no time to speculate on his own somewhat peculiar accomplishments. The bent wire flicked over the lock easily, as if he had done it a hundred times. The absence of oilskin trousers bothered him, but the boots were tremendous. They came well up over his thighs and the coat had a belt which took off and could be slipped through the boot-loops. The sou'-wester cap which fell out of the ensemble struck him as amusing, but he put it on and buttoned the coat up to his throat with deep relief.

Any incongruity in the costume did not occur to him. He was still moving with the simple directness of emergency. There was danger behind him and something tremendously important ahead. He was going away from the one and approaching the other. It appeared both sensible and elementary.

The row of doors still remained closed. There was no sound anywhere and no draught. The corridor was blank and quiet, but all the same it breathed. It was alive. He had no illusions about that. Wherever he was, whoever he was, drunk, mental, or dreaming, he was still wide awake enough to be able to tell a live building from an empty one. There were people about all right.

The door of the case imperfectly closed swung open again and startled him as it touched him. That was no good. That would give him away at once. If that crackling nurse put her head out of the ward that would be the first thing her pince-nez would light on. He thrust it back into its place, using far more force than he had intended. The thin glass splintered easily. The gentle clatter it made on the tiles was almost musical, but the automatic bell, which he had failed to notice above the case, was a different matter.

It screamed at him, sending every nerve in his body tingling to the roots of his hair. It bellowed. It raved. It shrieked, tremblingly hysterical in the night, and from every side, above him, and beneath him, other bells echoed it in a monstrous cacophony of alarum.

CHAPTER TWO

The building was alive all right. His senses had not deserted him. Doors swung open, rushing feet swept down on him, cries, sharp demands for information, raised anxious voices, they whirled round his head like bees from an overturned hive.

He ran for it, with his oilskin coat flapping and scraping round his hampered limbs. He passed the lift cages and sped on to the staircase. As he reached the second landing he collided with an elderly man in a white coat, who caught his sleeve.

"Can't wait, sir." The words escaped him as he wrenched himself free. "Look after your patients," he shouted as an afterthought as he took on the next flight.

Meanwhile the blessed bells continued. Their shrill clamour was inspiring. If only they kept it up until he made the ground.

He arrived in the main entrance hall sooner than he expected. Here too there was wild excitement. Someone had lowered most of the lights so that the large double doors could be thrown open, and a porter was exhorting everyone in sergeant-major tones to go quietly.

The man in the oilskins plunged across the tiled floor, guided instinctively by the nearest blast of cold air. A nurse stepped aside for him and a doctor touched his shoulder.

"Where is it, fireman?"

"Round the back. No danger. Keep them quiet. No danger at all." He succeeded in sounding wonderfully authoritative, he noticed. He had almost reached the threshold of the emergency doors when a girl slipped in front of him. As he dodged round her she spoke quietly.

"Is it by the gate?" she inquired idiotically.

He glanced at her over his shoulder and received a momentary impression of a heart-shaped face and disconcertingly intelligent brown eyes.

"The fire's at the back, Miss. Nothing serious," he said briefly and passed on.

It was a completely meaningless encounter and the girl might well have been half-witted for all he knew, but she left an uncomfortable doubt in his mind and he dived out into the darkness eagerly.

It was not a pitch-black night. There was a moon behind the thin coverlet of clouds and, as soon as his eyes became accustomed to the change, the shadowy greyness of the darkened town became fairly negotiable.

The scene meant nothing to him. He was in a large semi-circular drive in which a dozen cars were parked, while beyond roofs and spires rose up in velvet silhouette against the lighter sky.

He took the nearest car. It seemed the wisest thing to do at the time, although he had some difficulty in managing the controls, hampered as he was by the mighty boots. Still, the little runabout started and he took her gently down the slope to the open gates. He turned east when he reached the high road, mainly because it seemed more likely to be lucky than the other direction, and, treading hard on the accelerator, he rattled on down the dim ribbon of asphalt which was just visible in front of his single hooded headlight.

He had picked a terrible car. The discovery was particularly disconcerting because he fancied he was in the habit of driving something different altogether. Not only was this uncomfortable little machine cramped, but the steering was alarming, with a full turn play on the wheel at least, while somewhere behind him a suggestive clanking was growing noticeably louder.

The road, which was broad and lined with dim houses set back behind overgrown shrubberies, was quite new to him. It might have been any road in England for all he knew. There was no traffic and no street lamps. He drove anxiously, coaxing the unresponsive machine to further effort. Now it was a real nightmare, the familiar kind, in which one struggles down a dark tunnel with terror behind one and feet which become more and more laden at every step.

He had travelled half a mile or so before he met another vehicle and it was with relief that he saw a pair of darkened sidelights swaying down the road towards him. They turned out to belong to a bus. The interior was darkened, but as it came up with him he caught a glimpse of the dim number over the cab. It was a 15. The sight jolted him and for an instant recollection rushed at him in a great warm sweep of bright colours, only to recede again, leaving him desperate. Something was frighteningly urgent and important. There was something he had to do instantly and the responsibility concerned was tremendous.

For a moment he had had it almost within his brain's grasp and yet now it was all gone again, all lost. What he did know was bad enough, he recollected with something of a shock. The police were after him, apparently for murder. The clanking at the back of the car ceased to be ominous and became downright sinister. At any moment now the big-end must go and he would find himself stranded in the suburbs of an unknown town where his present costume would damn him the instant he was seen.

It was at this point that he became aware of the car behind. There was no way of telling its size or make, for its single eye was as dim and downcast as his own. He pulled in a little to allow it to pass, but the driver behind made no attempt to overtake and appeared to be content to keep at a distance of twenty-five yards or so. This was definitely alarming.

He estimated that he was doing a little over forty miles an hour at the outside, although from the way his machine was heaving and rolling her speed might well have been nearing three figures. Cautiously he slackened speed a trifle. The car behind slowed also and at the same time the death-rattle in his own back axle increased noticeably.

A smile of pure amusement twisted the mouth of the thin man in the oilskins. This was so disastrous that it was ridiculous. This was attempted cat burglary on roller-skates. The odds against him were immeasurably too great. He had no chance even to run for it in these colossal boots.

A side turning yawning in the darkness on his left decided him and he swung round into it for a final spurt. The driver behind him overshot the corner and a flicker of hope flashed through his mind, but before he had reached the next road junction the following car was back on his trail again.

The open country took him by surprise. The hospital must have been nearer the outskirts of the town than he had imagined. It was coming now, he supposed as he drove down a tunnel of bare trees into the lonely darkness beyond. They must make their arrest at any moment now, and he prepared himself for them to shoot past him and stop. But meanwhile there seemed no point in pulling up himself and he continued on through deeply wooded country with his silent attendant just behind him.

As the minutes passed his resignation gave place to nervous irritation and he drove squarely in the middle of the road. Whenever a convenient turning presented itself he took it, but always his companion followed him. If he eluded the car for a moment or so by some adroit piece of driving, invariably it put on speed and caught up with him again.

He seemed to travel for hours, even for weeks. It was bitterly cold and his mind, which was in darkness save for the one single pinpoint of illumination which was the immediate present, appeared to him for the first time as a machine independent of himself and about as unsatisfactory as the car he drove.

The dreadful thudding between the back wheels was now deafening. His speed had slackened considerably also and the engine was missing on at least one cylinder. A sudden dip in the road was his undoing. He hit the watersplash at the bottom without seeing it and a wall of spray rose up over him, rushed in through the radiator and obscured the windscreen. The engine coughed apologetically and died.

He sat where he was. After the crashing of the big-end the silence was sweet but uncanny. He waited. Nothing happened.

The clouds had cleared a little and in the moonlight he could see on either side of him low hedges, and beyond, the dark spikes of an osier bed. There was not a breath of wind, not a rustle. It was as still and cold as the bottom of the sea.

He turned his head cautiously and peered through the rear window. The other car was in its familiar place, a few yards behind him. It too was stationary and there was no telling who sat behind that single downcast headlamp.

Then, as he watched it, the car began to move. Very slowly it crawled down the road behind him, turned its long sleek body gently to one side, and, entering the water so quietly that there was hardly a ripple, it came up close to him so that the driving seat was on a level with his own.

CHAPTER THREE

The side windows of the two cars slid down simultaneously and the man in the fireman's coat braced himself to meet whatever was coming.

"Would you care for a lift by any chance?"

The question, put with a certain grave politeness, came quietly out of the darkness in a clear young voice which might have belonged to some nice child.

"Do you know where we are? We're relying on you. I hope you realize that."

The second voice, which was elderly and querulous besides being practically in his ear, startled half the life out of him, it was so close.

"Driving at night is difficult at the best of times," it rambled on hollowly, "and night comes so early this time of year. I must have hunted over this country as a young man, but that's many years ago. Many. I don't know what road we're on at all."

After a moment's incredulous silence the explanation of this apparent hallucination occurred to the fugitive with a second shock. Whoever these good people were they either knew him or his car very well indeed. He replied cautiously, relying on his voice to identify him or not as the case might be.

"I'm afraid this car has died," he said clearly and waited for their reaction.

"With a beautiful smile on its bonnet, no doubt." The young voice sounded gently reproachful. "Do you mind getting in the back? Mr. Anscombe is in the front with me. We shall all be rather late for dinner, I'm afraid, and I've phoned Lee once. Leave George's car where it is."

The man who could not remember pricked up his ears. There had been definitely a warning emphasis on the Christian name.

"Our George has a depraved taste in machinery," he remarked tentatively as he clambered out of the farther door and came round to the back of the second car. When he entered the warm darkness of the limousine the girl gave him the hint for which he had asked.

"It's not George's taste, poor child. It's his pocket," she said firmly. "Er—all undergraduates are a little trusting when confronted by a second-hand car salesman, aren't they? Still, it was very nice of him to lend it to you. I'm so sorry I missed you. I was waiting in the vestibule and only caught a glimpse of you as you shot through and you'd started off in George's car before I could catch you."

She let in the clutch as she spoke and they moved away into the darkness.

"I'm sorry, too. Very silly of me," murmured the man in the oilskins. He was feeling his way very cautiously. Clearly they were on dangerous ground and now was not the time for explanations. Whoever this blessed girl was she was certainly helpful and appeared to rely on him to play up to her.

He leant back among the cushions and strained his eyes in the darkness. Gradually he made out the two silhouettes against the windscreen. The girl was small but erect and the line of her shoulders was square, like a boy's. Of course! She was the young woman with the heart-shaped face and the disconcertingly intelligent light brown eyes who had spoken to him in the hospital vestibule. She must have been trying to tell him that this car was by the gate. No wonder she was treating him now as if he were mentally deficient. So he was, God help him. So he was.

The man who sat beside her was less definite in outline. He appeared to be a spreading bundle with a large head adorned by a flat cap which sat upon it like a lid. He turned presently and leant over the back.

"Rather a disturbing adventure," he remarked conversationally. His windy voice was old and foolish but it was also dangerously inquisitive.

The man in the back of the car hesitated.

"It was, in a way," he said at last.

"I know. I know." The old man was determined to talk, whatever the effort. "Still, you did your duty. There's a great comfort in that. Probably the only thanks you'll get out of it. A Good Samaritan . . ."

"Is his own reward," supplied the girl without moving her head. "All the same," she went on carefully, "I don't see what else you could have done. After all, if a stranger is polite enough to talk to one in a railway carriage and nutty enough to fall over one's bag and stun himself in getting out the least one can do is to take him to hospital."

"I can think of less," said the old man, grunting into his muffler. "Can't you, Campion?"

"Yes, yes, I can." The man in the back of the car was not thinking what he was saying. Campion. He seized on the name eagerly and tried to think that it was familiar. At first he was convinced that it was, and relief rushed over him. But the next moment he was not sure again and despair returned. It was an unnerving experience and he felt for a cigarette.

Finding that he had no pockets, he leant forward automatically and discovered in the dark a packet and a lighter tucked into the case at the back of the front seat. He was actually smoking before he realized the significance of his behaviour. He must have known the cigarettes were there. He had taken one as naturally as if he had done it a hundred times before. The explanation was obvious. He had. He was in his own car.

He lay back to think it over. His head was abominably sore but his mind was clear. It was only his memory which had deserted him and, if he could not remember, at least he could put together what facts he had.

The one clear conclusion to be drawn from present developments, he decided, was that he and the girl were up to something—or at least she certainly was. She was protecting him the whole time, feeding him with story after story and doing it very well, almost as though she were used to it. Perhaps she was.

The conviction that she was his wife came slowly. The more he thought of it the more likely it became. Here she was, driving his car, looking after him like a mother, lying for him like a heroine. George's car indeed! For the first time since he had recovered consciousness in the hospital ward he saw a ray of comfort in his prospect. The abysmal loneliness of his position was spanned. Apart from his tremendous relief he was also suddenly delighted and he peered at her again in the darkness.

She drove very well, with confidence and with an unusual sympathy for the machine. He appreciated that. So many people approached the petrol engine as if it were something vindictive, to be mastered with daring and a firm hand. He liked her voice too. It was clear and well bred, without being affected, and it was also engagingly immature. Her face he could only just remember from his brief glimpse of her in the entrance hall of the hospital, but he liked the carriage of her head and the courage and dignity in those small square shoulders.

His spirits rose. If she were his wife he was all right. It had gone through his mind once or twice that he might be a crook of some sort. The notion had so depressed him that he was inclined to discount it as unlikely on those very grounds. But he had opened the fire cupboard with the hairpin and there had been that mysterious remark about money made by the bobby to the nurse. Why should it have looked odd when he had been found with a lot of money on him? Why should the authorities have taken it for granted that he had slugged a policeman? Had anyone seen him do it? Had he done it? He did not feel a particularly violent man. What sort of person was he, anyway?

The final question pulled him up with a start. He had no idea. Physically he appeared to be fairly tall and he was thin. He had plenty of hair and his teeth were his own. Without a mirror he could tell no more.

His impression of the girl was that she was young, perhaps very young, and he considered the question of his own age thoughtfully. He was fit and, apart from a natural shakiness after his experience, which, whatever it had been, had left him with aching limbs and a reeling head, he felt fairly athletic. He wondered. He was clearly not a boy but, on the other hand, surely he was not old? Finally he plumped for twenty-nine. It was a nice age anyhow and he felt no more.

He began to feel better, almost adventurous. The big car was brushing aside the miles and he had half persuaded himself that the police-slugging episode was part of some past delirium when the elderly man stirred himself.

"I see where we are now," he said contentedly. "We must have come fifteen miles out of our way." He broke off abruptly and laughed, the silly little high-pitched giggle of a foolish old man. "I mean five miles, of course," he added clumsily. "I don't know what made me say fifteen."

The man who had been told that his name was Campion glanced up sharply in the darkness and the shadowy tide of anxiety rolled up into his mind once more.

"It's not far now, anyway." The girl's cool voice was comfortingly matter-of-fact. "If you don't mind, Mr. Anscombe, we'll put you down at your house and rush on to change. Aubrey has put the meal back to eight-thirty and we can't in all decency be late. We'll see you there, shan't we?"

"Yes, yes, I shall be there." The old man sounded enthusiastic. "I never miss an opportunity to dine at the Institute now that Aubrey is the skipper. I remember his predecessor, the great Doctor Hale. He was an able fellow but nothing like Aubrey. Lee Aubrey is one of the big men of our time."

"Yes," said the girl thoughtfully. "Yes, I think he may be. He's not afraid to surround himself with brains."

Anscombe grunted. "A particularly brilliant man on his own account," he announced didactically. "We were more than lucky to get him here at Bridge. I remember the famous session when his appointment was announced to the Secret Conclave. As Hereditary Secretary to the Society I was very much congratulated, but I said 'Don't thank me, Masters of Bridge'—that's the customary address, you know— 'Don't thank me. Thank the man himself for coming to us.'"

He settled himself in his seat and sighed. It was clear to Campion that he was talking of matters very near his heart. Pride and more than a touch of pomposity glowed from him.

Anscombe? The name meant nothing to Campion. But Bridge, and the Institute, struck a vaguely familiar note. He fancied that they were well-known terms, something he had heard about all his life.

Presently the old man spoke again.

"Aubrey is a wealthy man too, you know," he said. "It's not generally known, but he donates the whole of his two thousand pound salary to some scholarship fund in the north. His private income must be considerable. Still, it suits him, you know. He has a unique position which no money in the world could buy, and a house which is virtually a museum-piece, also not for purchase. You're comfortable there, aren't you?"

"Very. It's a glorious house, isn't it, Albert?"

It took Campion some seconds to realize that she was talking to him, but his response, when it did come, was manfully enthusiastic.

Mr. Anscombe turned in his seat.

"You're tired," he said. "That experience of yours took it out of you. That sort of thing often does. London is exhausting, too. What are you wearing? A mackintosh? I can hear something rustling but I can't see you. It's very warm in here. Why don't you take it off?"

"No. I don't think I will, thanks." To his horror he heard himself beginning to laugh, but again the girl came to his rescue.

"Leave him alone," she said. "He's in disgrace. He's taken the wrong car, led us miles out of the way, and now he dozes off smelling like a bicycle shop. You'll have to give up oilskins, Albert, at any rate for wear in a confined space. Still, we're practically there. This is your gate, isn't it, Mr. Anscombe? You wouldn't think it awfully rude of us if we didn't take the car into the drive, would you?"

"Oh of course not, of course not. I'm late myself. Thank you very much for all your kindness. I feel I forced myself on you this afternoon, but you've been so very good, so very good."

He was hoisting himself out of the low seat with difficulty as he spoke and his hollow foolish voice squeaked and trailed away as he landed himself safely on the pavement and closed the door. Through the window the remaining passenger caught a glimpse of him disappearing between high stucco pillars towards a steep dark house beyond.

"Silly little man," said the girl suddenly. "He's left his parcel. I shan't be a moment. I'll take it to him."

"That's all right, I'll do that," Campion said hastily, fumbling for the door handle.

"You can't in those clothes."

"Yes, I can. He won't see me. Or if he does he'll have to realize I'm an eccentric. Where's his baggage?"

She turned towards him in the darkness.

"It's books, I think," she said. "Here you are."

He took the square parcel and staggered out after the departing figure. It was brighter than he thought and he did not call to the man but came up the small drive quietly. The front door was already closed when he found it, and, rather than knock, he laid the package on the step and hurried down the drive to the waiting car again.

With the departure of Anscombe the very car seemed more comfortable. The girl let in the clutch softly and they slid away. The man, who was still trying to remember if his name really was Albert Campion, leant forward. Now that he was alone with this delightful if unrecognizable wife of his he felt unexpectedly embarrassed about coming to the vital point. She was having such an extraordinary effect on him. He was so very glad of her, so childishly content and happy to find her. He wished to God that she would take his head on her heart and let him go to sleep. It was ridiculous to have to ask her to tell him her name.

"It is all very difficult," he began awkwardly.

"I know." Her agreement was so heartfelt that it silenced him. "It's frightful, and there's absolutely no time to talk and get it straight. We're here already and we daren't be late, it'll look so fishy."

She swung the car up a steep incline and through a columned gateway as she spoke.

"I only found out where you were by a miracle. I'd been waiting down at the station as we arranged. I got rid of Anscombe until four o'clock, but after that I had to carry him around with me, telling him one dubious tale after another. I had to bring him because he insisted. He said he had to see his dentist and he asked Lee Aubrey if I'd give him a lift. Lee made a personal request of it and I couldn't refuse without sounding suspicious. So there he was."

The car had not stopped. As far as Campion could see they were rolling through some sort of park. The girl was still talking. She was nervous and a little breathless.

"He's a terrifying old boy, isn't he?" she demanded. "Flat mental deficiency for ninety-nine per cent of the time and single flashes of acuteness. You don't know whether it's silver showing through the disguising tarnish or the last few flecks of plate on the old tin spoon. Our only hope is to get down to the meal and behave normally. Have you got anything under that decontamination outfit? Can we leave it in the car?"

"It all depends where we're going," he said. "I'm in pyjamas . . . awful grey flannel things."

"What?" She stopped the car in her astonishment and turned to him. "What happened? You're not hurt?"

"Oh lord no," he said, warmed by her anxiety. "I'm all right really. I only got knocked out."

"Oh that was it, was it?" she said, much more relieved than he had expected her to be and far less surprised. "The man in the paper shop simply whispered 'hospital'. I didn't get an opportunity to talk to him at all. The place was full of people and there wasn't time. It was nearly five then and I had the wretched Anscombe inside. That old man knows something, I swear it."

"More than I do," said Campion grimly.

To his surprise she caught him up. "Yes," she said. "That's what I thought. We'll bear him in mind. I say, I am glad you're all right. It never went through my mind that you might have gone to the hospital as a patient. When I saw you charging out in the deep-sea-diver costume I thought some kind friend had lent it to you to hide the tramp's garbage. I've got your change in the luggage hatch. That's what was worrying me so when you didn't turn up before Anscombe returned. I didn't see how I was going to get it to you before he saw you. Well, it's silly to change now, isn't it? You'll have to smuggle yourself in."

The man laughed. She was charming and he was very tired.

"Anything you say, lady," he said. "Where do we go?"

"I think that side door," she said, "don't you? The one that leads up out of the yard where we leave the car. I know it's bad form for house guests to use the back stairs, but we'll just have to look badly brought up if we're seen. You could always shout 'Fire!' again of course, but that might not help in the long run."

He sat watching her silhouette as she manoeuvred the big car skilfully into a narrow entrance by the side of a large dim building. She was an astonishing young person, as practical and energetic as a child and utterly without affectation. He thought her voice was the coolest and most comforting sound he had ever heard.

She parked the car and he climbed out, stiff and unsteady, into a neat old-fashioned stableyard with cobbles under his feet and the low graceful lines of Georgian outbuildings just visible in the faint light. By the time he emerged she had already opened the luggage hatch and was tugging at a suitcase within.

He took it from her and would have put his free arm round her shoulders, but she did not notice his gesture and it occurred to him that he did not usually exhibit such open affection. He was wondering a little at himself when she called him from the house.

"Come on, Albert. It's awfully late."

He found her waiting for him in a dark arched doorway.

"Two steps up," she said. "Come on. It's got a blackout gadget which turns out the light when you open the door."

As the wood closed softly behind him the small passage in which they stood lit up and in a soft yellow glow the comfortable flagged and panelled interior of a perfect Georgian house emerged. A baize door opposite him clearly cut off the reception half of the establishment and a narrow flight of oak stairs on their left led to a similar door on the first floor. The girl made for this upper door and as she ran up the staircase he suddenly saw her and recognized her, the first real and familiar thing to emerge in the terrifying darkness of his mind. Her thin young back under the perfectly cut brown tweed of her suit, her red curls, and her small brown hand on the bannister were all suddenly well known and inexpressibly dear to him.

"Amanda!" he said.

"Yes?" She swung round on the top of the stairs and stood looking down at him, a picture of arrested movement, her light brown eyes questioning and every line of her heart-shaped face alive and young.

He laughed and came hurrying up the stairs after her.

"I only wanted to hear you answer to your name."

The smile faded from her face and he thought she looked a trifle embarrassed.

"I'm not really rattled," she murmured unexpectedly and as if he had reproached her. "It's only that it's all so horribly important and imminent. You've come back all carefree. Did something good happen?"

"No, I'm rather afraid it didn't. This is light-headedness," he said, and followed her through the second baize door into a small world of past elegance.

Amanda crossed the upper hall, where stripped pine panelling, Chinese carpet, and sage-green drapery made a Georgian setting without either the stuffiness or the full-blooded ostentation of that great period of nouveaux-riches, and opened a door under an archway.

"Yes, they've put your things out, thank God," she said, peering across another expanse of carpet. "Lee has got the servant problem taped, hasn't he? It's the combination of love *and* money, you know. They not only adore him but he pays them the earth. You get dressed and so will I. I'll give you ten minutes. We can't wash much: that's all there is to it. Then I'll come back. I must see you before we go down. Bless you."

She was gone before he could stop her, whisking into a room on the other side of the hall while her vivid friendly personality still warmed and comforted him like the glow of a coal fire.

Albert Campion went into the room that presumably was his own and looked at the dinner-jacket laid out neatly on his bed. The tailor's tab inside the breast pocket assured him that it was his and that he had bought it in the preceding spring. Now that he had been on his feet for some little time his weakness had become more apparent and, with the departure of Amanda, his earlier lost feeling returned. He began to dress carefully, moving slowly and with a certain amount of difficulty. After a minute or so he gave up trying to fathom any further deeper mysteries than those concerning the whereabouts of his underclothes and washing tackle. He had to hurry. Amanda was coming back in ten minutes and that was time enough to get all the serious questions settled. He clung to the thought of Amanda. As his wife she was the one satisfactory, friendly truth in a world of villainous fantasy.

Meanwhile the obvious thing to do was to get himself safely changed.

He accepted his reflection in the shaving mirror discovered in the adjoining bathroom without seeing it, as do most men every morning of their lives. His self-searching mood had disappeared and his sole anxiety was to get his chin smooth. The cool comfort of well-fitting clothes soothed him and he had tied his tie and was getting into his jacket when a knock sounded on the door. He sprang to open it with an eagerness which wrenched his stiff body unmercifully, and stepped back in blank disappointment an instant later. It was not Amanda, but a dinner-jacketed stranger who smiled at him familiarly and wandered into the room.

"My dear chap, I'm so glad you've got back," he said, revealing a voice several times deeper than the average, and so flexible that its charm was instantaneous. "Trouble all cleared up?"

Campion nodded without speaking. Even if some flicker of memory had not struggled to help him, he would have known the newcomer was his host as soon as he set eyes on him. The tall, big-boned figure, with its suggestion of elegant negligence, was impressive and went with the house. He recognized the type, or rather the species of original spirit, immediately.

Lee Aubrey was a personality; that is to say he exuded a force and a spiritual flavour as actual as if it had been warmth, or a small electric current. His big head was extravagantly moulded, the features fine but large and overdrawn, and his smiling eyes were kindly rather than friendly. The most striking thing about him was that he could not, apparently much to his regret, provide any stretch of common ground on which to walk with normal men. There was no suggestion of equality in his bearing but rather an exaggerated humility, as if he were in the habit of going down on mental all-fours to conduct any simple conversation. Now, as he stood lounging awkwardly against the mantelpiece, he was laughing a little, indulgently ashamed of himself for his clumsy efforts to relax.

"I was rather glad to put food off for half an hour," he said. "Fyshe from the War House has been down. Extraordinarily inferior mind.

A decent chap. Quite sound, of course, but thunderingly dull. It took Butcher all day to tell him what he wanted to know, while any intelligent undergraduate could have mastered the thing in a couple of hours. It's absurd, isn't it?"

He laughed again, half apologetically, for making the criticism.

"Absurd," said Campion.

It was coming back to him, or some of it was. This was the Principal's House in the Bridge Institute of General Research, that remarkable and ancient institution which, from being a provincial curiosity, part charity and part museum, for a hundred and fifty years, had blossomed forth in the early part of the century into one of the most valuable centres in the country. The recollection came as Amanda's name had come; not as a raising of the curtain of darkness which hung between the front and the back of his mind, but as a sudden rent in it which flashed a whole scene from the brightness within, only to close again a moment later as the folds resettled. It was all very confusing and alarming.

Lee Aubrey was looking at him intently.

"You're most frightfully tired," he said gently. "Or is something wrong?"

"No, no, I'm all right." Campion was surprised at his own vehemence, but it seemed desperately important to keep his secret.

"Oh that—that's fine." The other man was as hurt as a child. "Won't you come down? By the way, did you get your letters? There were two or three for you this morning. John should have brought them up here. He's probably left them in my study. I'll get them for you myself. Shall we go?"

He was lounging towards the door, self-conscious and uncomfortably gauche like an adolescent.

"No, I can't for a moment. I'm waiting for Amanda. We've got to talk to each other."

Even in his confused state the words appeared a little bald to Mr. Campion. Aubrey swung round and his eyes were suddenly sharp and frighteningly intelligent.

"Oh, I see," he said and immediately he became deeply if consciously kind again. "I see, I'll go down and hold the fort until you come."

He went out gently, and, it seemed to Mr. Campion, without compassion.

Left alone, the man in the bedroom returned to his earlier problems. He thrust the firefighting kit into the bottom of a wardrobe and was about to close the door on it when a sound behind made him turn.

It was Amanda. She was there just as he had expected her, in a long smooth white dress which seemed right and familiar and made her look about sixteen. She was wonderfully easy to look at. That discovery struck him as new and surprising and he felt irritated with himself that it should be so.

"Oh, that's grand," she said, nodding at him approvingly. "I was so afraid you might potter a bit, as you usually do. What are you up to? Admiring yourself?"

He glanced behind him and saw the point of her remark. The door of the armoire had swung open, revealing a dressing mirror within.

"No," he said and paused abruptly. He had just caught sight of himself and her standing beside him. He was older than he had thought. He saw a horrified man of thirty-five or so, tall and remarkably thin, with a lean wooden face on which there were far more lines than he had expected. She, on the other hand, might have been still at school.

"You look much more intelligent than usual," she remarked. "Don't you think so?"

"God help me, do I?" he said involuntarily. "I am rather shocked, as a matter of fact."

He saw the amusement die out of her face.

"That's not fair," she said unhelpfully.

"What isn't?" he said, turning to her and catching her hands.

To his surprise her embarrassment increased and she released herself slowly and stood before him, a steady determined young person, serious and annihilatingly frank.

"Albert," she said, "I know this isn't the time, and that all this business going on is far more serious at the moment, but I've got this on my mind and I want to clear it up. You know you were going to marry me next month?"

The information, coupled with the ominous form in which it was offered, appalled him. His disappointment and loneliness was so acute that it produced a physical chill and he stood looking at her without realizing that his face was a complete blank.

"Was I?" he said flatly.

She did not speak and he had the dreadful impression that he had struck her, or had behaved in some other disgraceful way quite out of character with himself or her.

She drew back from him and for a moment he felt panic-stricken that she was going to walk out and leave him.

"Don't," he said wildly. "I didn't mean that, Amanda. I'm completely at sea. I don't know where I am or who I am or what I'm doing."

"Oh I know." She was herself again, impulsive and warm and friendly. "I know and I'll see you through this. You can rely on me absolutely all the time. That is true. You do know that?"

She thrust her arm through his and he felt the urgent, nervous strength of her young body against his side.

"I'll do anything, Albert. This is desperate, the most important, the most serious business you've ever come up against, and I'm with you. I wouldn't be here if I wasn't. It's disgusting of me to talk about the marriage when you're nearly off your head with worry about the other thing, but you know how hopeless I am about hiding anything and I couldn't bear to behave like a hussy even for ten minutes. You see, we've never had a love affair, have we? I've just been going to marry you ever since I was seventeen. We've known each other so long, and quite frankly it was me who ever suggested getting married at all. You'd almost forgotten about it in the strain of this other business, hadn't you? My good ape, don't be polite about it. It's silly when we're so used to one another. Well now, I want to call all that off. I don't have to explain any more than that, do I?"

Albert Campion let the honest young pronouncement sink into his shuttering mind.

"How old are you?" he asked.

"Twenty-five."

"As old as that? And you've been going to marry me for eight years."

"Well, yes. Don't be silly, you know I have, more or less. We don't go talking like this as a rule but it's got to be mentioned some time. It wasn't really fixed by either of us and it was simply that I've never considered marrying anybody else. The question has never sort of come up, has it? But now, well, I thought I'd like to lay off, and like a complete mug I've come rushing in to tell you at this ungodly moment when you're exhausted and nearly off your head with worry about something which really is terrific. I'm sorry and ashamed, but anyway it's done. I've made it clear and that's all right."

"You've been going to marry me for *eight years*." He did not repeat the words aloud but they glowed at him from among the shadows and he strove helplessly to reconcile the information with the man he had so recently discovered himself to be. If he was a half-wit now, he seemed to have been a lunatic for some considerable time.

"And now you're not." Again he did not utter the phrase, but its finality petrified him. As he came to the surface he had a momentary flash of insight.

"Now you want a free hand?"

She glanced up at him and her brown eyes were level and truthful. "Yes," she agreed steadily. "I want a free hand. Come on, we must go down. Lee's waiting."

"Oh, just a moment." The appeal escaped him in desperation. "There are one or two things I've got to know. You see, when I got myself . . ." He paused with the words "knocked out" drying on his lips as he saw the pitfall and realized how she had forestalled him. He could hardly tell her now. To reveal his helplessness at this juncture would be both to plead weakness and to appeal to her pity, and to appeal to pity is very loathsome in love. He was appalled to discover how much love there was to be reckoned with. They seemed somehow to have achieved the mutual confidence of marriage without it, and now at a stroke it was destroyed; now, when probably for the first time he was realizing how much he had come to depend upon it.

"When you got yourself what?" she enquired.

"Nothing. It'll do later."

She put her hand in his. "You're a dear," she said with that sudden candour which he had rejoiced at in her. "I knew you'd be like this. You've always been rather magnificent, Albert, and you still are. Isn't it a mercy that you've never . . . I mean that you're a bit sensible, and . . . er . . . well, not exactly cold, but . . ."

"Fish-like," he said bitterly and let her lead him, lonely and wretched, downstairs towards that sinister "other thing" which was still lying like an ominous bundle behind the dark curtains of his mind.

CHAPTER FOUR

The drawing-room of the Principal's house at the Institute of Bridge was typical both of its owner and of the foundation; that is to say, it was a genuine period piece which had been considerably improved by modern austerity and modern money. Its fluted columns and Wedgwood plaques had been stripped and cleaned and each piece of furniture that it contained had been chosen with care and a splendid disregard of cost either one way or the other, so that an old fruitwood chair picked up for half a crown rubbed shoulders with Mozart's own spinet, acquired at considerable sacrifice.

When Campion followed Amanda in he walked into one of the few recognizable atmospheres of that nightmare evening. Intelligent academic formality, than which there is nothing more indestructible, closed over his head like a sea of glue.

Five people stood about sipping sherry from beautiful old apple-green glasses, and the soft light of candles in silver sticks flickered on determinedly unfashionable clothes and proud, clever, conservative faces.

Lee Aubrey came over to them at once, excusing himself briefly to the middle-aged woman with whom he had been talking. He smiled briefly at Amanda and turned to peer at her companion with one of his typical glances, as if he were humbly taking a little look at the soul and finding much to sympathize with there.

In the normal way Mr. Campion, who was acute in these matters, would have recognized the phenomenon and enjoyed it all for what it was worth, but tonight he was not himself and he felt suddenly savage.

Lee was disarming.

"This is fine," he said. "Now it's just Anscombe to come. I don't think you've met everyone, have you?"

He performed the introductions with casual efficiency and four faces, one male and three female, peered up into Mr. Campion's own in dreamlike succession. A pair of round dark eyes under grey brows registered on him as he bowed to the third masculine member of the party, and he received a blurred impression of a wedge of a man with a great chest and dwindling legs. But the women meant nothing to him. One was elderly, with an untidy white haircut and black eyes, but she barely spoke to him, fixing her attention entirely on Amanda.

Lee carried him over to the other side of the room, ostensibly to find some sherry.

"Rather a depressing assembly, I'm afraid," he murmured diffidently, "but it simply couldn't be helped. This is municipal intelligentsia, my dear chap. The Bridge Institute may do work of national importance but it's still the so-called philanthropic little plaything of the Masters of Bridge. There's something frightful about hereditary possession."

"I wonder the State doesn't take it over," said Campion and realized that the observation was idiotic as soon as he had made it.

Aubrey looked at him with bewildered incredulity.

"Naturally they'd like to," he said, "but it belongs to the town and it's pretty much of a financial asset, isn't it?"

"Yes, of course. I'd forgotten." In spite of his care the final word carried more emphasis than Campion had intended and again his host peered at him with concern.

"My dear good man, you're exhausted," he said. "For heaven's sake have a drink. Would you rather have something other than this? I don't want to be an infernal nuisance, but isn't there anything I can do?"

It went through Mr. Campion's mind to say "Yes, find out how I killed a policeman, old boy, and while you're about it have a squint to see if I've cracked my own skull," and to observe what happened, but he checked this irresponsibility. He felt as if he were just half drunk, he decided; sober enough to realize that it was definitely not wise to talk.

"Very kind of you," he said, "but I'm all right. A little tired, nothing else." He had spoken more loudly than he would normally have done and his host recoiled as the words sounded clearly in the hushed and frigid air.

"I see," he said very gently. "I see. Do forgive me. Oh yes, wait a minute, here are your letters. I brought them along."

He took a handful of mail out of the coat pocket of his loose dinner-jacket as he spoke and withdrew at once, with his odd self-conscious diffidence.

Campion glanced at the letters with a slowly growing sense of satisfaction. All but one were re-addressed to him from 17a Bottle Street, Piccadilly, and the sight of his name on several envelopes appeared to lend him, however unreasonably, a certain faith in his own identity.

He opened the letter which had not been re-addressed but had come to him direct at the Bridge Institute and stood looking at a clumsily typed sheet which no one but an executive who normally employed a secretary would have dared to send out. It was headed baldly: "My office. The Yard. Tuesday," and ran on: "Dear A.C. Interesting conversation this afternoon with Pugh, whom T. brought in. Fancy a man called Anscombe is your best bet. He is Secretary to the Masters. Old-ish, I think and with a sister. For God's sake get busy. Keep your eye on the calendar. The figures 15 turn my belly whenever I see or hear them. Nothing else this end. Saw the Minister again. Hardly recognized him. Enjoyed seeing fellow of that type exhibiting the weakness and humanity of the common bloke, but put the wind up me all the same. Forced to rely on you only now. Every other line has gone slack and the time is so short. If you fail, for my part I shall wait until the balloon actually does go up and then swim quietly out to sea. This is a tripey way of putting it but can't bring myself to put down what I really feel. If this thing happens it is the END and I mean that. I'm not a religious chap, as you know, but I'm praying now literally and if any blasted bobby on the beat wants to see me do it he's wel-

come to come in here and look at his Dep. Commish on his knees.
Damn you, succeed. S."

Mr. Albert Campion read the letter through twice. The words themselves were convincing enough but there was something else. Something about the note was more than ordinarily startling. Suddenly he
recognized what it was. Stanislaus did not write like that in the ordinary way. He accepted the name without realizing that it had not
been written in full and concentrated on the really alarming peculiarity. Stanislaus Oates was an old man, a prim, elderly policeman of
the oldest school, and he was hysterical. That was horrible, as dreadful as seeing a quarter of the Nelson Column sticking up raggedly
against a lowering sky. He crumpled the paper into a ball and thrust
it into his pocket until he should get near the fire to destroy it. There
were cold waves playing up and down his spine. This was truly frightful. Some terrible responsibility rested upon him and not only had he
no recollection of what it was but he was helpless, incapacitated by an
obscene mental weakness from doing anything about it.

Amanda's laugh on the other side of the room cut into his thoughts.
He looked across and saw her. She was talking to Lee Aubrey, who
was leaning towards her, his big-featured face young and revealing,
and a belated puppyishness apparent in his attitude. A servant was
at his elbow trying to attract his attention and Campion saw him come
out of his mood and turn with a startled expression to follow the
man out of the room.

Amanda glanced after him. She was radiant and excited, the entire
march of her magnificent common sense and reliability set aside for
the sweet, foolish fandango which any lesser woman can dance when
she is so minded. Campion stood looking at her and it seemed to
him that in that moment he actually struggled up and out of a whole
customary system of living and emerged a small naked essence of the
basic man. She should not do it. She should not desert him. Pride,
manners, custom, the habit of a lifetime, and the training of an ancient
system be damned. Amanda was his. He needed her, and God help the
man or the woman herself if there was any smashing up of that
combine.

He was walking over to her when Lee Aubrey came hurrying in and
accosted him. He listened to the murmured words with the sudden
chill which a vision of delay presents when an extra snag arises at a
time of crisis.

"The Police?" he repeated. "I can't see the Police now."

"But my dear chap . . ." Aubrey's deep voice was urgent, "please,
not here."

Campion followed him out into the wide hall and saw through an open doorway across an expanse of black and white flags the familiar gleam of silver and blue.

"The whole thing was some idiotic mistake and I can't spare the time," he said savagely.

Aubrey stared at him, his eyes surprised but shrewd.

"I don't know what you're talking about, Campion," he said patiently. "They've come about Anscombe. The poor old boy has just been found dead in his garden and you and Amanda appear to be the last people to have seen him alive."

CHAPTER FIVE

"Anscombe?"

As the echo escaped Campion, the personality of the old man as he remembered him slid into the front of his mind with startling vividness. He saw again the ragged silhouette with the flat cap atop as it had heaved towards him so ingratiatingly over the back of the car seat. The recollection of the crumpled letter in his pocket also became very clear before his eyes, like a close-up of a documentary on a movie screen. He could re-read the operative words: ". . . a man called Anscombe is your best bet."

His new mood of reckless determination, which he suspected was completely foreign to his nature, was still in complete possession of him.

"Dead?" he said aloud. "He would be."

Aubrey made no direct reply but Campion thought he saw the whites of his eyes for a second.

"All the same, my dear chap," he said at last, his tone only faintly reproving, "we must do what we can. There's a sister, and heaven only knows what other complications. Come on."

The immense blue great-coat containing the police sergeant moved out of the doorway as they approached and the bright room spread out before them. Lee Aubrey's private study was an impressive chamber at any time, with its arched bookcases, unexpected curios, and deep green hangings. It was a room with an air, a room used to soothing and entertaining people of widely different types and standards, a diplomat among rooms, gracious and superior, capable of stimulating as well as subduing, but none of its charm cut much ice with the man who stood waiting for them as he warmed the back of his legs before the open fire.

Campion knew he was a County C.I.D. Superintendent the moment he set eyes on him. He knew that as surely and in the same inspirational way that he had known Amanda's name or where to find a cigarette in the car. There was no mistaking that tall, bright-eyed, smiling superiority combined with a meticulous physical neatness. This last was a muscular and sartorial spit-and-polish, almost naval in its perfection. The stranger was the country policeman at his highest, an impressive specimen anywhere.

Aubrey, whose gaucherie had given place to a remarkable energy apparently engendered by the emergency, thrust his visitor forward.

"Superintendent Hutch," he said briefly. "This is Mr. Campion, Hutch. Here we are. What can we do?"

"That's a question, isn't it?" said the Superintendent, revealing an unexpectedly soft country accent, and Campion, glancing up sharply, became aware of the brightest eyes he had ever met smiling into his own with a startling intensity of horse-sense behind them.

The remark was clearly not intended to be taken at its face value. For an appalling instant it occurred to Campion that he had been betrayed and that Aubrey had got him to come quietly by a pretext. His face became wooden and he waited, his hands in his pockets, for the next move.

When it came it surprised him. Superintendent Hutch laughed a little. He might almost have been embarrassed. Glancing down at a disreputable piece of paper in his hand he said formally: "You are Mr. Campion, are you, sir?"

"It's a hundred to one on, I should think, God help me." Campion did not say the words aloud, but they came into his mind involuntarily and he smiled, only to freeze a moment later. The Superintendent, catching his expression, had echoed the grin, secretly, alarmingly. His manner then became uncomfortably informal and he spoke as important policemen are apt to speak to cornered delinquents, affably and as if they were part of the family.

"I just want the usual, you know," he said cheerfully. "A brief account of your last meeting with the deceased. Where did you leave him and when?"

He had a jaunty manner which sat well on his slightly comical countryman's face, with the long duck's-bill nose. He was evidently a local character and was very sure of himself.

Campion took the plunge without a pause. Hesitation, he felt, instinctively, was death.

"I last saw Anscombe at his own gate," he began glibly. "We'd come from—er—the town."

"What town?"

He had not the least idea. The shaky lands spread out before him and he wavered.

"I think we ought to have Amanda here."

"Amanda, sir?"

"Yes, my fiancée, Miss . . ." The hopeless pitfall loomed too late. Lee Aubrey was staring at him, but his surprise was not at Campion's astounding ignorance.

"I had rather hoped to keep Lady Amanda out of this as long as possible," he said briefly. He showed his annoyance and there was a suggestion of colour on his high cheekbones.

Lady Amanda? Lady Amanda who? The utter hopelessness of the situation might have defeated Campion at that moment had it not been for Aubrey's irritation. Who was Lee Aubrey to spare Amanda? What was this blasted proprietory talk? Damn him and his chivalry!

"Ah yes, of course, my mistake. That will be Lady A. Fitton, won't it?" murmured the Superintendent, glancing down at the slip in his hand.

"No. It's Lady Amanda. As the sister of a peer she takes her Christian name." Aubrey gave the snippet of information casually and the touch of schoolmaster came oddly from him. "Lady Amanda was driving this afternoon. She gave Mr. Anscombe a lift into Coachingford when she went to meet Mr. Campion off the London express. They were delayed and didn't get back until just after eight. These are the brief facts. Mr. Campion can give you anything else you need, I think. You won't need to trouble her at all, will you?"

The last words were barely a question. He spoke with the complete assurance of authority.

The Superintendent shifted his weight. He was not a young man and there was a deal of experience in his long head. Campion, who had been sidetracked momentarily by the two valuable names "Fitton" and "Coachingford", was now impressed by his hesitation and it dawned on him that as Principal of the Bridge Institute Aubrey was no ordinary power in the land.

"I think I ought to see her, sir, if you don't mind," Superintendent Hutch's soft voice was apologetic and he had a shy way of grinning, as if he had a secret joke on somewhere.

Campion, who was not at all sure that he had not, found the habit disconcerting.

Lee Aubrey clearly found his insistence astounding. He swung round on the policeman.

"Mr. Anscombe died naturally, surely?"

Hutch looked uncomfortable. "We're not absolutely certain, sir. He didn't do it himself, that's one sure thing. The Chief Constable is on his way over now. More I can't say, can I?"

"Good Lord!" Aubrey thrust his hands into the pockets of his loose dinner-jacket. Then he whistled and stood for a moment irresolute, staring at the blank wall. At length he turned abruptly. "I'll fetch her," he said. "Mr. Campion will tell you all he can. Apart from everything else this is rather unpleasant. The man lives on the Institute estate."

He went out, leaving Campion with the two policemen. Hutch said nothing. He stood studying his notes, his head bent earnestly over the small bundle of old envelopes and loose half-sheets of paper on which he appeared to have made them. His hesitation was unnerving. Campion was fully alive to the dangers of his position. Any question about the drive home from Coachingford must, if he stuck to the story Amanda had told Anscombe, introduce the suicidally dangerous subject of hospitals. It was the delay he dreaded most. He was getting a sufficiently clear angle on himself to realize that whatever he might or might not have done, it was no ordinary straightforward crime of violence, and meanwhile there was clearly something of importance for him to do, and to do immediately, if only he could get some sort of line on what it was. What troubled him particularly was that he had a growing conviction that he had been nearing success when disaster had overtaken him. There was a sensation of discovery in the back of his consciousness, an impression that things were moving. Moreover, the curtain between this misery of ignorance and a very clear vision indeed was tantalizingly thin.

Hutch was looking at him with his now familiar half-smile. He was waiting as though he expected Campion to speak first. The man who could not remember took a deep breath.

"How did Anscombe die?" he enquired.

The policeman grinned. There was no other word for the terrifying secret leer which spread over his face.

"We were going to ask you about that, Mr. Campion," he said.

In the moment of paralysed silence which followed, the step in the doorway behind them came as a merciful release to Campion, and the brisk new voice sounded comfortably commonplace.

"Hallo, Super. Mr. Aubrey here? Oh, it's you, is it, Campion? What a bad business, eh?"

It was the greeting of a familiar, anyway, and Campion turned towards the newcomer anxiously. He saw a heavy round man in early middle-age, with a distinctive ugly face and impudent eyes beneath brows as fierce and tufted as an Aberdeen's. He conveyed energy and efficiency and the sturdy decisiveness which goes with a simple point of view and no nerves. It occurred to Campion that he looked like a man who did not believe in ghosts, but for the rest he was as much a stranger as anyone else in this new and confusing world. At the moment he was very full of the story.

"I'm supposed to have dropped in for coffee," he said, "but the chap who let me in tells me you haven't started to eat yet. He told me this dreadful tale about Anscombe, too. Poor old boy! He couldn't face it, I suppose. Or am I letting cats out of bags?"

The Superintendent eyed him.

"It wasn't suicide, Mr. Pyne."

"*Wasn't* suicide?" The newcomer seemed first astounded and then embarrassed. "Well, I'm glad to hear it," he said. "What a *gaffe!* Lucky there were only you two to hear me. I'm always putting my foot in it like that. There's been a lot of gossip about, you know. You've heard it, haven't you, Super? About the Secretaryship of the Masters."

"Seems to me I did hear something." Hutch was very cautious.

"You must have done." Pyne's eyes were amused beneath his tremendous brows. "It's been told me in strictest confidence by everyone I've met in the last three months. I heard that the job, like all these hereditary offices, took a fine old packet to keep up, and that the old man was on the verge of a smash and had made up his mind to resign. Naturally, as soon as I heard he was a deader I thought he'd done it himself. One would. It breaks an old man's heart to give up a position carrying a bit of kudos like that, especially when it's been in the family for generations. The Bi-Annual Meeting of the Masters is sometime this week, too, isn't it?"

"Tomorrow."

"Is it? Very likely. They're such a secret high-and-mighty body that they don't trouble to publish a little thing like that." He laughed. "I like it," he said. "It appeals to the kid in all of us, that kind of mumbo-jumbo, even if it is only a sort of glorified parish council."

The Superintendent looked frankly scandalized and Pyne, catching Campion's eye, burst out laughing. It was a pleasant, open sound, a trifle high-pitched like his voice but full of limited humour.

"We're philistines, we Londoners," he said. "The Masters are sacrosanct down here in Bridge. I'm sorry, Super. I'm behaving disgustingly. Poor old Anscombe! I didn't know him well, of course. I'd only met him once or twice. You didn't know him at all, did you, Campion?"

"I appear to have been the last person to have seen him alive." The remark seemed to be the most cautious he could make in the circumstances, but it was not altogether fortunate. Amanda, who followed Aubrey into the room at that particular moment, heard it and said the first and natural thing to come into her head.

"I was there too," she said, "unless you saw him in the garden when you followed him in."

Everybody looked at Campion. Aubrey and Hutch looked because they knew where Anscombe had died and Amanda and Pyne looked because the others were looking.

"That's right," said Campion. "I followed him into the garden with a parcel he'd left in the car. I didn't catch him, though, so I put the package on the doorstep and went back."

There was another pause after he had spoken and again it was broken by Pyne.

"What an extraordinary thing to do, old boy," he said and laughed awkwardly.

Campion hesitated, remembering his reason for not ringing the door-bell, and meanwhile Amanda leapt to the rescue.

"We were so late," she explained. "I was jittering in the car in case we didn't have time to dress. I begged Albert not to be a moment and he wasn't."

"How long would you say you were, sir?" The Superintendent was making hieroglyphics on the back of one of his depressing envelopes.

"I don't know exactly. A minute and a half, perhaps. I went straight up the path and I came straight back again."

"You didn't meet anyone or hear anything?"

"No. What was there for me to hear?"

Hutch was magnificently deaf to the question.

"I think I'll ask you to step across with me, if you don't mind, sir," he said briskly. "I'd just like to see exactly where you put that parcel. We haven't come across it yet."

"I'll come too, shall I?" Amanda's young voice was eager, as usual, and Campion found it very comforting. She at least was definitely on his side.

The Superintendent was dampening, however.

"No, Miss—er—Lady Amanda. That'll be quite all right," he said firmly. "I won't disturb Mr. Aubrey's dinner party more than I can help. If I want any more from you I'll know where to find you, shan't I?"

"You'll come back later on, then, Hutch." Aubrey spoke for the first time since his return from the drawing-room and Campion, glancing at him, saw that he was annoyed by the whole situation. It was such an unexpected reaction that he noticed it and filed it for future reference. Such magnificent aloofness from the ordinary point of view was impressive. However, Aubrey caught his glance and evidently realized that he had betrayed a weakness, albeit a somewhat godlike one, for he smiled at Campion awkwardly and murmured apologetically, "It's absurd, but I believe I'm worrying about my wretched duties as a host. One finds oneself doing incredible things like that." His complete frankness was disarming, as also was his sudden return of gaucherie. All the same he did not change his mind and Campion saw himself delivered over to Hutch, alone and unprotected.

While he had someone with him to use as a stalking horse he felt he had at least an outside chance of getting by with his damning disability undiscovered, but alone he felt that the Superintendent must detect him in five minutes. Some of his old alarm must have shown itself in his face, for as he turned from Aubrey, Pyne suddenly laid a reassuring hand on his shoulder.

"I'll come along with you," he said. "Any reason why I shouldn't, Super?"

The touch of belligerence in the question was unmistakable and Campion was aware of Hutch's bright eyes regarding him curiously. He forced himself to meet them squarely and to his intense relief and surprise the policeman shrugged his shoulders.

"None at all," he said grudgingly. "We'll go at once if you don't mind. The Chief Constable will probably be there by now and we can't keep him waiting."

He led the way and they followed him, Pyne still holding Campion's shoulder.

As Campion passed Amanda she looked up at him and winked. It was such a swift gesture and her face remained so composed both before and after it that he was hardly sure it had happened. At the same moment Aubrey touched her arm and drew her back into the hall towards the dining-room.

The three men made the short journey on foot. It was a ghostly night. The moon had come out of the clouds and was riding high and serene, her blunt horns cutting into the sky, but the ground-mist had become thicker, so that the Superintendent, marching along in front, looked like a ridiculous bust of himself, his head and shoulders alone clearly defined in the cold light.

They passed down the drive with the gravel crunching under their

feet and out of the misty sea around them other buildings, some of
them very square and modern, rose up on either side in the middle
distance.

Pyne shook his head. "You can't help handing it to Aubrey," he
remarked, panting a little, for they were walking fast. "In seven years
he's turned this place from a museum into a living brain factory.
There's more valuable work done in these twelve acres than in any
other place in the country. He's got breadth of vision, that chap. I've
never met such a personality, have you? It gets me every time."

Campion hardly heard him, but his voice, friendly and matter of
fact at his elbow, was very reassuring. He wondered how long he had
known the man and what degree of friendship was theirs. It seemed
ridiculous to think of it but they might be partners, or school-friends,
or members of the same profession.

They passed through the wrought-iron gates and, turning on to an
old and narrow pavement made of the thin rectangular flags of other
days, they came up to the entrance through which Campion had last
seen Anscombe disappear. There were several cars drawn up against
the curb and a shadowy figure in uniform came out to challenge them.

While Hutch was talking to him, Campion grew acutely aware of
Pyne. The stocky man had become unnaturally still. He was standing
on the pavement looking up at one of the high stone pillars of the
gateway which rose up white in the moonlight.

"Interesting?" he murmured to Campion, and there was just a shade
more than the ordinary casual question in the remark.

Campion looked at the gate pillar and saw nothing more than the
heraldic leaden eagle on the top. It was a nice piece of period
decoration but too small and in no way remarkable.

"Charming," he said politely and turned back to the man. The
light was deceptive but he thought he saw a gleam die out of the
bright round eyes.

The Superintendent's minion had stepped aside by this time, however, and the little procession moved on into the dark garden. Just
before he passed behind it Campion glanced at the pillar again. He
caught it at an angle and saw upon its smooth surface something he
had not noticed before. His heart jolted violently and once again all
the old dark anxiety, which was mingled with an exasperated yet fearful curiosity, swept down on him, strangling him like a garotter's scarf.
In shallow relief, and now outlined by the shadow which the angle
gave it, the house number showed up clearly. It was a 15.

Campion's first reaction after the shock was one of complete relief
and his first impulse was to turn to Pyne as to a proven friend, a

brother in some misty conspiracy and the first man in whom he could confide, but second thoughts brought misgivings. The dead man, Anscombe, had also indicated that he attached some special significance to the number, and he had not been a friend—or at least Amanda had not seemed to think so. It occurred to Campion that he was pinning a lot of faith on to Amanda. Pyne was friendly and evidently knew him well, perhaps even better than the girl. He fancied he was accustomed to having many friends. He decided to await his opportunity and put out a feeler on the subject. God knew it was as well to go cautiously!

Just then there was not much time for investigation. As he entered the drive Hutch crossed over to him and walked by his side, while, to his intense discomfort, he found that the sergeant had come up at his other elbow, separating him from Pyne.

"Just show us exactly what you did, sir." Hutch spoke formally and it occurred to Campion that the words were very familiar, as if he had heard them many times before, which was absurd. He did what was required of him and pointed out the exact spot in the corner of the doorstep where he had deposited the bundle.

"It was not a big parcel," he said. "It measured about six by five, I should think. I took it that it was a couple of books."

Hutch seemed satisfied. "You just went away without ringing," he remarked.

It occurred to Campion that the literal truth, which was that he happened to be dressed up as a fireman and did not wish to be seen, might be misunderstood, so he repeated his original story about the hurry. The Superintendent made no comment.

"One does things like that every day," said Pyne, obviously with only the best intentions. "They only sound so jolly fishy when something happens. You're being damned mysterious, Superintendent. There's no question of foul play, is there?"

"There's always a question, sir." Hutch sounded reproachful. "I'd like you to see him, Mr. Campion. He's been taken into the house. Lead the way, will you, Sergeant?"

Even in his uncertain state Campion realized that the request was extraordinary from a policeman to a layman. It seemed hardly likely that Hutch had reverted to the ancient custom of confronting the suspected murderer with the body of his supposed victim, and it went through Campion's mind for one wild moment that he might himself be some sort of eminent pathologist, but he dismissed the theory immediately since the idea conjured up no answering memory.

Yet, as they stood in the brightly-lit bedroom, overcrowded with furniture and still full of the medicine bottles, books, and intimate personal impedimenta of the dead man, again Campion was touched with that sense of the familiar. He knew the scene was pathetic and expected it to be so. Moreover, he felt no qualms as he looked down at the body on the solid old-fashioned mahogany bed.

Anscombe was lying on his face and the pillows had been removed, so that his head received no support. He was still clothed in the light raincoat which he had worn in the car, and it and the suit beneath it had been cut to facilitate an examination of the larger vertebrae.

The four men, Campion and the Superintendent, Pyne and the sergeant, stood round the bed in complete silence. If Campion and the police were stolid, Pyne was rattled. His heavy cheeks were several shades paler and his paunch drooped. He whistled through his teeth.

"Horrible," he said. "He's broken his neck, hasn't he? How on earth did he do it?"

The Superintendent turned away from the sprawling body with the dreadful unnatural angle of the head and looked at Campion earnestly.

"There's a little bit of a lawn on the left of the drive," he said. "I don't know if you noticed it? It's very dark there, hidden from the road by the wall. Well, in the middle of this lawn there's a sort of ornamental basin, a lily-pond I think they call it. It's in a saucer-shaped hollow and there's a ring of very shallow brick and stone steps leading down to the actual water. We found him on his back, lying across the flight, if you see what I mean."

"As if he'd slipped on the lowest step and hit the back of his neck on the highest?" Campion put the question without noticing the clarity of the picture in his mind.

"Exactly," said Hutch and glanced meaningly at the body.

"What an astonishing thing to do!" The explosion came from Pyne. "In the first place what was he there for?"

"That's what we're hoping to find out, sir," said Hutch shortly and he looked again at Campion, who, catching the expression in his eyes, could not make up his mind if it was suspicion which he saw there or merely anxious enquiry.

At any rate he did not let it bother him. At that particular moment he had something even more alarming to consider. Ever since he had first seen the body he had felt less lost and more sure of himself, as if the dark curtain across his brain were already practically transparent, and now it had come to him up out of the shadows, but with all the conviction of certain knowledge, that he knew perfectly well how the man had been killed and what the weapon was which had murdered him. He did not attempt to argue with himself. He simply knew two things for facts, just as he knew that milk was white and ink was black. He knew that Anscombe had been struck from behind on the base of the skull by a man of full height and considerable strength. The blow must have dislocated the vertebrae and the actual cause of death was probably asphyxiation. Moreover, the murderer must have been experienced: that was the certainty which stood out in his mind. The murderer was an old hand, a killer, a professional. As for the weapon, it must have been a length of lead pipe, possibly stocking-covered since there was no mark on the man's collar.

Campion could see the thing quite distinctly in his mind, a long thin murderous bludgeon bound with bicycle tape as like as not.

The Superintendent's questioning eyes still resting upon him brought him out of his reverie with a jerk and he felt his clothes clinging clammily to his body as a possible solution to this new mystery presented itself. Suppose he *had* slugged the policeman? Suppose not only that, but that he had also slugged Anscombe? That was what had happened to Anscombe all right; he had been slugged.

Campion collected himself. It was absurd. He could not have done it. Even if his mind was not playing him monstrous tricks he could not have done it in the time. Amanda knew. Amanda had said distinctly that he had come back at once.

The Superintendent was waiting, his comic country face as grave as a judge's.

"We found him on the steps," he said. "The doctor's still waiting to think over his opinion. What would you say, Mr. Campion?"

The younger man stood still, moistening his dry lips with the tip of his tongue. At that moment, if it had not been for one thing, he would have made a complete statement of his condition and the terrors crowding through his head. The thing that prevented him was the letter in his pocket. A glimpse of Pyne's worried fat face had reminded him of it just in time. Pyne must know. After that deliberate question about the 15 on the gatepost, Pyne must know. He must get Pyne alone. He forced himself to eye Hutch calmly. It was a touchy business, God knew, like handling high-explosives in a fire.

"If Anscombe fell rigidly," he said, "arching his back to regain his balance, you know, then he just might have done it like that. Still, we're in the hands of the doctor, aren't we?"

He could have bitten out his tongue for using that "we". He had no idea why he'd done it. The moment it left his lips it stuck out like a signpost. However, if Hutch saw it he ignored it. He seemed relieved but unhappy.

"Yes," he said, sighing. "That about sizes it up. Would you care to see the steps?"

Since he had clearly made up his mind to show them, there was no way of avoiding the inspection, but as they crowded into the little pit of darkness at the side of the house and stared by the light of muffled torches at the meaningless jumble of stones and bricks, as unreal and confusing as pantomime scenery in the unnatural glow, Campion edged closer to Pyne. It was difficult to choose a sufficiently noncommittal opening but at last he ventured a sighting shot.

"Not much like the old days," he said heartily.

Pyne seemed engrossed with the exhibit, or at any rate he took some seconds to reply. Then his cheerful murmur came briskly out of the darkness.

"When we were in the States together, you mean?"

"Yes." Campion did not wish to be drawn into any further reminiscences until they had had time to talk, but it was not going to be so difficult after all. They were old friends; that was the main thing.

His immediate hopes were defeated a minute or two later, however, when they were all three walking back to the Principal's house together. At the Institute gates Pyne took his leave somewhat abruptly.

"I must get back at once," he said. "You know what work is, Superintendent, and you know where to find me if you want me, don't you? I'll see you in the morning, Campion. This is a bad business, Super. I believe it's turned me up a bit. I'm a novice, you know. I feel like a kid at the hunt who's been blooded."

He stumbled off down the road, the policeman looked after him and laughed soundlessly.

"I'm afraid we've upset that stomach of his," he said. "Serve him right for nosing in. Look here, Mr. Campion, I shan't come back with you now because I've got to wait for the Chief. I don't know what's delaying him. He ought to have been here hours ago. I only came along here because I wanted a word with you in private if I could get it. I wasn't quite accurate up at the house when I said we hadn't found the parcel. I wanted an excuse for getting hold of you. We had found it, of course, just exactly where you'd put it. I didn't want to go into it up there because in some ways it's rather peculiar, and I thought you might be particularly interested. Do you know what it contained?"

He bent closer and a trick of the light gave his face a menace which it did not normally possess.

"Close on four thousand pounds in cash," he said softly. "I found it interesting because we had another case earlier today in Coachingford when a lot of money cropped up. It's been a very funny business altogether over there, with one of our fellows laid out and an unknown in hospital. When I come along I'll tell you about it."

To Campion it seemed that the great starry arc of the sky above him reeled over and back like the lid of a bacon dish, but if the Superintendent knew what he said his game of cat and mouse was inhumanly effective. He gave no sign of meaning more than his actual words, but just before he turned on his heel and left his victim to go up the drive alone he made one further remark which was, if anything, even more annihilating than the first.

"I wonder at that fellow Pyne sticking to us like that," he said earnestly. "Curiosity seems to drive some people off their onion. He only met you three days ago. He told me that himself last night. And he doesn't know me at all. You wouldn't think any man would thrust himself forward like that, would you? I'll be seeing you later, then."

CHAPTER SIX

"I'm afraid Hutch has let us down. It's abominably late."

Lee Aubrey broke a long silence with the remark, which he delivered with an effort, as if he had been thinking of it for a long time. He, Campion, and Amanda were sitting round the fire in the drawing-room with the candles burning low and the uncomfortable silence of the night bearing down upon them. They had been there for perhaps an hour. Campion had returned from Anscombe's house just as the dinner guests were leaving and had found himself let in for a more or less formal *tête-à-tête*, his host the one person in the way.

He was more than anxious to talk to Amanda alone. Every time he set eyes on her she became clearer and dearer to him. Whatever other values were upset, whatever other mistakes he made in this new nightmare world of his, she was real and solid, a living part of that self which he was rediscovering so painfully.

She was sitting curled up in her chair between the two of them, very much alive but gloriously composed. She looked very young and very intelligent, but not, he thought with sudden satisfaction, clever. A dear girl. *The* girl, in fact. His sense of possession was tremendous. It was the possessiveness of the child, of the savage, of the dog, unreasonable and unanswerable. He glanced irritably at Aubrey.

The great man had risen and was leaning against the mantelpiece.

He was frowning at first but then once more that little smile of tolerant self-contempt curled his narrow lips. Suddenly he laughed.

"Well," he said, "we've thrashed it all out, haven't we? Anscombe appears to have fallen down and broken his neck: that's all it amounts to. I'll go up and see poor old Miss Anscombe in the morning. Until Hutch condescends to report we can't do anything else. You look fantastically tired, my dear fellow. Why don't you go to bed? Amanda and I will give the wretched Hutch another half hour. Don't you think so?"

The final question was put directly to Amanda and as he looked at her his expression softened so much that the change was positively theatrical. However, he seemed quite unconscious of betraying himself and it was as if he were not in the habit of considering himself objectively ever.

Amanda avoided his eyes and might almost, for the light was deceptive, have blushed. Her involuntary behaviour seemed to annoy her, however, for she looked at him squarely.

"Very well," she said.

Campion sat up. In the ordinary way he might well have been startled, for there are few hosts who send their guests to bed so blandly, but now, in his confused state, he was bewildered. Aubrey had spoken with authority, like—yes, that was it—like royalty, or a headmaster; not with rudeness, but as if he had special privileges.

At first Campion had every intention of refusing baldly and of forcing himself upon them, but Amanda swept the remaining ground from under his feet.

"Good night, Albert," she said.

He went up to his room and sat on his bed with the door open, as if he were a schoolboy in the throes of a first love affair. Until that moment he had not properly assimilated her announcement of earlier in the evening. So many things had happened since then and the dreamlike quality of his new existence had seemed to allow of lightning changes of front and back. Now, again, it returned to him that Amanda was real, and, being real, she was consistent, the one concrete thing in a world of fantasy. She meant what she said. She was not going to marry him. Beside this actual disaster all the other inconsistencies—the mad cat-and-mouse behaviour of the police, the too friendly Pyne who had tricked him into a betrayal and then disappeared on heaven knew what tortuous and subversive mission—faded into fantasy. On the top of his blinding desolation crept a new fear. It was a fear for Amanda. It occurred to him that it was the first completely unselfish thought he had had since the disaster, or, of course, ever in his life for all he knew. It was linked with something he knew about her, some vulnerability he had forgotten, and with something he knew about Aubrey. There was something from which he must protect her. She was a responsibility of his, quite as much a responsibility as that other which was rapidly assuming such enormous proportions. Apparently he was a responsible person. It seemed a pity he had lost half his mind.

He got off the bed and walked out into the upper hall. He strode up and down there for what seemed an eternity, his footsteps deadened by the heavy carpet. The lights were very bright, with the cold brilliance which seems to be a part of the middle of the night, and when the drawing-room door opened he walked over to the banister without hesitation and looked down.

"Good night, Amanda."

Aubrey's deep delightful voice was soft and packed with meaning. He was leaning against the doorpost with his head bent and a lock of his thick hair drooping boyishly forward. He had taken Amanda's hand and was swinging it backwards and forwards in the careless inarticulate fashion which Gerald du Maurier used to use so effectively in so many of his scenes. He was not a man who would ever appear handsome, but his whole pose was negligently graceful, which was odd in such a large-boned loosely constructed figure.

Campion got the impression that Amanda was a trifle flustered and also that the condition was hitherto unknown to her.

"Good night, Lee," she said, sounding positively schoolgirlish in an effort to be matter-of-fact. Then, turning away, she hurried upstairs, to arrive pink and a little breathless before Campion in the upper hall.

She was astounded to see him and obviously accepted the first explanation which came into her head.

"What's the matter?" she demanded. "What's happened?"

"I want to talk to you."

"All right. What is it? I say, nothing else awful, surely?" She appeared to expect disaster and hurried into his room as if she thought to find concrete evidence of it there.

He followed her and closed the door. Had there been bolts upon it he would have shot them.

"There's one thing you've got to tell me," he said. "I've been trying to find out all the evening."

"What?"

"What day is it?"

She stared at him. Her light brown eyes were wide with astonishment at first, but as he looked at her the fine brows came down in a straight line above them and the fiery colour spread over her face.

"Did you hang about on the staircase simply to ask me that? You're behaving rather extraordinarily, aren't you?"

He was, of course. He saw that the moment she pointed it out. To the uninstructed his behaviour and the all-important question could have only one explanation; that he was acting like a jealous child. He felt unreasonably angry with her for his own helplessness.

"I want to know the day and the date of today," he said doggedly. "You're the only person I dare ask. What is it?"

"It's the thirteenth, I think." She was furious, and the dignity which her control lent her was the coldest thing on earth.

"Friday, I suppose?"

"No. Tuesday. Now I think I'll go to bed."

Tuesday the thirteenth. That meant Thursday the fifteenth. A day. A day to do what?

Amanda moved over towards the door. He thought she was going out without a word and was helpless to stop her. He was completely unprepared, therefore, for what was evidence of one of the most lovable traits in her make-up. On the threshold she turned and quite suddenly grinned at him.

"I've gone all theatrical, Albert," she said. "What is up?"

He groaned. "God knows," he said truthfully.

Amanda came back into the room and sat down on the edge of the bed.

"Are you all right?" she demanded. "Don't forget you have had a dust-up. I don't want to fuss you—I know how you hate it—but you do look a bit green, you know. I've noticed it all the evening and haven't liked to mention it."

He cocked an eye at her. That was a piece of his own character slipping into place. He was one of those men with a horror of being fussed, was he? Yes, that was right; he felt he might be like that. She hadn't liked to fuss him. She was pretty marvellous. A great surge of desire for comfort from her broke over him. She was alive. She was his only link with reality. It was on his tongue to risk everything and come out with the awful truth when her next remark silenced him.

"I'm sorry I behaved so badly. I've got a bit self-centred. I thought you were playing the fool because I was falling in love with Lee." She spoke without any affectation and was free from any suggestion of the coyly blunt. Her eyes were as candid as her words.

"Are you?"

"I think so." There was a quiet softness in her voice, a gentle satisfaction which he knew he had never heard in it before.

"Why?"

She hesitated and finally laughed. "It's a thing I couldn't possibly tell you if you weren't yourself," she said, "I mean if I didn't know you as well as I know myself almost. He's like you, isn't he?"

"Is he?"

"I think so, very. Except for the one important thing."

"What's that?"

She looked up at him and there was a sort of rueful shyness in her young face.

"He loves me so. He's doing his best about it but it's bubbling out all over him and making him shy and silly, like an undergraduate or a peasant or something. And since he's a great man—because he is brilliant, you know—well, that makes it pretty irresistible." She paused and shook herself. "Let's not discuss it. It's not a bit in your line and things are getting up speed, aren't they? I feel disgusted with myself for getting—er—overtaken by this thing, but it's like that. It does— er—overtake. Tell me about Anscombe."

"He was murdered."

"What?" She sat staring at him. "But that's impossible! Who?"

"I don't know."

Amanda clasped her knees and her heart-shaped face looked small and worried as she rested her chin on them.

"Of course, I'm not competent to judge anything in this business," she said unexpectedly, "since I don't know the full strength."

"My dear," he said with elaborate deference, because he was still tingling from the blow which seemed to have hurt the secret forgotten part of himself even more than his conscious needy present, "I only wish I could tell you."

"Yes, well, you can't," she said briefly. "You're under oath and that's final. I don't mind. I know you well enough to work under sealed orders. Otherwise I'd hardly have done the unforgivable thing and got Lee to invite us down here without telling him you were working on something in the town. I've got your assurance that it's desperately important; that's good enough."

Campion was standing with his back to her and did not dare look round.

"Let's see," he said mendaciously, "how long have we known Lee?"

"You mean how long have I known him," objected Amanda. "You've known him three days, as you very well know. I came down here from Dell on some work on the new armour for the Seraphim planes. There was a man working at the Institute we had to get hold of. I made friends with Lee then."

She was talking gibberish, apart from the all-important dates, as far as Campion was concerned, and he wondered how far he dared press her for information. Fortunately she helped him unconsciously.

"Have you told anyone about the hospital episode this afternoon?"

"No."

"Nor have I. And I was thinking, Albert, I don't suppose Anscombe did. So suppose we stick to our original plan, which is, if you remember, that I took you into Coachingford on Sunday night to catch the London express. That was immediately after you had the wire which was waiting for you when we arrived. Then yesterday I was supposed to fetch you from the same station after your return. At dinner tonight I was very vague about our delay, but it was a sticky gathering anyway and didn't matter. Still, if it does come up we'll have to call it tyre trouble. How's that?"

"Excellent," he said dubiously and waited for her to continue.

"How did you get on at Coachingford?" she enquired at last.

He shrugged his shoulders and she nodded gloomily.

"Like that?" she said. "Never mind. It'll come suddenly. I don't like this Anscombe business, though. That's horrible. Just when we thought he knew something."

He turned on her. "What made you think he knew something?"

"I don't know. I just got that impression."

"Not—'fifteen'?"

"Fifteen?" She seemed surprised. "Fifteen what?"

"Fifteen men on a dead man's chest," he said and half wondered if he had invented the ringing phrase.

"Yo-ho-ho and some nice sound sleep," said Amanda. "You can't do any more tonight, anyway, if the whole world's at stake. You go to bed."

Campion leant heavily on the back of the chair which he had been fingering. His wooden face was haggard and he looked tired and frustrated.

"My God, I wonder if it is," he said.

She gave the question serious consideration.

"It seems a bit presumptuous, but it might be," she said.

Campion felt the beads of sweat break out on the line where his forehead met his hair.

"That's the kind of damned silly premonition I've got," he said.

Amanda smiled at him. "If it is, I'd rather it was in your hands than anybody's," she said honestly. "You've got all the cards, Albert, and fundamentally you're so . . ."

"So what?"

"So sort of sufficient at heart. So cold. You'll get by."

After she had gone he sat very still in the silent room and the strong light beat down upon him with chilly clarity. The warmth had gone out of the dream again and he was back in the familiar nightmare. He knew what it was like now. It was like one of those trick films wherein familiar objects are photographed from an unfamiliar angle. The strange shadows thus cast made vast secret shapes, forming a horror where there is none and, worse still, concealing a horror where horror lies.

Now that Amanda had gone he wondered why he had not confided in her. It was not only because of Lee and because he dreaded her pity as he dreaded insufferable pain. There was another reason. He reached down into the darkness in his mind and drew it out from its skulking place in all its hideousness. It was a fear. If she knew of his mental state, if she knew of that overheard conversation in the hospital, and had it presented to her with the facts as they both knew them about Anscombe's death, then would she still regard him with that candid trust which was the most precious thing about her? Or would the gleam of a doubt come creeping into her brown eyes before her loyalty doused it? That was the risk he had not dared to take. He was the man involved and he would not entirely trust himself.

The whistle cut into his thoughts. The low note, which was just sufficiently unlike a bird's to be uncanny, sounded twice before it brought him to his feet. He switched out the light and stood listening. It sounded again just beneath the window.

He pulled the heavy curtains aside, unlatched the old-fashioned shutters, and threw up the sash as quickly as he could.

The whistle began and ended suddenly and there was a long silence. The house cast a deep shadow and the space below the window was black as the pit.

"Is that you, sir?" The voice was very quiet and almost directly beneath him. "Are you ready? I've been waiting round the other side. I must have mistook your meaning. We'll have to get a move-on if we're to get the job done tonight. Can you come at once?"

"What? Yes, yes, all right, I'll be with you in a moment." Campion drew in his head, closed the windows, and replaced its various shroudings. Then he went downstairs with the soft-footed tread of a professional burglar. In his mind was a single unqualified question-mark, for the voice had been the utterly unmistakable one of Superintendent Hutch.

CHAPTER SEVEN

Campion came out of the front doorway noiselessly. He picked his way over the gravel to the silent turf of the lawn and stood waiting. If this was arrest the whole world was as light-headed as he was.

The Superintendent's jaunty figure emerged from the black shadows round the house and dropped into step beside him. He did not speak, but, taking Campion's arm, led him into the narrow line of darkness below the row of close-growing poplars which lined one side of the path. He walked very fast and did not open his mouth until they were a good two hundred yards from the window. Finally he sighed.

"Very nicely done, sir," he said with approval. "I didn't know you had come out until I set eyes on you. It's as well to be careful. We don't want to give a lot of fancy explanations. Once you start that game, it's my experience that you have to go on remembering what you've said for years afterwards."

Campion made no specific comment. He grunted noncommittally and pressed on towards the gateway.

As he had hoped, Hutch continued to talk. He revealed a friendly soul and a justifiable pride in his rise to eminence in the force.

"That's why I'm doing this little job myself," he remarked. "It's not that I haven't got half a dozen men I could trust to be both efficient and discreet, but I don't want them to take the risk, don't you see? When it's something unorthodox and a little delicate it's the Chief's job every time. Don't you agree?"

"Oh, every time," said Campion heartily. He wondered where in God's name they were going with such determined speed.

They turned away from Anscombe's house at the end of the drive and plunged off downhill in the opposite direction. Hutch kept to the shadowed side of the street and his long strides were silent as a ghost's. Most English country towns are picturesque in the moon's eye, but this winding hill was like a part of an old fairy story in the cold yellowish light. Tudor shops with overhanging upper storeys and windows like those on a galleon squeezed prim Queen Anne houses which wore shutters and graceful fanlights. There were mounting blocks and lantern posts at every dozen yards, and through carved archways occasional glimpses of cobbled courts and stone gardens. It was probably the most hackneyed picture-postcard subject in the world, but Campion saw it with the eyes of a child and its charm startled him. The crazy roofs were like witches' hoods huddling together for whispered consultations and the dark windows winked their panes at him from a bygone world.

Meanwhile the Superintendent's silence became oppressive and Campion ventured a leading question.

"Why exactly is this trip so delicate?"

"Perhaps that isn't the word I ought to have used." Hutch seemed a little put out and for a moment Campion was afraid that he had silenced him.

As they turned across a wide market square which might well have decorated any calendar the policeman opened out a little.

"I don't like to talk under windows," he said. "In a place like this everyone knows your voice, let alone your life story. You don't quite understand the position of the Masters in this town, do you?"

"No," said Campion truthfully, "I'm afraid I don't. Most of the offices are hereditary, aren't they?"

"All of them." Hutch appeared to respect the fact. "It's a very interesting survival," he announced, a touch of the professional guide creeping into his voice and mixing oddly with the confidential police low-down which was his natural manner. "Their records go back nearly five hundred years. This is the only example of what you might virtually call a free city in the British Isles—other than London, of course. We're in a funny position, you see, stuck here on a navigable river which yet isn't quite big enough to make us a port."

"Yes, of course." Campion held his breath. They were half-way across the Square now and in a moment or two windows would be over their heads again.

"That fellow Pyne," said Hutch, "he called the Masters a glorified municipal council, you may remember. So he can, but if he realized how glorified they are he'd keep his mouth shut like the rest of us. Do you know, Mr. Campion, there's not a man in this town selling so much as a packet of cigarettes who doesn't do his business solely at the direct discretion of the Masters? They're kings, that's what they are, little kings. Between 'em they own the whole place and the Institute makes 'em rich. Why do you think there's no cinema in the whole of Bridge? Because the Masters don't want to alter the character of the town. They own the land, they appoint the magistrates, they control the licences, and it's their say-so. Same with the trippers. You'll never see a charabanc in Bridge although it's the most famous beauty spot in the whole of the south-west. The Masters don't want charabancs. They know their townsfolk. In fact they are their townsfolk.

They're all related—the whole town is related—and charabancs aren't allowed."

He paused in his stride and lowered his voice.

"Of course, being so old and so rich and having all the ancient ceremonial and secrecy and so on, it makes them very powerful. They've got such a pull. They always put up a Member of Parliament and they subsidize a Chair at one of the Universities—oh, they've got a finger in all sorts of pies! They're thick as thieves with the Government and in fact I shouldn't be a bit surprised if they weren't one of the most powerful bodies in the whole country in their own quiet way."

"Quiet." Campion repeated the word aloud unconsciously. It was coming back to him, or rather it was all there now. He knew it all, just behind the shadows in his mind. The Superintendent's urgent words were like a new facet on some old stone which he knew well.

Hutch snorted. "They're quiet all right," he said. "There's never been a meeting of theirs discussed at a tea-table, let alone reported in the press. It's amazing what you can keep quiet if it's in your interest to do so. That's why I called our little job tonight delicate. We haven't got too much time either. This way, sir. It's quicker."

He took Campion's arm again as he spoke and drew him down a narrow alleyway between two dark houses whose sugarloaf roofs bowed to each other overhead.

"This brings us out directly into the Nag's Pykle," he said. "Round here."

Another sharp turn brought them out into the open moonlight again and Campion, still with his new child's eyes, was brought up short before what is perhaps one of the most dramatic natural pictures in England.

A broad road, still paved and flanked with squat houses, rises slowly to the Corn Exchange and the Nag's Head Inn. The hostelry, fourth oldest in the country, is three storeys high and its centre gable, gallant but drunken, leans appreciably westward, lending the whole structure a note of ancient and irresponsible festivity both laughable and endearing. Behind this, and behind the Corn Exchange and the low tower of St. Nicholas's Church, stands the Nag itself. The bare hill rises up stark and unexpected, like the head of the giant horse it is said to resemble. It is threadbare limestone and is entirely naked save for the double line of ragged pine trees on the crest which in Bridge are called The Mane. In broad sunlight it is impressive and even menacing, but that night, by the moon, it was breath-taking.

Even the Superintendent was tempted to comment.

"Extraordinary formation," he observed. "When you come on it like this you can almost believe the old tale about the bridge. You know that one, don't you? Oh well, if you don't, it's interesting," he added with some satisfaction. "It shows you how far back the name of the town goes. There's the river mouth behind there, as you know, and that other hill on the opposite bank is called The Manger. It's got a big hollow in the top. You can see it on a clear day. The story goes that there was a great flood here once that cut the town right off from the mainland. There was a terrible famine and no one could put out in a boat because of the storms. Right at the last moment, when everyone was practically dead, the Mayor—or local saint or somebody —said his prayers extra strong and lo! and behold, 'with a roar like a million drums', the Nag raised his head and shot out his great neck and put his nose in The Manger over on the other side of the river. Those who were still strong enough ran along his mane and brought back food for the rest. The Nag kept his head in The Manger until the floods went down and then one night, when everything was quiet and everyone was asleep, like it might be tonight, he drew it very quietly back again. That's the legend of how the town got its name, and there's certainly no bridge in the place except the little hump-backed one down by the mill on the Coachingford road."

He laughed a trifle self-consciously.

"I always think of it when I come along here at night," he said. "I like that bit about the 'roar like a million drums'. You can just imagine it, can't you? I don't know that there's much moral to the tale, unless it's that the Nag looks after Bridge. So he does, of course, to this day. Very much so. But it's remarkable how an old tale like that gets handed down. I wonder you hadn't heard it. It's very well known. One of the big composers wrote a bit of music about it. Holst, was it?"

Campion said nothing. The story, coupled with the unexpected sight, was strangely moving. He knew he must be hearing it much as a savage might, or as the early unsophisticated inhabitants of the town must have done. It was damnably convincing. He felt quite a thrill of superstitious fear.

Meanwhile, the Superintendent's attitude towards himself was growing more incomprehensible at every step. He was friendly, not to say obliging, and, moreover, the further they came the less certain of himself he appeared to be. But where they were going so fast and so secretly remained a complete and utter mystery.

Campion was naturally tempted to begin careful pumping operations, but he was alive to all the dangers. He knew so little about anything at all that the most innocent remark could easily prove a disaster. He ventured one little feeler.

"Mr. Aubrey rather expected you to come along earlier this evening," he said.

"I daresay he did, sir." Hutch became an official again. "I had one or two things to see to. I'd hardly left Mr. Anscombe's house when something else cropped up."

"Oh?" Campion tried to show interest without anxiety and the Superintendent rose to the fly.

"I had a call from Coachingford," he said briefly. "They're having a bit of a man hunt all round here tonight. As far as I could get it on the telephone the case seems to have all the usual features, but it's a worry in wartime. There was the stolen car abandoned on the high road and all the rest of it. They'll pick him up in the morning when they can see what they're doing. They're circulating a full description . . . here we are, sir, this way."

The final announcement was providential, since it covered Campion for the necessary moment. He had started like a cat, he noticed with concern, and he had a conviction that his nerves were not usually so unreliable.

They had passed the Inn now and had taken a side turning which ran round the eastern base of the Nag. This street was particularly ancient and here the buildings hung together, shrinking into the very sides of the hill. The shop before which Hutch had paused was a grocery and in its bow windows the familiar cartons of breakfast food, condensed milk, and sugar substitutes looked ridiculous. Such a place should have sold love philtres at least.

The Superintendent took Campion's elbow and led him into a minute alley which ran down between the shop and its neighbour. This passage was so narrow that they could not walk abreast and at one point, where the wall bulged, there was scarcely space for Campion's shoulders. Hutch was treading like a hunter. His tall figure passed like a shadow and his feet made no noise. Campion followed him with equal technique.

At the end of the alley they came into a yard. It was little more than a well, with the Nag rising sheer on one side and the building crowding down upon them on the other.

Hutch produced a torch no larger than a rifle cartridge. Its pin-point beam lit up a keyhole in a surprisingly modern door set in an ancient frame. A short key slid into position and the lock turned over. They passed inside into the spicy, slightly rancid atmosphere of a store-room. Campion followed the Superintendent blindly. His passage now had all the actual qualities of dreaming. He had no idea where he was and the velvet dark was warm and faintly anaesthetic.

They seemed to go on walking for some time and his impression was that they were following a narrow path amid all kinds of obstacles. Another door brought them to a flight of wooden stairs and a surprising change of atmosphere. It was still warm, but the air now smelt of paper and floor-polish and the gentle, exciting odour of old wood. It was a long climb and Hutch began to relax some of his elaborate caution.

"We're right in the hill now," he said unexpectedly. "You wouldn't think it, would you? We'll go right on up to the Council Chamber, shall we? There's nothing much down here."

"By all means." Campion spoke absently. He was struggling with incredulity. "Where are we?" he demanded, throwing caution to the winds. "In the Town Hall?"

Hutch laughed. He seemed to take the question as a witticism.

"That's about the size of it, really, isn't it?" he said. "The Masters run the show in Bridge, not the officials in Basket Street. At one time, you know, this used to be the only administrative headquarters in the town. I believe they used to hold the courts in the Council Chamber. It's very interesting if you're keen on ancient history. The whole place is formed from the natural caves in the hill. The air shafts are artificial but they're prehistoric. You'll be impressed by the room. I've only been in it once, and that was last year when I had to come up before the society and make a report. The carving is remarkable, I believe, to those who know."

"Is this the only entrance?" enquired Campion faintly.

"Not likely." Hutch paused in his stride. "You know about that, surely? Excuse me, sir, but don't you know your guidebook? I thought everyone knew about the Doors of Bridge, as they call them. It's one of the features of the place. It's my opinion that it's those four doors which give the Masters their peculiar fanciful quality. After all, there's nothing extraordinary in an ancient body meeting in a room built in a hill. In the old days it served as a fortress, and stood a long siege in the Jacobite rebellion. But those four doors, each one marked by an innocent-looking house, give it a sort of romantic touch, if you see what I mean."

"What houses?" enquired Campion, who appeared to have given up subterfuge.

"Well, there's the pub for one." Hutch was torn between astonishment and delight at the discovery of such ignorance. "The old Nag's Head is built across the main door. You can see it in the back room,

a lovely bit of carved wood. Takes up all one side. That's the ceremonial entrance where the Masters go in on a meeting night. Then
there's the Gate House, where Mr. Peter Lett lives. He's the hereditary
gatekeeper. That door leads out of his drawing-room and isn't often
used. His house is round the other side, in the Haymarket Road. The
third door is off the Rectory. It's a sort of gallery there, next to the
Church. And the fourth lies behind the Wain House, farther off down
the street. Mr. Phillips, who is the hereditary groom, lives there. It's
all very old-world and out of the ordinary, if you come to it new, but
of course when you're as used to it as we are you don't see anything
in it. It's just a custom, that's all."

Campion felt an absurd desire to sit down on the stairs. He wondered vaguely if all ancient history sounded as picturesque as this when
it was heard for the first time, and, if so, if most children lived in this
perpetual state of astonishment.

"We came in by a fifth door, then," he murmured.

"We came in by the back door," said Hutch firmly. "Not many
people know about it and I daresay it's comparatively recent—not
above seventy years old perhaps. Like everybody else the Masters have
to have cleaners and they have to have goods delivered. I imagine they
must have bought the shop at some period and installed a caretaker
there. It's an old-fashioned business. It's been in the same family for
years. I came in that way tonight because it seemed safest. I don't
want to have to give a lot of explanations and I'm sure you don't. This
is the last step, sir. Now to your right."

He produced a larger torch as he spoke and Campion was startled
by the height of the gallery in which they stood. It seemed to have no
ceiling but to go on up and up into infinity. There was a pleasant dull
sound of wood on wood, a faint squeak from a protesting hinge, and
then a great rush of cool air as they passed into the room within.

Hutch swept a broad beam of light round them and Campion
stepped back. The place was enormous. It was churchlike and colossal. He received a confused impression of black panelling, the lower
halves of mighty pictures, full-length portraits of heroic size, and, overhead, canopies of ragged banners, still bright and gallant after their
passage down the centuries. The centre-piece turned out somewhat
tamely to be a table. It was a mighty affair of glistening black oak and
it fitted snugly on a carpet which must have been very nearly the size
of a tennis court, but apart from this it was normal enough and almost
ordinary. Twenty-five chairs encircled it and at the head, before a seat
larger than the others, was a pile of papers and a very prosaic speaker's
water-bottle and glass.

The silence was remarkable. It hung over them like a smothering pall. There was not a breath anywhere, not a crackle of shrinking wood, not a scurry of dust upon the stone floor, nothing. Hutch sighed deeply. It was evident that he was about to make some pronouncement and Campion nerved himself to meet whatever might be coming.

The man's words when they arrived, however, took him completely by surprise.

"Well, sir." He sounded a trifle breathless. "Here you are. I've risked my warrant to get us in and I hope you'll forgive me if I say for God's sake get whatever you have to do done as soon as possible, so we can get out before the light. I don't like to think what would happen if we got caught. No one would lift a finger for us. But you know that even better than I do, I expect."

CHAPTER EIGHT

Campion did not move. The actor who drives up centre-stage in the middle of the big scene, and who stands there blankly with the urgent silence growing more acute at every second, feels much as he did then.

His first coherent thought was even more terrifying, however. Since he had evidently engineered this illegal entry himself, and had apparently persuaded a Superintendent of Police to break the dearest law in the British Constitution in order to achieve it, it must obviously have some vital importance and he himself must possess much more than ordinary influence. There was something he had to do here, more probably something he had to find out, and there was no knowing what stupendous matters hung upon his success. Already it was long past midnight. The morning of the fourteenth had begun. The fifteenth, as far as he knew, was zero-hour.

It came to him that he must lay his cards on the table and take the consequences. He turned to Hutch, prepared to speak, but as the first difficult words formed in his mind the Superintendent began again.

"I don't like to criticize," he said, his apology making the reproach a hundred times more poignant in the circumstances, "and I know men in your position have to keep their mouths shut, but, just as a question of policy, don't you think it would have made things a lot easier if your department had seen fit to trust the Chief Constable and myself with just a little more information? You can see how it is. We're quite blindfold, aren't we? We're instructed to give you every assistance, every assistance no matter what you ask, and so we will, but it would make things simpler if we had a glimmer of what you were up to."

He paused hopefully but, when the man before him did not reply, went on earnestly.

"Look at that business this evening, for instance. I haven't been in the Force for close on thirty years without being able to recognize a corpse which has been slugged when I see one. But what am I to do? There's a ready-made loophole there and we've got a young doctor. If I shut down on the enquiry I can let the whole investigation collapse without any trouble. But am I right in doing that? Is it in the country's interest or is it nothing to do with the case? I don't know. I'm asking you. I'm in the dark. I gave you every opportunity but you didn't give me any lead."

Campion pulled himself up as the solid ground gave way at his very feet.

"I can't tell you," he said helplessly. "Don't you understand? I am simply unable to tell you."

Hutch stiffened. He was like a soldier at attention.

"Very good, sir," he said. "I'm in your hands. Carry on."

Campion took the torch from him and advanced towards the table. It seemed the obvious thing to do. As he came up to it its enormous size became more apparent and panic seized him as he looked across that vast expanse of shining wood. It was so empty, so utterly uninformative.

He glanced towards the papers neatly arranged before the main chair and experienced his first ray of hope. They were not all the usual blanks. On the top of the pile was a fold of foolscap neatly headed "Agenda". Anscombe had done his last duty for the Masters.

By the light of the torch he read the list of items down for discussion at the morrow's meeting. It began archaically enough with "Prayers to Almighty God" and went on to the orthodox "Senior Master's Opening Remarks", "Minutes of the Last Meeting", and "Correspondence". But the third entry was more unusual. "Ceremony of the Bale of Straw", it stated simply, and continued, as though the one were the counterpart of the other, "Report on the New Sewage System for the Lower Town, temporarily suspended by War". The "Institute Report" followed and the fifth item recorded "Extraordinary Council: Resignation of John Robert Anscombe, Secretary".

The sixth heading brought Campion up short, his brows rising as he read the round characterless copperplate.

"*Suggested Purchase from the Government of the French,*" it ran briefly. "*Spice Island of Malaguama. 950,000,000 francs.*"

This somewhat staggering project brought him to the foot of the page and he turned it casually, unprepared for any further statement, but there, staring at him and in the same childish hand, was yet another consideration for the Masters of Bridge.

"*Main Business of the Evening,*" he read and saw underneath it, in a large carelessly drawn circle in red ink, the haunting figures 15.

Below were two further lines, clearly referring to some traditional closing ceremony: "(1) *The Oath*" and "(2) *The Toast Sec. 5. Perish All Those Who Doe Wrong Unto Us.*"

He refolded the sheet, put it back into position, and stepped back. His knees were trembling. It was all here, he felt certain, all under his hand, and yet he could not recognize it. The other half of the talisman was lying just out of his reach in the monstrous darkness of his own brain.

Hutch remained stiffly at his side. Campion could feel that the man was uneasy, alarmed at the enormity of his own share in storming this sacred fastness.

Campion peered round him in the gloom.

"There are other rooms, of course?"

"This is the only actual habitable room, sir. The others are only caverns. They go right on down to the Trough."

"The Trough?"

"Yes, sir. That's the local name of the big cave on the estuary bay. It runs a long way under the hill and the old river road leads past it. At one time it used to be a great place for picnics and so on, but the water comes right up to the entrance at high tide and there were so many cases of people getting caught down there that the Masters declared it shut and ran a railing across the entrance, which isn't very wide. A place like that gets very dirty and untidy if you leave it open to the public."

"I suppose so. Can you get down to it from here?"

"I don't know, sir. No one's allowed in here, you see. I don't think you can. As far as I know you can get on to a sort of gallery which looks down into the Trough, but I don't think there's any way down from that. When I was a boy we used to dare each other to get up into the Masters' store-rooms, but it was a terrific climb and you needed a rope. We never got very far."

"I see. I'd like to go on a bit, though. Is that possible?"

"It's possible, sir." Hutch did not add that it was also insane in his opinion, with the seconds racing by so dangerously.

A new doggedness had come over Campion and he hunched his shoulders.

"We'll have to risk it," he said.

Hutch was an experienced man and he worked quickly, but it was not an easy adventure since he was as ignorant of the geography of the place as was Campion, and their first need was to get out of the Council Chamber without stumbling inadvertently through any one of the Four Doors of Bridge.

They found the way by considering the formation of the cavern in which the chamber was set and came at first to an astonishingly efficient furnace-room with a chimney built up through a prehistoric airshaft in the hill. From there they passed on into a passage which had been roughly lined at some much earlier period, and thence an iron ladder took them down into the Masters' store-rooms.

These long caverns were unexpectedly well ventilated and confirmed Campion's suspicions that the whole Nag was nothing less than a fortress, probably dating back to Neolithic times.

A brief inspection disclosed that the main use to which the Masters put their space was the storage of wine. The first gallery contained rack after rack of dusty black bottles and a smile appeared on the Superintendent's strained face as he looked at them.

"They must have done themselves proud for generations," he said. "I bet there's a fortune here. As a matter of fact they do own vineyards all over the world, I've heard."

Campion did not comment.

At the end of the gallery the entrance to the next cavern was small and had been boarded up at some time. Hutch ran his torch beam over the edges of the torn wood lying in a neat pile on the uneven floor.

"This hasn't been down long," he remarked. "They've been making room for more liquor, I suppose."

It certainly looked like it. It seemed hardly credible, but the thin shafts from the Superintendent's two torches disclosed pile upon pile of small packing cases, each sealed and labelled with a grower's name and burnt with the same hieroglyphics. Most of it appeared to be hock and it was clear that the Masters had had the forethought to see that no European upheaval could interfere with their serious drinking.

Hutch gasped. "There's a cargo of it," he said, sounding thoroughly shocked. "A perishing cargo. Hallo, sir, what's the matter?"

Campion had paused in the middle of a step. His body had become rigid and he stood immovable, his head raised.

"Listen," he whispered.

Hutch became a rock. He had extinguished his torch and now both men waited in the suffocating darkness which filled the world about them like black wool.

"What was it, sir?" The Superintendent's agonized demand was only just audible.

"A petrol engine. Listen."

Very faint, so muffled that it was more of a sensation than a sound, the throbbing reached them.

"It's beneath us," said Campion briefly. "Come on."

"Sir . . ." Hutch was a good man and he knew his duty, but there is one State Department which does not recognize its servants if they make mistakes. He did not belong to it and thirty years' blameless record was at stake.

"Give me the torches. You stay where you are." It occurred to Campion briefly that it was odd that he should issue orders so naturally and should be so certain that they would be unquestioningly obeyed. He went on alone, moving like a wraith but very quickly, with a sure-footed stealth which betrayed long practice. He did not see the second iron ladder until he was almost upon it, and he paused with his heart in his mouth, peering down into the abyss.

The throbbing had ceased, but in the cold underground air there was a slight but unmistakable breath of exhaust. He went down the ladder for what seemed a very long way and found himself in a passage no wider than his outstretched arms.

Here the taint was stronger and he moved very cautiously, keeping the pin-point of light from the small torch on the ground at his feet. An abrupt right-angle turn brought him up with a start. The fumes were much stronger now and, mingling with them, was the fresh sharp tang of the sea.

He pressed on and came out suddenly into what felt like a vast open space. The air smelt like a garage and his tiny ray of light suddenly lengthened as the path ended in a yawning hole before his feet. He paused, breathless, and switched off the light.

There was no sound, no sign of life, nothing except the strong reek of petrol. He hesitated. If the place was occupied his presence must already be discovered. He took the Superintendent's larger torch in his left hand and, holding it at arm's length so that the beam should arise a good three feet away from him on the wrong side, switched it on.

What he saw was so unexpected that he almost dropped the torch. He was on a narrow ledge, high up on the rock wall of a cave which could only be the Trough of the Superintendent's description, for it stretched away to a narrow railed opening far away in the distance. This in itself was not altogether unexpected, but what was extraordinary was that directly below him, hidden from the entrance by a natural partition which jutted out into the main body of the cave, was a large pocket or alcove, snug and secret, which housed at the moment something under three hundred three-ton lorries of varying types and ages, but clearly in good running order and ready for the road.

Campion swung the torch over them and the finger of light rested on bonnets and cabs, on yawning bodies and solid wheels. The narrow shaft of light ran up one row and down the next, wavered dangerously, and swept on again.

Campion forced himself to finish his inspection, but that single glimpse at the end of the row had been enough. He had seen the face of a man, crouching back into the shelter of an overhanging cab. It had been a white face in the bright light and it had been familiar. It had flashed into his vision bringing a name with it; a name and a deep feeling of no enthusiasm, as someone once said so expressively. "Weaver Bea."

As he repeated it under his breath it sounded absurd and unlikely and yet in all the turmoil in his mind it remained familiar and unpleasant.

It was at this point that the full realization of his own utter inefficiency came home to him. The curious singleness of purpose which had hitherto characterized his condition was wearing thin and he began to take a more normal view of the situation in which he found himself, inasmuch as he began to suspect himself at every step. He saw himself making mountains out of molehills, and, what was even worse, pitfalls into mere depressions. Moreover, the physical effect of the experience had begun to tell on him again. His head ached maddeningly and he was not too certain of his legs.

He crept back the way he had come but, although he paused to listen when he reached the right-angle bend, there was still no sound from the great hidden garage he had left.

As he felt his way up the narrow iron ladder he tried to assimilate what he had seen since entering the Nag. It was both tantalizing and alarming. He had the uncomfortable feeling that it might all be very ordinary if seen with the clear eyes of a normally informed person. Any municipal stronghold of great antiquity could probably appear fantastic to the completely ignorant. Yet, on the other hand, every half-observed aspect of the place might well possess some all-important significance which he ought to recognize at once. There was the number 15 on the agenda: that must be of interest. And the man he had just seen: if his presence was normal, why had he hidden?

He struggled on and by the time he heard the Superintendent's heavy breathing just ahead of him he had made up his mind. There was only one course open to him which was not criminally negligent. He must get into touch with Oates at once. He ought to have done that immediately on receipt of the letter, of course. He wondered why he had ignored this obvious solution and suddenly remembered Anscombe and his own invidious position in that matter, which had focused his entire attention on the personal aspect. Hutch had only just explained that, of course. Good God, he was mad! Here he was, stumbling about in the dark seeing monsters where there were bushes and innocent shadows where there might be death-traps, and all the time the precious hours were racing past. He was a lunatic, very possibly a dangerous lunatic. Mercifully he was gradually getting the intelligence to recognize the fact.

The Superintendent was eager for news but even more eager to get out of his highly compromising position. He led the way back with alacrity and they passed across the Council Chamber like a couple of homing foxes.

"Lorries?" he said in astonishment when Campion had replied to his question. "How many?"

"Several." Campion could not explain his own urge towards caution.

Hutch shook his head. "I don't know anything about them," he said. "It's the Government work, I expect. They're doing a lot of experiments with synthetic juice up at the Institute—at least that's the gossip. The Masters own the Institute, and, come to think of it, the Trough wouldn't be a bad place to hide a lorry or two. You're suddenly in a great hurry, sir. You weren't seen, were you?"

"No," said Campion truthfully, "but I've got to get a move-on now."

The Superintendent opened his mouth to make an enquiry but the experience of long service saved him the indiscretion. Moreover, they were approaching the store-room behind the shop again.

They got out without incident but Hutch was not pleased to find it almost dawn. Fortunately it was misty and the two men plunged into the chilling vapour as thankfully as if it had been a smoke-screen especially provided for their benefit.

As they passed down the broad highway of the Nag's Pykle the squat houses blinked at them through the haze and the town of Bridge looked a little less like a fairy-tale than it had done by moonlight. It was old and very picturesque, but the unreality, the frankly fantastic atmosphere of the night before, had vanished with the moon.

Campion was relieved to see it and to credit his returning intelligence with the change. He felt definitely ill. His head was throbbing and his body ached. However, he knew what he had to do. Amanda was his card. Amanda must take him to Oates. It was odd that the very recollection of Amanda should wrap such comfort round him. He must get out of that, he supposed, if she had made up her mind, and yet . . . it was absurd. All that was ridiculous. Amanda was not only his: she *was* himself. Amanda . . . oh, he couldn't be bothered to work it out. He must go to her . . . get to her . . . get . . . to . . . her.

Hutch caught him as he stumbled, and as they stood swaying together on the cobbles Campion was aware of some inner reserve of strength like a separate person within his body reaching down, down, and dragging his submerging faculties to the surface again. It was a staggering experience, like being rescued from drowning in a dream.

The Superintendent's face, which had loomed very large, gradually resumed its normal proportions and his voice, which had receded to a distant hail, slipped back into tune.

"You've overdone it, sir, that's what you've done. We're just by the station. You'll have to sit down. You can't go on for ever without sleeping or eating; no one can."

The tone was plaintive and gently nagging.

"You'll go sick on your feet, and then where shall we be?"

He was leading his charge all the time with the firm efficiency of long practice and they advanced upon the unexpectedly modern Police Station, set among the Tudor scenery, in spite of his companion's incoherent protests.

A Police Sergeant met them on the doorstep and there was a muttered conference between him and his chief.

"Is there?" Hutch said at last. "I see. Yes. Yes, of course. Put it through at once. We'll take it in the Charge Room." He turned to Campion anxiously. "There's a personal call waiting for you, sir," he said. "It's from Headquarters. Can you manage it? Are you all right?"

Campion had no clear impression of his passage through the station. He came back to himself as he sat staring into the black mouthpiece of the shabby telephone.

"Yeo here, Mr. Campion," said a voice in his ear. It was so small and quiet that it might have been the whisper of conscience. "Yeo. Have you got the Chief with you?"

"Oates?" Campion's own voice was strong and apprehensive. It seemed to him that he was shouting.

"Yes, sir. He's gone. We can't find him. He left his room here in the small hours of yesterday morning and hasn't been heard of since. Is he with you?"

"No, he's not here."

There was a long pause. It seemed to stretch into centuries and shrink again into a minute's space. He had time to become aware of the light streaming in through the tall windows and of the green distemper on the wall at the end of the room.

The faraway voice spoke again.

"Then it's you alone now, sir. You're the only one now who can do anything. None of the rest of us here even know the full strength. I don't know if you think that's wise, sir. The Chief was in sole control of his agents."

Campion could not reply and after a pause the little voice came again.

"Any . . . luck, sir?"

Campion closed his eyes and opened them again as once more the secret reserve which lies in every human body was pumped up into his veins.

"Not yet," he said distinctly, "but there's still an hour or two."

Then he slipped forward across the table, his head in his arms.

CHAPTER NINE

He woke holding Amanda's hand. He was so relieved to find it there, so comforted to see her, alive, friendly, and gloriously intelligent, that for a blessed moment he remained mindless and content. He lay looking at her with placid, stupid eyes.

"You're ill," she said, her clear, immature voice frankly anxious. "I've been trying to wake you for hours. What shall I do? Phone Oates?"

That did it. That brought him back to the situation with a rush. Everything he knew, everything he had discovered or experienced since he had awakened in the hospital bed, sped past his conscious mind like a film raced through a projector at treble speed. The effect was catastrophic. It took his breath away and left him sweating.

"No," he said, struggling into a sitting position, while the whole top of his head seemed to slide backwards sickeningly. "No, that's no good. I mean don't do that. I'll get up at once."

"All right," she agreed and he looked at her with deep affection. She was quite obviously worried about him and in her opinion he should have stayed where he was, but he was the boss and she was not arguing. She was so pretty, too, so young and vividly sensible. He liked her brown eyes and wished she would kiss him. The reflection that he had probably lost her for ever was such an incredible disaster that he put it away from him, unconsidered, and tightened his grip on her hand childishly.

"How late am I?"

"About an hour." She released herself gently. "You start the tour of inspection at ten. I'll run you a bath and then go down and scrounge you some breakfast. You've got twenty minutes before you leave the house."

"Tour of inspection?" he said dubiously. "What—er—what do I wear?"

He had hoped for a clue but for once she was unobliging.

"Oh, just the simple uniform of an Admiral of the Fleet, I should think, don't you?"

Her voice floating back from the other room was followed by the roar of his bath water.

"Or you might stick to the old fireman's outfit, of course. That's bright and cheerful without being vulgar. I say," she added as she came in again, "what about those things? The servants here look as though they take a valet's interest in one's wardrobe. It'll look so bad if you come in and find them neatly laid out on the bed. Shall I take them down and stuff them in the toolbox of the car?"

"I wish you would. They're in the cupboard," he said. "You're very helpful, Amanda."

She did not answer for a moment, but when she emerged from the armoire with her arms full of oilskins her cheeks were bright.

"I'm still the Lieut.," she said, facing him squarely. "You get up and see to that bath or we'll have a flood. Time's very short."

Short! As the door closed behind him he realized how short time was and cursed himself for sleeping. He could only just remember the later events of the morning. Hutch had brought him home in a car and had put him to bed like a mother. Mercifully they had not given him alcohol at the Police Station. That might well have killed him with his head in its present condition. The Sergeant in charge had apologized, he remembered, and had substituted a stimulant fashionable in official circles at the moment, sweet weak tea. There had been gallons of it. The glucose had probably saved his life.

He said "probably" because getting out of bed proved to be a major operation. However, the sleep had done him good. Miraculously he had lost his terror of his disability. Now he was merely exasperated by it. He did not realize that this phenomenon was nothing less than a return of his original singleness of purpose and that it was a far more dangerous condition. He only saw that there was work to be done, and he was alone to do it, and that time was desperately short.

By the time he staggered downstairs he was fairly clear about his immediate plan of campaign. The Masters were his best bet. They knew the secret of 15 if anyone did, since they were making it their main business of the evening. Lee Aubrey must be persuaded to tell him all there was to be known about the Masters. For the rest, since they had obviously arranged a programme for himself when he had been in full possession of his senses, that programme must be part of his original plan and the only thing to do was to go through with it.

He found Aubrey waiting for him in a brown and yellow morning-room. He was standing by the window looking with tragedian's eyes at Amanda, who sat behind the silver. His greeting was gravely commiserating, as though he knew that lesser men had weaknesses and he could be tolerant and even a little envious of them.

Campion, watching him with his new child's eyes, saw what Amanda liked in him and sized it up like a General inspecting enemy fortifications before the commencement of hostilities.

He made a hurried breakfast and, only half-way through the meal, realized that it was Lee who was waiting for him.

"It's too bad we can't take you with us." Aubrey spoke to the girl with a frankness of regret which was almost indecent. "But I'm afraid it's impossible. We're not exactly wedded to the Government, but we're rather definitely under its protection, in the eighteenth-century sense, and my instructions only apply to Campion. It's all quite, quite mad, of course. I sometimes wonder if the fellows who set out these restrictions aren't using a little too broad a rule. There's not enough brains to go round, you know. That's the fundamental weakness in the Government and everywhere else."

"Oh, that's all right," said Amanda cheerfully. "I don't want to see your old Institute. The whole show sounds like a municipal school of conjuring to me."

Lee hesitated and it was only after a moment that his charming smile spread over his large curling features.

"You shocked me," he said with disarming naïveté. "I get very parochial down here. One does. To hear the Masters called 'municipal' gives me a sacrilegious thrill."

"They achieve almost international status, financially at any rate, don't they?" Campion's thought was running on spice islands and he spoke unguardedly.

Lee raised his head and gave him one of his surprisingly intelligent stares.

"They're very wealthy, of course," he said primly.

"Yes, well, there you are. A penny here and a penny there, it all mounts up over a period of years." Campion had intended to sound ignorant, but even he was unprepared for the degree of fatuous idiocy he managed to present.

Lee looked genuinely embarrassed and glanced at Amanda apologetically.

"When you're ready we'll go," he said, and later, as he and Campion walked across the turf together, he took it upon himself to explain gently, choosing his words carefully as though talking to a child. "Historically the Masters are amazingly interesting," he began, reproval in his pleasant voice. "The family which was the leading spirit at their foundation never completely rotted away. The Letts have never produced any great men, but nor have they had any downright wrong 'uns, and there's always been one moderately intelligent business man in every generation. The present fellow, Peter Lett, is just a good sound average brain like his uncle before him, and his grandfather and great-grandfathers before that. They've all been religious, respectable, and very parochial, while of course the curious hereditary and semisecret structure of the society has been a tremendous safeguard. Financially the Masters have had their bad periods but they've never gone quite under. Their basic line is so good."

"What's that?"

Aubrey seemed astounded. "Patents, of course," he said.

"Patents?"

"Well," he was laughing a little, "it was monopolies to begin with, naturally. Queen Elizabeth gave them their first big break. One of the kids in the little charity school they started up turned out to be the great Ralph Godlee, who invented the Godlee loom. The Masters got a monopoly on the manufacture of the things from the Queen and it revolutionized the wool-weaving industry over here, speeding up the production by about five hundred per cent and making the town's fortune. The word 'abridged' comes from it. It shortened the process. But you know all this as well as I do."

Campion coughed. "At the moment there are gaps in my education," he admitted modestly. "Do go on. I find this fascinating. They've continued like this, have they?—first educating and then fleecing the investor?"

Lee made a deprecatory grimace and quite openly thought for a moment or so. He was extraordinarily self-conscious in that one way. His thinking was obvious, almost pantomimic.

"That's not quite true," he said at last. "One must be fair. Let's say that instead of patronizing the arts they've always gone in for science and have been lucky in having been able to produce a few valuable inventors who have always made their own fortunes as well as adding to the general fund. The Masters had their great successes in the Victorian industrial age, naturally. It's only comparatively recently that they've become so very wealthy. They bought very sensibly at that time, always going for overseas property, tea plantations, and so on. At the moment I think the Institute gives more than value for money every time. Look at the facilities the chosen inventor gets here. Once his idea is approved, every mortal thing he needs is given to him gratis. His patents are acquired for him and he hands out a percentage. Just now things are more than booming, naturally. The Carter cheap process for extracting petrol from coal is going to be an enormous thing, and we've one or two pleasant little explosives on the carpet. The whisky bottle you can't refill is another one of ours too; that's a great money-maker."

Campion listened to him fascinated. He knew it, he had heard it all before, he was sure of that, and vaguely it was all coming back to him. It reminded him most of a rubbing of an old brass. Shadowy outlines of facts were coming up on the blank surfaces of his mind. If only he felt a little more sure of his legs, a little less as though he were ploughing through clouds of cotton-wool which gave beneath him!

"I don't approve of the Masters in principle," Lee was saying pedantically. "I don't like pockets of wealth like that in the country. But, to do these fellows justice, their little constitution does good work. The Ceremony of the Bale of Straw is a nice archaic idea, for instance. All the mummery of the fraternity is connected with the Nag, you know, and they have a ruling that at every half-yearly meeting the Masters shall 'put down a bale of straw in the Nag's stable'; that is to say they shall do something to improve the amenities of the town of Bridge. That's why the place is so luxuriously drained, watered, and lit. There's not a scrap of slum property in the area.

Fortunes are being spent on the place and the rates are negligible. Here we are. See the sentry? That's what working for the War House does for you."

They had come up over the ridge of high ground which stretched up behind the poplar trees and had reached the private road leading to the Institute, a cluster of roofs surrounded by a high moss-grown wall. The original building was now no more than a museum, but all around it clustered other houses, workshops, and laboratories, representing every phase of British architecture. There was the usual preponderance of Victorian-Gothic and a generous sprinkling of modern pillbox.

A soldier with fixed bayonet stood on guard before the ornamental iron gates. Lee Aubrey smiled at the man as they passed.

"Gloriously mad, isn't it?" he murmured. "There's something rather sweet and childlike about the modern world, don't you think? 'Halt. Give the countersign. Pass friend. Eena-deena-dina-do, you're a spy.' It's so monstrously young."

"Childish perhaps, but hardly sweet," said Campion absently. "Where do we go first?"

"My dear fellow, that's entirely up to you. My instructions are that I'm to show you anything that you care to see. Take your choice. On your left you have the bad-tempered but otherwise wholly delightful Carter working with his team of galley-slaves. They'll be polite because I'm by way of being the Headmaster, but they won't be hospitable."

Aubrey was enjoying himself. He was exaggeratedly proud of the place and its magnificent organization.

"On your extreme right, in that depressing building which looks like a Methodist chapel, is poor old Burgess. He'll talk all night. He's having trouble with his reaper. The late trials were nothing less than a fiasco and he may have struck a serious snag. Before you is the library, the office, the filing department, and the drafting rooms. And right over there, as comfortably distant as space will permit, is the star turn of the moment, the War House's little white-headed boy, our young Master Butcher, mucking about with Anderton's latest variety of potted hell fire. I have to keep an eye on him and see he controls his quantities. It's incredible stuff. Half a teaspoonful can make as much mess as a bucketful of T.N.T. Hence the sentry on the door."

He paused expectantly and Campion stood irresolute. This was a continuation of the frustration dream of the night before. As far as he could see, the whole thing was being handed to him on a plate and yet he could not put his finger on it.

"It's almost an embarrassment of riches," he said aloud, and added hastily: "What's in the dovecote?"

The building so unkindly described had caught his attention because of a certain amount of life going on before it. A lorry loading sacks was drawn up in front of the door.

Lee frowned and the man at his side was aware of the wave of irritation which passed over him. It was a physical thing, as if his personal magnetism had been switched off and on again.

"You've got a nose, haven't you?" he said, half laughing. "You're one of those people who always move the chair which covers the hole in the carpet and go straight to the cupboard where the dirty washing-up has been hidden. I offer you the exciting drawing-room exhibits and you go direct to the one dull ugly scullery in the place. That's our cross, the blot on our dignity. We've been compelled to shelter fifty beastly little amateur workers simply because we happen to have a lot of room. Think of it! In that sacred building Richardson perfected his adding machine, and now half a hundred little girls who can hardly write are addressing envelopes there for the Ministry of Health. As if there weren't five million other places in England which would do quite as well. I tell you, I have them shepherded in and out by a police matron and a stalwart from the Corps of Commissioners. Like to come and look at them?"

"Not very much," said Campion. They had reached the building by this time and through the long windows he could see rows of bent heads and piles of Government envelopes. It looked dull work, but in his present mood highly preferable to his own, and he envied them.

As they skirted the lorry a woman with untidy white hair came out of the arched doorway. She was faintly familiar and he recognized her at last as one of Aubrey's dinner guests of the night before. She was startled to see them and came up with that half-hesitant, half-eager humility which is more common in far younger women.

"We're getting on very nicely, Mr. Aubrey," she said appealingly and blushed.

Campion was surprised. Missing on four out of five cylinders though he was, he could still recognize those symptoms when he saw them, and she was not that kind of woman. A great many ladies who are old enough to know better frequently become hopelessly infatuated with brilliant middle-aged bachelors, but they are seldom of the experienced, intelligent type of gentlewoman which he saw before him. He recollected that she had been very interested in Amanda the last time he had seen her. He glanced at Aubrey, to find him frigid.

"Splendid, Mrs. Ericson," he said briefly and passed on, leaving a flavour of distaste in the air. "Patriotic voluntary work," he murmured under his breath to Campion as they turned the corner. "Intense stuff."

"She looked intelligent," said Campion and Lee considered the matter.

"Oh, she is," he agreed brightly. "She's a widow of the late holder of one of the Masters' minor offices and quite a power in the town. Very well read, you know, nice, educated, but emotionally unstable, I fancy. Now this is Butcher's domain, which I take it is your main interest. I say, I admire your magnificent reticence, Campion. It's impressive."

The final observation was made impulsively and as if he meant it.

Campion said nothing and hoped that his silence might pass for modest appreciation. There was a dull throbbing in the back of his head and he had begun to wonder if his vision was not a little deceptive. All the colours in the bright sunlight tended to blur together dangerously. He took hold of himself again. This was hopeless! There was something to be done and, as far as he could gather, only himself to do it. It was a fine thing if he was going to fall down on it through a god-damn silly bang on the head!

It was a longish walk to the square concrete tower at the far end of the Institute grounds and when they reached it their inspection was not illuminating. Butcher himself turned out to be a cheerful youngster with the face of a ploughboy and thick pebbled glasses. He had a youthful respect for Aubrey, whom he clearly admired, and was pleased to show his laboratories and workshops.

"These are the best of the bunch," he said, diving into a rough cupboard in a corner of the main room on the ground floor, which had been deserted and open to the path as they came up. "I keep them in their racks because they really are pretty sensational. We call 'em Phoenix Eggs. Don't drop it, old man, will you? It's quite safe unless you dig that pin out, of course, but it's as well not to bounce it about because it's only a specimen and you never know."

Campion looked down at the metal egg so suddenly thrust in his hand. It was a little larger than a hen's and unexpectedly light. Butcher was fondling another, fitting it lovingly into the hollow under his thumb.

"It's important to be able to chuck it a decent distance," he explained. "It's pretty powerful. The blast is colossal and they even make quite a crater. It's wonderful really. You can make almost any building look silly with only one of these. It's the Anderton variety of liquid air, but we've improved on it—or at least we've utilized every aspect of it. I could hit that old museum over there with this and after the balloon had gone up, oh boy, you wouldn't know it! This is refined warfare, that's what this is."

He retrieved Campion's specimen, juggled with the two of them absently, and replaced them in their nests.

"They're putting up the machines for these now," he said. "I've got some nice little aero models coming along in the basement, but we're still working on the detonators. Anything else in particular that you'd like to see?"

"No, I won't keep you from your work. You've given me more than fifteen minutes already."

The young man's expression did not change and Campion shook hands and turned away. A sixth sense, or rather that mysterious body-mind which so often seems to take charge when one's normal brain goes back on one, was looking after him. His reserve and noncommittal tone were far more impressive than any show of appreciation could ever have been and young Butcher retired to his underground laboratory wondering if the Authorities really put quite the trust in him which their behaviour so far had caused him to suspect.

It was Campion who led Aubrey out into the sun again. He had listened to a quantity of technical detail from Butcher, all of which might be important to an enemy but was not so to him. Whatever Butcher knew was also known already, presumably, by the War Office and was therefore none of Campion's business. What he must be looking for was something which was hitherto unknown to them. Fifteen? He must keep his mind clear and hang on to that. Fifteen: that was still his only definite clue. Fifteen, and the people who knew what it meant. Butcher was evidently not one of them, but there was someone else who was.

As he raised his eyes and looked down the narrow concrete path which ran like a chalk-line across the green turf, he saw the man he was thinking about. He appeared so quickly that it was difficult to say whether thought or vision came first. His jaunty roundness was recognizable at a tremendous distance and he came bouncing along towards them without haste.

CHAPTER TEN

"That fellow Pyne," said Campion.

"Really?" Aubrey's distinctive face clouded. "What on earth is the man doing wandering round here alone like this? They've let him in to look for me, I suppose. They mustn't do that, as they very well know. He's talked his way in, you see. How extraordinary these fellows are! I'm quite prepared to like him, but he mustn't make himself a nuisance. I loathe having to tell a man to clear out."

"Who is he?"

"Pyne? Oh, rather an interesting bird. Remarkably intelligent in his own way. Probably dishonest. Works like a fiend." Lee had dropped into his objective mood again. His remarks were quite free from affectation and he spoke with the judicial simplicity of an admittedly superior being. "He's evacuated his office down here. It's an amusing little organization and he makes a very good thing out of it. He calls it Surveys Limited. I suppose you've heard of it?"

"It's faintly familiar," said Campion not untruthfully. "What do they do? Arrange one's life for one?"

Lee laughed. "Only in part," he murmured. "They're an advice and information bureau. If you want to build a factory or start up a business in an unknown locality they'll get out all the dope on the place for you. They're remarkably thorough. Apart from the usual stuff, they tabulate the most intimate details, including some very shrewd work on public opinion and estimates of local wealth. In fact they'll sound every possible depth for you in strictest confidence. Pyne told me once that he had ten thousand agents all over England. That probably means that he's employed about half that number at some time or other during his career. I imagine any man to whom he's ever given five bob for personal views on local conditions is included in the aggregate, but still, to do him justice, he does seem to get the commissions. Mildly entertaining?"

Campion nodded briefly. He was not in the condition to be mildly entertained and Pyne was almost upon them.

By morning light he did not look quite so amiable and easy-going. At first Campion was inclined to blame his own unreliable observation on the night before for the change, but as soon as the newcomer began to speak he was not so sure. Pyne was still hearty, but now there was suppressed anxiety and a touch of antagonism there as well. He greeted them without preliminaries.

"Any developments?" he demanded as soon as he was within speaking distance.

"In which direction?" Campion was relieved to find that his own powers of controlling both his face and voice were considerable.

"Well, what about last night? What about Anscombe?" Pyne was keyed up and his round eyes were as shifty and inquisitive as a sparrow's.

A thin trickle of fear dribbled down Campion's spine. Until that moment he had entirely forgotten the incident. The enormity of the omission appalled him. Anscombe and his disturbing manner of dying had gone clean out of his mind. Good God! If he had forgotten that, what else had he overlooked? To his relief Lee looked faintly shame-faced also.

"Oh Lord! Miss Anscombe!" he said. "I *must* go down to see her. It's early yet, but what a merciful chance you reminded me. Once one gets behind this wall one passes into another world, you know. Don't you feel it, Campion? The mind simply settles down to consider ideas and their technical development. Poor old Anscombe. I knew him reasonably well, but in here and at the moment he's absolutely remote."

Pyne wiped his forehead. "You're lucky," he said drily. "I've been thinking of him all night. I don't like the look of that death. If the police are satisfied, of course, it's nothing to do with me, but I rather wondered if they were?"

There was a question in his last remark and Campion, who recollected just in time that no one present knew of his late night meeting with Hutch, ignored it. Lee Aubrey was less cautious.

"Anscombe was of the type who never commit suicide," he said didactically.

Pyne glanced at Campion.

"Murder was the thought in my mind," he said.

Lee coughed and moved on up the path. He was offended. His mouth was pursed and he looked shocked.

"My dear chap," he protested, giving the reproach just sufficient reproach to make it also a rebuke, "hysteria at this time in the morning is inexcusable. And there's one other thing while I think of it, Pyne. You really must not come in here unless I bring you personally. It's simply not allowed. The British Government has put its foot down on the subject. I don't want to know how you got yourself admitted, because I don't want to have to report the poor beast on the gate, but for heaven's sake don't do it again."

It was as near a schoolmaster's scolding as Campion had ever heard administered to a grown man. Pyne gave no sign that he had heard. He remained round, pink, and dangerously suspicious.

"There's been a man-hunt all over this district for the last twelve hours at least," he remarked presently as they walked on. "A fellow wanted by the police escaped from St. Jude's Hospital in Coachingford last night. He pinched an old car, abandoned it at the watersplash on the lower Bridge road, and disappeared. They're still searching for him. Doesn't that strike you as suspicious?"

Lee burst out laughing, an almost feminine spitefulness in his amusement.

"Oh, come," he said, "that's abominable thinking. Some wretched man is escaping from the police and therefore it's only natural to suppose that the first thing he does is to sneak into a garden and murder old Anscombe, who happened to be there. It's childish, Pyne. It won't wash. You're upset, my dear chap. That obtrusive stomach of yours is out of order."

The little fat man jerked in his belly, but his eyes did not lose their alarming shrewdness.

"I was thinking, Campion," he began, "you must have come over from Coachingford about the right time. You didn't see anything of this man, did you?"

"No," said Campion. His tone was mild, he noticed.

Lee sighed with exasperation. "My good Pyne," he said, taking the other man's arm with a weary familiarity which had in it the very essence of condescension, "you're making an unholy ass of yourself, you know."

"I don't believe I am, Aubrey."

"Then you must take my word for it." Lee was smiling dangerously. "Campion is personally known to me and I give you my word that (a) he gave no lift to any escaping suspect, and (b) that suspect did not reward him by bumping off poor old Anscombe in his own front yard. Moreover, that suggestion is ridiculous, it's absurd, it's mad, it's nuts. Forget it, and let the police do their own chores."

Pyne allowed himself to be led out of the Institute gates and across the turf towards the house. If Aubrey was offending him he did not show it.

"I don't know Mr. Campion well. If you do, I've nothing more to say," he remarked at last in a perfectly unruffled tone. "But have you read the description of the man the police are looking for?"

"No, I haven't. I don't think I want to particularly."

"I found it interesting." Pyne's placid obstinacy was insuppressible. "The man they want is thirty-five years old and six-foot-two high. He has a pale face and sleek blond hair, and his chief characteristics are that he is very thin and yet powerful." He paused and when no one spoke added ingenuously: "When last seen he was wearing fireman's oilskins."

Lee crowed with delight. "And a brass helmet as well?" he demanded. "This is lovely. Pyne, my poor friend, you're giving me an enormous amount of innocent pleasure. Do go on; I wouldn't stop you for the world."

The plump man turned to Campion.

"What do you think?" he enquired.

Campion appeared to give the matter serious consideration. They had reached the ridge of high ground and were now sauntering down towards the poplar trees. He had his hands in his pockets and they were clenched so that the nails dug into his palms. His heart was thudding in his side and before the dark curtain hung across his mind his conscious thoughts were as chaotic and useless as those behind it were lost. He was dithering, and that fact frightened him far more than this dangerous little man's questions.

"What name would you put to that description?" Pyne persisted.

He was waiting for an answer. He was waiting for an answer. He was waiting for an answer. A minute had gone by, a whole minute. A minute; perhaps another minute. Campion could not think. Good God, he could not *think*. This was horrible, terrifying. He could not think. The machinery for thinking had broken down. He was helpless, lost, at the mercy of this dreadful little creature with the cruel, predatory eyes of a bird.

What name? What name? What *name*?

"Almost any, I should say," he murmured, unaware that he sounded more bored than anything else. "John Smith, Albert Campion, Weaver Bea."

There was complete silence. It lasted so long that he was able to drag himself out of his floundering panic and glance round before anyone spoke.

Lee Aubrey was mooching along with his shoulders hunched under his sleek, almost foppishly cut jacket. He was clearly embarrassed by the personal turn which the conversation had taken. The ridiculous name which had slipped out so dangerously had not registered upon him.

But with Pyne it was very different. For the first time his shining composure was destroyed. He had changed colour and his eyes were no longer merely suspicious. He turned his head and looked the other man full in the face.

"I've obviously made an idiotic mistake, Mr. Campion," he said. "That scene last night unnerved me a bit, I expect. You and I ought to have a talk some time. Why don't you come down to my office? I think you'd be interested in it. We might have a spot of lunch together in the town."

"That's an idea," Lee cut in before Campion could reply. He spoke with the hearty relief of the host who thinks he sees a way of amusing the temporarily unwanted guest. "That business of his will entertain you, Campion. I found it fascinating. Pyne's a most amusing beggar when he's not being melodramatic or playing detectives."

Campion was silent. He had no illusions whatever about Pyne. The man was on the right track and knew it. It was a tight corner. Delay at this point was the one thing he knew would be fatal, and delay there certainly would be once the County Police discovered in him the particular man for whom they were scouring the country. Headquarters might back him up to the hilt, but there would have to be explanations first and explanations would lead to the discovery of his condition, whatever else they disclosed. Whatever else? That question was too alarming even to consider and he shrank from it.

With what was obviously a habit with him in difficult moments he looked around for Amanda. To his relief he actually saw her, turning the corner of the house. He was not surprised. That was the miraculous part of Amanda; she always seemed to materialize at the right moment. It was as though they were partners in some long practised game, with years of experience and cooperation behind them. She hailed him and with a muttered word of excuse he hurried over to meet her. She spoke quietly as he came up.

"I say, the Superintendent's here. He wants to see you alone, apart from Lee, I mean. He won't come in, and he's waiting round by the side door. Would you go to him?"

Would he! The idea of the lanky Hutch as a rescuing angel, robe, feathers, and all, did not seem in the least incongruous at that moment.

"Oh, bless you," he said so fervently that her brown eyes widened.

"Sticky?" she enquired under her breath.

"Not so hot, anyway," he admitted. "Stay with them, will you, my darling? Don't let Pyne open his heart to Aubrey."

He saw the faint flicker of astonishment in her expression and was puzzled by it until he realized that it was the heartfelt, grateful endearment which had surprised her. That was a revelation which brought him up with a jerk and his sudden sense of desolation was not lightened by the conviction that he deserved it.

He saw Hutch as soon as he turned into the yard. The plain-clothes man was sitting on the running-board of a huge old Buick and the sun shone down on the unexpectedly resplendent colours of his tweed suit. He rose as soon as Campion appeared and sauntered forward.

"Hallo!" Campion's greeting was unusually hearty. Here at least was an ally, however blindfold.

"Good morning." A guarded quality in the policeman's tone struck a warning note which set every nerve in his body on edge. "Can I have a few words with you, sir?"

"Of course. Why not? Carry on." Campion felt he was talking too much and could not stop himself. "What's the excitement?"

"No excitement, sir." Hutch eyed him curiously. "I'd just like you to take a look at this, if you will. We don't take any notice of these things as a rule, naturally, but in this case there are certain circumstances which made me think I'd bring it round to you."

Campion glanced at the sheet of paper which was thrust into his hand. It bore a short typewritten message.

"DEAR SUPERINTENDENT,—

"*When the Home Office issued you with instructions concerning Albert Campion, did they by any chance also send you a photograph? That's all. Think it over.*"

There was no signature and it was undated. Campion read it through twice. It was Pyne, of course; probably written the night before after his own idiotic slip when he had fallen into the little trap concerning their previous association in the U.S.

The inference was obvious. Pyne saw there was something fishy about him and suspected him of impersonation, impersonation of Albert Campion. That was pretty good, pretty funny. He could soon put a stop to that, anyway.

Could he, though? The new danger opened out like a morass in front of him.

He gave back the sheet of paper with a steady hand, but his head was hurting intolerably and he could feel the sweat on his forehead.

"Well?" he enquired.

Hutch produced another paper. This proved to be a police chit which detailed in the usual unenlightened phrases the chief physical characteristics of the man who had escaped in fireman's oilskins from St. Jude's Hospital, Coachingford.

Campion read them aloud.

"Well," he said again. The throbbing in the crown of his skull had turned to shooting pains of excruciating violence and the outlines of the Superintendent's jaunty figure were shimmering as though in a heat haze.

Hutch looked up. His eyes were searching and he took a long time to make up his mind to speak.

"I haven't got a warrant, of course," he said at last, "so I'd like to ask a favour of you. May I go over your room, sir, just to satisfy my own curiosity? I—well, to put it frankly, sir, when I was getting you to bed last night I noticed the whole room reeked of oilskins. I can't get that out of my head."

Campion laughed aloud. It was not a very convincing sound, but at least it was spontaneous.

"Search with pleasure," he said. "Search the whole house. I'll square you with Aubrey. How long have you been in the police, Hutch?"

"Twenty-eight years and two months, sir."

"Have you?" The implied criticism, as from a superior officer, had its effect. Campion felt rather than saw the man waver. He laughed again and with better humour. "You trot along and set your mind at rest," he said. "If you find the uniform bring it to me. I'd like to see myself in fireman's rig. If it shouldn't be in the bedroom, well, try the rest of the house and then the grounds."

Hutch shrugged. He was verging on the sheepish. He took a step towards the side door, changed his mind, and came back.

"Just answer me two questions, sir. Then I'll apologize."

This was more dangerous. Campion kept his tone light.

"Anything you like, Superintendent."

"What is the name of the C.I.D. in Room 49 at Headquarters?"

"Yeo." It was a shot in the dark but he had not hesitated. The name had been dragged up out of his mind as he forced himself to hear again the small voice on the telephone the night before.

Hutch stood looking at him oddly. There was no way of telling whether he had succeeded or failed.

"And the second?" Campion took the bold line. To pause, he felt, might be fatal, and whatever happened he could not be held up now.

Hutch moistened his lips and lowered his voice.

"What's your own S.S. number, sir?"

Campion smiled. He had no idea, no idea in the world.

"At the moment I rather fancy it's fifteen," he said and laughed.

He saw he had blundered badly. He saw the consternation slowly dawning on Hutch's pleasant face as the enormity of the situation dawned on him, since it included his own inexcusable deception and the incredible indiscretion he had committed in taking an unauthorized person on the visit of the evening before. Campion saw the next move, imminent and inescapable. He saw himself detained, held up helpless while the vital hours raced by. His tormented mind shuttered. It was as though the dark curtain became for a moment an open venetian-blind. It rattled, flickered, and was shut again.

He hit out.

His fist possessed a cunning he did not anticipate. It was a beautiful, expert's blow which rippled from his left shoulder with the entire weight of his body behind it.

Hutch, who was still reeling under the nervous shock, was taken completely unawares. He went down like a tree, the silly expression of astonishment still on his face.

Campion did not look at him. He was not aware of him. From that instant he moved automatically. He stepped into the Buick, trod on the accelerator which was also the starter, and leant back.

The car bounced in the air and he took the drive at sixty. At the gates he turned to the left as if he knew exactly what he was doing and drove with uncanny precision and great speed through the town, under the lowering Nag, over the small millbridge and on through twisting country roads, all without hesitation or any conscious thought. His mind was a peaceful blank. Never afterwards had he any recollection of the journey. He travelled as migrating birds seem to travel, with blind knowledge. The brain behind the curtain was in charge and the conscious man might well have been in an hypnotic trance. From first to last he was peculiarly dexterous.

He entered the big industrial town of Coachingford by the Roman road and negotiated the by-pass circus without difficulty. One or two policemen saluted the car, with its small priority notice in the corner of the windscreen. He drove without hesitation through a knot of tiny streets, paused correctly for the lights, and took the complicated turnings with precision.

At an open garage in a dizzy square he slowed, drove the car into a shelter, and climbed out. He did not feel his feet on the pavement and did not wait for his check. Moving with the unhesitating singleness of purpose which renders a man so natural that he is next best to invisible, he crossed the road, turned down an alley, came out of it into a busy but impoverished street, and pressed on until he paused before a small and dirty shop which possessed a row of empty display boards outside and a dreary collection of cigarettes and dusty sweets in the window. He glanced up and down the road and then went inside.

The cool darkness of the shop, with its characteristic smell of printer's ink and tobacco, brought him suddenly out of his state of somnambulism. He stopped dead and stood staring about him with startled eyes. He had no idea where he was, nor how or why he had come. A grey face peered at him from behind the back of the counter and the two men remained looking at one another in mutual doubt.

The shopkeeper, who was old and thin and ineffectual, seemed quite as bewildered to see his visitor as Campion was to see him.

After the first shock of returning intelligence Campion grew afraid. He was a man not used to fear in any form and its deep cold fingers gripped his stomach paralysingly.

The shopkeeper cleared his throat nervously and came edging round the counter.

"You'll want the boss," he said. "Come inside."

Campion moved forward unsteadily and the other man raised a greasy flap in the counter. The back of the shop was very small and dark and the two panels of frosted glass in the door which the old man indicated looked like some bright avenue of escape. Campion all but charged them, hurling himself into the room within, while the shopkeeper drew the door shut silently behind him. It was in many ways a dreadful little room, papered with sections of grey fruit and still furnished with all the misguided decorations of the eighties. Practically the entire floor space was taken up by a large table, covered first with a red cloth and then with several sheets of newspaper.

Sitting at this table, collarless and in shirt-sleeves, was a very remarkable person. He had a white melancholy face hung beneath a glistening bald skull, and his eyes, which were narrow and expressionless, were dull as coal-dust. At the moment he was engaged in cleaning and oiling a heavy service revolver which looked as if it had been well loved for many years. He raised his eyes as the door burst open, but did not move his head or speak. Campion said nothing. He leant back against the panels of the door. His ears were drumming and the beating of his heart seemed to keep time to the intolerable throbbing in his head.

The man at the table breathed heavily through his short nose.

"So you've come back, 'ave yer?" he said.

CHAPTER ELEVEN

Campion did not speak. The walls of the tiny room were converging on him. The air was too warm and too heavy to force open his lungs. The face of the man at the table swelled terrifyingly, widening and widening like the white of an egg in a pan. Soon it must fill the whole universe and suffocate him beneath its flabby weight.

Campion's lips moved in a final despairing cry of protest, but no sound came.

Across the red tablecloth the fat man gazed at him with new interest. Suddenly he laid aside the gun and slipped quietly to his feet with that surprisingly smooth agility only found in old fighting men.

He came round the room and peered into the newcomer's face.

"Eh," he said at last and the word was a grunt uttered deep in his throat. "Come here."

He lowered the young man on to a chair and propped his elbows on the table for him, while his own thick hands explored the scalp.

"You've 'ad a cosh, 'aven't yer? 'Ow bad are yer?"

His concern was genuine and intensely practical. He was also very gentle without being in the least soft. It was like being delivered into the hands of some gargantuan Roman matron, or perhaps a friendly female bear.

"Answer up," he commanded, prodding the nape of Campion's neck with a padded forefinger.

The injured man drew away from him wearily.

"Who the hell are you?" he murmured with just sufficient interest to drive home the genuineness of the enquiry.

"God Almighty!" The exclamation was no expletive but a direct and pious appeal to the Deity. The fat man plumped himself down on a chair and seized Campion's shoulders. His little black eyes were circular and a fine sprinkling of sweat appeared on his heavy face.

"Are you kiddin'? This isn't the ruddy time to play the goat, you know."

Campion let his head roll forward. The pain of movement was almost welcome, since it cut through the dreadful breathless sense of weight which was stifling him.

"Do you know 'oo you are yerself?" There was a tremor in the thick voice so near his ear.

"Campion . . . It's written in my suit."

"Lummel" There was a brief pause while the older man assimilated the salient facts. Then he took command. "Come on," he said. "Get yer collar orf and lie down. Don't try to use yer 'ead. It's no good to yer for a bit. You're all right. You're at 'ome. Don't start thinking. You're with yer own. Got that? With yer own. I'm goin' to put you on the sofa and cover you up while I get a crocus."

"No." Campion recognized the word without realizing that it was more than nine-tenths of his compatriots would have done. "Can't have a doctor. Can't have any officials. They're all after me by now."

" 'Oo?"

"The police."

"Rozzers? You've made a mistake. You're punch-drunk. What 'ave you done?"

"Slugged a copper. Two coppers. The last one was the local Super, a dear good chap, I can't have killed him."

"Killed 'im? 'Oo's talking of killing?" Generations of inbred fear of the one crime which is never forgiven to any man, however privileged, lay in the truculent demand.

"I am." It was a relief to Campion to talk freely at last. "Apparently I did kill the first one. Can't remember it. Woke up in hospital."

"Horspital?" The fat man's heavy eyelids lowered a fraction. "There was a man scarpered from the horspital in a fireman's outfit," he suggested.

"Yes. That was me. Now I've slugged a Superintendent of Police. I can't remember anything after that until I walked in here. Who are you?"

The other did not reply directly. He got up heavily and as if he had grown older.

"You come and lie down," he said. "I want to 'ave a look at you. I'll get you as right as I can and then we'll talk. We'd better," he added grimly.

Campion allowed himself to be led over to the dreadful imitation leather couch which took up practically all one side of the room, but the moment his head touched the clammy seat he struggled into a sitting position again.

"No time," he said, unaware that the words were slurred. "Tomorrow's the fifteenth. Must get on. No time for this."

"You'll 'ave all the time you want and more if you don't shut up. Lie still while I do a bit of doctoring."

The bald man moved towards the door as he spoke.

"I'll just drop a word to old Happy Fanny outside to keep 'is eyes skinned in case they take sights of us. You don't know if you was followed 'ere, do you? No, that's right, you don't 'ave to tell me. You don't know anything. You lie still. I'll see to yer."

It was warm and dark in the little room in spite of the time of day and the mean rickety french windows gave on to a weedy yard with a blank wall behind. Campion closed his eyes and was lost.

He came to himself to find artificial light burning painfully into his eyes. The fat man was on a chair, fitting a new bulb into a chandelier which hung over the table. It was a complicated arrangement of weights and pulleys decorated with distressing pink frosted glass shades.

He clambered down cautiously and, groping under the table, produced a cone-shaped contraption of black paper which he fixed round and over the lighting arrangements, so that a brilliant pool lay in the centre of the table alone while the rest of the room was in comparative darkness. Having complied with these black-out restrictions, he returned to his patient.

"That's right," he said with relief as he raised one of the pallid eyelids with a great thumb. "You're not so dead as you was. I got you warm, see? Now I'm not giving you spirits because they might finish you, but I've got some muck 'ere you'd better drink. I've cooked it meself so I know what's in it."

He went round the table and bent over a small grate where he had got a fire going. It was all very homely and grubbily comfortable.

Campion was puzzled by it, but not alarmed. The fat man, whoever he was, was a friend. He returned presently with a steaming jug which looked ominous but which turned out to contain nothing more extraordinary than strong old-fashioned beef tea, made according to Mrs. Beeton. Campion was surprised to find that instead of being repelled by it he could drink it with enjoyment, and its effect upon him was extraordinary. As its warmth spread over him he felt strength generating in him as clearly as if new blood was being pumped into his veins. It occurred to him that he had not eaten properly for a very long time. His head felt clearer too; that was a mercy. Everything which had happened recently stood out in his mind with stereoscopic vividness. The curtain was still there, though, heavy and dark as ever, with the great nagging worry lurking just behind it.

The other man took away the jug and hitched himself on the edge of the table.

"Now," he said, "you and me 'as got to 'ave a talk. You think you've slugged a big cop, don't you? A Super? How sure are you?"

"I'm certain of it. He was just getting on to me and I saw delay ahead and no way out of it, so I let him have it and bunked. I can't remember anything after that. But there's no time for talk now. How long have I been asleep?"

"What was the cop's name?"

"Hutch. Superintendent Hutch. A delightful bloke. He wanted my number."

"And you didn't know it?"

"Er—no."

"I see." He seemed more resigned than shocked. "Well, they ain't 'ere yet, that's one thing. Old Fanny in the shop is a good look-out. Lucky we kept this place so dark. This'll take a bit of getting away with. Do you remember anything at all before you got your cosh?"

"No. Nothing. That is, I remember odd things like people's names, and I remember the one thing, of course. I remember fifteen."

"Fifteen?" The little black eyes were suspicious. "That's more'n I do. That's something you never told me."

"Oh, my God!" Campion turned his face to the wall. It was back again, the damnable frustration-dream motif. He felt like a man in a stone maze.

"Don't you excite yerself or you'll go under again." His ally became the nurse once more. "Keep what little bit of common you 'ave got, for pity's sake. I've seen some of this sort of thing in my time and I know what it's like. You've got no bones broke and your eyes are re-acting all right. You've just forgot, that's all. There's nothing to get the serious wind-up about in that. Now, am I right? You feel as you do sometimes, when you first wake up in the morning in a strange bed. Just for a minute you've got a hold of yerself all right but you don't know where you are nor what's gone before. You're like a man living in that minute, aren't yer?"

This somewhat homely description was so apt that Campion turned to stare at his questioner. The stranger's white face was very grave and his eyes were intelligent.

He nodded. "Yes," he said, "that's just what I am like."

His questioner's reaction was not entirely comforting.

"I've known it go on for months and wear off gradual," he said un-happily, "and I've known it come back as quick as it went. We'd better get hold of Oates at once. You're fit for nothing now."

Campion explained the difficulty in that quarter and the other man's anxiety became acute.

"We're in the cart," he said. "In the cart good and proper." Campion groaned. "Who are we, anyway?" he demanded. "Who are you?"

The fat man did not reply for a minute. There was a curious half-smile which had nothing to do with amusement on his face. It was some little time before Campion recognized it for what it was. This odd stranger was deeply and sentimentally hurt.

"My name is Lugg," he said at last. "I've been a perishing servant of yours for seventeen years." There was an awkward pause and then he rose and stretched himself. "That's all right," he said magnificently, "you're not to blame. I'd 'ave told you at once only I was hoping it'd come back to you. 'Ullo, 'ullo, what's that?"

The lights flickered and a deep full-throated rumbling echoed through the house. Both men started.

"Thunder," Lugg pronounced as a whirlwind of heavy drops pattered against the glass behind the thick curtains. "It got me wondering. It always does nowadays. Oh well, let it snow if it feels like it. We've got more than we can carry anyway, so what does it matter what else piles up?"

"How late is it? I can't waste time." Campion was struggling to his feet as he spoke. "Tomorrow's the fifteenth. Must get on. God knows how."

"You stay where you are." Lugg had picked up his revolver and was playing with it carelessly. "Your head seems to 'ave gone so we'll 'ave to use mine for a ruddy change. Now look 'ere, we're in a very nasty position. I'm an accessory after the fact, don't forget that, so I'm going to tell you all you saw fit to let me know about the lark you're on before you lost your senses. You're going to listen, and we're both going to hope it's going to bring something back to you because if it don't we're both up the creek."

He was right, of course. Campion had the wits left to realize it even while every instinct warned him frantically against delay. The thing he had to avert was enormous and catastrophic.

"Avert." Once again it was a single word which arrested him. That was right. There was something he had to avert. Something tremendous.

Meanwhile Lugg was talking and his thick voice sounded comforting and sensible against the rumbling of the storm outside.

"I've only been by your side day and night for seventeen years and you couldn't trust me with the whole packet. Said you was under oath," he was observing. "If you hadda done, we shouldn't be in this mess, but I'm not reproaching you. That's not my way. Never 'as been. I've been here for five days and this is it, I should suppose. My instructions from you in London was that I should keep myself under cover 'ere and take all messages. Old Happy in the shop was to do all the front of the 'ouse stuff and I wasn't to show my face until I was told. Happy is quite okay, by the way. I picked this place of 'is my-

self. I used to know 'im years ago when 'e was one of the old Forty
Angels gang up at Hoxton. 'E's straight as a die to 'is own sort. 'E's
keeping the look-out now. There's been no one particular about since
you came. You must have given them the slip completely, punch-
drunk or not. Now listen. Since I've been 'ere you've only showed up
twice. The first time was the day before yesterday. You came in with a
portmanteau and that time you were wearing your ordinary clothes.
You changed here into some duds that even my old dad wouldn't
'ave worn and went off with a little fish-basket under yer arm, looking
as if you'd been on the tramp from one sick ward to the next for the
last five years. Don't you remember?"

"No, I don't. I'm sorry, it's gone completely."

"Never mind. Never mind. Don't strain it or you'll never get it.
Just listen. I may say something that'll bring the 'ole thing back." Lugg
was very earnest and the suppressed anxiety in his matt black eyes
belied his words. "The second time I saw you you came sneaking in
by these french doors 'ere, about three yesterday morning. I was sleeping where you're sitting now and I got up and fetched you a bit of
food. I asked 'ow things were going, but you didn't open out at all.
You seemed worried and distant-like, as though you was puzzled by
the way things was running."

"Was I—was I all right then?" Campion stirred as he spoke. This
was one of the most unnerving experiences of all.

"Oh yes. You'd got yer 'ead screwed on then. You was as bright as
I am. You just seemed sort of mystified, as though things weren't running the way you'd thought. About eleven in the morning you slipped
out again, still in yer old clothes, and that was the last time I saw you
right in the head."

It was an unfortunate way of putting it, but evidently Lugg was
one of those Britons without the celebrated national gift for euphemy.

"You left your little old basket," he said. "You locked it in the table
drawer, but you took one or two things out of it and put them in your
pockets. About tea-time yesterday Happy came in with a tale that 'e'd
picked up in the shop about you being mixed up in a row down at
the waterside. A rozzer had been killed and two or three men took to
horspital."

He paused hopefully, but Campion shook his head. In spite of the
sudden chill which this confirmation of his worst fears produced in
him, he still could not remember. Lugg breathed gustily.

"Never mind," he said again but without any sort of conviction.
"Never mind. It'll come back sudden. Then young Amanda called for

your suitcase with your good clothes in it," he went on, "and Happy told her some of what he'd heard—"

"Yes, I know. She came to the hospital." Campion spoke absently and did not see the small black eyes flicker.

"Oh, you've seen 'er, 'ave you? Did you recognize 'er?" The jealousy was very faint, but it was there and Campion noticed it.

"Not for a long time," he said. "I—er—like a fool I thought she must be my wife."

"So she will be in a week or two, if you're not strung up." Lugg's dreadful directness was irrepressible. The words came into his head and he said them.

A shadow passed over Campion's lean wooden face.

"I rather think that's off," he said shortly. "She—she didn't realize what had happened, you see. She doesn't know now and I don't particularly want her to, so, should you see her, for God's sake don't refer to it. She broke the engagement."

"*She* did?" Lugg was clearly incredulous. "Why? 'As she seen someone else?"

Campion writhed. The discussion was distasteful and also, he discovered, quite unbearable. (Ah, Amanda! Oh, my blessed smiling sweet! Oh, sensible, clear-eyed, unembarrassed beloved! Oh, dear God Almighty, what is to happen to me without you?)

Lugg took his silence for consent, apparently, for he pursed his mouth and jerked his head with resigned regret.

"I see that coming," he remarked brutally. "It was your fault for mucking about. Courting a woman's like cooking something. There comes a time when it's done. After that you had ought to eat it. If you don't, and keep it simmering on the side so to speak, you're apt to forget it and when you do come to look for it all the goodness is gorn away and you're left with nothing but a bit o' skin. And it annoys the young woman too. It doesn't do her any good."

He paused and glanced at the other man's face.

"Sorry, cock," he said abruptly.

Campion said nothing. Outside the storm was working itself up to fury and the rain hissed and spat against the windows like a host of serpents.

"Avert something tremendous." The command blazed at him suddenly, wrenching him out of his small private hell. "Hurry, hurry. Think, think. Pull yourself together. Get on with it."

"Where's the basket?" he said. "The whole story sounds nuts, but let's see it anyway. There may be something in it."

Lugg looked at him curiously. "Don't you know what's in it?"

"No, of course I don't. Do you?"

"I 'ad a look, naturally. I'm 'uman. The lock on the drawer could be turned with a bent pin."

"Oh, all right. What's in it?"

"I didn't touch anything, of course," he said, taking up a piece of wire which he kept conveniently on the mantelshelf. "It got me wondering, though."

He squatted down and poked at the lock. It was child's-play to open, as he had said, and he pulled out a wide drawer, revealing a fair-sized rush bag lying inside. Campion thrust his hand in the basket. An expression of blank amazement spread over his face and he shook the whole contents out on the table. A slippery, feathery heap of old one-pound and ten-shilling notes appeared before him.

"Six 'undred and eighty-four pounds exactly," said Lugg. "I counted it after you left."

Campion took up a bank note and rubbed it between his fingers. Then he held it up to the light. Britannia's head and trident shone out of the watermark at him. None of the notes appeared to be new. Their uniform shabbiness suggested months of circulation.

"Extraordinary," he said, looking blankly at the fish-basket. "I took some more out with me, you say?"

"Yes. About seventy quid. You didn't trouble to count it—what was that?"

Both men stood listening. At first they thought there was no sound but the storm, but an instant later there was a gentle thud outside the inner door and the shopkeeper put his head in.

"Take sights," he whispered. "They're all round the house. Plain-clothes. I'll watch the front."

Lugg swept the notes into the basket, thrust it into the drawer, and pulled back the tablecloth. The whole movement was as smooth as if it had been done by a conjuror. He thrust a gun into Campion's hand and produced another from his hip. He touched the sick man's arm and nodded towards the french doors, laying his finger on his lips. Campion nodded obediently and moved silently into the darkness at the back of the room.

The gentle knocking on the glass sounded like the Last Trump when it did come.

CHAPTER TWELVE

It was quiet, insistent tapping on the french windows. The gentle summons was very near and very intimate. It sped through the weeping of the storm and stood close to them.

They waited in silence and let it come again, still discreet but a fraction sharper, determined, inexorable.

Lugg glanced over his shoulder. Campion was well in the shadow, so he picked up his gun and advanced towards the window with all the easy confidence of an innocent householder expecting a visit from the police.

He drew back the curtains cautiously, as a good citizen should, allowing only the minimum of light to escape. For some seconds he stood peering into the darkness, alert as a dog at a rat-hole. Finally he unlatched the doors and pushed one of them open a few inches.

"'Ullo?" he demanded suspiciously.

There was no direct reply but there was a new movement out in the storm and Lugg became tense, his bald head with its fringe of greyish hair held oddly on one side.

Standing just below him in the driving rain was the figure he expected. The drab mackintosh and slouch hat of the plain-clothes man were there, but the stranger was not looking at him squarely. He peered up slyly out of the dark and from his white hand hung a large white handkerchief which fluttered significantly in the downpour. It was impossible to mistake its meaning.

Lugg backed slowly into the room and the newcomer came in after, holding the white rag ostentatiously before him.

He took up a position some little distance from the table and the heavy shade over the lights cut him off from the breast upwards as far as Campion was concerned. As soon as the window was closed behind him he held up his hands.

"You can take my gun," he said distinctly.

Lugg searched him promptly and efficiently, setting down the man's heavy Webley on the table well within the circle of light. Then with a glance at his visitor he produced his own gun and put it down beside the first. There was a long pause and then Campion also stretched out a hand in the darkness and added his weapon to the other two. He kept his face out of the light, however, as did the newcomer.

They made a curious headless group standing round the three guns, since all the light in the room focused on the weapons and on their three pairs of hands. Lugg and Campion maintained their advantage and waited for the visitor to make the first move.

"I've got a message for the man calling himself Campion," he announced at last. "That's you, isn't it?"

"Never mind which of us it is," corrected Lugg sharply. "What's the dope?"

"*He* knows." The stranger spoke meaningly, jerking a hand towards Campion. "It's up to him, that's all."

This was an unforeseen impasse. Campion's thin hands remained expressionless and Lugg's great ham-fists did not stir. The silence persisted. The room was hot and its very quiet was ominous and uncomfortable amid the bellowing of the storm which raged round the house. Lugg found it unbearable.

"The boys outside'll get wet," he observed pleasantly.

"I'm waiting."

"What do you think we're doing?"

"He's only got to make up his mind. He knows." The visitor had begun to reveal a personality. He was not a big man and his raincoat hung on him in concealing folds, yet he managed to convey an impression of wiry strength curiously and rather horribly allied to ill-health. His voice was not without culture of a sort, either, but it had a thin tinny ring to it and when he coughed, as he did frequently, his lungs wheezed and groaned dangerously. Yet he was a force in the room. There was no question but that he knew what he was doing and was determined to waste no time.

Since his head and shoulders were hidden, his hands were his only distinguishing feature and these were frankly repulsive, being woman-ish, degenerate, and quite abominably dirty.

A sixth sense warned Campion to hold his tongue. It was not that the half seen, headless figure was actually familiar, but the atmosphere of rank evil he brought with him was. Campion left the talking to Lugg, who seemed quite prepared to deal with it.

"Knowing's not always saying," the fat man remarked, managing to infuse a wealth of craft into the observation. "Your call, mate."

"*He* knows," the newcomer repeated and one of his repellent hands slid inside his raincoat.

The two others had their guns up off the table like one man. They waited, the two weapons levelled and the two barrels gleaming dully in the circle of light.

The visitor did not waver or hesitate. He went on with what he was doing smoothly. He seemed to have considerable experience of guns.

His hand came out of his coat with something in it. He laid his offering on the red tablecloth and they all looked at it. It was a thick packet of old banknotes secured with a rubber band.

"Two-fifty," he said, "and we ask no questions."

Lugg laughed. It was a genuine expression of surprised amusement and was entirely convincing. The newcomer was standing very still. Campion could feel him trying to pierce the shadow which shrouded both their heads. He made no movement himself and kept his gun steady.

Once again the dirty hand crept inside the sodden coat and presently another packet lay on top of the first. Once more the silence became suffocating.

The performance was very slow, definitely sinister, and, of course, in the circumstances entirely fantastic.

"Chicken feed," said Lugg thickly and a third packet of notes appeared on the table and finally a fourth.

"That's the limit," said the stranger at last. "Take it or leave it. Suit yourself."

"And supposing it's a deal?" Lugg was showing more finesse in an impossible situation than Campion would have expected from him.

"He quits his racket and gets out."

"Where to?"

"London. Hell. Anywhere. We're not fussy."

Campion's condition was making him slow-witted. It had taken him some minutes to realize that he was not dealing with the police, as he had expected. This man on the other side of the table, whose face he could not see, represented a new element in a complicated and terrifying predicament. He represented the element which until now had been maddeningly elusive. Here at last must be a definite materialization of the enemy. Campion's limping brain seized on the discovery and he struggled to make as many bricks as he might out of this meagre straw.

The stranger belonged to a very definite class. He was a thug, one of that mercifully small army of professional bullies who in previous ages were euphoniously called "soldiers of fortune"; men, that is, who would undertake violence for a fee. It did not occur to Campion that it was strange that he should recognize so much. He accepted the fact without thinking, as a natural deduction based on some past experience which he had forgotten. He went on with his reasoning. Since the man was what he was it argued that he possessed employers, some intelligent organization which had the sense to use professional servants. The question now was what sort of organization? It was obviously anti-social, but how large? How dangerous? How big? International importance?

The old phrase came into his head and he rejected it. It was not quite right. National importance? That was it. He had heard something like that described lately and in some connexion which, taken together, had had an extraordinary effect upon him. It was an amazing experience. He was remembering something not mentally but emotionally. The ghost of an emotional upheaval was returning to him. It was both terrifying and exhilarating. The whole thing was recent, too, very recent. Anger was coming back to him and with it something else, something new and overwhelming, a passion. That was it. Something deeper than affection, something more primitive and disturbing than love of women.

For a moment he felt it again, experienced it as he had done some time so very lately, a burning, raging, invigorating thing, the stuff of poetry and high imagining, the fountain-spring of superhuman endurance and endeavour.

Once again a fact came to him without recollection. He knew something suddenly as surely and clearly as if he had arrived at it by a long process of thought.

He belonged to a post-war generation, that particular generation which was too young for one war and most prematurely too old for the next. It was the generation which had picked up the pieces after the holocaust indulged in by its elders, only to see its brave new world wearily smashed again by younger brothers. His was the age which had never known illusion, the grimly humorous generation which from childhood had both expected and experienced the seamier side. Yet now, recently, some time very lately, so near in time that the tingle of surprise still lingered, something new had appeared on his emotional horizon. It had been something which so far he had entirely lacked and which had been born to him miraculously late in his life. He saw it for what it was. It was a faith, a spiritual and romantic faith. It had been there always, of course, disguised as a rejected illusion, and must have lain there for years like a girl growing to maturity in her sleep. Now it was awake all right and recognizable; a deep and lovely passion for his home, his soil, his blessed England, his principles, his breed, his Amanda and Amanda's future children. That was the force which was driving him. That was the fire which was crowding him on through and over the obscene obstacle of his own unnatural weakness.

He glanced towards the man with the filthy hands. This, then, this professional crook, this must be a hair on the hide of the Enemy, and, like the zoologists, from this one hair he must somehow reconstruct a whole beast. For God's sake what organization was he up against, and what particular machination was it engaged upon now?

He pulled himself up, despair facing him. He was annihilatingly helpless. He knew so horribly little, even about himself. For instance, what sort of man was he, if this enemy, which was shrewd enough in all conscience, should so confidently expect to be able to bribe him?

A possible explanation of that final question occurred to him. It was so absurd and yet so likely that he laughed outright. Bending forward suddenly, he allowed the full light from the chandelier to fall upon his face.

It succeeded. Miraculously the outside chance came home, proving him right beyond all question. The effect on the man was immediate and sensational. He drew in a gulping breath and there was a faint rattle from the dreadful lungs.

"Campion!" he ejaculated in a thin voice. "Campion. You *are* Campion."

He dived forward to snatch up his gun but Lugg was before him, bringing down his own revolver across the grimy wrist as it shot out over the cloth. It was a tremendous blow which might well have cracked the bone, and the sound it made was one of those ruthless noises which are inexplicably shocking in themselves.

The man sobbed once, deep in his throat, with pain, and then, before either of the others realized what he was doing, he turned and rushed from them, leaving gun and money still on the table. He threw himself at the window and burst out into the storm, leaving the curtains bellying behind him as a gust of rain surged into the room. Lugg stood gaping after him. Presently he went over and closed the window. He swore steadily for some little time.

"What d'you know about that?" he said at last. "Dirty little tyke! He made me sit up the moment I saw 'im. 'Oo's 'e working for?"

Campion felt himself giggling. The money and the gun and the ridiculous mistake were all absurdities out of a nightmare.

"I think I know that," he said, recovering himself. "I'm sure only one person could come to the conclusion that I was impersonating myself. Who was that man? I never saw his face clearly."

"That was no loss." Lugg was grimly amused. "I know 'im, and I'd like to know 'oo 'e's sold 'is mortgaged little soul to this time. You know 'im all right. That was Weaver, B."

He mistook Campion's blank expression for lack of recollection and hurried on to explain, all his old anxiety about the younger man's condition returning.

"You'll remember his brother better," he said coaxingly. "Weaver, T. A. They were both in the army together one time and they distinguished them like that, using the initials last. You remember them. I'll tell you 'oo they was both working for when we struck them last. Simister. The man we kept calling Ali Baba. Doesn't that ring a bell? Weaver, T. A., wasn't the class this chap is. He 'adn't the brains. He was killed with a tommy-gun when the Denver boys came over. This little sweep Weaver, B., went in for jam-jars afterwards. 'E's a wizard with a petrol engine. If 'e's in this there's something big going on in the car line. Does that bring anything 'ome?"

Campion thought of the fleet of trucks in the hidden garage under the crouching body of the Nag and he nodded. His brain was working feverishly. It was Pyne again, of course. Pyne was the man who had assumed that he was another crook trying to muscle in on a racket by impersonating Albert Campion. What about Pyne, then? What about his questions and his "amusing organization"? And his snooping about at the Institute?

He glanced at the pile of money on the table.

"They're not broke, anyway," he said.

"They are not." Lugg's heartfelt agreement was unexpected. He was very serious and his small black eyes were open to their widest extent. "They're a powerful crowd," he said. "Money to burn. There was a sort of share-out down here before we came, you know. The drunks filled every can in the place. Happy said 'e never saw anything like it. 'E reckons they're on to something colossal, something that'll need a lot of men from the way money has been splashing around."

He gathered up the cash on the table and rolled back the cloth.

"Wicked to waste it," he remarked virtuously.

The drawer was only just closed when the shopkeeper appeared behind them. His startled face came edging round the inner door.

"They've scarpered," he said, using the rhyming slang which still serves a fraternity needing a patois. "Only one of 'em left. He's leaning against the wall of a door or two down the road. What happened?"

"Nothing to interest you, my lad." Lugg was heavily jocular. "Someone came along to make what you might call an extravagant gesture, that's all."

"I don't like it." Their host was inclined to whine. "It's dangerous. There's some pretty funny chaps in this town just now. I saw 'Lily' Pettican walking down the street this morning."

"Lily?" Lugg was clearly astounded. "You've got the 'orrors," he said.

"If it wasn't Lily, it was 'is brother 'oo 'appened to 'ave lost the same eye," the old man persisted. "Chew on that."

"Go away." Lugg was not amused. His small eyes were frightened.

"All right, but I've got something for yer. What d'yer say to this lot?" He wriggled into the room through the smallest possible aperture and presented one of those long narrow ledger-books in which small shopkeepers often keep their orders. It was open at the last page and he pointed to the final entry made in his own wildest handwriting.

"A.C." it ran. "The White Hart, private sitting-room. Immediately. Come clean."

Both Lugg and Campion read the line and exchanged glances.

"Where the hell did you get that from?"

"From a woman." The shopkeeper did not seem particularly surprised. "She came in just before I shut the shop. I was just going to lock the doors after giving you the word the busies were about. She was about fifty, I suppose. Very respectable, you know. I hadn't never seen 'er before. She came up to the counter and said could I get 'er *Heartsease Novels* every week. I said I could and I got out my book to take 'er name. When I was ready she simply dictated that lot. After I'd written it down she said thank you very much and went out. A.C., that stands for you, doesn't it, Guv'nor? Albert Campion, that's your name."

Lugg turned to his employer. He was completely startled.

"But they were 'ere," he said stupidly. "They didn't know you were A.C. then. Lumme, see what it means? See what it means? It's someone else. It's not them at all. 'Come clean'? 'Oo the 'ell is it?"

The little shopkeeper looked at his excited face and shook his head.

"That's all I know, what I've told you," he began. "The White Hart's that big hotel in the middle of the town. Nothing could happen to you there, that's one thing mortal certain. It can't even be a try-on. More people know you than you know people."

"You're telling me," said Campion fervently.

CHAPTER THIRTEEN

"What are you going to do?"

The enquiry crept into the almighty muddle of confused thoughts and emotions in Campion's tortured mind and opened out like a great question-mark-shaped hole of nothingness.

He did not answer because both men were looking at him confidently and he saw that he should have no help from them in his decision. He was the Boss still; they relied on him.

He was trying to marshal some sort of order among his scattered forces when another secret question shot out at him. Just how ill am I? Just how serious is this damned injury? Am I going to curl up and die from it, and if so, how long have I got? He put that query from him impatiently. He guessed he'd find that out when the time came. Meanwhile, what *was* he going to do?

There was something just under his nose which he had missed. He felt it was there and he groped for it. When at last he found it it grinned at him with the dreadful cross-eyed leer of complete insanity. This was the fourteenth. Moreover this was the evening of the fourteenth. Therefore, all the arrangements for the catastrophe, or whatever it was which he was struggling so blindly to avert, must have been made already, and the thing itself be on the very point of happening. And yet Pyne, or the Enemy, whoever he was, had been prepared to try to buy him off even at this eleventh hour. That argued that he was still dangerous to this unknown. How? What could he do now, this minute? What was there to do?

He glanced at the remarkable message in the notebook and then at the man who had written it. The shopkeeper had come forward and the light was on his face. It was not so much that sterling honesty shone from his eyes. It didn't. He looked shifty and disreputable. But he was also puzzled. The message clearly fascinated him. He had no idea what it meant or from whom it came. He would like to have known. He, too, waited expectantly.

"I'll go down there," said Campion.

"I'll come with yer." Lugg was shaking off his carpet-slippers as he spoke. "You'll be less noticeable if we go together."

"I don't think so." Campion spoke frankly. If there is one human peculiarity which cannot be disguised it is fat. A fat man is distinctive at any distance. Lugg could scarcely hope to pass anywhere unobserved.

"There's a busy up the street, don't forget," said the shopkeeper.

"How do you know it's a busy?" Lugg was tolerantly contemptuous.

"Because I see 'is face and I know 'im. 'E's been round 'ere once or twice. The other lot went away. 'E didn't."

This was important information. The police were the one body who, so far as Campion knew for a fact, had definite cause to want to lay hands on him, but if they had actually located him it seemed highly peculiar that they should not come in and get him. The proba-

ble explanation was, of course, that they had not located him but
were keeping an eye on one of the others in case they should try to
contact him.

"I'll take you past the busy," said the shopkeeper unexpectedly. "I've
got my own way out. I'll go first, you come behind. I'll lead you right
to the White Hart. It's not easy to find if you don't know the town."

"I'm to stay 'ere?" Lugg enquired dubiously.

"Yes," said the shopkeeper.

Lugg looked at Campion silently. He was pathetic and Campion
could have murdered him. What right had he to lean like this, to sit
childlike and helpless, relying on a superior intelligence?—which, God
help them all, was no longer there. It was the original Campion's own
fault. The new Campion felt he had the grace to recognize that. He
had a vision of a damned superior young man who must always have
been laughingly tolerant, gloriously sure of himself. The new Campion turned from him with loathing. A fine chuckleheaded ass he
must have been to surround himself with dear, faithful, pathetic fol-
lowers incapable of independent thought; fawners, seekers after
orders.

"I'll give you a couple of hours," said Lugg, shattering the illusion.
"If you're not back then I'll come and save your ruddy life again.
It won't be the first time. Don't forget you're not right in the 'ead
now, either."

Campion set out with the shopkeeper. Both he and Lugg appeared
to have brought the art of avoiding police supervision to a high state
of perfection. Campion was provided with a shabby raincoat and a
peaked cap. It was no disguise but rather a badge of some unspecified
but respectable office. As he put them on he became just another
taxi-driver, bus conductor, chauffeur, St. John ambulance man, or gas
inspector hurrying home to get out of his working clothes.

The shopkeeper led him out of the back door into a minute yard
and out of that into another and another, all symmetrical and uniform as a section of a dusty egg-box.

They came out finally into an entirely different quarter of the town,
a solid residential district of ornate Victorian houses with transoms
over the doors and high surprised windows with little apartment cards
in them.

The shopkeeper scurried along in front. In his dirty overcoat and
dented bowler hat he looked as frail and negligible as a piece of sodden brown paper blown along by the bullying wind.

The storm itself had passed but there was still a lot of rain about.
There was just enough light to see one's way, but the going was not

too easy and the pavements looked washed and sticky, like pieces of half-sucked toffee.

Campion did not notice the town. It took every ounce of concentration which he still possessed to follow the little wisp of a figure in front. His legs were heavy and his head swam.

He was so intent on the mere physical task that he did not notice the carved portico of the White Hart until he was almost directly under the famous sign and was so close to the doorway that he was forced to turn straight in through the light-trap arranged over the double doors. He was walking quickly and stepped slap into a bright lounge full of people, most of whom turned and looked at him enquiringly.

Every town in England has one hostelry like the White Hart. It is always a grand old inn where either Charles Dickens or Queen Elizabeth spent a night and which modern motor traffic has made once more fashionable. In these ancient houses rooms are knocked together, beams are uncovered, mighty fireplaces are filled with false logs with red electric bulbs tucked under them, and in the roughcast walls mock casements show painted musical comedy settings through their diamond panes. The food is usually good, the service appalling, and the atmosphere about as cosy and cliquey as the school hall on prize-giving day. Practically every man in the room was in khaki on this occasion. Campion, who had no recollection of ever having seen anything like it before, was completely bewildered. Fortunately his astonishment fitted his somewhat unsuitable costume and no one among the little parties clustered round the small tables gave him a second look. A growing youth in a tail suit far too small for him hurried forward enquiringly, anxious to direct him to the saloon bar round the corner. Campion looked at him helplessly and said the first thing to come into his head.

"I want someone in a private room. I've been told to come here."

The boy regarded him dubiously and scuttled into a small office half hidden in a mass of oaken tracery far more suitable to the rood-screen for which it had originally been carved. He came out again with the landlord, a dapper elderly man with a military cut to his clothes and bored eyes.

"Yes?" he said.

"My name is Albert Campion."

"Really?" His surprise was genuine and terror seized the man who had just come in. What a fool thing to do? What a lunatic he was! What a benighted idiot! Both sections of society thirsting for his blood, no time to lose, disaster imminent, and he had to go and give

his name to the first stranger who raised an eyebrow at him. He was
so appalled that he hardly noticed the landlord until he realized that
the man had gone over to the foot of the main staircase and now
stood waiting for him to follow.

They went upstairs in silence and paused before a crooked door
with the fine thin panels of the Tudors. The landlord knocked and
bent his head to listen. Campion heard nothing, but presently the
other man seemed satisfied, for he threw open the door and announced "Mr. Albert Campion" as if he had been a flunkey.

Campion went in. It was a wide, low-ceilinged room, badly lit, possessing an uneven floor, antique furniture, and a genuine coal fire.
At first he thought he was alone and his misgivings rose up reproachfully. He turned to try the door but it was not even properly closed,
much less locked. As he moved somebody coughed on the other side
of the room.

It was a ladylike sound and he swung back just in time to see a
small figure rising up out of the shadows of a winged chair which he
had presumed to be empty. A little old woman stood before him.

He was astounded. She came nervously towards him, simpering a
little, and with two bright spots of embarrassment in her faded cheeks.
She held out her hand, but shyly, and as if she felt that she was being
forward.

"This is so awkward," she murmured. "I don't think we've met?"
Her voice trailed away and he became uncomfortably aware that she
was put out by his mackintosh and the peaked cap in his hand. Socially
the situation was absurd. Even factually it was peculiar.

They shook hands and stood looking at one another. The woman
was over seventy and frail. Her thin grey hair was parted demurely
and she wore a dark silk dress with bits of lace on it.

"You're not quite as I expected you," she said nervously. "Forgive
me, I don't quite mean that. I'm sure I'm very glad to meet you like
this. Sit down, will you? It's very cold, is it not?"

She was completely out of her element and very annoyed with herself for showing it. Suddenly she dabbed her eyes.

"It's all been such a shock," she said unsteadily, "but this is quite
unpardonable. So silly of me. I really ought never to have come."

"Oh Lord!" said Campion. He was under the impression that he
had spoken under his breath, but to his horror his voice, clear, brusque,
and unnaturally loud, echoed back at him from the shadowy walls.
An inner door which he had not noticed before opened at once and,
as though in direct answer to prayer, Amanda stood on the threshold.

Hallucination! The dreadful possibility shot into his mind and frightened every other consideration out of it. She looked so fine and fit and young and alive. Her brown suit matched her eyes and her head sat sanely on her shoulders. She was lovely, she was kind, she was friendly, a right thing in a ghastly unrealistic world. That was it; she was an oasis. No, of course, a mirage! One of those things you see before you die of thirst in a desert and the vultures come and pick your bones into decency before you decay.

"Oh beautiful," he said and had not spoken the words so guilelessly since he had first said them, leaning out of his go-cart to look at the sea.

Her fine eyebrows rose into arcs on her forehead.

"I heard your voice," she said. "I'm so sorry I wasn't here when you came. Have you and Miss Anscombe met?"

A great portion of the world slid into the horizontal again at the command of that cool voice and all the lovely machinery for living, like manners and introductions and calling-cards and giving up one's seat in the bus, began to whirr comfortingly in the background of the scene.

The old lady appeared to appreciate it as much as he did. She raised her head and smiled.

"I'm being very stupid, my dear," she said. "I hadn't realized how shaken I am. You must ask Mr. Campion to forgive me."

"I think he's been a bit shaken himself." There was warning as well as apology in Amanda's tone and she considered the forlorn figure in the tight mackintosh with interest. "I've got Miss Anscombe to come along herself to tell you one or two things, Albert," she went on. "Very kindly she came along to see me and . . ."

"I went to her because she looked so sensible and so sympathetic," interrupted the old lady. "I felt I ought to approach someone and naturally one has a horror of the police at such a time. I prefer to talk to a woman of course."

"Of course," said Campion so earnestly that again Amanda stared at him as if he were demented. He fought to get hold of the situation, but it was all hopeless. His memory had deserted him. He sighed. "Why?" he added disastrously.

"Well naturally, Albert." Amanda caught the dropping brick with both hands and struggled with it manfully. "I mean, since her brother's death she's been frightfully hurt and shaken, and she hasn't felt like talking to just anyone."

Her brother. Miss Anscombe. Of course! The name had not registered on him before. He understood at last. This must be the sister of the murdered man whom Lee Aubrey had kept talking about. It came into his head that Aubrey might have sent Amanda here now and the possibility irked him unreasonably.

The old lady tucked her handkerchief into her belt and leant forward purposefully.

"Mr. Campion," she said, "I'm a very strong-minded woman and all my life I've gone out of my way to do what I thought was right."

It was a formidable opening at the best of times and to Campion, who was not experiencing one of them, it sounded like a confession of early suicide. He nodded.

"Yes?" he said.

"Well, that's why I've come here now, to talk about poor Robert. We shall never know how he died. He was a very weak person in some ways and if he had taken his own life I should have been very sorry and very hurt, but I should not have been surprised."

Campion remained unimpressed. He knew how Anscombe had died and that information was enough to startle this old duck into screaming hysterics. It was only when he caught sight of Amanda watching him earnestly that he realized what the old woman was trying to tell him. Of course Anscombe had known! Anscombe had been the best bet. Oates had said so. He turned to the old lady so eagerly that he bewildered her.

"Was your brother frightened of something?" he demanded.

She bridled and he was aware of her rather hard blue eyes with their bald rims and wrinkled sockets.

"He had something on his conscience," she said. "I always felt he was just going to confide in me but he never did. I have a very rigid code," she added naïvely.

"Tell Albert about the money," put in Amanda.

Money? More money? This cash motif cropped up all the time. It frightened Campion. The Tory Englishman never underestimates the power of money as a weapon. It is his own, and when he sees it against him he feels betrayed as well as anxious.

Miss Anscombe cleared her throat. Having embarked on a distasteful duty she was determined to get every ounce of virtue out of it.

"He never told me that he was in financial difficulties, but it was very obvious some little time ago," she began. "I realized that he was hard put to it and I helped him to a certain extent. He was quite sick with worry, naturally, for we had a certain position in the town to keep up and he was a man who understood the importance of doing his duty to the community in that respect. Also he had the Secretaryship to think of. That is a very sacred responsibility, Mr. Campion."

"I suppose it is."

"Our family have thought so for seven generations," she said stiffly. "If you don't realize what it must have meant to him to resign that office, you can hardly appreciate anything I'm trying to tell you."

"He does understand," cut in Amanda hastily. "He's terribly tired and worried himself. Albert, for the love of Mike take off that awful mackintosh."

He obeyed her and realized as Miss Anscombe looked at him that his suit was crumpled and his linen grubby. What in God's name did it matter? The old lady exasperated him with her ridiculous niceties in the midst of this maelstrom. Why didn't she cut the cackle and come to the horses? What had Anscombe known? Didn't she realize that there was no time to waste? He could have shaken the facts out of her and was within an ace of telling her so when she spoke again.

"When my brother suddenly became comparatively wealthy again I was astounded," she said. "I knew then that things were not at all as they should be. We come of a class, Mr. Campion, which never acquires money suddenly, except by legacy. For a little while my brother was almost happy, but gradually a great change came over him. His conscience was haunting him."

Campion stared at her. In spite of his preoccupation some of the urgent tragedy in her story forced itself through to him. He saw her world vividly, with painful clarity. He saw the narrow, self-important old man clinging to his inherited privileges amid a snowstorm of falling shares, rising prices, fleecing taxes, whispers in the towns, nudges, older clothes, tradesmen waiting, and silly little economies which did no good.

"What did he do?" he said, his eyes reflecting some of the awe in her own.

"I'm not perfectly sure." Now that she was holding him she was less antagonistic. They had become fellow investigators, gossips with a licence. "For a long time I couldn't bring myself to consider it, but now that he's dead I feel I must tell all that I do know. I'm afraid poor Robert sold his honour and his integrity, Mr. Campion. I think he must have used his position as Secretary of the Masters to permit some sort of smuggling to go on in those caves under the Nag. And then later I think he changed his mind and was trying to expiate the sin he had committed. I don't know how he died. If it was an accident it was the hand of God, but if he took his own life, or if someone else killed him, I shouldn't be in the least surprised. I've lived through several wars and one can't do that without realizing that the world contains violent men."

Campion felt the muscles at the corners of his jaw contracting. This was truth. This was a break. At last a real break, if only he had the wits to assimilate it.

"Smuggling what?" he enquired.

"I don't know. I'm only guessing that," she reminded him quickly. "But there was a Mr. Feiberg who came to the house once or twice to see my brother. That was in the spring of 'thirty-nine, when my brother was most hard pressed for money. After he left Robert began to talk about the Nag and about the smuggling that was done there in the seventeenth century. He covered it up at once, of course, but I never forgot it. Mr. Feiberg came twice after that, but never after the war broke out. I mentioned him at once, of course, because he was an alien and my brother said definitely then 'We shan't see him again'."

"Had your brother acquired his new money then?"

"Yes," she said, "yes, he had, but it was after that that his conscience began to prick him."

"Long after?"

"No." She paused. There was uncertainty in her whole poise. She waited until he was exasperated with her and then, with an apologetic smile, came out with the one remark in the world which could have brought him up on his toes and re-kindled a flicker of hope in his heart.

"I mustn't mislead you," she said. "I think his conscience slept until he heard of fifteen."

"Fifteen?" His voice failed and he whispered the word.

She ignored the interruption.

"It must have been then that he saw his terrible mistake. I think he did everything he could after that. He decided to resign his Secretary-ship. He drew out every penny he had in the bank, and he was bringing it back with him yesterday when you drove him home. Also this morning his bank manager called on me and told me in confidence that Robert gave instructions for all his securities to be turned into cash and the money delivered to him."

"But that's extraordinary!" Amanda spoke before she saw the pit-fall, and, having seen it, went on sturdily. "I mean, that doesn't look like suicide. That suggests to me that he was going to clear out."

"Yes." Miss Anscombe was not offended. It was evident she held no very high opinion of her brother. "It does, doesn't it? Unless, you see, he meant to give it all back to someone. We shall never know and I prefer to be charitable."

Campion was not listening to them. His ears were still tingling from the shock of hearing that one most elusive, most tantalizing word of all, the keynote and symbol of the whole maddening enigma.

"Tomorrow is the fifteenth," he said stupidly.

"I didn't refer to the date." The old lady made the remark with complete conviction. "I don't know exactly what fifteen refers to, but it isn't a day of the month."

"How do you know?" Even then he did not believe her. The tension was still there, straining every nerve in his body, urging him to hurry.

"Because of the diary." She had been holding the little pocket-book all the time and he had not noticed. Now he would have snatched it from her, but she was not to be hurried. "Robert was a very un-methodical man," she remarked with exasperating deliberation. "I thought the book was empty at first but then I found just these two entries. Here's the first, just over a month ago. Look for yourself. It's almost as though the poor man bought the book just to write some-thing melodramatic in it. That would have been very like him."

Campion took the book and Amanda looked over his shoulder.

"Friday the 7th," they read. "Just heard of Minute Fifteen. See it all. What have I done?"

The following pages were blank until they came to the space al-lotted to the day before the one on which its owner had died.

"Done," he had written. "Done at last. Conscience clearer. Re-signed. Expiation must follow. Shall I see Henry Bull?"

On the following page, and right across the three days it repre-sented, two words had been scribbled large.

"Minute Fifteen."

Campion sat down. The train had snapped. He felt flat and ex-hausted. If the fifteenth was not a date there was no hurry. As he sat gazing at the page, however, the three printed dates stood out in re-lief. Sixteenth? Seventeenth? Eighteenth? Which? None of them or all of them?

The insufferable burden of anxiety returned more heavily than be-fore. Weaver, B.'s mission became more rational and therefore more serious. Fifteen itself was still a mystery. "Minute Fifteen" might mean anything.

Miss Anscombe rose to her feet.

"Where is Annie?" she enquired, looking at Amanda.

"In the next room, waiting for you. Are you sure she can take you home all right?"

"My dear, don't let her hear you say that." The old lady laughed as she spoke. "Annie used to be my personal maid. Now I think she's my guardian. She delivered the message safely to you, did she, Mr. Campion?"

"Eh? Oh yes, rather. Brilliantly. Was that your maid?" Campion was talking without thinking and he bundled his scattering thoughts together impatiently. "I'm afraid she must have thought it a rather unconventional method of approach," he said apologetically.

Miss Anscombe patted Amanda's hand.

"Not at all," she said unexpectedly. "These are unconventional times. We're not blind. It's no good being conventional in a world which is blowing up all round one. When the streets become a shambles one has to raise one's skirts. Good-bye. I don't know if I've been helpful, but at least I've cleared my conscience without giving poor miserable Robert's mistakes over to the police."

"Wait." Campion was still clinging to the pocket diary. "Who is Henry Bull?"

Both women stared at him. Miss Anscombe looked startled.

"Sir Henry is a Conservative and one of the Tey family," she said. "At the moment he's the Senior Master of Bridge and a Junior Lord of the Treasury."

"Don't be silly; you know that," said Amanda. "Besides, we met him, didn't we, at your sister's wedding?"

CHAPTER FOURTEEN

Amanda came back into the room after seeing Miss Anscombe and her maid out. She closed the door carefully behind her.

"I say, what's the matter with you?" she demanded.

He eyed her guiltily and got up to get away from her searching enquiry.

"I'm all right. When the wind is southerly I can tell a hawk from a handsaw."

The quotation escaped out of some shrouded cupboard in his mind without any context, so that he heard the words as though for the first time. They meant nothing to him now he considered them and left him considerably startled.

"That's good," said Amanda. "The fancy dress was a mistake," she added, picking up the peaked cap. "I told you to come clean. She's that sort of old pet. I thought that would warn you."

"Oh I see. I'm sorry. It never occurred to me to take the words literally. I didn't realize the message came from you, you see."

"You . . . ?" She swung round and stared at him. He did not understand her expression. She was astonished, but also, in some indefinable way, hurt. "But we've used that sort of language between ourselves for years and years," she said at last.

"Oh, yes," he agreed in horror as he saw the trap. "Yes, we have, haven't we? I forgot."

He expected her to be angry with him. Any woman would be. He was grateful that he had said it. Those intelligent young eyes terrified him. He needed her beside him with an unbearable urgency quite out of character. He was not the sort of man who ought ever to need the moral support of anyone else on earth with this dreadful sick anxiety. Once she knew the truth about him she'd stick to him with all that eager generosity which was her mainspring. She'd be so kind, so sorry. Pity, filthy humiliating weakening pity! Nauseating compassion! His soul retched at it—the ultimate concentrated essence of second-best.

His earlier determination to hold her at whatever cost shrank before that price. To have forced her into fidelity might have been admissible and even pleasurable, but to sneak it, to grovel round it, and prize it up this most repulsive of all ways, that was too much. He hadn't come to that yet.

He glanced across the room at her. She was sitting on the arm of a chair, looking half her age. Her short skirt showed her knees and her thin arms were folded on her chest. She grinned at him.

"You're up to something you don't want me to know about," she said. "That's all right. Don't fluff."

"I'm not fluffing." The protest sounded childish and he could have smacked her. She was so like that. They seemed to get on to schoolroom terms the moment they spoke together. He must have known her very well for a long time.

"Sorry," said Amanda. "To me you fluff. Miss Anscombe sounded as if she might have been being useful. Was she?"

"She was, very. I hope she keeps her mouth shut now. Aubrey suggested that you bring her along, did he?"

Campion was watching her very closely and he thought he saw her change colour.

"No," she said. "No, he didn't, as it happens. I rather edged her off Lee."

"I see. You're going back there now, are you?"

"If you think I ought to."

"My dear girl, that's your affair entirely." Campion hoped he was not bickering.

To his consternation she got up and came over to him.

"Look here, Albert," she said with unusual earnestness, "I'm not asking for any explanation, of course. Our usual arrangement stands. You know exactly what you're doing and I'm only out to be useful, but just at the moment I'm probably rather slow. I'm not too good. I've had a bit of a shock, as a matter of fact. I'll tell you about it later, when I'm better. But at the moment it's making me a bit ingrowing and slow on the uptake and I don't see what you're up to at all. I don't know what to look for. I don't even know if I've done the right thing about Hutch."

Hutch? Good heavens, of course! The Superintendent. Campion hoped that the sweat which had broken out on his face was not visible. The nightmare was riding him with a vengeance. It was bad enough to have one's previous life wiped clean off the slate on one's mind without developing this new propensity for forgetting any act of violence which came his way. First it had been Anscombe's murder and now it was his own attack on the unfortunate Superintendent.

"What did you do?" he enquired anxiously.

"Well, I convinced him that you were you, to start with. That took a bit of doing, but I got it into all their heads in the end. Then"— she coughed delicately—"then I said you were never afraid to take the unconventional line if the urgency of the job demanded it."

"How did they take that?"

"Not too well," she admitted. "You can't blame them, Albert. It was pretty drastic and high-hat, wasn't it? Very unlike you, too," she added after a pause. "You're not much like yourself at the moment. You'll find the police looking for you, by the way. They're not entirely satisfied and Hutch wants his car, for one thing."

Campion held his breath. He could just remember that there must have been a car, but what had happened to it or to himself between the moment when he had knocked out the Superintendent and had subsequently walked into the paper shop he had no idea.

This was dreadful. Amanda must find him out at any minute now. Her trust was heartrending, too. He wished she would not treat him with the blind faith of the silly little sister who follows her brother up the elm tree.

"You knew where to find me yourself," he remarked. "How was that?"

Again that look of hurt bewilderment.

"That was our arrangement, wasn't it?" She did not speak of the car again and he guessed that his reticence must be part of their arrangement also. Evidently she was his lieutenant. She offered any information she found but their plan of campaign was entirely his own.

"I must see Henry Bull," he said.

"Ye-es." Her hesitation was fractional but it infuriated him.

"What else can I do?" he demanded. "Stanislaus has disappeared and someone has got to explain this damned fifteen."

She sat up stiffly, her eyes widening.

"But I thought you knew. I thought you'd been given all the hush-hush dope and that you and Oates were holding the entire baby between you, because nobody dare risk any sort of leakage. I didn't realize that you were in the dark at all. No wonder you're so jittery."

He looked at her as she stood over him. His taut brown face was expressionless.

"Do you find me jittery?"

Amanda laughed. It was spontaneous amusement and her heart-shaped face was alive and sane and lovely.

"I find you theatrical, stinker," she said. "What's up?"

He took her hand and swung her arm to and fro. He had seen someone else do that. It had been Lee Aubrey. That was right; it had been that blighter Lee. He had done this, leaning against the doorpost, peering down.

"I can't look at you with great constipated cow's eyes," Campion said suddenly. His wretchedness had assembled the words and they were out of his mouth before he could censor them.

Amanda drew her hand away. Then she boxed his ears.

It was a gesture rather than a blow, very light and very quick. There was no smile on her face now and no animation. Her fine bones made a stamp, a die of quality, and she was as remote from him as if she had died.

He stumbled to his feet and stood looking at her wildly. At that moment every restraining consideration seemed utterly absurd. She was part of himself and she was lost. Her going would mean partial disintegration. He felt himself cracking hopelessly, shamefully, before her eyes.

The tap on the inner door came from another world. They both swung round to stare at the handle as it turned. Lugg came tip-toeing in, bouncing a little like a descending balloon.

"Watch out," he said. "They're on the doorstep."

"Who?" It was Amanda who spoke. She seemed perfectly normal and at ease.

"The busies are downstairs. The Inspector is in the lounge and 'e's got two men just outside on the door. The proprietor 'ere doesn't want any fuss on 'is premises, thank you, and the Inspector's being obliging." The fat man dominated the room and his little eyes were bright and excited under the jutting peak of his flat cap. "The back doors aren't 'ealthy either," he went on. "I see the Lily 'imself down there, not to mention Nervy Williams and one or two more. You got a hornet's nest on your tail and no mistake. Anyone'd think you was a classic race meeting."

"How did they find me here?" said Campion.

Lugg shrugged his shoulders. "Ask me another. The police followed young Amanda, I should say, and the other little syndicate of blossoms must have a tip-off in the police somewhere. I merely strolled down after you to satisfy myself that everything was okay and I walked right into it. The police don't know me 'ere, so I came in through the lounge, 'ad a drink in the saloon, and nipped up the first staircase I could find as soon as I 'ad a chance. I've been all over the 'ouse. There's no one upstairs at the moment. I tell you what, there's a cat-walk over the roofs if you want it, but I'd think twice before I took it with your 'ead."

Campion shot a glance at Amanda and turned the flat of his hand to Lugg. It was an entirely spontaneous gesture but miraculously the man seemed to understand in time.

"'E's 'ad a 'eadache," he said to the girl. "Still, it's up to 'im."

Amanda turned to Campion. "What are you going to do?"

She was as natural and polite as if Lugg had interrupted nothing more important than a tea-party. Her poise was imperturbable and he knew that she must always have possessed it.

"I must see Bull," he said. "You'll go back to Bridge, won't you? Lugg can wait at the paper shop. I'll try the roof. I must get on. It's so urgent, you see. If fifteen isn't a date the whole thing may cook up at absolutely any moment. I've got to stop it. Whatever it is I've got to stop it."

He saw that he was speaking with unusual violence, for they both looked at him under their eyelashes and there was an awkward pause when he finished.

"You'd better try it at once, then," said Lugg practically. "We don't want the busies coming up 'ere, do we?"

"Very well." Campion had no idea what he proposed to attempt nor if he could make any serious physical effort without collapsing. It was obviously the next move, that was all.

His programme was unfolding before him like sealed orders and there was only the passionate anxiety raging behind the dark curtain in his mind to drive him on to follow it.

Lugg went over to the inner door and opened it.

"You wait a second while I make sure the coast's still clear," he said over his shoulder.

Campion nodded and glanced at Amanda. She was looking at him and as he caught her eye she smiled with sudden frank generosity, her eyes dancing.

"The best of luck," she said. "You'll do it. How's the head?"

"Fine."

"Honest? Oh well then, that's all right. I'd back you to get to hell and home again. '*Begone! she stormed, Across the raging tide'*."

It was part of a couplet, of course, and he saw by her expression that she expected him to supply the missing line. It was doubtless some old joke they had shared since her childhood, something he knew so well that it should have come to his tongue without thinking. His mind remained obstinately blank. He could not remember ever having heard the melodramatic doggerel before. Amanda was waiting confidently, all her glorious natural friendliness ready to go back to him. He could snub and hurt her, or explain.

At that moment he saw his choice as clearly as if it had been presented to him in pictorial form, like one of the old morality pictures of the primrose path flanked with gin palaces on one side and the steep track amid the chasms on the other. It would be so easy to explain and so pleasant. Lugg was there to back him up and she was eager, too, forgiveness and intelligent understanding in every inch of her young body. Aubrey could be kicked out of her life as easily as if he'd been a hedgehog in the road. She would be so sorry, so abominably dutifully sorry . . .

He laughed. "I've forgotten my cue. I'll always be able to get in touch with you at Bridge, shan't I?" he said.

The last thing he saw of her was the smile fading out of her eyes.

CHAPTER FIFTEEN

"There you are. It's a straight drop to begin with and then you 'ave to start the fancy-work. Can you see anything at all?"

Lugg's whisper came gustily to Campion across the narrow corridor at the top of the old inn. The dark cul-de-sac in which they stood, bowing their heads to avoid the low ceiling, was warm and breathless and possessed a faint smell of dust and old wallpaper. Outside the narrow casement window the night was practically black, but the wet tiles showed occasional high lights under the far-away stars.

"I don't like you going off like this in the state your 'ead's in," the fat man whispered, "but I don't see what else you can do, do you? Besides, you can climb like a perishing cat, can't you?"

Campion sincerely hoped so, otherwise the project seemed suicidal. Lugg touched his arm. "I've brought this along," he said, thrusting a package into his hand. "It's some of that money out of the drawer. It never hurts to have plenty of cash on one. Then there's this little torch. It doesn't give no more light than a pin-'ead. Shade it with your 'and and nobody won't see it. Now listen, when you get to the ground make for the main road and turn down the hill. When you get to the bottom you'll see an archway on your right. There's a sort of alley through there. Take it and go up the steps at the end and there's the station right in front of you. You may 'ave to wait about a bit for a London train, but there's bound to be one for the mail even in these times. I'll sit tight until I 'ear from you."

He broke off abruptly. Someone was moving very close to them. Heavy footsteps rang out blithely on old boards and someone's sleeve brushed against panelling which might have been directly behind them. Lugg opened the window.

"Out yer get," he whispered. "These old places either 'ave walls eight feet thick or a thin slice of canvas between two sheets of wallpaper. Button that old raincoat round yer neck. Pity you left the cap but it can't be 'elped. Ready?"

Campion slipped through the narrow aperture and hung dangerously over the pit below.

To his relief, his muscles obeyed him miraculously. He was aware of them like a great webbing basket enclosing his bones. The discovery gave him first an enormous sense of relief and then of excitement. Ever since he had left Amanda alone with the unanswerable line on her lips a recklessness quite different from anything he ever remembered experiencing before had taken possession of him. He felt so bitterly free, and so much alone, that the night itself seemed to have taken on a new quality. The darkness had become an element, like water on air, treacherous but stimulating. The soft moist wind on his skin was invigorating and his dizziness had gone, leaving him super-sensitive, as though every nerve in his body had become exposed.

Lugg's white face loomed close above him.

"Don't forget," he whispered. "Police in the front and the gentry all round the back. Good luck."

Campion dropped. He landed very lightly on his toes and finger-tips. Good lord, he could climb like a cat! His own skill astounded him, but he thrust the astonishment away from him in panic lest it should destroy this instinctive efficiency.

The little torch proved invaluable. It shed only a pin-point of light, too small to be detected immediately from the street below.

He edged his way carefully up the sloping pantiles, paused a second astride a gable, and then slid down noiselessly the other side. He went most cautiously, allowing himself to lie full length against the sharp slope and feeling his way with his feet.

He was hanging there, supporting himself with remarkably little effort, when he heard the voices. There were two of them, male, and apparently directly beneath him. He lay motionless, pressing himself into the protecting blackness of the tiles.

The two men were keeping very quiet themselves. No words were distinguishable but the murmur was furtive and secret. Presently one of them spat and, at a whisper from the other, laughed aloud. He cut it off short immediately, but the sound had not been attractive. Campion was not sure that he recognized it but he had a warning instinct that he ought to do so. He gathered that he must be at the back of the building, probably looking down on some sort of semi-enclosed yard.

He hung there for a considerable time, the strain on his arms growing slowly intolerable.

The two men stirred at last and he heard their light footsteps moving away in the darkness. He saw the glow of a cigarette slowly disappearing into the gloom. Once it paused and they seemed to be settling. Campion felt he must lose his grip and come hurtling down on to the cobbles, but the moment passed, the men went on, and soon all was quiet.

Finally Campion let himself down into the guttering and edged along it perilously until he came to a gable and had to climb again. This time he was more lucky. On the other side of the mountain of tiles he came down quietly on to a perfectly good flat roof. It belonged to an old coach-house, reconditioned as a garage perhaps, and it was set back a few feet from a narrow side road. His eyes were becoming more and more accustomed to the darkness, and here, with a comparatively wide expanse of sky above him, he could almost see.

There was no traffic in the road below him, but farther away to the right he could hear an occasional car engine revving as its driver

changed gear. That must be the high road and the hill that Lugg had
spoken of, of course.

He came quietly across the leads and paused with his hands on the
low parapet. Beneath him was pitch darkness, but he could just see
a gleam of wet pavement on the far side of the narrow road opposite.
There was no movement, no sound, not a step on the stones.

He leant over the concrete ledge and flashed his torch. The little
beam was so small that it shed scarcely any glow.

He flicked it off at once. He had seen what he wanted to. Garage,
or coach-house, or whatever it was, the roof-high doors were ajar.

Lying on his stomach, with his thighs hooked over the parapet, he
leant down and pulled one door wider. It was unexpectedly well hung
and moved so easily that he almost overbalanced. He let it swing right
back until it rested across the angle made by the building on which
he lay and the blank wall of the next house. He waited.

There was not a breath from within, not a whisper, not a rustle.

Far away in the direction of the High Street a girl laughed foolishly
as though someone had tickled her and afterwards shouted something
which he could not catch, but here, close to him in the narrow alley,
there was nothing, only silence and the soft damp kisses of the rainy
wind.

He climbed on to the door and began to descend deftly by way of
the old harness pegs. He made no sound at all and when his foot
touched the paving stone it was very gently, as if he had been coming
down carpeted stairs.

He had just straightened himself when the door moved. It was
swung back forcefully as the man who had been standing hidden behind it saw his opportunity and leapt for it. Campion side-stepped
him with an instinctive swiftness nothing to do with his conscious
thoughts. It was instinct, too, which made him thrust his foot out at
the same moment that he struck blindly in the dark. He touched cloth
and a hard shoulder beneath it, but the man went down over the outstretched foot and as he fell his cosh rattled in the gutter.

Campion ran and again he experienced a shock of delight in his own
freedom of movement. All the unsteadiness of earlier in the day had
vanished under the tremendous pressure of this new excitement. His
illness had given place to a period of complete irresponsibility,
coupled, of course, with the *idée fixe* which had never left him. Physically, he was in perfect training. He moved like a whippet, easily, gracefully, and so lightly that his feet scarcely sounded upon the tarmac.

The High Street was dark and empty but as he turned down the hill
the row started behind him. Shouts and heavy footsteps echoed from

the side-streets, and these were answered by others outside the front of the hotel. He put on more speed so that the falling ground sped from under him.

Someone behind blew a police whistle. He ducked through the arch-way, just in time. It opened at his side like a huge mouth and he slid into it. The street was waking up behind him. He could hear cries and shouted enquiries and over his shoulder caught a glimpse of torches.

The lighting restrictions were on his side. His uncanny gift for find-ing his way in the dark, and above all his tremendous speed, were going to save him if he was lucky. He kept to the wall, found the stone steps, and emerged to find himself just across the road from a railway station. It was the only building in the town not quite in com-plete darkness and he found the entrance without difficulty. With re-markable presence of mind he took off his torn and dirty mackintosh and folded it over his arm as he walked in. He could hear a train pant-ing in the station, but his ears were still strained to catch any ominous sound behind him. They would find him, of course. It was such an obvious place to come. The police, who never make the mistake of neglecting the obvious, would certainly look for him here, if the others didn't.

The booking clerk put every other consideration out of his head, however.

"Last train just going," he said, slamming down the ticket and the change on the brass ledge.

Campion snatched it and fled. The collector at the top of the stairs did not wait to clip his ticket.

"Express right through. There she goes. There she goes," he shouted obligingly as he dragged the other man through the gates. "Might just do it. Run, sir."

The train, a great dark centipede with dead eyes, was already chug-ging away from the platform, gathering speed at every gasping breath. Campion sprinted after it and just managed to swing himself on to the footboard of the last coach.

Ignoring the warning shouts behind him, he got the door of the final compartment open, and, as stale leather-scented air gushed out to meet him, he clambered into a first-class smoker. He had just slammed the door behind him, congratulating himself that there was no corri-dor, and had flung himself into a corner under one of the small blue reading lights with relief in his heart, when the train stopped with a jerk.

They had caught him. That was his first thought. The police had followed him and stopped the train. He was trapped, caught as surely as if hands were already on his shoulder. He wondered if they would come up the line for him. If so, perhaps he had a chance if the farther door of the compartment was not locked. It was, of course. At the other window he made the unnerving discovery that the coach was still partly at the long platform. Moreover, there was no time to do anything. Flying feet and raised voices were bearing down upon him. He struggled with the door. At least he could make a dash for it. The darkness was on his side. Nothing else seemed to be helpful, however. The catch stuck and he was a moment wrenching it.

That delay defeated him. As the heavy door swung open a hurrying figure hurled itself in on top of him and as he caught a glimpse of it his arm, which had been upraised, dropped to his side.

"That's all right, that's all right. I'm quite all right. Very much obliged to you. Good night."

The newcomer spoke over his shoulder to someone in the darkness.

"Good night, sir. No trouble at all. Good night," an official voice answered deferentially and the guard's whistle sounded down the platform.

The train started with a jerk which unsteadied both men and Campion retired to his corner. It was another belated traveller; that was all. He was making a fool of himself. There was nothing to fear yet. He was still free. He leant back in his seat and closed his eyes. His body was chilled and clammy and he could feel his heart jolting painfully in his side.

The other man had settled himself diagonally opposite and was blowing gently in the semi-darkness. He was small and elderly and seemed taken up with his own near shave.

Campion dismissed him from his mind. There was plenty to think about. There had been no gun-play. That meant that somebody in charge of the crook element had issued very strict orders. In England gun-play invariably entails intensive police interest. It works like a charm. One shot produces forty policemen, endless enquiries, house-to-house visits, and more fuss than a football crowd can ever make over a foul. Someone was determined to get peace and quiet for his activities. Weaver, B.'s munificent offer proved that much, of course, but it was worth noticing.

Campion dug himself farther into the soft, old-fashioned upholstery and considered his chances. The train was an express. That should mean that he was safe until he got to a London terminus. There, of course, the Metropolitan Police would probably be waiting for him if the County Inspector knew his stuff, which seemed highly probable.

Well, that could wait. He'd cross that bridge when he came to it. Meanwhile, here at last was a breather, time to think if his mind would work.

With the grim determination of necessity he settled down to make it function. Very carefully he reviewed all the concrete evidence which the last thirty hours had produced. All of it was unexpected and most of it apparently entirely unrelated. Behind it all was this desperate urgency, this passionate instinct for haste. If only he knew the essentials. He was trying to fit together a jigsaw puzzle without knowing what sort of picture the pieces were expected to make. A few of them married, though. Pyne and his Surveys Limited. The professional crooks and the method of Anscombe's murder. These three shapes made a corner, anyway.

Then there had been Miss Anscombe's painfully vivid picture of her brother's last few weeks of life. She had been so clear with her story of the alien, the suspected smuggling under the Nag, and the suggestion that Anscombe had made up his mind to atone in some way.

That picture should fit in somewhere, although at the moment he had no idea where.

Then there were the Masters themselves, the fleet of lorries, Anscombe's sudden decision to draw all his money in cash. Then there was the cash which Campion had brought in to Lugg, the other cash which Weaver, B., had offered, the parcel of cash which Anscombe had forgotten to bring in from the car. Fifteen. Minute Fifteen. The fact that it wasn't a date.

His head reeled and he bent forward and rested his forehead in his hands and his elbows on his knees. The train's wheels grumbled and vibrated soothingly beneath him. It was a pause at any rate, a moment of peace and security in a breathless race through nightmare streets with police and crook alike his pursuers. He felt almost calm, almost at ease.

The other man in the compartment stirred. Campion could just see him in the blue mist which hung over the carriage like dusty limelight. As the younger man raised his head the stranger spoke, revealing a deep elderly voice, faintly suspicious as such voices often are.

"I've seen your face before," he said accusingly. "Where was that? Aren't you Albert Campion?"

CHAPTER SIXTEEN

Campion froze. Good God! Was the whole world after him? *Of course it was.* The recollection came like a scalding shower, shocking him back to reality. Of course it was. Hadn't he killed one policeman and assaulted another? Wasn't the whole countryside being scoured for him? He drew back in the shadows.

"No," he said huskily. "No. That's not my name. I don't think we've met."

"Oh? No? Perhaps not. Perhaps not." The voice sounded partially satisfied but its owner did not relax. Through the blue mist from the reading lamp Campion took careful stock of this new potential enemy. He was a neat little man, a character. His dark coat was sleek and unobtrusively expensive, but his hat was too large for him and his white hair was untidy beneath it. At the moment he was staring at Campion unwinkingly with unexpectedly shrewd eyes.

He had a small attaché case by his side and a walking-stick across his knees. He looked very English, very narrow and conventional.

It was quite possible that they had met, of course, in the far-off lucid days thirty-six hours ago. Campion began to feel for a name which he might give if asked point-blank. He saw the danger of that just in time, fortunately. Suppose if out of the dark presses of his mind he fished up some famous name. The only one to occur to him at that moment was Dick Turpin. He had a strong feeling there was something against it, yet it had a vaguely attractive sound.

Fortunately the question did not come but neither did the stare waver. It remained transfixing him, paralysingly steady and confident, for what seemed the best part of an hour. He moved uneasily under it, leaning back in the leathery darkness to escape it, but it did not falter. It had almost demoralized him before he realized that the man was not seeing him but was looking through him into some introspective unknown.

This discovery was a relief, but all the same it was not easy to think of anything else with those intelligent eyes glittering straight at one in the blue gloom. In the end he was forced to speak in sheer self-defence. He was so anxious to be entirely natural and he tried out many openings in his mind and finally succeeded in being gauche.

"Worried?" he enquired baldly, adding at once, as the glitter faded and astonishment took its place, "I mean, the—er—times are very disturbing, aren't they?"

The other man sat up. He was considerably flustered by the complete lack of ceremony. Campion could have kicked himself. Poor old boy. He was just a successful provincial business man chewing over the troubles of the day. There was nothing sinister about him, nothing to be frightened of. Surely his history as well as his character was written in his face. He looked tired, overworked, weighed down by the responsibilities of his job as the head of some firm or other. He was probably meticulously straight in his dealings, astute, too, in a narrow way, wealthy, and yet beset by problems. In fact, the great British public itself incarnate.

"Yes," he said at last, having decided to forgive the intrusion. "Not too easy, are they? I think we must face it that they're dangerous, damned dangerous."

It was odd how he managed to convey such consternation by saying so little. Campion wondered if his business had been badly hit. He saw it as something to do with wool. A fine old firm, probably generations old.

His own mind was running feverishly on the subject. He wanted the man to talk, to babble on reassuringly about ordinary things; anything, the war, the weather, sport, A.R.P., anything to keep him as he was now, a normal comprehensible fellow human-being and not a pair of fixed introspective eyes in the shadows.

"What worries you most?" Campion demanded, knowing the question was infantile but panic-stricken lest he should escape again.

The old man blinked at him. "Treachery," he said.

Campion wondered if he had heard the word. It was so unexpected, so melodramatic. The stranger was looking at him again, too, and the blue light shone in his eyes.

"You find it in your business?" Campion enquired.

"I do." The admission seemed to be wrenched out of the man. "I do, after fifty years. Treachery on a vast scale everywhere I look. Sometimes I wonder if my own eyes are deceiving me, but no, it's there and it's got to be faced."

He was silent and Campion took a liking to him. He looked such a dogged old chap, sitting there with his square hands gripping the stick across his knees.

There was a long pause and then the shrewd eyes rested on the younger man again.

"I could have sworn you were Albert Campion," he said. "It must be because I've been hearing about him tonight."

It came back. All Campion's apprehension of the past few hours returned with interest. He held himself together with an effort and forced his mind to go slow. It was too dangerous to ask questions. The old boy was too sharp. Besides, he had recognized him. The old fellow was not certain, of course. That was the one saving grace. The only hope was to take his mind off the subject and to talk of something else.

Campion searched wildly for a likely opening. What would interest a wool merchant, if the wretched man *was* in wool? Sheep, perhaps? No, that was absurd. He was losing his grip on reality altogether. This was madness. Oh God, what was he going to say next?

The old man leant back in his seat and crossed his short legs.

"We've always fought our wars with money," he remarked. "I wonder if it's going to save us now?"

Money! Of course. Campion could have laughed aloud. Why hadn't he thought of it before? Everybody was interested in money. It was a universal subject.

"I don't know," he said cautiously, choosing the safest lead. "It's not to be confused with wealth, of course."

"No," said the old man briefly, "no, it's not, but as it stands now, in its present position, it's a very important factor all the same."

He went on to talk fluently on the aspect of the struggle which evidently interested him. He appeared to be quite sound, but Campion made no attempt to follow him. He heard the voice and that was enough. He was soothed and reassured and it gave him a moment to think. Soon the train would come into the station. That was going to be a difficult moment. Detectives were almost certain to be there to meet it. They could hardly miss him, although they would be looking for a man alone and might with reasonable luck have only a telephoned description of him. If only there had been time he would have let them take him and have risked the enquiry. They could hardly hang him for murder in his present condition and almost anything would be preferable to this continuous hounding down. However, that was out of the question. He had a job to do and he must do it, at whatever cost.

Amanda came up in his mind and he thrust her out of it savagely.

"The unspeakable peril of forced inflation," droned the voice on the other side of the compartment. "The loss of faith in the country's essential soundness."

Campion smiled at the man and nodded to him without hearing. How comfortingly ordinary he was. What a blessed piece of solid and familiar ground in this new world of quicksands and blackouts. The intelligent thing to do was to stick to him, of course. It would be dangerous in a way, but at least it would ensure that he did not go trotting off to confide his suspicions to the first bobby he saw on the station.

Campion glanced at the man, to see that he had just finished speaking and now rose to his feet purposefully.

What was this? Campion grew cold. Was he going to turn out to be an elderly Chief Inspector after all? Was it a last-minute arrest? Campion seemed to remember having heard of something of the sort long ago. His face must have given him away because the old man was looking at him curiously.

"We're just coming in," he said. "Can't you feel us slowing down?"

"Of course." One crisis was over but another had arrived. "Of course," Campion repeated. "I hadn't noticed. I was so interested."

"Really? That's very gratifying." The old man was opening the carriage door and he was laughing a little. "I'm glad to hear that. Ah, thank you." The final remark was addressed to someone outside on the platform. "What's that?"

There was a muttering which Campion could not catch and then his travelling companion glanced over his shoulder.

"I'm afraid there's some trouble," he remarked. "The police are looking for someone on the train."

"Oh?" Now that it had come Campion was himself again. His thin face became wooden and his voice entirely natural. "What do they want us to do?"

Once again there was a murmur from the official in the darkness. The old man nodded briefly.

"Quite," he said. "Very sensible. They've shut off the main platform," he continued, turning to Campion. "This last coach is just outside the barrier. The fellow here suggests he takes our tickets for us and we go across the footway to the road. You'll want a cab, won't you?"

"Yes, please."

"Right. Well then, this is where we part. Good morning to you. I enjoyed our chat. I'm afraid it was all about nothing."

"Good morning, sir," said Campion and followed him into the grey darkness.

It was incredible. He had no time to realize his escape. It was like one of those wild rides in a switchback in a funfair. A blank wall looms up in front of the car. Nearer it comes, nearer and nearer, and then when the crash is imminent, when the impact and noise of it is almost a reality, the track swings away, the car swerves sickeningly, the corner is turned, and the delirious journey continues.

He stumbled across the platform, which was littered with goods trolleys, milk churns, and mailbags. On his right, beyond the police-lined barrier, there was all the usual confusion of arrival. The detectives were waiting farther on at the ticket gate, no doubt. Meanwhile his own getaway was made absurdly easy. No one took the least notice of him. The railway official led the old man and Campion followed the pair of them. That was all there was to it.

He thought he saw exactly what must have happened. His travelling companion was obviously a constant passenger on this particular train. Probably he had used it every day for the past ten years or more. Railway servants get to know a man like that and if he is a good tipper will go to endless trouble on his behalf. He must have been in the habit of using the final coach and doubtless this was his regular porter who was waiting to meet him.

They came out at last on to a narrow road on the goods side of the station. The old man's car was waiting for him and he nodded to Campion as he climbed into it. A taxi crawled forward out of the darkness.

"Where to, sir?"

"The Treasury," said Campion briefly and climbed inside.

The cab moved forward at once. There was no questioning, no delay, no pause at the station gates. He could hardly believe it. He had got away as neatly and smoothly as if he had been a ghost. It was an invigorating experience and he began to feel absurdly pleased with himself. The gods were on his side. He glanced out of the window and saw the chill grey outline of shabby old buildings, piled sandbags, and painted road-signs. The streets were practically deserted.

A sudden thought occurred to him and he rapped on the window. The taxi drew into the curb and the driver turned to peer through the glass screen.

"Yes, sir?"

"What time is it?"

"Just on a quarter before five, sir."

"In the morning?"

"Lumme! I 'ope so. Otherwise I've been drivin' back through Einstein ever since the pubs shut last night."

Campion ignored the pleasantry. He was thinking. Even if he was half-way down the straight to Colney Hatch he yet had enough sense to realize that no Cabinet Minister is liable to be available at his office before five in the morning.

"You'd better take me to a hotel," he said.

The driver, who was in a ferocious mood, shrugged his shoulders elaborately.

"Just as you say, sir. Got any particular place in mind?"

"No. Anywhere will do as long as it's open. I want to shave and get some breakfast."

The cabby beamed. He was an elderly cockney, with the bright little eyes and thin rodent's face of his race.

"Well," he said, "since you're not paying your income-tax for the moment, I see, what about the Ritz?"

"I've got no luggage."

" 'Strewth!" said the driver. "I'd better take you 'ome and give you a nice brush-up myself. Sorry, sir, it's the morning air on an empty stomach. What about this place 'ere? You're outside it; that's in its favour."

Campion looked at the gloomy façade across the pavement. A porter in shirt-sleeves was sweeping down the steps and at that moment a policeman sauntered over to speak to him.

"No." Campion did not mean to sound so vehement. "Somewhere more—more central."

"Right you are, sir." The cockney was looking at him very curiously. "It would help me if you'd give me an idea. Can't you think of anywhere you'd like to go, sir?"

"The Cecil would do." It was the first name to come into his mind and it was unfortunate.

"You're not by any chance Rip Van Winkle junior, are you, sir? The Cecil's been pulled down some little time now. Must be close on twenty years."

"Oh well, take me anywhere. Anywhere where there's a lot of people."

The policeman had given up chatting to the janitor and was looking their way. The driver cocked an eye at his fare and an indescribably cunning expression flickered over his face.

"You want a nice railway-station hotel, that's what you want," he said. "Leave it to me."

He drove off at a great rate and finally deposited Campion at a great terminus in Wyld Street, behind Charing Cross.

"You'll be safe and comfy 'ere," he said as he undressed himself to get change for a pound note. "Cosmopolitan that's what it is. Lost in a crowd, that's what you'll be." And he winked as he took the tip.

There was no mistaking his suggestion. As Campion saw him drive off his old panic returned. He had given himself away by flunking the first policeman. Of course he had! These damned Londoners were too smart. They saw too much. Their experience of human nature was boundless. Probably even now the fellow was scuttling away to the nearest police station to take a list of wanted persons. That ruled his hotel out and he'd have to go somewhere else.

Better not pick up another cab here, either.

He walked away and crossed Trafalgar Square, cutting down behind the National Gallery into the narrow streets beyond. The light was growing rapidly and the great friendly shabby old city was beginning to sit up and stretch itself like a tramp who has been asleep on a park bench.

He found a big tea-shop, finally, and went inside and bought himself some breakfast. The food restored him considerably. He was surprised to find how much he needed it and how much more intelligent he became after eating it. He began to see some things with painful clarity. If he was to get any help from Sir Henry Bull he must get it at once before any news from Bridge reached that distinguished gentleman. That was evident. The thing to do was to get hold of him at once, at his private house. If he turned out to be as worried as Oates had been then he should have the full story and the personal consequences could not be helped. The one vital consideration at the moment was to reach someone in real authority before the police held everything up by arresting him and letting the law take its majestic course.

There was a directory in the telephone booth at the entrance but the name was not in it, which was not extraordinary since public men do not often advertise their private numbers. Campion began to feel his disadvantage again. London confused him. The city had the same effect on him as Amanda had in the beginning. He knew that he knew it very well indeed. It smiled at him and comforted him. But its face was just outside his present powers of memory. Whole streets were gloriously familiar but they had no names for him and no definite associations. His only way of getting about was by taxi. The drivers knew the way if he did not.

It was confusing and it took a lot of time, but in the end he got what he wanted. He accepted his disability and set about circumnavigating it with a dogged patience which was characteristic of him. One cab took him to the nearest public library, where he consulted a battered *Who's Who*. The man was there all right. *BULL, the Rt. Hon. Henry Pattison, Kt. created* 1911, *M. P. Honorary Member of the Universities of Oxford, St. Andrews', Leeds. Senior Master of Bridge.*

Senior Master of Bridge. The words stared out of the tiny print at him, enlarging themselves before his eyes. What a fool! What a trebly mentally defective cretin! Of course. Miss Anscombe had told him that he already knew that the Masters were holding their meeting on the fourteenth. The man must have been there in the very town he himself had fled from. Probably even now he was tucked up in Mr. Peter Lett's best bed.

A sense of despair swept over him. He was beset, benighted, hagridden by his own horrible insufficiency. The gods were bouncing him on their great knees, saving him one minute, only to dash him within an inch of the abyss the next.

His eye travelled to the end of the paragraph, ignoring the impressive list of highlights in a useful career. The address was there, 52 Pytchley Square, W. He looked at it dubiously. It seemed scarcely worth while going there in the circumstances.

He decided to try it finally, because he could think of no alternative.

He reached the Square by taxi, which he dismissed as soon as he caught sight of the plane trees, continuing the journey on foot. The tall houses looked strangely virginal and unprotected without their iron trimmings. He could not understand what was missing at first, but when it came to him and he realized the reason for this nudity all the old fighting anger returned to his heart, coupled with the now familiar sense of impending disaster and the urge for haste. London's railings, her secret private little defences, were torn away to feed the big guns.

But what was this other danger which threatened her? What was this swift peril which drew so close and which he was floundering so desperately to defeat?

He saw the house across the corner. Very neat it was, and sober, with a polished number on the plum-coloured door and demure net curtains in the windows.

He was bearing down upon it when he saw the two men. One of them rose from the edge of the sandbin where he had been sitting under a tree in the Square and sauntered forward.

Police. Of course. All these public men's houses had police guards these days. Why should he have forgotten that?

He wondered if his description had already been circularized to every plain-clothes man in the country. He wished he were less conspicuous and less shabby from his roof climbing. The man was coming directly towards him. He was going to be stopped and questioned. He could see the fellow's face now clearly and he was grinning sheepishly, blast him. It was a "fair cop", was it? What should he do? Run for it and have all London at his heels?

It was the little mock salute which stopped him, that and the man's obvious embarrassment.

"Sergeant Cook, sir," said the stranger, his smile twisting wryly. "You've forgotten me, I expect. Any news of the Guv'nor, sir?"

The sincerity of his anxiety outweighed everything else. It had a force of its own which was sufficient to kindle an answering spark from Campion's imprisoned mind.

"Oates?" he enquired. "No, I haven't seen him."

The man shrugged his shoulders expressively. "I don't like it," he said. "I don't like it at all."

They stood there for a moment in silence and Campion glanced up at number 52.

"I want to see Sir Henry Bull," he said slowly, hardly trusting his voice. "Can you fix it?"

Sergeant Cook gave him an astonished glance and Campion saw that he had made a mistake. Obviously his right move would have been to have walked up to the front door and given his name in the ordinary way. He set about covering his tracks.

"I want a word or two with him in private. I don't have to explain, do I?" he said.

He sounded pretty mysterious to himself but to his relief the Sergeant responded, although he glanced at him sharply under his lashes.

"I get you, sir. There's a side door on the left of the area there. It leads through to the yard at the back. Will you wait in that passage?"

Campion followed him and entered the side gate. He was waiting in the little alley inside when at last the man reappeared. He came creeping in through the high latticed gate from the yard and beckoned.

"Okay," he said with some satisfaction. "Come round this way, will you, sir? Been tailed, sir?"

"I rather think so. Thank you. I—er—I shan't forget this, Sergeant."

"That's all right, sir. This way."

They passed through a warm little servants' hall, where a couple of maids eyed them inquisitively, ascended a back staircase, crossed a flagged inner hall, and finally reached a white-panelled door.

"He's having a late breakfast," whispered the Sergeant, "but he's alone. Lady Bull has just left him."

He knocked and listened.

"There you are, sir," he added and opened the door.

Campion went into a small bright room which glowed with flowers and smelt pleasantly of coffee. A breakfast table was set in the window and a man in a dressing-gown sat at it with his back to the door. He turned at the sound of the latch and smiled affably at his visitor.

"Hallo, my boy," he said. "I half expected you."

Campion said nothing. The world was reeling dangerously and he felt his scalp contract.

It was the old man he had met in the train coming up.

CHAPTER SEVENTEEN

The eyes which had glittered so disconcertingly in the blue reading-light in the train were equally shrewd and uncomfortably penetrating at the breakfast table. Campion looked at them helplessly. This was disaster. This was defeat.

He was taken so completely off his balance that he could not trust himself to speak. His lean tight-skinned face was expressionless.

The old man indicated a chair on the other side of the table.

"Sit down," he said. "Have some coffee. Don't look at me like that. I know I've been very obtuse."

Campion blinked. He began to feel impervious to surprise. He sat down obediently but did not dare to open his mouth.

Sir Henry Bull cleared his throat. He looked very uncomfortable.

"You've had a most nerve-racking experience, I don't doubt," he said. "Until we got into the terminus this morning I had no inkling of the extraordinary situation. You'll have to forgive me, my boy. You can't teach an old dog new tricks and I admit quite freely that I find it very difficult to get used to this—this transpontine world we suddenly seem to be living in."

He was quite incomprehensible to Campion, who gave up trying to save himself. His astonishment showed in his face. Sir Henry misunderstood it and laughed briefly in his embarrassment.

"Even the word belongs to another era," he said bitterly. " 'Transpontine.' Over the bridge. Over Waterloo Bridge to the Vic and the Surrey, the homes of melodrama. Blood tubs, we used to call them. That's the world we're living in today. I can't get into tune with it as fast as perhaps I ought. Enemy soldiers disguised as nuns, carrying machine-guns and portable bicycles, descending by parachute. Armed secret societies. Microphones in the walls of railway carriages—it's all boy's halfpenny paper stuff to me still. I can't force my mind to be on guard for its numberless ingenuities. I did no actual harm, I hope. The police got their man, no doubt."

Campion snatched at his scattering wits and faced the situation.

"Microphones in the walls of railway carriages"? Was it possible that the old boy actually thought . . . ? He did obviously. Having once convinced himself that the world had gone mad, he was evidently prepared to see lunacy everywhere.

The question remained unanswered and the man repeated it.

"Did they take the fellow?"

"No," said Campion. "No. Not that it matters."

"You don't think so? I'm very relieved to hear you say that." Sir Henry had turned in his chair. He looked an old man, very tired and very anxious. "I've been going over everything that passed and I realize I said nothing of value. Fortunately my training prevented me from being actually indiscreet. But I do realize I must have put you in a very awkward position. You see, when they stopped the train for me at Coachingford and I found you in my reserved carriage I immediately thought that you wanted a word with me in private. It never went through my head that you were there to look after me and that we might be overheard or overlooked. To be frank, I didn't understand your manner in the least, although it ought to have warned me. Then, when we arrived and the station people told me that the train was being searched, I saw the whole thing in a flash. This Fifth Column activity is incredible. They didn't get him, you say?"

"Not yet."

"They will." Sir Henry spoke with satisfaction. "They're wonderful people. They're probably on his track at this moment."

"More than probably," said Campion absently. He could hardly assimilate the facts even now when they were presented to him on a plate, but he forced himself to accept them without question. There was so much to do and so little time.

Meanwhile, Sir Henry was so unused to making mistakes that he was still offering explanations in his own defence.

"I usually stay the night after a meeting of the Masters," he said, "but it was imperative that I got back early today, so Peter Lett phoned the station-master and reserved me a carriage. Then we were held up on the road and I walked on to the platform to see the train starting. They held it for me but there was no time for explanations. I had no notion you were in the compartment until I saw you. I recognized you at once, of course, and then as I say I did not grasp the significance of the situation. I had been hearing from my fellow Masters that you were in the town and I simply thought you wanted a word with me. You see exactly how it happened, don't you?"

"I do," said Campion. "Exactly," he added after a pause. Obviously the Masters had not heard of the assault on Hutch and so far the man in front of him knew nothing of the St. Jude's Hospital episode. "I do want to see you," he went on hurriedly. "I want to talk about Anscombe."

"Anscombe?" Sir Henry frowned. "Poor fellow," he said. "I heard about him as soon as I arrived, of course. What do you want to know?"

"Why did Anscombe die wondering if he ought not to come to you? Why did he convert every halfpenny he possessed into cash and then debate in his own mind if he ought not to come and see you?"

"Did he?" Sir Henry was surprised but not bewildered. "He was a silly fellow. I've known him for years of course. He was too small a man altogether for his commitments. That's the weakness of these hereditary appointments. Old Anscombe ought to have been secretary of a cricket club, or a churchwarden perhaps. I always understood that personal finances were his difficulty. He ought to have been perfectly all right, but his father played Old Harry with the Secretaryship. That income was mortgaged out of hand and the children were left very modestly provided for. Anscombe himself was even more improvident. Between ourselves, we financed him over and over again, but finally we had to put a stop to it. So he converted what little money he had into cash, did he? What was he going to do? Try to make a dash from his local creditors?"

Campion shook his head. "His sister seems to have had a rather different idea," he said. "She suggests that he may have been going to make some sort of gesture. 'In expiation' were the words she used."

"To me? Really? What for?" Curiously enough, the suggestion did not seem to strike Sir Henry as entirely fantastic. "I see you don't understand," he said. "The Secretaryship of the Masters isn't quite the important office it sounds. The Secretary is the—how shall I say? —well, the steward of the club and the general clerk of the domestic arrangements. His office is comparatively modern. His main job is to look after the premises. It would not astonish me to hear that Anscombe had done anything. He was a remarkably silly man, one of those theatrical, hysterical types. What did you discover he had done? Filched a pound or two from the petty funds?"

"No, I don't think so. Miss Anscombe wondered if he had allowed the caverns in the Nag to be used for contraband."

"Really? I can't believe that. That would have been sacrilege. No, I don't think so. I fancy I know where that story comes from. I did hear something. What was it? Lett mentioned it. I think a great deal of wine was actually taken into the Nag some time before the war. It represented a sum of money which was due to us for the sale of our share of a Rhenish vineyard. The money could not be taken out of

Germany so we received its equivalent in wine. I don't know the full facts. Our Bursar would tell you that. Anscombe would probably be responsible for the storage of the wine. That was the kind of thing he did attend to. He had nothing to do with the main function of the Brotherhood."

"Which is?"

"The welfare of our country, young man." It was an oddly dignified answer, completely unaffected.

Once again Campion took a sudden liking to this canny old man with his dogged stance and the streak of unself-conscious patriotism which showed in him every so often.

"Our principal business is the Institute," Sir Henry added more specifically. "That place is a great national possession."

"National?"

The older man smiled with a depreciation which was very faint.

"The Masters of Bridge are the nation," he said, unaware of any naïveté. "That is, they're typical of the best of it. Is there anything else?"

"Yes." It was now or never and the ground was very uncertain. "Tell me about Minute Fifteen."

Once the question was out of his mouth the deepest misgivings seized him as he saw astonishment growing in the intelligent eyes.

"Minute Fifteen?" The man was not at ease. He seemed puzzled and slightly alarmed. "I don't know what I can tell you that you don't know already," he said at last. "The whole world will know about it tomorrow, or I sincerely hope so. As for details of the publicity, I understand that you were one of the few men who had known about that from the outset. What do you want from me? The financial details of the actual loan? The Chancellor of the Exchequer will be explaining them on the radio tomorrow evening."

"Why was the loan called Minute Fifteen?" he ventured.

"Ah, I see your difficulty. That *was* confusing." Sir Henry seemed relieved. "It wasn't. The Defence Loan had its own name, the Fifty Victory. Minute Fifteen simply covers the plan of its presentation. It was thought wisest to keep that anonymous since it was an innovation and secrecy was such an integral part of it, so it simply went under its own number on the agenda of the Cabinet meeting which approved it. However, this really isn't my pigeon at all. I can put you on to someone if you want details."

"I don't." Campion spoke desperately. "I want to know its exact importance. I mean," he added hastily, as a flash of bewilderment appeared in the older man's eyes, "in regard to every aspect of the immediate situation. Has it appreciated or decreased?"

"My dear boy," there was nothing but grimness in the old face now, "its success is imperative. I wish I had never used those words before. They're stale and inadequate. We must have no hitch whatever in raising the money. We are edging along such a precipice now that I hardly dare watch, and I am no coward where money is concerned. Use your common sense. Would we ever embark on a gigantic and drastic project like this, which virtually means that we are putting the British Empire on a company footing, with a personal invitation to every tax-payer to invest his all in it, if it wasn't absolutely vital? The forms which are going out tonight are, practically speaking, prospectuses. There is no other word for them. We're walking on the water. It's only the faith of the man in the street which is going to hold us from going under."

Campion sat very still. It was coming. Behind the curtain hanging across his mind like an arras something of tremendous importance was trying to shine through. He could feel the emotion belonging to it. It was fear.

"Nothing must go wrong," he said stupidly.

Sir Henry Bull pushed back his chair. He looked a dynamic figure, his white hair bristling and his long gown flowing round him.

"I said just now that I am never indiscreet," he said. "I am not. Both my training and my natural inclination are against it. But I am not made of wood. Now look here, Campion, I have heard whispers. Mind you, they have been little more than whispers, but they have come from most unexpected quarters and they are so terrible that I dare not even think of them. One of my informants named you as probably the only man who knew the full truth of the danger. I am not going to ask you for information, so you can take that blank expression off your face. I cannot and will not believe that the incredible story which I have heard has any reality, but, if it has, if it has, Campion, well then . . . the Dark Ages again, that's what it will mean."

There was silence for a moment or so and then the old man leant on the table and looked full at his visitor.

"I think I can tell you what you're hesitating to ask," he said. "It is true that at this moment Britain depends practically entirely on her faith in herself and on her own internal stability. If that could be destroyed suddenly, by a single stroke, there would come confusion, exhaustion, and finally decay. At this particular point in history everything hangs on Britain's faith. Europe is conquered; the New World is not yet prepared. So, should this thing happen, it means that there

will come once again the Dark Ages which followed Attila, and to-
morrow civilization is a thousand years away. It *could* happen; that is
the lesson of this generation. World barbarism is still possible. The
Beast is not dead. It has not even slept. All these years it has been
lying there watching with lidless eyes. To a man of my age that is the
most awful discovery that could ever have been made. That is what
you wanted to know, isn't it?"

The younger man did not speak and his host, with a little twist of
the lips which was alarming because his face was not one used to
weakness, demanded abruptly: "How bad is it?" Campion felt cold.
His fingers were numbed and there was a chill in the small of his back.
His determination to make a clean breast of his own disability, should
Sir Henry seem as alarmed as Oates had been, faded before the question in those anxious eyes.

It was the same story. Everyone was turning to himself for assurance. He dared not reveal the dreadful emptiness of his mind. Somehow he must struggle on, blind and half-witted though he was. There
was to be no outside help. He was quite alone.

"I don't know," he said slowly. "I don't know. These prospectuses,
or whatever they are, for Minute Fifteen; they go out tonight, do
they?"

"Yes. I can't understand why you didn't realize that. It hasn't been
possible to keep the thing a complete secret. Quite a number of important committees, including the Masters of Bridge who are going to
take up large portions of the loan, have had to be prepared for it. I
was talking to the Masters on the subject myself last night. Then the
Post Offices had to be warned that they will be expected to deal with
the enormous traffic, while the local tax authorities have had to put
the thing out. So a tremendous number of people know something
about it. Only taxpayers will be approached, of course, but that's half
the country. It must not fail, Campion. Nothing must happen to
make it fail or to . . ." He shook his head. "That eventuality won't
bear considering," he said.

Campion nodded. He was thinking fast. More corners of the jigsaw
were forming, although the whole picture was still obscure. Meanwhile the great missing portion was assuming an incredible shape. He
wondered how he could persuade Sir Henry to be more specific. It
was not going to be easy. The old man was very quick and already he
had been puzzled several times by little exhibitions of ignorance.

Campion thought he knew the man. He was a realist, a believer
of facts. A gambler, perhaps, but only in form, and that meant that
once he discovered his visitor's mental condition he would never take

a chance. Campion saw himself pushed into hospital again and not one word of anything he had to say believed or even considered until the doctors pronounced him lucid. The urgency of the situation would not make any difference to Sir Henry. Campion's disability would simply go down on the debit side.

He was interrupted by the arrival of the secretary, who came in with a word of apology and murmured to Sir Henry for some time in a deferential flow.

"Really?" The old man was surprised. "Where is he? In the house?"

"In the study, Sir Henry."

"Oh, I see. Yes, well, I shall have to give him a minute or two. You might warn him I'm overworked, vital information or not. I'll come down."

As the secretary went out he turned to Campion.

"I'm afraid I must see this fellow," he said. "He's a curious product, part genius, part crank, and one of the most influential men in the country in his own peculiar way. One moment he's doing untold service and the next he's trying to advance a hare-brained scheme for running the country. The trouble is one never knows which tack he's on until one's seen him. He's breathing mystery and disaster, Cuthbertson says. Don't go. I haven't finished with you yet. I shan't be more than five minutes."

He went out. The gentle latch did not quite slip home and the door swung open an inch or two behind him, so that Campion heard his voice as he entered the room across the hall.

"Hullo, Aubrey. What's this 'awful warning', my dear boy?"

Aubrey. Campion's hand closed over the door knob. Aubrey. Miss Anscombe. His own attack on Hutch. There was a complete line there. Aubrey had been going to see Miss Anscombe. She must have given him an account of her interview with himself and Amanda. Aubrey would be far too superior to go to the police direct. It would be so like him to attempt to stop the mischief at the head and to warn his distinguished Governor that a lunatic was at large.

There was nothing for it but flight again. It was the only way and this time he'd *got* to get away with it.

He stepped out into the hall and went straight from the house the way he had come. The maids eyed him as he passed them silently, but he nodded to them and walked by with the same odd singleness of purpose which had been his salvation before.

He came quietly out of a side gate, glanced sharply at the detective on the opposite side of the road, and, keeping well in so that he should not be seen from the windows of the house he had left, strode on down the side of the Square.

He was shaking with suppressed excitement. All the facts he had tumbled on in the last thirty-six hours were blazingly vivid in his mind. Minute Fifteen, representing the greatest war loan ever launched, was about to be presented at a time of trembling national emergency personally and privately to every taxpayer by post. That was the pivot. That was fact number one. All round it, gyrating like swing-boats round a tower, were the others. He went over them in his mind. The cases of wine in the Masters' store-rooms. The story of a foreign contraband before the war. The murder of Anscombe just before he "made expiation", obviously done by professional thugs probably employed by Pyne. The fleet of lorries under the Nag. The small army of well-paid crooks gathered together under Pyne's Surveys Limited. The activities in the Institute. There was something there he could not remember. What was it? Something he had seen with his own eyes and forgotten. The attempt of the Enemy to buy him off when they thought him a crook like themselves, and their subsequent decision to kill or capture him when they discovered who he was.

It was all there in his hand. He held it without knowing what it was. In his blindness he had discovered his objective. In his miserable ignorance he could not identify it.

He must get back to Bridge. That was the all-important factor. It must be now nearly eleven. He had, he suspected, until the provincial post went at about six in the evening, but he had to get back to Bridge and to do that he had to get across the City to the terminus.

Still he had a chance. For the first time he felt he had a chance.

He found a taxi and made the station in twenty minutes. Luck was with him and he discovered a Coachingford train actually waiting on the platform. He entered it in a state as near jubilation as he ever remembered. Amanda was the only dark spot on his horizon and he refused to think of her.

All through the journey he made his plans. It was going to be a near thing and abominably risky, and to get into the Nag by daylight would take some doing when every man's hand was against him. All the same, it had to be done and he had great faith in himself.

When at last the train carried him into the station at Coachingford he was already in his mind hurrying up the Nag's Pykle looking for the narrow passage by the side of the shop which should have sold love philtres. He was so engrossed with his project that he did not see the two plain-clothes men standing behind the ticket collector and did not realize their intention until their hands fell on his shoulders and he heard the strangely familiar form of arrest.

CHAPTER EIGHTEEN

Campion sat in a cell at the Waterhouse Street Police Station at Coachingford and prayed. He was a damned fool. He knew that. If only he had at least gone quietly and had given himself a chance. If only he hadn't lost his head in the station booking-office as they were taking him through. He saw himself now behaving like a lunatic, raving, expostulating, saying all the wrong things, citing all the wrong names.

That final attempt to make a dash for it just outside the present building! That had been a mistake, probably the worst of the lot. He was battered and dishevelled now and in the last condition in the world to inspire confidence in anyone, even to the extent of getting a message through to Lugg or Yeo.

They were leaving him here to cool his heels while they made out the charge. At any moment now they would come for him and take him out of this cold, disinfected tomb and march him into a big smelly charge-room, warm with breath and sweat. That was going to be his only chance. God knew what the charges against him were. As far as he knew, they might contain practically everything on the calendar. However, that aspect was trifling. Moreover, it belonged to another world. What was important was the time. Somehow or other he'd got to get out and get down to Bridge immediately.

An obvious idea which had occurred to him coming down in the train was torturing him. Very likely he had not got until the evening. More than likely the lorries had to spread their loads all over the country and were even now setting out on their journeys. England was such a little place. It would take so short a time to fan the poison out all over her lovely petite body.

He had given up worrying about the mystery. The actual facts of the Enemy's attack were still entirely beyond him. Even the identity of the Enemy himself had escaped him. All he knew were those things which were set out under his nose; the lorries, the date of the launching of the Minute Fifteen loan, the work at the Institute, and the wine cases in the Nag.

He must get out. Oh God, dear God, he must get out!

He was sweating when they came for him. The larger plain-clothes man, the one whose eye he had closed, was not present. The other one, the ratty specimen with the little moustache, gave him a wide berth and left the work to the old turnkey and the enormous young constable who would not normally have accompanied them.

Campion went quietly, meekly. He was so restrained that he felt they must notice that he was shaking and see that his hands were clenched to keep them down. They were all very gentle and so nervy that he guessed that they suspected him of mania. Very likely. God, what a situation! He would be in a strait-jacket with ice on his head when the blow fell, when the Enemy succeeded, when the knife slipped into her little green heart.

He was deferential to the Charge Sergeant. The man was a fool. He saw his great square head with the unnaturally grey face on one side of it nodding over the top of the high desk and was panic-stricken. He could hear the asinine jokes and heavy admonitions before they left the big mouth under the waterfall moustache. Yes, here they came. Here was the Charge Book. Here was the pronouncement.

"Wait," he said, and was hurt to find that even his own voice was going against him. It sounded strangled and hysterical. "Get in touch with Lady Amanda Fitton at the Principal's House at the Bridge Institute."

He saw they were surprised by something. It had not been the name, but the address had touched them. He seized the pause and hurried on.

"Also get hold of Yeo, of Scotland Yard. Find him. Tell him I'm here."

That made them laugh. Their great grins merged into one huge idiot face, like a mask of comedy on the ceiling of a theatre.

"All in good time, my lad," said the Charge Sergeant. "You shall have the Queen to see you if you don't hurry it. Meanwhile if you could wait a minute I'll just charge you, if you don't mind. We don't want to do anything against the book, do we?"

The clock with the face as big as a tea-tray leered over the Sergeant's shoulder. One o'clock. There was no time for anything. He must get to the Nag at once, within the half hour. The big hand moved while he looked at it.

"Send for Hutch," he implored in panic.

Hutch was at least intelligent. Angry and suspicious he probably was, but at least his mind worked. Perhaps he could be got to see the hideous urgency of the occasion.

"Here, that'll do, that'll do." The Charge Sergeant was scandalized.

"Superintendent Hutch has quite enough to do without bothering himself about you. If he wants to see you he'll come in his own time. Now then, Albert Campion. You are charged in that you did feloniously utter counterfeit banknotes to the value of one pound at the railway station booking office at . . ."

Campion ceased to hear. He went deaf and blind. A great avalanche of fury at their incompetence descended over him, sweeping away every shred of his control. Good God, they couldn't even charge him with something he'd done! They were going to hold him in this gimcrack police station on some drivelling mistaken or invented charge while the minutes rushed by. The door was open behind him and he did the fatal thing.

As he sprang for the rectangle of light the plain-clothes man seized him. Campion slung him off, pitching him half across the room. The turnkey shouted and the young constable raised a great fist, while a slow silly smile of surprised delight spread over his face. Campion took the blow just under the ear. The force of it lifted him off his feet and sent him sprawling across the boards towards the forms built in all round the room. The rounded edge of polished wood met his left temple with a crack which echoed round the building. He fell into complete darkness and lay still.

Albert Campion came to himself in the cell. He gathered where he was at once and sat up on the hard couch, smiling ruefully. A clock striking two somewhere in the town surprised him and he raised his eyebrows. To the best of his knowledge it must have been round about six in the evening when he had encountered the toughs down at the quayside. It was now daylight, so that if he had been out for round about twenty hours he must have taken a pretty severe blow. How extraordinarily like these country police to bring him into a cell and leave him to die while they found out who he was! So far they must have been singularly unsuccessful, the damned fools, and, while he was on that subject, where was Oates?

For the first time he felt a twinge of anxiety. Oates had certainly been with him. He remembered his own amused exasperation when the shambling figure, really astonishingly unfamiliar in the dirty flannels and threadbare greatcoat, had appeared at his elbow as he stepped out of Lugg's paper shop. Poor old Oates! He had been badly rattled. The thing was getting him down, as well it might of course, but it had been shocking to see him losing his grip and to hear his voice go husky as he admitted: "I wrote you last night, but I couldn't stick it. I simply couldn't sit up there and wait. I just walked out to see you. For God's sake, Campion, have you got a line?"

Well, he had, and he'd said so and they'd gone on together. The fight had been pretty sensational. Campion felt his head cautiously. Yes, there it was. A very nasty spongy little spot, by jiminy. There must have been five or six in the gang, all pro's and all using coshes, which had been fortunate. Had it been razors he might well have awakened to hear a harp quintet instead of the mouth-organ which some misguided amateur was playing in the street outside.

All the same, it had not been exactly a walk among the apple-blossoms. The money had drawn the gangsters, as he had hoped it would, and he had recognized them. He went over them in his mind. The Lily had been there, and the elder Weaver, and Williams, and the Glasshouse Johns, all C.R.O. boys as he suspected.

Who were the others? He could not remember at the moment.

He didn't feel too intelligent. He felt exhausted and somehow—yes, that was it, chastened. How off! He might have had some deep emotional experience rather than a bang on the head. He longed for a newspaper. He hadn't seen the news from the Front for seventeen hours. Anything might have happened. There was this business, too. The whole thing might have suddenly broken and what had been left of the ordered world be in chaos while he was sitting here.

He laughed at himself softly. He was getting jittery, like poor old Oates. It was having so much at stake, of course. Still, there was plenty of time. There would be no move until Minute Fifteen was about to be launched and that was several days away.

The clock struck the quarter and he admired its chimes. Some of these old towns had lovely chimes. Lovely corners, too. Bridge was a remarkably lovely place if only one could forget the calendars, the picture postcards, the ornamental biscuit-tins which made it hackneyed. Seen for the first time, Bridge must be staggering. Amanda was at Bridge and in a month they'd be married. A dear kid, Amanda. So young. Too young for him? Sometimes he was very much afraid so. His fine thin mouth twisted regretfully. One got so beastly self-sufficient as one grew older and there was the girl to think of. He'd hate to imprison her, to suppress her in any way.

A definite twinge, physical and yet bringing with it a sense of shame, stabbed his heart over. At the same time he saw Amanda in his mind's eye as clearly as if she stood before him. She was looking at him with a sort of stricken astonishment and reciting the first line of that silly old tag they had found together in the *Gentleman's Magazine* for 1860. "*Begone! she stormed, Across the raging tide.*"

The hallucination was so vivid, the pain in his side so acute, and the sense of self-disgust so strong that it brought him to his feet. He was ill. This blow on the head had affected him seriously. Good lord! Nothing like that must happen now. Things were a damned sight too serious. Of course they were, because no one *knew*. He and Oates were the only pair on earth who knew the full strength—and it was stupendous when you saw it in the round. It was criminally dangerous; he'd argued that from the beginning. Besides, where was Oates?

He went over to the judas-window in the cell door and peered through it into the empty passage outside. Not a soul, of course. He sighed and, putting his fingers to his mouth, gave a very reliable imitation of a police whistle. Five minutes' intensive effort produced the desired result.

The turnkey, puce in the face with fury, put his head in at the farther door.

"Shop," said Campion pleasantly. "Can I see the manager?"

"You'll be lucky if you see fresh air again, my lad. We've had to send Detective-Sergeant Doran to hospital."

(Hospital? Why should the word send a thrill of terror through him? He was ill, dangerously ill. He'd have to go and see old Todd of Wimpole Street, when he got back. Where had the old man evacuated himself to?)

"I'm sorry for Doran," he said aloud. "I can't say I recognize the name. Still, I sympathize with your domestic worries. And in the meantime, do you think you could make an effort to do a little business? This isn't the Central Coachingford Station, is it?"

The turnkey came farther into the passage, looking like a mystified bullpup.

"You've changed your tune, ain't you?" he demanded.

"I'm no longer unconscious, if that's what you mean," said Campion with gentle dignity. "And while we're on that subject, as a Metropolitan man I don't like to criticize your County arrangements, but, just to soothe my curiosity do tell me, when you bring in a concussion case do you usually leave it for the best part of a day and a night without medical attention?"

The turnkey gaped at him, his small eyes bewildered.

"You're crackers and you're impudent," he said. "That's what you are. You won't get anywhere by putting it on either. Shouting for a doctor now, are you? You'll be lucky if you see a magistrate the way you're going on."

Campion, whose face was pressed against the narrow slit in the door, frowned reprovingly.

"Just clear your mind," he said. "Save a little time by using the

brain with which I see a kind Government has issued you. Which of
the five Coachingford Police Stations is this one?"

"Waterhouse Street. You know that as well as I do, or ought to,
after the way you tore the road up coming here."

"Really? It's that sort of concussion, is it? Bits of bone sticking in
the grey matter. My hat, you don't look after your professional guests,
do you? Have you left me here since last night biting buttons off the
furniture?"

"Being difficult won't pay," said the turnkey and turned away in
disgust.

"Let us hope Superintendent Rose will accept your diagnosis,"
Campion murmured, reflecting that it was better to mention the regular police Superintendent rather than the C.I.D. man. What was his
name? Hutch, was it?

"Superintendent Rose?" The name appeared to have certain magic
properties. The turnkey was hesitating but at the last moment some
new consideration appeared to make up his mind for him. "Superintendent Rose doesn't bother himself with snide-panners who beat up
plain-clothes men. Besides, you've only been in an hour and a half.
What d'you think this is—a quick-lunch counter?" he said and went
out, locking the door behind him.

Campion was astounded. He had always found County Police
particularly intelligent. This type of crass idiocy was new to him. The
clock outside chimed another quarter hour and he cursed it. It had
lost its charm and was now irritating. The whole thing was really
damnably unfortunate. Besides, he'd got work to do. There was that
date with the C.I.D. Super to go over the Nag, and he wanted to have
a look at the Institute.

He had discovered the main game, he was sure of that. He had told
Oates so, definitely. He lay down on the hard bed and began to rearrange his mind. He seemed to have the afternoon before him. Oates
—and where was he, by the way?—had the wind-up. That was very
unlike him and argued that he must have had the importance of the
thing pretty hot and strong from the Cabinet itself.

Well then, to return to business. When Oates had borrowed him
from Headquarters and had first come out with this staggering tale of
thousands of counterfeit notes, so perfect that "one has to boil them
down to detect them," he had said that he thought the scheme was
on a colossal scale and might actually be aiming at some sort of sudden unofficial inflation, which would of course pitch the country's
whole economy into hell, destroy public confidence, pull down the
Government, and, if issued at the right moment, bring about the

moral collapse of the nation. Since Britain, as usual, seemed to have nothing absolutely ready to save her morals, the danger had seemed terrifying.

As he lay looking at the little barred window high in the wall, Campion reflected that so far he had been inclined to doubt the possibility of the scheme being so enormous. Oates had shown him the notes which had been found in two or three industrial towns. They had certainly been cracking good forgeries and could have been manufactured only in the official printing houses of an enemy power. Moreover, and the ingenuity of that move still took his breath away, they had been artificially dirtied most ingeniously.

Oates had put various picked men on to the job in different towns. All of them had drawn a blank save the man at Coachingford. He had reported the presence of some sort of crook organization, either in the town or at Bridge. Poor chap, he hadn't got much further. They'd fished him out of the estuary with a broken neck. It had been professional work, very neat and nasty, done with a lead pipe as like as not.

Campion stirred uncomfortably. There was something curious about that killing, something personal and near at hand. What was it? There was something on his mind that kept escaping him. It was probably nothing important but he found it irritating.

That damned clock again. That was a quarter to three, he supposed. He dismissed his irritation and went on dreamily with his reminiscences. Well, Oates had borrowed him and sent him to Coachingford. Amanda had got them both an invitation to stay at Bridge with Lee Aubrey, who was brilliant, he supposed. Everybody said so. Personally he suspected these academic dreamers. Still, let that pass. He had instated old Lugg in the town with a stock of the counterfeit and some old clothes. Then he had spent half a day at Bridge making arrangements, had come into Coachingford, changed into a tramp's outfit, and had gone off reconnoitring.

That had been an experience he would never forget. All the subversive element in the town was in a ferment. "Blokes were giving away cash—great wads of it." And the riff-raff of the place had been turned into a great greedy bulging-eyed secret society, getting rich quick as quids were handed to them behind doors, in doss houses, over greasy coffee-tables.

This had been a discovery, but it had been followed by another one. He had discovered that a whisper was going round to the effect that the great day was coming on the sixteenth. That was going to be milk-and-honey day, the day when it was going to be everybody's duty to spend and the wherewithal was going to be miraculously provided.

That had been a peculiarly uncomfortable discovery because the sixteenth was to be a red-letter day in other, more orthodox financial circles. On the sixteenth the Minute Fifteen Defence Loan was to be presented to the public. There was no doubt about it, the whole affair was alarming. If it was by any staggering chance as bad as Oates thought it was then it was hair-raising.

Leaning back on the bench Campion reflected on his subsequent actions. For a long time it had been impossible to locate any of these munificent agents and he had finally decided to take the bull by the horns and appear himself as one of them. That had drawn the flock. The whole bunch had turned up together, as he had known they would. Both he and Oates had been able to get a good look at them. They had made quite an impressive gathering and it had occurred to him then that it had taken someone with a real flair for organization to get that crew together.

Then there had been the fight and the police had come up. He remembered very little of the action save the sticky paving-stones of the quay and the awful mud-coloured water, thick with scum and rubbish.

Since the police had no idea who he and Oates were, either, they had been extraordinarily lucky to get away alive. That was why it had been so criminally dangerous for Oates to have come down and taken part himself. Suppose they had both been put out, then what might have happened? Of course, if Oates' theory of engineered inflation had anything in it at all he was justified in trusting as few people as possible, since any whisper of such a disaster might very easily start a scare nearly as bad as the thing itself. Good God, it was a horrible idea!

Campion pushed his hands through his hair and shivered. All the same, now he looked at it in cold blood he still maintained that the enormous scale of the plan as Oates saw it must be impossible because of the difficulties of distribution.

As long as the Enemy stuck to his present method of doling the money out by hand to the vagrant population the whole affair could be dealt with by the police. But a decisive blow of the kind Oates envisaged would demand instantaneous distribution of the stuff all over the country. Campion did not see how it could be done without the cooperation of the public. After all, the public had got to be induced first to take and then to spend the cash. It just was not possible. It is notoriously difficult to give away money by cash in the street. Generations of ordered living had taught the ordinary citizen that there is something very fishy and dangerous about banknotes which are not paid for in blood and sweat. No, the thing as Oates foresaw it could not happen, not on that scale, thank God.

And yet . . . yet . . .

He got up and walked irritably up and down the cell. This knock on the head was serious. It was having an extraordinary effect on him. The clock chiming another quarter sent an unexpected and unwarranted thrill of pure despair through him. Why was that? What the hell was the matter with him? There was a burden on his shoulders. Self-disgust leant on his arms. His feet were heavy with grief. Misery and the utter wretchedness of failure clung to him. This was terrible. This meant he was a . . . what was it? Manic depressive? Something like that. Perhaps he ought to try and sleep it off. After all, he must not go sick now. Today must be the fourteenth, by jove. And the six-teenth was the zero-hour. However, since he had located the actual men engaged the round-up should not take long. Fortunately the police had a few new powers under the Emergency Laws. They could finish this thing off quickly and release him to his work again. Perhaps there would be time to get married in the interim, if only . . . If only what?

Once again there was that physical tug at his heart, again that over-whelming sense of self-disgust, and again a definite picture in his mind of Amanda herself, hurt and puzzled, waiting for the other lines of a doggerel couplet. It was mania all right, obviously. Some variety of mental kink, probably irritatingly well known. The sooner he got him-self out of here and put himself into the hands of a reliable doctor the better. All very well to be gallantly negligent about a sore thumb or a lump on the skull, but mental trouble was a different caper al-together.

It wasn't going to be very easy to get out either, with this peculiarly obtuse specimen on the door. He must have been taken in completely by the vagrant's outfit; that and the money, of course. Those two taken together would be a difficult pill for any honest copper to swallow.

He glanced ruefully at his clothes and made a discovery which took him completely off his balance.

He was not wearing the suit in which he had had the quayside fight.

He stared into the cloth of his trouser knees and wrenched at the inside pocket of his jacket to find the tailor's label. It was his suit all right. He recognized it and knew too that it should have been hanging up in a wardrobe in his bedroom in Lee Aubrey's house in Bridge. Moreover, it was a new suit according to the date on the label, yet as he looked at it now he saw that it was dirty and crumpled and showed signs of having had hard wear for some little time.

The jolt to his nervous system was tremendous, the mental equivalent of a gigantic thump between the shoulder-blades. Then a frightful misgiving crept up close to him and laid its cold cheek on his heart. He had been here some time. How . . . long?

Out in the town the clock struck again, announcing that yet another quarter of an hour had passed.

CHAPTER NINETEEN

He saw Amanda through the judas-window. She came walking into the passage with the turnkey, completely unself-conscious and comfortably serene.

"Hullo," she said cheerfully as she caught sight of half his face through the slit. "They phoned your message to me, but they won't let me bail you out."

"What message?" The question was in his mouth but he did not put it. His eyes had narrowed and his thin face wore a startled expression. The instant he had seen Amanda it had come to him that something revolutionary, he was not at all sure that it was not evolutionary, must have taken place within him. He had grown old, or seen a great light, or else his blundering feet were on the ground at last. He thought he knew what it was all right. The symptoms were unmistakable. That sense of exasperated shame, that desire to kick himself or to cover his eyes with his great burning ears, all these indicated that his self-confidence had received a dangerous blow. A great weakness must have been uncovered. His misgivings increased and he remained staring at the girl through the judas-slit, with his eyes fixed and his forehead wrinkled.

Presently he realized what it was that he found so puzzling. He had known Amanda since she had been a child and yet now there was something new about her. He found out what it was. He was seeing her through some sort of mental curtain. His subconscious mind reached out for this infuriating barrier and drew it slowly aside like a wet page.

The complete picture lay before him.

He saw it all in a single dreadful moment of revelation. The whole kaleidoscopic history of the last thirty-six hours, painted with pitiless clarity and minute detail, unfolded before him in all its stark gravity; a mad, uncomic strip with himself wandering blindfold through it like a lost soul.

Then, as his two minds and personalities merged at last, as the new Campion's witless discoveries fitted over the old Campion's certain knowledge, the three-dimensional truth suddenly sprang out in blazing colours. He stood petrified. Good God Almighty! He knew now what the contraband was in those cases which the wretched Anscombe had been bribed to accept as honest Rhine wine! It could only be a counterfeit, the artificially dirtied indetectable counterfeit itself. Millions and millions of pounds' worth of lies and disruption. Anscombe had been murdered because he was preparing to salve his conscience and to confess to the contents of those packing-cases. Probably he intended to hand over his own small fortune in cash to the Treasury by way of a gesture after his confession.

Then there were the lorries. They were for the distribution, obviously. How this was going to be done, and what the magic password was which would make the sober, suspicious British public accept and spend this dynamite, was still a mystery. But the time, the hour of striking, was not. Anscombe had given that away by mentioning Minute Fifteen. Today *was* the fifteenth, and they were not going to wait until tomorrow. The hour was now. Perhaps this very minute. It had all come back to him. He knew where he was. He knew what he had got to do.

The danger was stultifying. His body winced inside. A year, six months, even three months ago such a gigantic project would have been fantastic, but tonight, in this beleaguered England, with all the tides of a new and diabolically astute barbary lapping at her feet, the plan was a sound weapon and it was poised squarely at her heart.

Panic possessed him and all but choked him. The time was almost gone and he was piteously helpless. He pressed his face to the judas-window.

"Amanda!"

"Yes?" She smiled at him quickly, reassuringly.

Campion took careful hold of himself and strove to compress and clarify the message he had to give her. Time had become as precious as a little drop of water in the bottom of a pannikin in the desert.

The clock chiming across the street was pure medieval torture.

"Look, my darling," he said, aware of the state of affairs between them, aware of his loss and its magnitude and thrusting it out of his mind because of the racing minutes and the disaster ahead, "I've got to get out of here immediately. Listen, Amanda, there was some sort of scrap on the quayside before I got into that hospital. One or two people may have got beaten up in it, but that's not the point . . ."

"'Ere, what are you saying?" The turnkey was very excited. "I'll 'ave to ask you to repeat that."

Amanda ignored the interruption. She leant forward to catch anything Campion might have to tell her.

"Oates was with me then," he said distinctly.

He saw her brown eyes widen and a flicker pass over her face. "Where is he?" he went on desperately. "I've got to get out, Amanda. I've got to get out and go down to the Nag immediately."

"Yes, I see," she said briefly. She turned on her heel at once and the turnkey had to hurry to keep up with her. She went so quickly that her going might have been desertion. The turnkey certainly put it down as that.

He came back a moment or so later, carrying a police memorandum. He was inclined to be amused by Amanda's exit, but very soon the description of the wanted person took up all his time and intelligence. He was a type mercifully rare in the Force, but every great organization had its minor blunders. He sat on the long bench which ran down the corridor wall opposite the cell and spelt out the points line by line. At every fresh item he got up and came over to peer at his victim through the slit. He was studiously deaf to every remark addressed to him and frequently returned to the beginning of his task, having forgotten how far he had got in it.

Campion began to suffer the tortures of the damned. The war, with all its noisy horror as he knew it in the battle zones, was very close to him. He could see and hear it over Britain, not merely as air raids but as invasion, and then, as well as these, he saw the whole country suddenly hit in the wind by an entirely unexpected blow. The magnificent jingle from the end of King John came into his mind: "Come the three corners of the world in arms, and we shall shock them: nought shall make us rue, if England to itself do rest but true." "But true": there was the talisman, there the strength, and there the danger. "But true." But confident of her own solidarity. "But true" . . .

Oh, God, let him get out! O sweet sanity! O ultimate honesty and the final triumph of the best! O faith in good as a force and an entity, let him get out in time!

The turnkey began to read the description again with cross-references.

"Yeller 'air . . . yeller 'air. Six foot two inches . . . well, just about. Very likely. 'Ere I say you in there, 'ow tall are you?"

"Yes, yes, that's a description of me." Campion's voice was shaking with his effort to control it. "I admit that. Don't worry about that any more. Now look here, this is serious. This is a million times more important and more urgent than any air raid siren. Either fetch me the most senior officer in the building or let me use the telephone at once. This is vital. Do you understand? It's so vital and so urgent that if you don't do it it won't much matter if you've discovered grounds for an arrest on that bit of paper or not. If you don't bring me someone in authority immediately I don't think you'll wake up in the same world tomorrow morning."

"Threats, eh?" said the turnkey with idiot satisfaction. "I'll 'ave to report all that. You want to be very careful what you say, my lad. This may not be the East Coast, but even so you can't be too careful these days. Fifth Column, that's what we're looking out for all the time."

"Listen." Campion's hands were sticky on the door of the cell. "I want to make a complete statement. I'm entitled to have a detective sergeant to take it down."

"In good time. In good time you shall have one of His Majesty's judges listening to you," said the turnkey without stirring. "In half a minute I'll take your statement myself."

This was a form of torture new to Campion. The Ordeal by Fool might well go down in the calendar, he felt. He swung away from the judas-window and walked down the cell. His agony of exasperation was so acute that it was physical, catching him in the throat and diaphragm, pressing on them until he could scarcely breathe. He sat down on the bunk and stared at the stone floor. His mind began to work over the situation feverishly. There was the plan itself. That was simple and terrible. There was only one last secret there: how was this devilishly convincing counterfeit to be distributed in sufficient quantities and in sufficiently short time to do the work of destruction? It was just possible that this snag had not been entirely overcome. If so, there was just a chance of salvation still. Yet it was madness to hope for a mistake or a weakness in the Enemy. That was absurd. That was criminal.

The clock chimed again. Each note beat through him in shivering pain. Outside in the passage the turnkey had risen and was peering at him through the judas-slit.

"Slim build . . ." he was muttering. "Slim build."

Campion's mind scurried on, tearing at the knots with nervy, unsteady fingers. His head still hurt him considerably and he felt weak and physically unreliable, but there was still a great reserve of raging nervous energy boiling within him. Everything was startlingly clear.

What he did know stood out in bright colours. What he did not know was defined and impenetrably black.

The whole scheme must have been Enemy Alien in the beginning; so much was obvious. The neatness and ingenuity of the arrangements all pointed to the same diabolically competent organization.

He went back to the judas-window and peered out at the policeman. As his eyes rested on that square, well-padded head, with its bald spot and fringe of oiled grey hair, it came to him with an overwhelming sense of finality that there was absolutely nothing he could say or do which would be of the slightest use.

Now that he had the whole picture in his mind he could see his own mistakes standing out like enemy flags on a map. That dash for freedom after they charged him, that had been suicidal. He knew from long experience of the police and their ways that nothing he did after that would make one ha'porth of difference. He knew what they were doing. They were letting him cool off. The more noise he made, the more he argued, the longer they would leave him. It was maddening, like being held at bay by one's own dog.

He had closed his eyes while he swallowed the inevitable and he stood now with his hands resting high up on the inside of the door and his blank face held to the judas-slit. There was no sound. Nothing concrete disturbed him, yet presently his eyes flickered open eagerly and he stood watching without moving.

The turnkey was sitting on the bench with his head raised and a foolish, startled expression on his face. His eyes were fixed on the farther door, the one which led to the corridor and the charge room, and he too was listening intently.

Campion realized that there was a judas-window in the farther door also and someone was watching the pair of them through it. It was a moment of intense excitement. Hope leapt up in him and he forced himself to hold his tongue. After what seemed an age of indecision the turnkey blundered to his feet and went to unlock the door.

Campion's fingernails cut into his hands and his mouth was dry. So much depended on this silly little question. So much. An Empire? Perhaps a civilization. All depending on who came into a prison corridor.

His first despairing impression was that the man was a stranger. He stooped to pass through the doorway and he was wearing a scarf wrapped round the lower part of his face. As he lifted his head, however, Campion knew him. It was Hutch.

The scarf took Campion off his guard. He knew quite well what it must be protecting but he had not expected it. He had not only never meant to hit so hard but in his present three-dimensional world the whole notion of doing such a thing at all savoured of madness.

It was the clock again which pulled him together. Its fifteen-minute chimes must have been a torture to any prisoner at any time, but to Campion they had become a scourge.

"Hutch," he said softly.

The man came over to the door and looked in through the window. He did not speak and his blue eyes were very bleak.

Campion took a deep breath.

"I must have a word with you," he said quietly. "I know there's a hell of a lot to explain. I've been walking around punch-drunk for the best part of two days. However, you shall have chapter and verse for everything in an hour or so. But just at the moment there's something that's got to be done. We've got to go to Bridge. We've got to get to the Nag at once. My dear fellow, you needn't let me out of your sight."

Still Hutch did not reply, nor did he alter his expression. Desperation made Campion very quiet and almost conversational.

"I can give you any bona fides you need," he said. "My S.S. number is twenty-seven. I've been lent to Chief Constable of the C.I.D. Mr. Stanislaus Oates. The work we're engaged on concerns Folio 6B and Minute Fifteen, but it's so damnably urgent now that I must insist . . ."

Hutch stepped back from the judas-window.

"For God's sake, man!" Campion's cry came from his soul and to his relief he heard the lock. The door swung wide and he stepped out to confront the Superintendent, who was still regarding him with a curious expression on the half of his face which showed above his muffler.

Campion opened his mouth to speak but got no farther. Hutch had turned to the wall and was scribbling a line or two on the back of an envelope taken from his pocket. The message was enlightening.

"Just located Oates. Has been St. Jude's Hospital unconscious since Tues. night. Has been under police guard in error. Was thought to have killed copper in street fight on quay. Police here b. fools. Oates just come round and Doc says thinks out of danger."

Understanding came to Campion. Of course! That explained it at last. The policeman and the nurse and that incredible conversation he had overheard from his bed in the huge deserted ward. They could never have been talking about himself. They must have been discussing poor old Oates, who was probably lying in a little private room leading off the main ward. Now he had his wits about him that much was obvious. When a police constable watches a man in bed he watches him from a chair at the foot of that bed and does not stand about in a passage. Yet it had all seemed very convincing at the time.

Hutch was still scribbling.

"Lady A. found him. Sent for me. You can leave here when you like. We'll square this lot. Understand it's urgent. She's outside with the car."

"Is she?" Campion leapt to the door. "You'll want twenty or thirty armed men," he said over his shoulder. "Bring them to the Nag at once. It's desperate. What's the time?"

"4.50." Hutch wrote the figures and Campion had to step back to look at them.

"What's the matter with you?" he demanded as the oddity of the proceeding suddenly occurred to him.

Hutch gave him a slow sidelong glance and his hand began to move again.

"You've cracked my ruddy jaw, blast you," he wrote. "Get on with it. I'm following."

CHAPTER TWENTY

Campion stepped out of the comparative calm of the police station into a world of exuberant speed. A tremendous wind had sprung up over the town, and low-lying clouds, like shoals of enormous blue-black sharks, swam across a brilliant sky. There was rain coming and the air felt damp and soft and exciting. Everywhere, from the scraps of wastepaper cartwheeling down the road to the flying patches of alternate sun and shadow which flickered over housetops and pavements, there was an impression of desperate urgency, of superhuman efforts to be quick.

The car was at the curb with the engine running and, as he appeared, the door swung open to meet him. Amanda slid out of the driving seat and handed over the wheel.

"That's good," she said with characteristic understatement. "I say, God bless Hutch. That man hasn't a grudge in his make-up, Albert. Rather a mercy in the circumstances, of course. He came at once when I phoned him from the hospital and Oates did the rest."

Campion climbed into the car and slammed the door.

"You found Oates pretty quickly," he remarked as he let in the clutch.

"Well, naturally." She was astonished. "You told me where he was. Why didn't you part up with the information before?"

"I hadn't got it."

"I thought you said he was with you in a fight before you went into hospital yourself? You were all right, you see, but he was knocked out completely. No one recognized him, as of course they wouldn't, and it was assumed he'd killed the copper." She shot a dubious glance at him from under her eyelashes. "Anyway, he's conscious and he's recovering," she added, "but he's practically out of his mind with worry. They were having to hold him down in the bed when I came away. He told me over and over again to impress it on you that every moment mattered. Turn here. We've got to go down to the paper shop."

"What for?"

"A message from Lugg," she said calmly. "I got him to go over to the Nag at once. I went straight to him when I left you. We didn't know what you wanted done there, so he's just going to scout round and phone the paper shop if there's anything to report."

Campion looked at her out of the corner of his eye. She was sitting placidly beside him with her slender brown hands folded in her lap. She might have been a self-possessed sixteen-year-old going to a race meeting. Her heart-shaped face was serene and her brown eyes clear and level. There was no telling what was going on in her mind. He must have taken her for granted for years now. The reflection sprang up in his head and shook him off his guard.

"That was remarkably bright of you," he said, and knew as soon as he had spoken that it was not so. Amanda always was bright. There was nothing remarkable about it. Amanda was God's own gift to anyone in a hole and always had been. He seemed to have become too used to it. However, she was entertained by the compliment.

"Praise is always welcome," she observed, grinning at him. "Nothing fulsome, of course. I say, it's pretty serious, isn't it?"

He nodded. "Not so hot. Time's short. That's the shop, isn't it, over there?"

"Yes. You wait. I'll get the message if there is one. Keep the bus running."

She was out before he reached the curb and he watched her disappear into the dark entrance between the empty newsboards. As he sat waiting the familiar chime of the fifteen-minute clock reached him from across the housetops. Fifteen minutes: Minute Fifteen. It was a ridiculous little coincidence but, once it had occurred to him, he could not get it out of his mind.

Fif-teen min-utes. Min-ute Fif-teen. Hur-ry hur-ry. Ding-dong. Ding-dong. Late. Late. Late. Late. Late.

He counted the strokes. Five of them. Too late.

He *was* too late.

The sudden and startling reflection came like another revelation. He felt as if he had just opened his eyes to find that he was staring down into a well. Good God, he was not going to pull it off! Hutch and his men could never get there in the time. The secretly unthinkable was actually going to occur. They were going to lose. The police, including himself, were licked. The ultimate disaster was going to come off.

"I say, don't look so terrified. It's bad for morale," said Amanda seriously. She had come back without him seeing her and now settled down beside him. "This is where we travel faster than light," she announced. "Lugg did phone, ten minutes ago. It was a message for you and the shopkeeper had the presence of mind to take it down verbatim. I'll read it to you while you concentrate on the road. He says 'The hornet's nest is round the back of the hill on the old coast road. I expect you know that but they are. A railing over the entrance to the hill cave has been took down and I see several hundred jams inside.' Is 'jams' right?"

Campion nodded. "Rhyming-slang. Jam-jar equals car. Go on."

Amanda continued obligingly, the message gaining in piquancy from her clear, well-bred young voice.

"'All our friends are there. Not half they are not and some more. There is strong signs of a move any minute now. The local rozzers have an idea that it is all some kind of Government work but it cannot be with all that gang on board or I am barmy. Have hid myself in garden of empty house bottom of coast road right side of hill. If you want to catch them, which I take it is what you are after, you will have to put your skates on. I am about as good as a bucket of nothing here alone.'"

Amanda folded the sheet and thrust it in her jacket pocket.

"Of course he is, poor old tortoise," she said. "Coming from him, that's by way of being an S O S, isn't it?"

"I'm afraid so." Campion was taking the last of the town at speed. He had had some wild journeys on this road to Bridge, which was so anonymous and difficult without its signposts, but this evening, with the yellow sun streaming behind him and the dark flying shapes overhead, it had an entirely new quality. For the first time for what seemed a lifetime he was in full possession of all his senses and the condition seemed to have its disadvantages.

For one thing he was acutely aware that Amanda was beside him. Her share in his recent nightmare was very vivid in his mind. He remembered, too, exactly how he had reacted to it. In his lonely and terrified ignorance she had emerged as a necessity, a lifeline, heaven-sent and indispensable. Now, with the full recollection of a long and sophisticated bachelor life behind him, and the most gigantic disaster of all time looking just ahead, he was startled to find that she remained just that; static and unalterable, like the sun or the earth.

The recollection of her confidences concerning Lee Aubrey made him feel physically sick. He had been in love, he remembered, many times. This was not much like it. To say that he was in love with Amanda seemed futile and rather cheap. To lose her . . . His mind shied at the idea and his body felt cold.

"Hurry," she said at his side. "Hurry and we'll do it."

He shook his head. "Sorry, old lady," he said heavily, "but to be honest I'm terribly afraid we're sunk."

"What?" She sat bolt upright in the seat beside him, her back stiff and her eyes scandalized. "But I say, Albert," she said, "you *must* pull it off. Oates made it so clear. He said everything depended on you. You can't say you're afraid we're sunk. You've got to stop it somehow. Everyone's relying on you. You can't fail and go on living."

Campion frowned and a faint colour spread over his face.

"Oh stow the heroics," he said unpardonably, because he was wretched. "Some things are impossible, and for poor old Lugg and me to stop three hundred crook-driven lorries without police assistance is one of them. I can't even appeal to the local Bridge police because the chances are that as soon as they see me they'll pounce on me and stuff me in jug again. It's all very well to be an optimist, my beautiful, but one doesn't want to be a dear little nut, does one?"

"Nonsense," said Amanda, unperturbed and without resentment. "All it means is that there are times when one has to do a miracle. This is one of those. You think one up."

Campion did not answer. The request seemed to him to be unreasonable. He allowed himself to think of Amanda for a moment or two. This attitude of hers was typical. She never had and never would get it into her dear head that anything was impossible. Her optimism was childlike and unbounded, her faith in himself embarrassing. At the moment she was exasperating. Things could hardly be worse. Time was certain to beat him. If he was honest with himself, he saw no way round it.

Unless . . .

An idea slid into his mind complete.

He sat gripping the wheel while the suggestion turned over and over in his head. It was wild and probably suicidal, but it did contain one very slender thread of hope.

"Are those gates where the sentry stands the only entrance to the Institute?" he enquired.

Amanda cocked an eye at him. "None of those sentries would ever stop *us*," she said, catching his thought. "There's only three of them. They take it in turns and they've all seen us about with Aubrey."

It was like her not to ask any questions. As usual, her only concern was to further the project whatever it might turn out to be.

Campion took hold of himself. Losing Amanda was going to be like losing an eye. Life would be a little less than half itself without her.

Meanwhile, however, the car was speeding down the narrow roads. The wind roared behind it and overhead the dark blue clouds streaked out across the sky like dirty finger trails. It was a wild ride, leading directly towards almost certain catastrophe. The rain in the air, the urgency of the wind, the tremendous drama of the skyscape, were all a fitting part of the great central situation. A spiteful energy rose up in Campion and he trod hard on the accelerator. If he was to go down it might as well be scrapping.

He drove straight to the Institute and, leaving the car outside the gates, went in past the sentry on foot. It was a ticklish moment but it went by successfully, Amanda creating a heaven-sent diversion by attempting to turn the car in a space six inches wider than its length. He left her graciously accepting both advice and assistance.

Five minutes later he came back, walking very fast. He was a little white round the cheekbones and he carried himself very carefully, but the new recklessness was still there and when she relinquished the wheel to him he took it eagerly.

He drove into the town with unusual caution and stopped at the top of the Pykle, the hill looming up over them dirty and grey in the evening light.

"You take the car," he said urgently. "Go and find old Lugg and tell him from me to get Hutch to block the coast road both ways as soon as he comes, at the same time avoiding the actual entrance to the hill. No single lorry must get out. When both barricades are up they can play Annie Laurie or something else appropriate on a police whistle, but not before. The one thing that really matters is that no lorry gets by."

"Right." She nodded and took the wheel again. "They probably won't get here in time," she said, catching his eye. "You've got a scheme in case of that, I take it?"

He grinned. His head was very sore and the prospects were about as bad as they could be.

"I've only got a lucky bean plus a profound and lovely faith in myself," he said.

She echoed his expression, her eyes as affectionately derisive as his own.

"Then I'll pray," she said cheerfully. "Good-bye. See you at dinner or in the Elysian Fields."

Campion hurried. Keeping one hand in his coat pocket, he swung down the narrow passage beside the little old-fashioned shop under the Nag where Hutch had taken him. It was not an easy journey to repeat in daylight, especially when any delay was certain to be disastrous and one was not at all sure one had not dreamt one's directions in the first place.

He found the storeroom door standing wide and walked straight in, nodding briefly to the startled boy who stood weighing dried fruit in the back of the building. The fatal thing, he realized, would be to lose his way. One moment's hesitation and he betrayed himself instantly.

He strode on, hoping devoutly for the best, and plunged down a dusty aisle lined with tea chests and bulging sacks of cereals. He heard the boy moving behind him, then a new step on the boards and a lot of whispering. He was going to be stopped. Now, at the eleventh hour, he was going to be held up, caught like a mouse, in a damned grocer's shop.

There was a bundle of long, old-fashioned soft brooms hanging from a hook in the ceiling and he snatched one of them. The door leading into the Masters' domain was unlocked, as before, and when he went through it he took the broom with him and wedged it between the door panel and the angle of the opposite wainscot. It was not a very effective barrier but it would certainly hold the door against the most determined shoulder for a minute or two, and it seemed most unlikely that any longer period was going to matter very much.

Once inside in the dark a new difficulty presented itself. He had no torch. Everything in his pockets except his cigarettes had been taken from him at the police station and was probably hanging up now in a little official bag outside the cell door.

He began to climb in the dark, praying against giddiness and keeping one hand tightly clasped over the things in his coat pocket. He was desperate with exasperation at his own slowness. Every moment counted. Every minute which galloped by might be the one which made all the difference between success and failure. His journey across the Council Chamber turned out to be a crawl through hell. Once he cannoned into the table, the hard wooden edge missing the burden in his pocket by inches, and all the time the seconds were racing by.

He found the farther door after what promised to be complete defeat, by observing a minute sliver of light showing just beneath it. He got it open, to discover that the corridor within was lit by a hurricane lantern standing at the entrance to the first of the Masters' storerooms. Although Campion was profoundly relieved to see it from one point of view, it presented another danger. He had no desire to run into anyone before he reached the Nag's Trough.

He went on, still with the same cautious haste which demanded every ounce of nervous discipline he possessed. His eyelids were sticky and his muscles hard and bunched against his bones.

There were lanterns in every vantage place and the damp stone had dried round them, indicating that they had been burning for some time. A great change had come over the Masters' storerooms. The packing cases were empty and the great caverns in confusion, as if an army had been at work there. There was so much debris about, so many dark corners and unexplained machines, that he hardly dared move, convinced that at any moment a living figure must detach itself from the chaos and bar his way.

He pushed on, feeling like a hurrying snail with all the world depending on his speed. The iron ladders required very cautious negotiation in the half-dark and he had his precious coat pocket to take care of during the descent.

He came down into the last narrow passage without being seen. Here the fumes of gasoline were almost suffocating and the throb of revving engines made the very heart of the hill vibrate.

He edged on towards the right-angled bend which would bring him out on to the ledge overlooking the whole Trough. At least some of the trucks were still there, although by the sound they were on the point of moving. The police could never have arrived in time, and even had they done so there could hardly have been enough of them. No one, not even Hutch in war time, could conjure up such a large army of police at five minutes' notice.

He turned the right-angled bend cautiously and looked out into the Nag's Trough. It made an amazing picture. The only light in the high cavern came from the masked headlamps of the vehicles themselves, so that the lorries and vans looked like great black humped insects trembling on a lampshade. There appeared to Campion's horrified eyes to be thousands of them, all loaded to capacity with bursting sacks.

He kept flat against the dark wall of rock and edged farther along, so that he could get a glimpse of the entrance round the protecting screen of the natural rock partition.

When at last he was able to get an uninterrupted view his heart jolted violently. There was a sacking curtain hanging over the single exit of the coast road, and the foremost truck was stationary a good twenty feet away from it. If he could do anything he was still in time.

The whole place was alive with people but voices were kept down and the roar of engines predominated. It was a ghostly inferno of a scene. He knew the trucks and vans must all be loaded up with financial dynamite, freight far more dangerous than ammunition. It was the counterfeit all right, that much was obvious, but inasmuch as its form of presentation and distribution was still undiscovered it remained a secret weapon, its degree of danger known only to the Enemy.

Campion strained his eyes through the gloom. Exhaust fumes were rising all round him and he was beginning to feel their effects. Was that Pyne in the far corner over by the sacking curtain? He thought it was. The man was calmly checking trucks over on a time-sheet as if he had been running a goods yard.

The fumes were growing worse up in the roof. Campion felt himself swaying and he put out his arms to steady himself. The sudden movement must have caught the attention of someone in the crowd below, for a shout went up and immediately the wide beam of a powerful torch began to rake the ledge on which he stood.

Campion made up his mind. He had no idea what the effect of his solitary "lucky bean" might be. From the beginning it had only been a forlorn hope, but now the time had come to take the risk.

As the torch beam came nearer he drew the little steel egg from his coat pocket and pulled out the pin. It had been really disgracefully easy to steal it from Butcher's workshop. That had simply been a question of walking in and lifting it from its rack in the cupboard. The whole proceeding could not have taken more than five minutes.

The phoenix egg nestled wickedly in the palm of his hand. Below him the trucks trembled and steamed. The torch beam was within a yard of him. He threw up his arm and stood spread-eagled against the wall.

"I hope you're praying," he said grimly to Amanda wherever she might be, "because this is our first attempt at a miracle and it's got to come off."

The egg sailed through the air to the goal he had chosen for it, low down on the left-hand side of the entrance to the Trough. At the same moment the torch beam got him and he dropped forward on his face as a bullet spat at him.

The next moment the world pancaked. It was no ordinary explosion. Campion's immediate thought was that Butcher was another of those damned maniacs with a passion for understatement.

There was very little noise, but it was as though some gigantic animal had placed its lips to the entrance to the Trough and had sucked in very sharply, only to blow out again immediately afterwards. There was a rumble and the exit to the coast road disappeared under several tons of earth and limestone sliding down from the Nag. The roar of fire followed as a score of petrol tanks exploded and the whole of the upper half of the cavern became a mass of flying paper.

Campion scrambled to his knees. Blood was trickling into his mouth and his body felt as if it had been through a clothes wringer, but he was alive and, as far as he knew, unwounded, save for the bullet graze across his face.

Below him, in the bowl of the Trough, there was a sea of blazing petrol and paper and the fumes of smouldering sacks. Millions of envelopes covered the place like a fall of brown snow. Injured men swore and died under their lorries, while others fought each other in their attempt to clamber on to the ledge. But the ladders which were normally used for this purpose had been smashed to matchwood and the bare sides of the rock provided no foothold.

Campion gathered up a handful of the letters which were still fluttering down over him as the hot air winnowed them up from the bonfire below, and, using every ounce of strength left in his body, he crawled painfully towards the mouth of the passage.

Hutch and his handful of men found him at the foot of the first iron ladder as they came swarming in through the Masters' storerooms to investigate the explosion, which had shaken the town. The sergeant and the constables went on at once to do what they could for the temporary staff of Surveys Limited trapped in the horrors of the Trough, but the Superintendent sat down by Campion on the stones and they looked at the envelopes together.

There is something unspeakably shocking about a very simple idea which, as well as being elementary, is also diabolical.

Both Campion and Hutch were highly sophisticated members of a generation which has had to learn to steel itself against ever being astonished by anything unpleasant, but there was a streak of frank bewilderment in both their expressions as they glanced at each other across the handful of envelopes.

The plan by which false inflation was to have been induced over-night in the most civilized island in the world was an exquisitely simple one. Each of the envelopes was of the familiar Government colour and pattern. *On His Majesty's Service* was printed across the front of each in the standard ink and type, as was also the black frank-mark, the familiar crown in the circle. Each envelope was, in fact, exactly the same as any of those others which were being circulated officially in millions on behalf of Minute Fifteen.

By the light of the Superintendent's torch Campion opened one of the packets. It was addressed to a Mr. P. Carter, 2 Lysander Cottages, Netherland Road, Bury-under-Lyne, and it contained seven of the spurious and artificially dirtied banknotes, as well as a buff-coloured printed slip, the text of which was masterly in its uncomplicated wickedness.

"The Ministry of Labour, Whitehall, London, S.W. SRG. 20539.

"Dear Sir/Madam,

"The enclosed sum of £7 os. od. has been awarded to you on the War Bonus Claims Committee's recommendation.

"This money is paid to you under the arrears of remuneration for Persons of Incomes Below Tax Level Board (O. in C. AQ430028), as has been announced in the public press and else-where.

"Note. *You will help your country if you do not hoard this money but translate it into goods immediately.*

"R. W. Smith,

"Compt."

The second envelope was directed to a Mr. Wild, or Wilder, of 13 Pond Street, Manchester, 4. It contained a copy of the same slip and four of the counterfeit notes.

The third should have gone to a Mrs. Edith somebody of Handel Buildings, Lead Road, Northampton, and contained, beside the familiar slip, nine pounds in spurious notes.

The addresses explained the scheme to the two men and they shiv-ered. It was very obvious. Someone had simply got hold of the regis-ters belonging to the various social service schemes functioning in the poorer districts of the industrial towns. These would contain between them the names of most of the permanently unemployed, those who had ever received help from State or local bodies, and all those thousand-and-one poorer folk whose names and addresses had ever been tabulated.

Campion held his breath. It all pointed directly to Pyne again. Lists of addresses of that kind would be just the thing in which Surveys Limited would have specialized. More than probably millions of addresses like these constituted the firm's main stock-in-trade. Many of them would be out of date, of course. The main bulk was bound to be damagingly correct.

The central idea lay revealed in all its destructiveness. Vast numbers of needy folk in all the poorer parts of the country were suddenly to be presented with a handful of money and instructions to spend it. The evil genius of the proposal lay in the fact that the windfall was to appear to come directly from the one authority from whom the recipients would accept money not only without question, but also with the dangerous assumption that it was in some inexplicable fashion their right to receive it.

As soon as Campion saw the scheme in its simple entirety he realized the overwhelming fact that in such circumstances the only thing any Government could hope to do was to admit the notes as legal tender and accept the consequences, however terrible they might turn out to be. It would be quite impossible to take the money back.

The practical arrangements had been a miracle of efficiency. The money had been inserted in the envelopes by a machine. The trucks were obviously due to spread out all over the country, posting their "Government mail" at main post offices all over the West of England. By synchronizing the plan with the launching of Minute Fifteen at a time when the authorities were prepared for an enormous influx of official letters, the G.P.O. was to be neatly tricked into rendering vital assistance and ensuring that the secret blow would fall at the same moment in every part of the land. The earlier, clumsier method of distributing the money must have been in the nature of a try-out to test the actual currency itself.

Campion wiped his face, which was still bleeding slightly. He felt sick with relief. Hutch leant close to him and his eyes were questioning. Campion guessed what he was asking and as suddenly knew the answer also. The whole vivid procession had brought them directly to Pyne, and Pyne was not convincing. The principal thing about him, the thing that overshadowed everything else, was that he was first and foremost an ordinary commercially-minded business man. There was no passion in him, no fanaticism, no emotional driving force. As a full-blown enemy agent he seemed unlikely; as a Quisling he was frankly absurd. From first to last he had behaved like a business man undertaking a delicate job for a client, and in that case who was his principal? Who? Who was employing Pyne? Who was it who had carried this half-prepared plan of the enemy's through to within an ace of success? Who had discovered the presence of the counterfeit and had then, either with or without direct contact with the enemy country, put the whole diabolical scheme into existence? That was the question.

The answer seemed to be contained in another. Who had the facilities for acquiring and accommodating a large army of local volunteer labour to address "Government envelopes"? Who would have had access to sufficient petrol, real or synthetic, to propel so many lorries?

Sir Henry Bull's description of Lee Aubrey came back very vividly to Campion.

"He's a curious product, part genius, part crank. One moment he's doing untold service and the next he's trying to advance a hare-brained scheme for running the country."

CHAPTER TWENTY-ONE

Campion leant against the wall in Lee Aubrey's gracious, comfortable study and considered the scene before him. It was one of those lucid, almost contemplative moments which sometimes arrive in the very heart of a crisis. Just for a moment he saw the whole history of the plan and its defeat in the round, as if it had been a play and this present moment the final scene.

The picture in front of him might easily have been on a stage. It was so brightly lit, so tense, so painfully dramatic. The room was very quiet. The two constables on the door stood stiffly. The distinguished company, with Oates himself in the middle looking like a grey corpse which had begun to fidget, was anxious and constrained. Sir Henry Bull, who had just arrived from London and was now surrounded by most of his fellow Masters, was glancing at the documents over which Hutch's Chief Inspector and an M.I.5 man were presiding.

The cupboard beneath the high bookcase stood open. So did every drawer in the room, as the squad of trained men methodically packed and docketed the papers they were taking away.

Lee Aubrey himself stood on the hearthrug with a plain-clothes man on either side of him. He looked astonished and faintly irritated, but there was no trace of alarm in his big-boned face and he was certainly far less gauche than usual.

It was the importance of the men which made the scene unique in Campion's experience. There was a note almost of domestic tragedy about the situation. It was like the disowning of the eldest son, the disgrace in the regiment, the expulsion from the school.

The Masters of Bridge were angry and horrified but also deeply hurt and ashamed. Even the police were not triumphant.

"The evidence against that fellow Pyne, who was killed, is of course conclusive," said Oates to Sir Henry. He spoke softly but included in his glance the thin, scandalized man who was Aubrey's solicitor and had only just arrived.

Sir Henry nodded grimly without speaking.

"I think there is no doubt that he must have been the moving spirit," the solicitor was venturing timidly when Aubrey interrupted from the hearthrug.

"My dear chap, don't be an ass," he said. "I employed Pyne because, not only was he obviously the right man for the job, but he had the right kind of organization at his fingertips. He was doing his work very efficiently until he was stopped."

"Take care." Oates turned on the man sharply, his haggard face unusually grim. In the background a detective-sergeant had begun to scribble in his notebook unobtrusively.

Aubrey's colour darkened and he threw out his long arms in an awkward gesture.

"My dear good people, this is all too absurd," he said, his deep pleasant voice flexible and persuasive as ever. "I'm perfectly willing to reserve my defence as you all advise so magnificently, but there's no point in making a mystery of the thing where none exists. It's quite *clear* what I've been doing. For heaven's sake see those fellows at my desk handle the green folders with care, because they contain the one vital scheme of government for this benighted country at the present time. I had to be unorthodox in my methods of forcing the Government to take it up, I admit that, but it was a case of necessity."

"Good God, Aubrey, do you realize what you're saying?" Sir Henry's face was as white as his hair.

"Yes, Bull, of course I do." The Principal of the Bridge Institute was at his most gently superior. "A great deal of the blame is yours. You made a very dangerous mistake last year when you failed to understand the importance of the financial scheme I put up to you then. All these Social Credit fellows, and Keynes and the rest, they have glimmerings of the idea, but they're none of them sufficiently drastic or far-reaching. My plan would have put the economic life of the country on an entirely new basis. Since I could not get a government to see reason by argument I realized I had to put them in a position in which they would be only too glad to listen to me. I had to smash their existing economy and create a chaos in which they would automatically turn to the one man who could save them. That's perfectly clear. There's nothing difficult to understand about that."

He was leaning against the mantelpiece now, lecturing academically from what he clearly felt to be an infinite height of intellectual superiority.

"Poor Campion here, who probably believes he's done his duty," he continued, "in reality he has betrayed his country and probably civilization by his interference. I had the whole little ingenuity completely in hand. It wasn't out of control. I knew Feiberg quite well. I met him in Frankfurt years ago. Quite an interesting mind. Extraordinarily meticulous over detail. I knew he was a Nazi agent when he turned up here, and in fact I think I probably suggested to him that the storerooms in the Nag would be an excellent place for his counterfeit. I may have mentioned too that the Masters were taking their money from the Rhenish vineyards in wine instead of cash and pointed out that such a shipment would give him a perfect opportunity to get his stuff into the country without query. I certainly put him on to Anscombe. I knew that man would be reasonable if properly approached. There's nothing to get excited about in that. I allowed it to happen because I knew it was perfectly safe. Last August I knew we had nothing to fear, because no foreign power on earth could have got the plan into operation once we were at war. I knew it was coming and Feiberg did not. He did not believe we should fight so soon. I saw that the money arrived and when war came I arranged for Feiberg to be interned. That left me with a weapon in my own hand if I needed it. I did not use it until I really was convinced that there was no other way. Then I saw that something had to be done, to be done quickly, and my plan was the only solution. So I found the man Pyne, who chose his own assistants, and through him I arranged to engineer the greatest crash in history, so that in picking up the pieces I could restore a decent order at last. You're following me, of course?"

They were. The whole room was hanging on his words with sick fascination. The old solicitor was in tears. He was an honest man with a wide reputation. He sat down abruptly in a corner and wiped his face again and again.

"God bless my soul," he was ejaculating in a soft regular monotone. "God bless my soul. Good Lord. God bless my soul."

Oates leant forward in his chair. He looked a very sick man and was out strictly against doctor's orders.

"You had the envelopes addressed at the Institute by voluntary labour?" he said. "That enormous undertaking was organized by a woman, wasn't it?"

"Mrs. Ericson?" A flicker of kindly regret passed over Aubrey's face. "Yes, she did all that for me and did it very well. She hadn't the faintest idea why I needed them, of course. She's one of those intense people who are simply very gratified in having a job to do at all. She made a religion of being discreet in the matter, as I knew she would. Pyne and his fellows, on the other hand, were arranging a private pool to clean up a packet on the crashing markets. That shows the different temperament. The mere fact that they did not think I knew, and they imagined they were being disloyal to me, satisfied the criminal streak which I recognized in them at once and made it safe for me to use them. They're both examples of what I mean by choosing the right people for the right job. It's a gift and an art. My whole scheme of government is based, virtually speaking, on just that main essential."

Sir Henry passed a stubby hand through his hair. His lips were grey. He looked very tired.

"You have not explained the part you were to play in this new government of yours," he said.

Aubrey turned on him. He seemed taller and leaner than ever, but there was a fire in his pale eyes.

"I should have to have exactly the same power in the country as I have here at the Bridge Institute, of course," he said. "That surely is obvious. When there is so much of passionate importance to be done quickly and ruthlessly then the man in charge must assume full responsibility."

As his voice ceased there was such a breathless, such an electric silence in the room, that the undertones of the pronouncement hung in the air. To Campion it was the most ghastly moment of them all. The man was brilliant, able, and in his own limited sphere doubtless extremely useful, yet as he stood there, smiling faintly at them, his mistaken belief in his own superiority cut him off from reality as completely as if he were living in a coloured glass jar.

He was utterly unaware of the enormity of his sin. He believed implicitly that he alone was capable of directing the Empire and had been fully prepared to destroy the whole structure of its economic life in order to get into command.

The men who had trusted and admired him remained looking at him and the same thought was in all their eyes: "This is not even the stuff dictators are made of, but this is the kind of madness which is often not found out until it is too late."

Campion pulled himself away from the wall and edged his way out. He had had so much emotional strain in the last three days that this final and objective example was too much for him. He felt physically ill. The house was alive with police. In the drawing-room across the hall a woman was crying wearily, her sobs sounding above the steady rumble of the interrogating officer. He guessed she was Mrs. Ericson.

He pushed on through the plain-clothes men, the influential friends, the M.I.5 personnel, and the Home Office experts and went out of the front door. It was another clear bright night with visibility nearly as good as day. The constable on duty on the door saluted him with such spontaneous deference that he knew he was already a nine-days' wonder in the west-country police force. He strode on across the grass, drawing the clean night air deep into his lungs and enjoying the moist wind on his skin.

Presently Amanda joined him. She materialized at his side as he passed under the shadow of the house and they walked on for some time without speaking. Campion had been thinking of her steadily for some hours. Ever since the answer to Hutch's unspoken question had come to him so decisively in the Masters' storerooms, her reaction to the affair had haunted him. The present situation was irretrievable as well as being so miserably awkward that, had she been anybody else in the world, the only possible thing to have done would have been to hurry back to one's job immediately and concentrate on other things with one's eyes, ears, and heart shut. Since she was Amanda, however, and not just an ordinary woman with whom one happened to be in love, that was not possible. She did not seem anxious to talk herself, but there was no constraint in her manner. She had taken his arm, as usual, and seemed content to wander and speculate much as he was doing.

They walked on for so long that his thought had time to settle and crystallize and become almost impersonal.

"I tell you one thing," he said suddenly. "Even if he hadn't turned out to be this particular kind of lunatic you would never have married him."

"No," she agreed frankly. "No, I wouldn't."

He looked down at her and caught her grinning to herself. It was an unexpected reaction and he wondered if the light was playing tricks.

"Are you laughing?" he demanded.

"Only at me," said Amanda with typical if devastating honesty. "Go on."

He looked ahead of them at the great silhouettes which the trees made against the moonlit sky. There was something on Campion's mind and he intended to say it, not because it might comfort her—if she was human and female it would probably infuriate her—but because she was Amanda and her education was important. She ought to know it and it might help some day.

"In spite of his brilliance and his staggering conceit, which throws his whole vision out of focus, that chap is a type," he began abruptly. "Did you ever notice that woman Mrs. Ericson?"

He thought he heard Amanda catch her breath. Then she chuckled. There was no other word for that murmur of mingled amusement and relief.

"Of course I did," she said. "I'm terrifically relieved you saw it too. I mean if you're trying to explain that Lee has a habit of making extravagant passes at people conveying that he's hopelessly in love with them, so that they'll respond and he'll have the flattering experience of declining their affections with sweet sympathetic understanding, I know about it. I don't think he works it out like that, of course, but it just keeps happening to him and one side of his mind finds it a delightful surprise to him every time while the other side attends to the machinery for making it come off. I was the complete mug. I was awfully surprised."

How like her. Not "I was wounded." Not "I was furious." Not "I was wretchedly degraded." Just "I was awfully surprised."

"When did all this happen?" he enquired.

"Just before I brought old Miss Anscombe to see you at that pub. I was going to tell you, because I was rather full of it, and—oh, you know how one is—rather sore and embarrassed. But it didn't seem to be quite the time for intimate revelations. You were a bit peculiar yourself, if you remember."

Peculiar! He did remember. He remembered her face, too, hurt and bewildered as the idiotic couplet hung unfinished between them. Another thought occurred to him and he turned to her in consternation.

"You had to come back here. I sent you back."

"Yes, I know," she said, "but it had to be done. Besides, it rubbed the whole thing in until I really did understand it. He enjoyed it so. I did get the whole thing clear and I *was* here when they phoned from Coachingford Police Station, so it was worth while."

Campion put an arm round her and held the small circle of her shoulder-bone. For the first time in his life he felt completely adult.

His hesitancy, his qualms, his intellectual doubts seemed suddenly the stuff of childhood.

"Let's get married early tomorrow," he said. "I've only got thirty-six hours' leave. A message came through tonight. I ought to have this conk on my head looked at too. It's time we got married."

"Yes," said Amanda, who never bothered with illusions. "It's time we got married."

They went back to the house to get hold of Oates, who could probably fix any licensing difficulty. Just before they reached the door Amanda turned to Campion.

"I'm sorry I boxed your ears," she said, "but you flicked me on the raw. You weren't quite like yourself, either, you know."

"My good girl, I was nuts," he began and hesitated. It was no good. He just did not want to tell her the full extent of his recent disability. The dreadful revelation of his helplessness and his need for her was still a vividly remembered pain.

Amanda waited a moment and finally laughed.

"Get it right this time, then," she commanded. " *'Begone!' she stormed. 'Across the raging tide!'* "

Campion grinned as the delightful cockney rhyme returned to him. He pulled her towards him.

" *'Dear Jove! Why did I go?'* " he quoted accurately, and kissed her as he finished with triumphant satisfaction the ecstatic Victorian anti-climax, so apt and so absurd, " *'I should have stiyed!'* "

The
Gyrth Chalice
Mystery

To Orlando

CHAPTER ONE

"Reward for Finder?"

"If you'll accept this, sir," said the policeman, pressing a shilling into the down-and-out's hand, "you'll have visible means of support and I shan't have to take you along. But," he added with a delightful hint of embarrassment, "I'll have to ask you to move on; the Inspector is due round any minute."

Percival St. John Wykes Gyrth, only son of Colonel Sir Percival Christian St. John Gyrth, Bt., of the Tower, Sanctuary, Suffolk, reddened painfully, thrust the coin into his trouser pocket, and smiled at his benefactor.

"Thank you, Baker," he said. "This is extraordinarily kind of you. I shan't forget it."

"That's all right, sir." The man's embarrassment increased. "You gave me five pounds the night you was married." He opened his mouth as though to continue, but thought the better of it, and the young man's next remark indicated clearly that he was in no mood for reminiscences.

"I say, where the devil can I sit where I shan't be moved on?"

The policeman glanced nervously up South Molton Street, whence even now the dapper form of the Inspector was slowly approaching.

"Ebury Square—just off Southampton Row," he murmured hastily. "You'll be as safe as houses there. Good night, sir."

The final words were a dismissal; the Inspector was almost upon them. Val Gyrth pulled his battered hat over his eyes, and hunching his shoulders, shuffled off towards Oxford Street. His "visible means of support" flopped solitarily in the one safe pocket of his suit, a suit which had once come reverently from the hands of the tailor whose shop he was passing. He crossed into Oxford Street and turned up towards the Circus.

It was a little after midnight and the wide road was almost deserted. There were a few returning revellers, a sprinkling of taxicabs, and an occasional late bus.

Val Gyrth chose the inside of the pavement, keeping as much in the shadow as possible. The summer smell of the city, warm and slightly scented like a chemist's shop, came familiarly to his nostrils and in spite of his weariness there was an impatience in his step. He was bitterly angry with himself. The situation was impossible, quixotic, and ridiculous. Old Baker had given him a shilling to save him from arrest as a vagrant on his own doorstep. It was unthinkable.

He had not eaten since the night before, but he passed the coffee-stall outside the French hat shop in the Circus without a thought. He had ceased to feel hungry at about four o'clock that afternoon and had been surprised and thankful at the respite. The swimming sensation which had taken the place of it seemed eminently preferable.

The pavement was hot to that part of his foot which touched it through the hole in an expensive shoe, and he was beginning to limp when he turned down by Mudie's old building and found himself after another five minutes' plodding in a dishevelled little square whose paved centre was intersected by two rows of dirty plane trees, beneath which, amid the litter of a summer's day, were several dilapidated wooden benches. There were one or two unsavoury-looking bundles dotted here and there, but there were two seats unoccupied. Val Gyrth chose the one under a street lamp and most aloof from its fellows; he sank down, realizing for the first time the full sum of his weariness.

A shiver ran through the dusty leaves above his head, and as he glanced about him he became obsessed with a curious feeling of apprehension which could not be explained by the sudden chill of the night. A car passed through the square, and from far off beyond the Strand came the mournful bellow of a tug on the river. None of the bundles huddled on the other seats stirred, but it seemed to the boy, one of the least imaginative of an unimaginative race, that something enormous and of great importance was about to happen, or was, indeed, in the very act of happening all round him; a sensation perhaps explainable by partial starvation and a potential thunderstorm.

He took off his hat and passed his fingers through his very fair hair, the increasing length of which was a continual source of annoyance to him. He was a thickset, powerful youngster in his early twenties, with a heavy but by no means unhandsome face and an habitual expression of dogged obstinacy; a pure Anglo-Saxon type, chiefly remarkable at the moment for a certain unnatural gauntness which accentuated the thickness of his bones.

He sighed, turned up his coat collar, and was about to lift his feet out of the miscellaneous collection of paper bags, orange skins, and cigarette cartons on to the bench, when he paused and sat up stiffly, staring down at the ground in front of him. He was conscious of a sudden wave of heat passing over him, of an odd shock that made his heart jump unpleasantly.

He was looking at his own name, written on a battered envelope lying face upwards among the other litter.

He picked it up and was astonished to see that his hand was shaking. The name was unmistakable. "P. St. J. W. Gyrth, Esq." written clearly in a hand he did not know.

He turned the envelope over. It was an expensive one, and empty, having been torn open across the top apparently by an impatient hand. He sat staring at it for some moments, and a feeling of unreality took possession of him. The address, "Kemp's, 32a Wembley Road, Clerkenwell, EC1", was completely unfamiliar.

He stared at it as though he expected the words to change before his eyes, but they remained clear and unmistakable. "P. St. J. W. Gyrth, Esq."

At first it did not occur to him to doubt that the name was his own, or that the envelope had been originally intended for him. Gyrth is an unusual name, and the odd collection of initials combined with it made it impossible for him to think that in this case it could belong to anyone else.

He studied the handwriting thoughtfully, trying to place it. His mind had accepted the astounding coincidence which had brought him to this particular seat in this particular square and led him to pick up the one envelope which bore his name. He hunted among the rubbish at his feet in a futile attempt to find the contents of the envelope, but an exhaustive search convinced him that the paper in his hand was all that was of interest to him there.

The hand puzzled him. It was distinctive, square, with heavy downstrokes and sharp Greek E's; individual handwriting, not easily to be forgotten. He turned his attention to the postmark, and the bewildered expression upon his young face became one of blank astonishment. It was dated the fifteenth of June. To-day was the nineteenth. The letter was therefore only four days old.

It was over a week since he had possessed any address. Yet he was convinced, and the fact was somehow slightly uncanny and unnerving, that someone had written to him, and someone else had received the letter, the envelope of which had been thrown away to be found by himself.

Not the least remarkable thing about a coincidence is that once it has happened, one names it, accepts it, and leaves it at that.

Gyrth sat on the dusty seat beneath the street lamp and looked at the envelope. The rustling in the leaves above his head had grown fiercer, and an uncertain wind ricocheted down the square; in a few minutes it would rain.

Once again he was conscious of that strange sensation of being just on the outside of some drama enacted quite near to him. He had felt it before to-night. Several times in the past few days this same uneasy feeling had swept over him in the most crowded streets at the height of noon, or at night in the dark alleyways of the city where he had tried to sleep. Experienced criminals recognize this sensation as the instinctive knowledge that one is being "tailed", but young Gyrth was no criminal, nor was he particularly experienced in anything save the more unfortunate aspects of matrimony.

He looked again at the address on the tantalizing envelope: "32a Wembley Rd., Clerkenwell." This was not far from where he now sat, he reflected, and the impulse to go there to find out for himself if he were not the only P. St. J. W. Gyrth in the world, or, if he was, to discover who was impersonating him, was very strong.

His was a conservative nature, however, and perhaps if the experience had happened to him in ordinary circumstances he would have shrugged his shoulders and taken no further active interest in the matter. But at the moment he was down-and-out. A man who is literally destitute is like a straw in the wind; any tiny current is sufficient to set him drifting in a new direction. His time and energies are of no value to him; anything is worth while. Impelled by curiosity, therefore, he set off across the square, the storm blowing up behind him.

He did not know what he expected to find, but the envelope fascinated him. He gave up conjecturing and hurried.

Clerkenwell in the early hours of the morning is one of the most unsavoury neighbourhoods in the whole of East Central London, which is saying a great deal, and the young man's ragged and dishevelled appearance was probably the only one which would not have attracted the attention of those few inhabitants who were still abroad.

At length he discovered a pair of policemen, of whom he inquired the way, gripping their colleague's shilling defiantly as he did so. They directed him with the unhurried omniscience of their kind, and he eventually found himself crossing a dirty ill-lit thoroughfare intersected with tramlines and flanked by the lowest of all lodging-houses, and shabby dusty little shops where everything seemed to be second-hand.

Number 32a turned out to be one of the few establishments still open.

It was an eating-house, unsavoury even for the neighbourhood, and one stepped down off the pavement a good eighteen inches to reach the level of the ground floor. Even Val Gyrth, now the least cautious of men, hesitated before entering.

The half-glass door of the shop was pasted over with cheap advertisements for boot polish and a brand of caramel, and the light from within struggled uncertainly through the dirty oiled paper.

Gyrth glanced at the envelope once more and decided that there was no doubt at all that this was his destination. The number, 32a, was printed on a white enamelled plaque above the door, and the name "Kemp's" was written across the shop front in foot-high letters.

Once again the full sense of the absurdity of his quest came over him, and he hesitated, but again he reflected that he had nothing to lose and his curiosity to appease. He turned the door-handle and stepped down into the room.

The fetid atmosphere within was so full of steam that for a moment he could not see at all where he was. He stood still for some seconds trying to penetrate the haze, and at last made out a long dingy room flanked with high, greasy pew seats, which appeared to be empty.

At the far end of the aisle between the tables there was a counter and a cooking-stove from which the atmosphere obtained most of its quality. Towards this gastronomic altar the young man advanced, the envelope clutched tightly in his coat pocket.

There was no one in sight, so he tapped the counter irresolutely. Almost immediately a door to the right of the stove was jerked open and there appeared a mountain of a man with the largest and most lugubrious face he had ever seen. A small tablecloth had been tied across the newcomer's stomach by way of an apron, and his great muscular arms were bare to the elbow. For the rest, his head was bald, and the bone of his nose had sustained an irreparable injury.

He regarded the young man with mournful eyes.

"This is a nice time to think about getting a bit of food," he observed more in sorrow than in anger, thereby revealing a sepulchral voice. "Everything's off but sausage and mash. I'm 'aving the last bit o' stoo meself."

Gyrth was comforted by his melancholy affability. It was some time since an eating-house keeper had treated him with even ordinary humanity. He took the envelope out of his pocket and spread it out on the counter before the man.

"Look here," he said. "Do you know anything about this?"

Not a muscle of the lugubrious face stirred. The mountainous stranger eyed the envelope for some time as if he had never seen such a thing before and was not certain if it were worth consideration. Then, turning suddenly, he looked the boy straight in the eyes and made what was in the circumstances a most extraordinary observation.

"I see," he said clearly, and with a slightly unnecessary deliberation, *"you take the long road."*

Gyrth stared at him. He felt that some reply was expected, that the words had some significance which was lost upon him. He laughed awkwardly.

"I don't quite follow you," he said. "I suppose I am tramping, if that's what you mean? But I came to inquire about this envelope. Have you seen it before?"

The big man ventured as near a smile as Gyrth felt his features would permit.

"Suppose I 'ave?" he said cautiously. "Wot then?"

"Only that it happens to be addressed to me, and I'm anxious to know who opened it," said Gyrth shortly. "Can you tell me who collected it?"

"Is that your name?" The big man placed a heavy forefinger upon the inscription. "I suppose you couldn't prove it, could yer?"

Gyrth grew red and uncomfortable. "I can't get anyone to identify me, if that's what you mean, and I haven't got a visiting-card. But," he added, "if you care to take my tailor's word for it there's the tab inside my coat here."

He unbuttoned the threadbare garment and turned down the edge of the inside breast pocket, displaying a tailor's label with his name and the date written in ink across it. In his eagerness he did not realize the incongruity of the situation.

The sad man read the label and then surveyed his visitor critically.

"I suppose it *was* made for yer?" he said.

Gyrth buttoned up his coat. "I've got thinner," he said shortly.

"Awright. No offence," said the other. "I believe yer—some wouldn't. Name o' Lugg meself. Pleased to meet yer, I'm sure. I got another letter for you, by the way."

He turned round ponderously, and after searching among the cups and plates upon the dresser behind him, he returned bearing a similar envelope to the one which Gyrth had put down upon the counter. It was unopened.

The young man took it with a sense of complete bewilderment. He was about to tear the seal when the gentleman who had just introduced himself with such light-hearted friendliness tapped him on the shoulder.

"Suppose you go and sit down," he observed. "I'll bring yer a spot o' coffee and a couple o' Zepps in a smoke screen. I always get peckish about this time o' night meself."

"I've only got a shilling—" Gyrth began awkwardly.

Mr. Lugg raised his eyebrows.

"A bob?" he said. "Where d'you think you're dining? The Cheshire Cheese? You sit down, my lad. I'll do you proud for a tanner. Then you'll 'ave yer 'visible means' and tuppence to spare for emergencies."

Gyrth did as he was told. He edged on to one of the greasy benches and sat down before a table neatly covered with a clean newspaper bill. He tore at the thick envelope with clumsy fingers. The smell of the place had reawakened his hunger, and his head was aching violently.

Three objects fell out upon the table; two pound notes and an engraved correspondence card. He stared at the card in stupefaction:

Mr. Albert Campion

At Home

—and underneath, in the now familiar square handwriting:

Any evening after twelve.

Improving Conversation.

Beer, Light Wines, and Little Pink Cakes.

Do come.

The address was engraved:

17, Bottle Street, W1

(Entrance on left by Police Station).

Scribbled on the back were the words: "Please forgive crude temporary loan. Come along as soon as you can. It's urgent. Take care. A.C."

Val Gyrth turned the card over and over.

The whole episode was becoming fantastic. There was a faintly nonsensical, Alice-through-the-Looking-Glass air about it all, and it did just cross his mind that he might have been involved in a street accident and the adventure be the result of a merciful anaesthetic.

He was still examining the extraordinary message when the gloomy but also slightly fantastic Mr. Lugg appeared with what was evidently his personal idea of a banquet. Gyrth ate what was set before him with a growing sense of gratitude and reality. When he had finished he looked up at the man who was still standing beside him.

"I say," he said, "have you ever heard of a Mr. Albert Campion?" The man's small eyes regarded him solemnly. "Sounds familiar," he said. "I can't say as I place 'im, though." There was a stubborn blankness in his face which told the boy that further questioning would be useless. Once again Gyrth took up the card and the two bank-notes.

"How do you know," he said suddenly, "that I am the man to receive this letter?"

Mr. Lugg looked over his shoulder at the second envelope. "That's yer name, ain't it?" he said. "It's the name inside yer suit, any'ow. You showed me."

"Yes, I know," said Val patiently. "But how do you know that I am the Percival St. John Wykes Gyrth—?"

"Gawd! It don't stand for all that, do it?" said Mr. Lugg, impressed. "That answers yer own question, my lad. There ain't two mothers 'oo'd saddle a brat with that lot. That's your invitation ticket all right. Don't you worry. I should 'op it—it's gettin' late."

Gyrth considered the card again. It was mad, of course. And yet he had come so far that it seemed illogical not to go on. As though to clinch the matter with himself he paid for his food out of his new-found wealth, and after tipping his host prodigally he bade the man good-night and walked out of the deserted eating-house.

It was not until he was outside the door and standing on the pavement that the problem of transportation occurred to him. It was a good three miles across the city to Piccadilly, and although his hunger was sated he was still excessively tired. To make the situation more uncomfortable it was very late and the rain had come in a sullen downpour.

While he stood hesitating, the sound of wheels came softly behind him.

"Taxi, sir?"

Gyrth turned thankfully, gave the man the address on the card, and climbed into the warm leather depths of the cab.

As he sank back among the cushions the old feeling of well-being stole over him. The cab was speeding over the glistening roads along which he had trudged so wearily less than an hour before. For some minutes he reflected upon the extraordinary invitation he had accepted so unquestioningly. The ridiculous card read like a hoax, of course, but two pounds are not a joke to a starving man, and since he had nothing to lose he saw no reason why he should not investigate it. Besides, he was curious.

He took the card out of his pocket and bent forward to read it by the light from the meter lamp. He could just make out the scribbled message: "Come along as soon as you can. It's urgent. Take care."

The last two words puzzled him. In the circumstances they seemed so ridiculous that he almost laughed.

It was at that precise moment that the cab turned to the right in Gray's Inn Road and he caught a glimpse of a quiet tree-lined Bloomsbury Square. Then, and not until then, did it dawn upon him with a sudden throb and quickening of his pulse that the chance of picking up a taxi accidentally at three o'clock in the morning in Wembley Road, Clerkenwell was one in a million, and secondly, that the likelihood of any ordinary cabman mistaking him in his present costume for a potential fare was nothing short of an absurdity. He bent forward and ran his hand along the doors. There were no handles. The windows too appeared to be locked.

Considerably startled, but almost ashamed of himself for suspecting a danger for which he was hardly eligible, he rapped vigorously on the window behind the driver.

Even as Gyrth watched him, the man bent over his wheel and trod heavily on the accelerator.

CHAPTER TWO

Little Pink Cakes

Val sat forward in the half-darkness and peered out. The old cab was, he guessed, travelling all out at about thirty-five miles an hour. The streets were rain-swept and deserted and he recognized that he was being carried directly out of his way.

On the face of it he was being kidnapped, but this idea was so ridiculous in his present condition that he was loth to accept it. Deciding that the driver must be drunk or deaf, he thundered again on the glass and tried shouting down the speaking tube.

"I want Bottle Street—off Piccadilly."

This time he had no doubt that his driver heard him, for the man jerked his head in a negative fashion and the cab rocked and swayed dangerously. Val Gyrth had to accept the situation, absurd though it might be. He was a prisoner being borne precipitately to an unknown destination.

During the past eighteen months he had discovered himself in many unpleasant predicaments, but never one that called for such immediate action. At any other time he might have hesitated until it was too late, but to-night the cumulative effects of starvation and weariness had produced in him a dull recklessness, and the mood which had permitted him to follow such a fantastic will-o'-the-wisp as his name on a discarded envelope, and later to accept the hardly conventional invitation of the mysterious Mr. Campion, was still upon him. Moreover, the kindly ministrations of Mr. Lugg had revived his strength and with it his temper.

At that moment, hunched up inside the cab, he was a dangerous person. His hands were knotted together, and the muscles of his jaw contracted.

The moment the idea came into his head he put it into execution.

He bent down and removed the heavy shoe with the thin sole, from which the lace had long since disappeared. With this formidable weapon tightly gripped in his hand, he crouched in the body of the cab, holding himself steady by the flower bracket above the spare seats. He was still prodigiously strong, and put all he knew into the blow. His arm crashed down like a machine hammer, smashing through the plate glass and down on to the driver's skull.

Instantly Gyrth dropped on to the mat, curling himself up, his arms covering his head. The driver's thick cap had protected him considerably, but the attack was so sudden that he lost control of his wheel. The cab skidded violently across the greasy road, mounted the pavement and smashed sickeningly into a stone balustrade.

The impact was terrific: the car bounded off the stonework, swayed for an instant and finally crashed over on to its side.

Gyrth was hurled into the worn hood of the cab, which tore beneath his weight. He was conscious of warm blood trickling down his face from a cut across his forehead, and one of his shoulders was wrenched, but he had been prepared for the trouble and was not seriously injured. He was still angry, still savage. He fought his way out through the torn fabric on to the pavement, and turned for an instant to survey the scene.

His captor lay hidden beneath the mass of wreckage and made no sound. But the street was no longer deserted. Windows were opening and from both ends of the road came the sound of voices and hurrying footsteps.

Gyrth was in no mood to stop to answer questions. He wiped the blood from his face with his coat-sleeve and was relieved to find that the damage was less messy than he had feared. He slipped on the shoe, which he still gripped, and vanished like a shadow up a side street.

He finished the rest of his journey on foot.

He went to the address in Bottle Street largely out of curiosity, but principally, perhaps, because he had nowhere else to go. He chose the narrow dark ways, cutting through the older part of Holborn and the redolent alleys of Soho.

Now, for the first time for days, he realized that he was free from that curious feeling of oppression which had vaguely puzzled him. There was no one in the street behind him as he turned from dark corner to lighted thoroughfare and came at last to the cul-de-sac off Piccadilly which is Bottle Street.

The single blue lamp of the Police Station was hardly inviting, but the door of Number Seventeen, immediately upon the left, stood ajar. He pushed it open gingerly.

He was well-nigh exhausted, however, and his shreds of caution had vanished. Consoling himself with the thought that nothing could be worse than his present predicament, he climbed painfully up the wooden steps. After the first landing there was a light and the stairs were carpeted, and he came at last to a full stop before a handsome linenfold oak door. A small brass plate bore the simple legend, "Mr. Albert Campion. The Goods Dept."

There was also a very fine Florentine knocker, which, however, he did not have occasion to use, for the door opened and an entirely unexpected figure appeared in the opening.

A tall thin young man with a pale inoffensive face, and vague eyes behind enormous horn-rimmed spectacles smiled out at him with engaging friendliness. He was carefully, not to say fastidiously, dressed in evening clothes, but the correctness of his appearance was somewhat marred by the fact that in his hand he held a string to which was attached a child's balloon of a particularly vituperant pink.

He seemed to become aware of this incongruous attachment as soon as he saw his visitor, for he made several unsuccessful attempts to hide it behind his back. He held out his hand.

"Doctor Livingstone, I presume?" he said in a well-bred, slightly high-pitched voice.

Considerably startled, Gyrth put out his hand. "I don't know who you are," he began, "but I'm Val Gyrth and I'm looking for a man who calls himself Albert Campion."

"That's all right," said the stranger releasing the balloon, which floated up to the ceiling, with the air of one giving up a tiresome problem. "None genuine without my face on the wrapper. This is me—my door—my balloon. Please come in and have a drink. You're rather late—I was afraid you weren't coming," he went on, escorting his visitor across a narrow hall into a small but exceedingly comfortable sitting-room, furnished and decorated in a curious and original fashion. There were several odd trophies on the walls, and above the mantelpiece, between a Rosenberg dry point and what looked like a page from an original "Dance of Death", was a particularly curious group composed of a knuckle-duster surmounted by a Scotland Yard Rogues' Gallery portrait of a well-known character, neatly framed and affectionately autographed. A large key of a singular pattern completed the tableau.

Val Gyrth sank down into the easy chair his host set for him. This peculiar end to his night's adventure, which in itself had been astonishing enough, had left him momentarily stupefied. He accepted the brandy-and-soda which the pale young man thrust into his hands and began to sip it without question.

It was at this point that Mr. Campion appeared to notice the cut on his visitor's forehead. His concern was immediate.

"So you had a spot of trouble getting here?" he said. "I do hope they didn't play rough."

Val put down his glass, and sitting forward in his chair looked up into his host's face.

"Look here," he said, "I haven't the least idea who you are, and this night's business seems like a fairy tale. I find an envelope addressed to me, open, in the middle of Ebury Square. Out of crazy curiosity I follow it up. At Kemp's eating-house in Clerkenwell I find a letter waiting for me from you, with two pounds in it and an extraordinary invitation card. I get in a taxi to come here and the man tries to shanghai me. I scramble out of that mess with considerable damage to myself, and more to the driver, and when I get here I find you apparently quite *au fait* with my affairs and fooling about with a balloon. I may be mad—I don't know."

Mr. Campion looked hurt. "I'm sorry about the balloon," he said. "I'd just come back from a gala at the Athenaeum, when Lugg phoned to say you were coming. He's out to-night, so I had to let you in myself. I don't see that you can grumble about that. The taxi sounds bad. That's why you were late, I suppose?"

"That's all right," said Val, who was still ruffled. "But it must be obvious to you that I want an explanation, and you know very well that you owe me one."

It was then that Mr. Campion stepped sideways so that the light from the reading-lamp on the table behind him shone directly upon his visitor's face. Then he cleared his throat and spoke with a curious deliberation quite different from his previous manner.

"*I see you take the long road, Mr. Gyrth,*" he said quietly.

Val raised his eyes questioningly to his host's face. It was the second time that night that the simple remark had been made to him, and each time there had been this same curious underlying question in the words.

He stared at his host blankly, but the pale young man's slightly vacuous face wore no expression whatsoever, and his eyes were obscured behind the heavy spectacles. He did not stir, but stood there clearly waiting a reply, and in that instant the younger man caught a glimpse of waters running too deep for him to fathom.

CHAPTER THREE

The Fairy Tale

Val Gyrth rose to his feet.

"The man at Kemp's said that to me," he said. "I don't know what it means—since it's obvious that it must mean something. What do you expect me to say?"

Mr. Campion's manner changed instantly. He became affable and charming. "Do sit down," he said. "I owe you an apology. Only, you see, I'm not the only person who's interested in you—I shall have to explain my interest, by the way. But if my rival firm got hold of you first—"

"Well?" said Val.

"Well," said Mr. Campion, "you might have understood about the Long Road. However, now that we can talk, suppose I unbosom myself—unless you'd like to try a blob of iodine on that scalp of yours?"

Val hesitated, and his host took his arm. "A spot of warm water and some nice lint out of my Militia Red Cross Outfit will settle that for you," he said. "No one can be really absorbed by a good story if he's got gore trickling into his eyes. Come on."

After ten minutes' first-aid in the bathroom they returned once more to the study, and Mr. Campion refilled his guest's glass. "In the first place," he said, "I think you ought to see this page out of last week's *Society Illustrated*. It concerns you in a way."

He walked across the room, and unlocking a drawer in a Queen Anne bureau, returned almost immediately with a copy of the well-known weekly. He brushed over the pages and folded the magazine at a large full-page portrait of a rather foolish-looking woman of fifty odd, clad in a modern adaptation of a medieval gown, and holding in her clasped hand a chalice of arresting design. A clever photographer had succeeded in directing the eye of the beholder away from the imperfections of the sitter by focusing his attention upon the astoundingly beautiful object she held.

About eighteen inches high, it was massive in design, and consisted of a polished gold cup upon a jewelled pedestal. Beneath the portrait there were a few lines of letterpress.

"A Lovely Priestess", ran the headline, and underneath:

"*Lady Pethwick, who before her marriage to the late Sir Lionel Pethwick was, of course, Miss Diana Gyrth, is the sister of Col. Sir Percival Gyrth, Bt., owner of the historic 'Tower' at Sanctuary in Suffolk, and keeper of the ageless Gyrth Chalice. Lady Pethwick is here seen with the precious relic, which is said to date from before the Conquest. She is also the proud possessor of the honorary title of 'Maid of the Cuppe'. The Gyrths hold the custody of the Chalice as a sacred family charge. This is the first time it has ever been photographed. Our readers may remember that it is of the Gyrth Tower that the famous story of the Secret Room is told.*"

Val Gyrth took the paper with casual curiosity, but the moment he caught sight of the photograph he sprang to his feet and stood towering in Mr. Campion's small room, his face crimson and his intensely blue eyes narrowed and appalled. As he tried to read the inscription his hand shook so violently that he was forced to set the paper on the table and decipher it from there. When he had finished he straightened himself and faced his host. A new dignity seemed to have enveloped him in spite of his ragged clothes and generally unkempt appearance.

"Of course," he said gravely, "I quite understand. You're doing this for my father. I ought to go home."

Mr. Campion regarded his visitor with mild surprise.

"I'm glad you feel like that," he said. "But I'm not assisting your father, and I had no idea you'd feel so strongly about this piece of bad taste."

Val snorted. "Bad taste?" he said. "Of course, you're a stranger, and you'll appreciate how difficult it is for me to explain how we"—he hesitated—"regard the Chalice." He lowered his voice upon the last word instinctively.

Mr. Campion coughed. "Look here," he said at last, "if you could unbend a little towards me I think I could interest you extremely. For Heaven's sake sit down and be a bit human."

The young man smiled and dropped back into his chair, and just for a moment his youth was apparent in his face.

"Sorry," he said, "but I don't know who you are. Forgive me for harping on this," he added awkwardly, "but it does make it difficult, you know. You see, we never mention the Chalice at home. It's one of these tremendously important things one never talks about. The photograph knocked me off my balance. My father must be crazy, or—" He sat up, a sudden gleam of apprehension coming into his eyes. "Is he all right?"

The pale young man nodded. "Perfectly, I believe," he said. "That photograph was evidently taken and given to the Press without his knowledge. I expect there's been some trouble about it."

"I bet there has." Val spoke grimly. "Of course, you would hardly understand, but this is sacrilege." A flush spread over his face which Mr. Campion realized was shame.

Gyrth sat huddled in his chair, the open paper on his knee. Mr. Campion sighed, and perching himself upon the edge of the table began to speak.

"Look here," he said, "I'm going to give you a lesson in economics, and then I'm going to tell you a fairy tale. All I ask you to do is to listen to me. I think it will be worth your while."

Val nodded. "I don't know who you are," he said, "but fire away."

Mr. Campion grinned. "Hear my piece, and you shall have my birth certificate afterwards if you want it. Sit back, and I'll go into details."

Val leant back in his chair obediently and Mr. Campion bent forward, a slightly more intelligent expression than usual upon his affable, ineffectual face.

"I don't know if you're one of these merchants who study psychology and economics and whatnot," he began, "but if you are you must have noticed that there comes a point when, if you're only wealthy enough, nothing else matters except what you happen to want at the moment. I mean you're above trifles like law and order and who's going to win the Boat Race." He hesitated. Val seemed to understand. Mr. Campion continued.

"Well," he said, "about fifty years ago half a dozen of the wealthiest men in the world—two Britons, an American, two Spaniards, and a Frenchman—made this interesting discovery with regard to the collection of *objets d'art*. They each had different hobbies, fortunately, and they all had the divine mania."

Once again he paused. "This is where the lesson ends and the fairy story begins. Once upon a time six gentlemen found that they could buy almost anything they wanted for their various collections, of which they were very fond. Then one of them, who was a greedy fellow, started wanting things that couldn't be bought, things so valuable that eminent philanthropists had given them to museums. Also national relics of great historical value. Do you follow me?"

Gyrth nodded. "I don't see where it's leading," he said, "but I'm listening."

"The first man," continued Mr. Campion, "whom we will call Ethel because that was obviously not his name, said to himself: 'Ethel, you would like that portrait of Marie Antoinette which is in the Louvre, but it is not for sale, and if you tried to buy it very likely there would be a war, and you would not be so rich as you are now. There is only one way, therefore, of getting this beautiful picture.' So he said to his servant George, who was a genius but a bad lot, I regret to say: 'What do you think, George?' And George thought it could be stolen if sufficient money was forthcoming, as he knew just the man who was famous for his clever thieving. And that," went on Mr. Campion, his slightly absurd voice rising in his enthusiasm, "is how it all began."

Gyrth sat up. "You don't expect me to take this seriously, do you?" he said.

"Listen," said his host sharply, "that's all I'm asking you. When Ethel had got the picture, and the police of four countries were looking everywhere for it except in Ethel's private collection at his country house, where they didn't go because he was an Important Person, Evelyn, a friend of his who was as wealthy as he was, and a keen collector of ceramics, came to Ethel's house, and Ethel could not resist the temptation of showing him the picture. Well, Evelyn was more than impressed. 'How did you get it?' he said. 'If you can get your picture of Marie Antoinette, why should I not obtain the Ming vase which is in the British Museum, because I am as rich as you?'

" 'Well,' said Ethel, 'as you are a friend of mine and will not blackmail me, because you are too honourable for that, I will introduce you to my valet George, who might arrange it for you.' And he did. And George did arrange it, only this time he went to another thief who was at the top of his class for stealing vases. Then Evelyn was very pleased and could not help telling his friend Cecil, who was a king in a small way and a collector of jewels in a large way. And of course, in the end they went to George and the thing happened all over again.

"After fifty years," said Campion slowly, "quite a lot of people who were very rich had employed George and George's successor, with the result that there is to-day quite a number of wealthy Ethels and Cecils and Evelyns. They are hardly a society, but perhaps they could be called a ring—the most powerful and the most wealthy ring in the world. You see, they are hardly criminals," he went on, "in the accepted sense. It is George, and George's friends, who meet the trouble when there is any, and they also pocket all the money.

"Besides, they never touch anything that can be bought in the open market. They are untouchable, the Ethels and the Cecils, because (a) they are very important people, and (b) nobody but George and George's successor ever knows where the treasures go. That is the strength of the whole thing. Now do you see what I mean?"

As his voice died away the silence in the little room became oppressive. In spite of the lightness of his words he had managed to convey a sense of reality into his story. Gyrth stared at him.

"Is this true?" he said. "It's extraordinary if it is. Almost as extraordinary as the rest of the things that have happened to me to-night. But I don't see how it concerns me."

"I'm coming to that," said Mr. Campion patiently. "But first of all I want you to get it into your head that my little fairy story has one thing only to mitigate its obvious absurdity—it happens to be perfectly true. Didn't the 'Mona Lisa' disappear on one occasion, turning up after a bit in most fishy circumstances? If you think back, several priceless, unpurchasable treasures have vanished from time to time; all things, you will observe, without any marketable value on account of their fame."

"I suppose some of the original members of—of this 'ring' died?" said Gyrth, carried away in spite of himself by the piquancy of the story.

"Ah," said Mr. Campion, "I was coming to that too. During the last fifty years the percentage of millionaires has gone up considerably. This little circle of wealthy collectors has grown. Just after the War the membership numbered about twenty, men of all races and colours, and the organization which had been so successful for a small number got a bit swamped. It was at this point that one of the members, an organizing genius, a man whose name is famous over three continents, by the way, took the thing in hand and set down four or five main maxims: pulled the thing together, and put it on a business basis, in fact. So that the society, or whatever you like to call it—it has no name that I know of—is now practically omnipotent in its own sphere."

He paused, allowing his words to sink in, and rising to his feet paced slowly up and down the room.

"I don't know the names of half the members," he said. "I can't tell you the names of those I do know. But when I say that neither Scotland Yard, the Central Office, nor the Sûreté will admit a fact that is continually cropping up under their noses, you'll probably see that Ethel and his friends are pretty important people. Why, if the thing was exposed there'd be a scandal which would upset at least a couple of thrones and jeopardize the governments of four or five powers."

Gyrth set his glass down on a small book-table beside him. "It's a hell of a tale," he said, "but I think I believe you."

The pale young man shot him a grateful smile. "I'm so glad," he said. "It makes the rest of our conversation possible."

Val frowned. "I don't see *how* they did it," he said, ignoring Campion's last remark. "The George in your fairy story: how did he set about it?"

Campion shrugged his shoulders. "That was easy enough," he said. "It was so simple. That's where the original gentleman's gentleman was so clever. That's what's made the business what it is to-day. He simply set himself up as a 'fence', and let it be known in the right quarter he would pay a fabulous sum for the article indicated. I dare say it sounds rather like a 'Pre-Raffleite' Brotherhood to you," he added cheerfully. "But you must take Uncle Albert's word for it. They pay their money and they take their choice."

Gyrth sighed. "It's extraordinary," he said. "But where do I come in? I'm not a famous crook," he added, laughing. "I'm afraid I couldn't pinch anything for you."

Mr. Campion shook his head. "You've got me all wrong," he said. "I do *not* belong to the firm. Don't you see why I've got you here?"

Val looked at him blankly for a moment, and then a wave of understanding passed over his face and he looked at Campion with eyes that were frankly horrified.

"Good heavens!" he said, "the Chalice!"

Mr. Campion slipped off the table. "Yes," he said gravely, "it's the Chalice."

"But that's impossible!" A moment's reflexion had convinced Val of the absurdity of any such suggestion. "I won't discuss it," he went on. "Hang it all! You're a stranger. You don't know—you can't know the absurdity of a story like this."

"My dear chump," said Campion patiently, "you can't protect anything unless you accept the reality of its danger. I've spent the last two weeks trying to find you because I happen to know for a fact that unless you do something the Gyrth Chalice will be in the private collection of a particularly illustrious Mohammedan within six months from to-day."

For a moment the boy was speechless. Then he laughed. "My dear sir," he said, "you're mad."

Mr. Campion was hurt. "Have it your own way," he said. "But who do you suppose went to the length of trying to kidnap you in a taxi? Why do you imagine there are at least four gentlemen at present watching my front door? You'll probably see them if you care to look."

The young man was still incredulous, but considerably startled. All the vagueness had for a moment vanished from his host's manner. Mr. Campion was alert, eager, almost intelligent.

Val shook his head.

"You're not serious," he said.

Campion took off his spectacles and looked his visitor straight in the eyes.

"Now, listen, Val Gyrth," he said. "You've got to believe me. I'm not nearly so ignorant of the position that the Gyrth Chalice holds in your family, *and in the country*, as you imagine. By warning you I am placing myself at direct variance with one of the most powerful organizations in the world. By offering you my assistance I am endangering my life." He paused, but went on again immediately after.

"Would you like me to tell you of the ceremony connected with the Chalice? Of the visits of the King's Chamberlain every ten years which have taken place regularly ever since the Restoration? Or of the deed by which your entire family possessions are forfeit to the Crown should the Chalice be lost? There's a great deal more I could tell you. According to your family custom you come of age on your twenty-fifth birthday, when there is a ceremony in the East Wing of the Tower. You'll have to go to Sanctuary for that."

Val took a deep breath. The last barriers of his prejudice were down. There was something in his host's sudden change from the inane to the fervent which was extraordinarily convincing.

Mr. Campion, who was pacing rapidly up and down the room, now turned.

"However you look at it, I think you and your family are in for a pretty parroty time. That's why I looked you up. 'Ethel' and his friends are after the Chalice. And they'll get it unless we do something."

Val was silent for some minutes, surveying his host with critical eyes. His colour had heightened, and the heavy muscles at the side of his jaw beneath his stubbly beard were knotted.

"The swine!" he said suddenly. "Of course, if this comes off it'll mean the end of us. As you know so much you must realize that this relic is the reason for our existence. We're one of the oldest families in England. Yet we take no part in politics or anything else much, simply devoting ourselves to the preservation of the Chalice."

He stopped dead and glanced at his host, a sudden suggestion of suspicion in his eye.

"Why are you interesting yourself in this affair?" he demanded.

Mr. Campion hesitated. "It's rather difficult to explain," he said. "I am—or rather I was—a sort of universal uncle, a policeman's friend, and master-crook's factotum. What it really boiled down to, I suppose, is that I used to undertake other people's adventures for them at a small fee. If necessary I can give you references from Scotland Yard, unofficial, of course, or from almost any other authority you might care to mention. But last year my precious uncle, His Grace the Bishop of Devizes, the only one of the family who's ever appreciated me, by the way, died and left me the savings of an episcopal lifetime. Having become a capitalist, I couldn't very well go on with my fourpence-an-hour business, so that I've been forced to look for suitable causes to which I could donate a small portion of my brains and beauty. That's one reason.

"Secondly, if you'll respect my confidence, I have a slightly personal interest in the matter. I've been practically chucked out by my family. In fact most of it is under the impression that I went to the Colonies ten years ago . . ."

Gyrth stopped him. "When you took off your spectacles a moment ago," he said, "you reminded me of . . ."

Mr. Campion's pale face flushed. "Shall we leave it at that?" he suggested.

A wave of understanding passed over the boy's face. He poured himself out another drink.

"I hope you don't mind," he said, "but you've treated me to a series of shocks and opened a bit of a chasm beneath my feet. You're a bit hard to swallow, you know, especially after the way you hooked me in here. How did you do it?"

"Conjuring," said Mr. Campion simply and unsatisfactorily. "It's all done with mirrors. As a matter of fact," he went on, becoming suddenly grave, "I've been looking for you for a fortnight. And when I spotted you I couldn't approach you, because 'George's' friends were interested in you as well, and I didn't want to put my head in a hornet's nest. You see, they know me rather better than I know them."

"I was followed?" said Val. "What on earth for?"

"Well, they wanted to get hold of you, and so did I," said Mr. Campion. "If a friend of mine had tapped you on the shoulder and led you into a pub, one of 'George's' friends would have come too. You had to come to me of your own volition, or apparently so. That explains why my people had to drop a score of envelopes under your nose before you'd rise to the bait. Lugg's been spending his evenings at Kemp's for the last fortnight. He's my man, by the way.

"You see," he added apologetically, "I had to get you to go down to Clerkenwell first just to make sure they hadn't already approached you. I fancy they wanted to see you in slightly more desperate straits before they came forward with their proposition." He paused and looked at his visitor. "Do you follow me?" he said.

"I'm trying to," said Gyrth valiantly. "But I don't see why they should want to get hold of me. Here am I, completely penniless. I'm no use to anyone. I can't even get a job."

"That," said the pale young man gravely, "is where we come to a personal and difficult matter. You are—estranged from your father?"

Val nodded, and the obstinate lines round his mouth hardened. "That's true," he said.

Mr. Campion bent forward to attend to the fire. "My dear young sir," he said, "as I told you, the practice of these collectors is to employ the most suitable agent for the job on hand. And although it might be perfectly obvious to anyone who knew you that the chance of buying your services was about as likely as my taking up barbola work, the dark horse who's taken on this job obviously hasn't realized this. Some people think a starving man will sell anything."

Val exploded wrathfully. The young man waited until the paroxysm was over and then spoke mildly.

"Quite," he said. "Still, that explains it, doesn't it?"

Val nodded. "And the 'long road'?" he said.

"A form of salutation between 'George's' friends."

Val sighed. "It's incredible," he said. "I'll put myself in your hands if I may. What are we going to do? Call in the police?"

Campion dropped into a chair beside his kinsman. "I wish we could," he said. "But you see our difficulty there. If we call in the police when nothing has been stolen they won't be very sympathetic, and they won't hang about indefinitely. Once the treasure has been stolen it will pass almost immediately into the hands of people who are untouchable. It wouldn't be fair do's for the policemen. I have worked for Scotland Yard in my time. One of my best friends is a big Yard man. He'll do all he can to help us, but you see the difficulties of the situation."

Val passed a hand over his bandaged forehead. "What happens next?" he said.

Mr. Campion reflected. "You have to patch things up with your father," he said quietly. "I suppose you've realized that?"

The boy smiled faintly. "It's funny how a single piece of information can make the thing that was worth starving for this morning seem small," he said. "I knew I should have to go down to Sanctuary in July. I'm twenty-five on the second. But I meant to come away again. I don't know how we're going to put this to Father. And yet," he added, a sudden blank expression coming into his face, "if this is true, what can we do? We can't fight a ring like this for ever. It's incredible; they're too strong."

"There," said Mr. Campion, "is the point which resolves the whole question into a neat 'what should A do?' problem. We've got just one chance, old bird, otherwise the project would not be worth fighting and we should not have met. The rules of this acquisitive society of friends are few, but they are strict. Roughly, what they amount to is this: all members' commissions—they have to be for things definitely unpurchasable, of course—are treated with equal deference, the best agent is chosen for the job, unlimited money is supplied, and there the work of 'George' and 'Ethel' ends until the treasure is obtained." He paused and looked steadily at the young man before him. "However—and this is our one loophole—should the expert whom they have chosen meet his death in the execution of his duty—I mean, should the owner of the treasure in question kill him to save it—then they leave well alone and look out for someone else's family album."

"If he's caught—?" began Val dubiously.

Mr. Campion shrugged his shoulders. "If he's caught he takes the consequences. Who on earth would believe him if he squealed? No, in that case the society lets him take his punishment and employs someone else. That's quite understandable. It's only if their own personal employee gets put out that they get cold feet. Not that the men they employ mind bloodshed," he added hastily. "The small fry— burglars, thugs, and homely little forgers—may die like flies. 'George' and 'Ethel' don't have anything to do with that. It's if their own agent gets knocked on the head that they consider that the matter is at an end, so to speak." He was silent.

"Who is the agent employed to get the Chalice?" said Gyrth abruptly.

Mr. Campion's pale eyes behind his heavy spectacles grew troubled. "That's the difficulty," he said. "I don't know. So you see what a mess we're in."

Gyrth rose to his feet and stood looking at Campion in slow horror.

"What you are saying is, in effect, then," he said, "if we want to protect the one thing that's really precious to me and my family, the one thing that must come before everything else with me, we must find out the man employed by this society, and murder him?"

Mr. Campion surveyed his visitor with the utmost gravity.

"Shall we say 'dispose of him'?" he suggested gently.

CHAPTER FOUR

Brush with the County

"The last time I come past 'ere," said Mr. Lugg sepulchrally, from the back of the car, "it was in a police van. I remember the time because I was in for three months hard. The joke was on the Beak, though. I was the wrong man as it 'appened, and that alibi was worth something, I can tell yer."

Campion, at the wheel, spoke without turning. "I wish you'd shut up, Lugg," he said. "We may be going to a house where they have real servants. You'll have to behave."

"Servants?" said Mr. Lugg indignantly. "I'm the gent's gent of this outfit, let me tell yer, and I'm not taking any lip. Mr. Gyrth knows 'oo I am. I told 'im I'd been a cut-throat when I shaved 'im this morning."

Val, seated beside Campion in the front, chuckled. "Lugg and Branch, my pater's old butler, ought to get on very well together," he said. "Branch had a wild youth, I believe, although of course his family have looked after us for years."

"'Is other name ain't Roger, by any chanst?" Mr. Lugg's voice betrayed a mild interest. "A little thin bloke with a 'ooked nose—talked with a 'orrible provincial accent?"

"That's right." Val turned round in his seat, amused surprise on his face. "Do you know him?"

Lugg sniffed and nodded. "The Prince of Parkhurst, we used to call 'im, I remember," he said, and dismissed the subject of conversation.

Val turned to Campion. "You are a fantastic pair," he said.

"Not at all," said the pale young man at the wheel. "Since we learned to speak French we can take our place in any company without embarrassment. They ought to quote Lugg's testimonial. I know he wrote 'em."

Val laughed, and the talk languished for a minute or so. They were speeding down the main Colchester road, some thirty-six hours after Gyrth had stumbled into Mr. Campion's flat off Piccadilly. Reluctantly he had allowed himself to be equipped and valeted by his host and the invaluable Lugg, and he looked a very different person from the footsore and unkempt figure he had then appeared. After his first interview with Campion he had put himself unreservedly into that extraordinary young man's hands.

Their departure from London had not been without its thrills. He had been smuggled out of the flat down a service lift into an exclusive restaurant facing into Regent Street, and thence had been spirited away in the Bentley at a reckless speed. He could not doubt that, unless his host proved to be a particularly convincing lunatic, there was genuine danger to be faced.

Mr. Campion's mild voice cut in upon his thoughts.

"Without appearing unduly curious," he ventured, "I should like to know if you anticipate any serious difficulty in getting all friendly with your parent. It seems to me an important point just now."

The boy shook his head. "I don't think so," he said. "It has really been my own pigheadedness that has kept me from going back ever since—" He broke off, seeming unwilling to finish the sentence.

Mr. Campion opened his mouth, doubtless to make some tactful reply, when he was forestalled by the irrepressible Lugg.

"If it's anything about a woman, you can tell 'im. 'E's been disappointed 'imself," he observed lugubriously.

Mr. Campion sat immovable, his face a complete blank. They were passing through one of the many small country towns on the road, and he swung the car to the side before an elaborately restored old Tudor inn.

"The inner Campion protests," he said. "We must eat. You go and lose yourself, Lugg."

"All right," said Mr. Lugg. He was very much aware of his *gaffe*, and had therefore adopted a certain defiance. "Whilst you're messing about with 'the Motorist's Lunch'—seven and a kick and coffee extra—I'll go and get something to eat in the bar. It's mugs like you wot changes 'The Blue Boar' into 'Ye Olde Stuck Pigge for Dainty Teas'."

He lumbered out of the car, opening the door for Campion but not troubling to stand and hold it. His employer looked after him with contempt.

"Buffoon," he said. "That's the trouble with Lugg. He's always got the courage of his previous convictions. He used to be quite one of the most promising burglars, you know. We'll go in and see what the good brewery firm has to offer."

Val followed the slender, slightly ineffectual figure down the two steps into the cool brick-floored dining-room, which a well-meaning if not particularly erudite management had rendered a little more Jacobean than the Jacobeans. The heavily carved oak beams which supported the ceiling had been varnished to an ebony blackness and the open fireplace at the end of the room was a mass of rusty spits and dogs, in a profusion which would have astonished their original owners.

"That spot looks good for browsing," said Mr. Campion, indicating a table in an alcove some distance from the other patrons.

As Val seated himself he glanced round him a little apprehensively. He was not anxious to encounter any old acquaintances. Mr. Campion looked about also, though for a different reason. But the few people who were still lunching were for the most part cheerful, bovine persons more interested in *The East Anglian* and their food than in their neighbours.

Mr. Campion frowned. "If only I knew," he said, "who they'll choose to do their dirty work."

Val bent forward. "Any fishy character in the vicinity ought to come in for a certain amount of suspicion," he murmured. "The natives don't get much beyond poaching."

The pale young man at his side did not smile. "I know," he said. "That makes it worse. I flatter myself that our grasping friends will do me the honour of picking on a stranger to do their homework for them. I'm afraid it may even be amateur talent, and that's usually illogical, so you never know where you are. I say, Val," he went on, dropping his voice, "to put a personal question, is your Aunt Diana—er—Caesar's wife, what? I mean you don't think they could approach her with flattery and guile?"

Val frowned. "My Aunt Diana," he said softly, "treats herself like a sort of vestal virgin. She's lived at the Cup House—that's on the estate, you know—ever since Uncle Lionel died, and since Father was a widower she rather took it upon herself to boss the show a bit. Penny has a dreadful time with her, I believe."

"Penny?" inquired Mr. Campion.

"My sister Penelope," Val explained. "One of the best."

Mr. Campion made a mental note of it. "To return to your aunt," he said, "I'm sorry to keep harping on this but is she—er—batty?"

Val grinned. "Not certifiable," he said. "But she's a silly, slightly conceited woman who imagines she's got a heart; and she's made copy out of that 'Maid of the Cup' business. Until her time that part of the ceremonial had been allowed to die down a bit. She looked it up in the records and insisted on her rights. She's a strong-minded person, and Father puts up with her, I think, to keep her quiet."

Mr. Campion looked dubious. "This 'Maid of the Cup' palaver," he said. "What is it exactly? I've never heard of it."

The young man reflected. "Oh, it's quite simple," he said at last. "Apparently in medieval times, when the menfolk were away fighting, the eldest daughter of the house was supposed to remain unmarried and to shut herself up in the Cup House and attend to the relic. Naturally this practice fell into abeyance when times got more peaceful, and that part of the affair had been obsolete until Aunt Diana hunted it all up as soon as she became a widow. She set herself up with the title complete. Father was annoyed, of course, but you can't stop a woman like that."

"No-o," said Mr. Campion. "Any other peculiarities?"

"Well, she's bitten by the quasi-mystical cum 'noo-art' bug, or used to be before I went away," Val went on casually. "Wears funny clothes and wanders about at night communing with the stars and disturbing the game. Quite harmless, but rather silly. I should think that if anyone put a fishy suggestion up to her she'd scream the place down and leave it at that."

A decrepit waiter brought them the inevitable cold roast beef and pickles of the late luncher, and shuffled away again.

Val seemed inclined to make further confidences. "I don't expect trouble with Father," he said. "You know why I walked out, don't you?"

Mr. Campion looked even more vague than usual. "No," he said. "You got into a row at Cambridge, didn't you?"

"I got married at Cambridge," said Val bitterly. "The usual tale, you know. She was awfully attractive—a Varsity hanger-on. There's a good lot of 'em, I suppose. I phoned the news to Dad. He got angry and halved my allowance, so—" he shrugged his shoulders, "she went off—back to Cambridge."

He paused a little, and added awkwardly: "You don't mind my telling you all this, do you? But now you're in it I feel I ought to tell you everything. Well, I came back to Sanctuary, and Hepplewhite, Dad's solicitor, was fixing up the necessary legal separation guff when I had a letter from her. She was ill, and in an awful state in London. Dad was bitter, but I went up and looked after her by selling up my flat and one thing and another, until she died. There was a filthy row at the time and I never went back. Hepplewhite tried to get hold of me several times for the old boy, but I wouldn't see him. Rather a hopeless sort of tale, I'm afraid, but you can see how it happened. Women always seem to muck things up," he added a trifle self-consciously.

Mr. Campion considered. "Oh, I don't know," he said, and then was silent.

They had been so engrossed in their conversation that they had not noticed a certain commotion at the far end of the room as a woman entered and saluted one or two acquaintances as she passed to her table. It was only when her high strident voice had drowned the subdued conversation in the room that the young men in the secluded corner observed her.

She was of a type not uncommon among the "landed gentry," but mercifully rare elsewhere. Superbly self-possessed, she was slightly masculine in appearance, with square flat shoulders and narrow hips. Her hair was cut short under her mannish felt, her suit was perfectly tailored and the collar of her blouse fitted tightly at her throat.

She managed to enter the room noisily and sat down so that her face was towards them. It was a handsome face, but one to which the epithet of "beautiful" would have seemed absurd. She was pale, with a strong prominent nose and hard closely-set blue-grey eyes. She hurled a miscellaneous collection of gloves, scarves, and papers into the chair in front of her and called loudly to the waiter.

It was evident that she was a personage, and that vague sense of uneasiness which invariably steals upon a room full of people when a celebrity is present was apparent in the stolid dining-room. Val averted his face hastily.

"Oh, Lord!" he said.

Mr. Campion raised his eyebrows. "Who is the rude lady?" he inquired casually.

Val lowered his voice. "Mrs. Dick Shannon," he muttered. "Surely you've heard of her? She's got a racing stable on Heronhoe Heath.

One of these damn women-with-a-personality. She knows me, too. Could you wriggle in front of me, old man? She's got an eye like a hawk."

Mr. Campion did his best, but as they rose to go, their path to the door led them directly past her table. His protégé was quick, but he was not quick enough.

"Val Gyrth!" The name was bellowed through the room until Mrs. Dick Shannon's victim felt as though the entire township must have heard it. The woman caught the boy's coat-sleeve and jerked him backward with a wrist like flexed steel.

"So you're back, eh? I didn't know you'd made friends with your father again." This piece of intimate information was also shouted. "When did this happen?" She ignored Mr. Campion with the studied rudeness which is the hall-mark of her type. He hovered for some moments ineffectually, and then drifted out into the corridor to settle the score.

Left unprotected, Val faced his captor and strove to make his excuses. He was quite aware that every ear in the room was strained to catch his reply. Gyrth was a name to conjure with in that part of the country.

Mrs. Dick seemed both aware and contemptuous of her audience. "I've just come down from the Tower," she said. "I'm trying to make your father sell me two yearlings. What does he want with race-horses? I told him he hadn't got the sense to train properly; and that man he's got is a fool. I saw your aunt, too," she went on, not waiting for any comment from him. "She gets sillier every day."

Val gulped and murmured a few incoherent words of farewell. Mrs. Dick gripped his hand and shook it vigorously.

"Well, good-bye. I shall see you again. You can tell your father I'm going to have those yearlings if I have to steal them. He's not capable of training 'em."

The boy smiled politely and a little nervously, and turned away.

"I heard your wife was dead—so sorry," bawled Mrs. Dick for the world to hear. Val fled.

His forehead was glistening with sweat when he came up with Campion on the broad doorstep of the inn.

"Let's get away from here," he said. "I loathe that woman."

" 'I did but see her passing by.' The rest of the song does not apply," said Mr. Campion. "That's her car, I suppose." He indicated a superb red and white Frazer Nash. "Hallo, here comes Lugg, looking like a man with a mission."

At that moment Mr. Lugg appeared from the doorway of the four-ale bar. His lugubrious face was almost animated.

"'Op in," he said huskily as he came up with them. "I got something to tell yer. While you've bin playing the gent, I've bin noticin'.'"

It was not until they were once more packed into the Bentley that he unburdened himself. As they shot out of the town he leant forward from the back seat and breathed heavily into Mr. Campion's ear.

"'Oo d'yer think I saw in the bar?" he mumbled.

"Some low friend of yours, no doubt," said his master, skilfully avoiding a trade van which cut in front of an approaching lorry.

"I should say!" said Lugg heavily. "It was little Natty Johnson, one of the filthiest, dirtiest, lousiest little race-gang toughs I've ever taken off me 'at to."

Mr. Campion pricked up his ears. "The Cleaver Gang?" he said. "Was he with anyone?"

"That's what I'm coming to," said Lugg reproachfully. "You're always 'urrying on, you are. 'E was talking to a funny chap with a beard. An arty bloke. I tell yer wot—'e reminded me of that Bloomsbury lot 'oo came to the flat and sat on the floor and sent me out for kippers and Chianti. They were talkin' nineteen to the dozen, sittin' up by theirselves in the window. I 'ad a bit o' wool in one ear or I'd 'ave 'eard all they was saying.

"'Owever, that's not the reely interestin' part. Where we come in is this. The artist chap, and some more like 'im, is staying at the Tower, Sanctuary. I know, because the barman told me when I was laughin' at 'em. Friends of Lady Pethwick's, they are, 'e said, as if that explained 'em."

Mr. Campion's pale eyes flickered behind his spectacles.

"That's interesting," he said. "And this man—"

"Yes," cut in Mr. Lugg, "'e was talkin' confidential with Natty Johnson. I know first-class dicks 'oo'd arrest 'im fer that."

CHAPTER FIVE

Penny: For Your Thoughts

The village of Sanctuary lay in that part of Suffolk which the railway has ignored and the motorists have not yet discovered. Moreover, the steep-sided valley of which it consisted, with the squat Norman church on one eminence and the Tower on the other, did not lie on the direct route to anywhere, so that no one turned down the narrow cherry-lined lane which was its southern approach unless they had actual business in the village. The place itself was one of those staggering pieces of beauty that made Morland paint in spite of all the noggins of rum in the world.

A little stream ran across the road dividing the two hills; while the cottages, the majority pure Elizabethan, sprawled up each side of the road like sheep asleep in a meadow. It is true that the smithy kept a petrol store housed in a decrepit engine boiler obtained from Heaven knows what dumping ground, but even that had a rustic quality. It was a fairy-tale village peopled by yokels who, if they did not wear the traditional white smocks so beloved of film producers, at least climbed the rough steps to the church on a Sunday morning in top hats of unquestionable antiquity.

The Three Drummers stood crazily with its left side a good two feet lower down the northern hill than its right side. It was of brown unrestored oak and yellow plaster, with latticed windows and a red tiled roof. It had three entrances, the main one to the corridor on the level of the road, the bar parlour up four steps upon the left, and the four-ale down two steps on the right.

It was at about five o'clock, when the whole village was basking in a quiet yellow light, that the Bentley drew up outside the Three Drummers and deposited Val Gyrth and Campion at the centre door. Lugg took the car across the road to the smithy "garage", and the two young men stepped into the cool, sweet-smelling passage. Val had turned up his coat collar.

"I don't want to be spotted just yet," he murmured, "and I'd like a chat with Penny before I see the Governor. If I can get hold of Mrs. Bullock, she'll fix everything."

He tiptoed down the passage and put his head round the door of the kitchen at the far end.

"Bully!" he called softly.

There was a smothered scream and a clatter of pans on a stone floor. The next moment the good lady of the house appeared, a big florid woman in a gaily patterned cotton dress and a large blue apron. Her sleeves were rolled above her plump elbows and her brown hair was flying. She was radiant. She caught the boy by the arm and quite obviously only just prevented herself from embracing him vigorously.

"You've made it up," she said. "I knew you would—your birthday coming and all."

She had a deep resonant voice with very little trace of accent in spite of her excitement.

"Won't you come into the bar and show yourself?—sir," she added as an afterthought.

Val shook his head. "I say, Bully," he said, "things aren't quite settled yet. Could you give my friend Mr. Campion here a room and find us somewhere we can talk? I'd like a note taken up to Penny if possible. How is everyone at the Tower? Do you know?"

Mrs. Bullock, who had sensed the urgency of his request, was wise enough to ask no questions. She had been the faithful friend and confidante of the children at the Tower ever since her early days as cook at that establishment, and their affairs were as always one of her chief concerns.

She led her visitors upstairs to a magnificent old bedroom with a small sitting-room leading out of it.

"You write your note, sir, and I'll bring you up something," she said, throwing open the window to let in the scented evening air. "You were asking about the folk, Mr. Val. Your father's well, but worried looking. And Penny—she's lovely. Oh, I can see your mother in her— same eyes, same walk, same everything."

"And Aunt?" said Val curiously.

Mrs. Bullock snorted. "You'll hear about your aunt soon enough," she said. "Having herself photographed with the Thing." She dropped her eyes on the last word as though she experienced some embarrassment in referring to the Chalice.

"I've heard about that," said Val quietly. "Otherwise—she's all right?"

"Right enough, save that she fills the whole place with a pack of crazy no-goods—strutting about in funny clothes like actors and actresses. Your Ma'll turn in her grave, if she hasn't done that already."

"The artists?" Val suggested.

"Artists? They ain't artists," said Mrs. Bullock explosively. "I know artists. I've 'ad 'em staying here. Quiet tidy little fellows—fussy about their victuals. I don't know what your aunt's got hold of—Bolsheviks, I shouldn't wonder. You'll find paper and pen over there, Mr. Val." And with a rustle of skirts she bustled out of the room.

Val sat down at the square table in the centre of the smaller room and scribbled a few words.

"*Dear Penny,*" he wrote, "*I am up here at 'The Drummers.' Can you come down for a minute? Love, Val.*"

He folded the paper, thrust it in an envelope and went to the top of the oak cupboard staircase. Mrs. Bullock's tousled head appeared round the door at the foot.

"Throw it down," she whispered, "and I'll send young George around with it."

Val went back to Campion. "I say," he said, "what about Lugg? He won't talk, will he?"

Mr. Campion seemed amused. "Not on your life," he said. "Lugg's down in the four-ale with his ears flapping, drinking in local wit and beer."

Val crossed to the window and looked out over the inn garden, a mass of tangled rambler roses and vivid delphiniums stretching down amid high old red walls to the tiny stream which trickled through the village.

"It seems impossible," he said slowly. "Up in your flat the story sounded incredible enough, but down here with everything exactly as it always was, so quiet and peaceful and miles away from anywhere, it's just absurd. By jove, I'm glad to get back."

Mr. Campion did not speak, and at that moment the door opened and Mrs. Bullock returned with a tray on which were two tankards, bread and butter, and a great plate of water-cress.

"It's home-brew," she said confidentially. "I only keep it for ourselves. The stuff the company sends down isn't what it used to be. You can taste the Government's hand in it, I say. I'll send Miss Penny up the moment she comes."

She laid a fat red hand on Val's shoulder as she passed him, an ineffably caressing gesture, and went out, closing the door behind her.

"Here's to the fatted calf," said Mr. Campion, lifting his tankard. "There's something so Olde English about you, Val, that I expect a chorus of rustic maidens with garlands and a neat portable maypole to arrive any moment. Stap me, Sir Percy! Another noggin!"

Val suddenly turned upon his companion, a shadow of suspicion in his eyes. "Look here, Campion," he said, "this isn't some silly theatrical stunt to get me back into the bosom of the family, is it? You're not employed by Hepplewhite, are you?"

Mr. Campion looked hurt. "Oh, no," he said. "I'm my own master now. No more selling my soul to commerce—not while Uncle's money lasts, anyhow. I'm one of these capitalistic toots. Only one in five has it."

Val grinned. "Sorry," he said. "But thinking it over in cold blood, I suppose you know that the Chalice is in the Cup House chapel, and that is burglar-proof. No ordinary thief could possibly touch it."

"No ordinary thief would want to," said Mr. Campion pointedly.

"You seem to have forgotten your fun in the taxicab. I suppose you know you bashed that chap up pretty permanently, and he didn't even mention to the hospital authorities that he had a fare on board? If someone doesn't try to murder one of us every two days you seem to think there's nothing up. Drink up your beer like a good boy, and old Uncle Al will find a nice crook for you to beat up. All I'm worrying about is if they've already got busy while we're hanging about. I say, I wish your sister would come. The Tower isn't far away, is it?"

"It's just up at the top of the hill," said Val. "You can't see it because of the trees. Hold on a moment—I think this is she."

There was a chatter of feminine voices on the staircase. Campion walked over to the bedroom.

"I'll stay here till the touching reunion is over," he said.

"Don't be a fool," said Val testily. He got no further, for the door opened, and not one but two young women came in, with Mrs. Bullock hovering in the background.

At first glance it was easy to pick out Val's sister. Penelope Gyrth was tall like her brother, with the same clear-cut features, the same very blue eyes. Her hair, which was even more yellow than Val's, was bound round her ears in long thick braids. She was hatless, and her white frock was sprinkled with a scarlet pattern. She grinned at her brother, revealing suddenly how extremely young she was.

"Hallo, old dear," she said, and crossing the room slipped her arm through his.

A more unemotional greeting it would have been difficult to imagine, but her delight was obvious. It radiated from her eyes and from her smile.

Val kissed her, and then looked inquiringly at her companion. Penny explained.

"This is Beth," she said. "We were coming down to the post office when young George met us with your note, so I brought her along. Beth, this is my brother, and Val, this is Beth Cairey. Oh, of course, you haven't heard about the Caireys, have you?"

The girl who now came forward was very different from her companion. She was *petite* and vivacious, with jet-black hair sleeked down from a centre parting to a knot at the nape of her neck. Her brown eyes were round and full of laughter, and there was about her an air of suppressed delight that was well-nigh irresistible. She was a few years older than the youthful Penny, who looked scarcely out of her teens.

Mr. Campion was introduced, and there was a momentary awkward pause. A quick comprehending glance passed between him and the elder girl, a silent flicker of recognition, but neither spoke. Penny sensed the general embarrassment and came to the rescue, chattering on breathlessly with youthful exuberance.

"I forgot you didn't know Beth," she said. "She came just after you left. She and her people have taken Tye Hall. They're American, you know. It's glorious having neighbours again—or it would be if Aunt Di hadn't behaved so disgustingly. My dear, if Beth and I hadn't conducted ourselves like respectable human beings there'd be a feud."

Beth laughed. "Lady Pethwick doesn't like strangers," she said, revealing a soft unexpectedly deep voice with just a trace of a wholly delightful New England accent.

Penny was plainly ill at ease. It was evident that she was trying to behave as she fancied her brother would prefer, deliberately forcing herself to take his unexpected return as a matter of course.

Campion watched her curiously, his pale eyes alight with interest behind his huge spectacles. In spite of her gaiety and the brilliance of her complexion there were distinct traces of strain in the faint lines about her eyes and in the nervous twisting of her hands.

Val understood his sister's restraint and was grateful for it. He turned to Beth and stood smiling down at her.

"Aunt Di has always been rather difficult," he said. "I hope Father has made up for any stupidity on her part."

The two girls exchanged glances.

"Father," said Penny, "is sulky about something. You know what a narrow-minded old darling he is. I believe he's grousing about the Professor—that's Beth's father—letting the Gypsies camp in Fox Hollow. It's rather near the wood, you know. It would be just like him to get broody about it in secret and feel injured without attempting to explain."

Beth chuckled. "The Gypsies are Mother's fault," she said. "She thinks they're so picturesque. But four of her leghorns vanished this morning, so I shouldn't wonder if your Dad's grievance would be sent about its business fairly soon."

Val glanced from one to the other of the two girls.

"Look here," he said after a pause, "is everything all right?"

His sister blushed scarlet, the colour mounting up her throat and disappearing into the roots of her hair. Beth looked uncomfortable. Penny hesitated.

"Val, you're extraordinary," she said. "You seem to smell things out like an old pointer. It doesn't matter talking in front of Beth, because she's been the only person that I could talk to down here and she knows everything. There's something awfully queer going on at home."

Mr. Campion had effaced himself. He sat at the table now with an expression of complete inanity on his pale face. Val was visibly startled. This confirmation of his fears was entirely unexpected.

"What's up?" he demanded.

Penny's next remark was hardly reassuring.

"Well, it's the Chalice," she said. There was reluctance in her tone as though she were loth to name the relic. "Of course, I may be just ultra-sensitive, and I don't know why I'm bothering you with all this the moment you arrive, but I've been awfully worried about it. You remember the Cup House chapel has been a sacred place ever since we were kids—I mean it's not a place where we'd take strangers except on the fixed day, is it? Well, just lately Aunt Diana seems to have gone completely mad. She was always indiscreet on the subject, of course, but now—well—" she took a deep breath and regarded her brother almost fearfully—"she was photographed with it. I suppose that's what's brought you home. Father nearly had apoplexy, but she just bullied him."

As Val did not respond, she continued.

"That's not the worst, though. When she was in London last she developed a whole crowd of the most revolting people—a sort of semi-artistic new religion group. They've turned her into a kind of High Priestess and they go about chanting and doing funny exercises in sandals and long white night-gowns. Men, too. It's disgusting. She lets them in to see the Chalice. And one man's making a perfectly filthy drawing of her holding it."

Val was visibly shocked. "And Father?" he said.

Penny shrugged her shoulders. "You can't get anything out of Father," she said. "Since you went he's sort of curled up in his shell and he's more morose than ever. There's something worrying him. He has most of his meals in his room. We hardly ever see him. And, Val"—she lowered her voice—"there was a light in the East Wing last night."

The boy raised his eyebrows in silent question, and she nodded.

Val picked up his coat.

"Look here," he said, "I'll come back with you if you can smuggle me into the house without encountering the visitors." He turned to Campion. "You'll be all right here, won't you?" he said. "I'll come down and fetch you in the morning. We'd better stick to our original arrangement."

Mr. Campion nodded vigorously.

"I must get Lugg into training for polite society," he said cheerfully.

He saw Penny throw a glance of by no means unfriendly curiosity in his direction as he waved the three a farewell from the top of the stairs.

Left to himself he closed the door carefully, and sitting down at the table, he removed his spectacles and extracted two very significant objects from his suitcase, a small but wicked-looking rubber truncheon and an extremely serviceable Colt revolver. From his hip-pocket he produced an exactly similar gun, save in the single remarkable fact that it was constructed to project nothing more dangerous than water. He considered the two weapons gravely.

Finally he sighed and put the toy in the case: the revolver he slipped into his hip-pocket.

CHAPTER SIX

The Storm Breaks

" 'Ere, wot d'you think you're doing?"

Mr. Lugg's scandalized face appeared round the corner of the door.

"Mind your own business," said Campion without looking up. "And, by the way, call me 'sir'."

"You've bin knighted, I suppose?" observed Mr. Lugg, oozing into the room and shutting the door behind him. "I'm glad that chap's gone. I'm sick o' nobs. As soon as I caught a bosso of 'im and 'is 'arem going up that street I come up to see what the 'ell you was up to—sir."

Mr. Campion resumed his spectacles. "You're a disgrace," he said. "You've got to make the 'valet' grade somehow before to-morrow morning. I don't know if you realize it, but you're a social handicap."

"Now then, no 'iding be'ind 'igh school talk," said Mr. Lugg, putting a heavy hand on the table. "Show us what you've got in yer pocket."

Mr. Campion felt in his hip-pocket and produced the revolver obediently.

"I thought so." Mr. Lugg examined the Colt carefully and handed it back to his master with evident contempt. "You know we're up against something. You're as jumpy as a cat. Well, I'm prepared too, in me own way." He thrust his hand in his own pocket and drew out a life-preserver with a well-worn handle. "You don't catch me carryin' a gun. I'm not goin' to swing for any challenge cup that ever was—but then I'm not one of the gentry. And I don't know wot you think you're up to swankin' about the cash your uncle left you. I know it paid your tailor's bill, but only up to nineteen twenty-eight, remember. You'll land us both in regular jobs workin' for a livin' if you're so soft-'earted that you take on dangerous berths for charity."

He was silent for a moment, and then he bent forward. His entire manner had changed and there was unusual seriousness in his little black eyes.

"Sir," he said, with deep earnestness, "let's 'op it."

"My dear fellow," said Mr. Campion with affable idiocy, "I have buttered my bun and now I must lie on it. And you, my beautiful, will stand meekly by. It is difficult, I admit. Gyrth's a delightful chap, but he doesn't know what we're up against yet. After all, you can't expect him to grasp the significance of the Société Anonyme all at once. You're sure that was Natty Johnson?"

"Wot d'you take me for—a private dick?" said Mr. Lugg with contempt. "Of course I saw 'im. As little and as ugly as life. I don't like it."

He glanced about him almost nervously and came a step nearer. "There's something unnatural about this business," he breathed. "I was listenin' down in the bar just now and an old bloke come out with a 'orrible yarn. D'you know they've got a blinkin' two-'eaded monster up at that place?"

"Where?" said Mr. Campion, considerably taken aback.

"Up at the Tower—where we've got to do the pretty. I'm not going to be mixed with the supernatural, I warn yer."

Campion regarded his faithful servitor with interest. "I like your 'fanny'," he said. "But they've been pulling your leg."

"All right, clever," said Mr. Lugg, nettled. "But it's a fac', as it 'appens. They've got a secret room in the east wing containin' some filfy family secret. There's a winder but there's no door, and when the son o' the house is twenty-five 'is father takes 'im in and shows 'im the 'orror, and 'e's never the same again. Like the king that ate the winkles. That's why they leave comin' of age till the boy is old enough to stand the shock." He paused dramatically, and added by way of confirmation: "The bloke 'oo was telling me was a bit tight, and the others was tryin' to shut 'im up. You could see it was the truth—they was so scared. It's bound to be a monster—somethin' you 'ave to feed with a pump."

"Lugg, sit down."

The words were rapped out in a way quite foreign to Mr. Campion's usual manner. Considerably surprised, the big man obeyed him.

"Now, look here," said his employer, grimly, "you've got to forget that, Lugg. Since you know so much you may as well hear the truth. The Gyrths are a family who were going strong about the time that yours were leaping about from twig to twig. And there is, in the east wing of the Tower, I believe, a room which has no visible entrance. The story about the son of the house being initiated into the secret on his twenty-fifth birthday is all quite sound. It's a semi-religious ceremony of the family. But get this into your head. It's nothing to do with us. Whatever the Gyrth's secret is, it's no one's affair but their own, and if you so much as refer to it, even to one of the lowest of the servants, you'll have made an irreparable bloomer, and I won't have you within ten miles of me again."

"Right you are, Guv'nor. Right you are." Mr. Lugg was apologetic and a little nervous. "I'm glad you told me, though," he added. "It fair put the wind up me. There's one or two things, though, that ain't nice 'ere. F'rinstance, when I was comin' acrost out of the garage, a woman put 'er 'ead out the door o' that one-eyed shop next door. She didn't arf give me a turn; she was bald—not just a bit gone on top, yer know, but quite 'airless. I asked about 'er, and they come out with a yarn about witchcraft and 'aunting and cursin' like a set o' 'eathens. There's too much 'anky-panky about this place. I don't believe in it, but I don't like it. They got a 'aunted wood 'ere, and a set o' gippos livin' in a 'ollow. Let's go 'ome."

Mr. Campion regarded his aide owlishly.

"Well, you have been having fun in your quiet way," he said. "You're sure your loquacious friend wasn't a Cook's Guide selling you Rural England by any chance? How much beer did it take you to collect that lot?"

"You'll see when I put in my bill for expenses," said Mr. Lugg unabashed. "What do we do to-night? 'Ave a mike round or stay 'ere?"

"We keep well out of sight," said Mr. Campion. "I've bought you a book of *Etiquette for Upper Servants.* It wouldn't hurt you to study it. You stay up here and do your homework."

"Sauce!" grumbled Mr. Lugg. "I'll go and unpack yer bag. Oh, well, a quiet beginning usually means a quick finish. I'll 'ave a monument put up to you at the 'ead of the grave. A life-size image of yerself dressed as an angel—'orn-rimmed spectacles done in gold."

He lumbered off. Mr. Campion stood at the window and looked over the shadowy garden, still scented in the dusk. There was nothing more lovely, nothing more redolent of peace and kindliness. Far out across the farther fields a nightingale had begun to sing, mimicking all the bird chatter of the sunshine. From the bar beneath his feet scraps of the strident Suffolk dialect floated up to him, mingled with occasional gusts of husky laughter.

Yet Mr. Campion was not soothed. His pale eyes were troubled behind his spectacles, and once or twice he shivered. He felt himself hampered at every step. Forces were moving which he had no power to stay, forces all the more terrible because they were unknown to him, enemies which he could not recognize.

The picture of Val and the two girls standing smiling in the bright old-fashioned room sickened him. There was, as Lugg said, something unnatural about the whole business, something more than ordinary danger: and the three young people had been so very young, so very ignorant and charming. His mind wandered to the secret room, but he put the subject from him testily. It could not have any significance in the present business or he would surely have been told.

Presently he closed the window and crossed to the table, where the best dinner that Mrs. Bullock could conjure was set waiting for him. He ate absently, pausing every now and then to listen intently to the gentle noises of the countryside.

But it was not until early the following morning, as he lay upon a home-cured feather bed beneath an old crocheted quilt of weird and wonderful design, that the storm broke.

He was awakened by a furious tattoo on his door and raised himself upon his elbow to find Mrs. Bullock, pink and horror-stricken.

"Oh, sir," she said, "as Mr. Val's friend, I think you ought to go up to the Tower at once. It's Lady Pethwick, sir, Mr. Val's aunt. They brought her in this morning, sir—stone dead."

CHAPTER SEVEN

Death in the House

The Tower at Sanctuary managed to be beautiful in spite of itself. It stood at the top of the hill almost hidden in great clumps of oak and cedar trees with half a mile of park surrounding it in all directions.

It was a mass of survivals, consisting of excellent examples of almost every period in English architecture.

Its centre was Tudor with a Georgian front; the west wing was Queen Anne; but the oldest part, and by far the most important, was the east wing, from which the house got its name. This was a great pile of old Saxon stone and Roman brick, circular in shape, rising up to a turreted tower a good sixty feet above the rest of the building. The enormously thick walls were decorated with a much later stone tracery near the top, and were studded with little windows, behind one of which, it was whispered, lay the room to which there was no door.

In spite of the odd conglomeration of periods, there was something peculiarly attractive and even majestic in the old pile. To start with, its size was prodigious, even for a country mansion. Every age had enlarged it.

The slight signs of neglect which a sudden rise in the cost of labour combined with a strangling land tax had induced upon the lawns and gardens had succeeded only in mellowing and softening the pretentiousness of the estate, and in the haze of the morning it looked kindly and inviting in spite of the fact that the doctor's venerable motor-car stood outside the square doorway and the blinds were drawn in all the front windows.

Val and Penny were standing by the window in a big shabby room at the back of the west wing. It had been their nursery when they were children, and had been regarded by them ever since as their own special domain. There were still old toys in the wide cupboards behind the yellow-white panelling, and the plain heavy furniture was battered and homely.

The view from the window, half obscured by the leaves of an enormous oak, led the eye down the steep green hill-side to where a white road meandered away and lost itself among the fields which stretched as far as the horizon.

The scene was incredibly lovely, but the young people were not particularly impressed. Penny was very pale. She seemed to have grown several years older since the night before. Her plain white frock enhanced the pallor of her face, and her eyes seemed to have become wider and more deep in colour. Val, too, was considerably shaken.

"Look here," he said, "I've sent word down for Campion to come up as we arranged before. It was just Aunt's heart, of course, but it's awkward happening like this. I thought she was disgustingly full of beans at dinner last night." He pulled himself up. "I know I ought not to talk about her like this," he said apologetically, "still, it's silly to pretend that we liked her."

He was silent for a moment, and then went on gloomily. "The village will be seething with it, of course. Being picked up in the Pharisees' Clearing like that. What on earth did she want to go wandering about at night for?"

Penny shuddered and suddenly covered her face with her hands.

"Oh, Val," she said, "did you see her? I was the first to go down into the hall this morning when Will and his son brought her in on a hurdle. That look on her face—I shall never forget it. She saw something dreadful, Val. She died of fright."

The boy put his arm round her and shook her almost roughly.

"Don't think of it," he said. "She'd got a bad heart and she died, that's all. It's nothing to do with—with the other thing."

But there was no conviction in his tone and the girl was not comforted, realizing that he spoke as much to reassure himself as to soothe her.

Their nerves were so taut that a tap on the door made them both start violently. It opened immediately to admit old Doctor Cobden, the man who had brought them both into the world, and whose word had been the ultimate court of appeal ever since they could remember.

He was a large, benign old gentleman with closely cropped white hair and immense white eyebrows and he was dressed in an unconventional rough tweed suit fitting snugly to his rotund form.

He advanced across the room, hand outstretched, exuding a faint aroma of iodoform as he came.

"Val, my boy, I'm glad to see you," he said. "You couldn't have come back at a better time. Your father and the estate have needed you very much lately, but never so much as now." He turned to Penny and patted her hand gently as it lay in his own. "Pull yourself together, my dear," he said. "It's been a shock, I know, but there's nothing to be afraid of. I'm glad I found you two alone. I wanted to have a chat. Your father, good man, is not much assistance in an emergency."

He spoke briskly and with a forthrightness that they had learned to respect. Val shot him a glance under his eyelashes.

"There'll have to be an inquest, I suppose, sir?" he said.

Doctor Cobden took out a pair of pince-nez and rubbed them contemplatively with an immense white handkerchief.

"Why no, Val. I don't think that'll be necessary, as it happens," he said. "I'm the coroner of this district, don't you know. And whereas I should perhaps have felt it was my duty to inquire into your aunt's death if I hadn't been in attendance on her quite so often lately, I really don't see any need to go into it all again." He paused and regarded them solemnly. "There was always a danger, of course. Any severe shock might have aggravated this aortic regurgitation, don't you know, but she was a nervy creature, poor soul, and I never saw any reason to frighten her."

"But, Doctor, something did frighten her. Her face—" Penny could not restrain the outburst. The old man's mottled face took on a slightly deeper tone of red.

"My dear," he said, "death is often ugly. I'm sorry you should have had to see your aunt. Of course," he went on hastily as he saw the doubt in their eyes, "she must have *had* a shock, don't you know. Probably saw an owl or trod on a rabbit. I warned her against this stupid wandering about at night. Your aunt was a very peculiar woman."

He coughed. "Sometimes," he added, "I thought her a very silly woman. All this semi-mystical nonsense was very dangerous in her condition. And that's where I come to the business I wanted to discuss with you. I don't want your father bothered. I've persuaded him to take things easily. It's been a great shock to him. He's in his own rooms and I don't want him disturbed. Now, Val, I want all this crowd of your aunt's friends out of the house before to-morrow." He paused, and his little bright eyes met the boy's inquiringly. "I don't know how many there are," he said, "or who they are. Some—ah— some Bohemian set, I understand. They've been getting on your father's nerves. I don't know what your aunt was doing filling the place with dozens of strangers."

Penny looked a little surprised.

"There's only seven visitors, and they're at the Cup House now," she said. "We don't see much of them. Aunt used to keep them to herself."

"Oh, I see." The doctor looked considerably relieved. "I understood from your father that there was an army of lunatics encamped somewhere. Oh, well, it won't be so difficult. I don't suppose they'll want to stay, don't you know."

The old man had brightened visibly. Clearly a weight was off his mind. "There's just one other thing," he went on rather more slowly than usual, evidently choosing his words with deliberation. "With regard to the funeral, I should—ah—get it over quietly, don't you know. As little fuss as possible. I don't think there's any necessity to fill the house with visitors. No last looks or any morbid rubbish of that sort. I'm sorry to speak frankly," he went on, directing his remarks to Val, "but it's your father we've got to think of. It's getting near your twenty-fifth birthday, you know, my boy, and that is a very trying time for both you and your father." He paused to let his words sink in, and then added practically: "There's no near relative that you'll offend, is there?"

Penny considered. "There's Uncle Lionel's brothers," she said dubiously.

"Oh, no need to worry about them. Write to them and leave it at that." The doctor dismissed the family of the late Sir Lionel Pethwick with a wave of his hand.

Penny laid her hand upon his arm affectionately.

"You dear," she said. "You're trying to hush it all up for us."

"My dear child!" The old man appeared scandalized. "I've never heard such nonsense. There's nothing to hush up. A perfectly normal death. I'm merely considering your father, as I keep on telling you. You young people are too eager to listen to the superstitious chatter of the country folk. There's no such thing as a look of horror on a dead face. It's death itself that is horrifying. A case of sudden end like this is always shocking. I'll make you up a sedative, Penny. One of the men can come down for it. Take it three times a day, and go to bed early.

"I'll speak to Robertson too, Val, as I go through Sudbury. You can leave everything to him. I should fix the funeral for Wednesday. Without appearing callous, the sooner you get these things over the better. You're modern young people. I'm sure you'll understand me. Now I'll go," he added, turning briskly towards the door. "Don't trouble to come down with me. I want to have a word with Branch on my way out. I believe that old rascal is more capable than the whole lot of you. Good-bye. I shall drop in to-morrow. Good-bye, Penny, my dear."

He closed the door firmly behind him and they heard him padding off down the parquetted corridor. Penny turned to her brother, her eyes wide and scared.

"Val, he suspects something," she said. "All this quiet funeral business—it's so unlike him. Don't you remember, Mother used to say that he was as proud at a funeral as if he felt he was directly responsible for the whole thing? He doesn't like the look of it. Poor Aunt Di, she was a thorn in the flesh, but I never dreamed it would all end so quickly and horribly as this. I'd give anything to be able to hear her explain her psychic reaction to sunset over Monaco again."

Val was troubled. "Do you mean you think it wasn't heart failure?" he said.

"Oh, nonsense," said Penny. "Of course it was. But I think the doctor feels, as I did, that she must have seen something terrible. There *is* something terrible down in Pharisees' Clearing. There's something round here that we don't understand—I've known it for a long time. I—"

A gentle knocking silenced her, and they both turned to see a pale ineffectual face half-hidden by enormous glasses, peering in at them from the doorway.

"Enter Suspicious Character," said Mr. Campion, introducing the rest of himself into the room. "By the way, I met an irate old gentleman downstairs who told me there was a goods train at 6.15 from Hadleigh. I hope that wasn't your father, chicks." He paused, and added awkwardly, "I heard a rumour in the village that something rather terrible had happened."

Val stepped forward to meet him. "Look here, Campion," he said, "it's all infernally mysterious and it is terrible. Aunt Di was brought in by two yokels. They found her in a clearing in the woods quite near here. She was dead, and they insist that she had an expression of absolute horror on her face, but of course we know that's impossible. That was the doctor you saw just now. He's giving a certificate, but I can't help feeling he wouldn't be so sanguine if he didn't know the family so well. Father has shut himself up in the library and the doc says we're to clear Aunt's crowd out as soon as we can."

He paused for breath.

"An expression of horror?" said Mr. Campion. "This is where we get out of our depth. I'm terribly sorry this has happened, Gyrth. How do you stand with your father?"

"Oh, that's all right." The boy spoke hastily. "I ought to have come home before. I had my own affairs too much on the brain. I think the old boy was worrying about me. Anyhow, he's very grateful to you. He wanted to send for you last night. I had to hint who you were— you don't mind that, do you? He seems to understand the situation perfectly. Frankly, I was amazed by his readiness to accept the whole story."

Campion did not answer, but smiled affably at the boy. Val seemed relieved.

"Now I'd better go round and politely turf out that Bohemian crowd," he said. "I don't suppose you want to interview them, Campion?"

The young man with the pleasant vacuous face shook his head.

"No," he said, "I think it would be better if we did not become acquainted, as it were. There's only one thing. Branch, I suppose, will superintend the luggage?"

"Why, yes, I suppose so." Val was almost impatient.

"Good," said Campion. "See that he does. By the way, he and Lugg were having an Old Boys' Reunion in the hall when I came up." He turned to the girl. "I say, while your brother's speeding the parting guests, I wonder if I could ask you to take me down to the clearing where they found Lady Pethwick?"

She shot him a glance of surprise, but his expression was mild and foolish as ever. "Of course I will," she said.

"Perhaps we could go by some back way that may exist?" Mr. Campion persisted. "I don't want my bad taste to be apparent."

Val glanced at his sister and hesitated. "We don't know the exact spot," he said awkwardly.

"Naturally," said Campion, and followed his guide out of the room.

They went down a shallow Elizabethan staircase, along a wide stone-flagged passage, and came out of a side door into a flower garden. As Mr. Campion stepped out blinking into the sunshine, the girl laid a hand upon his arm.

"Look," she said, "you can see the Cup House from here."

Her companion followed the direction of her eyes and saw a curious rectangular building which had been completely hidden from the front of the house by the enormous eastern wing.

It was situated in a little courtyard of its own, and consisted of what appeared to be two storeys built of flint cobbles reinforced with oak, the lower floor being clearly the Chapel of the Cup, while the upper section had several windows indicating a suite of rooms.

Mr. Campion regarded the structure, the sun glinting on his spectacles.

"Your aunt's artistic friends are upstairs, I suppose?" he said.

"Oh, yes," said Penny hastily. "The chapel is always kept locked."

Mr. Campion hesitated. "There's no doubt," he ventured, "that the relic is safe at the moment?"

The girl stared at him in astonishment. "Of course it is," she said. "I'm afraid all this talk of painting my aunt with the Chalice has given you a wrong impression. There were always two of the servants there at the time—Branch and someone else—and the relic was returned to its place and the doors locked after each sitting. There are three rooms up there over the chapel," she went on, "the Maid of the Cup's private apartments in the old days. Aunt had the big room as a sort of studio, but the two small ones are the bedrooms of the two men who have charge of this garden and the chapel building. There's an outside staircase to the first storey."

"Oh," said Mr. Campion.

They walked down the broad grass path towards a small gate at the end of the garden. For some time there was silence, and then the girl spoke abruptly.

"Mr. Campion," she said, "I made Val tell me about everything last night—I mean about the danger to the Chalice. You'll have to let me help. You'll find me quite as useful as he. For one thing," she added, dropping her voice, "I haven't got the shadow of The Room hanging over me. Besides," she went on with a wry little smile, "I'm the Maid of the Cup now, you know. I've got a right to come into this and you can count on me."

Mr. Campion's reply was unexpected. "I shall hold you to that," he said. "Now I think we'd better hurry."

They went through the garden gate and across the broad meadow on the other side. Here it was semiparkland with a great bank of trees upon their left, and presently they entered a small iron gate in the hedge surrounding the wood and struck a footpath leading down into the heart of the greenery.

"Pharisees' Clearing," said Penny, "is just through here. It's really a strip of grass which separates our wood from the other coppice which is the Tye Hall property where Beth lives."

"Ah," said Mr. Campion. "And where is Fox Hollow?"

She shot him a quick glance. "You remembered that? It's higher up on the other side of their woodlands. Dad really had cause for a grievance, you see, only Professor Cairey himself doesn't shoot, so you can't expect him to understand. And anyhow, he only wants asking. Dad's so silly that way."

"Professor?" said Campion thoughtfully. "What does he profess?"

"Archaeology," said Penny promptly. "But you don't think—?"

"My dear girl," said Mr. Campion, "I can't see the wood for trees. 'And in the night imagining some fear, how easy doth a bush appear a bear.' You see," he added with sudden seriousness, "if your aunt met her death by someone's design, I'm not only out of my depth, but I might just as well have left my water-wings at home." He paused and looked about him. "I suppose this is a happy hunting ground for poachers?"

Penny shook her head. "I don't think there's a man, woman or child in the whole of Sanctuary who'd come within a mile of Pharisees' Clearing after dark," she said. She hesitated for some seconds as if debating whether to go on. "I get on very well with the country folk," she added suddenly, "and naturally I hear a good deal of local chatter. They believe that this wood and the clearing are haunted—not by a ghost, but by something much worse than that. No one's ever seen it that I know of, but you know what country people are."

"I thought the breed had died out," said her companion. "Gone are the dimpled milkmaids and the ancient gaffers of my youth. You can't even see them on the pictures."

Penny smiled faintly. "We're very much behind the times here," she said. "We've even got a local witch—poor old Mrs. Munsey. She lives with her son in a little henhouse of a place some distance away from the village. They're both half-wits, you know, really, poor things. But there's a world of prejudice against them, and they're both so bad-tempered you can't do anything for them. Sammy Munsey is the village idiot, I suppose, but the old woman is a venomous old party. And that's why—" she hesitated, "you'll probably think I'm a fool for mentioning this, but she put a curse on Aunt Di at the last full moon, and it was full moon again last night."

She reddened and glanced furtively at her companion, whose pleasant vacant face conveyed nothing but polite interest. She looked absurdly modern in her smart white crêpe de Chine jumper suit, her bare brown arms hanging limply at her sides, and it was certainly odd to hear her speak of such an archaic practice as witchcraft as though she half believed in it.

"Now I've said it, it sounds stupid," she remarked. "After all, it may not even be true. It's only gossip."

Campion regarded her quizzically. "Did Mrs. Munsey ever curse anybody with such startling success before?" he said. "How did she build up her business, so to speak?"

The girl shrugged her shoulders. "I don't really know," she said, "except that there's a list of witches burnt in 1624 still in the Lady Chapel of the church—this village managed to escape Cromwell, you know—and every other name on the sheet is Munsey. It's partly that, and then—the poor old creature is perfectly bald. In the winter it's all right, she wears a bonnet of sorts, but in hot weather she goes about uncovered. Aunt Di was always trying to be kind to her, but she had an officious way and she annoyed the old biddy somehow. Do you think I'm mad?"

"My dear young lady," said her companion judicially, "there are lots of rum professions. There's nothing unusual about witchcraft. I used to be a bit of a wizard myself, and I once tried to change a particularly loathsome old gentleman into a seal on a voyage to Oslo. Certainly the vulgar creature fell overboard, and they only succeeded in hauling up a small walrus, but I was never sure whether I had done it or not.

They had the same moustaches, but that was all. I've often wondered if I was successful. I went in for wireless accessories after that."

Penny regarded him with astonishment, but he seemed to be perfectly serious. They were half-way through the wood by this time. The place was a fairyland of cool green arcades with moss underfoot, and a tiny stream meandering along among the tree roots.

She pointed to a patch of sunlight at the far end of the path. "That's the entrance to Pharisees' Clearing," she said. "Pharisee means 'fairy', you know."

Mr. Campion nodded. "Be careful how you talk about fairies in a wood," he said. "They're apt to think it disrespectful."

They walked on, and came at last to the edge of the clearing. It was a tiny valley, walled in by high trees on each side, and possessing, even at that hour of the morning, a slightly sinister aspect.

The grey-green grass was sparse, and there were large stones scattered about; a bare unlovely place, all the more uninviting after the beauty of the wood.

The girl paused and shivered. "It was here," she said quietly. "As far as I could gather from Will Tiffin, Aunt was lying quite close to this gateway—staring up with that awful look on her face."

Campion did not move, but stood regarding the scene, his pale face even more vacuous than usual. The girl took a deep breath.

"Mr. Campion," she said, "I've got to tell you something. I've kept quiet about it so far, but I think if I don't tell someone I shall go mad."

She was speaking impulsively, the quick colour rising in her cheeks.

"Will Tiffin told me early this morning, and I made him swear not to breathe it to another soul. When he found her she was lying here on her back, not twisted or dishevelled as she would have been if she had lain where she had fallen, but stiff and straight, with her hands folded and her eyes closed. Don't you see—" her voice quivered and sank to a whisper—"Will said it looked as if she had been laid out as a corpse."

CHAPTER EIGHT

The Professional Touch

"You'd be doing me a service, Mr. Lugg, if you'd refrain from referring to me as No. 705. Sir Percival did my father the honour of forgetting my little lapse twenty-five years ago."

Mr. Branch, a small dignified person in black tie and jacket, paused and regarded his shady old friend with something like appeal in his eyes.

"No good thinkin' o' that," he added, dropping his official voice and speaking with his natural Suffolk inflection.

Mr. Lugg, himself resplendent in black cloth, sniffed contemptuously. "'Ave it yer own way," he said. "Anyway, you nipped that lot out o' the satchel as if you still knew a thing or two."

He jerked his head towards a pile of water-colours and pencil sketches lying face downwards upon a bureau top. The two men were in one of the smaller bedrooms in the front of the mansion, at present in disuse.

The little man fidgeted nervously.

"I shan't be happy till they're out of the house," he said. "It's not my regular job to do the packing. The housekeeper would smell a rat immediately if any fuss was made."

"There won't be no fuss. 'Ow many more times 'ave I got to tell yer?" Mr. Lugg was irritated. "Mr. Gyrth and my young bloke said they'd take full responsibility. Livin' down 'ere on the fat of the land 'as made you flabby, my son."

Mr. Branch glanced under his eyelashes at the big man opposite him.

"Your Mr. Campion," he said. "I shouldn't be at all surprised if 'is real name didn't begin with a K. And figuring it all out, 'is Christian name ought to be Rudolph."

Mr. Lugg's large mouth fell open. "'Ow d'yer make that out?" he demanded.

His friend wagged his head knowingly. "A confidential family servant in a big 'ouse gets to know things by a sort of instinct," he observed. "Family likenesses—family manners—little tricks of 'abit, and so on."

Unwillingly, Mr. Lugg was impressed. "Lumme!" he said. "'Ow did you get a line on 'is nibs?"

"About an hour ago," said Branch precisely, "I went into Mr. Campion's bedroom to see if the maids had done their work. Quite by chance," he went on studiously, "I caught sight of 'is pyjamas. Light purple stripe—silk—come from Dodds. That didn't tell me much. But then I noticed a bit of flannel, sewed in by the firm, across the shoulder-blades. Now that's a silly idea, a woman's idea. Also I fancy I could lay me finger on the only woman 'oo could ever make Dodds do it. Then, a thing like that comes from 'abit—lifelong 'abit. It wouldn't be a wife. It'd 'ave to be a mother to fix it on a chap so's it 'ud last 'im all 'is life. I started thinkin' and remembered where I'd seen it before. Then of course I knew. The gilded bit of aristocracy 'oo comes down 'ere sometimes is just the chap to 'ave a little brother like your young bloke."

He paused and Mr. Lugg was mortified.

"Branch," he said, "who d'you make me out to be—Doctor Watson?"

It was evident that the butler did not follow him, and Lugg laughed. "You're smart, but you've got no education," he said complacently. "What's the point of all this knowledge of yours? What d'you use it for —graft?"

Branch was shocked, and said so. Afterwards he deigned to explain. "In the days when 'er Ladyship was alive and we used to entertain," he said, "it was as well to keep an eye on who was in the 'ouse. Oh, I was very useful to 'er Ladyship. She quite come to depend on me. First morning at breakfast when they come in, she'd raise 'er eyebrows at me, ever so faint, if there was any doubt, and if I knoo they was O.K., I'd nod."

"Yes?" said Lugg, fascinated by this sidelight into High Life. "And if you wasn't satisfied?"

"Then I'd ignore 'er," said Branch majestically.

Mr. Lugg whistled. "'Ard lines on a bloke with ragged pants," he observed.

"Oh no, you don't foller me." Branch was vehement. "Why, there's one pair of underpants that's been into this 'ouse reg'lar for the last fourteen years. Darned by the Duchess 'erself, bless 'er! I can tell it anywhere—it's a funny cross-stitch what she learnt in France in the 'fifties. You see it on all 'er family's washin'. It's as good as a crest." He shook his head. "No, this 'ere knowledge of mine comes by instinc'. I can't explain it."

"Well, since you're so clever, what about this lot that's just off?"

said Lugg, anxious to see if the remarkable attribute could be turned to practical account. "Anything nobby in the way of darns there?"

Branch was contemptuous.

"Fakes!" he said. "Low fakes, that's what they were. Nice new outfits bought for the occasion. 'Something to show the servants,'" he mimicked in a horribly refined voice. "Not every pair of legs that's covered by Burlington Arcade first kicked up in Berkeley Square, you can take it from me."

Mr. Lugg, piqued by this exhibition of talent, was stung to retort.

"Well, anyway, 'ere's your watch back," he said, handing over a large gold turnip, and gathering up a sheaf of drawings he strode out of the room.

He padded softly down the corridor and tapped upon a door on his left. Penny's voice bade him enter, and he went in to find himself in a small sitting-room elaborately decorated in the dusty crimson and gold of the later Georges.

Mr. Campion and the daughter of the house were standing beside the window, well hidden from the outside by heavy damask curtains. The young man, who had turned round as Lugg entered, raised his eyebrows inquiringly.

"I've got the doings, sir," Lugg murmured huskily, the faded splendours of the old mansion combined with Penelope's beauty producing a certain respect in his tone. "Just like what you thought."

"Good," said Mr. Campion. "Hold hard for a moment, Lugg. I'm watching our young host and your friend Branch, who I see has just come out to him, packing the intelligentsia into a couple of cars."

"Ho." Mr. Lugg advanced on tiptoe and stood breathing heavily over his master's shoulder. They could just see a group of weirdly dressed people surrounding a venerable Daimler and a still more ancient Panhard, both belonging to the house, which were stationed outside the front door.

Lugg nudged his master. "That's the chap I saw with Natty," he rumbled. "That seedy looking bloke with the ginger beard. It was 'is traps that this lot come out of." He tapped the pile of papers in his hand.

"Do you recognize any of the others?" Mr. Campion spoke softly.

Mr. Lugg was silent for some moments. Then he sniffed regretfully.

"Can't say I do," he said. "They look genuine to me. They've got that 'Gawd-made-us-and-this-is-'ow-'e-likes-us' look."

Penny touched Mr. Campion's arm.

"Albert," she said, "do you recognize that man with the ginger beard?"

Mr. Campion turned away from the window and advanced towards the table in the centre of the room.

"Rather," he said. "An old employee of mine. That's why I'm so glad he didn't see me. His trade name before he took up art and grew a beard was Arthur Earle. He's a jeweller's copyist, and one of the best on the shady side of the line." He turned to Penny and grinned. "When Lady Ermyntrude gives her dancing partner the old Earl's jewelled toodle-oo clock to keep the wolf from the door, the old Earl is awakened every morning by a careful copy of our Arthur's making. Likewise Lady Maud's ruby dog collar and the necklace Sir George gave little Eva on her twenty-first. They're all copies of the originals made by our Arthur. Arthur, in fact, is one of the lads who make Society what it is to-day." He took the pile of papers from Lugg. "This, I fancy, is some of his handiwork. Now we'll see."

There had been a sound of wheels in the drive, and Val came in almost immediately afterwards.

"Well, they've gone," he said. "Hullo, what have you got there?"

Mr. Campion was busy spreading out the drawings. "A spot of Noo-Art," he said. "When they discover they've lost this lot they'll realize we're not completely in the dark, but we can't help that."

The brother and sister bent forward eagerly. There were about a dozen drawings in all, each purporting to be a portrait of Lady Peth-wick. In each drawing the Chalice figured. In fact the Chalice was the only subject which the artist had attempted to treat with any realism, whilst the drawings of the lady were ultra-modern, to say the best of them.

Mr. Campion chuckled. "There's not much about the treasure that our friend missed," he said. "It's a miracle your aunt didn't spot what he was up to. Look, here's the Chalice from the right side, from the left, from the top—see, he's even jotted down the measurements here. And I should fancy he had a pretty good idea of the weight. That's what I call thoroughness."

Val looked at him questioningly. "I don't quite see the idea," he said.

"My dear old bird," said Mr. Campion, "our Arthur was a con-scientious workman in spite of his murky reputation. He must have been a bit of an actor, too, by the way, to deceive your aunt like that. These are plans"—he waved his hand to the drawings on the table—"working diagrams, in fact. I should say that, given the materials, our Arthur could turn you out a very good copy of the Chalice from these."

"But if they could make a copy that would deceive us, why not let his Mohammedan client have it?" said Val testily.

Mr. Campion was shocked. "My dear fellow, have you no respect for a collector's feelings?" he said. "Arthur couldn't make anything that would deceive an expert."

"So they were going to exchange it?" It was Penny who spoke, her eyes blazing with anger and her cheeks flushed. "To give them plenty of time to get the real thing out of the country before we spotted anything. Pigs! Oh, the insufferable farmyard pigs! Pigs in the French sense! Why don't we wire down to the station and get the man arrested?"

"I shouldn't do that," said Mr. Campion. "We've spiked his guns pretty effectively anyhow. And after all, I don't see what we could charge him with. He might retort that we'd pinched his drawings, which would be awkward. Lugg's record would come out and we'd all be in the soup. Besides," he went on gravely, "Arthur is very small fry—just about as small as Natty Johnson, in fact. That's what's worrying me," he added with unusual violence. "The place is swarming with minnows, but there's not a trout in the stream. And the big man is the only one who's any good to us at all. I wish I knew what your aunt saw last night."

He gathered up the drawings and tore them neatly across and across. "Now you can go and play bonfires, Lugg," he said, handing him the pieces.

It was growing dark in the room, and at any moment the dinner gong might sound.

The little party was disturbed by the sudden entrance of Branch, who came in without ceremony, his usual composure completely gone.

"Mr. Val, sir," he burst out, "would you step across the passage? There's a stranger peering in through the chapel window."

With a smothered exclamation Val started after the butler into the spare bedroom on the opposite side of the corridor, followed by the entire company. The window afforded a perfect view of the Cup House.

"There!" said Branch, pointing down towards the old flint building. It was almost dusk, but the watchers could easily make out the figure of a man balanced upon a pile of loose stones peering in through one of the narrow lattice windows of the chapel. He was hidden by a yew hedge from the lower windows of the house, and apparently thought himself completely secluded. He had a torch in his hand with which he was trying to penetrate the darkness inside the building.

As they watched him, fascinated, the hastily improvised pedestal on which the intruder stood collapsed beneath his weight, and he stumbled to the ground with a rattle of stones. He picked himself up hastily and shot a single startled glance up at the house.

Even at that distance the features were dimly visible, revealing a handsome little man of sixty odd, with a sharp white vandyke beard and a long nose.

The next moment he was off, streaking through the flower garden like a shadow.

Penny gasped, and she and the butler exchanged glances. When at last she spoke, her voice trembled violently.

"Why, Branch," she said, "that—that looked very like Professor Gardner Cairey."

Branch coughed. "Begging your pardon, miss," he said, "that *was* him."

CHAPTER NINE

The Indelicate Creature

If the extreme unpopularity of Lady Pethwick produced in her immediate household an emotion more akin to quiet shock than overwhelming grief at her death, the village of Sanctuary seethed with excitement at the news of it, and the most extravagant gossip was rife.

Mr. Campion wandered about the vicinity in a quiet, ineffectual fashion, his eyes vague and foolish behind his spectacles, but his ears alert. He learnt within a very short space of time, and on very good authority in every case, that Lady Pethwick had been (*a*) murdered by Gypsies; (*b*) confronted by the Devil, who had thereupon spirited her away at the direct instigation of Mrs. Munsey, and (*c*) according to the more prosaic wiseacres, had died in the normal way from drink, drugs, or sheer bad temper.

Even the rational Mrs. Bullock held no belief in the doctor's verdict.

On the afternoon of the funeral he absented himself, and spent that day and part of the night pursuing and finally interviewing his old friends Jacob Benwell and his mother, Mrs. Sarah, mère and compère of the Benwell Gypsy tribe, who had seen fit for obvious reasons to remove from Fox Hollow on the morning on which Lady Pethwick was found in Pharisees' Clearing.

It was early afternoon of the following day, after a luncheon at which Sir Percival did not appear, that Mr. Campion was standing at the nursery window regarding the flower garden attentively when Lugg came to him, an expression of mild outrage upon his ponderous face.

"A party 'as just come visitin'," he remarked. "Tourists on 'orseback. Day after the funeral—get me? Not quite the article, I thought."

This announcement was followed almost immediately by the entrance of Penny. Her eyes were dark and angry.

"Albert," she said, "have you ever heard such cheek? Mrs. Dick Shannon has just arrived with two complete strangers. She has the nerve to say that she has come to pay a call of condolence, and incidentally, if you please, to show her two beastly friends the Chalice. We open the chapel to visitors on Thursday as a rule—it's part of the Royal Charter—but this is a bit stiff, isn't it?"

She paused for breath.

"Mrs. Dick Shannon?" said Mr. Campion. "Ah, yes, I remember. The megaphonic marvel. Where is she now? I suppose your father is doing the honours?"

"Father can't stand her," said Penny. "She's trying to make him sell her some horses—that's the real reason why she's come. Look here, you'd better come downstairs and support us. Father likes you. If you could get rid of them he might offer you my hand in marriage or put you up for his club. Anyway, come on."

She went out of the room and Campion followed. Almost immediately Mrs. Dick's penetrating voice met them from the hall below.

"Well, of course, drink's better than lunacy in a family, as I told the mother."

The phrase met them as they descended the stairs.

Penny snorted. "I bet she's talking about one of our relatives," she whispered. "It's her idea of making conversation."

Mrs. Dick, backed by her two friends, who to do them justice looked considerably embarrassed, was standing with her feet planted far apart in the centre of the huge lounge-hall. All three were in riding kit, Mrs. Dick looking particularly smart in a black habit.

Once again Mr. Campion was conscious of the faint atmosphere of importance which her dashing personality seemed to exude.

Colonel Sir Percival Gyrth, supported by his son, stood listening to the lady. He was a sturdy old man of the true Brass Hat species, but there was about him a suggestion that some private worry had undermined his normal good-tempered simple character. At the moment he was quite obviously annoyed. His plump hands were folded behind his back, and his eyes, blue and twinkling like his children's, had a distinctly unfriendly gleam. He was a by no means unhandsome man, with curling iron-grey hair, and a heavy-featured clean-shaven face. He glanced up hopefully as Campion entered.

"Ah," he said, "let me present you. Mrs. Shannon, this is a young friend of Val's. Mr. Campion—Mr. Albert Campion."

Mrs. Dick's cold glance wandered leisurely over the young man before her. Had she spoken, her contempt could not have been more apparent. Finally she honoured him with a slight but frigid bow. Then she turned to her companions.

"Major King and Mr. Horace Putnam," she said, and then quite patently dismissed all of them as negligible.

Major King proved to be a large, florid and unhappy-looking person, slightly horsey in appearance and clearly not at his ease. Mr. Putnam, on the other hand, was a small man with little bright eyes and a shrewd, wrinkled face. He too was clearly a stranger to his surroundings, but was not letting the fact worry him.

"Well?" Mrs. Dick whipped the company together with the single word. "Now, Penny Gyrth, if you'll take us over to the museum, we'll go. I'm afraid the horses may be getting bored. You still maintain your complete unreasonableness about those two yearlings, Colonel?"

It said a great deal for Sir Percival's upbringing that his tone when he replied was as charming as ever.

"My dear lady, I don't want to sell. And just at the moment," he added simply, "I'm afraid I don't feel much like business of any sort."

"Oh, of course. Poor Diana." Mrs. Dick was not in the least abashed. "I always think it best to face things," she went on, bellowing the words like a bad loudspeaker. "Mawkishness never did anyone any good. The only wonder to my mind is that it didn't happen years ago. Cobden's such an old fool. I wouldn't let him vet me for chilblains."

By this time the entire Gyrth family were smarting. Only their inborn politeness saved Mrs. Dick and her protégés from an untimely and undignified exit. Mr. Campion stood by smiling foolishly as though the lady had irresistible charm for him.

Mrs. Dick moved towards the door. "Come on," she said. "I'm not very interested in these things myself, but Mr. Putnam is amused by all this ancient rubbish."

Penny hung back. "The Chalice is veiled," she said. "It always is, for ten days after a—" The word "death" died on her lips as Mrs. Dick interrupted her.

"Then unveil it, my dear," she said. "Now come along, all of you— we can't keep the horses waiting. How you've let this place go down since your wife's time, Colonel! Poor Helen, she always believed in making a good show."

Impelled by the very force of her vigorous personality, the little company followed her. At least three of the party were bristling at her outrageous monologue, but she was superbly oblivious of any effect she might create. It was this quality which had earned her the unique position in the county which she undoubtedly occupied. Everybody knew her, nobody liked her, and most people were a little afraid of her. Her astounding success with any species of horseflesh earned her a grudging admiration. Nobody snubbed her because the tongue capable of it had not yet been born. Her rudeness and studied discourtesy were a byword for some fifty square miles, yet she came and went where she pleased because the only way of stopping her would have been to hurl her bodily from one's front door, no mean feat in itself, and this method had not yet occurred to the conservative minds of her principal victims.

Outside on the gravel path there was still a very marked reluctance on the part of the members of the household to continue towards the Cup House, but at last the Colonel, realizing that there was no help for it, decided to get the matter over as soon as possible. Branch was dispatched for the keys and the little procession wandered round the east wing, through a small gate at the side, and came out into the flower garden. Mrs. Dick still held forth, maintaining a running commentary calculated to jade the strongest of nerves.

"A very poor show of roses, Colonel. But then roses are like horses, you know. If you don't understand 'em, better leave 'em alone."

She stood aside as Branch advanced to unlock the heavy oak and iron door of the chapel. The lock was ancient and prodigiously stiff, so that the little butler experienced considerable difficulty in inserting the great key, and there was a momentary pause as he struggled to turn it.

Before Val could step forward to assist the old man, Mrs. Dick had intervened. She thrust Branch out of her way like a cobweb, and with a single twist of her fingers shot the catch back. Major King laughed nervously.

"You're strong in the wrist," he observed.

She shot him a single withering glance. "You can't be flabby in my profession," she said.

The unpleasant Mr. Putnam laughed. "That's one for you, Major," he said. "I was watching Mrs. Shannon dealing with Bitter Aloes this morning. That mare will beat you," he added, turning to the lady. "She's got a devil in her. I thought she was going to kill you. A bad woman and a vicious mare, they're both incorrigible. Lose 'em or shoot 'em, it's the only way."

He turned to the rest of the party, who were unimpressed.

"There was Bitter Aloes rearing up, pawing with her front feet like a prizefighter," he said, "and Mrs. Shannon hanging on to the halter rope, laying about with a whip like a ring-master. She got the brute down in the end. I never saw such a sight."

It was with this conversation that the unwelcome visitors came into the ancient and sacred Chapel of the Cup.

It was a low room whose slightly vaulted ceiling was supported by immensely thick brick and stone columns, and was lit only by narrow, diamond-paned windows set at irregular intervals in the walls, so that the light was always dim even on the brightest day. The floor was paved with flat tombstones on which were several very fine brasses. It was entirely unfurnished save for a small stone altar at the far end of the chamber, the slab of which was covered with a crimson cloth held in place by two heavy brass candlesticks.

Let into the wall, directly above the centre of the altar, was a stout iron grille over a cavity in the actual stone, which was rather ingeniously lit by a slanting shaft open to the air many feet above, and sealed by a thick sheet of glass inserted at some later period than the building of the chapel.

At the moment the interior of the orifice was filled by a pyramid of embroidered black velvet.

Colonel Gyrth explained.

"Immediately a death occurs in the family," he murmured, "the Chalice is veiled. This covering was put on here three days ago. It is the custom," he added, "not to disturb it for at least ten days." He hesitated pointedly.

Mrs. Dick stood her ground. "I suppose the grille opens with another key," she said. "What a business you make of it! Is there a burglar alarm concealed in the roof?"

Quite patently it had dawned upon the Colonel that the only way to get rid of his unwelcome visitors was to show them the Chalice and have done with it. He was a peace-loving man, and realizing that Mrs. Dick would not shy at a scene, he had no option but to comply with her wishes. He took the smaller key which Branch handed him, and bending across the altar carefully unlocked the grille, which swung open like a door. With reverent hands he lifted the black covering.

Mr. Campion, whose imagination ran always to the comic, was reminded irresistibly of a conjuring trick. A moment later his mental metaphor was unexpectedly made absolute.

There was a smothered exclamation from the Colonel and a little scream from Penny. The removal of the black cloth had revealed nothing more than a couple of bricks taken from the loose pedestal of one of the columns.

Of the Chalice there was no sign whatever.

Mrs. Dick was the only person who did not realize immediately that some calamity had occurred.

"Not my idea of humour." Her stentorian voice reverberated through the cool, dark chapel. "Sheer bad taste."

But Val stared at Mr. Campion, and his father stared at Branch, and there was nothing but complete stupefaction and horror written on all their faces.

It was Colonel Gyrth who pulled himself together and provided the second shock within five minutes.

"Of course," he said, "I had quite forgotten. I'm afraid you'll be disappointed to-day, Mr. Putnam. The Chalice is being cleaned. Some other time."

With remarkable composure he smiled and turned away, murmuring to Val as he passed him: "For God's sake get these people out of the house, my boy, and then come into the library, all of you."

CHAPTER TEN

Two Angry Ladies

Colonel Sir Percival Gyrth walked up and down the hearthrug in his library, while his two children, with Mr. Campion and Branch, stood looking at him rather helplessly.

"Thank God that woman's gone." The old man passed his hand across his forehead. "I don't know if my explanation satisfied her. I hope so, or we'll have the whole country buzzing with it within twenty-four hours."

Val stared at his father. "Then it really has gone?"

"Of course it has." There was no misunderstanding the consternation in the Colonel's voice. "Vanished into thin air. I veiled it myself on Sunday evening, just after you said that busybody Cairey was fooling about in the courtyard. It was perfectly safe then. I brought the keys back and put them in my desk. Branch, you and I, I suppose, are the only people who knew where they were kept."

Branch's expression was pathetic, and his employer reassured him.

"Don't worry, man. I'm not accusing anybody. It's ridiculous. The thing can't have gone."

For a moment no one spoke. The suddenness of the loss seemed to have stunned them.

"Hadn't I better send someone for the police, sir? Or perhaps you'd rather I phoned?" It was Branch who made the suggestion.

Sir Percival hesitated. "I don't think so, thank you, Branch," he said. "Anyway, not yet. You see," he went on, turning to the others, "to make a loss like this public entails very serious consequences. We are really the guardians of the Chalice for the Crown. I want the chapel locked as usual, Branch, and no mention of the loss to be made known to the staff, as yet."

"But what shall we do?" said Val breathlessly. "We can't sit down and wait for it to reappear."

His father looked at him curiously. "Perhaps not, my boy," he said. "But there's one point which must have occurred to all of you. The Chalice is both large and heavy, and no stranger has left the house since I locked it up myself. No one except ourselves could possibly have had access to it, and we are all very particularly concerned in keeping it here."

"According to that argument," said Val bluntly, "it can't have gone. And if so, where is it? Can't you send for the Chief Constable? He used to be a friend of yours."

His father hesitated. "I could, of course," he said, "though I don't see what he could do except spread the alarm and question all the servants—search the house, probably, and make a lot of fuss. No, we must find this thing ourselves."

There was an astonishing air of finality in his tone which was not lost upon the others.

"I'm not calling in the police," he said, "not yet, at any rate. And I must particularly ask you not to mention this loss to anyone. I'm convinced," he went on as they gasped at him, "that the relic is still in the house. Now I should like to be left alone."

They went out, all of them, except Val, who lingered, and when the door had closed behind the others he went over to the old man, who had seated himself at his desk.

"Look here, Dad," he said, "if you've hidden the Cup for some reason or other, for Heaven's sake let me in on it. I'm all on edge about this business, and frankly I feel I've got a right to know."

"For Heaven's sake, boy, don't be a fool." The older man's voice was almost unrecognizable, and the face he lifted towards his son was grey and haggard. "This is one of the most serious, most terrifying things I have ever experienced in my whole lifetime," he went on, his voice indubitably sincere. "All the more so because, as it happens, we are so situated that at the moment it is impossible for me to call in the police."

He looked the boy steadily in the eyes. "You come of age in a week. If your birthday were to-day perhaps I should find this easier to explain."

Early the following morning Mr. Campion walked down the broad staircase, through the lounge-hall, and out into the sunlight. There seemed no reason for him to be particularly cheerful. So far his activities at Sanctuary seemed to have met with anything rather than conspicuous success. Lady Pethwick had died mysteriously within eight hours of his arrival, and now the main object of his visit had disappeared from almost directly beneath his nose.

Yet he sat down on one of the ornamental stone seats which flanked the porch and beamed upon a smiling world.

Presently, as his ears detected the sound for which he was listening, he began to stroll in a leisurely fashion down the drive. He was still sauntering along the middle of the broad path when the squawk of a motor-horn several times repeated made him turn to find Penny, in her little red two-seater sports car, looking at him reprovingly. She had had to stop to avoid running him over. He smiled at her foolishly from behind his spectacles.

"Where are you going to, my pretty maid?" he said. "Would you like to give a poor traveller a lift?"

The girl did not look particularly pleased at the suggestion.

"As a matter of fact," she said, "I'm running up to Town to see my dressmaker. I'll give you a lift to the village if you like."

"I'm going to London too," said Mr. Campion, climbing in. "It's a long way from here, isn't it?" he went on with apparent imbecility. "I knew I'd never walk it."

Penny stared at him, her cheeks flushing. "Surely you can't go off and leave the Tower unprotected," she said, and there was a note of amusement in her voice.

"Never laugh at a great man," said Mr. Campion. "Remember what happened to the vulgar little girls who threw stones at Elisha. I can imagine few worse deaths than being eaten by a bear," he added conversationally.

The girl was silent for a moment. She was clearly considerably put out by the young man's unexpected appearance.

"Look here," she said at last, "I'm taking Beth with me, if you really want to know. I'm meeting her at the end of the lane."

Mr. Campion beamed. "That's all right," he said. "I shan't mind being squashed. Don't let me force myself on you," he went on. "I shouldn't dream of doing that, but I've got to get to London somehow, and Lugg told me I couldn't use the Bentley."

The girl looked at him incredulously. "What is that man Lugg?" she said.

Her companion adjusted his spectacles. "It depends how you mean," he said. "A species, definitely human, I should say, oh yes, without a doubt. Status—none. Past—filthy. Occupation—my valet."

Penny laughed. "I wondered if he were your keeper," she suggested.

"Tut, tut," said Mr. Campion, mildly offended. "I hope I'm going to enjoy my trip. I don't want to be 'got at' in a parroty fashion all the way up. Ah, there's your little friend waiting for us. Would you like me to sit in the dickey?"

"No!" said Penny, so vehemently that he almost jumped. She bit her lip as though annoyed with herself and added more quietly, "Sit where you are. Beth can squeeze in."

She brought the car to a standstill against the side of the road where Beth Cairey, smart and coolly attractive in navy and white, stood waiting. She seemed surprised to see Mr. Campion and her greeting was subdued.

"This appalling creature has insisted on our giving him a lift," said Penny. "I do hope you won't be squashed in front here."

Mr. Campion made way for her between himself and the driver.

"I couldn't very well refuse him," Penny added apologetically to Beth. "We shall have to put up with him."

Mr. Campion continued to look ineffably pleased with himself. "What a good job there's no more for the Skylark, isn't it?" he remarked as he shut the door on the tightly packed little party. "I love riding in other people's motor-cars. Such a saving of petrol, for one thing."

"Silly and rather vulgar," said Penny, and Mr. Campion was silent.

"I suppose I can eat my sandwiches and drink my ginger beer so long as I don't throw the bottle on the road?" he said meekly after they had progressed a couple of miles without speaking. "I've got a few oranges I could pass round too if you like."

Penny did not deign to reply, although Beth looked upon him more kindly. Unabashed, Mr. Campion continued.

"I've got a rattle to swing in the big towns," he said. "And a couple of funny noses for you two to wear. If we had some balloons we could tie them on the bonnet."

Penny laughed grudgingly. "Albert, you're an idiot," she said.

"What do you think you're doing here, anyhow? Where are you going to in London?"

"To buy a ribbon for my straw hat," said Mr. Campion promptly. "The thing I've got now my Aunt knitted. It's not quite the article, as Lugg would say."

Penny slowed down. "You're just being offensive," she said. "I've a good mind to make you get out and walk."

Mr. Campion looked apprehensive. "You'd regret it all your life," he said warningly. "The best part of my performance is to come. Wait till you've heard me recite—wait till I've done my clog dance—wait till the clouds roll by."

"I should turn him out," said Beth stolidly. "We've come a long way, it would do him good to walk back."

They were, it happened, in one of the narrow cross-country lanes through which Penny was threading in her descent upon the main Colchester motor-way, some distance from a house of any kind, and the road was deserted.

"Don't turn me out," pleaded Mr. Campion. "I knew a man once who turned such a respectable person out of his car after giving him a lift for a long way just like you and for the same reason, all because he'd taken a sudden dislike to him. And when he got home he found that his suitcase, which had been in the back of the car, was missing. Suppose that happened to you? You wouldn't like that, would you?"

Penny stopped the car, engine and all. Both girls were scarlet, but it was Penny who tried to rescue what was obviously an awkward situation.

"How silly of me," she said. "You'll have to get out and start her up. The self-starter isn't functioning."

Mr. Campion moved obediently to get out, and in doing so contrived to kneel up on the seat and grasp one end of the large suitcase which protruded from the open dickey. His next movement was so swift that neither of the two girls realized what was happening until he had leapt clear of the car and stood beaming in the road, the suitcase in his arms. In fact Penny had already trodden on the self-starter and the car was in motion before she was conscious of her loss.

Mr. Campion put the suitcase on the bank and sat down on it. Penny stopped the car, and she and Beth descended and came down the road towards him. She was white with anger, and there was a gleam of defiance in Beth's brown eyes that was positively dangerous.

"Mr. Campion," said Penny, "will you please put that case back in the car at once? Naturally, I can't offer you a lift any farther, and if ever you have the impudence to appear at the Tower again I'll have you thrown out."

Mr. Campion looked dejected, but he still retained his seat. "Don't be unreasonable," he begged. "You're making me go all melodramatic and slightly silly."

The two girls stared at him fascinated. He was juggling with a revolver which he had taken from his hip-pocket.

Penny was now thoroughly alarmed. "What do you think you're doing?" she demanded. "You can't behave like this. Another car may come along at any moment. Then where will you be?"

"Then where will *you* be?" said Mr. Campion pointedly.

With his free hand he slipped open the catches of the suitcase. There was a smothered scream from Beth.

"Please—please leave it alone," she whispered.

Mr. Campion shook his head. "Sorry," he said. "Dooty is dooty, miss. Hullo! Is that a car?"

The inexperienced ladies were deceived by the old trick. They turned eagerly, and in the momentary respite Mr. Campion whipped open the suitcase and exposed a large bundle wrapped lightly in a travelling rug.

Beth would have sprung at him, but Penny restrained her. "It's no good," she said, "we're sunk."

And they stood sullenly in the road with pink cheeks and bright eyes regarding him steadily as he unwrapped and produced to their gaze the eighteen inches of shining glory that was called the Gyrth Chalice.

CHAPTER ELEVEN

Mr. Campion Subscribes

For some moments Mr. Campion stood at the side of the glittering flint road with the bank of green behind him, and the shadows of the beech leaves making a pattern on his face and clothes. The Chalice lay in his arms, dazzling in the sunshine.

Penny and Beth stood looking at him. They were both crimson, both furious, and a little afraid. Penny was fully aware of the enormity of the situation. It was Campion who spoke first.

"As amateurs," he said judicially, "you two only serve to show what a lot of undiscovered talent there is knocking about."

He re-wrapped the Chalice and put it back into the suitcase.

All this time there was an ominous silence from Penny, and glancing at her he was afraid for one horrible moment that she was on the verge of tears.

"Look here," he said, smiling at her from behind his spectacles, "I know you think I've butted into this rather unwarrantably, but consider my position. In this affair I occupy the same sort of role as the Genie of the Lamp. Wherever the Chalice is I am liable to turn up at any moment."

Penny's expression did not change for some seconds, and then, to his relief, a faint smile appeared at the corners of her mouth.

"How on earth did you know?" she said.

Mr. Campion sighed with relief.

"The process of elimination," said he oracularly as he picked up the suitcase and trudged back to the car with it, "combined with a modicum of common sense, will always assist us to arrive at the correct conclusion with the maximum of possible accuracy and the minimum of hard labour. Which being translated means: I guessed it." He lifted the case into the dickey once more, and held the door open for Penny and her companion.

She hung back. "That's not fair," she said. "Suppose you explain?"

Mr. Campion shrugged his shoulders. "Well, it wasn't very difficult, was it?" he said. "In the first place it was obvious that the chapel had not been burgled. Ergo, someone had opened the door with the key. Ergo, it must have been you, because the only other two people who could possibly have known where it was were your father and Branch, and they, if I may say so, are both a bit conservative on the subject of the Chalice."

Penny bit her lip and climbed into the driving seat. "Anyway," she said, "I'm the 'Maid of the Cup'."

"Quite," said Mr. Campion. "Hence your very natural feeling of responsibility." He hesitated and looked at her owlishly. "I bet I could tell you what you were going to do with it."

"Well?" She looked at him defiantly.

Mr. Campion laid his hand on that part of the suitcase which projected from the dickey. "You were going to put this in Chancery Lane Safe Deposit," he said.

Penny gasped at him, and there was a little smothered squeak from Beth. Mr. Campion went on.

"You had relied on the ten days' veiling of the Chalice to keep its loss a secret, and I have no doubt you intended to confess the whole matter to Val and your father before they had any real cause for worry. Unfortunately, Mrs. Shannon upset the apple-cart and you had to get busy right away. And that's why I was waiting for you this morning. Now shall we go on?"

Penny sat staring at him in bewilderment. "It's not fair of you to look so idiotic," she said involuntarily. "People get led astray. I suppose you won't even be particularly bucked to know that you've guessed right?"

The young man with the simple face and gentle ineffectual manner looked uncomfortable.

"All this praise makes me unhappy," he said. "I must admit I wasn't sure until I was in the car this morning that you had the treasure in the suitcase. It was only when you were so anxious for me not to sit beside it that I knew that the rat I saw floating in the air was a bona fide rose to nip in the bud."

Penny drew a deep breath. "Well," she said, "I suppose we turn back."

Mr. Campion laid a hand on the driving wheel.

"Please," he said pleadingly, with something faintly reminiscent of seriousness on his face, "please listen to me for a little longer. You two have got to be friends with me. We're all in the soup together. Consider the facts. Here we are, sitting in the middle of a public highway with a highly incriminating piece of antiquity in the back of the car. That's bad to start with. Then—and this is much more worthy of note—if I was bright enough to spot what you were up to, what about our nosy friends who are out for crime anyhow?"

"You mean you think they might actually come down on us on the way?" said Penny apprehensively. This aspect of the case had clearly never occurred to her. "And yet," she added, a flash of suspicion showing in her blue eyes, "it's perfectly ridiculous. How is any outside person to know that the Chalice isn't still in the Cup House? Only Father, Val, Branch, you and I know it's gone."

"You forget," said Mr. Campion gently. "You had visitors yesterday, and the unpleasant Mr. Putnam, who is making use of your retiring little friend Mrs. Shannon, had a face vaguely familiar to me."

Penny's eyes flickered. "That revolting little man?" she said. "Is he the—the big fellow you were talking about? You know, when you said the stream was full of minnows and there were no big fish about."

Mr. Campion regarded her gravely. "I'm afraid not," he said. "But he's certainly in the dab class. I fancy his real name is Matthew Sanderson. That's why I kept so quiet; I was afraid he might spot me. I

don't think he did, but he certainly noticed that the Chalice had disappeared. Hang it all, he couldn't very well miss it. Anyhow, if he is
the man I think he is, then I'm open to bet that he's not twenty
miles away from here now."

Penny looked at him helplessly. "I've been a fool," she said. "We'll
go back at once."

Campion hesitated. "Wait a minute," he said, and glanced at Beth.
"I don't know if we ought to drag Miss Cairey into all this—"

An expression of determination appeared upon the elder girl's face,
and her lips were set in a firm hard line.

"I'm in this with Penny," she said.

To her surprise he nodded gravely. "I told Val you'd be game,"
he said. "He should be waiting for us at a little pub called 'The Case
is Altered' just outside Coggeshall."

"Val?" Penny was startled. "What does he know about it?"

"Just about as much as I do," said Mr. Campion, considering.
"While you were shouting your travelling arrangements over the
phone in the hall last night, he and I were discussing fat stock prices
and whatnot in the smoking-room. I told him what I thought, and I
persuaded him to let you carry on the good work and smuggle the
thing out of the house for us."

"Then you think it's a good idea—the safe deposit?" said Beth anxiously. "I told Penny I was sure that was the only certain way of
keeping it safe."

Mr. Campion did not answer her immediately. He had resumed
his place in the car and sat regarding the dashboard thoughtfully as
though he were making up his mind how much to say.

"Well, hardly, to begin with," he ventured finally. "Although perhaps it may come to that in the end. In the meantime I wondered
if we couldn't beat our friend Arthur Earle at his own game. There's
an old firm in the city—or rather the last remaining member of an old
firm—who'd turn us out a first-rate copy of the Chalice, and somehow
I'd rather be playing hide-and-seek with that than with the real one.
I fancy we shall have to show a bait, you see, to catch the big fish."

"Just one thing," said Penny. "What about Father? Does he know
anything? I seem to have made a pretty prize fool of myself."

Mr. Campion looked if possible more vague than ever. "Your father,
I regret to say," he murmured, and Penny was convinced that he was
lying, "I thought it best to keep in the dark. You left your own excuses. Val no doubt left mine and his own. But," he went on gravely,
"that is hardly the most important point to be considered at the mo-

ment. What we have to arrange now is the safe conveyance of the Chalice to London."

Penny swung the car up the narrow white road.

"I don't know if I'm going to agree with all this," she said warningly, "but I'd like to see Val. Of course, you're not really serious about this attack on the road, are you?"

Mr. Campion regarded her solemnly. "The chivalry of the road," he said, "is not what it was when I used to drive my four-in-hand to Richmond, don't you know. Natty Johnson is no Duval, but he might make a very fine Abbershaw, and old Putnam Sanderson can level a first-class blunderbuss. On the whole, I should think we were certainly in for fun of some sort."

"But if this is true," said Beth indignantly, "why are we going on? How do you know we shan't be held up before we get to Coggeshall?"

"Deduction, dear lady," explained Mr. Campion obligingly. "There are two roads from Sanctuary to Coggeshall. You might have taken either. After Coggeshall you must go straight to Kelvedon, and thence by main road. I fancy they'll be patrolling the main road looking for us."

In spite of herself Penny was impressed. "Well, you're thorough, anyway," she said grudgingly.

"And clean," said Mr. Campion. "In my last place the lady said no home was complete without one of these—hygienic, colourful, and only ten cents down. Get Campion-conscious to-day. Of course," he went on, "I suppose we could attempt to make a detour, but considering all things I think that the telephone wires are probably busy, and at the same time I'm rather anxious to catch a glimpse of our friends in action. I think the quicker we push on the better."

Penny nodded. "All right," she said without resentment. "We leave it to you."

The Case is Altered was a small and unpretentious red brick building standing back from the road and fronted by a square gravel yard. Mr. Campion descended, and cautiously taking the suitcase from the dickey, preceded the ladies into the bar parlour, an unlovely apartment principally ornamented by large oleographs of "The Empty Chair", "The Death of Nelson", and "The Monarch of the Glen", and furnished with vast quantities of floral china, bamboo furniture, and a pot of paper roses. The atmosphere was flavoured with new oilcloth and stale beer, and the motif was sedate preservation.

Val was standing on the hearthrug when they entered, a slightly amused expression on his face. Penny reddened when she saw him, and walking towards him raised her face defiantly to his.

"Well?" she said.

He kissed her.

"Honesty is the best policy, my girl," he said. "Have some ginger beer?"

Penny caught her brother's arm. "Val, do you realize," she said, "here we are, miles from home, with the—the *Thing* actually in a portmanteau. I feel as if we might be struck by a thunderbolt for impudence."

Val put his arm round her shoulders. "Leave it to Albert," he said. "He spotted your little game. He seems to have one of his own."

They turned to Campion inquiringly and he grinned. "Well, look here," he said, "if you don't want to play darts or try the local beer or otherwise disport yourselves, I think the sooner we get on the better. What I suggest is that we split up. Penny, you and I will take the precious suitcase in the two-seater. Val and Miss Cairey will follow close behind to come to our assistance if necessary. Have you got enough petrol?" Penny looked at him in surprise. "I think so," she said, but as he hesitated she added, laughing, "I'll go and see if you like."

Mr. Campion looked more foolish than before. "Twice armed is he who speeds with an excuse, but thrice is he whose car is full of juice," he remarked absently.

Penny went out, leaving the door open, and was just about to return after satisfying herself that all was well, when the young man came out of the doorway bearing the suitcase.

"We'll get on, if you don't mind," he said. "Val's just squaring up with the good lady of the establishment. They'll follow immediately."

Penny glanced about her. "Where is the other car?" she demanded. There was a Ford trade van standing beside the bar entrance, but no sign of a private car.

"Round at the back," said Campion glibly. "There's a petrol pump there."

He dropped the suitcase carefully into the back of the car and sprang in beside the girl. "Now let's drive like fun," he said happily. "How about letting me have the wheel? I've got testimonials from every magistrate in the county."

Somewhat reluctantly the girl gave up her place, but Mr. Campion's driving soon resigned her to the change. He drove with the apparent omnipotence of the born motorist, and all the time he chattered happily in an inconsequential fashion that gave her no time to consider anyone or anything but himself.

"I love cars," he said ecstatically. "I knew a man once—he was a relation of mine as a matter of fact—who had one of the earliest of the breed. I believe it was a roller-skate to start with, but he kept on improving it and it got on wonderfully. About 1904 it was going really strong. It had gadgets all over it then: finally I believe he overdid the thing, but when I knew it you could light a cigarette from almost any pipe under the bonnet, and my relation made tea in the radiator as well as installing a sort of mechanical picnic-basket between the two back wheels. Then one day it died in Trafalgar Square and so—" he finished oracularly—"the first coffee-stall was born. Phoenix-fashion, you know. But perhaps you're not liking this?" he ventured, regarding her anxiously. "After all, I have been a bit trying this morning, haven't I?"

Penny smiled faintly at him.

"I don't really dislike you," she said. "No, go on. Some people drive better when they're talking, I think, don't you?"

"That's not how a young lady should talk," said Mr. Campion reprovingly. "It's the manners of the modern girl I deplore most. When I was a young man—years before I went to India, don't you know, to see about the Mutiny—women were women. Egad, yes. How they blushed when I passed."

Penny shot a sidelong glance in his direction. He was pale and foolish-looking as ever, and seemed to be in deadly earnest.

"Are you trying to amuse me or are you just getting it out of your system?" she said.

"Emancipated, that's what you are," said Mr. Campion, suddenly dropping the Anglo-Indian drawl he had adopted for the last part of his homily. "Emancipated and proud of yourself. Stap my crinoline, Amelia, if you don't think you're a better man than I am!"

Penny laughed. "You're all right, really," she said. "When does the fun begin?"

"Any time from now on," said Mr. Campion gaily, as he swung the little car into the main road. Penny glanced nervously over her shoulder.

"There's no sign of the others yet," she said.

Her companion looked faintly perturbed.

"Can't help that," he said.

It was now about half-past eleven o'clock, and although a Friday morning, the road was not as crowded as it would become later in the day. Mr. Campion drove fiercely, overtaking everything that presented itself. On the long straight strip outside Witham he once more broke into his peculiar brand of one-sided conversation.

"Then there's poetry," he said. "Here is to-day's beautiful thought:

There was an ex-mayor in a garden
A-playing upon a bombardon,
His tunes were flat, crude,
Broad, uncivic, rude,
And—

"I don't like the look of that car which has just passed us. It's an old Staff Benz, isn't it? Sit still, and whatever you do don't try and hit anybody. If you lose your head it doesn't matter, but don't try to hit out."

On the last word he jammed on the brakes and brought the car to a standstill only just in time, as the old German staff car, heavy as a lorry and fast as a racer, swerved violently across the road in front of them and came to a full stop diagonally across their path so that they were hemmed in by the angle. The whole thing was so neatly timed that there was no escape. It was only by brilliant driving that Mr. Campion had succeeded in pulling up at all.

What took place immediately afterwards happened with the speed and precision of a well-planned smash-and-grab raid. Hardly were the two cars stationary before five men had slipped out of the Benz, the driver alone remaining in his seat, and the sports car was surrounded. The raiding party swarmed over the little car. There was no outward show of violence, and it was only when Penny glanced up into the face of the man who had stationed himself on the running-board at her side that she fully realized that the newcomers were definitely hostile.

She shot a sidelong terrified glance at Mr. Campion, and saw that the man upon his side had laid a hand in an apparently friendly fashion on the back of his neck, the only untoward feature of the gesture being that in the hand was a revolver.

A third man leaned negligently against the bonnet, his hand in the pocket of his coat, while a fourth, with remarkable coolness, stood by the back of the Benz to signal that all was well to any passing motorist who might stop, suspecting a smash.

They were all heavy, flashily dressed specimens of the type only too well known to the race course bookmaker.

Penny opened her mouth. She was vaguely conscious of other cars on the road. The man at her side gripped her arm.

"Hold your tongue, miss," he said softly. "No yelping. Now then, where is it?"

Penny glanced at Albert. He was sitting very still, his expression a complete blank.

"No—no," he said, in a slightly high-pitched voice, "I do not wish to subscribe. I am not a music lover. Go and play outside the next house."

The stranger's hand still rested caressingly on the back of his neck. "Now then, no acting 'crackers'," he said. "Where is it?"

"You should take glycerine for your voice and peppermints for your breath, my friend," continued Mr. Campion querulously. "Don't bellow at me. I'm not deaf."

His interlocutor summoned the man who leant so negligently against the bonnet. "There's nothing in the front of the car," he said. "Have a squint into the dickey."

"No!" Penny could not repress a little cry of horror.

The man with the gun, who seemed to be in charge of the proceedings, grinned. "Thank you kindly, miss," he said sarcastically. "A girl and a loony. It's like stealing a bottle from a baby."

"There's only my lunch in there," said Mr. Campion, but Penny noticed that his voice betrayed nothing but nervousness.

"Is that so?" The third man lifted out the suitcase. "This is it," he said. "It weighs a ton. The rest of the car is empty, anyhow."

Too terror-stricken to speak, Penny glanced wildly up the road only to see a Rolls-Royce and a van being waved on by their persecutors.

"'Ere, these locks 'ave been bunged up," said a voice behind her. "Give us yer knife."

The man with the gun glanced down the road, apprehensively it seemed to Penny. "Stick it in the bus," he said. "There's nothing else here, anyhow. Now then, boys, scarpa!"

His four satellites were back in the Benz with the precious suitcase within ten seconds. The driver swung the car back with a roar, and the man with the gun gave up his position and leapt for it as it passed. They had chosen a moment when the coast was clear, and the whole astounding episode was over in a space of time a little under five minutes.

Mr. Campion freed his brakes and started the engine, but instead of turning and following the retreating raiders as Penny had half hoped, half feared he would, he sent the car careering down the road towards London, and the speedometer finger crept round the dial like a stop watch.

It was not until they reached Witham and crawled through the narrow street that Mr. Campion permitted himself a glance at his companion. Before then the car had occupied his whole attention. To his horror she was in tears. For the first time that day his nerve failed him.

CHAPTER TWELVE

Holding the Baby

"*And he never stopped once to beg pardon,*" said Mr. Campion, as he swung the sports car neatly into the big yard at the back of the Huguenot's Arms at Witham and brought it to a stop within a yard of the pump.

Penny hastily dabbed away her tears. "What on earth are you talking about?"

"Poetry," said Mr. Campion. "The highest within me. Soul juice, in fact. It's the last line of the Neo-Georgian sonnet I was declaiming to you when the rude gentleman with the acquisitive instinct stopped us. Don't you remember—about the civic person in the garden? I'd better recite the whole thing to you."

Penny put out her hand appealingly. "Don't," she said. "It's awfully good of you to try to cheer me up, but you can't realize, as a stranger, what this means. That suitcase contained the one thing that matters most in the world. I'm afraid I've lost my nerve completely. We must get to the police."

Mr. Campion sat perfectly still, regarding her with owlish solemnity.

"You're the first person I've met to feel so sensibly about a couple of bottles of bitter," he said. "I had no idea you'd get het-up like this."

Penny stared at him, the truth slowly dawning upon her.

"Albert," she said, "you—"

He laid a hand upon her arm. "Don't spoil the fun," he said. "Look."

Even as he spoke there came the roar of an engine from outside and a trade van jolted slowly into the yard. The cab was facing them, and a gasp of mingled amusement and relief escaped Penny.

Val sat at the steering wheel, a peaked cap pulled well down over his eyes and a cheap yellow mackintosh buttoned tightly up to his throat. He had a strap buckled across one shoulder which suggested admirably the presence of a leather cash satchel. A pencil behind his ear finished the ensemble. The metamorphosis was perfect. Anyone would have been deceived.

The *chef-d'œuvre* of the outfit, however, was Beth. She had pushed her smart beret on to the back of her head, reddened her lips until they looked sticky, plastered a kiss-curl in the middle of her forehead, and had removed the jacket of her three-piece suit so that she was in a blouse and skirt. She was smiling complacently, her big dark eyes dancing with amusement. And in her arms, clasped tightly against her breast, was a precious bundle swaddled in white shawls with a lace veil over the upper part.

"There," said Mr. Campion. "All done with a few common chalks. Our young Harry taking his missus and the kid for a trip during business hours. 'Domesticity versus Efficiency', or 'All His Own Work'."

Penny chuckled. "You're wonderful," she said. "And the baby, of course—?"

"Is worth his weight in gold. Let's leave it at that," said Mr. Campion. "Now, since this trip seems to have degenerated into a pub-crawl, suppose we go into the private room which Val I hope has booked on the phone and we'll shuffle and cut again."

Ten minutes later, in a small and stuffy room on the first floor of the old road house, Mr. Campion made his apologies to Penny.

"I've behaved like a common or garden toot," he said with real penitence in his eyes. "But you see, there wasn't time to go into full explanations at Coggeshall—and then you might not have agreed. And I did so want to get a squint at Uncle Beastly's boy friends in action. I didn't think there'd be any real danger, and there wasn't, you know. Will you forgive me?"

Penny sat down in a rickety wicker arm-chair. "That's all right," she said weakly. "What happens next?"

Beth, who was standing before the mirror over the fireplace re-arranging her make-up, turned to her friend.

"When we passed you and the man who was holding you up signed to us to go on, I thought I'd die," she said.

"If this had been a real baby I'd have squeezed the life out of it. They didn't suspect us for a moment, though, and later on, when you passed us again, we knew it was all right."

Penny passed a hand over her forehead. "Who worked it all out?" she said. "I suppose you had the shawls and stuff with you, Val?"

Her brother nodded. "When you went out to see if there was enough petrol we swapped the—contents of the suitcase for a couple of quart bottles of bitter, and then I explained to Beth. She's been wonderful."

He cast an admiring glance at the little dark-haired girl. Beth changed the subject.

"Did you find out what you wanted to know about the gangsters, Mr. Campion?" she said. "I mean—did you recognize any of them?"

"Yes and no, as they say in legal circles," said Mr. Campion. "The unsavoury little object who leant on our bonnet, Penny, was our Natty Johnson, an old thorn in Lugg's flesh. Two others were 'whizz boys' —pickpockets or sneak-thieves, you know—and the gentleman who did the talking and tickled my neck with a gun muzzle is 'Fingers' Hawkins, an old associate of 'Putnam' Sanderson. All sound reliable workmen whose services can be obtained for a moderate fee. The driver I was unable to see, although his was a nice professional piece of work. They're now probably swigging the beer and playing 'who says the rudest word'. That's why we needn't fear reprisals at the moment. They've got no personal animosity, if you get me. They'll wait for instructions before they do anything else. It doesn't tell us much, unfortunately."

Val lounged forward. "Now I suppose we send these two kids home?" he said.

"A remark that might have been better put," said Mr. Campion mildly. "What I was hoping we could persuade our two young female friends to do is to catch the twelve-thirty to Hadleigh from the station opposite, while we sally forth to the city in their car with their treasure." He looked from one to the other of the two girls dubiously. "I suppose you're going to be furious?" he inquired.

Penny looked disappointed, but Beth chuckled. "I'll say they've got a nerve," she said. "Still, I guess we'll have to let them have their own way. This is strong man's work." She imitated Val's somewhat unctuous delivery, and the boy laughed.

"She's been getting at me all the way along," he said. "You wait till this thing's over and I'll show you the lighter side of country life."

Beth smiled. "It's had its moments already," she said, and placed the shawl-wrapped bundle in his arms.

"How about the van?" said Penny.

"That's all right," said Val. "I arranged with the man to leave it. It belongs to Mudds', of Ipswich. Now, suppose we get along?"

He insisted that he would accompany the girls to the station opposite, while Mr. Campion got out the car and invested in another suitcase.

"When will you be back?" inquired Penny in the doorway.

"To-morrow, if all goes well." Campion spoke lightly. "In the meantime rely on Lugg, my other ego. I don't think there's a chance of any trouble, but should the worst happen he's as good as a police force and about as beautiful. He's going to the nation when I die. Tell him not to wear my socks, by the way. Also my pullover in the School colours. I have spies everywhere."

She laughed and went out. Mr. Campion looked after her reflectively. "Such a nice girl," he observed to the world at large. "Why in Heaven's name couldn't Marlowe Lobbett have waited a bit and picked on her instead of Biddy?"

He and Val were on the road again within twenty minutes. The younger man seemed much more cheerful than before.

"Do you know," he confided after a long period of silence, "there's something quite different about that girl, Beth. She's got a sort of charm. I've hated women for so long," he went on diffidently, "that it's marvellous to find one who breaks down your prejudices. In spite of your being such a funny bird you must know what I mean."

"You forget I am wedded to my art," said Mr. Campion with great solemnity. "Since I took up woodcraft women have had no place in my life."

"I mean seriously," said Val, a little nettled.

A slightly weary expression entered Mr. Campion's pale eyes behind his enormous spectacles. "Seriously, my dear old bird," he said, "Ophelia married Macbeth in my Hamlet. Now, for Heaven's sake get your mind on the business in hand."

Val leant back in the car. "You drive magnificently," he said. "I'm not sure if it's her voice or her eyes that are most attractive—which would you say?" he added irrelevantly.

Mr. Campion did not reply immediately, and the little car sped on towards the city.

"We'll go straight there if you don't mind." It was almost an hour later when he spoke again as he turned the car deviously through Aldgate and made for that ancient and slightly gloomy section of the city which is called Poultry.

Val sat forward.

"Not at all—good idea," he said. "Although, I say, Campion, you're sure it's safe?"

Mr. Campion shrugged his shoulders. "Melchizadek's safe enough," he said. "Patronized by all the best people since the first George, don't you know. And as silent as the grave. An old friend of mine, too. But, of course, I don't suppose he's bullet-proof if it comes to that. Still, I'd like his opinion on the chances of getting an indetectable copy made. Frankly, Val, how far back does this Chalice date?"

The younger man hesitated. "It's hard to say, really," he said at length. "It's pre-Conquest, anyhow."

Mr. Campion all but stopped the car, and the face he turned towards his passenger was blank with astonishment. "Look here," he said, "you don't mean to say this thing we've got in the suitcase is a thousand years old, do you?"

"My dear fellow, of course it is." Val was a little hurt. "You know the legends about it as well as I do."

Mr. Campion was silent, and the other went on. "Why the amazement?" he demanded.

"Nothing," said his companion. "The idea suddenly struck me all of a heap, that's all. Here have we been playing 'body in the bag' with it all the morning and its importance suddenly came home to me. Here we are, by the way."

He turned the car dexterously into a narrow blind alley and pulled up outside a small old-fashioned shop, or rather a building with a shop window which had been half covered over with gold and black paint so that it resembled one of the many wholesale businesses with which the neighbourhood abounded. The heavy door with its shining brass trimmings stood ajar, and Mr. Campion dismounted, and lifting out the new suitcase walked into the building. Val followed him.

A small brass plate with the name "I. Melchizadek" engraved upon it was fixed directly beneath the old-fashioned bell-pull. Val noticed that there was no sign of any other business in the building. He followed Campion into a large outer office with a flimsy wooden barrier across it. It all seemed very quiet and deserted, and save for two or three small showcases containing beautifully worked replicas of obscure medals and diplomatic jewellery there was no indication of the business of the firm.

Immediately upon their arrival a slight, suave young man rose from behind a roll-top desk set in the far corner behind the barrier and came towards them. Mr. Campion took a card from his pocket and handed it to him.

"Will you ask Mr. Melchizadek if he can spare me a few moments?" he asked.

The young man took the card and repeated the name aloud.

"Mr. Christopher Twelvetrees."

"Hullo," said Val, "you've made—"

To his astonishment Mr. Campion signalled to him to be quiet and nodded to the clerk. "That's all right," he said. "Mr. Melchizadek knows me."

As the young man disappeared Campion turned an apologetic face to his friend. "I ought to have warned you about my many *noms de guerre*," he said. "It's just so that my best friends can't tell me. You won't forget, will you? I'm Christopher Twelvetrees until we get outside."

Considerably bewildered, Val had only just time to nod in silent acquiescence when the door of the inner office through which the clerk had disappeared re-opened to admit one of the most striking-looking old men he had ever seen.

Mr. Israel Melchizadek was that miracle of good breeding, the refined and intellectual Jew. Looking at him one was irresistibly reminded of the fact that his ancestors had ancestors who had conversed with Jehovah. He was nearing seventy years of age, a tall, lean old fellow with a firm delicate face of what might well have been polished ivory. He was clean-shaven and his white hair was cut close to his head. He came forward with outstretched hand.

"Mr. Twelvetrees," he said, "I am pleased to see you."

His voice had a luxurious quality which heightened the peculiar Oriental note of his whole personality. Campion shook hands and introduced Val.

The boy was conscious of little shrewd black eyes peering into his face, summing him up with unerring judgement. In spite of himself he was impressed. Mr. Melchizadek glanced at the suitcase.

"If you'll come into my office, Mr. Twelvetrees," he said, "we can speak without being overheard or interrupted."

He led the way through the second doorway down a short corridor, and ushered them into a small luxurious room which served as a perfect frame for his remarkable personality.

The floor was covered with an ancient Persian rug, while the walls were hung with fine paintings; a David, a Zoffany, and, over the mantel, the head of a very beautiful woman by de Laszlo.

An immense table desk took up most of the room, and after setting chairs for his clients Mr. Melchizadek sat down behind it.

"Now, Mr. Twelvetrees," he said, "what can I do for you?" He hesitated. "You wish me to make a copy, perhaps? Perhaps of a certain very famous chalice?"

Mr. Campion raised his eyebrows.

"Taking the long road, sir?" he inquired affably.

The old man shook his head and for a moment his thin lips parted in a smile.

"No, my friend," he said. "I have too many clients to follow any road but my own."

Campion sighed. "Thank Heaven for that," he said. "Well, of course, you're right. I see you appreciate the gravity of the situation. What we've got here is nothing more nor less than the Gyrth Chalice."

He picked up the suitcase and laid it reverently upon the desk. The old man rose and came forward.

"I have never seen it," he said, "although of course its history—or rather its legend—is quite well known to me. Really, this is going to be a most delightful experience for me, Mr. Gyrth," he added, glancing at Val. "In the last two hundred years we have been privileged to handle many treasures, but even so this is a memorable occasion."

"Over a thousand years old," said Mr. Campion profoundly, and, Val thought, a little foolishly, as if he were particularly anxious to impress the date on the old man's mind. "Over a thousand years."

He carefully unlocked the suitcase, and having first removed the motor rug, produced the Chalice, still in its wrapping of shawls.

Mr. Melchizadek was surprised and even a little shocked, it seemed to Val, by this unconventional covering. However, he said nothing until Mr. Campion took off the last shawl and placed the golden cup in his hands.

The picture was one that Val never forgot. The tall, austere old man appraising the magnificent workmanship with long delicate fingers. He turned the relic over and over, peering at it through a small jeweller's glass; glancing beneath it, inside it, and finally setting it down upon the desk, and turned to his visitors. He seemed a little puzzled, ill at ease.

"Mr. Twelvetrees," he said slowly, "we are old friends, you and I."

Mr. Campion met his eyes.

"Mr. Gyrth here, and I," he said with apparent irrelevancy, "can swear to you that that is the Gyrth Chalice. What can you tell us about it?"

For the first time Val sensed that something was wrong, and rising from his chair came to stand beside the others.

Mr. Melchizadek picked up the Chalice again.

"This is a beautiful piece," he said. "The workmanship is magnificent, and the design is almost a replica of the one in the church of San Michele at Vecchia. But it is not medieval. I am not sure, but I believe that if you will allow me to look up our records, I can tell you the exact date when it was made."

An inarticulate cry escaped Val, and he opened his mouth to speak angrily. Mr. Campion restrained him.

"Hang on a bit, old bird," he murmured. "This thing's getting more complicated every minute. I fancy we're on the eve of a discovery."

The silence which followed was broken by Mr. Melchizadek's quiet voice. "I would rather you did not take my word for it, Mr. Twelvetrees," he said. "I should like a second opinion myself. I am an old man, and remarkable freaks of period do occur. I wonder, therefore, if you would allow me to introduce a friend of mine into this discussion? Quite by chance I have in the next room one of the most famous experts on this subject in the world. He was calling on me when you arrived, and did me the honour to wait until I should be disengaged. What do you say?" He turned from Campion to Val. The boy was scarlet and frankly bewildered. Mr. Melchizadek coughed.

"You can rely upon his discretion as you would upon mine," he murmured.

"Oh, certainly," said Val hurriedly, and Campion nodded to the old expert, who went silently out of the room.

Val turned to Campion. "This is madness," he said huskily. "It—"

Mr. Campion laid a hand upon his shoulder. "Hold on," he said, "let them do the talking. I believe I'm getting this thing straight at last."

He had no time for further confidences as Mr. Melchizadek reappeared, and behind him came a slight, agile little man, with a high forehead and a pointed vandyke beard. His appearance was familiar to both of them, and they had recognized him even before Mr. Melchizadek's opening words.

"This, gentlemen, is Professor Gardner Cairey, a great American authority. Professor Cairey, allow me to present to you Mr. Gyrth and Mr. Christopher Twelvetrees."

CHAPTER THIRTEEN

"I. Melchizadek Fecit"

There was a considerable pause after the introductions. Professor Cairey stood looking at the two young men, a slightly dubious expression in his eyes, and Val, for the first time, took good stock of him.

He was a little dapper old man, with the same delightful air of suppressed enjoyment that was so noticeable in his daughter. His face was keen and clever without being disconcertingly shrewd, and there was a friendliness about him which impressed the two immediately.

He was the first to speak, revealing a quiet, pleasant voice, with a definite transatlantic intonation which somehow underlined his appreciation of the oddity of the situation. He smiled at Mr. Melchizadek. "This is a whale of a problem," he said. "Luck has caught me out. I'm not on speaking terms with Mr. Gyrth's folk, and I owe him an apology, anyway."

Then he laughed, and instantly the tension relaxed. Val would have spoken had not Campion rested a hand on his arm, and Professor Cairey continued.

"I've been what my daughter would call a Kibitzer," he said. "In fact, I even went so far as to trespass in your garden a day or two back, Mr. Gyrth. I didn't think I was seen, but in case I was perhaps I'd better explain."

Val could not be restrained. "I'm afraid we did see you, Professor," he said. "You were looking into the chapel."

The old man grimaced. "I was," he said. "I was half-way through my new book, *The Effect of the Commonwealth on East Anglian Ecclesiastical Decoration*, and I don't mind telling you I was hoping— well, to get some assistance from you folk. But I got myself in wrong with your Pa somehow, and I was as far off from the inside of your chapel as I should have been if I'd stayed at home in Westport, N.J." He hesitated and glanced at them with bright, laughing eyes. "I stuck it as long as I could," he went on, "and then the other night, before I heard of your trouble, I felt I'd attempt to have a look and finish my chapter if it meant being chased by a gardener's boy."

Val reddened. "I haven't been at home," he said. "And, of course, I'm afraid my poor aunt made things rather difficult. I'd be delighted to take you over the place any time. As a matter of fact," he added transparently, "I came up to Town part of the way with your daughter."

Mr. Campion, who had been silent so far during the interview, regarded the Professor with eyes that laughed behind his spectacles.

"Professor Cairey," he said, "you're the author of *Superstition before Cotton Mather*, aren't you?"

Professor Cairey positively blushed. "That's so, Mr. Twelvetrees," he said, laying particular stress on the name. "I didn't think anyone on this side took any stock of it."

Val had the uncomfortable impression that these two were getting at one another with a certain playfulness which he did not understand.

Mr. Campion's manner then became almost reverential. "I owe you an apology, sir," he said. "I don't mind telling you we thought you were a bird of a very different feather. In fact," he added with alarming frankness, "we thought you were out after the Chalice."

Mr. Melchizadek looked horrified and muttered a word of protest. The Professor soothed him with a smile.

"So I was," he said, "in a way." He turned to Val and explained himself. "Of course, I've been familiar with the history of your great treasure, Mr. Gyrth. It's one of the seven wonders of the world, in my estimation. I was naturally anxious to get a glimpse of it if I could. I had heard that there was one day in the week when it was displayed to the public, and I'd have availed myself of that, only, as I say, the Cup was hidden behind bars in a bad light and there was this mite of trouble between your aunt and Mrs. Cairey, and while I was hoping that the little contretemps would blow over, your poor aunt met her death, and naturally I could hardly come visiting."

Val, who seemed to have fallen completely under the spell of the old man's charming personality, would have launched out into a stream of incoherent apologies for what he knew instinctively was some appalling piece of bad manners from the late Lady Pethwick, when Mr. Melchizadek's suave gentle voice forestalled him.

"I think," he ventured, "that if you would allow Professor Cairey to examine the Chalice on the table he could give an opinion of interest to all of us."

"By all means." Mr. Campion stepped aside from the desk and revealed the Cup. The Professor pounced upon it with enthusiasm. He took it up, turned it over, and tested the metal with his thumb.

"I'll take the loan of your glass, Melchizadek," he said. "This is a lovely thing."

They stood watching him, fascinated. His short capable fingers moved caressingly over the ornate surface. He appraised it almost movement for movement as Mr. Melchizadek had done. Finally he set it down.

"What do you want to know about it?" he said.

"What is it?" said Mr. Campion quickly, before Val could get a word in.

The Professor considered. "It's a church Chalice," he said. "The design is Renaissance. But the workmanship I should say is of much later date. It's about a hundred and fifty years old."

Val looked at Campion dumbly, and Mr. Melchizadek took the treasure.

"I thought so," he said. "If you will permit me, Mr. Gyrth, I think I could prove this to you. I didn't like to suggest it before in case I was mistaken."

He took a small slender-bladed knife from a drawer, and after studying the jewelled bosses round the pedestal of the cup through his lens for some minutes, finally began to prise gently round the base of one of them. Suddenly an exclamation of gratification escaped him, and putting down the instrument he unscrewed the jewel and its setting and laid it carefully on the desk. As the others crowded round him he pointed to the tiny smooth surface that was exposed.

There, only just decipherable, was the simple inscription, engraved upon the metal:

I. Melchizadek fecit

1772

"My great-grandfather," said Mr. Melchizadek simply, "the founder of this firm. He invariably signed every piece that he made, although at times it was necessary for him to do so where it would not be seen by the casual observer."

"But," said Val, refusing to be silenced any longer, "don't you see what this means? This is what has passed for the last—well, for my own and my father's lifetime—as the Gyrth Chalice."

For a moment the Professor seemed as stupefied as Val. Then a light of understanding crept into his eyes. He crossed over to Mr. Campion.

"Mr. Twelvetrees," he murmured, "I'd like to have a word with you and Mr. Gyrth in private. Maybe there's somewhere where we could go and talk."

Mr. Campion regarded him shrewdly from behind his heavy spectacles. "I was hoping that myself," he said.

Meanwhile Val, still inarticulate and bewildered, was standing staring at the handiwork of the Melchizadek great-grandparent as if he had never seen it before. Professor Cairey took the situation in hand. He bade farewell to the old Jew, with whom he seemed to be on intimate terms, the Chalice was repacked in the suitcase, and ten minutes later all three of them were squeezed into the two-seater worming their way from the City to the West End.

It did just occur to Val that this acceptance of Professor Cairey was a little sudden, to say the least of it. But the Professor was so obviously bona fide, and his disposition so kindly, that he himself was prepared to trust him to any lengths within ten minutes of their first meeting. However, Mr. Campion had never struck him as being the possessor of a particularly trusting spirit, and he was surprised.

Before they had reached Piccadilly Campion had reintroduced himself with charming naïveté, and by the time they mounted the stairs to the flat they were talking like comparatively old friends.

Val, who had been considerably astonished by the open way in which Campion had approached the place, now glanced across at him as he set a chair for their visitor.

"Last time I came here," he remarked, "I understood from you that I was liable to be plugged at any moment if I went outside the door. Why no excitement now?"

"Now," said Mr. Campion, "the damage is done, as far as they're concerned. It must be obvious by this time to everyone interested that you and I are on the job together. To put a bullet through you would

be only wanton destructiveness. The good news has been brought from
Aix to Ghent, as it were. Your father knows there's danger, Scotland
Yard knows, every 'tec in the country may be on the job. 'George's'
minions may be watching outside, but I doubt it."

Professor Cairey, who had been listening to this conversation, his
round brown eyes alert with interest and his hands folded across his
waist, now spoke quietly.

"I haven't been able to help gathering what the trouble is," he remarked.

Val shrugged his shoulders. "After Mr. Melchizadek's discoveries,"
he said slowly, "the trouble becomes absurd. In fact, the whole thing
is a tragic fiasco," he added bitterly.

The Professor and Campion exchanged glances. It was the old man
who spoke, however.

"I shouldn't waste your time thinking that, son," he said. "See here,"
he added, turning to Campion, "I'll say you'd better confess to Mr.
Gyrth right now, and then perhaps we can get going."

Val looked quickly at Campion who came forward modestly.

"The situation is a delicate one," he murmured. "However, perhaps
you're right and now is the time to get things sorted out. The truth is,
Val, I had my doubts about the Chalice the moment I saw the photograph of it. Before I looked you up, therefore, I paid a visit to my old
friend Professor Cairey, the greatest living expert on the subject, who,
I discovered, was staying next door to the ancestral home. This is not
the coincidence it sounds, you see. The Professor has confessed why
he rented the next place to yours. He couldn't tell me for certain from
the photographs, although he had very grave doubts." He paused, and
the American nodded. Campion continued:

"Since there was a little friction between your aunt and her neighbours, I couldn't very well introduce the Professor into the bosom of
the family right away. I regret to say, therefore, that I called on him,
and begged him to meet me up at Melchizadek's. You see, I knew it
would take more than one expert opinion to convince you that the
Chalice wasn't all it set itself up to be." He paused and stood looking
hesitantly at the younger man. "I'm awfully sorry," he said apologetically. "You see, I was going to persuade you to bring it up to be copied,
and then the girls pinched it so obligingly for us."

Val sank down in a chair and covered his face with his hands. "It's
beyond me," he said. "It seems to be the end of everything."

The Professor leant forward in his chair, and the expression upon his
wise, humorous face was very kindly.

"See here," he said, "I don't want to upset any family arrangement whereby you're told certain things at a certain age. Also I appreciate the delicacy of the matter I'm presuming to discuss. But, if you'll permit me, I'd like to tell you certain facts that occur to me as they might to anyone who looked at this matter from the outside without being hampered by a lifelong association with one idea."

He paused, and Val, looking up, listened to him intently.

"If you ask me," went on the Professor, "I'd say that that very lovely piece which you have in the case there, and which has been in your chapel for the last hundred and fifty odd years, is what might be called a 'mock chalice'. You see," he continued, warming up to his subject, "most ancient ideas were simple, obvious notions; uncomplicated methods of preserving the safety of a treasure. Now in my opinion that 'mock chalice', as we'll call it, is the last of many such—probably all different in design. The real Chalice has always been kept in the background—hidden out of sight—while the show-piece took its place to appease sightseers and thieves and so forth."

Val took a deep breath. "I follow you," he said, a glimmer of hope appearing in his eyes. "You mean that the real Chalice is too valuable to be on show?"

"Absolutely—when there were marauders like your great patriot Cromwell about." The Professor spoke with the hint of a chuckle in his voice. "There are two or three examples of this happening before. I've made a study of this sort of thing, you know. In fact," he added, "I could probably tell you more about the history of your own Chalice than anyone in the world outside your own family. For instance, in the time of Richard the Second it was said to have been stolen, and again just after the Restoration. But the Gyrths' lands were never forfeited to the Crown as they would certainly have been had the real Chalice been stolen. Queen Anne granted another charter, ratifying, so to speak, your family's possession of the genuine thing."

He paused at the boy's surprise, and Campion grinned.

"The Professor's a true son of his country—he knows more about ours than we do," he remarked.

Val sat back in his chair. "Look here," he said, "if this is the 'mock chalice', as you call it, why can't we let these infernal thieves, whoever they are, have it, and say no more about it?"

Mr. Campion shook his head. "That's no good," he said. "In the first place they'd spot it from the thing itself, just as we have; and in the second place, unless this forfeiting business of lands and whatnot was at any rate discussed, they'd know they hadn't got the real thing and they wouldn't be happy until they had. Infernally tenacious beg-

gars, 'Ethel' and 'George'. No, our original scheme is the only one.
We've got to find the big fish and hook him."

"You see, Mr. Gyrth," the Professor put in slowly, "everything that
I have told you this morning would be perfectly obvious to an intelligent thief. I imagine the people you have to deal with are men of
taste and discrimination. Once they had handled this Chalice themselves they'd be bound to come to the same conclusion as I have. Unfortunately it has been described by several ancient writers. Modern
delinquents have much more opportunity of finding out historical facts
than their medieval counterparts."

"My dear old bird," said Mr. Campion, "don't look so funereal.
They don't know this yet, rest assured of that. There are probably only
five people in the world at present aware of the existence of the second
Chalice, and in order to preserve the secret of the real one we must
hang on to the 'mock chalice' like a pair of bull pups."

"Yes, I see that." Val spoke slowly. "But where is the real Chalice
—buried somewhere?"

The Professor cleared his throat. "As an outsider," he began, "I
hardly like to put forward the suggestion, but it seems perfectly obvious
to me—allowing for the medieval mind—that that point will be made
quite clear to you on your twenty-fifth birthday."

Val started violently. "*The Room!*" he said. "Of course."

For a moment he was lost in wonderment. Then his expression
changed and there was something that was almost fear in his eyes.

"But that's not all," he said huskily. It was evident that the subject
so long taboo had rankled in his mind, for he spoke with eagerness,
almost with relief, at being able at last to speak his pent-up suspicions.

"The room in the east wing," he said solemnly, "contains something
terrible. Do you know, Campion, I may be crazy, but I can't help feeling that it's no ordinary museum exhibit. All my life my father has been
overshadowed by something. I mean," he went on, struggling vainly
to express himself, "he has something on his mind—something that's
almost too big for it. And my grandfather was the same. This is not a
subject that's ever spoken of, and I've never mentioned it before to a
soul, but there *is* something there, and it's something awe-inspiring."

There was a short silence after he had spoken, and the Professor
rose to his feet. "I don't think there's any doubt," he said quietly, "that
the real Chalice, which is made of English red gold, and is probably
little bigger than a man's cupped hand, has a very terrible and effective guardian."

CHAPTER FOURTEEN

Fifty-seven Varieties

"All these things are ordained, as the old lady said at the Church Congress," observed Mr. Campion. "Everything comes to an end, and we're certainly getting a bit forrader. We shall have another expert opinion in a moment or so. My friend Inspector Stanislaus Oates is a most delightful cove. He'll turn up all bright and unofficial and tell us the betting odds."

He sank down in an arm-chair opposite Val and lit a cigarette. His friend stirred uneasily.

"We *are* having a day with the experts, aren't we?" he said. "I say, I like the Professor. Why did you keep him up your sleeve so long?"

Mr. Campion spread out his hands. "Just low cunning," he said. "A foolish desire to impress. Also, you must remember, I didn't know you very well. You might not have been the sort of young person for him to associate with. Besides that, Mrs. Cairey—a most charming old dear, by the way—and your aunt were playing the old feminine game of spit-scratch-and-run among the tea-cups. Sans 'purr' seems to have been your aunt's motto."

Val frowned. "Aunt Di," he said, "was what Uncle Lionel's brother Adolphe used to call a freak of Nature. I remember him saying to me: 'Val, my boy, you never get a woman who is a complete fool. Many men achieve that distinction, but never a woman. The exception which proves that rule is your Aunt Diana'. He didn't like her. I wonder what she said to Mrs. Cairey. Something offensive, I'll bet."

"Something about the 'Pilgrim Fathers being Nonconformists, anyhow,' I should think," said Mr. Campion judicially, as he adjusted his glasses. "Hullo," he added, pricking up his ears, "footsteps on the stairs. 'And that, if I mistake not, Watson, is our client.' He's early. As a rule they don't let him out till half-past six."

He did not trouble to rise, but shouted cheerfully: "Enter the Byng Boy! Lift the latch and come in."

A long silence followed this invitation. Mr. Campion shouted again. "Come right in. All friends here. Leave your handcuffs on the hook provided by the management."

There was a footstep in the passage outside, and the next moment the door of the room in which they sat was pushed cautiously open, and a small white face topped by a battered trilby hat peered through the opening. Mr. Campion sprang to his feet.

"Ernie Walker!" he said. "Shoo! Shoo! Scat! We've got a policeman coming up here."

The pale unlovely face split into a leer. "That's all right," he said. "I'm out on tick. All me papers signed up proper. I got something to tell yer. Something to make yer sit up."

Mr. Campion sat down again. "Come in," he said. "Shut the door carefully behind you. Stand up straight, and wipe the egg off your upper lip."

The leer broadened. "I can grow a moustache if I like, can't I?" said Mr. Walker without malice. He edged into the room, revealing a lank, drooping figure clad in dingy tweeds grown stiff with motor-grease. He came towards Campion with a slow self-conscious swagger.

"I can do you a bit o' good, I can," he said. "But it'll cost yer a fiver."

"Just what they say in Harley Street, only not so frankly," said Mr. Campion cheerfully. "What are you offering me? Pills? Or do you want to put me up for your club?"

Ernie Walker jerked his thumb towards Val. "What about 'im?" he demanded.

"That's all right. He's the Lord Harry," said Campion. "No one of importance. Carry on. What's the tale?"

"I said a fiver," said Ernie, removing his hat, out of deference, Val felt, to the title his friend had so suddenly bestowed upon him.

"You'll never get a job on the knocker like that," said Mr. Campion reprovingly. "Get on with your fanny."

Ernie winked at Val. "Knows all the words, don't 'e?" he said. "If 'e was as bright as 'e thinks 'e is 'e'd 'ave spotted me this morning."

Mr. Campion looked up. "Good Lord! You drove the Benz," he said. "You'll get your papers 'all torn up proper' if you don't look out."

"Steady on—steady on. I wasn't doin' nothin'. Drivin' a party for an outin'—that's wot I was up to." Ernie's expression was one of outraged innocence. "And if you don't want to know anything, you needn't. I'm treatin' yer like a friend and yer start gettin' nasty." He put on his hat.

"No need to replace the divot," said Mr. Campion mildly. "You were hired for the job, I suppose?"

"That's right," said Ernie. "And I thought you might pay a fiver to find out who hired me."

Mr. Campion sighed. "If you've come all this way to tell me that

Matthew Sanderson doesn't like me," he said, "you're a bigger fool than I am, Gunga Din."

"If it comes to callin' names," said Mr. Walker with heat, as he struggled to repress his disappointment, "I know me piece as well as anybody."

Campion raised a hand warningly. "Hush," he said, indicating Val. "Remember the Aristocracy. Is that all you have to offer?"

"No, it ain't. Certainly Matt Sanderson engaged me, but he's working for another feller. While I was tuning up the car I kept me ears open and I 'eard 'im talkin' about the big feller. You never know when a spot of information may be useful, I says to meself."

Mr. Campion's eyes flickered behind his big spectacles. "Now you're becoming mildly interesting," he said.

"It's five quid," said Ernie. "Five quid for the name o' the bloke Sanderson was workin' for."

Mr. Campion felt for his note-case. "It's this cheap fiction you read," he grumbled. "This thinking in terms of fivers. Your dad would come across for half a crown." He held up five notes like a poker hand.

"Now," he said, "out with it."

Ernie became affable. "You're a gent," he said, "that's what you are. One of the nobs. Well, I 'eard Sanderson say to a pal of 'is—a stranger to the game—'I shall 'ave to answer to The Daisy for this.' That was when we was drinkin' up the beer you left in the bag. Mind yer—I didn't know it was you until I saw yer in the car. You 'ad the laugh of 'em all right. They was wild."

"The Daisy," said Mr. Campion. "Are you sure?"

"That was the name. I remember it becos Alf Ridgway, the chap they used to call The Daisy, was strung up two years ago. At Manchester, that was."

"Oh," said Mr. Campion, and passed over the notes. "How's the car business?"

"As good as ever it was." Mr. Walker spoke with enthusiasm. "I sold a lovely repaint in Norwood last week. My brother pinched it up at Newcastle. Brought it down to the garage and we faked it up lovely —registration book and everything. I was the mug, though. The dirty little tick I sold it to—a respectable 'ouseholder, too—passed a couple o' dud notes off on me. Dishonest, that's what people are half the time."

"Hush," said Mr. Campion, "here comes Stanislaus."

Ernie pocketed the notes hastily and turned expectantly towards the doorway. A moment later Inspector Stanislaus Oates appeared. He was a tall, greyish man, inclined to run to fat at the stomach, but nowhere else.

"Hullo," he said, "do you always leave the front door open?" Then, catching sight of Ernie, he added with apparent irrelevancy: "O—my —aunt!"

"I'm just off, sir." Indeed, Ernie was already moving towards the door. "I come up 'ere visitin'. Same as you, I 'ope," he added, cocking an eye slyly at his host.

Campion chuckled. "Shut the door behind you," he said pointedly. "And remember always to look at the watermark."

"What's that?" said Inspector Oates suspiciously. But already the door had closed behind the fleeting figure of the car thief, and they were alone.

Campion introduced Val, and poured the detective a whisky-and-soda. The man from Scotland Yard lounged back in his chair.

"What are you doing with that little rat?" he demanded, waving his hand in the direction of the door through which Mr. Ernest Walker had so lately disappeared. He turned to Val apologetically: "Whenever I come up to see this man," he said, "I find someone on our books having a drink in the kitchen or sunning himself on the mat. Even his man is an unreformed character."

"Steady," said Mr. Campion. "The name of Lugg is sacred. I'm awfully glad you've turned up, old bird," he went on. "You're just the man I want. Do you by any chance know of a wealthy, influential man-about-the-underworld called 'The Daisy'?"

"Hanged in Manchester the twenty-seventh of November, 1928," said the man from Scotland Yard promptly. "Filthy case. Body cut in pieces, and whatnot. I remember that execution. It was raining."

"Wrong," said Mr. Campion. "Guess again. I mean a much more superior person. Although," he added despondently, "it's a hundred to one on his being an amateur."

"There are fifty-seven varieties of Daisy that I know of," said Mr. Oates, "if you use it as a nickname. But they're small fry—very small fry, all of 'em. What exactly are you up to now? Or is it a State Secret again?"

He laughed, and Val began to like this quiet, homely man with the twinkling grey eyes.

"Well, I'm taking the short road, as a matter of fact," said Mr. Campion, and added, as his visitor looked puzzled, "as opposed to the long one, if you get my meaning."

The Inspector was very silent for some moments. Then he sighed and set down his glass. "You have my sympathy," he said. "If you go playing with fire, my lad, you'll get burnt one of these days. What help do you expect from me?"

"Don't you worry," said Mr. Campion, ignoring the last question. "I shall live to be present at my godson's twenty-first. Nineteen years hence, isn't it? How is His Nibs?"

For the first time the Inspector's face became animated. "Splendid," he said. "Takes that Mickey Mouse you sent him to bed with him every night. I say, you understand I'm here utterly unofficially," he went on hurriedly. "Although if you haven't already lost whatever you're looking after why not put it in our hands absolutely, and leave it at that?" He paused. "The trouble with you," he added judicially, "is that you're so infernally keen on your job. You'll get yourself into trouble."

Mr. Campion rose to his feet. "Look here, Stanislaus," he said, "you know as well as I do that in ninety-nine cases out of a hundred the police are the only people in the world to protect a man and his property. But the hundredth time, when publicity is fatal, and the only way out is a drastic spot of eradication, then the private individual has to get busy on his own account. What I want to talk to you about, however, is this. You see that suitcase over there?" He pointed to the new fibre suitcase resting upon a side table. "That," he said, "has got to be protected for the next few days. What it contains is of comparatively small intrinsic value, but the agents of our friends of the long road are after it. And once they get hold of it a very great State treasure will be in jeopardy. Do you follow me?"

The Inspector considered. "Speaking officially," he said, "I should say: 'My dear sir, put it in a bank, or a safe deposit, or the cloakroom of a railway station—or give it to me and I'll take it to the Yard'."

"Quite," said Mr. Campion. "But speaking as yourself, personally, to an old friend who's in this thing up to the hilt, then what?"

"Then I'd sit on it," said the Inspector shortly. "I wouldn't take it outside this door. This is about the safest place in London. You're over a prominent police station. I'd have a Bobby on the doorstep, a couple in old Rodriguez's cookshop, and a plain-clothes man on the roof. You can hire police protection, you know."

"Fine," said Mr. Campion. "How do you feel about that, Val? You stay up here with the suitcase with a small police force all round you, while I go down to Sanctuary and make an intensive effort to get a line on The Daisy?"

Val nodded. "I'll do anything you like," he said. "I'm completely in your hands. There's one thing, though. You've only got four days. Next Wednesday is the second."

"That's so," said Mr. Campion. "Well, four days, then. Can you fix up the body guard, Stanislaus?"

"Sure." The Inspector picked up the telephone, and after ten minutes' intensive instruction set it down again. "There you are," he said. "Endless official forms saved you. It'll cost you a bit. Money no object, I suppose, though? By the way," he added, "hasn't an order come through to give you unofficially any assistance for which you may ask?"

Campion shot him a warning glance and he turned off the remark hastily. "I probably dreamt it," he said. He looked at Val curiously, but the boy had not noticed the incident.

"That's settled, then," said Mr. Campion. "I'll wait till you're all fixed up, and go back to Sanctuary to-morrow morning. You'll find everything you want here, Val. I suppose it'll be all right with your pater?"

Val grinned. "Oh, Lord, yes," he said. "He seems to have taken you for granted since the first time he heard of you, which is rather odd, but still—the whole thing's incomprehensible. I've ceased to marvel."

The Inspector rose and stood beside his friend. "Take care," he said. "Four days isn't long to nail down a chosen expert of *Les Inconnus* and write full-stop after his name. And besides," he added with unmistakable gravity, "I should hate to see you hanged."

Mr. Campion held out his hand. "A sentiment which does you credit, kind sir," he said. But there was a new solemnity beneath the lightness of his words, and the pale eyes behind the horn-rimmed spectacles were hard and determined.

CHAPTER FIFTEEN

Pharisees' Clearing

When Mr. Campion sailed down the drive of the Tower at about ten o'clock the next morning, Penny met him some time before he reached the garage. She came running across the sunlit lawn towards him, her yellow hair flopping in heavy braids against her cheeks.

Campion stopped the car and she sprang on to the running-board.

He noticed immediately a certain hint of excitement in her manner, and her first words were not reassuring.

"I'm so glad you've come," she said. "Something terrible has happened to Lugg."

Mr. Campion took off his spectacles as though to see her better. "You're joking," he said hopefully.

"Of course I'm not." Penny's blue eyes were dark and reproachful. "Lugg's in bed in a sort of fit. I haven't called the doctor yet, as you said on the phone last night that you'd be down early."

Mr. Campion was still looking at her in incredulous amazement. "What do you mean? A sort of fit?" he said. "Apoplexy or something?"

Penny looked uncomfortable and seemed to be debating how much to say. Eventually she took a deep breath and plunged into the story. "It happened about dawn," she said. "I woke up hearing a sort of dreadful howling beneath my window. I looked out, and there was Lugg outside on the lawn. He was jumping about like a maniac and bellowing the place down. I was just going down myself when Branch, whose room is over mine, you know, scuttled out and fetched him in. No one could do anything with him. He was gibbering and raving, and very puffed." She paused. "It may seem absurd to say so, but it looked to me like hysterics."

Mr. Campion replaced his glasses. "What an extraordinary story," he said. "I suppose he hadn't found the key to the wine cellars, by any chance?"

"Oh, no, it wasn't anything like that." Penny spoke with unusual gravity. "Don't you see what happened? He'd been down to Pharisees' Clearing. He saw what Aunt Di saw."

Her words seemed to sink into Mr. Campion's brain slowly. He sat motionless in the car in the middle of the drive staring in front of him.

"My hat," he said at last. "That's a step in the right direction, if you like. I only meant to keep the old terror occupied. I had no idea there'd be any serious fun toward."

He started the car and crawled slowly forward, the girl beside him.

"Albert," she said severely, "you didn't tell him to go down there at night, did you? Because, if so, you're directly responsible for this. You didn't believe me when I told you there was something fearful there. You seem to forget that it killed Aunt Di."

Mr. Campion looked hurt. "Your Aunt Diana and my friend Magersfontein Lugg are rather different propositions," he said. "I only told him to improve the shining hour by finding out what it was down there. I'll go and see him at once. What does Branch say about it?"

"Branch is very discreet," murmured Penny. "Look here, you'd better leave the car here and go straight up."

Mr. Campion raced up the narrow staircase at the back of the house which led to the servants' quarters, the expression of hurt astonishment still on his face. He found Branch on guard outside Mr. Lugg's door. The little old man seemed very shaken and his delight at seeing Campion was almost pitiful.

"Oh, sir," he said, "I'm so glad you've come. It's all I can do to keep 'im quiet. If 'e shouts much louder we shan't 'ave a servant left in the 'ouse by to-night."

"What happened?" said Mr. Campion, his hand on the door knob.

"I doubt not 'e went down to Pharisees' Clearing, sir." The Suffolk accent was very apparent in the old man's voice, and his gravity was profound. Mr. Campion opened the door and went in.

The room was darkened, and there was a muffled wail from a bed in the far corner. He walked across the room, pulled up the blind, and let a flood of sunshine into the apartment. Then he turned to face the cowering object who peered at him wildly from beneath the bed quilt.

"Now, what the hell?" said Mr. Campion.

Mr. Lugg pulled himself together. The sight of his master seemed to revive those sparks of truculence still left in his nature. "I've resigned," he said at length.

"I should hope so," said Campion bitterly. "The sooner you clear out and stop disgracing me the better I shall like it."

Mr. Lugg sat up in bed. "Gawd, I 'ave 'ad a night," he said weakly. "I nearly lost me reason for yer, and this is 'ow yer treat me."

"Nonsense," said Campion. "I go and leave you in a respectable household, and you bellow the place down in the middle of the night and generally carry on like an hysterical calf elephant."

The bright sunlight combined with the uncompromising attitude of his employer began to act like a tonic upon the shaken Lugg.

"I tell yer what, mate," he said solemnly, "I lost me nerve. And so 'ud you if you'd seen what I seen. Lumme, what a sight!"

Mr. Campion remained contemptuous. "A couple of owls hooted at you, I suppose," he observed. "And you came back and screamed the place down."

"A couple o' blood-curdling owls," said Mr. Lugg solemnly. "And some more. I'll tell you what. You spend the night in that wood and I'll take you to Colney 'Atch in the morning. That thing killed Lady Pethwick, the sight of it, that's what it did. And she wasn't no weakling, let me tell yer. She was a strong-minded woman. A weak-minded one would 'ave burst."

In spite of his picturesque remarks there was an underlying note of deadly seriousness in Mr. Lugg's husky voice, and his little black eyes were frankly terror-stricken. Secretly Mr. Campion was shocked. He and Lugg had been through many terrifying experiences together, and he knew that as far as concrete dangers were concerned his aide's nerves were of iron.

"Just what are you driving at?" he said, with more friendliness than before. "A white lady with her head under her arm tried to get off with you, I suppose?"

Mr. Lugg glanced about him fearfully.

"No jokin' with the supernatural," he said. "You may laugh now, but you won't later on. What I saw down in that wood last night was a monster. And what's more, it's the monster that chap in the pub was tellin' me about. The one they keep in the secret room."

"Shut up," said Campion. "You're wrong there. I told you to forget that."

"All right, clever," said Mr. Lugg sulkily. "But what I saw wasn't of this world, I can tell you that much. For Gawd's sake come off yer perch and listen to this seriously or I'll think I've gone off me onion."

Such an appeal from the independent, cocksure Lugg was too much for Campion. He softened visibly.

"Let's have it," he suggested. "Animal, vegetable, or mineral?"

Mr. Lugg opened his mouth to speak, and shut it again, his eyes bulging, as he attempted to recall the scene of his adventure.

"I'm blowed if I know," he said at last. "You see, I was sittin' out in the clearing, like you said, smoking me pipe and wishin' it wasn't so quiet like, when I 'eard a sort of song—not church music, you know, but the sort of song an animal might sing, if you take me. I sat up, a bit rattled naturally. And then, standin' in the patch of light where the moon nipped in through the trees, I see it." He paused dramatically. "As filfy a sight as ever I clapped eyes on in all me born days. A great thin thing with little short legs and 'orns on its 'ead. It come towards me, and I didn't stay, but I tell yer what—I smelt it. Putrid, it was, like somethink dead. I lost me 'ead completely and come up to the 'ouse at forty miles an hour yelping like a puppy dawg. I expec' I made a bit of a fool of meself," he added regretfully. "But it 'ud put anyone into a ruddy funk, that would."

Mr. Campion perched himself on the edge of the bedrail. Lugg was glad to see that his animosity had given place to interest.

"Horns?" he said. "Was it a sort of animal?"

"No ordin'ry animal," said Lugg with decision. "I'll tell yer what, though," he conceded, "it was like a ten-foot 'igh goat walkin' on its 'ind legs."

"This has an ancient and fishlike smell," said Mr. Campion. "Are you sure it wasn't a goat?"

"You're trying to make me out a fool. I tell you this thing was about nine foot 'igh and it 'ad 'uman 'ands—because I saw 'em. Standin' out black against the sky."

Mr. Campion rose to his feet. "Lugg, you win," he said. "I apologize. Now get up. And remember, whatever you do, don't breathe a word of this to the other servants. And if they know you saw a ghost, well, it was nothing to do with the room, see? Don't you breathe a word about that. By the way, I met a friend of yours in Town. Ernie Walker."

"Don't you 'ave nothin' to do with 'im." The last vestige of Mr. Lugg's hysteria disappeared. "No soul above 'is work—that's the sort of bloke Ernie is. A dirty little shark 'oo'd squeal on 'is Ma for a packet o' damp fags."

Mr. Campion grinned. "It seems as if you can't see a ghost in the place without my getting into bad company in your absence, doesn't it?" he said affably. "Now get up and pretend you've had a bilious attack."

"Oi, that's not quite the article," said Mr. Lugg, shocked. "'Eart attack, if you don't mind. I 'ave my feelings, same as you do."

Campion went out and stood for a moment on the landing, the inane expression upon his face more strongly marked than ever. He went to Sir Percival's sanctum on the first floor, and remained there for twenty minutes or so. When he came out again he was more thoughtful than ever. He was about to set off downstairs when a figure which had been curled up on the windowsill at the far end of the corridor unfolded itself and Penny came towards him.

"Well?" she said. "I hope you're convinced about Lugg now."

To her astonishment Mr. Campion linked her arm through his.

"You are now, my dear Madam, about to become my Doctor Watson," he said. "You will ask the inane questions, and I shall answer them with all that scintillating and superior wisdom which makes me such a favourite at all my clubs. They used to laugh when I got up to speak. Now they gag me. But do I care? No, I speak my mind. I like a plain man, a straightforward man, a man who calls a spade a pail."

"Stop showing off," said Penny placidly, as they emerged into the garden. "What are you going to do?"

Mr. Campion stopped and regarded her seriously. "Look here," he said, "you haven't quarrelled with Beth or anything?"

"Of course not. Why? I was on the phone to her last night. She naturally wanted to know all about Val staying in Town. They seem to have got on astoundingly well together, you know."

"Quite old friends, in fact," said Mr. Campion. "I noticed that yesterday. Oh, I'm not so bat-eyed as you think. A youthful heart still beats beneath my nice new chest-protector and the locket containing the old school cap. No, I only asked about Beth because we are now going to visit her father, who is a very distinguished person in spite of the fact that he is a friend of mine. I ought to have told you that before, but there you are."

"Be serious," the girl begged. "You seem to forget that I don't know as much about things as you do."

"We're going to see Professor Cairey," continued Mr. Campion. "Not charioted by Bacchus and his pards but via the footpath. You see," he went on as they set off across the lawn, "you're getting a big girl now, and you may be useful. The situation is roughly this. I've got three days before Val's birthday. Three days in which to spot the cause of the trouble and settle up with him. The only line I've got on the gent in question is that his pet name is 'The Daisy'."

Penny looked dubious. "It's hardly possible, is it?" she said.

Mr. Campion did not answer her, but proceeded equably. "It's perfectly obvious to me," he continued, "and probably to you, my dear Watson, that there's something fishy in Pharisees' Clearing—something very fishy if Lugg is to be believed. I have a hunch that if we can lay that ghost we'll get a line on The Daisy."

"But," said Penny, "if The Daisy, as you call him, is responsible for the ghost and Aunt Di was frightened intentionally, why should the creature go on haunting?"

"That," observed Mr. Campion, "is the point under consideration. Of course Lugg may have gone batty and imagined the whole thing."

Penny shot a quick glance at him. "You don't believe that," she said.

Mr. Campion met her gaze.

"You," he said, "believe it's something supernatural."

The girl started violently and the colour came into her face.

"Oh," she burst out suddenly, "if you only knew as much about the country folk as I do, if you'd been brought up with them, listened to their stories and heard their beliefs, you wouldn't be so supercilious about things that aren't, well, quite right things. Of course," she went on after a pause, "I'm not saying anything definite. I don't know.

But ever since Aunt Di's death more and more Gypsies have been pouring into the district. They say there's a small army of them on the heath."

Mr. Campion raised his eyebrows. "Good old Mrs. Sarah," he said. "Always do all you can for the Benwell tribe, Penny; the finest chals and churls in the world."

Penny was mystified. "You seem to know something about everything," she said. "Why are we going to see the Professor?"

"Because," said Mr. Campion, "if our bogle in Pharisees' Clearing is a genuine local phenomenon you can bet your boots Professor Cairey knows all there is to know about it. Besides that, when dealing with the supernatural there's nothing quite so comforting as the scientific mind and a scientific explanation."

They found the Professor at work in a green canvas shelter in the garden of his attractive Tudor house, whose colour-washed walls and rusty tiled roof rose up in the midst of a tangle of flowers. The old man rose to meet them with genuine welcome in his face.

"This is delightful. You've come to lunch, I hope? Mrs. Cairey is somewhere in the house and Beth with her."

Penny hesitated awkwardly, and it was Mr. Campion who broached the all-important matter in hand.

"Professor," he said, "I'm in trouble again. We've come to you for help."

"Why, sure." The Professor's enthusiasm was indubitable. "Judge Lobbett, one of my greatest friends, owes his life to this young man," he added, turning to Penny. "Now what can I do for you two?"

"Have you ever heard of the ghost in Pharisees' Clearing?" said Penny, unable to control her curiosity any longer.

The Professor looked from one to the other of them, a curious expression in his round, dark eyes.

"Well," he said hesitantly, "I don't know what you'll think of me, but I've got a sort of idea that I've a photograph of it. Come into the library."

CHAPTER SIXTEEN

Phenomenon

In the depths of the Professor's study, a cool old-fashioned room with stamped plaster walls striped with unstained oak beams, Penny and Mr. Campion listened to an extraordinary story.

"I don't want you to get me wrong," said the Professor, as he knelt down before an exquisite old lowboy and unlocked the bottom drawer. "I admit I've been poking my nose into other people's business and I've been trespassing. Way over across the water we don't mind if we do set our feet in a neighbour's back garden," he added slyly.

Penny looked profoundly uncomfortable. "Don't tease us about that, Professor," she said pleadingly. "That was just an unfortunate accident. Aunt Di made it awkward all round, and Father was silly about the Gypsies."

The Professor paused with his hand on the drawer handle.

"You don't say it was that?" he said. "Well, your father had one up on me that time. I've lost half a dozen pedigree hens to those darn hobos. I sent them off my land yesterday morning when I saw they were back again."

Penny hardly heard him. "The—the ghost," she said. "Is it a real one?"

The Professor looked at her curiously and did not answer directly. "You'll see," he said. "As I was saying, I've been trespassing. I heard this yarn of a ghost long before your poor aunt passed over, and naturally I was interested. You see, I'm something of an authority on medieval witchcraft and magic—it's my hobby, you know—and there were certain peculiarities about the tales I heard that got me interested. I sat up waiting in your father's wood for several nights and I can't say I saw anything. Still, I had a gun with me and maybe that had something to do with it."

He paused and looked at Penny searchingly. "You probably know these stories better than I do," he said.

She nodded. "I've heard several things," she admitted. "But the photograph—?"

"I was coming to that," said the Professor. "I don't know if you know it, but there's a way that folks have for setting a trap to photograph animals at night. It's a dandy little arrangement whereby the animal jerks a string stretched across its path, that releases a flashlight and snaps open the camera lens. I set a thing like this two or three nights, and finally, about a fortnight back, I got a result. Now I'll show you."

He rose to his feet carrying a big envelope. While they watched him he raised the flap and produced a large shiny reproduction.

"I had it enlarged," he said. "It's not good—I warn you it's not good, but it gives you an idea."

Mr. Campion and Penny bent forward eagerly. As in all flashlight photographs taken in the open at night, only a certain portion of the plate bore a clear picture, and the snapshot conveyed largely an impression of tangled leaves and branches shown up in vivid black and white. But on the edge of the circle of light, and largely obscured by the shadows, was something that was obviously a figure turned in flight.

It was horned and very tall. That was all that was clear. The rest was mostly hidden by the undergrowth and the exaggerated shadows thrown by the foliage. In the ordinary way the photograph might have been dismissed as a freak plate, an odd arrangement of light and shadow, but in view of the Professor's story and Lugg's horrific description it took on a startling significance. Seen in this light, every blur and shadow on the figure that might have passed as accidental took on a horrible suggestion of unnamable detail.

Campion looked at the Professor.

"Have you got a nice satisfying explanation for all this?" he said.

Professor Cairey's reply was guarded. "There is a possible explanation," he said, "and if it's the right one it'll be one of the most interesting examples of medieval survival I've ever heard of. Naturally I haven't cared to bring this matter up, nor to go trespassing lately. You'll appreciate that the situation was a little delicate."

"Well," said Mr. Campion, straightening his back, "first catch your ghost. A cheery night's work for our little Albert."

The Professor's face flushed with enthusiasm. "I'm with you," he said. "I've been itching to do just that for the last month."

There was something boyish in the old man's heartiness which Penny hardly shared. "Look here," she said quietly, "if you really mean to go wandering about in Pharisees' Clearing to-night I think I can put you on to the man to help you. Young Peck. He works for you, doesn't he, Professor? He and his father know more about the countryside than all the rest of Sanctuary put together."

Professor Cairey beamed.

"I was just about to suggest him myself," he said. "As a matter of fact, old Peck has been my chief source of information in this affair. A fine old chap," he added, turning to Mr. Campion. "It took me three weeks to find out what he was talking about, but we get on famously now. He has a cottage on the edge of my willow plantation, and he spends all his days sitting in the sun 'harkening in', as he calls it. His son's put him up a radio. See here," he went on, "if you'll stay to lunch we'll go down there afterwards and get the youngster on the job."

"Oh, we can't force ourselves on you like this," Penny protested. But the luncheon gong silenced her and the Professor bore them off in triumph to the dining-room.

Mrs. Cairey, a gracious little woman with grey eyes and white shingled hair, received the unexpected addition to her luncheon table with charming equanimity. Whatever her quarrel with Lady Pethwick had been, she did not allow its shadow to be visited upon the young people. Mr. Campion appeared to be an old favourite of hers, and Penny was a friend of Beth's. By her pleasant personality the meal was made a jolly one in spite of the sinister business which lay in the background of the minds of at least three of the party.

"I'm real glad Albert is no longer a secret," said she as they settled themselves at the fine Georgian table in the graceful flower-filled room. "Beth and I kept our promise to you," she went on, smiling at the young man. "Not a word about us knowing you has passed our lips. I thought this was a quiet old-fashioned county. I never dreamed I'd have so much mystery going on around me."

The Professor grinned. "Mother likes her mysteries kept in the kitchen," he said.

His wife's still beautiful face flushed. "Will I never hear the end of this teasing, Papa?" she said. "He's making game of me," she added, turning to the visitors, "because when I came over here and saw this house I was so charmed with the old brick oven and the pumps and the eighteenth-century brew-house that I just made up my mind I wouldn't have the electric plant we planned, but I'd set up house-keeping as they did in the old days, and I'd bake and brew and I'd make Devonshire cream in the right old-fashioned way." She paused and spread out her hands expressively. "I had six girls in the kitchen before I'd finished, and not one of them could I get to do the necessary chores."

The Professor chuckled. "We bought a brewing licence down at the Post Office," he said. "But do you think one of the lads on the farm would drink the homemade stuff? Not on your life. They'd rather have their fourpence to go to the pub with."

"It was the refrigerator that did it," said Beth.

Little Mrs. Cairey laughed. "How you manage to exist without ice I don't know," she said to Penny. "I stuck it out for a long time, just so Papa wouldn't get the laugh on me. Then one day Beth and I went into Colchester and got just what we wanted—all worked by paraffin. Half the village came to see it, and the tales we heard about illnesses that could only be cured by an ice cube you wouldn't believe."

Penny grinned. "They're terrible," she said. "For goodness' sake don't let yourself in for too much fairy godmothering. You see," she went on, "all the little villages round here are really estates that have got too big and too expensive for the Squires to take care of. Death duties at ten shillings in the pound have rather spoilt the feudal system. But the people still expect to be looked after. If they live on your land they consider themselves part of the family."

"You can get very fond of them, though," said Mrs. Cairey placidly. "Although they like their 'largesse', as they call it."

The meal passed, and as they rose and went out on to the lawn Penny felt as though a peaceful interlude in a world of painful excitement had passed.

The Professor had a word with Campion in private under the pretence of showing him a magnificent rambler.

"I guess we ought to keep the ladies out of this," he said.

Mr. Campion nodded. "Emphatically," he agreed. "But I don't know about Penny. She's a strong-minded young woman, and, as I take it, an old friend of the worthy gentleman we're just about to visit. I don't think she'll want to come ghost hunting, but her influence with the Pecks may be useful."

The Professor hesitated. "If it's what I think it is," he said, "it's no business for a woman. Still, as you say, Miss Gyrth may be a deal of help just at first. If you'll excuse me I'll have a word with Mother."

Five minutes later the remarkable old gentleman had succeeded in allaying both the fears and the curiosity of the feminine part of his establishment, and the three walked down the shady gravel path of his flower garden and through a tiny wicket gate into a broad green meadow beyond, which was a belt of marshy land where a clump of slender willows shook their grey leaves in the sunlight.

They were unusually silent for the best part of the way but just before they entered the clearing Penny could contain her fears no longer.

"Professor," she said, "you know something. Tell me, you don't think this—phenomenon, I suppose you'd call it—is definitely supernatural?"

The old man did not answer her immediately.

"My dear young lady," he said at last, "if it turns out to be what I think it is, it's much more unpleasant than any ghost."

He offered no further explanation and she did not like to question him, but his words left a chill upon her, and the underlying horror which seems always to lurk somewhere beneath the flamboyant loveliness of a lonely English countryside in the height of summer, a presence of that mysterious dread, which the ancients called panic, had become startlingly apparent.

Peck's cottage was one of those picturesque, insanitary thatched lath-and-plaster dwellings which stir admiration and envy in the hearts of all those who do not have to live in them. The thatch was moss-covered, and the whole building almost obscured by the high grass and overgrown bushes with which it was surrounded. A weed-grown brick path led up to the front door which stood open, revealing an old man in a battered felt hat seated on a low wooden chair beside an atrocious loud-speaker, which was at this moment murmuring a nasal reproduction of the advertising gramophone music from Radio Paris.

The old man cocked an eye at their approach, and rising with evident regret, switched off the instrument. Mr. Peck senior was by no means an unhandsome old man, with a skin like red sandstone and a rugged toothless face, on the lower promontory of which he had raised a very fine tuft of bristly white hair. He was dressed in an odd assortment of garments, chiefly conspicuous among which were a pair of well-patched white canvas trousers and a red and green knitted waistcoat, obviously designed for a much larger man. His knuckles were swollen with rheumatism, and the backs of his hands were almost as furry as bears' paws.

"Old Man 'Possum," said Mr. Campion, *sotto voce*.

"Be quiet," said Penny reprovingly, and went forward to greet her friend. He touched his hat to her solemnly. "Mornin', miss," he said.

"Good morning," replied Penny politely but inaccurately. "Is your son anywhere about?"

Mr. Peck glanced over his shoulder. "Perce!" he bellowed. "Gentry be 'ere."

"I'm now comin'," a voice replied from the depths of the cottage, and the next moment a tall, loose-limbed young countryman appeared from an inner doorway. He was in shirt-sleeves and waistcoat, and was collarless. Smiling and unembarrassed, he indicated the seats in the cottage porch.

"If you don't mind settin' there, sirs," he said, "I'll get Miss Penny a chair."

They sat down, and instantly the little gathering took on the air of a conspiracy. Young Perce hovered behind his father's chair, his quick brown eyes watching their visitors, waiting for them to come to the object of their call.

"My j'ints be bad," Mr. Peck senior put forward as an opening gambit.

"I'll send you down some of cook's linament," Penny offered.

"Huh," said Mr. Peck, without pleasure or reproach.

"Don't take no notice on 'im," said Percy, reddening for his father's delinquencies. "'E's as right as ever 'e was, ain't yer, Father?"

"No I ain't," returned his father uncompromisingly, and added irrelevantly, "I 'ear that were a quiet buryin'. Yer aunt was pison to some on us. Still, I 'on't speak ill o' the dead."

A violent kick at the back of his chair almost upset him, and he sat quiet, mumbling, his lips together. His two subjects of conversation having been turned down, he was inclined to let people speak for themselves.

The formalities of the call being over, it was Penny who broached the all-important matter in hand.

"Percy," she said, "I want you to take Mr. Campion and Professor Cairey down to Pharisees' Clearing to-night. They think there's—there's an animal there wants snaring. Do you understand? You wouldn't be afraid, would you?"

"No, miss. I shouldn't be scared." The boy spoke readily enough, but a shadow had passed over his face.

His father grunted. "That ain't no animal, miss," he said. "That's a spirit, like I told Master Cairey."

His tone was so matter-of-fact that Mr. Campion shot an inquiring glance at him. The Professor spoke hastily.

"Of course, we won't want any tales told about this, Peck, you understand?"

The boy laughed. "Us don't talk, sir," he said. "Was you thinkin' of trappin' that, now, or do you want to shoot ut?"

"Oh, trap it certainly," said the Professor firmly.

Penny looked up.

"Percy," she said, "do you remember when Val and I were kids we helped you and young Finch to catch an old ram that had gone wild down in Happy Valley?"

"That was with a stack net, warn't ut?" The idea evidently appealed to Mr. Peck junior. "Yes, us could do that. Allowin' that's real," he added, practically.

"You 'on't catch nothin'," observed his father, accepting a fill of tobacco gratefully from the Professor's pouch. "That's a spirit. You'll drop a net, and that'll go right through ut, like that was water. You can make fules of yourselves ef you like: that ain't nothin' to me. Oi won't hurt."

"Look here," said Mr. Campion, breaking into the conversation for the first time. "Is the ghost in Pharisees' Clearing a new affair or has it been going on for some time?"

The elder Peck considered. "There's allus been summat strange down there," he said. "It ain't been reg'lar. Off and on, as you might say. I mind when I was a boy the whole village were quaggly about ut. Then that died down. Then about five years agoo someone seen un, and there ain't no one been there of a night time sence. I reckon that's a spirit."

Penny looked at the younger man. "What do you think about it?" she said.

"I don't know, miss." The boy was puzzled. "I never rightly thought on ut. That never interfered with me. But I never were there at night. That's a mystery, that's what that is. Still," he added cheerfully, "I ain't afraid of ut. I fixed up that wireless for the old 'un and if I can rule that I can rule any ghost. Seems like that's magic," he observed naïvely, indicating the mass of crazy looking machinery behind the old man's chair.

The Professor rose. "Then you'll be down at Tye Hall at about eleven-thirty, with a stack net?" he said.

Mr. Peck junior touched an imaginary hat. "I will, sir."

"I 'on't," said his father complacently. "I'll be harkening to a band then from Germany; they don't be so set on the Sabbath as we are 'ere, the 'eathens. And if you're wise," he added with sudden vigour, "you'll stay in yer beds, same as I do. There be more goes on at night than us thinks on. You stay out of ut, miss. That ain't no wild sheep down in Pharisees. And whatever comes on ut," he concluded solemnly, "it won't be no good."

"I'll be there," said his son, escorting them down the path. As they turned into the field the strains of the Soldiers' Chorus came floating to them across the tangled garden.

CHAPTER SEVENTEEN

The Stack Net

"If that owl cries again I shall have hysterics," said Beth nervously. There were all four of them, the two girls, Professor Cairey and Mr. Campion, seated in the candle-lit library at Tye Hall, waiting for half-past eleven and the arrival of young Perce with his stack net. Mrs. Cairey had retired, but nothing the Professor or Mr. Campion could say would persuade the two girls to follow her example.

Earlier in the evening Campion had been pleasantly fatuous, but now, as the actual moment approached, even he seemed to have become sobered by the eeriness of the occasion. The Professor was the virtual leader of the party. His boyish enthusiasm of earlier in the day had given place to a brisk, commanding mood, and he prepared for the expedition in a business-like manner.

"Torch, travelling rug, and a hip flask," he said, setting them on the table. "I shouldn't take a gun in case you're tempted to loose off. I wish you two girls would go to bed and keep out of it."

"Nonsense," said Beth stoutly. "We're going to hold the fort for you. Whether you see a ghost or not you'll be glad of something hot when you come in."

Mr. Campion, who had been standing in the window, turned. "We shall have a little moon," he said. "I wish I knew what you were getting at, Professor. Am I to expect a wailing manacled figure, or are chains distinctly *passé?*"

The Professor shook his head. "I'm not going to make guesses," he said, "in case my hunch is absolutely wrong. However, the girls will be all right up here. There won't be any clutching hands or spooks blowing out the candles. It's extraordinary how these old houses do creak at night, though," he observed involuntarily.

Beth perched herself on the arm of Penny's chair. "We shall hold each other's hands till you come back," she said. "It's hot to-night, isn't it?"

As soon as she had spoken, the oppressive warmth of the night seemed to become almost unbearable. It was a breathless evening, and the garden outside was uncannily silent, so that when an owl screamed it sounded almost as if the terrifying noise were in the room.

Long awkward silences fell on the company as they waited, and even the most casual sentence seemed jerky and nervous.

A sharp tap on the window startled them violently, and it was only when a husky Suffolk voice outside remarked confidentially: "I be 'ere, sir," that they realized that the party was complete.

Next moment Mr. Peck junior's head and shoulders appeared in the open half of the casement. He looked a little distrait himself, and his grin was inclined to be sheepish. He had paid special attention to his coiffure in honour of going ghost hunting with the gentry, with the result that his brown curling locks were brushed up to a stupendous quiff on the top of his head, which gave him the startling appearance of having his hair standing on end with fright.

"I see a light, so I come 'ere, sir," he said. "Not wishin' to startle the maids, like. Am I right for time?"

It was evident that he was endeavouring to appear as calm as though the trip were the most usual one in the world. The Professor hastily gathered his things together.

"We'll go out by the side door," he said to Campion. "Wait there a minute, will you, Peck? We'll come round to you."

"Good luck," said Penny.

Mr. Campion followed the alert and still youthful Professor out into the stone-flagged corridor and down to the half-glass garden door. They stepped out on to a soft lawn and the Professor led the way round to the side of the house, where young Peck's gaunt figure stood silhouetted against the window. As they approached, something stirred in the darkness at their feet.

" 'Tis Neb, sir," said Peck in reply to the Professor's muttered exclamation. "My owd dog. I reckoned I'd bring 'un with me. For company, like. He'll be as quiet as a meece, won't you, boy?" The last words were addressed to the dog, as he stooped and patted a shape that was rapidly becoming visible as their eyes grew accustomed to the darkness. Neb turned out to be a large, lank creature with a huge head, no tail, and ears like a calf. He moved like a shadow behind his master, being trained with that astonishing excellence that is often regarded with suspicion in those parts of the country where men preserve game.

"Have you got the net?" said Mr. Campion as they crossed the grass and made for the footpath to the coppice.

" 'Ere it be, sir. 'Tis a piece of an old 'un. I reckoned we couldn't manage a whole heavy 'un." He half-turned, showing a large and heavy roll of stout interlaced cords which he carried slung over his shoulder.

"I brought a hurricane with me, too," he added, turning to the Professor, "but I didn't light 'un by the house."

"You can leave that," said the Professor. "I've got a torch."

Mr. Peck clung to his lantern.

"I reckon I'll keep that, if you don't mind, sir," he said.

As they went through the darkness, the heavy silence closed in upon them, broken only by the rustle of their own feet in the grass.

Presently young Peck detailed his idea of their procedure.

"Since you left the trappin' of ut to me, sirs," he ventured, "I thought maybe you'd like to know how I be settin' out. I reckoned I'd find a good tree with a branch stickin' out on ut, and I'd set on that with the net, and when the thing come beneath then I'd drop that over ut."

The simplicity of this plan seemed to fill the young man with pride and delight. Mr. Campion and the Professor were hardly so struck by it.

"Suppose it doesn't come under your tree?" said Mr. Campion.

But the younger Peck was prepared for this emergency. "I doubt not that will, sir," he said. He paused, and after a moment or two of consideration volunteered an enlightening remark. "That chases people, sir. I was talking to the old 'un, tea-time. 'E told I that, and I thought ut out that if I was up the tree, sir, you could sort of lead that under I. Of course," he went on cheerfully, "us can't tell if that'll be there, can us?"

Mr. Campion chuckled. "I see," he said. "We're the bait and the poor fish too."

Mr. Peck shook with silent mirth at this sally. "That's so, sir," he whispered. "Now, if you don't mind, us'll keep quiet. I'll go first, if you please."

He slipped in front of them, treading silently as a cat, and behind him the great mongrel picked his way furtively. For some time they plodded on in silence. Mr. Campion had removed his spectacles, a habit of his when action was indicated. The heat had become almost unbearable. There was only a waning moon visible, although the stars shone brightly enough.

The belt of trees which they were rapidly approaching was ink black and curiously uninviting, and the little Belgian owls with which that part of the country is infested hooted dismally from time to time. They followed the path and entered the Professor's wood, which corresponded to the larger one belonging to the Tower on the opposite side of the clearing, and through which Penny had conducted Mr. Campion on the morning of Lady Pethwick's death only a week before.

Young Peck straightened himself and pushed on doggedly as the branches over his head rendered his path almost completely black. Suddenly Neb began to snuffle, his great head bowed to his master's heels. Presently he stopped dead and emitted a suppressed whinnying sound which brought the youth to a standstill.

"What is ut, boy?" whispered Peck. The dog turned silently from the path and disappeared into the darkness, to return a moment or so later with something hanging from his jaw. The youth squatted down on his heels and lit a match. The tiny flare showed the great yellow dog with a young rabbit in his mouth. The animal was quite dead, a piece of wire drawn tightly round its neck.

Peck took it from the dog and the Professor produced his torch.

"Ah," whispered the boy contemptuously as he threw the rabbit down. "There's someone about don't fear no ghosts. That ain't been snared above a 'alf-hour."

He rose to his feet, and with the dog walking obediently behind him set off once more into the silent depths of the wood. The path was one left by woodcutters in the winter, and led directly through the scrub into open space beyond.

Pharisees' Clearing was uncanny enough in the daytime, but at night it was frankly awe-inspiring. The narrow stony strip between the woods was ghostly in the starlight, and here, hemmed in between the long line of trees, the air was suffocating.

The Professor nudged Mr. Campion's arm. "Almost too good to be true," he murmured.

Campion nodded. "So much for background," he whispered. "This is the place and the hour all right. When does the performance begin?"

But if Campion could be light-hearted, Mr. Peck was certainly not in the same mood. As they halted in the shadows on the edge of the clearing his voice came to them husky and alarmed.

"Reckon this is the place. You draw that under 'ere and I'll catch un," he murmured, indicating the oak beneath which they stood. Then he disappeared like a shadow into the blackness, and they heard the soft scrape of his rubber shoes on the bole of the tree. He climbed like a monkey, no mean feat in the darkness with two stone of ropes tied round him, and they heard him grunt softly as he pulled himself up. A few moments later a whisper came from just above their heads.

"I'll rest 'ere time that comes."

"Where's the dog?" said the Professor softly.

"That's at the foot of the tree. That won't move."

Mr. Peck seemed to have made his arrangements complete.

"What does A do now?" murmured Mr. Campion.

There were faint, almost indetectable sounds all round them in the wood, minute rustlings like stifled breathings in the dark. Neither was insensible to the eeriness of the moment, but each man had his own particular interest in the matter.

"I think," the Professor whispered, "that if you'll work round the left side I'll go round the right. I got my photograph from the point where the Colonel's woodpath reaches the clearing. If we all three wait at equal distances round the oval, our quarry can't very well escape us, if it appears at all."

"I wish I'd brought my twig of rowan," said Mr. Campion with apparent feeling, as he set off in the direction indicated. He moved along the side of the wood, keeping well in the shadow of the overhanging trees. Apart from the breath-taking moment when he disturbed a hare at his very feet, there were no thrills until he reached a spot about thirty yards, or so he judged, from the entrance to the Tower Wood. Here he sat down in the long grass and waited.

From the absolute silence in the clearing he guessed that the Professor had reached his point of vantage somewhere across the faintly lit stretch opposite him. The thought that there were three men and a dog watching anxiously for something unknown to appear among those loose stones and sparse clumps of coarse grass in front of him made the scene slightly more terrifying. He hunched his knees to his chin and composed himself for a long wait. He had not underestimated his vigil.

The minutes passed slowly. Once or twice a sleepy squawk sounded from the wood behind him, and, as his ears became attuned to the quietness, somewhere far away in the Tower garden a nightjar repeated its uncouth cry like an old-fashioned policeman's rattle.

And then, for the first time, Mr. Campion became conscious that someone was moving clumsily in the depths of the wood behind him. He turned his head and listened intently. There was certainly nothing supernatural about this. The movements were those of a man, or some animal quite as heavy. For a minute or so he was puzzled, but a single sound reassured him, the sharp metallic click of a spring trap being set.

He listened to the rustling going farther and farther away, with occasional pauses as other traps were set. Someone evidently paid very little respect to the horror which had killed Lady Pethwick and driven Lugg into hysterics.

Once again all was silent. The illuminated hands on his watch showed half-past twelve. He sighed and settled down once more. His face in the darkness still wore his habitual expression of affable fatuity. His eyes were half-closed.

"Angels and ministers of grace defend me, I hope," he remarked under his breath, and turned up his coat to obscure the whiteness of his collar.

The oppressive warmth of the night was giving place to the first cool breath of dawn when his senses, which had gradually become drowsy, were startled into tingling life by one of the most terrible sounds he had ever heard. It was not very loud, but its quality made up for any deficiency on that score.

It was a noise that could only be described as a gentle howling, coming swiftly through the trees, and he was reminded unpleasantly of Mr. Lugg's description, "the sort of song an animal might sing". Not even among native races, of whom he had some little experience, had he ever heard anything quite so blood-curdling. Quite the most terrifying point about the noise was that the sound was rhythmic. It rose and fell on a definite beat, and the pitch was high and quavering.

The sound came nearer and nearer, and quite suddenly he saw the figure.

It had advanced not from the Colonel's path, as they had expected, but from the narrow opening at the northern end of the clearing, and now stood silhouetted against the lightening sky.

Mr. Campion rose to his feet, only vaguely aware of his numbed and aching limbs. The creature, whatever it was, certainly had points of elemental horror about it. It was immensely tall, as Lugg had said, and almost inconceivably thin. Long caprious horns crowned its head, and its body showed grotesque and misshapen.

It advanced down the clearing, still wailing, and Campion caught a clearer glimpse of the front of it as it came nearer.

He felt suddenly sick, and his scalp tingled.

Almost at the same moment the creature came to windward of him, and he was aware of the aroma of putrefaction, strong and unclean in his nostrils.

He darted out of his hiding-place. The figure halted and turned towards him. As it did so he caught sight of a single dead eye, blank and revolting.

Mr. Campion stood his ground, and the figure came nearer. From somewhere beyond it Peck's dog had begun to howl piteously. Mr. Campion gave way cautiously, edging round towards the sound, allowing the apparition to gain a little upon him as he did so. Every time it came a step forward he retreated, leading it unerringly towards the trap.

Suddenly it made a rush at him, and he turned and ran for the opening, his long thin figure a picture of terror in the night. The horned thing padded after him.

He passed the whimpering dog, and for a giddy moment the creature seemed almost upon him. There was a rustle above his head and something seemed to hover for an instant in the air like a great bat. Then the weighty stack net dropped over his pursuer and a terrible half human howl went shattering through the leaves.

"Call off the dog!" shouted the Professor as he came running up. "For God's sake call off the dog!"

CHAPTER EIGHTEEN

Survival

As he levelled his torch, the Professor's hand shook violently.

The dog, after its first frenzied attack, crouched cowering by the tree trunk, while Mr. Campion bent over the struggling mass in the heavy net.

The almost blinding beam of light after the intense darkness seemed paradoxically to add to the confusion. The creature, whatever it was, had ceased to struggle and lay motionless in the net, shapeless and hairy under the tangle of ropes.

The fact that the "ghost" actually lay captured at their feet brought home to both men how slender their hopes of success had been the previous evening. Yet there it lay, still incomprehensible, a grotesque and reeking mass.

Peck dropped to the ground from his branch, and they caught a glimpse of his face, pale, and glistening with great beads of sweat. "Lumme," he kept whispering to himself pathetically. "Lumme."

The Professor bent over the net, and when he spoke there was more excitement than horror in his tone.

"I knew it," he said. "I'm right. This is one of the most remarkable survivals I've ever heard of. Do you know what we've got here?"

"A woman," said Mr. Campion.

"A witch," said the Professor. "Look out—gently now. I'm afraid she has collapsed."

Very carefully he began to lift off the net. Young Peck, fighting his terror with what was, in the circumstances, real heroism, set about lighting the hurricane with hands that trembled uncontrollably.

Mr. Campion and the Professor gently removed the tangle of cords. The figure on the ground did not move.

"Lands sakes! I hope the shock hasn't killed her!" There was real concern in the Professor's voice. "Bring that lantern over here, will you, Peck? That's fine. Now hold this torch."

And then, as the light fell uninterruptedly upon their captive, the horror of Pharisees' Clearing lay exposed.

In many respects it differed from the conventional ghost, but chiefly it did so in the fact that none of its horror was lost when it was clearly seen.

The figure was that of a woman, old, and scarcely clad at all save for great uncured strips of goatskin draped upon her gaunt yellow form. Her headdress was composed of the animal's skull to which the hair still clung, and her face was hidden by a mask of fur, slits having been cut for the eye-holes. Her bony arms appeared to have been smeared with blood and the effect was unspeakable.

The Professor bent down and removed the headdress, picking it up gingerly by the horns. Mr. Campion turned away for a moment, sickened. When he looked again a fresh shock awaited him. The woman's head lay exposed, and above her closed eyes her forehead seemed to stretch back unendingly. She was perfectly bald.

Young Peck's voice, husky with relief, answered the question in both their minds.

" 'Tis owd Missus Munsey," he said. "The old 'un said she were a witch, but I never took no heed on ut. Lumme, who'd 'a' thought ut? I never believed them tales."

The Professor produced his travelling rug. "Since we know who it is, it makes it much simpler," he said. "Where does she live? Alone, I suppose?"

"She lives with 'er son, sir—Sammy," put in Mr. Peck, whose courage was reviving apace at the discovery that the "spirit" had human substance. " 'E's a natural. They ain't neither on 'em right."

"Can you lead us to the cottage?" said Campion. "Is it far? We shall have to carry this woman."

"No, that ain't no distance. One thing, that's some way from any other house."

The Professor in the meantime had succeeded in disengaging the old woman from her grisly trappings and had wrapped her in the rug.

"It occurs to me," he said, "that if we could get this poor thing to her house before we attempt to revive her it may be better for all con-

cerned. The discovery of herself still out here surrounded by her re-
galia—and us—might send her raving."

Young Peck, who had stolen off some moments before, now reappeared with a light wooden hurdle, part of the boundary fence between the two estates. "I thought I seen this," he observed. "Now, if
you're ready, sirs, our best way is to set 'er on 'ere and cut through the
clearin'. It ain't above a 'alf mile."

They lifted the repellent figure on to the rough stretcher and set
out. Since the first outburst no one had spoken. This extraordinary
finish to an extraordinary expedition had silenced them for the time
being. Peck took the head of the procession. The hurricane clanked
at his side, throwing a fitful distorted light on his path. His dog ran
behind him, beneath the hurdle, and the Professor and Campion
brought up the rear, stumbling along on the uneven ground.

For some time the Professor seemed lost in thought, but as the
track led them up through the northern exit from the clearing he
glanced at Campion.

"Do you get it?" he said.

"Vaguely," said Campion. "I shouldn't believe it if I hadn't seen it."

"I suspected it all along," the older man confided. "The goat horns,
and those yarns of the curious chantings put the idea in my head at
once. It's an interesting case. There hasn't been one approaching it
for fifty years that I know of. It's an example of a blind spot. Modern
civilization goes on all over the country—all over the world—and yet
here and there you come across a patch that hasn't been altered for
three hundred years. This woman's a lunatic, of course," he added
hastily, as he became aware of Peck's large red ears strained back to
catch every word. "But there's no doubt at all in my mind that she's
descended from a regular line of practising witches. Some of their beliefs have been handed down to her. That costume of hers, for instance, was authentic, and a chant like that is described by several experts. She's a throw-back. Probably she realizes what she's doing only
in a dim, instinctive sort of fashion. It's most interesting—most interesting."

"Yes, but *why?*" said Campion, who was more rattled than he cared
to admit. "Had she any motive? Did any one put her up to it?"

The Professor considered. "We must find that out," he said. "I
should say, since her nocturnal trips were so frequent, she must have
had some very powerful reason. But doubtless that will emerge. Of
course," he went on almost hopefully, "this may have gone on for
years. Her mother may have done the same sort of thing. You'd be
astonished to discover what a lot of witchcraft has been practised in

this country, and my own, in the last three hundred years. It wasn't so long ago that the authorities stopped burning 'em. A couple of years before I was born, D. D. Home was expelled from Rome as a sorcerer. A lot of it survives to this day in one superstition or another. You come across extraordinary stories of this sort in the police court reports in local newspapers."

"Still, this is a bit unusual, isn't it?" said Mr. Campion, indicating the shrouded figure on the hurdle they carried.

"Oh, this?" said the Professor. "I'd say so. This is a survival of one of the early forms of witchcraft, but, after all, if you find these country folk sitting on three-hundred-year-old chairs and using Elizabethan horn spoons to mix their puddings, why shouldn't you find them—very, very rarely, I admit—practising the black rites of three or four centuries back? We'll learn a lot more when we get her home, no doubt."

"I hate to be unfeeling," said Mr. Campion, straightening his back and changing his grip on the hurdle, "but I certainly wish the good lady had provided herself with a broomstick."

"We're now there," observed Peck, joining naturally in the conversation. "That's just over this rise."

Five minutes' plodding brought them to the top of the field. It was now nearing dawn, and in the east the sky was almost white. The light from the hurricane lantern was beginning to yellow.

The old woman's cottage was faintly visible, therefore. It was a mere shed of a building, quite obviously an outhouse belonging to a cottage that had long since collapsed. As they came nearer they could make out the heterogeneous collection of boards, mud and tarred sheeting of which it was composed. It was surrounded by a patch of earth trodden bare, upon which several lean fowls nestled uneasily. Some six feet from the door young Peck turned.

"Reckon us 'ad better set un down 'ere, sir," he suggested, "while us find out if Sammy's t'home. Will you wait 'ere?"

He set his end of the hurdle down gratefully, and they followed suit, easing their strained backs. Mr. Peck, lantern in hand, advanced towards the crazy door, his dog at his heels. He tapped upon it softly, and receiving no answer, opened it and entered.

Almost immediately there was a terrified twittering sound from within, and a figure fled out of the doorway and disappeared into the shadows round the back of the hut. The incident was so unexpected that it jolted the nerves of the two who waited, almost more than any of the foregoing adventures of the night.

"Gee! what was that?" said the Professor huskily.

He was answered by Peck, who appeared a little shamefacedly in the doorway. "That's Sammy," he said. "That didn't 'alf give I a turn. Shall us carry 'er in? 'Tis a wonderfully dirty place."

Between them they lifted the hurdle once more and bore it into the dwelling. Peck hung the lantern from a hook in the roof and it shed its uncertain light on one of the most squalid of all human habitations.

A poverty-stricken collection of furniture was strewn about the low-ceilinged room. There was a bed in one corner, and a door leading into another apartment revealed a second couch. A fireplace in which there were still the relics of a fire was built in the outer wall on the left of the door, and the floor was strewn with debris.

The Professor looked about him with distaste. "I'll say this shouldn't be allowed," he said. "Though it's hard to interfere always, I know. If you'll help me, Campion, I'll put her on the couch here."

They lifted the ragged old creature, still in the rug, and set her down on the tousled bed.

"Whose land is this?" he inquired.

"That don't rightly belong to anyone, sir," volunteered Peck. " 'Tis a bit o'waste, as you might call ut. They've lived 'ere years, she and 'er mother afore 'er. There ain't nobody 'ereabouts as can do anything with 'er."

The Professor produced his flask, and pouring a little brandy into the cupped top, forced it between the old woman's lips. She stirred uneasily and mumbled a few unintelligible words.

"Take care, sir. I doubt not she'll curse you." Peck could not repress the warning.

The Professor grinned. "I doubt not," he said.

It was at this point that a shadow appeared in the doorway, and they were conscious of a white, frightened face with a straggling growth of beard on its chin peering in at them.

"Come in," said Mr. Campion in a quiet, matter-of-fact voice. "Your mother fainted in the wood."

Sammy Munsey came into the room shyly, moving from side to side like a timid animal. Finally he paused beneath the light, revealing himself to be an undersized, attenuated figure clad in ragged misshapen garments. He stood smiling foolishly, swinging his arms.

Suddenly a thought seemed to occur to him, and he whimpered: "You seen 'er—you seen 'er in the wood. Don't you touch me. I won't 'ave 'em after me. I ain't done nothin'."

He exhausted himself by this outburst, and Mr. Peck, who had been poking about the cabin, suddenly came forward with a pair of scarcely cold hares in his hand. Sammy snatched them from him and put them behind his back like a child, and he stood there quivering with fear and a species of temper.

"Snared," said Mr. Peck with righteous indignation. "That's why they don't do no work," he added, turning to the Professor. "It's been a miracle down in the village how they lived."

Sammy looked round for some means of escape, but his path to the doorway was blocked by his accuser. He swore vehemently for some moments, and then as though he realized his helplessness, he turned wildly to the figure on the bed.

"Mother, they've found us!" he shouted, shaking the old creature. "They've found us out!"

The old woman opened her eyes, pale, and watery, with bloodshot rims.

"I'll curse 'em," she murmured with sudden venom. "They don't none of 'em dare come near me." She turned her head and caught sight of the Professor, and raising herself upon an elbow she let out such a stream of filthy abuse that in spite of his interest he was quite obviously shocked. As he did not fly before her, however, her mood changed.

"Leave I alone," she wailed. "I ain't hurt ye. I ain't done nothin'. I 'on't hurt ye, if ye go."

It was Sammy who cut in upon her wailings, and his fear was piteous. "They've found us out," he repeated. "They've found us out."

The words seemed to sink into the old creature's mind only after some moments. She began to moan to herself.

"I couldn't 'elp ut."

It dawned upon Mr. Campion that she was by no means the mental case that her son was. There was a glimmer of intelligence in the old red-rimmed eyes. As they rolled round they seemed to take in the situation pretty completely.

"Did you frighten people out of Pharisees' Clearing so that your son could poach in the wood?" he said.

She looked at him shrewdly. "You 'on't take un away if I tell ye?"

"I won't touch him," said Mr. Campion. "I only want to know why you dressed up like that."

The guileless expression upon his face seemed to lull the old creature's suspicions, for her voice grew quieter. " 'E ain't right," she said. " 'E couldn't catch nothing if 'e was interfered with. 'E don't know 'ow to take care of 'isself. 'E warn't afraid of I. But the others—I scared 'em." She laughed, sucking the breath in noisily between her gums.

The Professor bent over her. "Who taught you to do this?" he said.

She seemed to scent a challenge in his remark, for she snarled at him. "I larnt ut when I were young. I know more'n you think. Where be my robe?"

The Professor started. "If you mean your goatskins, they're in the wood."

The old woman attempted to stumble out of bed. "I must get they," she insisted. "There be power in they—more than you know on."

"Soon," promised Mr. Campion. "Soon. Lie down now, till you're stronger."

Mrs. Munsey lay back obediently, but her glance roved suspiciously about the room, and her mouth moved without words.

Mr. Campion bent forward again. "Why did you set upon Lady Pethwick?" he said. "She wouldn't have stopped anyone poaching."

The old woman sat bolt upright, making a fearsome picture with her bald head and her toothless gums bared like an animal's.

"I di'nt," she said huskily.

"Then perhaps it was Sammy?" suggested Mr. Campion quietly.

Mrs. Munsey's red-rimmed eyes became positively venomous. She rose up in her bed and stood there, towering above them, clutching the rug about her attenuated form.

"I curse ye," she said with concentrated hatred in her voice which was uncommonly disconcerting. "I curse ye be a right line, a crooked line, a simple and a broken. By flame, by wind, by water, by a mass, by rain, and by clay. By a flying thing, by a creeping thing, by a sarpint. By an eye, by a hand, by a foot, by a crown, by a crost, by a sword and by a scourge I curse ye. *Haade, Mikaded, Rakeben, Rika, Rita lica, Tasarith, Modeca, Rabert, Tuth, Tumch.*"

As the last word left her lips she sank down upon the bed again, where she lay breathing heavily.

The Professor, who had listened to this wealth of archaic invective with unabashed delight, took a small note-book from his pocket and scribbled down a few words.

Mr. Campion, who had received the full brunt of the lady's ill-wishes, stood his ground. Now that she was proving herself strong enough for the interview he felt more at ease.

"You frightened Lady Pethwick to death," he said, speaking with slow, careful deliberation as though he were talking to a child. "Afterwards, when you saw what you had done, you folded her hands and closed her eyes. Why did you do it? If it was an accident, tell us."

Sammy, who had been listening to this harangue with his mouth hanging open, now spoke in a misguided effort to exonerate his mother from what he realized vaguely was a serious charge.

"She hid from the gentry afore Daisy told 'er about 'er Ladyship. Afore then she only chased the country folk."

"Don' you listen to un!" screamed his mother, dancing up and down on the bed in her fury. "'E don't know nothin'. 'E's lyin' to 'ee."

But Mr. Campion had heard quite enough to interest him.

"Who's Daisy?" he demanded, repressing every shade of interest in his voice. "Now, Sammy?"

"You can't blame Daisy!" shouted Mrs. Munsey. "She didn't mean for her to die. She said for to frighten 'er, so's maybe she'd take to 'er bed for a day or two. She ain't done nothin'."

"Who *is* Daisy?" persisted Mr. Campion. His pale eyes were hard, and for once there was no vacuity in his face.

"You can't blame Daisy." Mrs. Munsey repeated the words vehemently. "I made the image on 'er Ladyship, I named ut, and I burnt ut."

She made this startling announcement without pride or remorse, and the Professor caught his breath.

"Was it a clay image or a wax image?" he said involuntarily.

"It was mud," said Mrs. Munsey sulkily.

Mr. Campion did not hear this part of the conversation: his mind was entirely taken up with Sammy. Once again he repeated his question.

The half-wit would not look at him, but bending his head, he mumbled a few almost unintelligible words.

"That's Miss Daisy she means," he said. "My father worked for 'er one time when 'e was alive."

It was Peck who came forward and supplied the final startling piece of information.

"Excuse me, sir," he said. "That's Mrs. Daisy 'e means. Mrs. Daisy Shannon, as keeps the 'orses. 'Er they call Mrs. Dick."

"Damn!" said Mr. Campion, for once taken aback.

CHAPTER NINETEEN

"What Should A Do?"

"I'd say that's one of the most remarkable experiences of my life," remarked the Professor to Mr. Campion, as they walked back over the fields together from Mrs. Munsey's cottage to the Tye Hall. "Of course, it mustn't come out," he went on. "I understand that all right. There'd be endless complications. But I shall cite you as a witness if ever I write a book of reminiscences. I suppose that boy Peck will hold his tongue?"

Mr. Campion seemed to drag his thoughts back from some vague and foolish calculation. "Eh?" he said, recalling the old man's last words to his mind with a conscious effort. "Oh, Lord, yes, he'll be as silent as the grave. In the first place, I don't think he believes it happened. Besides," he added as his eye caught the top of the Tower rising above the trees in the distance, "they're used to keeping secrets round here. Old Mr. Peck may hear something, but no one else."

They walked on in silence for some moments. It was now full dawn and the air was fresh and cool, and the heavy dew made the myriads of tiny cobwebs with which the grass was covered stand out in delicate tracery.

"A genuine case," the Professor repeated. "Did you hear what she said about her robe, and the image she'd made? The notion of making a clay figure of an enemy and breaking or maiming it to ensure that the same evils fall on the human is one of the oldest ideas in the world, an authentic traditional practice. And that curse she put upon you, Campion. Pure traditional magic. Each symbol, the right line and the 'sarpint' and so on—each represents a different evil spirit. I shall set that down if I can when I get in."

Mr. Campion shrugged his shoulders. "You might counteract it with a suitable blessing while you're about it," he said. "I hope to goodness it doesn't come off. If it does, I'm for a parroty time, as far as I remember. And just at the moment I need the angels on my side."

The Professor shot him a sly glance. "That remarkable accusation against a lady called Shannon," he said. "You're not taking that seriously, are you?"

The pale young man at his side vouchsafed no reply. His face was as expressionless as ever, and he seemed if anything a little tired. The Professor shook his head.

"A woman like Mrs. Munsey might say anything," he said, and went on thoughtfully: "You can see just how it happened. There they were, friendless and practically destitute, and the boy not wise enough to go trapping satisfactorily unless he was completely undisturbed. Then his mother thinks out in that twisted, tortuous brain of hers how best she can help him, and there comes to her the memory of what her mother had taught her when she was a girl—all the old beliefs, the peculiar power of the goat. The strange half-forgotten shibboleths come crowding back into her mind, and instinctively she turns it to her own use. It wasn't the keepers she had to fear, you see. I don't preserve, so there was no man patrolling my wood. It was the other poachers. Every man's hand was against Sammy. This isn't the first or last country community that has no sympathy with the weak-minded." He laughed shortly. "It's a real primitive story, illustrating, probably, one of the earliest reasons for witchcraft—the terrorization of the strong by the weak. Most interesting."

"What'll happen to them?" said Mr. Campion.

"I've been thinking that out." The Professor's face was very kindly. "The parson down here is a very decent old man. His name's Pembroke. He and I get on very well together. He's a scholar, but a man who hasn't let the teachings of the spirit blind him to a knowledge of the world. I'll see him about these two. Maybe something can be done for them. They want looking after, and they must be looked after. Lands sakes! If Mother had seen that woman it might have scared her out of her wits. I guessed more or less what was coming, but it gave me a turn."

"A turn?" said Mr. Campion. "I was dizzy before we'd finished. Poor old Lugg! One more shock like that and he'll sign the pledge. I wonder why Mrs. Munsey took so much trouble to rearrange Lady Pethwick's body?"

"Instinct again," said the Professor. "That old woman scarcely thinks. She works by instinct and superstition. There's an old belief that if you leave the dead with their eyes wide open they watch you ever after."

They had reached the lattice gate at the end of the garden by this time. "We'll keep most of this story to ourselves," he remarked.

"Of course," Mr. Campion agreed. "I'll collect Penny and go back to the Tower."

There was a fire in the library when they went in, and a scratch meal appeared upon the table. Beth and Penny were burning with excitement, but their hollow eyes and pale cheeks betrayed that their vigil had not been without its terrors. Beth kissed her father.

"Golly, I'm glad you're back," she said. "When it got so late Penny and I were afraid the ghost had decamped with you. Did you find anything?"

The Professor contented himself with a very brief outline of the story.

"It was simply an old woman wandering around trying to frighten folks so her son could do a bit of poaching," he said, accepting the coffee she handed to him with gratitude. "Nothing to get alarmed about."

"Mrs. Munsey?" said Penny quickly.

The Professor raised his eyebrows. "What gives you that idea?" he murmured.

"It sounded like her," said Penny cryptically.

"It sounds rather flat to me," remarked Beth, a tinge of disappointment in her voice. "If you'd seen the things that we've *imagined* sitting up here alone you'd have a different tale to tell."

Mr. Campion rose to his feet. "I think, Penny," he observed, "you and I had better get back to the Tower. To come to lunch and stay till breakfast next morning is not quite the article. Lugg will be shocked. His book of etiquette considers over-long calls definitely low."

Penny agreed readily. "I'll come at once," she said, and in spite of the Professor's protestations they gently insisted on returning.

The Professor shook Campion's hand in the hall. "You can leave all this to me," he murmured. "I'll see to it."

As they passed out of the garden Penny turned to Mr. Campion suspiciously. "Now," she said, "out with it. What really did happen?"

"Undue curiosity in females should be curbed on all occasions as the evidences of it are invariably distressing to the really well-bred," said Mr. Campion morosely. "That's in the etiquette book, too. Page four. It's illustrated."

"How dare you behave like this," said the girl with sudden spirit, "when you both came in looking as though you'd been through hell fire together? Mrs. Munsey, was it? Did she go for Aunt Di of her own volition, or did someone put her up to it?"

Mr. Campion eyed her speculatively. "It wasn't nice," he said. "Even Peck's dog was shocked. It was frightened to death and kept howling about the place like an old lady at a wake. The Professor was strong and silent, of course, but Mrs. Munsey's sartorial efforts blanched even his cheek. We took her to her residence, whereupon she told my fortune, in a rather pessimistic vein, I thought. Then we shook hands all round and came home. There you are, there's the whole story, hot from the horse's mouth."

"All right," said Penny, "I'll find out all the details. You needn't worry."

"I bet you will," said Campion with contempt. "Beth will worm the lurid story from her poor doting father, and you two, little Annie Mile and little Addie Noid, will gloat over them together like the two little nasties you are."

Penny was silent for some time.

"Anything about The Daisy?" she ventured at last.

Mr. Campion shot a quick glance at her. "I say," he said. "I forgot I'd told you about that. Look here, Penny, this is deadly serious. By the bones of my Aunt Joanna and her box, swear to me that you will never breathe a word about The Daisy to a living soul, especially not to Beth and her father. Because although Mrs. Munsey gave your aunt the scare that killed her, it was The Daisy who engineered the whole thing. I don't think murder was intended, but . . . I don't know."

There was an unusual earnestness in his face and Penny, regarding him steadily, was surprised and a little flustered to see an almost imploring expression in his eyes.

"Promise," he repeated.

"All right," she said ungrudgingly. "You found out something, then?"

Campion nodded. "It may or may not be important," he said. "Frankly, I hope it isn't."

Penny did not reply, but walked along beside him, her hands clasped behind her and her yellow head bent.

"I say," he said suddenly, "when I had a word with your father yesterday to assure him that Val would be home for his birthday the day after to-morrow he didn't say anything about the general procedure. What usually happens on these occasions?"

Penny considered. "It was a great day, years ago, I believe," she said dubiously. "The family was quite wealthy in my grandfather's time, you know. Mother used to tell us that on Father's twenty-fifth birthday they had a terrific set-out with a Church service, theatricals, a house party, and a dance for the tenants in the evening. Daddy had to keep out of the fun, though, because of the midnight ceremony of the Room, when his father and the chaplain initiated him into the secret. Of course," she said quickly, "we don't talk about that."

"I see," said Mr. Campion slowly. "I suppose they dispense with a chaplain these days?"

"Well, we haven't got a private chaplain, if that's what you mean," she said, grinning; "although old Mr. Pembroke, the vicar here, had rooms in the east wing when Father was away at the War. That was when we were children. I think he'll dine with us on the birthday night. There won't be any other celebrations, partly because we haven't got much money, and also because of poor Aunt Di. Of course," she went on, "I dare say you think Father has been rather curious about this whole terrible business—the way he's kept out of it all—but you can't possibly understand about him if you don't realize that he is a man with something on his mind. I mean," she added, dropping her voice, "I wouldn't say this to anyone but you, but the secret absorbs him. Even when he thought the Cup was missing it didn't seem to rouse him to frenzy. You do follow me? That's why he's so odd and reserved and we see so little of him."

She paused and looked at Campion appealingly. The young man with the pale face and absent air turned to her.

"I'm not nearly the mutt I look," he said mildly.

A wave of understanding passed over her face. "I believe you and Father are pretty thick," she said. "Usually he loathes strangers. Do you know, you're quite the most remarkable person I've ever met?" She looked up at him with all the admiration of her age showing in her young face.

"No vamping me," said Mr. Campion, nervously. "My sister—her what married the Squire—would be ashamed of you."

"That's all right," said Penny cheerfully. "I haven't got any designs on you. I think Val and Beth are heading for the altar, though. Val seemed to have got over his anti-woman complex with a vengeance last time I saw him."

"You'll be a danger," said Mr. Campion, "in a few years' time. I'll come and sit at the back of the church when you're married and weep violently among all the old maids. I always think a picturesque figure of that sort helps a wedding so. Don't you?"

Penny was not to be diverted from the matter in hand.

"You've got something on your mind," she said.

She linked her arm through his with charming friendliness.

"In the words of my favourite authoress: 'Is it a woman, my boy?' Or aren't you used to late hours?"

To her surprise he stopped dead and faced her. "My child," he said with great solemnity, "in the words of the rottenest actor I ever heard on mortal stage: 'The man who raises his hand against a woman save in the way of kindness is not worthy of the name.' Which is to say: 'Don't knock the lady on the head, Daddy, or the policeman will take you away.' This is the most darned awkward situation I've ever been in in my life."

Penny laughed, not realizing the significance beneath the frivolous words. "I should give it her," she said, "whoever she is. I'll stand by you."

Mr. Campion permitted himself a dubious smile.

"I wonder if you would?" he murmured.

CHAPTER TWENTY

Trunk Call

"'Ere, wake up, sir. Inspector Stanislaus Oates, 'imself and personal, on the phone. Now we shall 'ave a chance of seein' that lovely dressin'-gown o' yours. I've bin wondering when that was comin' out."

Mr. Lugg put his head round the door of his master's room and spoke with heavy jocularity. "'E's bin ringin' you all day," he added, assuming a certain amount of truculence to hide his apprehension. "There's a couple o' telegrams waitin'. But I didn't like to rouse yer. Let 'im 'ave 'is beauty sleep, that's what I said."

Mr. Campion bounded out of bed, looking oddly rakish in the afternoon light. "Good Heavens," he said, "what's the time?"

"Calm yerself—calm yerself. 'Alf-past four." Mr. Lugg came forward bearing a chastely coloured silk dressing-gown. "Pull yerself together. You remind me o' Buster Keaton when you're 'alf awake. Brush yer 'air before yer go down. There's a lady 'elp what's taken my fancy 'anging on to the phone."

Mr. Campion bound the dressing-gown girdle tightly round his willowy form and snatched up his spectacles.

"What's this about phoning all day?" he said. "If this is true I'll sack you, Lugg."

"I've got to keep you alive. My job depends on it," observed his valet sententiously. "Staying out all night ghost 'untin' ain't done you no good. You look like an 'arf warmed corpse as it is. That's right—knock me about," he added, as Mr. Campion brushed past him and pattered down the stairs to the side hall where the phone was situated.

The chubby little servant girl, evidently a captive to the charms of Mr. Lugg, was clinging to the receiver, which she relinquished to

Campion. She stood back and would have remained at a respectful distance, if by no means out of earshot, had not Mr. Lugg waved her majestically kitchenwards.

"Hallo," said a faint voice at the far end of the crackling wire, "is that you? At last. I was on the point of coming to you. I'm terribly sorry, old boy, but they've got it."

Mr. Campion remained silent for some moments, but in response to a sharp query from the other end of the phone he said weakly: "Oh, yes, I can hear you all right. What do you want—congratulations?"

"Go easy," came the distant voice imploringly. "It was a most ingenious stunt. You'd have been sunk yourself. About two o'clock this morning a whole pack of drunks got hauled into Bottle Street Station, and about thirty of their friends arrived at the same time. There was a terrific fight, and the man on duty on your doorstep joined in, like a mutt. In the confusion someone must have peeled up your stairs and raided the flat. I've been trying to get on to you ever since. What have you been doing? Dabbling in the dew?"

In spite of the lightness of his tone it was evident to Mr. Campion that his old friend was desperately worried. "We're doing all we can," came the voice, "and some more. Can you give us a line?"

"Half a minute," said Mr. Campion. "What about young Hercules?"

"Oh, Gyrth? That's half the trouble," whispered the distant voice. "They knocked him on the head, of course, but the moment our man on the roof dropped through the skylight he pulled himself together and shot down after his property. Frankly, we can't find him. There was a free fight going on in the street, you see, and you know what a hopeless place it is. We've rounded up the usuals, but they don't seem to know anything. We've got a dozen or so of the rowdies too. Clever men most of 'em. Have you got anything we can go on?"

Mr. Campion considered. He was now fully awake. "Have you got a pen there?" he said. "Listen. There's two whizz-boys, Darky Farrell and a little sheeny called Diver. They may or may not be concerned, but I've seen them in the business. Oh, you've got them, have you? Well, put them through it. Then there's Natty Johnson, of course. The only other person I can think of is Fingers Hawkins, the Riverside one. How's that?"

"A nasty little list." The far-away voice spoke with feeling. "Righto, leave it to us. You'll stay there, will you? I'll ring you if anything happens. We're pretty sick up here, of course. They're a hot lot; all race-gang people, I notice."

"That had occurred to me," said Mr. Campion. "Don't get your head bashed in for my sake. Oh, and I say, Stanislaus . . . kiss that Bobby on the door for me."

He replaced the receiver and turned wearily away from the instrument to come face to face with his aide, the sight of whom seemed to fill him with sudden wrath.

"Now you've done it," he said. "If we muck this whole thing up it'll be directly due to your old-hen complex. Bah! Go and keep mushrooms!"

Mr. Lugg remained unabashed.

"You've mixed us up with a nice set, 'aven't yer?" he said. "I've known ticket o' leave men who'd blush to 'ear theirselves associated with them names you've mentioned over the phone. Fight with razors and broken bottles, they do. It's the class o' the thing I object to. No one can call me a snob—not reely—but a gent 'as to draw 'is line somewhere."

But for once Mr. Campion was not mollified by this attitude.

"Put on a bath, get out the car, find a map, and go and lose yourself," he said, and stalked off upstairs, leaving Mr. Lugg speechless and startled out of his usual gloomy truculence.

A little over an hour later Penny, seated by herself in the spacious faded drawing-room whose broad lattice-paned windows overlooked the drive, was somewhat surprised to hear the door of her father's room across the hall close softly, and to see Mr. Campion in a motoring coat and hatless run down the steps from the open front door, and, climbing into his car which stood waiting for him, hurtle off down the drive at an alarming speed.

She had imagined that he would have been down shortly to take tea with her, and she was just about to put her pride in her pocket and ring for Lugg and information, when Branch appeared carrying a bulky envelope on a salver.

"Mr. Campion was wishful for me to give you this, miss," he said, and withdrew.

With her curiosity considerably piqued, Penny tore open the stout manilla and shook its contents out upon the Chesterfield beside her. To her astonishment there lay disclosed upon the faded brocade a folded sheet of paper, another envelope, and a small bag made of cheap red silk. The paper was closely written in broad distinctive writing.

Dear Penny, I have gone to pay a friendly call to show off my new suit. I may be so welcome that they won't want to part with me, so don't expect me until you see me. I leave Lugg with you as

*a sort of keepsake. Three meals a day, my dear, and no alcohol.
I wonder if you would mind giving him the enclosed note,
which I have stuck down to show my ill-breeding. No doubt he
will show it to you. But I don't want him to have it until I am
safely on my journey, since he is trained to follow a car. The
rather garish bag, which you will see is not made to open, contains,
as far as I know, a portion of the beard of a very old friend of
mine (a prophet in a small way). That is for Lugg too.*

*Remember your promise, which only holds good while I'm
alive, of course. Don't get the wind up whatever happens. If in
doubt, apply to the Professor, who is a mine of information and
the best sort in the world.*

*Such clement weather we are having for the time of year, are
we not? "The face is but the guinea's stamp. The heart's the
heart for a' that."*

> *Believe me, Sincerely yours, W. Shakespeare.*
> *(Bill, to you.)*

The girl sat turning the paper over on her knee until Branch re-
entered with the tea-wagon. But although she was burning with curiosity, it was not until a good half-hour had elapsed that she sent for
Lugg. Colonel Gyrth never took tea, and she was still alone when the
door opened to admit the troubled face and portly figure of Mr.
Campion's other ego.

The big man had a horror of the drawing-room, which he crossed
as though the floor were unsteady.

"Yes, miss?" he said suspiciously.

Penny handed him the envelope in silence. He seized upon it
greedily, and, quite forgetting all Branch's training of the past few
days, tore it open and began to read, holding the paper very close to
his little bright eyes.

"There," he said suddenly. "Wot did I tell yer? Now we're for it.
'Eadstrong, that's what 'e is."

He caught sight of Penny's face, and, remembering where he was,
was about to withdraw in an abashed and elephantine fashion when
she stopped him.

"I had a letter from Mr. Campion too," she said. "He said I was
to give you this." She handed him the red silk bag, and added
brazenly: "He said you'd probably show me your letter."

Mr. Lugg hesitated at first, but finally seemed relieved at the thought
of having a confidante.

"There you are," he said ungraciously. "That'll show yer what a caution 'e is." He tossed the note into her lap. "It may be a bit above yer 'ead."

Penny unfolded the missive and began to read.

> *Unutterable Imbecile and Cretin. Hoping this finds you as it leaves me—in a blue funk. However, don't you worry, cleversides. Have had to resort to the Moran trick. If I am not back by tomorrow morning get somebody to take the beard of the prophet to Mrs. Sarah on Heronhoe Heath. Don't have hysterics again, and if the worst comes to the worst don't forge my name to any rotten references. You'd only be found out. Leave the Open Sesame to Sarah and the Chicks. Yours, Disgusted.*

Penny put the note down. "What does it all mean?" she said.

"Ask me another," said Mr. Lugg savagely. "Sneaked off on me, that's what 'e's done. 'E knew I'd 'ave stopped 'im if 'e didn't. This 'as torn it. I'll be readin' the Situations Vacant before I know where I am. 'E ain't even left me a reference. Lumme, we are in a mess."

"I wish you'd explain," said Penny, whose patience was beginning to fail her. "What's the Moran Trick, anyhow?"

"Oh, that," said Mr. Lugg. "That was silly then. It's sooicide now. We was up against a bloke called Moran, a murderer among other things, 'oo kep' a set o' coloured thugs around 'im. What did 'Is Nibs do when we couldn't get any satisfaction from 'im but walk into 'is 'ouse as cool as you please—forcin' 'em to kidnap 'im, so's 'e could find out what they was up to. 'Curiosity'll kill you, my lad,' I said when I got 'im out. 'A lot of satisfaction it'll be to you when you're 'arping to 'ave a pile of evidence against the bloke who's bumped you off.'"

Penny sprang to her feet. "Then he knows who it is?" she said.

"O' course 'e does," said Mr. Lugg. "Probably known it from 'is cradle—at least, that's what 'e'll tell you. But the fac' remains that we don't know. Gorn off in a silly temper and left me out of it. If I ever get 'im back from this alive I'll 'ave 'im certified."

The girl looked at him wildly. "But if the Cup's safe with Val, what's he doing it for?" she wailed.

Lugg cocked a wary eye at her. "Depend upon it, miss, there's a lot o' things neither of us 'ave been told. All we can do is to carry out 'is orders and 'ope fer the best. I'll tell yer wot, though, I'll get my lucky bean out to-night—blimey if I don't."

Penny returned to the letter. "Who is Mrs. Sarah?" she demanded.

"The Mother Superior of a lot o' gippos," said Mr. Lugg disconsolately. "It's either nobs or nobodies with 'im, and I loathe the sight o' both of 'em—begging yer pardon, miss."

Penny looked up quickly. "We'll take the token together to-morrow morning," she said. "Heronhoe Heath is about five miles from here across country. Mrs. Shannon has her racing stables on the far side of it. We'll drive over."

Lugg raised an eyebrow. "Mrs. Shannon? Is that the party as come snooping round 'ere the day after yer aunt died?" he said. "Powerful voiced, and nippy like?"

"That's right," said Penny, smiling in spite of herself.

Mr. Lugg whistled. "I 'ate women," he said, with apparent irrelevance. "Especially in business."

CHAPTER TWENTY-ONE

The Yellow Caravan

Heronhoe Heath, a broad strip of waste land bordered by the Ipswich road on one side and Heronhoe Creek on the other, was half covered with gaudy broom bushes when Mr. Lugg and Penny bumped their way across it in the two-seater on the morning after Mr. Campion's departure. The sunshine was so brilliant that a grey heat haze hung over the creek end of the heath, through which the flat red buildings of Mrs. Shannon's stables were faintly discernible. There was not another house for three miles either way.

The Gypsy encampment was equally remote from the world. It lay sprawled along the northern edge of the strip like a bright bandana handkerchief spread out upon the grass by the side of a little ditch of clear water which ran through to the creek.

When they were within hailing distance of the camp the track, chewed up by many caravans' wheels, became unnegotiable. Penny pulled up. "We'll have to walk this bit," she said.

Mr. Lugg sighed and scrambled out of the car, the girl following him. They made an odd pair.

Penny was in a white silk jumper suit and no hat, while Mr. Lugg wore the conventional black suit and bowler hat of the upper servant, the respectability of which he had entirely ruined by tilting the hat over one eye, thereby achieving an air of truculent bravado which was not lessened by the straw which he held between his teeth. He grumbled in a continuous breathy undertone as he lumbered along.

"Look at 'em," he said. "Vagabonds. 'Ut dwellers. Lumme, you wouldn't catch me spendin' my life in a marquee."

Penny surveyed the scene in front of her with approval. The gaily painted wagons with their high hooped canvas tops, the coloured clothes hanging out on the lines, and the dozens of little fires whose smoke curled up almost perpendicularly in the breathless air were certainly attractive. There was squalor there, too, and ugliness, but on the whole the prospect was definitely pleasing, the sunlight bringing out the colours.

What impressed the girl particularly was the number of wagons and caravans; there seemed to be quite forty of them, and she noticed that they were not settled with the numerous little odd tents and shacks around them as is usual in a big encampment, but that the whole gathering had a temporary air which was heightened by the presence of a huge old-fashioned yellow char-à-banc of the type used by the people of the fairs.

Although she had known the Gypsies since her childhood she had never visited them before. Their haunts had been forbidden to her, and she knew them only as brown, soft-spoken people with sales methods that would put the keenest hire-system traveller to shame.

It was with some trepidation, therefore, that she walked along by the disconsolate Lugg towards the very heart of the group. Children playing half-naked round the caravans grinned at her as she approached and shouted unintelligible remarks in shrill twittering voices. Mr. Lugg went on unperturbed.

A swarthy young man leaning over the half-door of one of the vans, his magnificent arms and chest looking like polished copper against the outrageous red and white print of his shirt, took one look at Lugg and burst into a bellow of delight that summoned half the clan. Heads popped out from every conceivable opening, and just for a moment Penny was afraid that the reception was not going to be wholly friendly.

Mr. Lugg stood his ground. "Party, name o' Mrs. Sarah," he demanded in stentorian tones. "I got a message for 'er. Private and important."

The name had a distinctly quietening effect upon the crowd which was gathering, and the young man who had heralded their arrival opened the low door of his wagon and clattered down the steps.

"Come here," he said, and led them across the uneven turf to the very heart of the assembly, where stood a truly magnificent caravan, decorated with a portrait of the King and Queen on one side and four dolphins surrounding a lurid representation of the Siamese Twins on

the other. The brasswork in the front of this exquisitely baroque char-
iot was polished until it looked like gold. It formed a little balcony
in front of the wagon, behind which, seated in the driver's cab, was a
monstrously fat old woman, her head bound round with a green and
yellow cotton scarf, while an immense print overall covered her
capacious form. She was smiling, her shrewd black eyes regarding the
visitors with a species of royal amusement.

Their guide made a few unintelligible remarks to her in some peculiar "back slang" which the girl did not follow. The old woman's
smile broadened.

"Come up, lady," she said, throwing out a hand to indicate the
coloured steps which led into the darkness of the wagon. As she did so
the sunlight caught the rings on her hand, and the blaze of real stones
dazzled in the heat.

Penny clambered up the steps and took the seat opposite the old
woman, while Mr. Lugg lumbered after her and perched himself gingerly on the topmost step of the ladder. The crowd still hung about
inquisitively. Penny was aware of eager derisive brown faces and shrill
chattering tongues making remarks she could not hope to understand.

The monstrous old lady, who appeared to be Mrs. Sarah, turned
upon the crowd, her smile gone. A few vitriolic sentences, at the sense
of which Penny could only guess, dispersed them like naughty children. With the ease of a duchess Mrs. Sarah then returned to her
guests.

"Who sent you, lady?" she said in her sibilant persuasive, "party"
voice.

Mr. Lugg produced the red silk bag, which he handed to Penny,
who in turn gave it to the old lady. The plump brown fingers seized
upon it, and with her long blackened finger-nails Mrs. Sarah jerked at
the cotton which bound the topmost edge of the bag. Next moment
the contents lay in her hand.

Penny regarded it with curiosity. It was an old-fashioned hair ring,
made of countless tiny plaits woven together with microscopic intri-
cacy. She held it up and laughed.

"Orlando!" she said with evident delight. "Don't worry, lady. Sarah
knows. To-morrow," she went on slowly. "Yes, he said the day after.
Very well. We shall be ready. Good-bye, lady."

Penny, considerably mystified, looked startled. "Orlando?"

Mr. Lugg nudged her. "One of 'is names," he said sepulchrally.
"Come on. The court is adjourned."

He was obviously right: the old woman smiled and nodded but did
not seem disposed to converse any further. Penny had the impression

that their hostess had received a piece of information for which she had been waiting. As the girl descended the steps, however, the affable old goddess leaned forward.

"You've got a lucky face, my dear," she said. "You'll get a nice husband. But you won't get Orlando."

Considerably startled by this unexpected announcement, Penny smiled at her and started after Lugg, who was making for the little car as fast as his dignity would permit.

" 'E calls 'isself Orlando among the gippos," he said. "A funny old party, wasn't she? See 'er groinies?—Rings, I mean. Close on a thousand quid's worth there, I reckoned. All made from poor mugs like us. One of 'em told my fortune once. A journey across the water, she said. I was in Parkhurst inside of a month."

Penny was not listening to him. "But what does it mean?" she said. "What's he got them to do?"

Mr. Lugg made an exaggerated gesture of despair. "They're old friends of 'is," he said. " 'E goes off with 'em sometimes. 'E don't take me—leaves me at 'ome to mind the jackdaw. That's the sort of man 'e is. You got to face these things. I can see a rough 'ouse afore we've finished."

They had reached the car by this time, and Penny did not answer, but as she climbed into the driver's seat yet another caravan passed them heading for the camp. She glanced across the heath to where the stables lay just visible in the distance. For a moment a gleam of understanding appeared in her eyes, but she did not confide her thoughts to Lugg.

They drove home through the winding lanes to Sanctuary.

" 'Ere! Wot's this we're in?" said Mr. Lugg, after some seventeen sharp turns. "A blinkin' maze?"

Penny, who had grown used to his artless familiarity, smiled. "It's a long way round by road, I know," she said. "It's only five miles across the fields. This road dates from the time when one had to avoid the wealthy landowners' property."

As they passed Tye Hall Beth and the Professor were at the gate. They waved to her, and Penny pulled up and got out.

"Look here," she said to Lugg, "you take the car back to the Tower. I'll walk home."

Still grumbling a little, Mr. Lugg obeyed, and Penny went back along the white dusty road to where her friends were waiting.

"We're waiting for the post," said Beth cheerfully. "Where's your funny little friend this morning?"

"Goodness only knows," said Penny awkwardly. "He went off last night, leaving a note to say he was going visiting. I believe he knows something."

The Professor, very coolly and sensibly dressed in yellow shantung and a panama hat, stroked his neat little beard with a thin brown hand. "Is that all he said?" he inquired. "I'll say that sounds very odd."

"To walk out at a time like this," said Beth. "It's not like him."

"I think he's up to something," said Penny, anxious to dispel any wrong impression. "He left Lugg and me a most extraordinary errand to do. That's where we've been. We've taken a red silk bag to an old lady who looked like that figure of Hotei in your drawing-room, Professor, all wrapped up in coloured print. She's a sort of Gypsy Queen, I suppose. There's a whole crowd of them camping on Heronhoe Heath."

The Professor's round brown eyes widened perceptibly. "Well, now, isn't that strange?" he said, and appeared to relapse in deep thought.

"She seemed to understand what it was all about, anyhow," Penny went on, "which was more than I did. And she said something about to-morrow, as if he'd made a date or something. He's an extraordinary person, you know."

Beth opened her mouth to agree, but she was silenced by an apparition which had just appeared leaning over the field gate which split the high hedge directly opposite the Tye Hall drive. A startled exclamation escaped her, and all three of them turned and stared at the dishevelled figure which clutched the topmost bar of the gate for support.

"Val!" Beth darted across the road, the other two behind her. The young man was deathly pale. He looked ill, and as he made a move towards them he swayed drunkenly. The Professor unhooked the gate, and, hitching the boy's arm round his own shoulder, half led, half dragged him across the road and up the path to the house.

"Don't chatter to him now, girls." The Professor spoke firmly, silencing a chorus of questions. "He looks real bad to me. Beth, cut up to the house and get out some brandy and ice water. Penny, my dear, give me a hand with his other arm."

"I'm all right," said Val weakly. "I've been doped, I think. Only just came to myself—heard you talking and staggered out. I'm a silly ass, that's what I am."

"Hold on. Don't talk for a bit," the Professor advised, as he led the little party into the house by the side door from the lawn. "No, it's all right," he said to an excited maidservant who met them. "Don't alarm Mrs. Cairey. Young Mr. Gyrth has come over a bit faint, that's all."

The girl vanished with a startled "yessir," and the Professor turned his charge into the library, where Beth was already waiting with the brandy and water.

Val would not be silenced any longer. "I asked for it and I got it," he said, as he sank down gratefully into a deep saddleback. "Gosh! I've got a head like fifty champagne suppers."

"But what's happened?" said Penny and Beth in chorus. "And," added his sister as the thought suddenly burst upon her, "where's the Cup?"

Val's clouded eyes grew hard for a moment, and he tried to struggle to his feet as the recollection returned to him. Next moment, however, he had sunk back again helplessly.

"They've got it," he said apathetically. "Where's Campion?"

Penny made an inarticulate noise in her throat and then sat down by the table, white and trembling.

Beth seemed more concerned about Val than any Chalice, however. Beneath her kindly ministrations the boy began to recover rapidly. He looked at her gratefully.

"I'm giving you an awful lot of trouble," he said. "I don't know how I got in that field. I woke up and heard you talking and staggered out, and here I am."

"Now, my boy," said the Professor, "what happened? Can you remember?"

Val considered. "I was at Campion's flat," he said. "I sat up late, reading, with the Chalice in the suitcase actually on my lap. A damn silly place to put it, I suppose. I hadn't undressed—I didn't mean to go to bed. Early in the morning, about two or three I suppose it was, I heard a fiendish noise going on outside. I looked out of the window and saw a sort of free fight in progress round that Police Station downstairs. I was wondering what was up when I heard someone in the flat behind me. He must have had a pass-key, I suppose."

He paused reflectively as he tried to piece together the jumbled events in his mind. "Oh well, then," he said at last, "—curse this headache, it's blinding me—then I got a crack over the skull, but not before I'd caught a glimpse of the fellow who swatted me. I recognized him. When I was down and out," he added awkwardly, "I went into all sorts of low eating-houses. And there was one off Berwick Street, in Soho, just by the market, you know, where I used to see a whole lot of odd fishy characters going in and out. I think they had a room at the back. Well, this chap who hit me was a man I'd seen there often. I spotted him at once. He'd got a most obvious sort of face with a curious lumpy nose."

He stopped again and the Professor nodded comprehendingly. "Then you were knocked out?" he suggested.

"That's right," Val agreed. "But I don't think I was out more than a couple of minutes at the most. I remember getting in a hell of a temper and charging downstairs; the only thing clear in my mind was that dirty little dive off Berwick Street. Outside there was still a young battle going on, and I charged through it. I think I sent a bobby flying in the process. Of course, I ought to have taken a few of them with me, but that didn't occur to me at the time. They had their hands full, anyhow."

"And when you got to Berwick Street?" said Beth, who had listened to this recital of her hero's with wide-eyed enthusiasm.

"Well, that was about all," said Val. "I charged into the place like a roaring bull and asked the proprietor chap for the man I wanted. He took me into the back room, where I waited, fuming, until a great lout of a fellow came in and before I knew what had happened I got a towel full of ether or chloroform or something in my face. That's all I remember, until I found myself sitting in the hedge in the field outside here, feeling like a half resuscitated corpse.

"I say," he added suddenly, "what's to-day? I mean—?"

"You're twenty-five to-morrow," said the Professor. "By the look of you you've been lying in that hedge since early this morning. Thank goodness it's dry weather."

"How did I get there?" said Val in bewilderment. "I tell you, I was laid out in a filthy little dive off Berwick Market last night—no, it couldn't have been last night. The night before, then. I suppose they injected something. Chloroform wouldn't have kept me under all that time. Here—where's Campion? I must let him know. Although," he added morosely, "I suppose he's heard all about it from the police by now."

"Albert's gone," wailed Penny. "And we've lost the Chalice. And yet," she added, suddenly sitting up, "that accounts for it. Someone was phoning Albert up all day yesterday. I was in bed at the time, but Mary told me this morning. That's why he went off. He didn't want to scare Father or me, I suppose."

She was interrupted by the arrival of Mrs. Cairey, who put her head round the door.

"Papa dear," she said, "the postman's here. There's that special mail you've got to pay for, and I wondered if you'd like your letters too, Penny, my dear. He'll give them to you if you come. Lands above!" she added, coming into the room, all her motherly instincts aroused, "you do look ill, Mr. Gyrth. Is there anything I can do for you?"

Penny went out with the Professor almost mechanically. Her brain was whirling with the complications of this new and apparently final development. Why on earth could no one realize that the Chalice had gone?

The postman, a scarlet-faced and perspiring East Anglian, was standing at the front door leaning gratefully on his bicycle.

"Two letters for you, miss," he remarked, as he completed his transaction with the Professor. "Your brother ain't 'ere by any chance, is 'e?" he added, raising a hopeful blue eye in her direction.

"He is, as a matter of fact," said Penny, considerably startled by the coincidence of such a question.

"Ain't that lucky? The only other thing for the Tower is this parcel for 'im. If you wouldn't mind, miss—?" The man was already unbuckling the prodigious canvas bag on his carrier, and the next moment he had dumped a large and heavy parcel in her arms. "It's lucky you got it," he said. "It feels like it's over the regulation weight to me. Good morning, miss."

He touched his ridiculous hat and swung on to the bicycle.

Penny, with the parcel in her arms, walked slowly back to the study. Just as she entered the room something about the weight and size of her burden sent a curious thrill through her.

"Val," she said breathlessly, "open this. I think—oh, I don't know —anyhow, open it."

There was something so imperative in her tone that the boy's interest was roused.

"What in the name of—" he began. "Oh, it's my birthday to-morrow. It's probably something stupid from one of the relations."

Nevertheless he accepted the knife Beth handed him and ripped up the cords, displaying a stout cardboard box of the type usually used to pack large bottles. Something of his sister's excitement seemed to be conveyed to him, for the hand that unfastened the slotted end of the carton shook violently.

Next moment he had pulled out a wad of straw packing and an exclamation escaped him. The Professor, Mrs. Cairey and Beth bent forward, and very gently he drew out the long, slender golden cup that Mr. Melchizadek's great-grandfather had made.

"The Chalice!" said Penny, a sob in her voice. "Oh, Val, it's all right."

The faces of the other two women reflected her delight, but the Professor and Val exchanged glances.

"How—?" said Val breathlessly. "This is incredible. Is there any message? Who addressed it?"

A frenzied search revealed that there was no other enclosure, and that the address was printed in block capitals. The postmark was illegible.

The Professor cleared his throat. "I guess I can understand this," he said, tapping the relics of the parcel. "But how you arrived in that field this morning is completely beyond my comprehension. Who set you there, and why? It doesn't make sense."

Penny, who had been staring at her brother during the last few minutes, suddenly stretched out her hand.

"Val!" she said. "Your buttonhole!"

Instinctively the boy put up his hand to the lapel of his collar and an expression of astonishment came into his face as he detached a drooping wild flower bud from the slit and stared at it.

"Funny," he said. "I certainly don't remember putting it there. It's fairly fresh, too."

Penny snatched it from him. "Don't you see what it is?" she said, her voice rising. "There's hundreds of them in that field where you woke up. It's a white campion. There's only one person on earth who would think of that."

CHAPTER TWENTY-TWO

The Three-Card Trick

Mr. Campion stopped his car among the high broom bushes on Heronhoe Heath that evening and sniffed the air appreciatively. He seemed if anything a little more inane than usual, and in spite of his evident anxiety, there was something about him which conveyed that he was definitely pleased with himself.

Although he had been driving most of the day there was no trace of weariness in his tall loose-limbed figure. He locked the car, slipped the key into his pocket, and stood for a moment with his hand on the bonnet. "The highwayman's farewell to his horse," he remarked aloud to the empty air, and then, turning abruptly, strode off across the springy turf.

Behind him the lights of the Gypsy camp glowed in the dusk, and for a moment he hesitated, half drawn by their inviting friendliness. He turned away resolutely, however, and contented himself by hailing them with a long drawn-out whistle that might easily have come from one of the myriad seabirds on the creek. He paused to listen, the heath whispering and rustling around him. Almost immediately the cry was returned, two melodious whistles that sounded pleasantly reassuring. Mr. Campion appeared satisfied and strode on his way almost jauntily.

Mrs. Dick's stables were only just discernible, a dark rectangular patch in the greyness. He had miscalculated the distance a little, and the walk was longer than he had anticipated. When he reached the buildings at last he stood for a moment in the shadow of a high wall listening intently. There was no sound from within, and convinced that his approach had not been observed, he began to work slowly round the walls, moving silently and using his torch at intervals.

The building was much as he had expected. A high red wall enclosed the whole of the establishment, forming a large rectangular block, only one side of which was skirted by the rough private track which he had been so careful to avoid in his journey from the main road.

The large iron gates which formed the entrance from the track were locked. Peering cautiously through them, he was relieved to find the place in darkness. The dwelling-house and garden took up the western third of the rectangle. Directly in front of him was a square court with a cottage on his left, while the stables occupied the remaining portion of the whole block. They were built on all four sides of a square, two storeys high, with big wooden gates to the courtyard and a second entrance giving on to the heath on the eastern side, at right-angles to the creek. The drive led on a gentle curve past the front door of the house to the wooden gates of the stable yard.

Alone in the darkness, Mr. Campion became suddenly intensely alert. Somewhere in the house he fancied he could hear the murmur of voices. He made no attempt to enter until he had been all round the buildings, however, and by the time he had returned to the front gates once more he was considerably wiser.

The place was in appalling repair and many of the bricks had begun to fluke badly under the influence of the salt air. Mr. Campion put his spectacles in his pocket, and, having chosen a suitable spot by the kitchens of the house where an overgrown creeper hung down, began to climb. It was by no means an easy ascent, for the wall was high, and it was surmounted by broken glass which the creeper only just masked. He accomplished it, however, and slid noiselessly to the ground on the other side. Once again he paused to listen, holding his breath. Still there was no noise but the continued murmur of voices somewhere on the opposite side of the house.

Having replaced his spectacles, he set off once more on his perambulation. There were no dogs nor grooms to be seen, and after careful inspection of the stable yard, the wooden doors of which stood ajar, Mr. Campion was convinced that the information which he had gathered on one of his many visits that afternoon in London was substantially correct. Mrs. Dick's racing stables could hardly be regarded as a going concern. Although there were boxes for twenty horses, only one of them appeared to be occupied.

The cottage by the stable gates was empty also, and evidences of decay were on all sides. Only the lawn and the courtyard were trim. The garden was a wilderness.

Very cautiously he approached the one lighted aperture in the whole establishment; two glass doors giving out on to the lawn. He had been careful to avoid the beam of light which they shed on to the lawn, but now he ventured up to it, the grass deadening his footsteps.

There was a thin net curtain over the windows, but the light inside rendered it transparent as he came nearer. In the relics of what had once been a fine room, five men and a woman were grouped round a table at which a hand of poker was in progress.

"Not a nice lot," Mr. Campion reflected as he glanced from face to face. There was Matthew Sanderson, looking more astute than ever as he dealt the cards; the horse-faced "Major", and Fingers Hawkins, who had held him up on the road, a little ill at ease among his social superiors, but nevertheless in shirt-sleeves. Then there was a grey-headed, narrow-eyed man he did not recognize, and a little insignificant Japanese half-caste that he did, and whose presence bewildered him.

Mrs. Dick dominated the group by sheer force of personality. As usual, she was strikingly smart; her black and white dress contrived to be almost theatrical in its extreme yet austere fashionableness. Her white face was twisted in a half-smile. Her hair was close-cropped like a man's, displaying her curiously lobeless ears. A heavy rope of barbaric crimson beads was coiled round her throat, and the feminine touch looked bizarre upon her angular, masculine form.

"Not staying, Major?" she said, as the red-faced man threw down his cards. "You never have the courage to see a thing through. Sandy, I've been watching you. You're playing all you know."

Sanderson threw down his cards. "I wonder someone hasn't strangled you, Daisy," he said, with more admiration than resentment in his tone.

Mrs. Dick was unabashed. "My husband tried," she observed.

"You got him first, I suppose?" said the Major, laughing.

The woman fixed him with her peculiarly insolent stare. "He used to say the whisky wasn't strong enough," she said. "I often think it was the methylated spirits we used to pep it up with that killed him."

Sanderson turned away. "You put the wind up me," he said. "The way you talk I wonder you're not afraid of the 'Blacking'."

Mrs. Dick laughed. "I'd like to see any man who's got the guts to blackmail me," she said. "Make it five, Tony."

"No 'Blacking'," said Fingers Hawkins from the other side of the table. "But we'll get our do's."

"You'll get your dues and more." Mrs. Dick was inclined to be contemptuous. "I'll make it the limit, Tony. You won't stay? Thanks. Mine."

She threw down her hand as Mr. Campion tapped on the window.

The gentle noise startled everyone save Mrs. Dick, who hardly looked up from the cards she was collecting. "Open that window, Fingers," she murmured. "There's something scratching on it."

The big man went forward cautiously, and, raising the catch, jerked the half-door open, jumping smartly sideways as he did so.

Mr. Campion, pale, smiling and ineffably inane, was revealed on the threshold.

"Good evening, everybody," he said, coming into the room. "Anybody got a good tip for the Ascot Gold Cup?"

Fingers Hawkins side-stepped behind him and passed out into the darkness. "'E's alone," he remarked, and coming back into the room, relocked the window.

At this piece of information the spirits of the company, which had been momentarily uncertain, now became almost uproarious. Sanderson began to laugh.

"All on his own," he said. "Isn't that sweet and confiding? We were telling Daisy she ought to invite you for a nice quiet rest until the fun was over, and here you are."

"Look out. P'raps there's a cartload of busies outside," said the half-caste nervously.

Sanderson turned on him. "Shut up, Moggie," he said viciously. "How many times have I told you the police aren't in this business? What d'you think they're going to get you for—being alive?"

"Well, I could understand that," remarked Mr. Campion affably. "Still, everyone to his taste, eh, Mrs. Shannon?"

Mrs. Dick did not deign to look in his direction. "What have you come here for?" she said, reshuffling the cards. "I don't think I know you."

"Nonsense," said Mr. Campion. "We met at the dear Vicar's. You must remember. I was passing round the biscuits. You took two. Then we both laughed heartily."

Mrs. Dick raised her eyes and regarded him coldly. "You seem to be even more of a fool than I took you for at first," she said, her stentorian tones blaring at him across the card table. "What are you doing here?"

"Calling," said Mr. Campion firmly. "That must be obvious to the meanest intelligence."

"Sandy," said Mrs. Shannon, "put this creature out."

"Not on your life." Sanderson spoke with enthusiasm. "Daisy underestimates you, Campion. I shall feel all the safer with you as a guest here for the next few days. Got a gun?"

"No," said Mr. Campion. "I don't like firearms. Even pea-shooters are dangerous in my opinion."

"No fooling. I've got mine trained on you."

Mr. Campion shrugged his shoulders and turned to Fingers. "Do your stuff," he said, raising his arms above his head. "I love to see a professional at work."

"You stow it," said the pickpocket uneasily. Nevertheless he complied with Mr. Campion's request, and stood back a moment or so later shaking his head.

Sanderson's amusement increased.

"Well, this *is* friendly," he said. "What d'you think you're doing? You've done some balmy things in your life, but now you've stepped clean over the edge. What's the idea?"

"You look out for 'im," said the gentleman addressed as Moggie. "'E's as slippery as an eel. 'E's got something up his sleeve, you betcher life. Probably that great bull pup Lugg's about somewhere."

"Write that down, sign it, send it to our head office, and we present you with a magnificent fountain pen absolutely free," said Mr. Campion. "Every testimonial, however humble, is docketed and on view at any time."

Mrs. Dick stacked the cards up neatly and turned in her chair to survey her visitor once more. "Why have you come here, young man?" she said. "You're beginning to bore me."

"Just you wait," said Mr. Campion. "Wait till I get my personality over. I do hope you don't mind. I've been looking over your stables. There's one thing I didn't quite get. So many boxes but only 'a' horse. I suppose the pretty creature has a different home each day, like Alice at the mad tea party."

The woman's expression did not change, but her strong bony hands ceased to play with the cards.

"Perhaps you had better stay here for a day or two," she said. "Lock him up in one of the boxes, Sandy, and then for Heaven's sake stick to the game."

"We'd better see if he *is* alone, first," said Sanderson. "I shan't be surprised if he is. He's conceited enough for anything."

"If you find anyone outside he's nothing to do with me," said Mr. Campion. "Absolutely no connexion with any other firm. No; as I told you before, I'm making a perfectly normal formal call. I climbed the wall by a honeysuckle bush. Up and down, quite unaided. Moggie couldn't have done it better. Frankly," he went on, turning towards that worthy, "I don't see what a cat burglar is doing in this."

"You don't have to," cut in Sanderson quickly. "You don't have to think about us. It's your own skin you've got to watch. Fingers, you and the Major go and have a scout round."

"That's right," said Mr. Campion. "And whistle all the time. Then we'll know it's you. Meantime, perhaps I could show you some card tricks?" he added, eyeing the pack on the table wistfully. "Or I'll tell your fortune, Mrs. Shannon. You've got a lucky face."

To everyone's surprise Mrs. Dick threw the pack in his direction. Mr. Campion picked them up and shuffled with great solemnity.

"You cut three times towards me and wish," he said. His pale eyes were mild and guileless, and there was an infantile expression upon his face. She cut the cards, the half-amused, half-derisive smile still twisting her small thin mouth.

Mr. Campion set about arranging the cards with a portentous air. "I see a lot of knaves about you," he remarked cheerfully. "One fat one," he added, eyeing the retreating form of the "Major".

Sanderson laughed. "You're a cool customer," he said, a tinge of admiration in his voice. "Carry on."

"I see a great understanding," said Mr. Campion, planking down the cards one after the other. "And a lot of trouble. Oh, dear, dear, dear! All black cards. It looks as if there's a hanging in it for somebody."

"Shut up," said Sanderson, stretching out a hand as if to sweep the cards off the table. "He's playing for time, or something."

"Hush," said Mr. Campion. "I'm going to have my palm crossed with silver for this—I hope. Now here's a whole stack of money—I might almost say a pot of money. Ah, don't be led astray by riches, lady. Here comes the luck card. It's very close but it doesn't quite touch. There's a fair young man in between. I should watch out for him, Mrs. Dick."

He prattled on, apparently oblivious of his surroundings.

"There's an old woman and her son who'll give the game away if you don't take care—a silly old woman and a sillier son. You'll have a lot to answer for there," he said presently, and was interrupted by the return of the two searchers.

"All the gates fast. Not a soul on the heath. He's alone," said the Major. "Shall we take him along now?"

"Don't interrupt," said Mr. Campion reprovingly. "The gentleman is suffering from second sight and must not be disturbed until the fit is passed. Now, let me see." He sat for a moment looking at the cards which he had arranged in a half circle on the table. They lay so that one broken end faced Mrs. Dick and the other was beneath his hand.

"Oh, yes," he said at last, as though a new thought had occurred to him. "And then there's journeys." He bent across the table and planted a single card before the woman some distance from the rest, so that the whole formation resembled a rough question mark.

"I see a far journey," he remarked. "Why yes, most certainly. *You take the long road.*" And then, as she stared at the table, he swept the cards carelessly aside and rose to his feet.

"The seance is ended," he said. "Any more for the information bureau? Sanderson, let me tell you your past."

An explosive giggle from the "Major" was silenced by a single savage glance from the gentleman addressed.

"You'll stop mucking about," Sanderson said. "Where shall I put him, Daisy? In the loft, I suppose."

"Looks to me as though he's askin' for it a bit obvious," said Moggie. "What price we chuck 'im out on 'is ear?"

It was Mrs. Dick who settled the discussion. "Put him in the gate loft," she said. "Let him cool his heels for a couple of days."

Sanderson grinned. "I thought you'd see reason," he remarked complacently. He put his hand on Campion's shoulder and jerked him towards the door. Fingers Hawkins seized his other arm, and thus, with all ignominy, was Mr. Campion escorted to the stables which he had so lately examined; but although he protested the whole way, it should perhaps be recorded that on the whole he felt distinctly satisfied.

CHAPTER TWENTY-THREE

"Madame, Will You Talk?"

At eight o'clock on the evening of July the second, Val Gyrth's twenty-fifth birthday, Mr. Campion languished in the room over the gateway of Mrs. Shannon's stable-yard. It was an effective prison. The windows were barred to prevent an entry rather than an exit, but they were equally efficient in either case. The two doors which led into other first storey rooms on either side were locked. Even had he desired to escape, the process would have been difficult.

The atmosphere was suffocating under the low penthouse roof, and his couch, which consisted of a blanket thrown over a heap of straw, was not altogether comfortable. Yet he was by no means disheartened. He had had frequent visitors during the day, but so far the one person he had come to see had studiously avoided him.

While Sanderson seemed fidgety with curiosity, Mrs. Dick had not yet appeared.

This was the one factor in his plans that had so far miscarried, and here he was completely in the dark. And he realized clearly that upon Mrs. Dick's character everything depended.

During the day he had ascertained that there were considerably more men at the lady's command than he had encountered at the poker game, but he felt grateful at the thought of the yellow caravan across the heath.

He rose to his feet and glanced out of the window. Great dark blue streaks of cloud were beginning to creep across the golden sky in the west. A clatter in the yard sent him over to the opposite window, and he stood looking down at just such a scene as Sanderson had described to the uninterested little group in the Cup House on the day after Lady Pethwick's death.

Mrs. Dick, assisted by a terrified stable-boy and the equally unhappy "Major", was engaged in transferring her remaining pedigree mare from one box to another. They made an extraordinary picture; the woman, tall, angular and more mannish than ever in her rat-catcher riding-breeches and gaiters, and her white shirt buttoned tight to her neck and finished with a high stock tie of the same colour. Her cropped head was bare, and the evening light fell upon her pale, distorted face. The beast, a beautiful creature with a coat like black satin save for a single white stocking, was both nervous and bad-tempered. She was as heavy as a hunter and very tall, and as she moved the great muscles rippled down her shoulders like still water ruffled by the wind.

She refused the second box, and reared, pawing savagely with her forefeet. Mrs. Dick, one hand gripping the bridle rein, lashed out with her whip. Again and again the mare refused, clattering over the yard till the bricks echoed. But the woman was indomitable; a dozen times she seemed to save herself by sheer skill and the single steel wrist by which she held the animal.

Mr. Campion remembered the horse's name, "Bitter Aloes". As the words came back to him the battle outside came to a sudden end. The mare, charging savagely at her mistress, had been rewarded by a vicious punch on her velvet nose from a small but very forceful feminine fist, and as she clattered back from this unexpected attack the woman seized her opportunity and ran her back unprotesting into the box. Mrs. Dick emerged a moment later, grim and triumphant, superbly conscious of her victory. She accepted the "Major's" clumsy congratulations with a tart bellow of "Don't be a fool," which reached Mr. Campion clearly in his prison, and once again the yard was deserted.

He remained standing by the window for some time, vaguely troubled. The presence of Moggie, the little Japanese half-caste, puzzled him. And there was the grey-headed man too. There was no telling to what particular branch of the profession he might belong.

For the rest, however, he was content to wait. If Mrs. Dick had any spark of femininity in her make-up she would come to see him after the fortune-telling episode. He was a little surprised that she had not come before. The burning question of the moment, as far as he was concerned, and the sole reason for his present position, was the problem of whether Mrs. Dick was alone the employee of the "Société Anonyme", the amateur who, with the professional assistance of Matthew Sanderson and his associates, was directly responsible for the whole adventure of the Gyrth Chalice, the employee whose death according to the rules of the society would constitute the only reason for the abandonment of the quest.

For his own sake as much as hers Mr. Campion trusted fervently that this was not the case. Both he and Val had mentally shelved this aspect of the affair, concentrating doggedly on the immediate protection of the Chalice. But always this question had been lurking in the background, and now, it seemed to Campion, it clamoured for recognition.

In spite of himself he shied away from the subject and turned his thoughts towards the Tower. He imagined the sedate and rather solemn little dinner-party now in progress; Sir Percival at the head of the table with Val on his right, Penny opposite her brother, and Pembroke, the old parson, beside her. The conversation would be constrained, he felt sure, in spite of the intimate nature of the gathering. The shadow of the secret room would hang over them all relentlessly; the secret room which held the real Gyrth Chalice, and something else, that something which never seemed to leave Sir Percival's thoughts. He wondered if Val would react in the same way as his father had done, or if the sharing of the secret would lighten the burden on the old man's mind.

He was disturbed in his reflexions by the sound of a motor engine in the courtyard, and, glancing out of the opposite window to that by which he had been standing, he saw Sanderson bringing out a car from the garage.

Something about this most ordinary action alarmed him unreasonably.

There was a storm blowing up, and the heat, which had been oppressive all day, was now positively unbearable. Sanderson went into the house, and Campion was able to stare at the car at his leisure. Lying over the front seat he saw a coil of very flexible rope, knotted at intervals. He was puzzled, and his pale face peering through the bars of the window wore an expression of almost childlike discomfort. There was a distinct atmosphere of preparation abroad; something was about to happen.

The sound of a key turning in a lock behind him made him spin round.

Mrs. Dick stepped briskly into the room. She wore the costume in which he had seen her in the yard, and the short-handled whip was still in her hand. She stood with her back to the door, her legs slightly straddled, and regarded him insolently.

Immediately Mr. Campion sensed the extreme force of her personality, for the first time, directed upon him alone. He had met forceful and unpleasant personalities before in the course of a short and somewhat chequered career, but never in a woman, and it was this fact which robbed him for the moment of his usual urbanity.

"You haven't shaved this morning," she said suddenly. "I like men to be clean. I don't want you in this loft any longer. Get in here, will you?"

Mr. Campion looked hurt as he complied with her command, and suffered himself to be driven through a succession of similar lofts until he came to a full stop in a hay-strewn apartment which was, if anything, more hot and dusty than the one he had just left, in spite of the fact that there was a small open grating overlooking the heath in lieu of a window in the outer wall.

Mrs. Dick followed him into the room and shut the door behind her. "I want you in here because both doors bolt on the outside," she remarked. "Now, young man, what did you come here for?"

Mr. Campion considered. "You hurt me about not being shaved," he said. "None of your friends would trust me with a razor. I used to have a beard once. I called it 'Impudence'—'Persuasion' out of 'Cheek', you see. Rather neat, don't you think?"

Mrs. Dick permitted herself one of her sour smiles.

"I've been hearing about you," she said. "Impudence seems to be your strong point. I'm sorry you've got yourself mixed up in this. You might have been amusing. However," she went on, "since you've evidently got nothing to say, it's quite obvious to me what you're doing here. Since you are a prisoner like this, it gives you an excellent excuse to explain to your employers why you've failed. I recognize that fact."

Mr. Campion grinned. "I say," he said, "that's a good idea. How did you come to that startling conclusion?"

Mrs. Dick remained unmoved. "It was quite clever," she said judicially. "What a pity you'll never be able to use it. Sandy thinks you know much too much to get away with it. I've never paid blackmail, and I'm certainly not going to begin."

"It must be the people you associate with," said Mr. Campion with dignity. "My Union doesn't allow blackmail. I had no idea I was going to be a perpetual guest," he added cheerfully. "I do hope you won't expect me to wear an iron mask."

Mrs. Dick raised her eyebrows expressively, but she did not speak, and he went on.

"I suppose your present intention is to keep me here until you fix everything up with your London agents?"

The woman shot a penetrating glance at him. "You know very well we haven't succeeded yet," she said. "You were very clever, Mr. Campion, making all that fuss about your spurious Chalice. A little childish, perhaps, but quite effective. You made us waste a lot of time."

Mr. Campion's pale eyes flickered behind his spectacles. The blow had gone home.

"So you've found that out, have you?" he said. "You've been pretty quick. Little Albert has been taking things too easily, I see. Dear, dear,

dear! What are you going to do next? Have a lovely treasure hunt and give prizes? I'll come and tell you when you're getting warm."

"I'm not amused by nonsense," said Mrs. Dick. "In fact," she added with devastating frankness, "I have very little sense of humour."

"Well, that's original, I can't say fairer than that," said Mr. Campion politely. "May I make you a suggestion? Take the Chalice you already have. It has been in the Cup House at the Towers ever since it was made. Present it to your employers. If they cavil at it you can answer sincerely that as far as you know it is the only Gyrth Chalice in existence. I fancy that they'd pay up."

"Now you're beginning to be genuinely amusing," said Mrs. Dick. She lit a cigarette from a yellow packet which she drew from her breeches' pocket. "You don't seem to be very well informed. The spurious cup was sent back to the Tower the day before yesterday. I know perfectly well where the real Chalice is and I'm going to get it."

"With Matt Sanderson, Fingers Hawkins, Natty Johnson, the Major, old Uncle Tom Moggie and all," said Mr. Campion. "You won't get much of a look-in on the pay roll, will you? Mother, is it worth it? Father's got to have his share, you know."

Mrs. Dick stopped smoking, the cigarette hanging limply between her thin lips.

"I'm managing this," she said. "I was approached and the responsibility as well as the reward is entirely mine."

Mr. Campion was silent for some moments. Then he coughed, and raising his eyes to hers, he regarded her solemnly. "If you're really responsible for this little lot," he said gravely, "the situation becomes exceedingly uncomfortable and difficult. In fact, to put it crudely, to end the matter satisfactorily, one or both of us will have to retire from the picture pretty effectively."

"That," said Mrs. Dick absently, "has already occurred to me. You won't get out of here alive, my friend."

"Threats!" said Mr. Campion, his light-heartedness returning. "Isn't it time you hissed at me? You have an advantage over me by being dressed for the part, you know. Give me a pair of moustachios and I'll be a villain too."

The light was gradually going, though he could still distinguish her white face across the loft, but he felt himself all the more at a disadvantage inasmuch as the finer shades of expression on it were lost to him.

"It would interest me," she said suddenly, "to know who employed you. The Gyrths, I suppose. How did they get wind of it in the first place? Well, I'm sorry they've wasted their money. Heaven knows they've got little enough."

"I suppose you need money yourself," said Campion quietly.

"Naturally. I've spent two fortunes in my time," said Mrs. Dick without boast or regret. "That's why I've got to get hold of another. You don't think I'm going to allow a little rat like you to interfere?"

"You underestimate me," said Mr. Campion with firm politeness. "Manly courage, intelligence and resource are my strong points."

He raised his voice during the last words for the first time during the interview. Instantaneously there was a clatter of hoofs beneath his feet, followed by several thunderous kicks on the woodwork which shook the building.

"Bitter Aloes," said Mrs. Dick significantly. "She's in the box beneath here. You're in good company. Keep your voice down, though . . . she's vicious with strangers."

"Not too matey with the lady of the house," observed Mr. Campion more quietly. "I saw you playing together in the yard like a pair of kittens. I thought she'd get you with her forefeet."

"She killed a boy last year." Mrs. Dick's voice was brisk but expressionless. "I was supposed to have her shot but I wangled out of it. The little beast came on her unexpectedly. I saw it happen. It wasn't a pretty death. Those forefeet of hers were like steel hammers."

Mr. Campion hunched his shoulders. "You have a curious taste in pets," he observed. "Fingers Hawkins and Bitter Aloes make a very fine pair. But suppose we cut the melodrama and come back to business? In the first place—merely as a matter of curiosity, of course— how do you hope to get away with it?"

"What can prevent me?" said Mrs. Dick with placid assurance. "You seem to forget why I was invited to enter into the business at all. My position is unassailable. I can go where I like with impunity, and surround myself with as many rough customers as I like without rousing any suspicion. That's the advantage of a profession and a reputation like mine."

"I see," said Mr. Campion. "And this reputation of yours plus the state of your financial affairs which rendered you practically desperate, you got the contract, as we say in big business? But what I meant was, how do you expect to get clear away—go on living here, for example?"

"Why not? Mere suspicion can't upset a standing like mine. Even if the police arrested me, what possible reason could I have for stealing a gold cup? It isn't saleable, you know, and I'm not the sort of person to collect drawing-room ornaments. The police are not the people to press the question of my employers. Once I have hold of it I can do exactly as I please. The Gyrths daren't blare their loss abroad. Frankly, I don't see how the police would come into it, and ordinary county feeling has long since ceased to affect me. I assure you I've come through worse scandals than this will ever cause."

Mr. Campion was silent, and she shot him an inquisitive glance through the gloom. "Well?" she said.

"I was thinking how clever they are, these employers of yours," he said slowly. "You're right. You're unassailable. In fact, there's only one danger point in your whole scheme."

"And that?"

"Me," said Mr. Campion modestly. "You see, I know the rules of the society as well as you do. You, I take it," he went on quietly, "are thinking of killing me?"

"It would be absurd of me to let you interfere with my affairs," said Mrs. Shannon. "You might possibly have been useful to me, but as it is you're a damned little nuisance. I'm not thinking of killing you. I'm preparing to kill you."

"So this is Suffolk," said Mr. Campion. "Commend me to Chicago. I hate to keep raising objections, but won't you find my body about the place more than just a social nuisance? I know the police are forgiving, friendly people, but they do draw the line at a body. Perhaps you're going to bury me in the garden or throw me in the creek? Do tell."

The woman made no reply, and he went on.

"Before you get busy, however, I must do my singing exercises. Listen to this for an E in Alt."

He threw back his head, and the shrill bird cry that had sounded over the heath the previous evening now echoed through the little room. The grating above Mr. Campion's head was open to the heath, and the sound escaped clearly to the sky beyond. Again he shouted, and the horse below clattered and kicked violently in her stable.

Mrs. Dick began to laugh.

"If you've been relying on that pack of Gypsies," she said, "it's kindest to tell you that I had sent them off the heath this morning. You're alone. You seem to have played your cards very badly. In fact," she added with sudden seriousness, "you're such a damn failure that you're beginning to irritate me."

Mr. Campion's eyes were hard and anxious behind his spectacles, but his expression of charming inanity had never wavered.

"Talking of failures," he said, "where's your success? You're no better off than when you started. You haven't got the Chalice."

"It's perfectly obvious where it is," said Mrs. Dick slowly. "I was a fool not to think of it before. In that secret room in the east wing they make such a fuss about, of course. That was clear to me as soon as I found the cup in the chapel was spurious. I shall have the Chalice to-night."

She spoke with complete assurance, a tone that dismissed any other possibility as absurd. Mr. Campion stiffened.

"I see," he said softly.

He took off his spectacles and put them in his pocket. It was growing very dark in the loft, and although he was not altogether unprepared for what followed, the suddenness of her attack caught him unawares. He saw the flash of the woman's arm in its white shirt-sleeve upraised, and the next moment the thong of her whip caught him full across the face and sent him staggering back against the wall beneath the grating.

He was vaguely aware of voices outside, but he had no time to think clearly. Mrs. Dick was lashing at him with the same cool skill and deadly accuracy with which she had subdued the mare who was trampling wildly in the box beneath them. He threw up his arms to shield his face, and reeled backward as she drove him into the corner.

She came after him, feeling in the hay-strewn floor with her foot. At last she found what she sought. With a single vicious twist of her heel she shot back the iron bolt of the hay-shoot, precipitating the young man into the maelstrom of flying hoofs below.

Instinctively he threw out his hands to save himself, and his fingers caught at the edge of the trap.

For a sickening moment he swung suspended in the air, Mrs. Dick, bending down to draw up the trap again, kicked his fingers from their grasp as if she were flicking a stone out of her way.

Then she drew up the door by the slack rope and slipped the bolt home.

CHAPTER TWENTY-FOUR

Bitter Aloes

Bitter Aloes was as frightened by the sudden intrusion into her box as was Mr. Campion by his equally sudden descent. She started back,

THE GYRTH CHALICE MYSTERY

rearing and screaming, her forefeet beating wildly in the air. It was this momentary respite which saved Mr. Campion's life.

Set across the corner of the stable, some four feet below the ceiling, was an old-fashioned iron hay-basket, just low enough to allow the horse to pull out mouthfuls of fodder as she desired, while saving the bulk from being fouled on the ground or in the manger.

When Mrs. Dick kicked Mr. Campion's fingers from their grasp, he dropped, and was actually in the low wooden manger when Bitter Aloes reared above him. Pressing himself back into a corner to save himself as much as possible from the flying hoofs, his head brushed against the bars of this hay-basket. The mare, frenzied with fear and with bad temper, rose up on her hind legs once more, pawing frantically in the gloom.

Campion leapt for the iron basket, drawing himself up into it, and at last crouched, his head and shoulders battened down beneath the rebolted trap and Bitter Aloes snapping at him not six inches below his feet. Even at that moment he could not help marvelling at the simple villainy of Mrs. Dick's arrangements. A stranger found savaged to death and probably unrecognizable in a racehorse box would convey only one thing to a jury's mind, especially if the lady supplied any necessary details to show that he had entered the stable for some nefarious purpose. Twelve good Suffolk men and true would consider it a case of poetic justice.

With his head and shoulders still smarting from her whip and his body growing numb in its unnatural position, which he knew he could not hold for long, he listened intently. Bitter Aloes had quietened considerably, but he could still hear her snorting angrily and the swishing of her tail in the darkness. Outside he was vaguely aware of a bustle in the yard. Mrs. Dick and her party of raiders were about to set out. He realized that she must have some very definite plan of action, and his heart failed him as he thought of the Tower completely unprotected save for Val and a handful of servants, all of whom would be taken by surprise. It would not only be robbery with violence, but robbery by a group of picked men, each a master in his own particular line. Such a party could hardly fail, since they had such a very good notion where to look for their spoil. The difficulty of tracing them once the coup was made would be unsurmountable even for Scotland Yard, since the treasure itself could never be traced.

Savage with himself as much as with the woman, Campion raised himself cautiously in his perilous cradle and tried to force the trapdoor up, against the hinge, by the whole strength of his head and shoulders. There was an ominous creak and he felt to his horror that it was the staples that supported the hay basket and not the trapdoor which were giving.

He ceased his futile efforts and crouched down once more, while Bitter Aloes, alarmed by the noise, reared again.

It was at this moment that he became aware of footsteps above his head. Someone was moving stealthily across the loft. He crouched back in the corner, fearing for an instant that Mrs. Dick had returned to make sure that the mare had done her work. His alarm increased as the bolt of the trap was shot safely back and the door began to descend.

The next moment a shaft of light from an electric torch cut through the gloom and sent Bitter Aloes rearing and kicking against the outer wall of the stable. Mr. Campion remained very still, racked by a thousand cramps.

The trap opened a little wider, and a soft American voice murmured:

"Say, Campion, are you there?"

The young man started so violently that the staples creaked beneath him.

"Professor Cairey!" he whispered.

"Oh, you're there, are you?" The torch was turned full on his face. "I thought she'd got you. Hold on a minute while I let this door down. Then you can pull yourself up."

The trapdoor descended, Mr. Campion keeping his head low. A minute later, assisted by the Professor, he was dragging himself up into the loft once more. The American pulled up the trap behind him and shot the bolt.

"I'll say it was time I dropped in," he remarked. "What's happened to your face? Did the horse do that?"

"No, that's its mistress," said Mr. Campion bitterly. "You've saved my life, Professor. How on earth did you land here?"

The old man rose to his feet and dusted his knees before replying. It was lighter in the loft than in the stable, and Campion could see his dapper little figure, still in his shantung suit, and the sharp triangle made by his white vandyke beard.

"Something occurred to me," he remarked softly. "A point I thought maybe you'd overlooked. So I just came along on a bicycle on the offchance of finding you." He paused. "I figured out where you were when Penny told me she'd been to see those Gypsies. I trailed around the heath until I found your car. Then I was sure. By the way, your tyres have been slashed."

Mr. Campion was still looking at him as if he could hardly believe his eyes, and the Professor's voice continued with the same gentle precision, for all the world as if he had been carrying on a most normal conversation in his own library.

"I called on the lady this afternoon," he went on. "Sent in my card and said I'd come about some yearlings that I thought might interest her. She sent word that she couldn't see me, and the man I saw let me out of the front door. Fortunately there was no one around. I guessed they'd keep you a prisoner, and looking at the stables I thought what a grand prison they'd make. So I nipped into an empty loose box. I've been here about two hours." He paused, and then added quietly: "You see, in my opinion it's vitally necessary for you to go back to the Tower to-night."

"How did you get *here?*" said Campion, still amazed by the astounding matter-of-fact attitude of the old gentleman.

The Professor chuckled. "I waited in a horse-box until I saw that woman fooling about with a horse. Land sakes! I thought she was going to put it in on top of me. So I nipped up a ladder on to the top floor, and I hadn't been waiting there above fifteen minutes when I heard you talking to her in here. My hearing isn't altogether what it used to be and I didn't quite make out what either of you was up to. But I heard you fall through the trap and I heard her go out. Then I had some difficulty getting the door open and it wasn't for some time that I realized where you were. The rest you know. I don't like to be disrespectful to ladies, but that woman seems an honest to God hell-cat to me."

Mr. Campion felt the weal on his face. "I'm inclined to agree with you," he said.

The Professor touched his arm. "You must hurry," he said. "Don't worry about me. I'll get back all right. If they're going to make an attack on the genuine Chalice they'll do it to-night. That's why I came along. There's a bit of tradition that it occurred to me you might not know. I'm interested in these things; that's why it stayed in my mind. Old Peck put me wise months ago. I meant to tell you before, but what with one thing and another it slipped my mind."

He lowered his voice still more. "That secret room at the Tower has a window, but no apparent door, as you know. Now, on the night of the heir's twenty-fifth birthday there's a light burns in the window from sunset to cockcrow. You see," he hurried on, ignoring Campion's smothered exclamation, "in the old days there was always a big party on, so that every window in the house would be ablaze, but this time there isn't any party. The position of that room will be clear to anyone who cares to look from ten o'clock till dawn. Get me? That's not all, either," he added. "There's sure to be special preparations made to disclose the door to-night. If anyone raided the Tower now they'd find pretty clear indications of where the Room was, I'm thinking, provided they knew on what floor and in what direction to look. It may be thirty years before this opportunity occurs again. I think you ought to be on hand."

Mr. Campion was silent for some moments. "I guessed there'd be a light, of course," he said at last, "but it never dawned on me it'd be on for so long. I didn't know the tradition. You're right. It's the time I've misjudged." He hurried to the window. "I suppose they've gone already."

The stable-yard was deserted, but he caught a glimpse of the big car still standing before the house. "We must get out," he said. "We'll go the way you came in."

The Professor led the way down the ladder in the adjoining loft and into the empty box below. Next moment an exclamation of annoyance escaped him.

"We're bolted in," he said. "We shall have to nip back and get round on the top storey. If we're fixed in here we're sunk."

"There's a window in that front room over the gate," said Campion thoughtfully. "I've been locked in there all day. I could get out of that, I think."

Fortunately, the communicating doors between the two storey lofts were unlocked, and they pushed right round the square until they emerged once more into the room over the gateway. Here Mr. Campion stopped dead, and the Professor, panting a little, caught up with him. From somewhere outside there had arisen a most extraordinary noise.

"Heck!" said the Professor. "What's that?"

But Mr. Campion was already at the window.

"Good old Mrs. Sarah!" he said breathlessly. "I thought that was all guff about turning them off the heath." He caught the Professor's arm and dragged him to the window. Together they looked out over the scene below.

The sight was an extraordinary one. The remains of a lurid sunset still blazed across the heath and the wind was rising. At the moment when they first peered through the window together an immense dark object silhouetted against the sky was bearing down upon the buildings at an ever-increasing rate. As it came nearer they were just able to discern what it was. The decrepit char-à-banc which Penny had noticed in the Gypsy encampment the morning before charged upon the stables, bristling with an overload of wildly gesticulating figures.

They disappeared from the view of the watchers from the window beneath the outer wall, but the next moment a shattering crash echoed through the buildings as the iron gates were burst open. The char-à-banc swung into sight, churning off the near wheel of the Delage in its path and coming to a full stop in the gateway above which they stood. The noise was fiendish, the shrill Gypsy voices, their musical sibilance entirely vanished, mingled with the shrieking of brakes and the infuriated swearing of the members of Mrs. Dick's peculiar house-hold who came swarming out to attack the invaders.

Pandemonium broke loose. In her stable Bitter Aloes added to the increasing confusion by kicking at the woodwork in a frenzy. Innumer-able figures tumbled out of the juggernaut and swarmed over the house and stables.

Mrs. Dick's adherents defended themselves and their property from this unexpected attack with a savagery of their kind. The Professor, with his hands on the bars of the window and his eyes glued to the pane, whistled under his breath.

"Gee, this is the dirtiest fighting I've ever seen," he said.

Mr. Campion did not reply at once. He was wrestling with the other window whose fittings he had tentatively loosened during the day.

"They got my signal," he said at last, between vigorous wrenches at the bars. "I put them on to this weeks ago. I never dreamed they'd do the thing so thoroughly. When they got the signal they were to attack. If there was no signal then they were to arrive at ten. Lugg took them the sign yesterday, so they've been waiting all day. They're old enemies of this lot. Gypsies and race gangs hate each other."

"I haven't heard any guns," said the Professor as he watched the battle with almost boyish enthusiasm.

"They don't use guns." Mr. Campion had to raise his voice as the crashing of windows and splitting woodwork was added to the turmoil. "They've a prejudice against them. Makes it worse if they're caught. Their own methods are quite as effective and slightly more filthy. Who's winning?"

"Hard to tell," said the Professor. "They all look alike to me. It's smashed up the attack on the Tower all right, I should think. I don't see Mrs. Shannon anywhere."

He broke off abruptly as a pistol shot sounded above the general uproar.

"That's Sanderson, I bet," said Mr. Campion. "That man'll get hanged before he's finished."

"Whoever it is," said the Professor, "they've got him." He paused. "Can you hear a car?"

"Can't hear anything through this din," Campion grunted as he detached a bar from the window. "Sounds like an early Christian idea of hell to me."

"Say, Campion," said the Professor, suddenly turning for a moment, "there's murder going on outside. Won't your Gypsy friends have some difficulty in getting away with it?"

"More disabling than killing." Mr. Campion was edging himself through the window as he spoke. "You don't know Gypsies, Professor. There won't be a trace of them in the morning. They'll have split up and scattered to every corner of the country by dawn. Some of them just live for fighting. This is one of their gala nights. Look here," he added, as he prepared to lower himself out of the narrow aperture, "your best plan is to stay here. I'll unbolt the door downstairs and let you out. If anything happens to me, you're Orlando's friend, and any Gypsy will see you clear. Don't forget, *Orlando*. I'm going after Mrs. Dick. I'll never forget what you've done for me to-night, Professor."

The old man returned to his window. "Boy, I wouldn't miss this for a fortune," he said. "It's an education."

"Going down," sang Mr. Campion, and disappeared.

He dropped into the very centre of the char-à-banc, which was at the moment an oasis amid the tumult, and groped about him for a weapon. He kicked against something hard on the floor of the vehicle, and putting his hand down came across a bottle. He bound his handkerchief round his hand and seized the glass club by the neck. Then, still keeping low, he dropped gently out of the car and slipped back the bolt of the stairway to the lofts.

"All clear, Professor," he called softly up into the darkness. Then, stepping out gingerly once more, he was just about to work his way round to the house when he caught sight of a figure bearing down upon him, hand upraised. Campion put out his arm to ward off the blow and spoke instinctively.

"Jacob?" he said sharply.

The arm dropped to the man's side. "Orlando?"

"Himself," said Mr. Campion, and added, drawing the Gypsy into the protecting shadow of the box: "Where's the donah?"

"Scarpered," said the Gypsy promptly. "Went off in a little red motor. The finger with the gun was going with her, but we got him."

"Scarpered?" said Mr. Campion. "Alone?"

The man shrugged his shoulders. "I don't know. I think not; she went in a red motor that was standing by the side door when we came in. Been gone ten minutes. Took a coil of rope with her. Some of the boys started after her, I think, but she's away."

Mr. Campion's scalp tingled. Mrs. Dick had nerves of iron. She had nothing to lose, and once the genuine Chalice was in her possession she was safe. Moreover, the calmness with which she had attempted to dispose of him dispelled any doubts of personal squeamishness on her part. There was nothing she might not do.

He returned to the Gypsy. "I'm going after them," he said, "though Heaven knows how. I say, Jacob, there's an old finger upstairs, a great friend of Orlando's. See he gets out. Give Mrs. Sarah my love. I'll see you all at Hull Fair, if not before. Round up this lot now and scarpa yourselves."

The Gypsy nodded and disappeared silently up the stairs to carry out his instructions as far as the Professor was concerned.

Most of the fighting had by this time spread into the house whither the majority of the gang had retreated.

Mr. Campion sped across the yard, which was now a mass of broken bottles, blood, and odd portions of garments, and made for the heath. It was still far from dark outside the walls. The wind was rushing great wisps of cloud across the pale sky and the stars seemed very near.

As he passed the groom's cottage a dark figure detached itself from the shadows and leapt at him. He swung his weapon which he still held and brought it down on something hard. His assailant went down. He was vaguely aware of the "Major's" red face gaping at him from the ground, but he hurried on, one thought only clear in his mind: Mrs. Dick and a coil of rope.

He stepped hopefully into the garage and looked about. To his dismay it was empty, save for the recumbent and unconscious figure of Matt Sanderson. The Delage, now completely beyond repair, and the red Fraser Nash, in which Mrs. Dick was speeding towards the Tower he had no doubt, were the only vehicles it had contained. His own car, besides being some distance off across the heath, was, according to the Professor, completely out of action, and the char-à-banc in which the Gypsies had arrived would take the concerted efforts of at least a dozen men to get out of the yard. There remained the Professor's bicycle, which was hardly fast enough even could it have been found.

The problem of transport seemed insoluble, and speed mattered more than anything in the world. Even telephoning was out of the question, as he knew from experience that to cut the wires was the first care of raiding Gypsy parties. It dawned upon him that the only chance he had was to make for the camp and borrow a horse from Mrs. Sarah.

He set off across the heath towards the camp at a good steady pace, taking a diagonal course towards the north-east. Almost immediately he was conscious of footsteps behind him. He stopped and turned.

A man leading a horse was coming swiftly up. Mr. Campion's lank form and spectacled face were recognizable in the faint light. "Orlando!" the man called softly.

"Who's that? Joey?" Campion recognized the voice as that belonging to Mrs. Sarah's son Joey, the horse expert of the Benwell tribe. He came up.

"Jacob sent me after you. The old finger with him said you wanted to get off. I'll lend you this." The Gypsy indicated the horse with a jerk of his head. "Careful with her. She's all right for half an hour. She may be a bit wild after that. Lovely bit, though, ain't she?"

Mr. Campion understood the insinuation perfectly. Joey, who had ever more an eye for business than for warfare, had taken the opportunity to raid Mrs. Dick's stables, an act in which he had been detected by his kinsman, and straightaway dispatched to Campion's assistance.

As he turned gratefully to take the bridle, forgetting for the moment the impoverished state of the lady's stables, a white stocking caught his eye. Instinctively he started back.

"Good Lord, you've got a nerve," he said. "This is Bitter Aloes. They keep her as a sort of executioner," he added grimly.

"She's all right," Joey insisted. "Run like a lamb for half an hour. You can trust me. I've fixed her with something."

Mr. Campion glanced at the proud silky head with the ears now pricked forward, and the wild eyes comparatively mild. The mare was saddleless. It seemed madness to attempt such a ride.

The Gypsy handed him a broom-switch.

"Hurry," he whispered. "Turn her loose when you've done with her. I'll come after her with something in me hand that she'll follow for miles. To Sanctuary you're goin', ain't you?"

Mr. Campion looked over the heath. Sanctuary was five miles as the crow flew. Even now Mrs. Dick might have reached her goal. He returned to the Gypsy.

"Thank you, Joey," he said quietly. "Sanctuary it is," and he vaulted lightly on to the gleaming back of Bitter Aloes.

CHAPTER TWENTY-FIVE

The Window

It was a light summer's night with a strong wind blowing. Strips of
indigo cloud scored the pale star-strewn sky, and the air was cool after
the intense heat of the day.

The heath ticked and crackled in the darkness, and the broom
bushes rustled together like the swish of many skirts.

It was not a night for staying indoors: everything seemed to be
abroad and the wind carried sounds for great distances, far-off sheep
cries, voices, and the barking of dogs.

Most of these things were lost upon Mr. Campion as he thundered
across the countryside. Whatever horse-witchery Joey had practised
upon Bitter Aloes, her temper had certainly subsided, but she was
still very nervy and inclined to be erratic, although for the moment
her innate savagery was subdued. Campion, his long thin legs wrapped
round her sleek sides, trusted devoutly that for the promised half-hour,
at any rate it would remain so.

After the first breath-taking dash across the heath he forgot her
vagaries and concentrated upon his goal. As he reached the road, a
church clock from Heronhoe village struck eleven, and he abandoned
his original intention of sticking to the road. Time was too precious.
He turned the mare at the hedge which bordered one of the wide
stretches of pasture-land which lay between him and the Tower. Bitter
Aloes took the jump like a cat. As she rose beneath him the notion
flashed into Campion's mind that she probably enjoyed the hazardous
journey. Her curious twisted temperament was best pleased by danger.

He had no illusions about what he was doing. To ride a Gypsy-
doctored horse over a tract of unfamiliar land in the half-darkness was
more than ordinarily foolhardy. Trusting devoutly that they would not
come up against any insurmountable object, and praying against wire
—the recollection that this was a hunting district relieved him considerably on that score—he kept the mare's head in the direction of
Sanctuary and urged her on to further efforts.

She had her moments of difficulty. A nesting partridge disturbed
under her feet sent her rearing dangerously, and once when a sheep

lumbered out of their path she plunged continuously for some seconds and all but unseated him.

Luck and his unerring sense of direction brought them safely over the meadows to the brow of Saddlehill, and as they galloped up the steep grassland Campion suddenly saw the end of his quest, the gaunt east wing of the Tower of Sanctuary standing up against the sky on the other side of the valley.

In the Tower, high in the topmost storey, was a lighted window. It stood out quite clearly, a little circular spot of red light in the blackness.

Although he had expected it, it startled him. It was higher than he had supposed the windows would come, and he identified it suddenly in his mind with the curious circular decoration over the centre window of the wing, an orifice which had looked like a plaque of deeply indented stone work from the ground.

As he stared at the Tower, something in the grounds attracted his attention, and he looked down to see a car's headlights turn in to the trees at the far end of the drive. Even as he looked they vanished. A panic seized him. He drove his heels gently into the mare's sides and she leapt forward quivering.

For a moment he thought he had lost control, but she quietened as the long gallop down the slope exerted her. He took her over a ditch into the lane at the foot of the hill, and they continued down the narrow road, her hoofs striking sparks from the ragged flints. The little white gate at the end of the home meadow she took almost in her stride and the steep incline hardly affected her pace: the effect of Joey's treatment was wearing off and she jerked her head angrily from time to time as though she were irritated by the reins.

Campion barely noticed her changing mood. He flung himself off her back at the end of the flower garden, and she kicked out at him as he disappeared through the gate and ran up the grass path towards the house.

There were beads of sweat on his forehead, and the expression on his pale face was no longer inane. A car had turned into the drive and had instantly switched off its lights; that was fifteen minutes ago at least, he reckoned. Even allowing for reckless driving, Mrs. Dick could hardly have traversed the twelve miles of winding lane in less time than that would account for.

Therefore she was in the grounds now. He was prepared for anything. Mrs. Dick's possibilities were numberless.

He glanced up at the Tower across the wide lawn. The single red eye, a significant and silent witness to the thousand rumours concerning the Gyrths' secret, glared down upon him. Behind that eye lay the

Chalice, protected by something unknown, the intangible and perhaps terrible guardian upon which probably only three men living had ever looked. He had heard dozens of "genuine explanations"; men referred to it guardedly in famous clubs, well-known books of reminiscense hinted darkly at unprintable horrors. Val himself had seemed a little afraid to consider what it might be.

He wondered how many anxious eyes were fixed on the Tower that evening. Mrs. Dick's band of experts had been put out of action, certainly. But there would surely be others waiting to bear the treasure to safety. The lady herself, he fancied, would keep out of it for fear of being recognized, but would general the attack from somewhere outside.

At present all was peaceful. There were only two other lights in the whole building, both in the west wing, in the drawing-room and in the library. The servants' quarters were dark; the staff had been sent to bed early, no doubt. Campion imagined Penny alone in the drawing-room, and Val seated with his father and the old Rector in the study. And somewhere in the darkness a group of watchers, utterly without fear or scruple, eyeing, even as he, the single glaring window in the Tower.

He advanced across the lawn, keeping carefully to the deep shadow. The uncanny silence of the garden around him filled him with apprehension. He could have sworn that there was no one moving amid the belts of trees and shrubs which surrounded the lawn. Once again he paused and stood rigid. Somewhere there had been a movement. Instinctively he glanced up. The old house stood out black against the night sky. His eyes were drawn irresistibly to the circular window. Then he started. Just above it, standing out clearly over the battlements of the east wing, there was a figure.

He waited, silent, hoping against hope that it was Val or his father, but, even as he watched, something slender, snake-like, slid down across the circle of crimson light. As he strained his eyes to make it out, the truth came slowly home to him. It was a fine flexible rope, knotted at intervals.

Instantly the question which had been rankling at the back of his mind was made blindingly clear to him. The raiders were going to make sure of the exact whereabouts of their prize before they risked an open attack. The half-caste cat burglar's part in Sanderson's scheme became obvious. He was to have been the spy, possibly even their thief, if the window were negotiable. The simplicity of it appalled him. It would be so easy. Although the Tower was about a hundred and twenty feet high, a man with nerve could make a descent to the win-

dow once its whereabouts was made clear to him. It would be dangerous, but by no means impossible, to a man of Moggie's experience.
Then he remembered that Moggie was lying in the garage with
Sanderson on Heronhoe Heath. Who, then, was the climber who was
about to take his place? There was an answer to this question, but
his mind shrank from considering it.

He raced for the house. His first impulse was to alarm the Colonel,
but as he reached the base of the east wing the intruder's means of
entry was instantly apparent. One of the narrow latticed windows
stood open. He climbed through it without hesitation and crept across
the flagged state dining-room within to the centre hall, where a huge
wooden spiral staircase, one of the showpieces of the county, reared
its way up into the darkness.

He crept up the steps, the wood creaking terrifyingly beneath his
weight. It was a long climb in the darkness. The stairs wound up the
whole height of the Tower. At last they began to narrow and presently he felt the cool night air upon his face.

Suddenly the faint light from the open doorway above his head
warned him that he was reaching the roof. He paused to listen. There
was no sound in the house. All was quiet and ghostly in the gloom.
He moved silently up the last half-dozen stairs, and emerged at last
from the little central turret on the flat stone roof of the Tower.

For a moment he looked about him, prepared for instant attack.
As far as he could see the place was deserted. Keeping his back to
the wall he worked his way round the turret. Then a chill feeling of
horror crept over him. He was quite alone.

A movement almost like the passing of a shadow just in front of
him made him start forward, and in doing so his thigh brushed against
something stretched tightly from the central flagstaff and disappearing
over the edge of the battlements. He touched it with his hand. It was
a rope with knots in it. In that moment he realized that the one
eventuality which he had never foreseen had taken place. Whoever
was undertaking the theft of the Chalice was doing it alone.

Beads of sweat stood out on his forehead. There was only one person living who would have the nerve to make such an attempt, only
one person who would consider the prize worth the risk. He moved
to the edge of the Tower and drew out his torch, which he had been
careful not to use until now.

"Hold on," he said firmly, "you'd better come back."

His voice sounded strained and theatrical to him after the silence,
the words inadequate and ridiculous. He listened intently, but the
reply was loud, almost as if the speaker had been standing beside him.

"I'll see you in hell first," said Mrs. Dick.

Following the rope, he bent over the parapet and switched his torch downwards. Although he had expected it, the sight sickened him. She lay against the side of the Tower like a fly on a wall, her steel hands gripping the rope which supported her as she picked her way down with easy precision. Not more than two feet below her the round window gleamed dully on to the cord as it squirmed and flopped against the stone work. In the daytime the height was sickening; at night it was impossible to see the ground, and Campion was glad of it.

He leant on the parapet looking down at her. He could see her distinctly, still in the riding costume in which she had interviewed him only that afternoon. As he stared, a thought forced itself into his mind. Mrs. Dick was the employee of the society; the responsibility lay upon her shoulders alone. Should she meet with her death the danger to the Chalice would end automatically.

The rope, which alone supported her from a hundred foot drop on to the flags beneath, lay under his hand. If the cord should slip its mooring round the flagstaff . . .

He leant on the parapet and kept his eyes fixed upon her. He could find plenty of moral justification in his own mind for this execution, and he did not flinch from the fact that it would be an execution. There were passages in Mrs. Dick's past that no English jury would have excused in spite of their notorious leniency towards women. He gripped the stones, his knuckles showing white in the faint light.

"Come back," he said distinctly, turning the light full on her bent head. "Come back before you look in that room, or I swear I'll cut this rope."

As soon as he had spoken the meaning of his own words startled him. Once Mrs. Dick, the agent for the most influential syndicate in the world, saw the prize she sought, no power on earth could save it from her. She must be prevented from reaching the window.

"I'll cut the rope," he repeated.

She looked up at him unflinchingly, and the merciless light revealed the twisted smile on her small, hideous mouth.

"You wouldn't dare," she said. "You haven't the courage. Get back; I'll deal with you later."

She descended another step deliberately.

"Come back!" Campion's voice was menacing. "Hold tight. I'm going to draw you up." He gripped the rope and took the strain, but she was a heavy woman, and he knew instinctively that in spite of the knots the task would be beyond him.

Mrs. Dick, who had remained motionless on the rope, steadying herself for any such attempt, jeered at him openly.

"Mind your own business," she said. "If you must interfere, go downstairs and call a servant to help you."

Her voice sounded a little farther away, and he knew that she was climbing down. Again he bent over the parapet. He caught sight of her feet reflecting the red glare from the window.

"Come back!" he called hoarsely. "Come back, for God's sake!"

"Just a moment." The words came softly to him as she deliberately lowered herself another foot, and adjusting her position, peered into the window.

There was a pause which seemed like an age. The man bending forward with his torch directed upon the hunched figure on the rope received some of the tremor which shot through her body. The red light was on her face, and he saw her shoulders twitch as she hung there, apparently fascinated by what she saw. In that moment the world seemed to have paused. It was as if the Tower and garden had held their breath.

Then from somewhere beneath him he fancied he heard a faint, almost indetectable sound. It was a sound so intangible that it did not convey anything concrete to his mind, so soft that he questioned it immediately afterwards. The effect upon Mrs. Dick, however, was instantaneous.

"No!" she said distinctly, "no!"

The last word was smothered by a shuddering intake of breath, and she swung round on the rope, hanging to the full length of her arms. Her face was turned up to the man on the Tower for an instant. He saw her lips drawn back over her teeth, her eyes wide and expressionless with fear, while a thin trickle of saliva escaped at one corner of her mouth. He bent forward.

"Hold on," he said, not realizing that he was whispering. "Hold on!"

But even as he looked, her limp fingers relinquished their grip, he heard the sickening hiss of the rope as it raced through her hands, and she receded with horrible slowness down, down, out of the range of his torch into the darkness below.

The body crunched as it hit the flags, and then—silence. The guardian of the Gyrth Chalice had protected its treasure.

Mr. Campion, sick and trembling uncontrollably in the cold wind, reeled unsteadily to the turret and went quietly downstairs.

CHAPTER TWENTY-SIX

Mr. Campion's Employer

The East Suffolk Courier and Hadleigh Argus for
July 7th

SAD FATALITY AT SANCTUARY

Coroner Comments on Curiosity

An inquest was held on Saturday last at the Three Drummers
Inn, Sanctuary-by-Tower, before Doctor J. Cobden, Coroner for
the district, on Daisy Adela Shannon (44) of Heronhoe Stables,
Heronhoe, who fell from the tower in the east wing of the mansion of Colonel Sir Percival Gyrth, Bt., on the night of July 2nd
while a birthday party was in progress.

The body was discovered by Mr. Alfred Campion, a guest at
the Tower. Mr. Campion, 17 Bottle Street, London, W1, said
that on Thursday evening he was walking across the lawn at
about 11.25 p.m. when he noticed someone moving on the top of
the east wing tower. He thought that it was a member of the
household, and hailed them. Receiving no reply he became
alarmed, a state of mind which increased when he perceived that
one of the dining-room windows stood open. He ran into the
house and climbed the staircase to the top landing, coming out
at last upon the roof. The jury subsequently viewed the staircase, which is one of the showpieces of Suffolk.

Mr. Campion, continuing, said that when he reached the roof
of the Tower he found himself alone. Running downstairs again
he discovered the deceased lying on the flagstones at the foot of
the Tower. He immediately summoned the household.

Corroborative evidence was given by Roger Arthur Branch,
butler to Sir Percival, and by the Rev. P. R. Pembroke, of The
Rectory, Sanctuary, who was visiting the Tower at the time of
the accident.

Dr. A. H. Moore, of Sanctuary Village, said that death was
due to contusion of the brain following fracture of the skull.
Death was instantaneous.

Evidence of identification was given by W. W. Croxon, Veterinary Surgeon, of The Kennels, Heronhoe.

P. C. Henry Proudfoot deposed that he was summoned to the Tower at 11.45 p.m. on the night in question. He climbed to the top of the Tower and there discovered a length of rope (produced) attached to a flagpole on the summit.

David Cossins, of 32 Bury Road, Hadleigh, dealer, identified the rope as having been sold to the deceased on the 18th or 19th June last. When asked if in his opinion this rope was sufficiently strong to bear the weight of a human body, witness opined that it undoubtedly was.

Sir Percival, asked by the Coroner if he could offer any explanation for deceased's presence on his estate at so late an hour, replied that he was at a total loss to account for it. He was only casually acquainted with the deceased, and she was not a guest at his son's coming-of-age party, which was necessarily an intimate affair in view of the recent bereavement in the family.

By P. C. Proudfoot, recalled: A red two-seater Fraser Nash motor-car, later identified by registration marks as the property of deceased, was found drawn up against some bushes in the drive later in the evening. Lights were extinguished, and it was reasonable to suppose that this was done by deceased.

Questioned, Proudfoot suggested that the deceased had attempted to lower herself on to the centre window-sill of the fourth floor of the Tower, where, according to popular superstition, some festivities took place on the occasion of a birthday in the family. Proudfoot apologized to the Court for the intrusion of common superstition and gossip, but opined that the deceased had attempted her giddy descent in the execution of a wager with some third party who had not come forward. Deceased was a well-known sporting character of the district, and had been known to enter into undertakings of this sort in the past. Witness cited the occasion of the Horse v. Automobile race in 1911, when deceased challenged Captain W. Probert, the well-known motorist, over a distance of twenty miles across country.

The Coroner told the jury that he was inclined to accept the Constable's very intelligently reasoned explanation as being as near the truth as they were likely to arrive. In her attempt to carry out this unparalleled piece of foolhardy daring in a woman of her age, the deceased had undoubtedly suffered from an attack of vertigo and so had fallen.

The Coroner added that it would be a lesson to all on the evils of undue curiosity and the undesirability of entering into foolish sporting contracts which might endanger life or limb. The Coroner said he could not express himself too strongly on the subject. He regretted, as must all those in Court, that such an unfortunate accident should have visited itself upon Colonel Sir Percival Gyrth and his family, who were already suffering from a very recent bereavement. He instructed the jury, therefore, to bring in a verdict according to the evidence. The jury returned a verdict of Accidental Death, the Foreman (Mr. P. Peck, senr.) remarking that they would like to second the Coroner's expressions of regret.

The funeral will take place at Heronhoe to-morrow, Tuesday. A short obituary notice appears in another column with a list of the deceased's sporting awards. It is understood that the deceased died intestate, and her property, which is in very bad repair, few of the windows being whole and many of the doors off their hinges, was in the hands of the Police when our Representative called yesterday.

"A very intelligently reasoned explanation indeed," remarked Mr. Campion, putting down the paper. "Mark my words, Val. We shall have old Proudfoot a sergeant before we know where we are. And rightly so, as they say on the soap-box."

He lay back in his deck-chair and put his arms behind his head. They were all four of them, Penny, Beth, Val and himself, seated beneath the trees at the far corner of the lawn on a brilliant morning some days after the events so ably recorded by the *Argus*. The adventures of the preceding weeks had left their marks on the young people, but there was a distinct hint of relief in the manner which told plainly of a tension that had relaxed.

Val had assumed a new air of responsibility during the few days since his coming of age. He seemed, as Penny remarked, to have grown up. She and Beth were frankly happy; as they lay in the comfortable chairs they looked like a couple of schoolgirls with their bare arms and long thin legs spread out to the sunlight which dappled through the leaves.

Mr. Campion alone bore concrete marks of battle. His face was still scored by the weals of Mrs. Dick's whip, but apart from this slightly martial disfigurement, he looked even more amiably fatuous than ever.

"They're nearly as bright about the Gypsies," Penny observed as she took up the paper from the grass. "Apparently 'a raid was thought to have been made by van dwellers on a party of undesirables camping on Heronhoe Heath. The van dwellers have since disappeared, and some of the injured campers have been taken to the Police Infirmary.' I believe you managed that, Albert. Oh, to think that it's all all right!" She sighed luxuriously. "To look back upon it's like a welsh rarebit nightmare with you as the hero."

"With me as the rabbit," said Mr. Campion feelingly. "The Professor was the hero. Lugg's painting an illuminated address that we're going to present to him. It begins 'Hon. Sir and Prof.' and goes on with all the long words he's ever heard from the Bench. All about Depravity, Degradation, and Unparalleled Viciousness. He's turning them into the negative, of course. It'll be a stupendous document when it's finished. Perhaps the Professor will let you two have a copy of it for a wedding present." He grinned at Val and Beth, who were quite blatantly holding hands between their deck-chairs. They smiled at each other and Mr. Campion went on.

"Had it not been for the Professor, Mr. 'Alfred Campion' would doubtless have figured in another role, and some crueller Coroner than old Doctor Cobden would be moralizing on the dangers of putting strange animals in other people's stables. The Professor's a stout fellow, as we say in the Legion. How are the two papas to-day, by the way?"

"Splendid," said Penny. "I saw a sweet sight as I came past the library window. You know they retired to discuss deep archaeological secrets? Well, when I came past there were two armchairs drawn up by the open window, two little curls of cigar smoke, and there was Daddy deep in *The New Yorker*—a most indelicate young woman on the cover, my dears—and the Professor regaling himself with *Punch*. Too sweet."

"Hands across the sea, in fact," said Campion. "I shall hear the tinkle of little silver bells in a minute."

Beth laughed. "The way they forgave each other for the Gypsies and your Aunt Di's *faux pas* was rather cute," she said.

"I know," said Penny. " 'My dear sir!' 'Nonsense! *My* dear sir!' 'Come and shoot partridges!' 'Rubbish. Come and pick my roses.' All boys together. What delightful neighbours we are, are we not? Do you know, this is the first time I've felt this summer was worth living? By the way, Albert, when did you arrange everything so neatly with your fat friend, Mrs. Sarah? I was trying to work it out in bed last night."

"Irreverent hussy," said Mr. Campion, shocked. "She'd put a spell on you for that. Then you'd know all about it. I called upon the lady in question, as a matter of fact, on the night before I came home to find Lugg so curiously indisposed. I'd previously seen her, of course, very early on in the proceedings. I guessed I might need a spot of assistance sooner or later, so I asked them to hang around. As Mr. Sanderson was staying at Heronhoe, it occurred to me that the heath was very conveniently situated. I pointed this out to Mrs. Sarah and she had no doubts in her mind as to where the fun would arise."

"Then you knew about Mrs. Dick?" said Val. "From the beginning?"

"Well, yes and no," said Mr. Campion. "I thought she might be in it, but I did so hope she wouldn't be in it alone. Mrs. Munsey almost convinced me, but just before I visited Mrs. Dick, I inquired about her in all the likely quarters, and after that, well it seemed desperately likely. She was head over heels in debt, and on the verge of all sorts of unkind attention from the Jockey Club Stewards. I asked my own pet turf expert about her over the phone and the Exchange cut us off long before he got into his stride. My hat! She had a nerve, though."

Val looked at him in astonishment. "You talk as though you admired her," he said.

"She had a way of compelling admiration," said Mr. Campion, stroking his face thoughtfully. "If you ask me, there weren't two hoots to choose between her and her horse. They were both vicious and both terrifying, both bad lots, but oh, boy! they both had Personality."

Val grimaced. "I never liked her," he said. "By the way, I never saw why she set Mrs. Munsey on to Aunt Di. What was the point of it?"

Mr. Campion considered. "That took me off my balance at the beginning," he admitted, "but the local witch herself put me on to the truth. You see, Val, your aunt, silly as she was, never let the Chalice out of her sight for a second except when it was in its niche, half-hidden behind iron bars. Arthur Earle, her artist friend, probably complained to Headquarters that his hostess was a nuisance in this respect, and Mrs. Dick, knowing of Mrs. Munsey's peculiarities, and your aunt's propensity for wandering about at night, hit on the idea of giving her Ladyship a shock that would keep her indisposed for a day or two, during which time the disappointed artist, deprived of his sitter, might easily get permission to continue his portrait of the Chalice. You see," he went on, "a man like Arthur would want to weigh it and examine it really thoroughly, which he could hardly do with your aunt about. Unfortunately for all concerned, Mrs. Munsey was too much for your aunt and the whole scheme came unstuck."

Penny sighed. "It was bad luck on Aunt Di," she said. "Mr. Pembroke's looking after the Munseys. Did you know? They'll have to go into a home, he says, poor things."

Val's mind still dwelt upon the mechanism of Mrs. Dick's original scheme. "I suppose," he said bitterly, "they set out with the idea of bribing me to swap a copy for the cup? We owe a lot to you, Campion."

His friend did not appear to hear the last part of his remark.

"I think that was it," Campion agreed. "Later, the 'Major' and Sanderson came to spy out the nakedness of the land themselves. I believe that the 'Major' was the expert who decided that the Chalice in the Cup House was not the real one, once they got hold of it. I've never felt so sick in my life as I did when Stanislaus phoned me to tell me they'd got the copy. That was a darn clever raid of theirs. It was only sheer bad luck on Stanislaus' part that they were successful, though. If that bobby on the door had been an older hand it wouldn't have happened."

Penny grinned at him from where she lay basking like a kitten in the heat. "Thinking it over, Albert," she remarked, "it has occurred to me that you don't work up your publicity properly at all. Modesty is all very sweet and charming but it doesn't get you anywhere. According to your account of the whole thing to Daddy you haven't done anything at all worth talking about."

Mr. Campion blinked at her from behind his spectacles.

> "Beauty is truth, truth beauty, and these three
> Hover for ever round the gorbal tree—

Ovid," he said. "Like Sir Isaac Newton and his fishing-rod, I cannot tell a lie."

"Still," said Penny, unimpressed, "you might have put it a bit better. For instance, about Val being kidnapped. When you're asked for an explanation you simply say you called for him at a garage, and brought him back and put him in a field because you were in a hurry to get back to London to see a bookmaker. You must learn to work up your stories more. A yarn like that gets you nowhere."

"But all quite true," said Mr. Campion mildly. "And not really extraordinary. When Inspector Oates told me over the phone that Val had gone charging after the gentleman who had stolen his suitcase, it was perfectly obvious to me that if he had caught the thief he would have returned with him, and if he hadn't caught him, then the thieving gentleman's friends had caught Val. Therefore," he went on, beaming at them from behind his spectacles, "Val was the unwelcome guest of someone who was probably Mr. Matthew Sanderson or one of his associates. They didn't want to keep him about the place, you see. They thought they'd got their prize, and once they had disposed of it in the right quarter, they had nothing to fear. I guessed they'd plant him somewhere and say no more about it."

Beth's brown eyes opened wide. "But they might have killed him," she said.

"Hardly," said Campion judicially. "There is no one who is more anxious to avoid an unpleasant death in the house than your English crook. You see, in England, in nine cases out of ten, if there's a body there's a hanging. That rather cramps their style when disposing of people. Working all this out with lightning speed, what did Our Hero do? He got out his little motor-car and went-a-visiting." He paused.

"It may have dawned on you people that all my friends are not quite the article. So, sure enough, in one of their back-yards I found our juvenile lead lying happily on a lot of old motor tyres waiting to be dropped somewhere where he could be 'found wandering'. I relieved the gentleman in charge of his guest, admired his wife's new frock, kissed the baby and came home. It was so abominably easy that I hadn't the face to tell you all, even if I had had time, so I left him where I thought Beth might find him and went on to see our lady friend, who was beginning to worry me.

"You were at Ernie Walker's garage, as a matter of fact, Val. He specializes in that sort of thing. It was the second place I looked. No, Penny, I regret to say that in this case I do not find myself wearing my laurel wreath with that sense of righteous satisfaction which is my wont. The Professor and the Benwells get all the credit. The way they cleared up that bunch and scarpered fills me with a sense of my own clumsiness."

"Ah," said Beth, "that was the word. 'Scarpa'. Father was awfully interested in your Gypsy friend, who had some most extraordinary words. What does that one mean?"

"'Bunk' is the best English translation," said Mr. Campion. "To bunk, that is—to clear off, scat, vamoose, beat it, make a getaway, hop it, or more simply, 'to go'. Jacob is a great lad, but Joey is the wizard. That horse was quite manageable when I rode her over, so bang goes your last illusion, Penny, of me as a second Dick Turpin. Joey must have had his eye on Bitter Aloes for days, and as soon as the opportunity offered he left the fight and slipped into her box with some filthy concoction of his own. The crooks use a hypodermic, but I fancy he has other methods."

"I haven't got any illusions about you," said Penny. "I think you ought to go into a Home. When I heard someone had fallen off the Tower, I took it for granted it was you. Yes, a good comfortable home with Lugg to dress you, and plenty of nice kind keepers who would laugh at your remarks. In the first place, I happen to know for a fact that that story about your coming into a fortune from your Uncle the

Bishop is all rubbish. Lugg says he left you a hundred pounds and a couple of good books."

Mr. Campion looked uncomfortable. "Curse Lugg," he said. "So much for my efforts to appear a gilded amateur. I'm sorry, Val, but this nosy little creature will have to be told. Yes, Angel-face, the poor vulgar gentleman is a Professional. I was employed, of course."

He lay back in his chair, the sunlight glinting on his spectacles. The three young people stared at him.

"Employed?" said Val. "Who employed you? It couldn't have been the Old Boy, because—I hate to be fearfully rude, but you must be—er well, awfully expensive."

"Incredibly," said Mr. Campion placidly. "Only the highest in the land can possibly afford my services. But then, I need an immense income to support my army of spies, and my palatial offices, to say nothing of my notorious helot, Lugg."

"He's lying," said Penny, yawning. "I wish you had been employed, though. You've done such a lot for us. I feel you ought to get something out of it. I'd offer you my hand if I thought I could bear you about the house. Ooh!" she added suddenly, "look!"

Her exclamation had been occasioned by the appearance of a magnificent limousine, whose long grey body gleamed in the sunlight as it whispered expensively up the drive to the front door. Val and Penny exchanged glances.

In the car, seated behind the chauffeur, was a single slim aristocratic figure, with the unmistakable poker back of the old regime.

"There he is," said Penny. "That's why if you stay to lunch, Beth, you'll have to have it with Albert and me in the morning room. That's why Branch is in his show swallowtails and we've got the flag flying. Here comes the honoured guest."

Beth leant forward in her chair. "Is that *him*?" she said. "No top hat? I haven't seen a good top hat since I came to England."

"Very remiss," said Mr. Campion sternly. "Coming down here representing the Crown without a top hat—why, the thing's absurd. Hang it, when a policeman brings a summons, which is a sort of invitation from the Crown, he wears a top hat."

"No?" said Beth.

"No," said Mr. Campion. "Still, the principle's the same. I don't think it's cricket to come down on a special formal occasion in an ordinary trilby that any man might wear. Look here, Val, you'd better wear yours at lunch just to show him. We keep the old flag flying, dammit."

Beth was puzzled. "Why don't you get lunch with this Lord whatever he is?"

"Because it's an ancient ceremony," said Penny. "Not the lunch—unless cook's muffed it—but the whole business. We shall be expected to be all voile and violets at tea-time."

"Leaving the Honourable Gentleman out of the question," said Val, "and returning to your last sensational announcement, Campion, in which you stated that you were not enjoying our shooting and hunting, as it were, for private but for professional reasons, may I ask, if this is so, who put you on to it, and where is your hope of reward?"

"Oh, I shall get my fourpence, don't you worry, young sir," said Mr. Campion. "The gent who put me up to this is a real toff." He paused. Coming across the lawn towards them, sedate, and about as graceful as a circus elephant, was Mr. Lugg. As he came nearer they saw that his immense white face wore an almost reverent expression.

" 'Ere," he said huskily as he approached his master, "see oo's come? Orders are for you to nip into the 'ouse and report in the library. Lumme," he added, "you in flannels, too. I believe there's an 'ole comin' in the sole of them shoes."

Mr. Campion rose to his feet. "Don't worry, Lugg," he said. "I shouldn't think he'd go into that."

In the general astonishment it was Penny whose curiosity found voice.

"You?" she said. "He wants to see you? Whatever for?"

Mr. Campion turned a mildly reproachful eye in their direction. "I thought you'd have got it a long while before now," he said. "He is my employer. If all goes well I shall be able to treat you to a fish-and-chip supper to-night."

CHAPTER TWENTY-SEVEN

There were Giants in those Days

At half-past three in the afternoon, with the strong sunlight tracing the diamond pattern of the window panes on the polished floor of the Colonel's library, lending that great austere room some of the indolent warmth of the garden, five men surrounded the heavy table desk on which the yellow length of an historic document was spread.

The great house was pleasantly silent. There were birds singing in the creeper and the droning of a bumble bee against the panes, but the thick walls successfully shut out any sounds of domestic bustle. The air was redolent with the faint mustiness of old leather-bound books, mingling delightfully with the scent of the flowers from the bed outside the windows.

The distinguished stranger, a tall, grey-headed man with cold blue eyes and a curious dry little voice, coughed formally.

"There's really no need for me to read all this through, Colonel," he said. "After all, we've read it through together several times before. It makes one feel old. Every reading means another decade gone."

He sighed and shot a faint, unexpectedly shy smile at Campion and the Professor, who were standing side by side. The old American was alert and deeply interested, but his companion stood fingering his tie awkwardly, an almost imbecile smile on his mild, affable face. Val stood at his father's elbow, his young face deadly serious, a distinct hint of nervousness in his manner. The memory of his first excursion to the secret room on the night of Mrs. Shannon's death was still clear in his mind. Sir Percival himself was more human than Campion or the Professor had ever seen him before. In sharing the secret of the Room with his son he seemed to have halved a burden that had been a little over-heavy for him alone.

"I think this one clause will be sufficient," the visitor continued, placing a forefinger on a rubric at the foot of the sheet. He cleared his throat again and began to read huskily and without expression.

"'And the said representative of Her Gracious Majesty or Her Heirs shall go up into the chamber accompanied by the master and his eldest son, providing he be of sufficient age, and they shall show him and prove to his satisfaction that the treasure which they hold in the stead of the Crown be whole and free from blemish, that it may be known to Us that they have kept their loyal and sacred trust. This shall be done by the light of day that neither use of candle or lamp shall be needed to show the true state of the said vessel.

"'Further, We also command that in times of trouble, or such days as the House of Gyrth may be in danger, that the master allow two witnesses to go with them, strong men and true, sworn to keep faith and all secrecy as to the Treasure and the manner of its keeping.

"'Given under Our Hand and Seal, this day . . .' and so on. I think that covers the matter, Colonel."

His quiet voice died away, and rolling up the parchment he returned it to his host who locked it in a dispatch-box on the table.

The visitor turned to Campion and the Professor.

"Strong men and true," he said, smiling at them. "Of course, I understand, strictly speaking, my dear Albert, that 'such days as the House of Gyrth may be in danger' are past. But I certainly agree with the Colonel that in the circumstances we might stretch a point in this —er—archaic formula. It seems the only courtesy, Professor, that we can extend to you for your tremendous assistance in this unfortunate and distressing affair."

The Professor made a deprecatory gesture. "There's nothing I would consider a greater honour," he said.

Mr. Campion opened his mouth to speak, but thought better of it, and was silent.

The Colonel took a small iron instrument which looked like a tiny crowbar from his desk and led the way out of the room. They followed him through the hall and down the long stone corridor into the seldom used banqueting room in the east wing. They passed no one in their journey. Branch had gathered his myrmidons in their own quarters at the back of the west wing, while Penny and Beth remained discreetly in the drawing-room.

In the cool shadow of the great apartment the Colonel paused and turned to them, a slightly embarrassed expression in his very blue eyes. The visitor relieved him of an awkward duty.

"The Colonel and I," he began prefacing his remark with his now familiar cough, "feel that we should adhere to tradition in this matter. The entrance to the—er—chamber is, and always has been, a closely guarded secret, known only to my predecessors and the Colonel's. I feel sure that I shall offend neither of you if I ask you to lend me your handkerchiefs and allow me to blindfold you just until we approach the treasure."

The Professor took out a voluminous silk bandanna which proved more suitable than Mr. Campion's white cambric. The blindfolding was accomplished with great solemnity.

On any other occasion such an incident might have been absurd, but there was a deadly earnestness in the precaution which no one in the group could ignore after the terrifying events of the preceding weeks. Val's hand shook as he tied the knot behind Campion's head and some of his nervousness was conveyed to the other man. After all, they were about to share a secret of no ordinary magnitude. Campion had not forgotten the expression upon Mrs. Shannon's face when she had looked up for a moment after peering into the window of the grim treasure house.

The Professor, too, was unusually apprehensive. It was evident that in spite of his vast store of archaic knowledge he had no inkling of what he was to expect.

The visitor's voice came to them in the darkness. "Val, if you'll take Campion's arm I'll look after Professor Cairey. Colonel, will you go first?"

Val linked his arm through Campion's, and he felt himself being led forward, the last of a little procession.

"Look out," Val's voice sounded unsteadily in his ear. "The stairs begin here."

They ascended, and once more the wood creaked beneath his feet. They went up in silence for what seemed a long time. There were so many turns that he lost his sense of direction almost immediately. He had suffered many odd experiences in his life, but this strange halting procession was more unnerving than anything he had ever known. Curiosity is the most natural of human emotions, but there came a point in the journey when he almost wished that the mystery might remain unsolved, for him at any rate, for ever. He could hear the Professor breathing hard in front of him, and he knew that it was not the steepness of the stairs which inconvenienced the old man.

Val's pressure on his arm increased. "Wait," he said so softly that he was scarcely audible. Then followed a period of silence, and they went on again. The stairs had ended and they were crossing a stone floor. Then again there was a halt. The air still smelt fresh and the song of the birds sounded very near.

"Step," whispered Val, as the procession restarted. "Keep your head down. I shall have to come behind you."

Mr. Campion felt himself clambering up a narrow stone spiral staircase, and here the air was scarcer and there was a faint, almost intangible smell of spices. He heard the grating of iron on stone and stepped forward on to a level floor. Val was close behind him, and once again there was the grating of the iron, and then complete silence. He felt his scalp tingling. He sensed that he was in a very small space, and with them he was certain, in the instinctive fashion that one is conscious of such things, there was something else, something incredibly old, something terrible.

"Take off the bandages."

He was never sure whether it was the Colonel or the visitor who had spoken. The voice was unrecognizable. He felt Val's icy fingers pulling at the knot behind his head. Then the cambric slipped from his eyes.

The first thing of which he was conscious as he blinked was the extraordinary crimson light in the room, and he turned instinctively to its source, the circular window with the heavy stone framework which had been sealed at some time with blood-red glass. The sunlight outside was very strong so that the tiny cell seemed full of particles of glittering red dust.

Campion turned from the window and started violently. The Gyrths' secret lay revealed.

Set immediately below the window so that the light fell directly upon it was a little stone altar, and kneeling before it, directly in front of the huddled group, was a figure in full Tourney armour.

As Campion stared, a pulse in his throat throbbing violently, the light seemed to concentrate on the figure.

It was that of a giant, and at first he thought it was but an immense suit of black armour only, fashioned for a man of legendary stature, but as his eye travelled slowly down the great gyves to the wrists, he caught sight of the human hands, gnarled, yellow, and shapeless like knotted willow roots. Between them, resting on the slab, was the Gyrth Chalice, whose history was lost behind the veils of legend.

It was a little shallow bowl of red gold, washed from the English mountain streams before the Romans came. A little shallow bowl whose beaten sides showed the marks of a long-dead goldsmith's hammer, and in whose red heart a cluster of uncut rubies lay like blood, still guarded by the first Messire Gyrth who earned for Sanctuary its name.

Campion raised his eyes slowly to the head of the figure and was relieved to find that the visor was down. The head was thrown back, the mute iron face raised to the circular window through which Mrs. Dick had peered.

There was utter silence in the little cell with its ancient frescoes and dust-strewn floor of coloured flags. The door by which they had entered was hidden in the stonework. Turning again, Campion saw the great sword of the warrior hanging on the wall behind the kneeling figure, the huge hilt forming a cross behind its head.

The Professor was gazing at the Chalice with tears in his eyes, a spontaneous tribute to its beauty which he did not attempt to hide.

As Campion stared at the figure he was obsessed by the uncanny feeling that it might move at any moment, that the mummified hands might snatch the sword from the wall and the great figure tower above the impious strangers who had disturbed his vigil. It was with relief that he heard the Colonel's quiet voice.

"If you are ready, gentlemen—"

No other word was spoken. Val retied the handkerchief and once again there was the grating of metal and the procession started on its return journey. The Professor stumbled once or twice on the stairs, and Campion felt that his own knees were a little unsteady. It was not that the sight had been particularly horrible, although there had been a suggestion about the hands that was not pleasant; nor did the idea of the lonely watcher keeping eternal vigil over the treasured relic he had won fill him with repugnance. But there had been something more than mortal about this ageless giant, something uncanny which filled him with almost superstitious awe, and he was glad that Penny did not know, that she could live and laugh in a house that hid this strange piece of history within its walls, unconscious of its existence.

They were still silent when once more they stood in the daylight in the old banqueting hall. The Colonel glanced at his watch.

"We meet the ladies for tea on the lawn in fifteen minutes," he said. "Mrs. Cairey promised me she'd come, Professor."

The old man dusted his hands abstractedly. There were plaster and cobwebs on all their clothes. Campion carried the Professor off to his room, leaving his host to attend to the other visitor.

No word of comment had been made, nor did anyone feel that any such remark was possible.

In Mr. Campion's pleasant Georgian room the tension relaxed.

"Lands sakes," said the Professor, subsiding into a little tub chair by the window. "Lands sakes."

Mr. Campion glanced over the lawn. The white table surrounded by garden chairs was set under the trees. Branch was already half-way towards it with a tea-wagon on which glittered the best silver, and a service which had been old when Penny's grandmother was a girl. Mrs. Cairey, Beth and Penny, looking cool and charming, their flowered chiffon frocks sweeping the lawn, were admiring the flower-beds in the far distance. It was a graceful, twentieth-century picture, peaceful and ineffably soothing, incredibly removed from the world they had just left. The tinkle of china came pleasantly to them as Branch began to arrange the table.

They were interrupted by the unceremonious entrance of Lugg with a tray bearing glasses, a siphon and a decanter.

"Branch sent me up with this lot," he remarked. "I should 'ave it. A b and s will do yer good any time o' day."

Even the Professor, who restricted himself to one whisky-and-soda a day out of deference to his wife's principles, accepted the proffered drink gratefully. Lugg hung about, apparently seeking an opening for conversation.

"They ain't 'alf doing 'Is Nibs proud downstairs," he said. "I've bin 'elping that girl I took a fancy to to clean the silver all the afternoon.

Old Branch didn't take 'is eyes off me the 'ole time. If 'e counted them spoons once 'e counted 'em a dozen times. I couldn't 'elp pinchin' this." He laid a delicate pair of Georgian sugar-tongs on the dressing-table with a certain pride.

His master looked at him in disgust. "Don't lay your filthy bone at my feet," he said. "What do you expect me to do with it?"

"Put it back for me," said Mr. Lugg unabashed. "It won't look so bad if you get noticed. I've got me record to think of. There's nothing in writin' against you."

"Go away," said Campion. "I'm going to sell you to a designer of children's cuddle-toys. You can pack my things after tea, by the way. We go back to Town to-morrow morning."

"Then you've finished?" said the Professor, looking up.

Campion nodded. "It's over," he said. "They'll stick to their rules, you know. Their employee is dead; that finishes it. I was talking to old poker-back downstairs. He's convinced we shall hear no more from them. The Maharajah has had his turn. They're connoisseurs more than criminals, you see. This is so definitely not one of their successes that I should think they'll turn their attention to Continental museums again for a bit."

"I see." The Professor was silent for some moments. Then he frowned. "I wonder—" he began, and hesitated.

Campion seemed to understand the unspoken thought, for he turned to Lugg.

"You can go back to Audrey," he said. "Any more thieving, and I'll tell her about the picture of Greta Garbo you keep under your pillow."

As the door was closed behind the disconsolate and still inquisitive Lugg, the Professor remained silent, and Campion went on.

"I couldn't understand why my precious boss downstairs hadn't told me about the second Chalice at the beginning," he said. "I see it now. He's a man of very conservative ideas, and after the awe-inspiring oath of secrecy I suppose he thought he had no alternative but to let me find it out for myself. That complicated things at the start, but I'm not sure it didn't make it easier for us in the long run."

The Professor nodded absently. His mind was still dwelling upon the experience of the afternoon.

"What a lovely, lovely thing," he said. "I may sound a bit inhuman, but when I looked at that Chalice to-day, it occurred to me that probably in the last fifteen hundred years it cost the lives of Heaven knows how many thieves and envious people, by looking at it. Campion, do you know, I thought it was worth it."

Mr. Campion did not answer. The thought in his mind was one that had rankled ever since he had stood with the others in that little painted cell, looking in at the Chalice and its guardian. What had Mrs. Dick seen when she had looked in the window that had differed from their own experience? She had been no easily frightened woman, nor was hers an imaginative nature. He spoke aloud, almost without realizing it.

"What exactly did she see when she looked through that window? Why did she say 'no'? Who did she say it to? Just what was it that made her let go?"

He paused. Outside on the lawn the chatter of feminine voices was coming nearer. Mr. Campion was still puzzled.

"I don't understand it," he said.

The Professor glanced up at him. "Oh, that?" he said. "That's quite obvious. The light was shining directly upon the figure. The head was raised to the window, if you remember."

"Yes, but—" said Mr. Campion, and was silent.

"Yes," said the Professor thoughtfully, "I think it's perfectly clear. On the night of the birthday, when she looked in, the visor was up. She saw his face . . . I'm afraid it may be a very shocking sight."

"But she spoke," said Mr. Campion. "She spoke as if she was replying to someone. And I heard something, I swear it."

The Professor leant forward in his chair and spoke with unusual emphasis. "My very dear boy," he said, "I'll say this. It doesn't do to dwell on these things."

The gentle clangour of the gong in the hall below broke in upon the silence.